A T for Blood

A Taste for Blood

Fifteen Great Vampire Novellas

Edited by
Martin H. Greenberg

BARNES
&NOBLE
BOOKS
NEW YORK

This edition published by Barnes & Noble, Inc.,
by arrangement with Martin H. Greenberg.

1993 Barnes & Noble Books

Book design by Charles Ziga, Ziga Design

ISBN 1-56619-280-3

Printed and bound in the United States of America

M 9 8 7 6 5 4 3 2

Acknowledgments

Grateful acknowledgment is made to the following for permission to reprint their copyright material:

"Murgunstrumm" by Hugh B. Cave—Copyright 1932 by The Clayton Magazines, Inc. Reprinted by permission of The Pimlico Agency, Inc.

"The Hills of the Dead" by Robert E. Howard—Copyright 1930 by Popular Fiction Publishing Company. Reprinted by permission of Glenn Lord.

"Black Thirst" by C. L. Moore—Copyright 1934, renewed © 1961 by C. L. Moore. Reprinted by permission of Don Congdon Associates, Inc.

"The Shunned House" by H. P. Lovecraft—Copyright 1939, 1943 by August Derleth and Donald Wandrei. Reprinted by permission of the Scott Meredith Literary Agency, Inc., 845 Third Avenue, New York, NY 10022.

"The Feasting Dead" by John Metcalfe—Copyright 1954 by Arkham House, Inc. Reprinted by permission of Arkham House, Inc.

"Pages from a Young Girl's Journal" by Robert Aickman—Copyright © 1973 by Mercury Press, Inc. First appeared in THE MAGAZINE OF FANTASY AND SCIENCE FICTION. Reprinted by permission of The Pimlico Agency, Inc.

"Beyond Any Measure" by Karl Edward Wagner—Copyright © 1982 by Stuart David Schiff. Reprinted by permission of the author.

"Carrion Comfort" by Dan Simmons—Copyright © 1982 by Dan Simmons; © 1983 by Omni Publications International Ltd. Reprinted by permission of the author.

"The Yougoslaves" by Robert Bloch—Copyright © 1986 by TZ Publications, Inc. Reprinted by permission of the Scott Meredith Literary Agency, Inc., 845 Third Avenue, New York, NY 10022.

"Bite-Me-Not, or, Fleur de Fur" by Tanith Lee—Copyright © 1984 by Davis Publications, Inc. First appeared in ISAAC ASIMOV'S SCIENCE FICTION MAGAZINE. Reprinted by permission of the author.

"The Lost Art of Twilight" by Thomas Ligotti—Copyright © 1986, 1989 by Thomas Ligotti. Reprinted by permission of Robinson Publishing Ltd., London.

"Blood Disease" by Patrick McGrath—Copyright © 1988 by Patrick McGrath. Reprinted by permission of Poseidon Press, a division of Simon & Schuster, Inc.

"Midnight Mass" by F. Paul Wilson—Copyright © 1990 by F. Paul Wilson. Reprinted by permission of the author.

"Son of Celluloid" by Clive Barker—Copyright © 1984 by Clive Barker. Reprinted by permission of The MacDonald Group, London.

Contents

Introduction   ix

Carmilla   1
J. Sheridan Le Fanu

Murgunstrumm   71
Hugh B. Cave

The Hills of the Dead   153
Robert E. Howard

Black Thirst   172
C. L. Moore

The Shunned House   208
H. P. Lovecraft

The Feasting Dead   234
John Metcalfe

Pages from a Young Girl's Journal   296
Robert Aickman

Beyond Any Measure   331
Karl Edward Wagner

Carrion Comfort   380
Dan Simmons

The Yougoslaves   420
Robert Bloch

Bite-Me-Not, or, Fleur de Fur   441
Tanith Lee

The Lost Art of Twilight
Thomas Ligotti
467

Blood Disease
Patrick McGrath
484

Midnight Mass
F. Paul Wilson
502

Son of Celluloid
Clive Barker
554

Introduction

There is no more durable monster in all of horror fiction than the vampire. Though preceded into print by the ghost and superseded by many more viscerally imagined creatures in frightfulness, the vampire continues to fascinate readers around the world almost 200 years after its debut. One need only see how the other classic monsters of supernatural fiction have fared in recent years to appreciate the vampire's enduring achievement. The ghost has been reduced to an unthreatening symbol of the power of memory; the werewolf supplanted by the psychopath; and the mummy usurped by the zombie as a reminder that death may *not* be the end. The vampire, however, continues to flourish virtually untouched by time in an increasing number of short stories, bestselling novels, and popular films.

The stories in *A Taste for Blood* are a testament to the vampire's long and illustrious history. Spanning more than a century, they explore vampire fiction on a time scale extending from the Middle Ages to an indeterminate future, and follow an itinerary that includes New England, France, Italy, Africa, and the planet Venus. If nothing else, they show how easily the vampire acclimates itself to the demands of different eras and milieus.

But in fact, these stories show something more. In their breadth and magnitude, they reveal the secret of the vampire's literary immortality: adaptability. The vampire tale began as a folk legend that, like all folk tales, was shaped to serve the needs of each community where it was told. What those needs might have been was scarcely important to British and European writers of the nineteenth century when they began importing the vampire into their Gothic fiction. What mattered was that in this malignant creature they found a vehicle perfectly suited to carry their own cultures' fears and dreads.

The traditional image of the vampire with which most readers are familiar is that of Dracula, the bloodthirsty Transylvanian count from Bram Stoker's 1897 novel. So potently realized was

Stoker's creation, and so memorably interpreted for the movie screen by Bela Lugosi in 1931, that all of the paraphernalia surrounding him—daytime slumber in a coffin, nighttime thirst for blood, the ability to transform into a bat, the repelling power of the cross, the destructive use of the sharpened stake—are accepted as the rules every genuine vampire story must follow. In fact, Stoker was no different from any other writer of vampire stories in his selective shaping of superstitions handed down (in this case, those surrounding the fifteenth-century Wallachian warlord Vlad Tepes) into a tale of supernatural menace appropriate for his time. By the artistic liberties he took with his source material, Stoker set the stage for unconventional additions to the vampire tradition.

Like *Dracula*, the stories in *A Taste for Blood* are vampire tales that take liberties. No two portray the vampire in the same light. Each stretches the conventional image of the vampire—omitting here, embellishing there—to reflect the interests of the time and place in which it was written. Collectively, these stories increase our appreciation of vampire fiction, even as they call into question the parameters by which we define such fiction.

Of all the stories included, J. Sheridan Le Fanu's "Carmilla" is perhaps the most traditional, and with good reason. Serialized between 1871 and 1872, "Carmilla" appeared in print twenty-five years before *Dracula* and made a strong impression on the young Bram Stoker's imagination. One sees many elements in Le Fanu's tale, particularly its climactic death scene, that would later ossify into the durable clichés of the vampire myth. More important, though, is the sexual subcurrent that flows through the story. Presented as the deposition of a naive young girl barely aware of the dangers to which she is exposed, "Carmilla" renders the theme of imperiled innocence that typifies the vampire tale through the veil of an implied lesbian relationship. Though daring by Victorian standards, Le Fanu's tale was not intended to shock or titillate. Rather, the "unnatural" desires of its vampire were meant to reinforce her supernatural character. Considering the prevailing values of the day, it is hardly surprising that Le Fanu's narrator complains of "tumultuous excitement that was pleasurable . . . mingled with a vague sense of fear and disgust" in her response to the Countess Carmilla's attentions. "Carmilla" was the first story to delineate in this way the mutually attractive and repulsive qualities that distinguish the vampire.

The difference between Le Fanu's refined vampire tale and Hugh B. Cave's gruesome thriller "Murgunstrumm" is the difference between the classic British tale of the supernatural and the American pulp horror story. Created in 1896, the pulp magazines served as the major source of cheap, popular fiction in the United States up through the 1950s. The success of any pulp title was determined by how much escapism it could provide, so it's not surprising that a significant number catered to tastes for fantasy and horror. "Murgunstrumm" appeared in the seventh and final issue of the short-lived *Strange Tales* in 1933. Prior to its publication, very few vampire tales had been set on American soil; those that were usually employed vampires with conspicuously European accents. But Cave's rural Gray Toad Inn proved a natural substitute for the vampire-infested Gothic castle, and his Jazz Age lounge lizards provided the perfect species of indigenous American nightlife to assume the duties of the Undead. Told in the fast-paced adventure mode, "Murgunstrumm" was the quintessential vampire story of its time, one that helped to open the American landscape up to a vampire invasion.

That invasion was to come in the pages of *Weird Tales*, the most famous of all pulp horror magazines. Over the course of its thirty-one-year existence, *Weird Tales* published perhaps a hundred vampire tales, most of which were fairly routine. Some, however, were quite distinguished and a few changed forever the way we look at the vampire story.

Robert E. Howard, one of the most popular of all pulp fiction authors, wrote a number of vampire tales for *Weird Tales* and other magazines of the day, but none so memorable as his 1930 story "The Hills of the Dead." Howard is best known as the creator of sword-and-sorcery, a style of fiction epitomized by his tales of Conan the Barbarian in which the historical adventure is imbued with elements of fantasy and horror. His several heroic sagas include the exploits of Solomon Kane, a footloose Puritan soldier-of-fortune during the age of Cromwell. Kane's travels frequently take him to exotic locales whose enchantments test his faith, a challenge to be expected in "The Hills of the Dead"—which presents a land where vampires are not an anomaly, but one of the dominant species. The tale's ingenious ending is an example of how early twentieth-century writers were already seeking to stretch the vam-

pire myth through variations on the usual methods of destroying
vampires.

Like Howard, C. L. Moore seemed to be of the opinion the
discover-and-dispatch scenario of the conventional vampire tale
had become stale and deserving of reformulation. Moore burst
upon the fantasy scene in 1933 with the highly acclaimed "Sham-
bleau," in which the intergalactic gunslinger Northwest Smith en-
counters a medusa-like Venusian whose race may have served as
the prototype for earthly legends of the vampire. She continued
this exploration of horror motifs with her second tale of Northwest
Smith, "Black Thirst," which presupposes an ancient species that
cultivates and feeds vampirishly off the beauty of its victims. Not
content to stop with so original an idea, Moore extended the theme
of this story even further by suggesting that beauty itself often
exhibits a vampiric voraciousness. "You must have noticed the
vacuity that accompanies perfect beauty in so many women," ob-
serves her vampire overlord, "the force so strong that it drives out
all other forces and lives vampirishly at the expense of intelligence
and goodness and conscience and all else." In its implicit condem-
nation of the standards by which we measure and quantify beauty,
Moore's tale is a rare example of a pulp story that criticized, rather
than supported, the sexual politics of its time.

Quite possibly the most original vampire story to appear in
Weird Tales was H. P. Lovecraft's "The Shunned House," published seven months after his death in 1937. Lovecraft, however, is
recognized today as the most important writer of horror fiction in
the twentieth century precisely because he jettisoned the vampire
and all other carryovers from the Gothic tradition as inadequate
for supporting weird fiction written in the age of modern scientific
rationalism. His best stories suggest instead that such creatures of
superstition are merely fairy tales concocted by human beings to
give an understandable shape to the incomprehensible forces that
govern the universe. Approaching horror fiction from this perspective, Lovecraft was able to combine the best elements of the
vampire tale and haunted house story in "The Shunned House,"
and to suggest an ancient evil more foul than would have been
yielded by the sum of its parts.

The reinterpretation of vampirism pioneered by Lovecraft became essential to the vampire story's survival in the years immediately following the Second World War, when the scientific sophis-

tication of a readship familiar with the atom bomb all but consigned supernatural horror to the dustbin of literature. Inaugurating a trend that would continue into the vampire fiction of today, John Metcalfe resuscitated the vampire in his 1954 novella "The Feasting Dead" by deflecting attention from the vampire to its victims, who struggle to make sense of their ordeal as a perfectly rational explanation. So much of Metcalfe's story happens offstage that we can only assume the pernicious influence of the vampire on the narrator's son from his growing disaffection with his father—an ambiguous response that might just as easily be explained as the natural behavior of a growing child.

Implicit in Metcalfe's story is one possible explanation for the vampire's continuing appeal: the recognition that there are normal life situations for which the vampire-victim relationship is an appropriate metaphor. Certainly this is the case in Robert Aickman's 1973 story "Pages from a Young Girl's Journal." Although generally a master of ambiguity, Aickman leaves no question in the reader's mind that his innocent young narrator has been visited in the night by a vampire lover. Unequipped with the knowledge to recognize this, though, she views her nocturnal guest without the prejudice of superstition, and thus is aware only that he has brought about a fundamental change in her perception of herself. Seen in this light, "Pages from a Young Girl's Journal" is as much a tale of a young woman's sexual awakening and coming of age as a vampire story.

The fact that half of the stories in A Taste for Blood date from the 1980s is a tribute not only to the vampire's tenacious hold on the imagination but also the explosive growth of contemporary horror fiction. Fueled in part by the enormous popularity of Stephen King and Robert R. McCammon (each of whom has written a vampire novel) and the novels of Anne Rice, whose bestselling "Vampire Chronicles" trilogy has almost singlehandedly reinvented the vampire for the modern era, the modern horror movement in the last decade has produced as large a volume of weird fiction as what was published in the preceding century. Not surprisingly, the vampire tale forms a significant percentage of this output, the result of writers familiar with the heritage seeking new ways to reach modern readers.

There are noticeably classic overtones in Karl Edward Wagner's 1982 story "Beyond Any Measure," which develops through the slow accumulation of incident and detail one associates with the traditional tale of the supernatural, even though set in London's punk rock decade. However, just as Howard turned the sword-and-sorcery tale inside out through his critically acclaimed stories of Kane, an amoral anti-hero, Wagner also presents a completely different sort of vampire tale here. It is one that both elaborates an aspect of the vampire myth never adequately explained and also speculates on the intriguing complications that might occur in a world where vampirism and reincarnation are equally possible.

An even more modern sensibility is at work in Dan Simmons' "Carrion Comfort," published in 1983. Here, Simmons strips the vampire myth to its bones, asking what unique characteristic of this ancient figure has resonance with our modern fears. Looking beyond the threat of physical harm which virtually every supernatural creature poses, he locates the source of our dread in the vampire's exercise of absolute power over its victim. Dispensing with the accouterments of traditional vampire stories, Simmons imagines a race of psychic vampires in our midst, indistinguishable from ourselves except for their pitiless manipulation of human pawns to commit the random acts of violence on which they feast.

In 1989, Simmons expanded "Carrion Comfort" into a novel that shuttled between the concentration camps of World War II and modern urban ghettoes in search of vampiric forces at work wherever individual freedom of choice was suppressed. But he was not the first to see this modern analog for the vampire tale. In his 1986 story "The Yougoslaves," Robert Bloch, author of many traditional vampire stories, notes a parallel between the vampire's control over its victims and the enslavement of a gang of street youths by a morally delinquent adult. The result is a neat inversion of the traditional vampire story, in which a stand-in for the original Count Dracula comes off as not only more respectable but more worthy of reader sympathy than his human antagonists.

Untraditional depictions of the vampire as a sympathetic character are almost entirely a contemporary phenomenon in horror fiction, an inevitable response of writers to the perception of predatory motives behind much of normal human behavior. Such portrayals tend either to present the vampire as a tragic victim of circumstance or someone whose nefarious capabilities are greatly exceeded by the evil that *men* do. An example of the latter is Tanith

Lee's 1984 story "Bite-Me-Not, or, Fleur de Fur," which tells of the love that develops between an ill-treated scullery maid and an inhumanely tortured vampire king when they are cast out of their respective societies. The high fantasy of Lee's story contrasts sharply with the oblique horror of "The Lost Art of Twilight," Thomas Ligotti's 1986 portrait of the vampire as a young artist. Here, a mortal child tainted while in his vampire mother's womb —thus forever trapped between the world of the living and the dead—finds himself endowed with a special aesthetic sensitivity. The sad fate that befalls him at the hands of relatives can be read as both a commentary on the conforming pressures of the family and a subtle criticism of the banality of the good-versus-evil scenarios that serve as the foundation for the traditional vampire story.

If a sympathetic portrait of the vampire is possible, then can a whimsical treatment be far behind? Just as tales like Lee's and Ligotti's neutralize the horror of the vampire by focusing on its fundamental humanity, so does the subgenre of humorous vampire fiction deflate the vampire's potential for fright by exaggerating its all-too-human fallibility. Patrick McGrath's 1988 story "Blood Disease" provides an example of sardonic vampire humor that is unique in its complete lack of a supernatural vampire. His story succeeds as a vampire tale by benefit of the many forms of natural life—human included—which he portrays as depending for their survival upon vampiric sustenance. In this dismantling of the Gothic vampire tale, a true vampire would not only be unthreatening but faced with stiff competition.

The increasing use of the vampire in the modern horror story to reflect on the essence of humanity comes full circle in F. Paul Wilson's short novel, "Midnight Mass," published in 1990. Using as his starting point the premise of Richard Matheson's renowned science fiction/horror novel I Am Legend (1954), which presented a future in which vampires outnumber mortals and rule the world by night, Wilson proposes that a vampire's bite might not alter the conduct of the victim for the worse so much as remove the moral restraints that have kept his misanthropic personality as a mortal in check. Although ultimately a story of redemption through faith, "Midnight Mass" has a darkness at its core with the suggestion that vampirism originates less with a bite than with a penchant for anti-social behavior.

If the measure of any vampire tale is how well it reflects the time in which it was written, then Clive Barker's "Son of Celluloid," published in 1984, is surely a mirror image of its age. It is no coincidence that the modern vampire story has achieved its greatest popularity in a world confronted daily with the reality of cancer and other consumptive diseases, and it would have been enough for Barker to simply point out the obvious parallels. But Barker's ambition is to peel back the facade of our world and show that virtually all of its elements—not only blood and tissue, but even fantasy and desire—can serve as sustenance for strange appetites. Though in "Son of Celluloid" one looks in vain for a traditional blood-drinking creature of the night, Barker's delineation of an infinitely consumable world may be the last word in vampire fiction.

But surely not. It is the privilege of each generation to assume that it has extrapolated an idea to its ultimate extreme, and as the stories in *A Taste for Blood* demonstrate, a timeless theme is open to infinite interpretation. Two centuries of vampire stories in the English language have yet to exhaust the vampire's potential as food for the imagination, or satiate the thirst of readers for more. The stories that follow offer a summary of what has been achieved in vampire literature, and though they may not offer a clue as to the territory the next generation's vampire stories will cover, they do assure that such tales will be written. Though mortals die and books crumble, the vampire lives.

—Stefan Dziemianowicz
New York, 1992

Carmilla

J. Sheridan Le Fanu

Upon a paper attached to the narrative which follows, Doctor Hesselius has written a rather elaborate note, which he accompanies with a reference to his Essay on the strange subject which the Manuscript illuminates.

This mysterious subject he treats, in that Essay, with his usual learning and acumen, and with remarkable directness and condensation. It will form but one volume of the series of that extraordinary man's collected papers.

As I publish the case, in this volume, simply to interest the "laity," I shall in no way forestall the intelligent lady who relates it; and, after due consideration, I have determined, therefore, to abstain from presenting any *précis* of the learned Doctor's reasoning, or extract from his statement on a subject which he describes as "involving, not improbably, some of the profoundest arcana of our dual existence, and its intermediates."

I was anxious, on discovering this paper, to re-open the correspondence commenced by Doctor Hesselius, so many years before, with a person so clever and careful as his informant seems to have been. Much to my regret, however, I found that she had died in the interval.

She, probably, could have added little to the Narrative which

she communicates in the following pages, with, so far as I can
pronounce, such a conscientious particularity.

An Early Fright
I

Although we are by no means magnificent people, we inhabit a
schloss, a castle in Styria. A small income, in that part of the
world, goes a great way. Eight or nine hundred a year does wonders. Scantily enough ours would have answered among wealthy
people at home. My father is English, and I bear an English name,
although I never saw England. But here, in this lonely and primitive place, where everything is so marvelously cheap, I really don't
see how ever so much more money would at all materially add to
our comforts, or even luxuries.

My father was in the Austrian service, and retired upon a pen-
sion and his patrimony, and purchased this feudal residence, and
the small estate on which it stands, a bargain.

Nothing can be more picturesque or solitary. It stands on a
slight eminence in a forest. The road, very old and narrow, passes
in front of its drawbridge, never raised in my time, and its moat,
stocked with perch, and sailed over by many swans, and floating
on its surface white fleets of water-lilies.

Over all this the schloss shows its many-windowed front; its
towers, and its Gothic chapel.

The forest opens in an irregular and very picturesque glade
before its gate, and at the right a steep Gothic bridge carries the
road over a stream that winds in deep shadow through the wood.

I have said that this is a very lonely place. Judge whether I say
truth. Looking from the hall door towards the road, the forest in
which our castle stands extends fifteen miles to the right, and
twelve to the left. The nearest inhabited village is about seven of
your English miles to the left. The nearest inhabited schloss of any
historic associations, is that of old General Spielsdorf, nearly
twenty miles away to the right.

I have said "the nearest *inhabited* village," because there is, only
three miles westward, that is to say in the direction of General
Spielsdorf's schloss, a ruined village, with its quaint little church,
now roofless, in the aisle of which are the moldering tombs of the
proud family of Karnstein, now extinct, who once owned the

equally-desolate château which, in the thick of the forest, over-looks the silent ruins of the town.

Respecting the cause of the desertion of this striking and melancholy spot, there is a legend which I shall relate to you another time.

I must tell you now, how very small is the party who constitute the inhabitants of our castle. I don't include servants or those dependents who occupy rooms in the buildings attached to the schloss. Listen, and wonder! My father, who is the kindest man on earth, but growing old; and I, at the date of my story, only nineteen. Eight years have passed since then. I and my father constituted the family at the schloss. My mother, a Styrian lady, died in my infancy, but I had a good-natured governess, who had been with me from, I might almost say, my infancy. I could not remember the time when her fat, benignant face was not a familiar picture in my memory. This was Madame Perrodon, a native of Berne, whose care and good nature in part supplied to me the loss of my mother, whom I do not even remember, so early did I lose her. She made a third at our little dinner party. There was a fourth, Mademoiselle De Lafontaine, a lady such as you term, I believe, a "finishing governess." She spoke French and German, Madame Perrodon French and broken English, to which my father and I added English, which, partly from patriotic motives, we spoke every day. The consequence was a Babel, at which strangers used to laugh, and which I shall make no attempt to reproduce in this narrative. And there were two or three young lady friends besides, pretty nearly of my own age, who were occasional visitors, for longer or shorter terms; and these visits I sometimes returned.

These were our regular social resources; but of course there were chance visits from "neighbors" of only five or six league's distance. My life was, notwithstanding, rather a solitary one, I can assure you.

My elders had just so much control over me as you might conjecture such sage persons would have in the case of a rather spoiled girl, whose only parent allowed her pretty nearly her own way in everything.

The first occurrence in my existence, which produced a terrible impression upon my mind, which, in fact, never has been effaced, was one of the very earliest incidents of my life which I can recollect. Some people will think it so trifling that it should not be recorded here. You will see, however, by-and-by, why I mention it. The nursery, as it was called, though I had it all to myself, was a large room in the upper story of the castle, with a steep oak roof. I can't have been more than six years old, when one night I awoke, and looking round the room from my bed, failed to see the nursery-maid. Neither was my nurse there; and I thought myself alone. I was not frightened, for I was one of those happy children who are studiously kept in ignorance of ghost stories, of fairy tales, and of all such lore as makes us cover up our heads when the door creaks suddenly, or the flicker of an expiring candle makes the shadow of a bed-post dance upon the wall, nearer to our faces. I was vexed and insulted at finding myself, as I conceived, neglected, and I began to whimper, preparatory to a hearty bout of roaring; when to my surprise, I saw a solemn, but very pretty face looking at me from the side of the bed. It was that of a young lady who was kneeling, with her hands under the coverlet. I looked at her with a kind of pleased wonder, and ceased whimpering. She caressed me with her hands, and lay down beside me on the bed, and drew me towards her, smiling; I felt immediately delightfully soothed, and fell asleep again. I was wakened by a sensation as if two needles ran into my breast very deep at the same moment, and I cried loudly. The lady started back, with her eyes fixed on me, and then slipped down upon the floor, and, as I thought, hid herself under the bed.

I was now for the first time frightened, and I yelled with all my might and main. Nurse, nursery-maid, housekeeper, all came running in, and hearing my story, they made light of it, soothing me all they could meanwhile. But, child as I was, I could perceive that their faces were pale with an unwonted look of anxiety, and I saw them look under the bed, and about the room, and peep under tables and pluck open cupboards; and the housekeeper whispered to the nurse: "Lay your hand along that hollow in the bed; some one *did* lie there, so sure as you did not; the place is still warm."

I remember the nursery-maid petting me, and all three examining my chest, where I told them I felt the puncture, and pronouncing that there was no sign visible that any such thing had happened to me.

The housekeeper and the two other servants who were in charge of the nursery, remained sitting up all night; and from that time a servant always sat up in the nursery until I was about fourteen.

I was very nervous for a long time after this. A doctor was called in, he was pallid and elderly. How well I remember his long saturnine face, slightly pitted with smallpox, and his chestnut wig. For a good while, every second day, he came and gave me medicine, which of course I hated.

The morning after I saw this apparition I was in a state of terror, and could not bear to be left alone, daylight though it was, for a moment.

I remember my father coming up and standing at the bedside, and talking cheerfully, and asking the nurse a number of questions, and laughing very heartily at one of the answers; and patting me on the shoulder, and kissing me, and telling me not to be frightened, that it was nothing but a dream and could not hurt me.

But I was not comforted, for I knew the visit of the strange woman was *not* a dream; and I was *awfully* frightened.

I was a little consoled by the nursery-maid's assuring me that it was she who had come and looked at me, and lain down beside me in the bed, and that I must have been half-dreaming not to have known her face. But this, though supported by the nurse, did not quite satisfy me.

I remember, in the course of that day, a venerable old man, in a black cassock, coming into the room with the nurse and housekeeper, and talking a little to them, and very kindly to me; his face was very sweet and gentle, and he told me they were going to pray, and joined my hands together, and desired me to say, softly, while they were praying, "Lord, hear all good prayers for us, for Jesus' sake." I think these were the very words, for I often repeated them to myself, and my nurse used for years to make me say them in my prayers.

I remember so well the thoughtful sweet face of that white-haired old man, in his black cassock, as he stood in that rude, lofty, brown room, with the clumsy furniture of a fashion three hundred years old, about him, and the scanty light entering its shadowy atmosphere through the small lattice. He kneeled, and the three women with him, and he prayed aloud with an earnest quavering voice for, what appeared to me, a long time. I forget all my life preceding that event, and for some time after it is all obscure also; but the scenes I have just described stand out vivid as the isolated pictures of the phantasmagoria surrounded by darkness.

A Guest
II

I am now going to tell you something so strange that it will require all your faith in my veracity to believe my story. It is not only true, nevertheless, but truth of which I have been an eyewitness.

It was a sweet summer evening, and my father asked me, as he sometimes did, to take a little ramble with him along that beautiful forest vista which I have mentioned as lying in front of the schloss.

"General Spielsdorf cannot come to us so soon as I had hoped," said my father, as we pursued our walk.

He was to have paid us a visit of some weeks, and we had expected his arrival next day. He was to have brought with him a young lady, his niece and ward, Mademoiselle Rheinfeldt, whom I had never seen, but whom I had heard described as a very charming girl, and in whose society I had promised myself many happy days. I was more disappointed than a young lady living in a town, or a bustling neighborhood can possibly imagine. This visit, and the new acquaintance it promised, had furnished my day dream for many weeks.

"And how soon does he come?" I asked.

"Not till autumn. Not for two months, I dare say," he answered. "And I am very glad now, dear, that you never knew Mademoiselle Rheinfeldt."

"And why?" I asked, both mortified and curious.

"Because the poor young lady is dead," he replied. "I quite forgot I had not told you, but you were not in the room when I received the General's letter this evening."

I was very much shocked. General Spielsdorf had mentioned in his first letter, six or seven weeks before, that she was not so well as he would wish her, but there was nothing to suggest the remotest suspicion of danger.

"Here is the General's letter," he said, handing it to me. "I am afraid he is in great affliction; the letter appears to me to have been written very nearly in distraction."

We sat down on a rude bench, under a group of magnificent lime trees. The sun was setting with all its melancholy splendor behind the sylvan horizon, and the stream that flows beside our home, and passes under the steep old bridge I have mentioned, wound through many a group of noble trees, almost at our feet, reflecting in its current the fading crimson of the sky. General Spielsdorf's letter was so extraordinary, so vehement, and in some places so self-contradictory, that I read it twice over—the second time aloud to my father—and was still unable to account for it, except by supposing that grief had unsettled his mind.

It said, "I have lost my darling daughter, for as such I loved her. During the last days of dear Bertha's illness I was not able to write to you. Before then I had no idea of her danger. I have lost her, and now learn *all*, too late. She died in the peace of innocence, and in the glorious hope of a blessed futurity. The fiend who betrayed our infatuated hospitality has done it all. I thought I was receiving into my house innocence, gaiety, a charming companion for my lost Bertha. Heavens! what a fool have I been! I thank God my child died without a suspicion of the cause of her sufferings. She is gone without so much as conjecturing the nature of her illness, and the accursed passion of the agent of all this misery. I devote my remaining days to tracking and extinguishing a monster. I am told I may hope to accomplish my righteous and merciful purpose. At present there is scarcely a gleam of light to guide me. I curse my conceited incredulity, my despicable affectation of superiority, my blindness, my obstinacy—all—too late. I cannot write or talk collectedly now. I am distracted. So soon as I shall have a little recovered, I mean to devote myself for a time to enquiry, which may possibly lead me as far as Vienna. Some time in the autumn, two months hence, or earlier if I live, I will see you—that is, if you permit me; I will then tell you all that I scarce dare put upon paper now. Farewell. Pray for me, dear friend."

In these terms ended this strange letter. Though I had never seen Bertha Rheinfeldt, my eyes filled with tears at the sudden intelligence; I was startled, as well as profoundly disappointed.

The sun had now set, and it was twilight by the time I had returned the General's letter to my father.

It was a soft clear evening, and we loitered, speculating upon the possible meanings of the violent and incoherent sentences which I had just been reading. We had nearly a mile to walk before reaching the road that passes the schloss in front, and by that time the moon was shining brilliantly. At the drawbridge we met Madame Perrodon and Mademoiselle De Lafontaine, who had come out, without their bonnets, to enjoy the exquisite moonlight.

We heard their voices gabbling in animated dialogue as we approached. We joined them at the drawbridge, and turned about to admire with them the beautiful scene.

The glade through which we had just walked lay before us. At our left the narrow road wound away under clumps of lordly trees, and was lost to sight amid the thickening forest. At the right the same road crosses the steep and picturesque bridge, near which stands a ruined tower, which once guarded that pass; and beyond the bridge an abrupt eminence rises, covered with trees, and showing in the shadow some grey ivy-clustered rocks.

Over the sward and low grounds, a thin film of mist was stealing like smoke, marking the distances with a transparent veil; and here and there we could see the river faintly flashing in the moonlight.

No softer, sweeter scene could be imagined. The news I had just heard made it melancholy; but nothing could disturb its character of profound serenity, and the enchanted glory and vagueness of the prospect.

My father, who enjoyed the picturesque, and I, stood looking in silence over the expanse beneath us. The two good governesses, standing a little way behind us, discoursed upon the scene, and were eloquent upon the moon.

Madame Perrodon was fat, middle-aged, and romantic, and talked and sighed poetically. Mademoiselle De Lafontaine—in right of her father, who was a German, assumed to be psychological, metaphysical, and something of a mystic—now declared that when the moon shone with a light so intense it was well known that it indicated a special spiritual activity. The effect of the full moon in such a state of brilliancy was manifold. It acted on dreams, it acted on lunacy, it acted on nervous people; it had marvelous physical influences connected with life. Mademoiselle related that her cousin, who was mate of a merchant ship, having taken a nap on deck on such a night, lying on his back, with his face full in the light of the moon, had awakened, after a dream of an old woman clawing him by the cheek, with his features horribly drawn to one side; and his countenance had never quite recovered its equilibrium.

"The moon, this night," she said, "is full of odylic and magnetic influence—and see, when you look behind you at the front of the schloss, how all its windows flash and twinkle with that silvery splendor, as if unseen hands had lighted up the rooms to receive fairy guests."

There are indolent states of the spirits in which, indisposed to talk ourselves, the talk of others is pleasant to our listless ears; and I gazed on, pleased with the tinkle of the ladies' conversation.

"I have got into one of my moping moods tonight," said my father, after a silence, and quoting Shakespeare, whom, by way of keeping up our English, he used to read aloud, he said:

> " 'In truth I know not why I am so sad:
> It wearies me; you say it wearies you;
> But how I got it—came by it.'

"I forget the rest. But I feel as if some great misfortune were hanging over us. I suppose the poor General's afflicted letter has had something to do with it."

At this moment the unexpected sound of carriage wheels and many hoofs upon the road, arrested our attention.

They seemed to be approaching from the high ground overlooking the bridge, and very soon the equipage emerged from that point. Two horsemen first crossed the bridge, then came a carriage drawn by four horses, and two men rode behind.

It seemed to be the travelling carriage of a person of rank; and we were all immediately absorbed in watching that very unusual spectacle. It became, in a few moments, greatly more interesting, for just as the carriage had passed the summit of the steep bridge, one of the leaders, taking fright, communicated his panic to the rest, and, after a plunge or two, the whole team broke into a wild gallop together, and dashing between the horsemen who rode in front, came thundering along the road towards us with the speed of a hurricane.

The excitement of the scene was made more painful by the clear, long-drawn screams of a female voice from the carriage window.

We all advanced in curiosity and horror; my father in silence, the rest with various ejaculations of terror.

Our suspense did not last long. Just before you reach the castle drawbridge, on the route they were coming, there stands by the roadside a magnificent lime tree, on the other stands an ancient stone cross, at the sight of which the horses, now going at a pace that was perfectly frightful, swerved so as to bring the wheel over the projecting roots of the tree.

I knew what was coming. I covered my eyes, unable to see it out, and turned my head away; at the same moment I heard a cry from my lady-friends, who had gone on a little.

Curiosity opened my eyes, and I saw a scene of utter confusion. Two of the horses were on the ground, the carriage lay upon its side, with two wheels in the air; the men were busy removing the traces, and a lady, with a commanding air and figure had got out, and stood with clasped hands, raising the handkerchief that was in them every now and then to her eyes. Through the carriage door was now lifted a young lady, who appeared to be lifeless. My dear old father was already beside the elder lady, with his hat in his hand, evidently tendering his aid and the resources of his schloss. The lady did not appear to hear him, or to have eyes for anything but the slender girl who was being placed against the slope of the bank.

I approached; the young lady was apparently stunned, but she was certainly not dead. My father, who prided himself on being something of a physician, had just had his fingers to her wrist and assured the lady, who declared herself her mother, that her pulse, though faint and irregular, was undoubtedly still distinguishable. The lady clasped her hands and looked upward, as if in a momentary transport of gratitude; but immediately she broke out again in that theatrical way which is, I believe, natural to some people.

She was what is called a fine-looking woman for her time of life, and must have been handsome; she was tall, but not thin, and dressed in black velvet, and looked rather pale, but with a proud and commanding countenance, though now agitated strangely.

"Was ever being so born to calamity?" I heard her say, with clasped hands, as I came up. "Here am I, on a journey of life and death, in prosecuting which to lose an hour is possibly to lose all. My child will not have recovered sufficiently to resume her route for who can say how long. I must leave her; I cannot, dare not, delay. How far on, sir, can you tell, is the nearest village? I must leave her there; and shall not see my darling, or even hear of her till my return, three months hence."

I plucked my father by the coat, and whispered earnestly in his ear, "Oh! papa, pray ask her to let her stay with us—it would be so delightful. Do, pray."

"If Madame will entrust her child to the care of my daughter and of her good governess, Madame Perrodon, and permit her to remain as our guest, under my charge, until her return, it will confer a distinction and an obligation upon us, and we shall treat her with all the care and devotion which so sacred a trust deserves."

"I cannot do that, sir, it would be to task your kindness and chivalry too cruelly," said the lady, distractedly.

"It would, on the contrary, be to confer on us a very great kindness at the moment when we most need it. My daughter has just been disappointed by a cruel misfortune, in a visit from which she had long anticipated a great deal of happiness. If you confide this young lady to our care it will be her best consolation. The nearest village on your route is distant, and affords no such inn as you could think of placing your daughter at; you cannot allow her to continue her journey for any considerable distance without danger. If, as you say, you cannot suspend your journey, you must part with her tonight, and nowhere could you do so with more honest assurances of care and tenderness than here."

There was something in this lady's air and appearance so distinguished, and even imposing, and in her manner so engaging, as to impress one, quite apart from the dignity of her equipage, with a conviction that she was a person of consequence.

By this time the carriage was replaced in its upright position, and the horses, quite tractable, in the traces again.

The lady threw on her daughter a glance which I fancied was not quite so affectionate as one might have anticipated from the beginning of the scene; then she beckoned slightly to my father and withdrew two or three steps with him out of hearing; and talked to him with a fixed and stern countenance, not at all like that with which she had hitherto spoken.

I was filled with wonder that my father did not seem to perceive the change, and also unspeakably curious to learn what it could be that she was speaking, almost in his ear, with so much earnestness and rapidity.

Two or three minutes at most, I think, she remained thus employed, then she turned, and a few steps brought her to where her daughter lay, supported by Madame Perrodon. She kneeled beside her for a moment and whispered, as Madame supposed, a little benediction in her ear; then hastily kissing her, she stepped into her carriage, the door was closed, the footmen in stately liveries jumped up behind, the outriders spurred on, the postilions cracked their whips, the horses plunged and broke suddenly into a furious canter that threatened soon again to become a gallop, and the carriage whirled away, followed at the same rapid pace by the two horsemen in the rear.

We Compare Notes
III

We followed the *cortège* with our eyes until it was swiftly lost to sight in the misty wood; and the very sound of the hoofs and wheels died away in the silent night air.

Nothing remained to assure us that the adventure had not been an illusion for a moment but the young lady, who just at that moment opened her eyes. I could not see, for her face was turned from me, but she raised her head, evidently looking about her, and I heard a very sweet voice ask complainingly, "Where is mamma?"

Our good Madame Perrodon answered tenderly, and added some comfortable assurances.

I then heard her ask:

"Where am I? What is this place?" and after that she said, "I don't see the carriage; and Matska, where is she?"

Madame answered all her questions in so far as she understood them; and gradually the young lady remembered how the misadventure came about, and was glad to hear that no one in, or in attendance on, the carriage was hurt; and on learning that her mamma had left her here, till her return in about three months, she wept.

I was going to add my consolations to those of Madame Perrodon when Mademoiselle De Lafontaine placed her hand upon my arm, saying:

"Don't approach, one at a time is as much as she can at present converse with; a very little excitement would possibly overpower her now."

As soon as she is comfortably in bed, I thought, I will run up to her room and see her.

My father in the meantime had sent a servant on horseback for the physician, who lived about two leagues away; and a bedroom was being prepared for the young lady's reception.

The stranger now rose, and leaning on Madame's arm, walked slowly over the drawbridge and into the castle gate.

In the hall the servants waited to receive her, and she was conducted forthwith to her room.

The room we usually sat in as our drawing-room is long, having four windows, that looked over the moat and drawbridge, upon the forest scene I have just described.

It is furnished in old carved oak, with large carved cabinets, and the chairs are cushioned with crimson Utrecht velvet. The walls are covered with tapestry, and surrounded with great gold frames, the figures being as large as life, in ancient and very curious costume, and the subjects represented are hunting, hawking, and generally festive. It is not too stately to be extremely comfortable; and here we had our tea, for with his usual patriotic leanings he insisted that the national beverage should make its appearance regularly with our coffee and chocolate.

We sat here this night, and with candles lighted, were talking over the adventure of the evening.

Madame Perrodon and Mademoiselle De Lafontaine were both of our party. The younger stranger had hardly lain down in her bed when she sank into a deep sleep; and those ladies had left her in the care of a servant.

"How do you like our guest?" I asked, as soon as Madame entered. "Tell me all about her."

"I like her extremely," answered Madame, "she is, I almost think, the prettiest creature I ever saw; about your age, and so gentle and nice."

"She is absolutely beautiful," threw in Mademoiselle, who had peeped for a moment into the stranger's room.

"And such a sweet voice!" added Madame Perrodon.

"Did you remark a woman in the carriage, after it was set up again, who did not get out," inquired Mademoiselle, "but only looked from the window?"

No, we had not seen her.

Then she described a hideous black woman, with a sort of colored turban on her head, who was gazing all the time from the carriage window, nodding and grinning derisively towards the ladies, with gleaming eyes and large white eyeballs, and her teeth set as if in fury.

"Did you remark what an ill-looking pack of men the servants were?" asked Madame.

"Yes," said my father, who had just come in, "ugly, hangdog looking fellows, as ever I beheld in my life. I hope they mayn't rob the poor lady in the forest. They are clever rogues, however; they got everything to rights in a minute."

"I dare say they are worn out with too long travelling," said Madame. "Besides looking wicked, their faces were so strangely lean, and dark, and sullen. I am very curious, I own; but I dare say the young lady will tell us all about it tomorrow, if she is sufficiently recovered."

"I don't think she will," said my father, with a mysterious smile, and a little nod of his head, as if he knew more about it than he cared to tell us.

This made me all the more inquisitive as to what had passed between him and the lady in the black velvet, in the brief but earnest interview that had immediately preceded her departure.

We were scarcely alone, when I entreated him to tell me. He did not need much pressing.

"There is no particular reason why I should not tell you. She expressed a reluctance to trouble us with the care of her daughter, saying she was in delicate health, and nervous, but not subject to any kind of seizure—she volunteered that—nor to any illusion; being, in fact, perfectly sane."

"How very odd to say all that!" I interpolated. "It was so unnecessary."

"At all events it *was* said," he laughed, "and as you wish to know all that passed, which was indeed very little, I tell you. She then said, 'I am making a long journey of *vital* importance'—she emphasized the word—'rapid and secret; I shall return for my child in three months; in the meantime, she will be silent as to who we are, whence we come, and whither we are travelling.' That is all she said. She spoke very pure French. When she said the word 'secret,' she paused for a few seconds, looking sternly, her eyes fixed on mine. I fancy she makes a great point of that. You saw how quickly she was gone. I hope I have not done a very foolish thing in taking charge of the young lady."

For my part, I was delighted. I was longing to see and talk to her; and only waiting till the doctor should give me leave. You who live in towns, can have no idea how great an event the introduction of a new friend is, in such a solitude as surrounded us.

The doctor did not arrive till nearly one o'clock; but I could no more have gone to my bed and slept, than I could have overtaken, on foot, the carriage in which the princess in black velvet had driven away.

When the physician came down to the drawing-room, it was to report very favorably upon his patient. She was now sitting up, her pulse quite regular, apparently perfectly well. She had sustained no injury, and the little shock to her nerves had passed away quite harmlessly. There could be no harm certainly in my seeing her, if we both wished it; and, with this permission, I sent forthwith, to know whether she would allow me to visit her for a few minutes in her room.

The servant returned immediately to say that she desired nothing more.

You may be sure I was not long in availing myself of this permission.

Our visitor lay in one of the handsomest rooms in the schloss. It was, perhaps a little stately. There was a somber piece of tapestry opposite the foot of the bed, representing Cleopatra with the asp to her bosom; and other solemn classic scenes were displaced, a little faded, upon the other walls. But there was gold carving, and rich and varied color enough in the other decorations of the room, to more than redeem the gloom of the old tapestry.

There were candles at the bed side. She was sitting up; her slender pretty figure enveloped in the soft silk dressing-gown, embroidered with flowers, and lined with thick quilted silk, which her mother had thrown over her feet as she lay upon the ground.

What was it that, as I reached the bedside and had just begun my little greeting, struck me dumb in a moment, and made me recoil a step or two from before her? I will tell you.

I saw the very face which had visited me in my childhood at night, which remained so fixed in my memory, and on which I had for so many years so often ruminated with horror, when no one suspected of what I was thinking.

It was pretty, even beautiful; and when I first beheld it, wore the same melancholy expression.

But this almost instantly lighted into a strange fixed smile of recognition.

There was a silence of fully a minute, and then at length *she* spoke; *I* could not.

"How wonderful!" she exclaimed. "Twelve years ago, I saw your face in a dream, and it has haunted me ever since."

"Wonderful indeed!" I repeated, overcoming with an effort the horror that had for a time suspended my utterances. "Twelve years ago, in vision or reality, *I* certainly saw you. I could not forget your face. It has remained before my eyes ever since."

Her smile had softened. Whatever I had fancied strange in it, was gone, and it and her dimpling cheeks were now delightfully pretty and intelligent.

I felt reassured, and continued more in the vein which hospitality indicated, to bid her welcome, and to tell her how much pleasure her accidental arrival had given us all, and especially what a happiness it was to me.

I took her hand as I spoke. I was a little shy, as lonely people are, but the situation made me eloquent, and even bold. She pressed my hand, she laid hers upon it, and her eyes glowed, as, looking hastily into mine, she smiled again, and blushed.

She answered my welcome very prettily. I sat down beside her, still wondering; and she said:

"I must tell you my vision about you; it is so very strange that you and I should have had, each of the other so vivid a dream, that each should have seen, I you and you me, looking as we do now, when of course we both were mere children. I was a child about six years old, and I awoke from a confused and troubled dream, and found myself in a room, unlike my nursery, wainscoted clumsily in some dark wood, and with cupboards and bedsteads, and chairs, and benches placed about it. The beds were, I thought, all empty, and the room itself without any one but myself in it; and I, after looking about me for some time, and admiring especially an iron candlestick, with two branches, which I should certainly know again, crept under one of the beds to reach the window; but as I got from under the bed, I heard someone crying; and looking up, while I was still upon my knees, I saw *you*—most assuredly you—as I see you now; a beautiful young lady, with golden hair and large blue eyes, and lips—your lips—you, as you are here. Your looks won me; I climbed on the bed and put my arms about you, and I think we both fell asleep. I was aroused by a scream; you were sitting up screaming. I was frightened, and slipped down upon the ground, and, it seemed to me, lost consciousness for a moment; and when I came to myself, I was again in my nursery at home. Your face I have never forgotten since. I could not be misled by mere resemblance. You *are* the lady whom I then saw."

It was now my turn to relate my corresponding vision, which I did, to the undisguised wonder of my new acquaintance.

"I don't know which should be most afraid of the other," she said, again smiling. "If you were less pretty I think I should be very much afraid of you, but being as you are, and you and I both so young, I feel only that I have made your acquaintance twelve years ago, and have already a right to your intimacy; at all events, it does seem as if we were destined, from our earliest childhood, to be friends. I wonder whether you feel as strangely drawn towards me as I do to you; I have never had a friend—shall I find one now?" She sighed, and her fine dark eyes gazed passionately on me.

Now the truth is, I felt rather unaccountably towards the beautiful stranger. I did feel, as she said, "drawn towards her," but there was also something of repulsion. In this ambiguous feeling, however, the sense of attraction immensely prevailed. She interested and won me; she was so beautiful and so indescribably engaging.

I perceived now something of languor and exhaustion stealing over her, and hastened to bid her goodnight.

"The doctor thinks," I added, "that you ought to have a maid to sit up with you tonight; one of ours is waiting, and you will find her a very useful and quiet creature."

"How kind of you, but I could not sleep, I never could with an attendant in the room. I shan't require any assistance—and, shall I confess my weakness, I am haunted with a terror of robbers. Our house was robbed once, and two servants murdered, so I always lock my door. It has become a habit—and you look so kind I know you will forgive me. I see there is a key in the lock."

She held me close in her pretty arms for a moment and whispered in my ear, "Goodnight, darling, it is very hard to part with you, but goodnight; tomorrow, but not early, I shall see you again."

She sank back on the pillow with a sigh, and her fine eyes

followed me with a fond and melancholy gaze, and she murmured again, "Goodnight, dear friend."

Young people like, and even love, on impulse. I was flattered by the evident, though as yet undeserved, fondness she showed me. I liked the confidence with which she at once received me. She was determined that we should be very dear friends.

Next day came and we met again. I was delighted with my companion; that is to say, in many respects.

Her looks lost nothing in daylight—she was certainly the most beautiful creature I had ever seen, and the unpleasant remembrance of the face presented in my early dream, had lost the effect of the first unexpected recognition.

She confessed that she had experienced a similar shock on seeing me, and precisely the same faint antipathy that had mingled with my admiration of her. We now laughed together over our momentary horrors.

Her Habits—A Saunter
IV

I told you that I was charmed with her in most particulars.
There were some that did not please me so well.

She was above the middle height of women. I shall begin by describing her. She was slender, and wonderfully graceful. Except that her movements were languid—*very* languid—indeed, there was nothing in her appearance to indicate an invalid. Her complexion was rich and brilliant; her features were small and beautifully formed; her eyes large, dark, and lustrous; her hair was quite wonderful, I never saw hair so magnificently thick and long when it was down about her shoulders; I have often placed my hands under it, and laughed with wonder at its weight. It was exquisitely fine and soft, and in color a rich very dark brown, with something of gold. I loved to let it down, tumbling with its own weight, as, in her room, she lay back in her chair talking in her sweet low voice, I used to fold and braid it, and spread it out and play with it. Heavens! If I had but known all!

I said there were particulars which did not please me. I have told you that her confidence won me the first night I saw her; but I found that she exercised with respect to herself, her mother, her history, everything in fact connected with her life, plans, and people an ever-wakeful reserve. I dare say I was unreasonable, perhaps I was wrong; I dare say I ought to have respected the solemn injunction laid upon my father by the stately lady in black velvet. But curiosity is a restless and unscrupulous passion, and no one girl can endure, with patience, that hers should be baffled by another. What harm could it do anyone to tell me what I so ardently desired to know? Had she no trust in my good sense or honor? Why would she not believe me when I assured her, so solemnly, that I would not divulge one syllable of what she told me to any mortal breathing.

There was a coldness, it seemed to me, beyond her years, in her smiling melancholy persistent refusal to afford me the least ray of light.

I cannot say we quarreled upon this point, for she would not quarrel upon any. It was, of course, very unfair of me to press her, very ill-bred, but I really could not help it; and I might just as well have let it alone.

What she did tell me amounted, in my unconscionable estimation—to nothing.

It was all summed up in three very vague disclosures.

First.—Her name was Carmilla.

Second.—Her family was very ancient and noble.

Third.—Her home lay in the direction of the west.

She would not tell me the name of her family, nor their armorial bearings, nor the name of the estate, nor even that of the country they lived in.

You are not to suppose that I worried her incessantly on these subjects. I watched opportunity, and rather insinuated than urged my inquiries. Once or twice, indeed, I did attack more directly. But no matter what my tactics, utter failure was invariably the result. Reproaches and caresses were all lost upon her. But I must add this, that her evasion was conducted with so pretty a melancholy and deprecation, and so many, and even passionate declarations of her liking for me, and trust in my honor, and with so many promises, that I should at last know all, that I could not find it in my heart long to be offended with her.

She used to place her pretty arms about my neck, draw me to her, and laying her cheek to mine, murmur with her lips near my ear, "Dearest, your little heart is wounded; think me not cruel because I obey the irresistible law of my strength and weakness; if your dear heart is wounded, my wild heart bleeds with yours. In the rapture of my enormous humiliation I live in your warm life, and you shall die—die, sweetly die—into mine. I cannot help it; as I draw near to you, you, in your turn, will draw near to others, and learn the rapture of that cruelty, which yet is love; so, for a while, seek to know no more of me and mine, but trust me with all your loving spirit.''

And when she had spoken such a rhapsody, she would press me more closely in her trembling embrace, and her lips in soft kisses gently glow upon my cheek.

Her agitations and her language were unintelligible to me.

From these foolish embraces, which were not of very frequent occurrence, I must allow, I used to wish to extricate myself; but my energies seemed to fail me. Her murmured words sounded like a lullaby in my ear, and soothed my resistance into a trance, from which I only seemed to recover myself when she withdrew her arms.

In these mysterious moods I did not like her. I experienced a strange tumultuous excitement that was pleasurable, ever and anon, mingled with a vague sense of fear and disgust. I had no distinct thoughts about her while such scenes lasted, but I was conscious of a love growing into adoration, and also of abhorrence. This I know is paradox, but I can make no other attempt to explain the feeling.

I now write, after an interval of more than ten years, with a trembling hand, with a confused and horrible recollection of certain occurrences and situations, in the ordeal through which I was unconsciously passing; though with a vivid and very sharp remembrance of the main current of my story. But, I suspect, in all lives there are certain emotional scenes, those in which our passions have been most wildly and terribly roused, that are of all others the most vaguely and dimly remembered.

Sometimes after an hour of apathy, my strange and beautiful companion would take my hand and hold it with a fond pressure, renewed again and again; blushing softly, gazing in my face with languid and burning eyes, and breathing so fast that her dress rose and fell with the tumultuous respiration. It was like the ardor of a lover; it embarrassed me; it was hateful and yet overpowering; and with gloating eyes she drew me to her, and her hot lips travelled along my cheek in kisses; and she would whisper, almost in sobs, "You are mine, you *shall* be mine, and you and I are one for ever." Then she has thrown herself back in her chair, with her small hands over her eyes, leaving me trembling.

"Are we related," I used to ask; "what can you mean by all this? I remind you perhaps of some one whom you love; but you must not, I hate it; I don't know you—I don't know myself when you look so and talk so."

She used to sigh at my vehemence, then turn away and drop my hand.

Respecting these very extraordinary manifestations I strove in vain to form any satisfactory theory—could not refer them to affectation or trick. It was unmistakably the momentary breaking out of suppressed instinct and emotion. Was she, notwithstanding her mother's volunteered denial, subject to brief visitations of insanity; or was there here a disguise and a romance? I had read in old story books of such things. What if a boyish lover had found his way into the house, and sought to make advances in masquerade, with the assistance of a clever old adventuress. But here were many things against this hypothesis, highly interesting as it was to my vanity.

I could boast of no little attentions such as masculine gallantry delights to offer. Between these passionate moments there were long intervals of commonplace, of gaiety, of brooding melancholy, during which, except that I detected her eyes so full of melancholy fire, following me, at times I might have been as nothing to her. Except in these brief periods of mysterious excitement her ways were girlish; and there was always a languor about her, quite incompatible with a masculine system in a state of health.

In some respects her habits were odd. Perhaps not so singular in the opinion of a town lady like you, as they appeared to us rustic people. She used to come down very late, generally not till one o'clock, she would then take a cup of chocolate, but eat nothing; we then went out for a walk, which was a mere saunter, and she seemed, almost immediately, exhausted, and either returned to the schloss or sat on one of the benches that were placed, here and there, among the trees. This was a bodily languor in which her mind did not sympathize. She was always an animated talker, and very intelligent.

She sometimes alluded for a moment to her own home, or mentioned an adventure or situation, or an early recollection, which indicated a people of strange manners, and described customs of which we knew nothing. I gathered from these chance hints that her native country was much more remote than I had at first fancied.

As we sat thus one afternoon under the trees, a funeral passed us by. It was that of a pretty young girl, whom I had often seen, the daughter of one of the rangers of the forest. The poor man was walking behind the coffin of his darling; she was his only child, and he looked quite heartbroken. Peasants walking two-and-two came behind, they were singing a funeral hymn.

I rose to mark my respect as they passed, and joined in the hymn they were very sweetly singing.

My companion shook me a little roughly, and I turned surprised.

She said brusquely, "Don't you perceive how discordant that is?"

"I think it is very sweet, on the contrary," I answered, vexed at the interruption, and very uncomfortable, lest the people who composed the little procession should observe and resent what was passing.

I resumed, therefore, instantly, and was again interrupted. "You pierce my ears," said Carmilla, almost angrily, and stopping her ears with her tiny fingers. "Besides, how can you tell that your religion and mine are the same; your forms wound me, and I hate funerals. What a fuss! Why, *you* must die—*everyone* must die; and all are happier when they do. Come home."

"My father has gone on with the clergyman to the churchyard. I thought you knew she was to be buried today."

"*She?* I don't trouble my head about peasants. I don't know who she is," answered Carmilla, with a flash from her fine eyes.

"She is the poor girl who fancied she saw a ghost a fortnight ago, and has been dying ever since, till yesterday, when she expired."

"Tell me nothing about ghosts. I shan't sleep tonight if you do."

"I hope there is no plague or fever coming; all this looks very like it," I continued. "The swineherd's young wife died only a week ago, and she thought something seized her by the throat as she lay in her bed, and nearly strangled her. Papa says such horrible fancies do accompany some forms of fever. She was quite well the day before. She sank afterwards, and died before a week."

"Well, *her* funeral is over, I hope, and *her* hymn sung; and our ears shan't be tortured with that discord and jargon. It has made me nervous. Sit down here, beside me; sit close; hold my hand; press it hard—hard—harder."

We had moved a little back, and had come to another seat.

She sat down. Her face underwent a change that alarmed and even terrified me for a moment. It darkened, and became horribly livid; her teeth and hands were clenched, and she frowned and compressed her lips, while she stared down upon the ground at her feet, and trembled all over with a continued shudder as irrespressible as ague. All her energies seemed strained to suppress a fit, with which she was then breathlessly tugging; and at length a low convulsive cry of suffering broke from her, and gradually the hysteria subsided. "There! That comes of strangling people with hymns!" she said at last. "Hold me, hold me still. It is passing away."

And so gradually it did; and perhaps to dissipate the somber impression which the spectacle had left upon me, she became unusually animated and talkative; and so we got home.

This was the first time I had seen her exhibit any definable symptoms of that delicacy of health which her mother had spoken of. It was the first time, also, I had seen her exhibit anything like temper.

Both passed away like a summer cloud; and never but once afterwards did I witness on her part a momentary sign of anger. I will tell you how it happened.

She and I were looking out of one of the long drawing-room windows, when there entered the courtyard, over the drawbridge, a figure of a wanderer whom I knew very well. He used to visit the schloss generally twice a year.

It was the figure of a hunchback, with the sharp lean features that generally accompany deformity. He wore a pointed black beard, and he was smiling from ear to ear, showing his white fangs. He was dressed in buff, black, and scarlet, and crossed with more straps and belts than I could count, from which hung all manner of things. Behind, he carried a magic-lantern, and two boxes, which I well knew, in one of which was a salamander, and in the other a mandrake. These monsters used to make my father laugh. They were compounded of parts of monkeys, parrots, squirrels, fish, and hedgehogs, dried and stitched together with great neatness and startling effect. He had a fiddle, a box of conjuring apparatus, a pair of foils and masks attached to his belt, several other mysterious cases dangling about him, and a black staff with copper ferrules in his hand. His companion was a rough spare dog, that followed at his heels, but stopped short, suspiciously at the drawbridge, and in a little while began to howl dismally.

In the meantime, the mountebank, standing in the midst of the courtyard, raised his grotesque hat, and made us a very ceremonious bow, paying his compliments very volubly in execrable French, and German not much better. Then, disengaging his fiddle, he began to scrape a lively air, to which he sang with a merry discord, dancing with ludicrous airs and activity, that made me laugh, in spite of the dog's howling.

Then he advanced to the window with many smiles and salutations, and his hat in his left hand, his fiddle under his arm, and with a fluency that never took breath, he gabbled a long advertisement of all his accomplishments, and the resources of the various arts which he placed at our service, and the curiosities and entertainments which it was in his power, at our bidding to display.

"Will your ladyships be pleased to buy an amulet against the vampire, which is going like the wolf, I hear, through these woods," he said, dropping his hat on the pavement. "They are dying of it right and left, and here is a charm that never fails; only pinned to the pillow, and you may laugh in his face."

These charms consisted of oblong slips of vellum, with cabalistic ciphers and diagrams upon them.

Carmilla instantly purchased one, and so did I.

He was looking up, and we were smiling down upon him, amused; at least, I can answer for myself. His piercing black eye, as he looked up in our faces, seemed to detect something that fixed for a moment his curiosity.

In an instant he unrolled a leather case, full of all manner of odd little steel instruments.

"See here, my lady," he said, displaying it, and addressing me, "I profess, among other things less useful, the art of dentistry. Plague take the dog!" he interpolated. "Silence, beast! He howls so that your ladyships can scarcely hear a word. Your noble friend, the young lady at your right, has the sharpest tooth—long, thin, pointed, like an awl, like a needle; ha, ha! With my sharp and long sight, as I look up, I have seen it distinctly; now if it happens to hurt the young lady, and I think it must, here am I, here are my file, my punch, my nippers; I will make it round and blunt, if her ladyship pleases; no longer the tooth of a fish, but of a beautiful young lady as she is. Hey? Is the young lady displeased? Have I been too bold? Have I offended her?"

The young lady, indeed, looked very angry as she drew back from the window.

"How dares that mountebank insult us so? Where is your father? I shall demand redress from him. My father would have had the wretch tied up to the pump, and flogged with a cartwhip, and burnt to the bones with the castle brand!"

She retired from the window a step or two, and sat down, and hardly lost sight of the offender, when her wrath subsided as suddenly as it had risen, and she gradually recovered her usual tone, and seemed to forget the little hunchback and his follies.

My father was out of spirits that evening. On coming in he told us that there had been another case similar to the two fatal ones which had lately occurred. The sister of a young peasant on his estate, only a mile away, was very ill, had been, as she described it, attacked very nearly in the same way, and was now slowly but steadily sinking.

"All this," said my father, "is strictly referable to natural causes. These poor people infect one another with their superstitions, and so repeat in imagination the images of terror that have infested their neighbors."

"But that very circumstance frightens one horribly," said Carmilla.

"How so?" inquired my father.

"I am so afraid of fancying I see such things; I think it would be as bad as reality."

"We are in God's hands; nothing can happen without His permission, and all will end well for those who love Him. He is our faithful creator; He had made us all, and will take care of us."

"Creator! *Nature!*" said the young lady in answer to my gentle father. "And this disease that invades the country is natural. Nature. All things proceed from Nature—don't they? All things in the heaven, in the earth, and under the earth, act and live as Nature ordains? I think so."

"The doctor said he would come here today," said my father,

after a silence. "I want to know what he thinks about it, and what he thinks we had better do."

"Doctors never did me any good," said Carmilla.

"Then you have been ill?" I asked.

"More ill than ever you were," she answered.

"Long ago?"

"Yes, a long time. I suffered from this very illness; but I forget all but my pain and weakness, and they were not so bad as are suffered in other diseases."

"You were very young then?"

"I dare say; let us talk no more of it. You would not wound a friend?" She looked languidly in my eyes, and passed her arm round my waist lovingly, and led me out of the room. My father was busy over some papers near the window.

"Why does your papa like to frighten us?" said the pretty girl, with a sigh and a little shudder.

"He doesn't, dear Carmilla, it is the very furthest thing from his mind."

"Are you afraid, dearest?"

"I should be very much if I fancied there was any real danger of my being attacked as those poor people were."

"You are afraid to die?"

"Yes, every one is."

"But to die as lovers may—to die together, so that they may live together. Girls are caterpillars while they live in the world, to be finally butterflies when the summer comes; but in the meantime there are grubs and larvae, don't you see—each with their peculiar propensities, necessities and structure. So says Monsieur Buffon, in his big book, in the next room."

Later in the day the doctor came, and was closeted with papa for some time. He was a skilful man, of sixty and upwards, he wore powder, and shaved his pale face as smooth as a pumpkin. He and papa emerged from the room together, and I heard papa laugh, and say as they came out:

"Well, I do wonder at a wise man like you. What do you say to hippogriffs and dragons?"

The doctor was smiling, and made answer, shaking his head—

"Nevertheless, life and death are mysterious states, and we know little of the resources of either."

And so they walked on, and I heard no more. I did not then

know what the doctor had been suggesting, but I think I guess it now.

A Wonderful Likeness
V

This evening there arrived from Gratz the grave, dark-faced son of the picture-cleaner, with a horse and cart laden with two large packing-cases, having many pictures in each. It was a journey of ten leagues, and whenever a messenger arrived at the schloss from our little capital of Gratz, we used to crowd about him in the hall, to hear the news.

This arrival created in our secluded quarters quite a sensation. The cases remained in the hall, and the messenger was taken charge of by the servants till he had eaten his supper. Then with assistants, and armed with hammer, ripping chisel, and turnscrew he met us in the hall; where we had assembled to witness the unpacking of the cases.

Carmilla sat looking listlessly on, while one after the other the old pictures, nearly all portraits, which had undergone the process of renovation, were brought to light. My mother was of an old Hungarian family, and most of these pictures, which were about to be restored to their places, had come to us through her.

My father had a list in his hand, from which he read, as the artist rummaged out the corresponding numbers. I don't know that the pictures were very good, but they were, undoubtedly very old, and some of them very curious also. They had, for the most part, the merit of being now seen by me, I may say, for the first time; for the smoke and dust of time had all but obliterated them.

"There is a picture that I have not seen yet," said my father. "In one corner, at the top of it, is the name, as well as I could read, 'Marcia Karnstein,' and the date '1698'; and I am curious to see how it has turned out."

I remembered it; it was a small picture, about a foot and a half high, and nearly square, without a frame; but it was so blackened by age that I could not make it out.

The artist now produced it, with evident pride. It was quite beautiful; it was startling; it seemed to live. It was the likeness of Carmilla!

"Carmilla, dear, here is an absolute miracle. Here you are, living, smiling, ready to speak, in this picture. Isn't it beautiful, papa? And see, even the little mole on her throat."

My father laughed, and said "Certainly it is a wonderful likeness," but he looked away, and to my surprise seemed but little struck by it, and went on talking to the picture-cleaner, who was also something of an artist, and discoursed with intelligence about the portraits of other works, which his art had just brought into light and color, while I was more and more lost in wonder the more I looked at the picture.

"Will you let me hang this picture in my room, papa?" I asked.

"Certainly dear," said he, smiling, "I'm very glad you think it so like. It must be prettier even than I thought it, if it is."

The young lady did not acknowledge this pretty speech, did not seem to hear it. She was leaning back in her seat, her fine eyes under their long lashes gazing on me in contemplation, and she smiled in a kind of rapture.

"And now you can read quite plainly the name that is written in the corner. It is not Marcia; it looks as if it was done in gold. The name is Mircalla, Countess Karnstein, and this is a little coronet over it, and underneath A.D. 1698. I am descended from the Karnsteins; that is, mamma was."

"Ah!" said the lady, languidly, "so am I, I think, a very long descent, very ancient. Are there any Karnsteins living now?"

"None who bear the name, I believe. The family were ruined, I believe, in some civil wars, long ago, but the ruins of the castle are only about three miles away."

"How interesting!" she said, languidly. "But see what beautiful moonlight!" She glanced through the hall door, which stood a little open. "Suppose you take a little ramble round the court and look down at the road and river."

"It is so like the night you came to us," I said.

She sighed, smiling.

She rose, and each with her arm about the other's waist, we walked out upon the pavement.

In silence, slowly we walked down to the drawbridge, where the beautiful landscape opened before us.

"And so you were thinking of the night I came here?" she almost whispered. "Are you glad I came?"

"Delighted, dear Carmilla," I answered.

"And you asked for the picture you think like me, to hang in your room," she murmured with a sigh, as she drew her arm closer about my waist, and let her pretty head sink upon my shoulder.

"How romantic you are, Carmilla," I said. "Whenever you tell me your story, it will be made up chiefly of some one great romance."

She kissed me silently.

"I am sure, Carmilla, you have been in love; that there is, at this moment, an affair of the heart going on."

"I have been in love with no one, and never shall," she whispered, "unless it should be with you."

How beautiful she looked in the moonlight!

Shy and strange was the look with which she quickly hid her face in my neck and hair, with tumultuous sighs, that seemed to sob, and pressed in mine a hand that trembled.

Her soft cheek was glowing against mine. "Darling, darling," she murmured, "I live in you; and you would die for me, I love you so."

I started from her.

She was glazing on me with eyes from which all fire, all meaning had flown, and a face colorless and apathetic.

"Is there a chill in the air, dear?" she said drowsily. "I almost shiver; have I been dreaming? Let us come in. Come, come; come in."

"You look ill, Carmilla; a little faint. You certainly must take some wine," I said.

"Yes, I will. I'm better now. I shall be quite well in a few minutes. Yes, do give me a little wine," answered Carmilla, as we approached the door. "Let us look again for a moment; it is the last time, perhaps, I shall see the moonlight with you."

"How do you feel now, dear Carmilla? Are you really better?" I asked.

I was beginning to take alarm lest she should have been stricken with the strange epidemic that they said had invaded the country about us.

"Papa would be grieved beyond measure," I added, "if he thought you were ever so little ill, without immediately letting us know. We have a very skilful doctor near this, the physician who was with papa today."

"I'm sure he is. I know how kind you all are; but, dear child, I

am quite well again. There is nothing ever wrong with me but a
little weakness. People say I am languid; I am incapable of exertion; I can scarcely walk as far as a child of three years old; and
every now and then the little strength I have falters, and I become
as you have just seen me. But after all I am very easily set up again;
in a moment I am perfectly myself. See how I have recovered."

So, indeed, she had; and she and I talked a great deal, and very
animated she was; and the remainder of that evening passed without any recurrence of what I called her infatuations. I mean her
crazy talk and looks, which embarrassed, and even frightened me.

But there occurred that night an ᴠent which gave my thoughts
quite a new turn, and seemed to startle even Carmilla's languid
nature into momentary energy.

A Very Strange Agony
VI

When we got into the drawing-room, and had sat down to our
coffee and chocolate, although Carmilla did not take any, she
seemed quite herself again, and Madame, and Mademoiselle De-
Lafontaine, joined us, and made a little card party, in the course of
which papa came in for what he called his "dish of tea."

When the game was over he sat down beside Carmilla on the
sofa, and asked her, a little anxiously, whether she had heard from
her mother since her arrival.

She answered "No."

He then asked her whether she knew where a letter would reach
her at present.

"I cannot tell," she answered, ambiguously, "but I have been
thinking of leaving you; you have been already too hospitable and
too kind to me. I have given you an infinity of trouble, and I
should wish to take a carriage tomorrow and post in pursuit of
her; I know where I shall ultimately find her, although I dare not
yet tell you."

"But you must not dream of any such thing," exclaimed my
father, to my great relief. "We can't afford to lose you so, and I
won't consent to your leaving us, except under the care of your
mother, who was so good as to consent to your remaining with us
till she should herself return. I should be quite happy if I knew
that you heard from her; but this evening the accounts of the

progress of the mysterious disease that has invaded our neighborhood, grow even more alarming; and my beautiful guest, I do feel
the responsibility, unaided by advice from your mother, very
much. But I shall do my best; and one thing is certain, that you
must not think of leaving us without her distinct direction to that
effect. We should suffer too much in parting from you to consent
to it easily."

"Thank you, sir, a thousand times for your hospitality," she
answered, smiling bashfully. "You have all been too kind to me; I
have seldom been so happy in all my life before, as in your beautiful château, under your care, and in the society of your dear
daughter."

So he gallantly, in his old-fashioned way, kissed her hand, smiling, and pleased at her little speech.

I accompanied Carmilla as usual to her room, and sat and chatted with her while she was preparing for bed.

"Do you think," I said, at length, "that you will ever confide
fully in me?"

She turned round smiling, but made no answer, only continued
to smile on me.

"You won't answer that?" I said. "You can't answer pleasantly; I
ought not to have asked you."

"You were quite right to ask me that, or anything. You do not
know how dear you are to me, or you could not think any confidence too great to look for. But I am under vows, no nun half so
awfully, and I dare not tell my story yet, even to you. The time is
very near when you shall know everything. You will think me
cruel, very selfish, but love is always selfish; the more ardent the
more selfish. How jealous I am you cannot know. You must come
with me, loving me, to death; or else hate me, and still come with
me, and *hating* me through death and after. There is no such word
as indifference in my apathetic nature."

"Now, Carmilla, you are going to talk your wild nonsense
again," I said hastily.

"Not I, silly little fool as I am, and full of whims and fancies; for
your sake I'll talk like a sage. Were you ever at a ball?"

"No; how you do run on. What is it like? How charming it must
be."

"I almost forget, it is years ago."

I laughed.

"You are not so old. Your first ball can hardly be forgotten yet."

"I remember everything about it—with an effort. I see it all, as divers see what is going on above them, through a medium, dense, rippling, but transparent. There occurred that night what has confused the picture, and made its colors faint. I was all but assassinated in my bed, wounded *here*," she touched her breast, "and never was the same since."

"Were you near dying?"

"Yes, very—a cruel love—strange love, that would have taken my life. Love will have its sacrifices. No sacrifice without blood. Let us go to sleep now; I feel so lazy. How can I get up just now and lock my door?"

She was lying with her tiny hands buried in her rich wavy hair, under her cheek, her little head upon the pillow, and her glittering eyes followed me wherever I moved, with a kind of shy smile that I could not decipher.

I bid her goodnight, and crept from the room with an uncomfortable sensation.

I often wondered whether our pretty guest ever said her prayers. I certainly had never seen her upon her knees. In the morning she never came down until long after our family prayers were over, and at night she never left the drawingroom to attend our brief evening prayers in the hall.

If it had not been that it had casually come out in one of our careless talks that she had been baptized, I should have doubted her being a Christian. Religion was a subject on which I had never heard her speak a word. If I had known the world better, this particular neglect or antipathy would not have so much surprised me.

The precautions of nervous people are infectious, and persons of a like temperament are pretty sure, after a time, to imitate them. I had adopted Carmilla's habit of locking her bedroom door, having taken into my head all her whimsical alarms about midnight invaders, and prowling assassins. I had also adopted her precaution of making a brief search through her room, to satisfy herself that no lurking assassin or robber was "ensconced."

These wise measures taken, I got into my bed and fell asleep. A light was burning in my room. This was an old habit, of very early date, and which nothing could have tempted me to dispense with.

Thus fortified I might take my rest in peace. But dreams come through stone walls, light up dark rooms, or darken light ones, and their persons make their exits and their entrances as they please, and laugh at locksmiths.

I had a dream that night that was the beginning of a very strange agony.

I cannot call it a nightmare, for I was quite conscious of being asleep. But I was equally conscious of being in my room, and lying in bed, precisely as I actually was. I saw, or fancied I saw the room and its furniture just as I had seen it last, except that it was very dark, and I saw something moving round the foot of the bed, which at first I could not accurately distinguish. But I soon saw that it was a sooty-black animal that resembled a monstrous cat. It appeared to me about four or five feet long, for it measured fully the length of the hearth-rug as it passed over it; and it continued to-ing and fro-ing with the lithe sinister restlessness of a beast in a cage. I could not cry out, although as you may suppose, I was terrified. Its pace was growing faster, and the room rapidly darker and darker, and at length so dark that I could no longer see anything of it but its eyes. I felt it spring lightly on the bed. The two broad eyes approached my face, and suddenly I felt a stinging pain as if two large needles darted, an inch or two apart, deep into my breast. I awoke with a scream. The room was lighted by the candle that burnt there all through the night, and I saw a female figure standing at the foot of the bed, a little at the right side. It was in a dark loose dress, and its hair was down and covered its shoulders. A block of stone could not have been more still. There was not the slightest stir of respiration. As I stared at it, the figure appeared to have changed its place, and was now nearer the door; then, close to it, the door opened, and it passed out.

I was now relieved, and able to breathe and move. My first thought was that Carmilla had been playing me a trick, and that I had forgotten to secure my door. I hastened to it, and found it locked as usual on the inside. I was afraid to open it—I was horrified. I sprang into my bed and covered my head up in the bedclothes, and lay there more dead than alive till morning.

Descending
VII

I t would be vain my attempting to tell you the horror with which, even now, I recall the occurrence of that night. It was no such transitory terror as a dream leaves behind it. It seemed to deepen by time, and communicated itself to the room and the very furniture that had encompassed the apparition.

I could not bear next day to be alone for a moment. I should have told papa, but for two opposite reasons. At one time I thought he would laugh at my story, and I could not bear its being treated as a jest; and at another, I thought he might fancy that I had been attacked by the mysterious complaint which had invaded our neighborhood. I had myself no misgivings of the kind, and as he had been rather an invalid for some time, I was afraid of alarming him.

I was comfortable enough with my good-natured companions, Madame Perrodon, and the vivacious Mademoiselle Lafontaine. They both perceived that I was out of spirits and nervous and at length I told them what lay so heavy at my heart.

Mademoiselle laughed, but I fancied that Madame Perrodon looked anxious.

"By-the-by," said Mademoiselle, laughing, "the long lime tree walk, behind Carmilla's bedroom window, is haunted!"

"Nonsense!" exclaimed Madame, who probably thought the theme rather inopportune, "and who tells that story, my dear?"

"Martin says that he came up twice, when the old yard-gate was being repaired before sunrise, and twice saw the same female figure walking down the lime tree avenue."

"So he well might, as long as there are cows to milk in the river fields," said Madame.

"I dare say; but Martin chooses to be frightened, and never did I see a fool *more* frightened."

"You must not say a word about it to Carmilla, because she can see down that walk from her room window," I interposed, "and she is, if possible, a greater coward than I."

Carmilla came down rather later than usual that day.

"I was so frightened last night," she said so soon as we were together, "and I am sure I should have seen something dreadful if it had not been for that charm I bought from the poor little hunchback whom I called such hard names. I had a dream of something black coming round my bed, and I awoke in a perfect horror, and I really thought, for some seconds, I saw a dark figure near the chimney piece, but I felt under my pillow for my charm, and the moment my fingers touched it, the figure disappeared, and I felt quite certain, only that I had it by me, that something frightful would have made its appearance, and perhaps, throttled me, as it did those poor people we heard of."

"Well, listen to me," I began, and recounted my adventure, at the recital of which she appeared horrified.

"And had you the charm near you?" she asked, earnestly.

"No, I had dropped it into a china vase in the drawingroom, but I shall certainly take it with me tonight, as you have so much faith in it."

At this distance of time I cannot tell you, or even understand, how I overcame my horror so effectually as to lie alone in my room that night. I remember distinctly that I pinned the charm to my pillow. I fell asleep almost immediately, and slept even more soundly than usual all night.

Next night I passed as well. My sleep was delightfully deep and dreamless. But I wakened with a sense of lassitude and melancholy which, however, did not exceed a degree that was almost luxurious.

"Well, I told you so," said Carmilla, when I described my quiet sleep, "I had such delightful sleep myself last night; I pinned the charm to the breast of my nightdress. It was too far away the night before. I am quite sure it was all fancy except the dreams. I used to think that evil spirits made dreams, but our doctor told me it is no such thing. Only a fever passing by, or some other malady, as they often do, he said, knocks at the door, and not being able to get in, passes on, with that alarm."

"And what do you think the charm is?" said I.

"It has been fumigated or immersed in some drug, and is an antidote against the malaria," she answered.

"Then it acts only on the body?"

"Certainly; you don't suppose that evil spirits are frightened by bits of ribbon, or the perfumes of a druggist's shop? No, these complaints, wandering in the air, begin by trying the nerves, and so infect the brain; but before they can seize upon you, the antidote repels them. That I am sure is what the charm has done for us. It is nothing magical, it is simply natural."

I should have been happier if I could quite have agreed with Carmilla, but I did my best, and the impression was a little losing its force.

For some nights I slept profoundly; but still every morning I felt the same lassitude, and a languor weighed upon me all day. I felt myself a changed girl. A strange melancholy was stealing over me, a melancholy that I would not have interrupted. Dim thoughts of death began to open, and an idea that I was slowly sinking took gentle, and, somehow, not unwelcome possession of me. If it was sad, the tone of mind which this induced was also sweet. Whatever it might be, my soul acquiesced in it.

I would not admit that I was ill, I would not consent to tell my papa, or to have the doctor sent for.

Carmilla became more devoted to me than ever, and her strange paroxysms of languid adoration more frequent. She used to dote on me with increasing ardor the more my strength and spirits waned. This always shocked me like a momentary glare of insanity.

Without knowing it, I was now in a pretty advanced stage of the strangest illness under which mortal ever suffered. There was an unaccountable fascination in its earlier symptoms that more than reconciled me to the incapacitating effect of that stage of the malady. This fascination increased for a time, until it reached a certain point, when gradually a sense of the horrible mingled itself with it, deepening, as you shall hear, until it discolored and perverted the whole state of my life.

The first change I experienced was rather agreeable. It was very near the turning point from which began the descent of Avernus.

Certain vague and strange sensations visited me in my sleep. The prevailing one was of that pleasant, peculiar cold thrill which we feel in bathing, when we move against the current of a river. This was soon accompanied by dreams that seemed interminable, and were so vague that I could never recollect their scenery and persons, or any one connected portion of their action. But they left an awful impression, and a sense of exhaustion, as if I had passed through a long period of great mental exertion and danger. After all these dreams there remained on waking a remembrance of having been in a place very nearly dark, and of having spoken to people whom I could not see; and especially of one clear voice, of a female's, very deep, that spoke as if at a distance, slowly, and producing always the same sensation of indescribable solemnity and fear. Sometimes there came a sensation as if a hand was drawn softly along my cheek and neck. Sometimes it was as if warm lips kissed me, and longer and more lovingly as they reached my throat, but there the caress fixed itself. My heart beat faster, my breathing rose and fell rapidly and full drawn; a sobbing, that rose into a sense of strangulation, supervened, and turned into a dreadful convulsion, in which my senses left me, and I became unconscious.

It was now three weeks since the commencement of this unaccountable state. My sufferings had, during the last week, told upon my appearance. I had grown pale, my eyes were dilated and darkened underneath, and the languor which I had long felt began to display itself in my countenance.

My father asked me often whether I was ill; but, with an obstinacy which now seems to me unaccountable, I persisted in assuring him that I was quite well.

In a sense this was true. I had no pain, I could complain of no bodily derangement. My complaint seemed to be one of the imagination, or the nerves, and, horrible as my sufferings were, I kept them, with a morbid reserve, very nearly to myself.

It could not be that terrible complaint which the peasants call the vampire, for I had now been suffering for three weeks, and they were seldom ill for much more than three days, when death put an end to their miseries.

Carmilla complained of dreams and feverish sensations, but by no means of so alarming a kind as mine. I say that mine were extremely alarming. Had I been capable of comprehending my condition, I would have invoked aid and advice on my knees. The narcotic of an unsuspected influence was acting upon me, and my perceptions were benumbed.

I am going to tell you now of a dream that led immediately to an odd discovery.

One night, instead of the voice I was accustomed to hear in the dark, I heard one, sweet and tender, and at the same time terrible, which said, "Your mother warns you to beware of the assassin." At the same time a light unexpectedly sprang up, and I saw

Carmilla, standing, near the foot of my bed, in her white night-dress, bathed, from her chin to her feet, in one great stain of blood.

I wakened with a shriek, possessed with the one idea that Carmilla was being murdered. I remember springing from my bed, and my next recollection is that of standing on the lobby, crying for help.

Madame and Mademoiselle came scurrying out of their rooms in alarm; a lamp burned always on the lobby, and seeing me, they soon learned the cause of my terror.

I insisted on our knocking at Carmilla's door. Our knocking was unanswered. It soon became a pounding and an uproar. We shrieked her name but all was vain.

We all grew frightened, for the door was locked. We hurried back, in panic, to my room. There we rang the bell long and furiously. If my father's room had been at that side of the house, we would have called him up at once to our aid. But, alas! he was quite out of hearing, and to reach him involved an excursion for which we none of us had courage.

Servants, however, soon came running up the stairs; I had got on my dressing-gown and slippers meanwhile, and my companions were already similarly furnished. Recognizing the voices of the servants on the lobby, we sallied out together; and having renewed, as fruitlessly, our summons at Carmilla's door, I ordered the men to force the lock. They did so, and we stood, holding our lights aloft, in the doorway, and so stared into the room.

We called her by name; but there was still no reply. We looked round the room. Everything was undisturbed. It was exactly in the state in which I left it on bidding her good night. But Carmilla was gone.

Search
VIII

At sight of the room, perfectly undisturbed except for our vio-lent entrance, we began to cool a little, and soon recovered our senses sufficiently to dismiss the men. It had struck Mademoiselle that possibly Carmilla had been wakened by the uproar at her door, and in her first panic had jumped from her bed, and hid herself in a press, or behind a curtain, from which she could not, of course, emerge until the majordomo and his men had withdrawn.

We now recommenced our search, and began to call her by name again.

It was all to no purpose. Our perplexity and agitation increased. We examined the windows, but they were secured. I implored of Carmilla, if she had concealed herself, to play this cruel trick no longer—to come out, and to end our anxieties. It was all useless. I was by this time convinced that she was not in the room, nor in the dressing-room, the door of which was still locked on this side. She could not have passed it. I was utterly puzzled. Had Carmilla discovered one of those secret passages which the old housekeeper said were known to exist in the schloss, although the tradition of their exact situation had been lost. A little time would, no doubt, explain all—utterly perplexed as, for the present, we were.

It was past four o'clock, and I preferred passing the remaining hours of darkness in Madame's room. Daylight brought no solution of the difficulty.

The whole household, with my father at its head, was in a state of agitation next morning. Every part of the château was searched. The grounds were explored. Not a trace of the missing lady could be discovered. The stream was about to be dragged; my father was in distraction; what a tale to have to tell the poor girl's mother on her return. I, too, was almost beside myself, though my grief was quite of a different kind.

The morning was passed in alarm and excitement. It was now one o'clock, and still no tidings. I ran up to Carmilla's room, and found her standing at her dressing-table! I was astounded. I could not believe my eyes. She beckoned me to her with her pretty finger, in silence. Her face expressed extreme fear.

I ran to her in an ecstasy of joy; I kissed and embraced her again and again. I ran to the bell and rang it vehemently, to bring others to the spot, who might at once relieve my father's anxiety.

"Dear Carmilla, what has become of you all this time? We have been in agonies of anxiety about you," I exclaimed. "Where have you been? How did you come back?"

"Last night has been a night of wonders," she said.

"For mercy's sake, explain all you can."

"It was past two last night," she said, "when I went to sleep as usual in my bed, with my doors locked, that of the dressing-room and that opening upon the gallery. My sleep was uninterrupted, and, so far as I know, dreamless; but I awoke just now on the sofa in the dressing-room there, and I found the door between the rooms open, and the other door forced. How could all this have happened without my being awakened? It must have been accompanied with a great deal of noise, and I am particularly easily wakened; and how could I have been carried out of my bed without my sleep having been interrupted, I whom the slightest stir startles?"

By this time, Madame, Mademoiselle, my father, and a number of the servants were in the room. Carmilla was, of course, overwhelmed with inquiries, congratulations, and welcomes. She had but one story to tell, and seemed the least able of all the party to suggest any way of accounting for what had happened.

My father took a turn up and down the room, thinking. I saw Carmilla's eye follow him for a moment with a sly, dark glance.

When my father had sent the servants away, Mademoiselle having gone in search of a little bottle of valerian and sal-volatile, and there being no one now in the room with Carmilla except my father, Madame, and myself, he came to her thoughtfully, took her hand very kindly, led her to the sofa, and sat down beside her.

"Will you forgive me, my dear, if I risk a conjecture, and ask a question?"

"Who can have a better right?" she said. "Ask what you please, and I will tell you everything. But my story is simply one of bewilderment and darkness. I know absolutely nothing. Put any question you please. But you know, of course, the limitations mamma has placed me under."

"Perfectly, my dear child. I need not approach the topics on which she desires our silence. Now, the marvel of last night consists in your having been removed from your bed and your room without being wakened, and this removal having occurred apparently while the windows were still secured, and the two doors locked upon the inside. I will tell you my theory, and first ask you a question."

Carmilla was leaning on her hand dejectedly; Madame and I were listening breathlessly.

"Now, my question is this. Have you ever been suspected of walking in your sleep?"

"Never since I was very young indeed."

"But you did walk in your sleep when you were young?"

"Yes; I know I did. I have been told so often by my old nurse.

My father smiled and nodded.

"Well, what has happened is this. You got up in your sleep, unlocked the door, not leaving the key, as usual, in the lock, but taking it out and locking it on the outside; you again took the key out, and carried it away with you to some one of the five-and-twenty rooms on this floor, or perhaps upstairs or downstairs. There are so many rooms and closets, so much heavy furniture, and such accumulations of lumber, that it would require a week to search this old house thoroughly. Do you see, now, what I mean?"

"I do, but not all," she answered.

"And how, papa, do you account for her finding herself on the sofa in the dressing-room, which we had searched so carefully?"

"She came there after you had searched it, still in her sleep, and at last awoke spontaneously, and was as much surprised to find herself where she was as anyone else. I wish all mysteries were as easily and innocently explained as yours, Carmilla," he said, laughing. "And so we may congratulate ourselves on the certainty that the most natural explanation of the occurrence is one that involves no drugging, no tampering with locks, no burglars, or poisoners, or witches—nothing that need alarm Carmilla, or any one else, for our safety."

Carmilla was looking charmingly. Nothing could be more beautiful than her tints. Her beauty was, I think enhanced by that graceful languor that was peculiar to her. I think my father was silently contrasting her looks with mine, for he said:—

"I wish my poor Laura was looking more like herself"; and he sighed.

So our alarms were happily ended, and Carmilla restored to her friends.

The Doctor
IX

As Carmilla would not hear of an attendant sleeping in her room, my father arranged that a servant should sleep outside her door so that she could not attempt to make another such excursion without being arrested at her own door.

That night passed quietly; and next morning early, the doctor, whom my father had sent for without telling me a word about it, arrived to see me.

Madame accompanied me to the library; and there the grave little doctor, with white hair and spectacles, whom I mentioned before, was waiting to receive me.

I told him my story, and as I proceeded he grew graver and graver.

We were standing, he and I, in the recess of one of the windows, facing one another. When my statement was over, he leaned with his shoulders against the wall, and with his eyes fixed on me earnestly with an interest in which was a dash of horror.

After a minute's reflection, he asked Madame if he could see my father.

He was sent for accordingly, and as he entered, smiling, he said:

"I dare say, doctor, you are going to tell me that I am an old fool for having brought you here; I hope I am."

But his smile faded into shadow as the doctor, with a very grave face, beckoned him to him.

He and the doctor talked for some time in the same recess where I had just conferred with the physician. It seemed an earnest and argumentative conversation. The room is very large, and I and Madame stood together, burning with curiosity, at the further end. Not a word could we hear, however, for they spoke in a very low tone, and the deep recess of the window quite concealed the doctor from view, and very nearly my father, whose foot, arm, and shoulder only could we see; and the voices were, I suppose, all the less audible for the sort of closet which the thick wall and window formed.

After a time my father's face looked into the room; it was pale, thoughtful, and, I fancied, agitated.

"Laura, dear, come here for a moment. Madame, we shan't trouble you, the doctor says, at present."

Accordingly I approached, for the first time a little alarmed; for, although I felt very weak, I did not feel ill; and strength, one always fancies, is a thing that may be picked up when we please.

My father held out his hand to me as I drew near, but he was looking at the doctor, and he said:

"It certainly *is* very odd; I don't understand it quite. Laura, come here, dear; now attend to Doctor Spielsberg, and recollect yourself."

"You mentioned a sensation like that of two needles piercing the skin, somewhere about your neck, on the night when you experienced your first horrible dream. Is there still any soreness?"

"None at all," I answered.

"Can you indicate with your finger about the point at which you think this occurred?"

"Very little below my throat—*here*," I answered.

I wore a morning dress, which covered the place I pointed to.

"Now you can satisfy yourself," said the doctor. "You won't mind your papa's lowering your dress a very little. It is necessary, to detect a symptom of the complaint under which you have been suffering."

I acquiesced. It was only an inch or two below the edge of my collar.

"God bless me!—so it is," exclaimed my father, growing pale.

"You see it now with your own eyes," said the doctor, with a gloomy triumph.

"What is it?" I exclaimed, beginning to be frightened.

"Nothing, my dear young lady, but a small blue spot, about the size of the tip of your little finger; and now," he continued, turning to papa, "the question is what is best to be done?"

"Is there any danger?" I urged, in great trepidation.

"I trust not, my dear," answered the doctor. "I don't see why you should not recover. I don't see why you should not begin *immediately* to get better. That is the point at which the sense of strangulation begins?"

"Yes," I answered.

"And—recollect as well as you can—the same point was a kind of center of that thrill which you described just now, like the current of a cold stream running against you?"

"It may have been; I think it was."

"Ay, you see?" he added, turning to my father. "Shall I say a word to Madame?"

"Certainly," said my father.

He called Madame to him, and said:

"I find my young friend here far from well. It won't be of any great consequence, I hope; but it will be necessary that some steps be taken, which I will explain by-and-by; but in the meantime, Madame, you will be so good as not to let Miss Laura be alone for one moment. That is the only direction I need give for the present. It is indispensable."

"We may rely upon your kindness, Madame, I know," added my father.

Madame satisfied him eagerly.

"And you, dear Laura, I know you will observe the doctor's direction."

"I shall have to ask your opinion upon another patient, whose symptoms slightly resemble those of my daughter, that have just been detailed to you—very much milder in degree, but I believe quite of the same sort. She is a young lady—our guest; but as you say you will be passing this way again this evening, you can't do better than take your supper here, and you can then see her. She does not come down till the afternoon."

"I thank you," said the doctor. "I shall be with you, then, at about seven this evening."

And then they repeated their directions to me and to Madame, and with this parting charge my father left us, and walked out with the doctor; and I saw them pacing together up and down between the road and the moat, on the grassy platform in front of the castle, evidently absorbed in earnest conversation.

The doctor did not return. I saw him mount his horse there, take his leave, and ride away eastward through the forest. Nearly at the same time I saw the man arrive from Dranfeld with the letters, and dismount and hand the bag to my father.

In the meantime, Madame and I were both busy, lost in conjecture as to the reasons of the singular and earnest direction which the doctor and my father concurred in imposing. Madame, as she afterwards told me, was afraid the doctor apprehended a sudden seizure, and that, without prompt assistance, I might either lose my life in a fit, or at least be seriously hurt.

This interpretation did not strike me; and I fancied perhaps luckily for my nerves, that the arrangement was prescribed simply to secure a companion, who would prevent my taking too much exercise, or eating unripe fruit, or doing any of the fifty foolish things to which young people are supposed to be prone.

About half-an-hour after, my father came in—he had a letter in his hand—and said:

"This letter had been delayed; it is from General Spielsdorf. He might have been here yesterday, he may not come till tomorrow, or he may be here today."

He put the open letter into my hand; but he did not look

pleased, as he used to when a guest, especially one so much loved as the General, was coming. On the contrary, he looked as if he wished him at the bottom of the Red Sea. There was plainly something on his mind which he did not choose to divulge.

"Papa, darling, will you tell me this?" said I suddenly laying my hand on his arm, and looking, I am sure, imploringly in his face.

"Perhaps," he answered, smoothing my hair caressingly over my eyes.

"Does the doctor think me very ill?"

"No, dear; he thinks, if right steps are taken, you will be quite well again, at least on the high road to a complete recovery, in a day or two," he answered, a little drily. "I wish our good friend, the General, had chosen any other time; that, is, I wish you had been perfectly well to receive him."

"But do tell me, papa," I insisted, "*what* does he think is the matter with me?"

"Nothing; you must not plague me with questions," he answered, with more irritation than I ever remember him to have displayed before; and seeing that I looked wounded, I suppose, he kissed me, and added, "You shall know all about it in a day or two; that is, all that *I* know. In the meantime, you are not to trouble your head about it."

He turned and left the room, but came back before I had done wondering and puzzling over the oddity of all this; it was merely to say that he was going to Karnstein and had ordered the carriage to be ready at twelve, and that I and Madame should accompany him; he was going to see the priest who lived near those picturesque grounds, upon business, and as Carmilla had never seen them, she could follow, when she came down, with Mademoiselle, who would bring materials for what you call a picnic, which might be laid for us in the ruined castle.

At twelve o'clock, accordingly, I was ready, and not long after, my father, Madame and I set out upon our projected drive. Passing the drawbridge we turn to the right, and follow the road over the steep Gothic bridge westward, to reach the deserted village and ruined castle of Karnstein.

No sylvan drive can be fancied prettier. The ground breaks into gentle hills and hollows, all clothed with beautiful wood, totally destitute of the comparative formality which artificial planting and early culture and pruning impart.

The irregularities of the ground often lead the road out of its course, and cause it to wind beautifully round the sides of broken hollows and the steeper sides of the hills, among varieties of ground almost inexhaustible.

Turning one of these points, we suddenly encountered our old friend, the General, riding towards us, attended by a mounted servant. His portmanteaus were following in a hired wagon, such as we term a cart.

The General dismounted as we pulled up, and, after the usual greetings, was easily persuaded to accept the vacant seat in the carriage, and send his horse on with his servant to the schloss.

Bereaved
X

It was about ten months since we had last seen him; but that time had sufficed to make an alteration of years in his appearance. He had grown thinner; something of gloom and anxiety had taken the place of that cordial serenity which used to characterize his features. His dark eyes, always penetrating, now gleamed with a sterner light from under his shaggy grey eyebrows. It was not such a change as grief alone usually induces, and angrier passions seemed to have had their share in bringing it about.

We had not long resumed our drive, when the General began to talk, with his usual soldierly directness, of the bereavement, as he termed it, which he had sustained in the death of his beloved niece and ward; and he then broke out in a tone of intense bitterness and fury, inveighing against the "hellish arts" to which she had fallen a victim, and expressing with more exasperation than piety, his wonder that Heaven should tolerate so monstrous an indulgence of the lusts and malignity of hell.

My father, who saw at once that something very extraordinary had befallen, asked him, if not too painful to him, to detail the circumstances which he thought justified the strong terms in which he expressed himself.

"I should tell you all with pleasure," said the General, "but you would not believe me."

"Why should I not?" he asked.

"Because," he answered testily, "you believe in nothing but

what consists with your own prejudices and illusions. I remember when I was like you, but I have learned better."

"Try me," said my father; "I am not such a dogmatist as you suppose. Besides which, I very well know that you generally require proof for what you believe, and am, therefore, very strongly predisposed to respect your conclusions."

"You are right in supposing that I have not been led lightly into a belief in the marvelous—for what I have experienced is marvelous—and I have been forced by extraordinary evidence to credit that which ran counter, diametrically, to all my theories. I have been made the dupe of a preternatural conspiracy."

Notwithstanding his professions of confidence in the General's penetration, I saw my father, at this point, glance at the General, with, as I thought, a marked suspicion of his sanity.

The General did not see it, luckily. He was looking gloomily and curiously into the glades and vistas of the woods that were opening before us.

"You are going to the Ruins of Karnstein?" he said. "Yes, it is a lucky coincidence; do you know I was going to ask you to bring me there to inspect them. I have a special object in exploring. There is a ruined chapel, isn't there, with a great many tombs of that extinct family?"

"So there are—highly interesting," said my father. "I hope you are thinking of claiming the title and estates?"

My father said this gaily, but the General did not recollect the laugh, or even the smile, which courtesy exacts for a friend's joke; on the contrary, he looked grave and even fierce, ruminating on a matter that stirred his anger and horror.

"Something very different," he said, gruffly. "I mean to unearth some of those fine people. I hope, by God's blessing, to accomplish a pious sacrilege here, which will relieve our earth of certain monsters, and enable honest people to sleep in their beds without being assailed by murderers. I have strange things to tell you, my dear friend, such as I myself would have scouted as incredible a few months since."

My father looked at him again, but this time not with a glance of suspicion—with an eye, rather, of keen intelligence and alarm.

"The house of Karnstein," he said, "has been long extinct: a hundred years at least. My dear wife was maternally descended from the Karnsteins. But name and title have long ceased to exist.

The castle is a ruin; the very village is deserted; it is fifty years since the smoke of a chimney was seen there; not a roof left."

"Quite true. I have heard a great deal about that since I last saw you; a great deal that will astonish you. But I had better relate everything in the order in which it occurred," said the General. "You saw my dear ward—my child, I may call her. No creature could have been more beautiful and only three months ago none more blooming."

"Yes, poor thing! when I saw her last she certainly was quite lovely," said my father. "I was grieved and shocked more than I can tell you, my dear friend; I knew what a blow it was to you."

He took the General's hand, and they exchanged a kind pressure. Tears gathered in the old soldier's eyes. He did not seek to conceal them. He said:

"We have been very old friends; I knew you would feel for me, childless as I am. She had become an object of very dear interest to me, and repaid my care by an affection that cheered my home and made my life happy. That is all gone. The years that remain to me on earth may not be very long; but by God's mercy I hope to accomplish a service to mankind before I die, and to subserve the vengeance of Heaven upon the fiends who have murdered my poor child in the spring of her hopes and beauty!"

"You said, just now, that you intended relating everything as it occurred," said my father. "Pray do; I assure you that it is not mere curiosity that prompts me."

By this time we had reached the point at which the Drunstall road, by which the General had come, diverges from the road which we were travelling to Karnstein.

"How far is it to the ruins?" inquired the General, looking anxiously forward.

"About half a league," answered my father. "Pray let us hear the story you were so good as to promise."

The Story
XI

With all my heart," said the General, with an effort; and after a short pause in which to arrange his subject, he commenced one of the strangest narratives I ever heard.

"My dear child was looking forward with great pleasure to the visit you had been so good as to arrange for her to your charming daughter." Here he made me a gallant but melancholy bow.

"In the meantime we had an invitation to my old friend the Count Carlsfeld, whose schloss is about six leagues to the other side of Karnstein. It was to attend the series of fêtes which, you remember, were given by him in honor of his illustrious visitor, the Grand Duke Charles."

"Yes; and very splendid, I believe, they were," said my father.

"Princely! But then his hospitalities are quite regal. He has Aladdin's lamp. The night from which my sorrow dates was devoted to a magnificent masquerade. The grounds were thrown open, the trees hung with colored lamps. There was such a display of fireworks as Paris itself had never witnessed. And such music—music, you know, is my weakness—such ravishing music! The finest instrumental band, perhaps, in the world, and the finest singers who could be collected from all the great operas in Europe. As you wandered through these fantastically illuminated grounds, the moonlighted château throwing a rosy light from its long rows of windows, you would suddenly hear these ravishing voices stealing from the silence of some grove, or rising from boats upon the lake. I felt myself, as I looked and listened, carried back into the romance and poetry of my early youth.

"When the fireworks were ended, and the ball beginning, we returned to the noble suite of rooms that was thrown open to the dancers. A masked ball, you know, is a beautiful sight; but so brilliant a spectacle of the kind I never saw before.

"It was a very aristocratic assembly. I was myself almost the only 'nobody' present.

"My dear child was looking quite beautiful. She wore no mask. Her excitement and delight added an unspeakable charm to her features, always lovely. I remarked a young lady, dressed magnificently, but wearing a mask, who appeared to me to be observing my ward with extraordinary interest. I had seen her, earlier in the evening, in the great hall, and again, for a few minutes, walking near us, on the terrace under the castle windows, similarly employed. A lady, also masked, richly and gravely dressed, and with a stately air, like a person of rank, accompanied her as a chaperon. Had the young lady not worn a mask, I could, of course, have been much more certain upon the question whether she was really watching my poor darling. I am now well assured that she was.

"We were now in one of the *salons*. My poor dear child had been dancing, and was resting a little on one of the chairs near the door; I was standing near. The two ladies I have mentioned had approached, and the younger took the chair next my ward; while her companion stood beside me, and for a little time addressed herself, in a low tone, to her charge.

"Availing herself of the privilege of her mask she turned to me, and in the tone of an old friend, and calling me by my name, opened a conversation with me, which piqued my curiosity a good deal. She referred to many scenes where she had met me—at Court, and at distinguished houses. She alluded to little incidents which I had long ceased to think of, but which, I found, had only lain in abeyance in my memory, for they instantly started into life at her touch.

"I became more and more curious to ascertain who she was, every moment. She parried my attempts to discover very adroitly and pleasantly. The knowledge she showed of many passages in my life seemed to me all but unaccountable; and she appeared to take a not unnatural pleasure in foiling my curiosity, and in seeing me flounder, in my eager perplexity, from one conjecture to another.

"In the meantime the young lady, whom her mother called by the odd name of Millarca, when she once or twice addressed her, had, with the same ease and grace, got into conversation with my ward.

"She introduced herself by saying that her mother was a very old acquaintance of mine. She spoke of the agreeable audacity which a mask rendered practicable; she talked like a friend; she admired her dress, and insinuated very prettily her admiration of her beauty. She amused her with laughing criticisms upon the people who crowded the ballroom, and laughed at my poor child's fun. She was very witty and lively when she pleased, and after a time they had grown very good friends, and the young stranger lowered her mask, displaying a remarkably beautiful face. I had never seen it before, neither had my dear child. But though it was new to us, the features were so engaging, as well as lovely, that it was impossible not to feel the attraction powerfully. My poor girl did so. I never saw anyone more taken with another at first sight, unless indeed, it was the stranger herself, who seemed quite to have lost her heart to her.

"In the meantime, availing myself of the license of a masquerade, I put not a few questions to the elder lady.

" 'You have puzzled me utterly,' I said laughing. 'Is that not enough? Won't you, now consent to stand on equal terms, and do me the kindness to remove your mask?'

" 'Can any request be more unreasonable?' she replied. 'Ask a lady to yield an advantage! Besides, how do you know you should recognize me? Years make changes.'

" 'As you see,' I said, with a bow, and, I suppose, a rather melancholy little laugh.

" 'As philosophers tell us,' she said; 'and how do you know that a sight of my face would help you?'

" 'I should take chance for that,' I answered. 'It is vain trying to make yourself out an old woman; your figure betrays you.'

" 'Years, nevertheless, have passed since I saw you, rather since you saw me, for that is what I am considering. Millarca, there, is my daughter; I cannot then be young, even in the opinion of people whom time has taught to be indulgent, and I may not like to be compared with what you remember me. You have no mask to remove. You can offer me nothing in exchange.'

" 'My petition is to your pity, to remove it.'

" 'And mine to yours, to let it stay where it is,' she replied.

" 'Well, then, at least you will tell me whether you are French or German; you speak both languages so perfectly.'

" 'I don't think I shall tell you that, General; you intend a surprise, and are meditating the particular point of attack.'

" 'At all events, you won't deny this,' I said, 'that being honored by your permission to converse, I ought to know how to address you. Shall I say Madame la Comtesse!'

"She laughed, and she would, no doubt, have met me with another evasion—if, indeed, I can treat any occurrence in an interview every circumstances of which was prearranged, as I now believe, with the profoundest cunning, as liable to be modified by accident.

" 'As to that,' she began; but she was interrupted, almost as she opened her lips, by a gentleman, dressed in black, who looked particularly elegant and distinguished, with this drawback, that his face was the most deadly pale I ever saw, except in death. He was in no masquerade—in the plain evening dress of a gentleman;

and he said, without a smile, but with a courtly and unusually low bow:—

" 'Will Madame la Comtesse permit me to say a very few words which may interest her?'

"The lady turned quickly to him, and touched her lip in token of silence; she then said to me, 'Keep my place for me, General; I shall return when I have said a few words.'

"And with this injunction, playfully given, she walked a little aside with the gentleman in black, and talked for some minutes, apparently very earnestly. They then walked away slowly together in the crowd, and I lost them for some minutes.

"I spent the interval in cudgelling my brains for conjecture as to the identity of the lady who seemed to remember me so kindly, and I was thinking of turning about and joining in the conversation between my pretty ward and the Countess's daughter, and trying whether, by the time she returned, I might not have a surprise in store for her, by having her name, title, château, and estates at my fingers' ends. But at this moment she returned, accompanied by the pale man in black, who said:

" 'I shall return and inform Madame la Comtesse when her carriage is at the door.'

"He withdrew with a bow."

A Petition
XII

Then we are to lose Madame la Comtesse, but I hope only for a few hours,' I said, with a low bow.

" 'It may be that only, or it may be a few weeks. It was very unlucky his speaking to me just now as he did. Do you now know me?'

"I assured her I did not.

" 'You shall know me,' she said, 'but not at present. We are older and better friends than, perhaps, you suspect. I cannot yet declare myself. I shall in three weeks pass your beautiful schloss about which I have been making inquiries. I shall then look in upon you for an hour or two, and renew a friendship which I never think of without a thousand pleasant recollections. This moment a piece of news has reached me like a thunderbolt. I must set out now, and travel by a devious route, nearly a hundred miles, with all the dispatch I can possibly make. My perplexities multiply. I am only deterred by the compulsory reserve I practice as to my name from making a very singular request of you. My poor child has not quite recovered her strength. Her horse fell with her, at a hunt which she had ridden out to witness, her nerves have not yet recovered the shock, and our physician says that she must on no account exert herself for some time to come. We came here, in consequence, by very easy stages—hardly six leagues a day. I must now travel day and night on a mission of life and death—a mission the critical and momentous nature of which I shall be able to explain to you when we meet, as I hope we shall, in a few weeks, without the necessity of any concealment.'

"She went on to make her petition, and it was in the tone of a person from whom such a request amounted to conferring, rather than seeking a favor. This only in manner, and, as it seemed, quite unconsciously. Than the terms in which it was expressed, nothing could be more deprecatory. It was simply that I would consent to take charge of her daughter during her absence.

"This was, all things considered, a strange, not to say, an audacious request. She in some sort disarmed me, by stating and admitting everything that could be urged against it, and throwing herself entirely upon my chivalry. At the same moment, by a fatality that seems to have predetermined all that happened, my poor child came to my side, and, in an undertone, besought me to invite her new friend, Millarca, to pay us a visit. She had just been sounding her, and thought, if her mamma would allow her, she would like it extremely.

"At another time I should have told her to wait a little, until, at least, we knew who they were. But I had not a moment to think in. The two ladies assailed me together, and I must confess the refined and beautiful face of the young lady, about which there was something extremely engaging, as well as the elegance and fire of high birth, determined me; and quite overpowered, I submitted, and undertook, too easily, the care of the young lady, whom her mother called Millarca.

"The Countess beckoned to her daughter, who listened with grave attention while she told her, in general terms, how suddenly and peremptorily she had been summoned, and also of the arrangement she had made for her under my care, adding that I was one of her earliest and most valued friends.

"I made, of course, such speeches as the case seemed to call for, and found myself, on reflection, in a position which I did not half like.

"The gentleman in black returned, and very ceremoniously conducted the lady from the room.

"The demeanor of this gentleman was such as to impress me with the conviction that the Countess was a lady of very much more importance than her modest title alone might have led me to assume.

"Her last charge to me was that no attempt was to be made to learn more about her than I might have already guessed, until her return. Our distinguished host, whose guest she was, knew her reasons.

" 'But here,' she said, 'neither I nor my daughter could safely remain for more than a day. I removed my mask imprudently for a moment, about an hour ago, and, too late, I fancied you saw me. So I resolved to seek an opportunity of talking a little to you. Had I found that you *had* seen me, I should have thrown myself on your high sense of honor to keep my secret for some weeks. As it is, I am satisfied that you did not see me; but if you now *suspect*, or, on reflection, *should* suspect, who I am, I commit myself, in like manner, entirely to your honor. My daughter will observe the same secrecy, and I well know that you will, from time to time, remind her, lest she should thoughtlessly disclose it.'

"She whispered a few words to her daughter, kissed her hurriedly twice, and went away, accompanied by the pale gentleman in black and disappeared in the crowd.

" 'In the next room,' said Millarca, 'there is a window that looks upon the hall door. I should like to see the last of mamma, and to kiss my hand to her.'

"We assented, of course, and accompanied her to the window. We looked out, and saw a handsome old-fashioned carriage, with a troop of couriers and footmen. We saw the slim figure of the pale gentleman in black, as he held a thick velvet cloak, and placed it about her shoulders and threw the hood over her head. She nodded to him, and just touched his hand with hers. He bowed low repeatedly as the door closed, and the carriage began to move.

" 'She is gone,' said Millarca, with a sigh.

" 'She is gone,' I repeated to myself, for the first time—in the

hurried moments that had elapsed since my consent—reflecting
upon the folly of my act.

" 'She did not look up,' said the young lady, plaintively.

" 'The Countess had taken off her mask, perhaps, and did not
care to show her face,' I said: 'and she could not know that you
were in the window.'

"She sighed and looked in my face. She was so beautiful that I
relented. I was sorry I had for a moment repented of my hospitality, and I determined to make her amends for the unavowed churl-
ishness of my reception.

"The young lady, replacing her mask, joined my ward in per-
suading me to return to the grounds, where the concert was soon
to be renewed. We did so, and walked up and down the terrace
that lies under the castle windows. Millarca became very intimate
with us, and amused us with lively descriptions and stories of
most of the great people whom we saw upon the terrace. I liked
her more and more every minute. Her gossip, without being ill-
natured, was extremely diverting to me, who had been so long out
of the great world. I thought what life she would give to our
sometimes lonely evenings at home.

"This ball was not over until the morning sun had almost
reached the horizon. It pleased the Grand Duke to dance till then,
so loyal people could not go away, or think of bed.

"We had just got through a crowded saloon, when my ward
asked me what had become of Millarca. I thought she had been by
my side, and she fancied she was by mine. The fact was, we had
lost her.

"All my efforts to find her were vain. I feared that she had
mistaken, in the confusion of momentary separation from us, other
people for her new friends, and had, possibly, pursued and lost
them in the extensive grounds which were thrown open to us.

"Now, in its full force, I recognized a new folly in my having
undertaken the charge of a young lady without so much as knowing her full name; and fettered as I was by promises, of the reasons
for imposing which I knew nothing, I could not even point my
inquiries by saying that the missing young lady was the daughter
of the Countess who had taken her departure a few hours before.

"Morning broke. It was clear daylight before I gave up my
search. It was not till near two o'clock next day that we heard
anything of my missing charge.

"At about that time a servant knocked at my niece's door, to say that he had been earnestly requested by a young lady, who appeared to be in great distress, to make out where she could find the General Baron Spielsdorf and the young lady, his daughter, in whose charge she had been left by her mother.

"There could be no doubt, notwithstanding the slight inaccuracy, that our young friend had turned up; and so she had. Would to Heaven we had lost her!

"She told my poor child a story to account for her having failed to recover us for so long. Very late, she said, she had got into the housekeeper's bedroom in despair of finding us, and had then fallen into a deep sleep which, long as it was, hardly sufficed to recruit her strength after the fatigues of the ball.

"That day Millarca came home with us. I was only too happy, after all, to have secured so charming a companion for my dear girl."

The Woodsman
XIII

There soon, however, appeared some drawbacks. In the first place, Millarca complained of extreme languor—the weakness that remained after her late illness—and she never emerged from her room till the afternoon was pretty far advanced. In the next place, it was accidentally discovered, although she always locked her door on the inside, and never disturbed the key from its place, till she admitted the maid to assist at her toilet, that she was undoubtedly sometimes absent from her room in the very early morning, and at various times later in the day, before she wished it to be understood that she was stirring. She was repeatedly seen from the windows of the schloss, in the first faint grey of the morning, walking through the trees, in an easterly direction, and looking like a person in a trance. This convinced me that she walked in her sleep. But this hypothesis did not solve the puzzle. How did she pass out from her room, leaving the door locked on the inside. How did she escape from the house without unbarring door or window?

"In the midst of my perplexities, an anxiety of a far more urgent kind presented itself.

"My dear child began to lose her looks and health, and that in a manner so mysterious, and even horrible, that I became thoroughly frightened.

"She was at first visited by appalling dreams; then, as she fancied by a specter, something resembling Millarca, sometimes in the shape of a beast, indistinctly seen, walking round the foot of the bed, from side to side. Lastly came sensations. One not unpleasant, but very peculiar, she said, resembled the flow of an icy stream against her breast. At a later time, she felt something like a pair of large needles pierce her, a little below the throat with a very sharp pain. A few nights after, followed a gradual and convulsive sense of strangulation; then came unconsciousness."

I could hear distinctly every word the kind old General was saying, because by this time we were driving upon the short grass that spreads on either side of the road as you approach the roofless village which had not shown the smoke of a chimney for more than half a century.

You may guess how strangely I felt as I heard my own symptoms so exactly described in those which had been experienced by the poor girl who, but for the catastrophe which followed, would have been at that moment a visitor at my father's château. You may suppose, also, how I felt as I heard him detail habits and mysterious peculiarities which were, in fact, those of our beautiful guest, Carmilla!

A vista opened in the forest; we were on a sudden under the chimney and gables of the ruined village, and the towers and battlements of the dismantled castle, round which gigantic trees are grouped, overhung us from a slight eminence.

In a frightened dream I got down from the carriage, and in silence, for we had each abundant matters for thinking; we soon mounted the ascent, and were among the spacious chambers, winding stairs, and dark corridors of the castle.

"And this was once the palatial residence of the Karnsteins!" said the old General at length, as from a great window he looked out across the village, and saw the wide, undulating expanse of forest. "It was a bad family, and here its blood-stained annals were written," he continued. "It is hard that they should, after death, continue to plague the human race with their atrocious lusts. That is the chapel of the Karnsteins, down there."

He pointed down to the grey walls of the Gothic building, partly visible through the foliage, a little way down the steep. "And I hear the axe of a woodsman," he added, "busy among the trees that surround it; he possibly may give us the information of which I am in search, and point out the grave of Mircalla, Countess of Karnstein. These rustics preserve the local traditions of great families, whose stories die out among the rich and titled so soon as the families themselves become extinct."

"We have a portrait, at home, of Mircalla, the Countess Karnstein; should you like to see it?" asked my father.

"Time enough, dear friend," replied the General. "I believe that I have seen the original; and one motive which has led me to you earlier than I at first intended, was to explore the chapel which we are now approaching."

"What! see the Countess Mircalla," exclaimed my father; "why, she has been dead more than a century!"

"Not so dead as you fancy, I am told," answered the General.

"I confess, General, you puzzle me utterly," replied my father, looking at him, I fancied, for a moment with a return of the suspicion I detected before. But although there was anger and detestation, at times, in the old General's manner, there was nothing flighty.

"There remains to me," he said, as we passed under the heavy arch of the Gothic church—for its dimensions would have justified its being so styled—"but one object which can interest me during the few years that remain to me on earth, and that is to wreak on her the vengeance which, I thank God, may still be accomplished by a mortal arm."

"What vengeance can you mean?" asked my father, in increasing amazement.

"I mean, to decapitate the monster," he answered, with a fierce flush, and a stamp that echoed mournfully through the hollow ruin, and his clenched hand was at the same moment raised, as if it grasped the handle of an axe, while he shook it ferociously in the air.

"What!" exclaimed my father, more than ever bewildered.

"To strike her head off."

"Cut her head off!"

"Aye, with a hatchet, with a spade, or with anything that can cleave through her murderous throat. You shall hear," he answered, trembling with rage. And hurrying forward he said: "That beam will answer for a seat; your dear child is fatigued; let her be seated, and I will, in a few sentences, close my dreadful story."

The squared block of wood, which lay on the grass-grown pavement of the chapel, formed a bench on which I was very glad to seat myself, and in the meantime the General called to the woodsman, who had been removing some boughs which leaned upon the old walls; and, axe in hand, the hardy old fellow stood before us.

He could not tell us anything of these monuments; but there was an old man, he said, a ranger of this forest, at present sojourning in the house of the priest, about two miles away, who could point out every monument of the old Karnstein family and, for a trifle, he undertook to bring him back with him, if we would lend him one of our horses, in little more than half-an-hour.

"Have you been long employed about this forest?" asked my father of the old man.

"I have been a woodsman here," he answered in his dialect, "under the forester, all my days; so has my father before me, and so on, as many generations as I can count up. I could show you the very house in the village here, in which my ancestors lived."

"How came the village to be deserted?" asked the General.

"It was troubled by ghosts, sir; several were tracked to their graves, there detected by the usual tests, and extinguished in the usual way, by decapitation, by the stake, and by burning; but not until many of the villagers were killed.

"But after all these proceedings according to law," he continued —"so many graves opened, and so many vampires deprived of the horrible animation—the village was not relieved. But a Moravian nobleman, who happened to be travelling this way, heard how matters were, and being skilled—as many people are in his country—in such affairs, he offered to deliver the village from its tormentor. He did so thus: There being a bright moon that night, he ascended, shortly after sunset, the tower of the chapel here, from whence he could distinctly see the churchyard beneath him; you can see it from that window. From this point he watched until he saw the vampire come out of his grave, and place near it the linen clothes in which he had been folded, and glide away towards the village to plague its inhabitants.

"The stranger, having seen all this, came down from the steeple, took the linen wrappings of the vampire, and carried them up to

the top of the tower, which he again mounted. When the vampire
returned from his prowlings and missed his clothes, he cried furiously to the Moravian, whom he saw at the summit of the tower,
and who, in reply beckoned him to ascend and take them. Where-
upon the vampire, accepting his invitation, began to climb the
steeple, and so soon as he had reached the battlements, the Moravian, with a stroke of his sword, split his skull in two, hurling him
down to the churchyard, whither, descending by the winding
stairs, the stranger followed and cut his head off, and next day
delivered it and the body to the villagers, who duly impaled and
burnt them.

"This Moravian nobleman had authority from the then head of
the family to remove the tomb of Mircalla, Countess Karnstein,
which he did effectually, so that in a little while its site was quite
forgotten."

"Can you point out where it stood?" asked the General, eagerly.

The forester shook his head and smiled.

"Not a soul living could tell you that now," he said; "besides
they say her body was removed; but no one is sure of that either."

Having thus spoken, as time pressed, he dropped his axe and
departed, leaving us to hear the remainder of the General's strange
story.

The Meeting
XIV

My beloved child," he resumed, "was now growing rapidly
worse. The physician who attended her had failed to produce
the slightest impression upon her disease, for such I then supposed it to be. He saw my alarm, and suggested a consultation. I
called in an abler physician, from Gratz. Several days elapsed before he arrived. He was a good and pious, as well as a learned
man. Having seen my poor ward together, they withdrew to my
library to confer and discuss. I, from the adjoining room, where I
awaited their summons, heard these two gentlemen's voices
raised in something sharper than a strictly philosophical discussion. I knocked at the door and entered, I found the old physician
from Gratz maintaining his theory. His rival was combating it
with undisguised ridicule, accompanied with bursts of laughter.

This unseemly manifestation subsided and the altercation ended on my entrance.

" 'Sir,' said my first physician, 'my learned brother seems to think that you want a conjuror, and not a doctor.'

" 'Pardon me,' said the old physician from Gratz, looking displeased, 'I shall state my own view of the case in my own way another time. I grieve, Monsieur le Général, that by my skill and science I can be of no use. Before I go I shall do myself the honor to suggest something to you.'

"He seemed thoughtful, and sat down at a table, and began to write. Profoundly disappointed, I made my bow, and as I turned to go, the other doctor pointed over his shoulder to his companion who was writing, and then, with a shrug, significantly touched his forehead.

"This consultation, then, left me precisely where I was. I walked out into the grounds, all but distracted. The doctor from Gratz, in ten or fifteen minutes, overtook me. He apologized for having followed me, but said that he could not conscientiously take his leave without a few words more. He told me that he could not be mistaken; no natural disease exhibited the same symptoms; and that death was already very near. There remained, however, a day, or possibly two, of life. If the fatal seizure were at once arrested, with great care and skill her strength might possibly return. But all hung now upon the confines of the irrevocable. One more assault might extinguish the last spark of vitality which is, every moment, ready to die.

" 'And what is the nature of the seizure you speak of?' I entreated.

" 'I have stated all fully in this note, which I place in your hands, upon the distinct condition that you send for the nearest clergyman, and open my letter in his presence, and on no account read it till he is with you; you would despise it else, and it is a matter of life and death. Should the priest fail you, then, indeed, you may read it.'

"He asked me, before taking his leave finally, whether I would wish to see a man curiously learned upon the very subject, which after I had read his letter, would probably interest me above all others, and he urged me earnestly to invite him to visit him there; and so took his leave.

"The ecclesiastic was absent, and I read the letter by myself. At another time, or in another case, it might have excited my ridicule. But into what quackeries will not people rush for a last chance, where all accustomed means have failed, and the life of a beloved object is at stake?

"Nothing, you will say, could be more absurd than the learned man's letter. It was monstrous enough to have consigned him to a madhouse. He said that the patient was suffering from the visits of a vampire! The punctures which she described as having occurred near the throat, were, he insisted, the insertion of those two long, thin, and sharp teeth which, it is well known, are peculiar to vampires; and there could be no doubt, he added, as to the well-defined presence of the small livid mark which all concurred in describing as that induced by the demon's lips, and every symptom described by the sufferer was in exact conformity with those recorded in every case of a similar visitation.

"Being myself wholly skeptical as to the existence of any such portent as the vampire, the supernatural theory of the good doctor furnished, in my opinion, but another instance of learning and intelligence oddly associated with some hallucination. I was so miserable, however, that, rather than try nothing, I acted upon the instructions of the letter.

"I concealed myself in the dark dressing-room, that opened upon the poor patient's room, in which a candle was burning, and watched there till she was fast asleep. I stood at the door, peeping through the small crevice, my sword laid on the table beside me, as my directions prescribed, until, a little after one, I saw a large black object, very ill-defined, crawl, as it seemed to me, over the foot of the bed, and swiftly spread itself up to the poor girl's throat, where it swelled, in a moment, into a great, palpitating mass.

"For a few moments I had stood petrified. I now sprang forward, with my sword in my hand. The black creature suddenly contracted toward the foot of the bed, glided over it, and, standing on the floor about a yard below the foot of the bed, with a glare of skulking ferocity and horror fixed on me, I saw Millarca. Speculating I know not what, I struck at her instantly with my sword; but I saw her standing near the door, unscathed. Horrified, I pursued, and struck again. She was gone! and my sword flew to splinters against the door.

"I can't describe to you all that passed on that horrible night. The whole house was up and stirring. The specter Millarca was gone. But her victim was sinking fast, and before the morning dawned, she died."

The old General was agitated. We did not speak to him. My father walked to some little distance, and began reading the inscriptions on the tombstones; and thus occupied, he strolled into the door of a side chapel to pursue his researches. The General leaned against the wall, dried his eyes, and sighed heavily. I was relieved on hearing the voices of Carmilla and Madame, who were at that moment approaching. The voices died away.

In this solitude, having just listened to so strange a story, connected, as it was, with the great and titled dead, whose monuments were moldering amongst the dust and ivy round us, and every incident of which bore so awfully upon my own mysterious case—in this haunted spot, darkened by the towering foliage that rose on every side, dense and high above its noiseless walls—a horror began to steal over me, and my heart sank as I thought that my friends were, after all, not about to enter and disturb this sad and ominous scene.

The old General's eyes were fixed on the ground, as he leaned with his hand upon the basement of a shattered monument.

Under a narrow, arched doorway, surmounted by one of those demoniacal grotesques in which the cynical and ghastly fancy of old Gothic carving delights, I saw very gladly the beautiful face and figure of Carmilla enter the shadowy chapel.

I was just about to rise and speak, and nodded smiling, in answer to her peculiarly engaging smile; when, with a cry, the old man by my side caught up the woodsman's hatchet, and started forward. On seeing him a brutalized change came over her features. It was an instantaneous and horrible transformation, as she made a crouching step backwards. Before I could utter a scream, he struck at her with all his force, but she dived under his blow, and unscathed, caught him in her tiny grasp by the wrist. He struggled for a moment to release his arm, but his hand opened, the axe fell to the ground, and the girl was gone.

He staggered against the wall. His grey hair stood upon his head, and a moisture shone over his face, as if he were at the point of death.

The frightful scene had passed in a moment. The first thing I recollect after, is Madame standing before me, and impatiently repeating again and again, the question, "Where is Mademoiselle Carmilla?"

I answered at length, "I don't know—I can't tell—she went there," and I pointed to the door through which Madame had just entered; "only a minute or two since."

"But I have been standing there, in the passage, ever since Mademoiselle Carmilla entered; and she did not return."

She then began to call "Carmilla" through every door and passage and from the windows, but no answer came.

"She called herself Carmilla?" asked the General, still agitated.

"Carmilla, yes," I answered.

"Aye," he said; "that is Millarca. That is the same person who long ago was called Mircalla, Countess Karnstein. Depart from this accursed ground, my poor child, as quickly as you can. Drive to the clergyman's house, and stay there till we come. Begone! May you never behold Carmilla more; you will not find her here."

Ordeal and Execution
XV

As he spoke, one of the strangest-looking men I ever beheld entered the chapel at the door through which Carmilla had made her entrance and her exit. He was tall, narrow-chested, stooping, with high shoulders, and dressed in black. His face was brown and dried in with deep furrows; he wore an oddly-shaped hat with a broad leaf. His hair, long and grizzled, hung on his shoulders. He wore a pair of gold spectacles, and walked slowly, with an odd shambling gait, and his face sometimes turned up to the sky, and sometimes bowed down toward the ground, seemed to wear a perpetual smile; his long thin arms were swinging, and his lank hands, in old black gloves ever so much too wide for them, waving and gesticulating in utter abstraction.

"The very man!" exclaimed the General, advancing with manifest delight. "My dear Baron, how happy I am to see you, I had no hope of meeting you so soon." He signed to my father, who had by this time returned, and leading the fantastic old gentleman, whom he called the Baron, to meet him. He introduced him formally, and they at once entered into earnest conversation. The stranger took a roll of paper from his pocket, and spread it on the worn surface of a tomb that stood by. He had a pencil case in his fingers, with which he traced imaginary lines from point to point on the paper, which from their often glancing from it, together, at certain points of the building, I concluded to be a plan of the chapel. He accompanied, what I may term his lecture, with occasional readings from a dirty little book, whose yellow leaves were closely written over.

They sauntered together down the side aisle, opposite to the spot where I was standing, conversing as they went; then they began measuring distances by paces, and finally they all stood together, facing a piece of the side-wall, which they began to examine with great minuteness; pulling off the ivy that clung over it, and rapping the plaster with the ends of their sticks, scraping here, and knocking there. At length they ascertained the existence of a broad marble tablet, with letters carved in relief upon it.

With the assistance of the woodsman, who soon returned, a monument inscription, and carved escutcheon, were disclosed. They proved to be those of the long lost monument of Mircalla, Countess Karnstein.

The old General, though not I fear given to the praying mood, raised his hand and eyes to heaven, in mute thanksgiving for some moments.

Then turning to the old man with the gold spectacles, whom I have described, he shook him warmly by both hands and said:

"Baron, how can I thank you? How can we all thank you? You will have delivered this region from a plague that has scourged its inhabitants for more than a century. The horrible enemy, thank God, is at last tracked."

My father led the stranger aside, and the General followed. I knew that he had led them out of hearing, that he might relate my case, and I saw them glance often quickly at me, as the discussion proceeded.

My father came to me, kissed me again and again, and leading me from the chapel, said:

"It is time to return, but before we go home, we must add to our party the good priest, who lives but a little way from this; and persuade him to accompany us to the schloss."

In this quest we were successful: and I was glad, being unspeakably fatigued when we reached home. But my satisfaction was changed to dismay, on discovering that there were no tidings of Carmilla. Of the scene that had occurred in the ruined chapel, no explanation was offered to me, and it was clear that it was a secret which my father for the present determined to keep from me.

The sinister absence of Carmilla made the remembrance of the scene more horrible to me. The arrangements for that night were singular. Two servants and Madame were to sit up in my room that night; and the ecclesiastic with my father kept watch in the adjoining dressing-room.

The priest had performed certain solemn rites that night, the purport of which I did not understand any more than I comprehended the reason of this extraordinary precaution taken for my safety during sleep.

I saw all clearly a few days later.

The disappearance of Carmilla was followed by the discontinuance of my nightly sufferings.

You have heard, no doubt, of the appalling superstition that prevails in Upper and Lower Styria, in Moravia, Silesia, in Turkish Serbia, in Poland, even in Russia; the superstition, so we must call it, of the vampire.

If human testimony, taken with every care and solemnity, judicially, before commissions innumerable, each consisting of many members, all chosen for integrity and intelligence, and constituting reports more voluminous perhaps than exist upon any one other class of cases, is worth anything, it is difficult to deny, or even to doubt the existence of such a phenomenon as the vampire.

For my part I have heard no theory by which to explain what I myself have witnessed and experienced other than that supplied by the ancient and well-attested belief of the country.

The next day the formal proceedings took place in the Chapel of Karnstein. The grave of the Countess Mircalla was opened; and the General and my father recognized each his perfidious and beautiful guest, in the face now disclosed to view. The features, though a hundred and fifty years had passed since her funeral, were tinted with the warmth of life. Her eyes were open; no cadaverous smell exhaled from the coffin. The two medical men, one officially present, the other on the part of the promoter of the inquiry, attested the marvelous fact, that there was a faint but appreciable respiration, and a corresponding action of the heart. The limbs were perfectly flexible, the flesh elastic; and the leaden coffin floated with blood, in which to a depth of seven inches, the body lay immersed. Here then, were all the admitted signs and proofs of vampirism. The body, therefore, in accordance with the ancient practice, was raised, and a sharp stake driven through the heart of the vampire, who uttered a piercing shriek at the moment, in all respects such as might escape from a living person in the last agony. Then the head was struck off, and a torrent of blood flowed from the severed neck. The body and head were next placed on a pile of wood, and reduced to ashes, which were thrown upon the river and borne away, and that territory has never since been plagued by the visits of a vampire.

My father has a copy of the report of the Imperial Commission with the signatures of all who were present at these proceedings attached in verification of the statement. It is from this official paper that I have summarized my account of this last shocking scene.

Conclusion
XVI

I write all this you suppose with composure. But far from it; I cannot think of it without agitation. Nothing but your earnest desire so repeatedly expressed, could have induced me to sit down to a task that has unstrung my nerves for months to come, and it induced a shadow of the unspeakable horror which years after my deliverance continued to make my days and nights dreadful, and solitude insupportably terrific.

Let me add a word or two about that quaint Baron Vordenburg, to whose curious lore we were indebted for the discovery of the Countess Mircalla's grave.

He had taken up his abode in Gratz, where, living upon a mere pittance, which was all that remained to him of the once princely estates of his family, in Upper Styria, he devoted himself to the minute and laborious investigation of the marvelously authenticated tradition of vampirism. He had at his fingers' ends all the great and little works upon the subject. *Magia Posthuma, Phlegon de Mirabilibus, Augustinus de curâ pro Mortuis, Philosophicae et Christianae Cogitationes de Vampiris*, by John Christofer Herenberg; and a thousand others, among which I remember only a few of those which he lent to my father. He had a voluminous digest of all the judicial cases, from which he had extracted a system of principles that appear to govern—some always, and others occasionally only

—the condition of the vampire. I may mention, in passing, that the deadly pallor attributed to that sort of *revenants*, is a mere melodramatic fiction. They present, in the grave, and when they show themselves in human society, the appearance of healthy life. When disclosed to light in their coffins, they exhibit all the symptoms that are enumerated as those which proved the vampire-life of the long-dead Countess Karnstein.

How they escape from their graves and return to them for certain hours every day, without displacing the clay or leaving any trace of disturbance in the state of the coffin or the cerements, has always been admitted to be utterly inexplicable. The amphibious existence of the vampire is sustained by daily renewed slumber in the grave. Its horrible lust for living blood supplies the vigor of its waking existence. The vampire is prone to be fascinated with an engrossing vehemence, resembling the passion of love, by particular persons. In pursuit of these it will exercise inexhaustible patience and stratagem, for access to a particular object may be obstructed in a hundred ways. It will never desist until it has satiated its passion, and drained the very life of its coveted victim. But it will, in these cases, husband and protract its murderous enjoyment with the refinement of an epicure, and heighten it by the gradual approaches of an artful courtship. In these cases it seems to yearn for something like sympathy and consent. In ordinary ones it goes direct to its object, overpowers with violence, and strangles and exhausts often at a single feast.

The vampire is, apparently, subject, in certain situations, to special conditions. In the particular instance of which I have given you a relation, Mircalla seemed to be limited to a name which, if not her real one, should at least reproduce, without the omission or addition of a single letter, those, as we say anagrammatically, which compose it. *Carmilla* did this; so did *Millarca*.

My father related to the Baron Vordenburg, who remained with us for two or three weeks after the expulsion of Carmilla, the story about the Moravian nobleman and the vampire at Karnstein churchyard, and then he asked the Baron how he had discovered the exact position of the long-concealed tomb of the Countess Millarca. The Baron's grotesque features puckered up into a mysterious smile; he looked down, still smiling on his worn spectacle-case and fumbled with it. Then looking up, he said:

"I have many journals, and other papers, written by that remarkable man; the most curious among them is one treating of the visit of which you speak, to Karnstein. The tradition, of course, discolors and distorts a little. He might have been termed a Moravian nobleman, for he had changed his bode to that territory, and was, beside, a noble. But he was, in truth, a native of Upper Styria. It is enough to say that in very early youth he had been a passionate and favored lover of the beautiful Mircalla, Countess Karnstein. Her early death plunged him into inconsolable grief. It is the nature of vampires to increase and multiply, but according to an ascertained and ghostly law.

"Assume, at starting, a territory perfectly free from that pest. How does it begin, and how does it multiply itself? I will tell you. A person, more or less wicked, puts an end to himself. A suicide, under certain circumstances, becomes a vampire. That specter visits living people in their slumbers; *they* die, and almost invariably, in the grave develop into vampires. This happened in the case of the beautiful Mircalla, who was haunted by one of those demons. My ancestor, Vordenburg, whose title I still bear, soon discovered this, and in the course of the studies to which he devoted himself, learned a great deal more.

"Among other things, he concluded that suspicion of vampirism would probably fall, sooner or later, upon the dead Countess, who in life had been his idol. He conceived a horror, be she what she might, of her remains being profaned by the outrage of a posthumous execution. He has left a curious paper to prove that the vampire, on its expulsion from its amphibious existence, is projected into a far more horrible life; and he resolved to save his once beloved Mircalla from this.

"He adopted the stratagem of a journey here, a pretended removal of her remains, and a real obliteration of her monument. When age had stolen upon him, and from the vale of years he looked back on the scenes he was leaving, he considered, in a different spirit, what he had done, and a horror took possession of him. He made the tracings and notes which have guided me to the very spot, and drew up a confession of the deception that he had practiced. If he had intended any further action in this matter, death prevented him; and the hand of a remote descendant has, too late for many, directed the pursuit to the lair of the beast."

We talked a little more, and among other things he said was this: "One sign of the vampire is the power of the hand. The slender

hand of Mircalla closed like a vise of steel on the General's wrist
when he raised the hatchet to strike. But its power is not confined
to its grasp; it leaves a numbness in the limb it seizes, which is
slowly, if ever, recovered from."

The following Spring my father took me on a tour through Italy.
We remained away for more than a year. It was long before the
terror of recent events subsided; and to this hour the image of
Carmilla returns to memory with ambiguous alternations—sometimes the playful, languid, beautiful girl; sometimes the writhing
fiend I saw in the ruined church; and often from a reverie I have
started, fancying I heard the light step of Carmilla at the drawing-
room door.

Murgunstrumm

❧❀❧

Hugh B. Cave

3 a.m.

I

The night hours are terrifying in that part of the country, away from traveled roads and the voices of sane men. They bring the moan of lost winds, the furtive whisper of swaying trees, the agony wail of frequent storms. They bring madness to men already mad, and fear and gibbering and horrible screams of torment. And sometimes peals of wild hideous laughter a thousand times worse.

And with the dread of darkness, that night, came other fears more acute and more terrifying, to clutch viciously at the man who sought to escape. Macabre horrors of the past, breeding anew in the slough of his memory. Visions of the future, huge and black before him. Grim dread of detection!

The square clock at the end of the long corridor, radium-dialed for the guard's benefit, told him silently that the hour was 3 A.M. The hour when darkness deepens before groping dawn; when man is so close to that other-world of mystery that a mere closing of his eyes, a mere clutching of the subconscious, brings contact with nameless shapeless entities of abhorrent magnitude. The hour when the night watch in this grim gray structure, and the solitary guard on the outer walls, would be least alert. *His* hour, for which he had waited seven months of eternity!

His eyes were wide, staring, fearful. He crept like a cat along the corridor, listening for every separate sound. Somewhere in the tiers above him a man was screeching violently, thumping on a locked door with frenzied fists. That would be Kennery, whom they had dragged in only a week ago. They had warned him to be still at night, poor devil. In the morning he would learn the awful loneliness and silence of solitary confinement. God! And men like that had to go on living, had to wait for death, slowly!

He prowled forward again, trembling, hugging the wall with thin fingers. Three more corridors now and he would be in the yard. He clutched the key feverishly, looking down at it with hungry eyes. The yard, then the last great gate to freedom, and then. . . .

His groping hands touched a closed door. He stopped abruptly. Over his head hung the number 23. The V. D. ward. And he shuddered. Someone was mumbling, laughing, inside—Halsey, the poor diseased idiot who had been here eighteen endless years. He would be on hands and knees, crawling over the floor, searching for beetles. He would seek and seek; and then, triumphant at last, he would sit for hours on his cot, holding a terrified insect cupped in his huge hands while he laughed gleefully at its frantic struggles.

Sickness surged over the fugitive's crouching body. He slunk on again quickly. God, he was glad when that mad caterwauling was smothered by a bend in the corridor! It clung in his brain as he tiptoed to the end of the passage. He fingered the key savagely. Eagerness glared in his eyes.

That key was his. His own! His own cunning had won it. During the past month he had obtained an impression of every separate lock between him and escape. Furtively, secretly, he had taken chewing-gum forms of every infernal slot. And no one knew. No one but Martin LeGeurn, Ruth's brother, who had come once each week, on visiting day, and carried the impressions back to the city, and had a master key made. A master key! Not successful at first. But he himself, with a steel nail file, had scraped and scraped at the thing until it fitted. And now, tonight. . . .

He descended the staircase warily, feeling his way every step. It was 3:10 now. The emergency ward would be open, with its stink of ether and its ghastly white tables on wheels. He could hide there until the guard passed. Every move according to schedule!

The door was open. He crept toward it, reached it, and stopped to peer anxiously behind him. Then he darted over the threshold and clung silently to the wall, and waited.

Hours passed. Frantic hours of doubt and uncertainty. Strange shapes came out of nowhere, out of his distorted mind, to leer and point at him. God! Would those memories never die? Would the horrors of that hour of madness, seven months gone, torment him forever, night after night, bringing back visions of those hideous creatures of living death and the awful limping thing of the inn? Was it not enough that they had already made a soul-twisted wreck of him and sent him to his black house of dread? Would they—

Footsteps! They were audible now, approaching down the corridor outside. They came closer, closer. They scuffed past with an ominous *shf-shf-shf*, whispering their way. With them came the muffled clink of keys, dangling from a great ring at the guard's belt. And the sounds died away.

The fugitive straightened up and stepped forward jerkily. And then he was running wildly down the passage in the opposite direction. A massive door loomed before him. He flung himself upon it, thrusting his own key into the lock. The door swung open. Cold, sweet air rushed into his face. Outside lay the yard, bleak, empty, and the towering walls that barred the world beyond.

His terror was gone now. His movements were mechanical and precise. Silently he locked the barrier behind him and slunk sideways along the wall of the building. If he made the slightest sound, the slightest false move, those glaring, accusing, penetrating searchlights would clank on and sweep the enclosure from one end to the other. The great siren would scream a lurid warning for miles and miles around, howling fiendishly that Paul Hill had escaped.

But if he went cautiously, noiselessly, he would be only a part of the darkness. There was no moon. The night was like pitch. The guard on the wall would not see.

A step at a time he moved along the stone, hesitating before each venture. Now a hundred feet lay between him and the gate. Now fifty; and the guard had not heard. Now twenty. . . .

His breath caught in his throat as he darted across the final ten feet. Flat against the last barrier of all, he fumbled with the huge lock. His fingers turned the key with maddening slowness, to muffle any fatal thud. Then, putting his shoulder to the mass, he pushed. The big gate inched outward.

Without a sound he squeezed through the narrow aperture. His teeth were clenched; his lips tasted of blood. But he was out, outside! No one had seen him! Feverishly he pushed the great block of iron back into place. On hands and knees he crawled along the base of the wall, crawled and crawled, until the guard's turret was only a grim gray blur against the black sky. Then, rising abruptly to his feet, he stumbled into the well of darkness beyond.

"Thank God!" he whispered hoarsely. And then he was hacking, slashing his way through tangled black underbrush, with huge trees massed all about him and the inky sky blotted out overhead.

Armand LeGeurn
II

No one, that night, saw the disheveled gray-clad figure that stumbled blindly from the woods and slunk silently, furtively down the state road. No one saw the unholy lust for freedom in his eyes, or the thin whiteness of his compressed lips.

He was violently afraid. He turned continually to glance behind him. But his fists were clenched viciously. If that hideous siren sounded now, when he was so close to ultimate freedom, they would never take him back there alive. Never! Once before, during his seven hellish months of confinement, the siren had screamed. That was the time Jenson—foolish, idiotic Jenson, mad as a hatter —had scaled the walls. The bloodhounds had uncovered his hiding place in the heart of the woods, and he had been dragged back, whimpering, broken.

But not this time! This time the escaped fugitive was no madman. Horror, not madness, had thrust him into that den of cackling idiots and screeching imbeciles. Stark horror, born of an experience beyond the minds of men. Horror of another world, a world of death and undead demons. And to-night, at four o'clock, Martin LeGeurn would be waiting at the crossroads, with a car. Martin would not be late.

Paul Hill began to run. On and on he ran. Once he turned abruptly and plunged into the edge of the woods as a passing bus roared up behind him. Then, as the bus bellowed past, he leaped to the shoulder of the road again, racing frantically.

A sob of relief soughed through his lips as he rounded the last sharp bend and saw, far ahead, a pair of stationary headlights glaring dimly toward him. He stumbled, caught himself. His legs were dead and heavy and aching sullenly, but he lurched on. And then he was gripping the side of the car with white nerveless hands, and Martin LeGeurn was dragging him into the seat.

There was no delay now. Everything had been arranged! The motor roared sharply. The roadster jerked forward and gathered momentum. The clock on the dash said five minutes past four. By five o'clock they would be in the city. The city, and Ruth, and—and then he would be free to finish it in his own way. Free to fight!

He fumbled with the leather bag under his feet.

"Why didn't Ruth come to see me?"

"Listen!" Martin LeGeurn said sibilantly.

Paul stiffened. He heard it. The sound was a moaning mutter, trembling on the still air, somehow audible above the drone of the motor. It rose higher, clearer, vibrating like a living voice. Paul's fingers dug cruelly into the leather seat cushion. The color seeped out of his face.

He knew that sound. It was a lurid screaming now, filling the night with shrill significance. The night watch had discovered his absence. He had blundered somewhere. Some door left open; some twist of unforeseen fate—and now, up there in the tower, a black-faced fiend was whirling the handle of the great siren faster and faster, gloating over its hellish voice. The same awful wail had seared the countryside when Jenson had fled into the woods, four months ago.

A terrible shudder shook Paul's body. He cringed against his companion. Courage left him. Incoherent mumblings came from his mouth.

"They know," Martin said jerkily. "In ten minutes the road will be patrolled. Every car will be stopped. Get into your clothes. Quick!"

Paul stiffened. Suddenly he sat erect, fists clenched savagely.

"They'll never take me back! I'll kill them! Do you hear? I'll kill them all!"

Then he was tearing at the leather bag between his knees. He got it open, dragged out the light brown suit and tan shirt, the necktie and shoes. Feverishly, as the car rushed on at reckless speed with Martin LeGeurn hunched over the wheel, he ripped off his asylum garb and struggled into the other. Deliberately he stuffed the gray clothes into the bag, and snapped the lock.

"Get off this road. Take the first right."

Martin glanced at him quickly, frowning.

"It's madness. If we hurry, they may not—"

"We can't make it. The state police will—"

"But if we turn off—"

"I know the way, I tell you! Let me drive!"

Martin's foot jammed on the brake. Even before the car had trembled to a stop, Paul snapped his door open and leaped out. And he was no longer a ghastly spectre in gaunt gray as he stumbled in the glare of the headlights. He was a lean, powerful young man, decently dressed, resolute and determined and fighting viciously to overcome his own natural terror. He slid behind the wheel without a word. The car shot forward again under more expert hands. Roaring over the crest of the hill, it swerved suddenly to the right and lumbered into a narrow sub-highway of dirt and gravel.

And the siren screeched behind it. The whole of creation was vibrant with that infernal moan. It would throb and throb all through the night, flinging its message over an unbelievable radius. It would never stop!

But Paul paid no attention to it. He said curtly: "Heave that bag out. They'll never find it in here." And later, when Martin had obeyed, he said abruptly, scowling: "Why didn't Ruth come to see me?"

"She—she just couldn't, Paul."

"Why?"

"You wouldn't understand."

"She's waiting for me now. Is she?"

"I"—Martin stared straight at the windshield, biting his lips—"I don't know, Paul."

"She never tried to help me," Paul said bitterly. "Good God, she knew why I was in there! She could have gone to Kermeff and Allenby and made them listen."

"They left the city," Martin mumbled.

"That's a lie."

"She—"

"I know," Paul said heavily. "She went to them and they wouldn't listen. They're not supposed to listen. Doctor Anton Kermeff and Doctor Franklin Allenby,"—the words were bitter as acid—"that's who they are. Too big to believe the truth. Their job was to put me away and sign a statement that I was mad. That's all they cared."

"I don't think Ruth went to see them, Paul."

Paul's hands tightened on the wheel. The stiffening of his body was visible, so visible that Martin said abruptly, as the car lurched dangerously to the side of the road and jerked back again:

"You—you don't understand, Paul. Please! Wait until you've talked to Father."

"Father?" And the voice was tinged with sudden suspicion. "Why not Ruth?"

"You'll know everything soon, Paul. Please."

Paul was silent. He did not look at his companion again. A vague dread caught at him. Something was wrong. He knew it. He could feel it, like a lurking shape leering and grinning beside him. Like those other lurking undead demons of seven months ago. But Martin LeGeurn could not tell him. Martin was his friend. Someone else would have to blurt out the truth.

The big roadster droned on through the night.

It was daylight when they reached the city. Murky, sodden daylight, choked with drizzling rain. Street lights still smirked above drooling sidewalks. The elevated trestle loomed overhead, a gleaming, sweating mastodon of steel. Silence, which had held sway for the past hour over black country roads, gave way to a rumble of sound.

"Better let me take the wheel," Martin LeGeurn said dully. And when Paul had swung the car to the curb: "We're safe now. They won't look for you here. Not yet."

Not yet! Paul's laugh was mockery. Before the day was over, the news of his escape would be in every headline, glaring over town. Newsboys would be shrilling it. News flashes on the radio would blurt it to millions of listeners. "Special Journal Dispatch! At an early hour this morning, Paul Hill, twenty-three-year-old inmate of the State Insane Asylum, escaped. . . ."

The car moved on again through slanting rain. The windshield wiper clicked monotonously, muttering endless words to the beat of Paul's brain. "Police of this state and neighboring states are conducting an unceasing search for the escaped madman who eluded the dragnet last night. . . ."

"You want to go straight to the house?" Martin LeGeurn said suddenly.

"Of course. Why shouldn't I?"

"I'm not going in with you."

"Why?"

"I've got something to do. Got to go to Morrisdale, and get there before night. But Father's waiting for you. You can talk to him."

He drove on. The streets were deserted, here in the lower downtown sector. The roadster picked its way through intricate short cuts and sideways, and emerged presently on the South Side, to purr softly along glistening boulevards.

"You're going to Morrisdale?" Paul frowned.

"Yes."

"What for?"

"For—Ruth," Martin said grimly. "It's your own idea, Paul. Your method of escape. Just what I couldn't think of myself, though I sat up night after night, half mad."

"What do you mean?"

"I'll tell you—when it's over," Martin muttered. He was staring through the crescent of gleaming glass before him. His lips were tight, bloodless. "We're almost there," he said abruptly.

They were entering the residential sector of the South Side. The car groped its way more slowly. Paul stared on both sides, remembering the houses, the great church on the corner, the rows of stores: things he had forgotten during the past months. And presently Martin swung the wheel. The roadster skidded into a tree-lined road. Lovely homes with immaculate driveways and wide lawns loomed gray in the drizzle. The car slowed to an awkward stop. Martin turned abruptly, thrusting out his hand.

"Good-by, Paul. Don't worry."

"But—"

"I've got to go. Got to reach Morrisdale on time to-night. Talk to Father, Paul. And trust me."

Paul gripped the outstretched hand. Then he was out of the car, hurrying up the drive. And the car was roaring down the road again, into the murk, like a great greyhound.

Paul's fingers pressed the bell. He waited, nervously. The door opened. Old Armand LeGeurn, Ruth's father, stood there on the sill, arms outthrust.

After that, things blurred. The door closed, and Paul was pacing down the thick carpet with LeGeurn's arm around him. Then he was in the luxurious library, slumped in a huge chair, folding and unfolding his hands, while Old LeGeurn talked slowly, softly.

"She couldn't come to see you, Paul. They've sent her away. The same two physicians, Kermeff and Allenby. Less than a week after they sent you. Mad, they said. They're big men, Paul. Too big. She never returned here after leaving the hospital at Marssen. They took her straight from there to Morrisdale."

"Morrisdale," Paul muttered feebly. Suddenly he was on his feet, eyes wide and body tense. "That's where Martin's gone!"

"He's been often, Paul. That's how you got your letters. He mailed them from here. She didn't want you to know."

"But there *must* be some way of getting her out."

"No, Paul. Not yet. We've tried. Tried everything—money, influence, threats. Kermeff and Allenby are bigger than that, boy. They put their names to the paper. No power on earth can convince them they're wrong. No power on this earth—yet."

"Then she's got to stay?" Paul pleaded. "She's got to. . . ." He relaxed again with a heavy shudder. "It's not right, Mr LeGeurn! It's horrible! Why, those places are—are. . . ."

"I know what they are, boy. We're doing all we can. But we must wait. She still remembers those other things: Murgunstrumm and the awful creatures of the inn. They rush upon her. They affect her—queerly. You understand, boy. You know what it means. Until she's forgotten all that, we can only wait. No physician in the country would disagree with Kermeff and Allenby. Not with such evidence. In time she'll forget."

"She'll never forget, in there!" Paul cried harshly. "At night, in the dark, the whole thing comes back. It's awful. Night after night it haunted me. I could hear that horrible laughter, and the screams. And those inhuman shapes would come out of nowhere, grinning and pointing and leering. She'll never forget. If we don't get her away. . . ."

"Escape, son?"

"Yes! Escape!"

"It won't do. She couldn't face it. She's not strong enough to be hunted down as you'll be."

Paul stood up savagely, pushing his fingers through his hair. He stared mutely at the man before him. Then his nerves gave way. He buried his face in his hands, sobbing.

"You'll stay here to-night, Paul?" he heard Armand LeGeurn asking.

Paul shook his head heavily. No, he couldn't stay here. The first place they'd look for him would be here in Ruth's home. As soon as they discovered that he had wriggled through their unholy dragnet, they'd come here and question, and search, and watch.

"I want to think," he said wearily. "It's all so tangled. I want to be alone."

"I know, son." Armand LeGeurn rose quietly and offered his hand. "Let me know where you are, always. If you need money or help, come here for it. We believe in you."

Paul nodded. He didn't need money. There was a wallet in the pocket of the coat Martin had given him. He could go and get a room somewhere, and think the thing out alone. More than anything else he wanted to be by himself.

"I'll go to the North End," he said, "and—"

But Armand LeGeurn was pacing to the door. When he returned, he carried a small suit-case in his hand.

"Take this," he advised. "It won't do for you to go prowling about the stores, getting what you need. Everything is here. And—be careful, Paul."

Paul took the suit-case silently. Abruptly he thrust out his hand. Then he hurried down the hall and went out the front door.

"To Rehobeth"
III

Paul found lodgings in a third-rate rooming house, deep in the twisted cobblestoned streets of the North End slums. There, late in the afternoon, he sat on the slovenly bed and stared fixedly at the single window. The suit-case, open but not unpacked, lay between his feet; and on top, grinning up at him like a black beetle nestling in the clean white folds of the shirt beneath it, lay a loaded revolver. Armand LeGeurn, acting evidently on the spur of the minute, had dropped it there just before clicking the bag shut.

It was raining. A drooling porous mist fogged the window pane. The room was a chill, dark, secluded retreat high above the muttering side street below. A radio, somewhere in the bowels of the house, mumbled dance music and crooning voices.

Paul sat motionless. He was not afraid of realities any more. It was not fear of tangible things that kept the color out of his face and made him sit rigid. The police would never look here for him, at least not until they had combed the rest of the city first. He was in no immediate danger. He had money, clothes, and friends if he needed them.

But the torment had returned—torment a hundred times more vicious than fear of capture. Macabre shadows stalked the room. Nameless voices laughed horribly. Fingers pointed at him. Red, red lips, set fiendishly in chalk-colored dead-alive faces, curled back over protruding teeth to grin malignantly. A significant malicious name hissed back and forth, back and forth, never ceasing. *Murgunstrumm! Murgunstrumm!*

Ruth was in the asylum at Morrisdale. Martin LeGeurn had gone there. Something was wrong. Martin had seemed preoccupied, mysterious. He hadn't wanted to talk. Now he was gone. Only Armand LeGeurn was left, and Armand had tried every method possible; had tried to convince Kermeff and Allenby that she was not mad.

Paul's fists clenched. He mouthed the two names over and over, twisting them bitterly. Kermeff and Allenby. It was their fault! He jerked to his feet, clutching at the wooden bed-post with both hands, cursing loudly, violently.

Then he sat down again, staring at the black revolver which leered up at him. A truck rumbled over the cobblestones, far below. Someone was turning the dials of the radio, bringing in snatches of deep-throated music and jangling voices. Paul reached down slowly and took the revolver in his hands. He fingered it silently, turning it over and over. Then he sat very still, looking at it.

Ten minutes later, without a word, he stood up and put the revolver in his pocket. He bent over the suit-case. Very quietly he walked to the door. His lips were thin and tight, and his eyes glaring.

He paced noiselessly down the narrow stairs to the lower hall. The street door opened and closed. He hurried out into the rain, along the sidewalk.

Suit-case in hand, he groped his way through the maze of

gleaming streets, avoiding the lighted thoroughfares as much as possible, yet bearing ever toward the uptown sector. He glanced neither to right nor left, but strode along without hesitating, carried forward recklessly by the hate in his heart and the sudden resolution which had come to him. Not until he reached the outskirts of the slums did he consider his own peril again. Then he stopped, stepped quickly into a black doorway, and stared furtively about him.

He was mad, walking through the streets like this. What if the police down here had been given his description? What if they were even now looking for him? Probably they had and they were. If he stepped on a bus or boarded a street car, or even hailed a cab, he would be playing squarely into their hands. He couldn't reach the LeGeurn home that way. And he couldn't go on walking, like a blind fool, waiting for some stranger to peer suddenly into his face and scream an alarm.

He studied the street in both directions. A hundred yards distant, on the corner, a red-and-white electric sign, blinking in the drizzle, designated a drugstore. Warily Paul crept out of the doorway and moved along the sidewalk. He was afraid again now, and nervous. He kept his face hidden when hurrying men and women brushed past him. Reaching the drugstore, he slipped inside without attracting attention and looked quickly for a telephone booth. An instant later, with a little gasp of relief, he swung the booth door behind him and groped in his pockets for a coin.

The nickel jangled noisily. With stiff fingers Paul dialed the LeGeurn number and waited fretfully until the resultant hum clicked off.

A masculine voice, Armand LeGeurn's, answered almost inaudibly.

"Mr LeGeurn," Paul said slowly, fumbling for the right thing to say. "I want to—"

His words had a surprising effect. LeGeurn, instead of waiting for him to finish, interrupted with a hearty laugh and sputtered quickly:

"Hello, Frank, hello! By the Lord, man, it's a downright joy to hear that voice of yours. I'm all tied up here. Police watching the house, and the phone wires tapped in the bargain. Damned inconvenient, I'm telling you! What's up? What d'you want?"

Paul's reply choked on his lips. He stiffened, and his fingers tightened on the receiver. Phone wires tapped! Police at the house! Then abruptly he understood Armand LeGeurn's ruse. Regaining his composure, he answered with assumed astonishment:

"Police? Why, what's wrong?"

"What's wrong! Don't you read the papers?"

"You don't mean," Paul said, frowning, "it's about that chap who got away from the nut house? Good Lord, what's that got to do with you?"

"Plenty. Tell you later, when you're sober."

"I'm sober now. That is, almost."

"What's on your mind then?"

"Nothing much." Then Paul added quickly: "That is, nothing but the fact that I'm getting thoroughly soaked and I'm stranded in the slums without a sou in my pocket, old man. I was going to demand your car to escort me home, if your pugilistic chauffeur isn't asleep or something. But if you're tied up. . . ."

"The car, eh? Where'd you say you were?"

"Down in the heart of the most miserable, sloppy, filthy section of this confounded city, my boy." Paul flung back desperately. "And not enjoying it a bit."

"Really? Well, you can have the car. Welcome to it. Where'll I send it?"

Paul named the streets hurriedly. As an afterthought he said as carelessly as he could: "Tell Jeremy to pull up at the dinky little drugstore just around the corner of Haviland. Yeah, I'll be in there getting my feet dry. And say—thanks, mister. Thanks a lot. I appreciate it."

The telephone clicked ominously. Releasing it, Paul leaned against the side of the booth, limp, frightened, with cold sweat trickling down his face. It was another moment before he could steel himself to open the door and step out. Then, with a forced slouch, he picked up his bag, pushed the door wide, and strode across the tile floor.

He couldn't wait in the store. That would be dangerous. The police might see fit to check the call and send someone to investigate. But he could wait outside, in some convenient doorway a short distance up the street. And then, when he saw the car coming, he could walk casually toward it without being seen.

Outside, with the rain beating in his face, he sought a suitable niche and found one. Huddled there, he wondered if his plan was plausible. It wasn't. The element of risk was too great. If the police came to the drugstore, seeking him, they would be suspicious when they found him gone. They too would wait for the car. Then, if he stepped out. . . .

But the car, coming from the suburbs, would have to pass along the avenue before turning into Haviland Street. That was it! Paul knew the machine by sight—a long low black roadster, inconspicuous among others, but easily discerned by one who knew it intimately. And it would have to cross the avenue intersection, have to pass the lights.

Very quickly Paul slipped out of the doorway and hurried into the rain.

He had to wait long when he reached the square. While he waited, leaning against the wall of a building, with his coat collar pulled high above his neck and face, he watched the lights blink from red to green and green to red, endlessly. Slow lights they were, and the corner was a dangerous one, choked with traffic and scurrying pedestrians. The cars that snaked past, scintillating and gleaming, were like huge moving gems as they groped their way with sluggish caution.

The whole square was bright with illumination. Brilliant store windows threw out walls of color. Sparkling electric signs twinkled overhead. Street-lamps glared accusingly, sullenly, striving to penetrate the rain. It was maddening to stand there, waiting and waiting. . . .

Once a policeman, in rustling rubber coat, swung past with mechanical steps. Paul stiffened and watched him. But pedestrians were waiting at the same time for the traffic lights to become red and yellow; and the policeman paid no attention. He passed on idly, and Paul relaxed with a shudder.

Five minutes passed, and ten. And then the car came. The lights were against it. It slowed cautiously as it approached; and as it stopped, Paul darted forward across the gleaming avenue. Skirting two intervening machines, he leaped to the running-board and clawed the door open. And then he was in the seat beside the lean, wiry form of Matt Jeremy, and muttering harshly:

"I prayed for that light, Jeremy, prayed it would be red when you came. If you hadn't stopped. . . ."

Jeremy glanced at him quickly, bewildered.

"What's wrong, sir? I was going to the drugstore, like you told Mr LeGeurn. I thought you wanted—"

The light changed. Paul clutched the man's arm and said abruptly, thickly:

"Turn right. Get out of here quickly!"

Jeremy grunted. The car jerked forward, hesitated an instant to nose its way through cross traffic, and swung sharply off the avenue. Gaining speed, it droned on through the rain, leaving the clamor and congestion of the main thoroughfare behind.

"You'll have to get home the best way you can," Paul said evenly, a little later. "I've got to have the machine."

"That's what Mr LeGeurn said, sir," Jeremy nodded.

"He'll understand. That's why I phoned."

"Yes, sir. He understands all right. He said for me to go with you."

"What?"

"I'm to stick with you, sir. That's what he said. If you want me."

Paul drew a deep breath and stared squarely into the man's grinning face.

"Want you! Jeremy, I—"

"I might come in handy, maybe," Jeremy shrugged. "Trouble's my middle name, sir. Where to?"

"To Rehobeth," Paul said grimly. "To Rehobeth and the Gray Toad Inn. And the rest is up to God, if there is a God in that unholy place."

"They Don't Come Out, Sir."
IV

For years, old Henry Gates had squeezed a meager existence out of the ancient Rehobeth Hotel. For years he had scuffed quietly about the village, minding his own affairs and seldom intruding, but wise in his knowledge of what went on about him. For years he had lived in silent dread of what might some day happen.

To-night he stood silently on his veranda, gazing down into the deepening dusk of the valley below. The air was cold and sweet with the smell of rain-soaked earth. Darkness was creeping in on all sides, hovering deep and restless above the village.

Across the way a light blinked, announcing that Tom Horrigan's boy was working in the stables. Other lights, feeble and futile, winked on either side. Beyond them the woods were still and dark, and the leaden sky hung low with threatening rain.

"A night of evil," Gates mumbled, sucking his pipe. "There'll be doin's to-night. There'll be laughin' and screamin' on the Marssen Road."

The light across the way went out suddenly. A boy appeared, framed in the stable doorway. The door creaked on rusty wheels, jarring shut. The boy turned, glanced toward the hotel, waved his hand.

"Hi there, Mr Gates! A fair black night it'll be, hey? I was walkin' to town."

"Ye've changed your mind, I'm thinkin'," Gates retorted.

"That I have. I'll be goin' home and to bed, and lockin' my windows this night."

The boy hurried away. Other lights blinked out. Henry Gates gazed into the valley again, muttering to himself.

"There'll be screamin' and laughin' in the old inn to-night."

He turned and hobbled inside. The door closed; the bolt thudded noisily. The village of Rehobeth was dormant, slumbering, huddled and afraid, waiting for daylight to arouse it.

An hour later the black roadster purred softly out of the darkness. The car was a dusty gaunt shape now, after three hours travel over sixty-odd miles of paved highways and black, deserted country roads. Matt Jeremy hung wearily over the wheel. Paul Hill, slumped beside him, stretched arms and legs with a grumble of complaint, and opened the door.

Shadows filled the valley below. Here the road, after climbing steadily for five miles, rested in the uncouth little hamlet before venturing the last mile or so over the ridge into the next state. And Rehobeth had not changed since that day, more than seven months past, when Paul Hill had stood in this same spot—stood here with Ruth LeGeurn and laughed, because they were marooned with a broken-down car and had to spend the night in the ancient hotel beside them.

No, Rehobeth had not altered. It was still the same lonely isolated village, looking down upon a world all its own—a shadowed gray world, blanketed with bleak snow during the long winter months, swathed in murky sunlight through the summer. Only sixty miles from the big city, only twenty-odd miles from civilization, but in reality a million miles from anywhere, sordid, aloof, forgotten.

"Well, what do you think?" Paul said with a shrug. "Like the place?"

"Not much, sir," Jeremy confessed. "Still, I reckon it's a pretty good hide-away, and it ain't so far you can't keep track of things."

"I'm not hiding, Jeremy."

"No? Then what are we doin' here, sir? I thought"—Jeremy released the wheel and slid out—"I thought we were just goin' to lay low and wait."

Paul climbed the hotel steps slowly. The door was locked. Evidently it was bolted on the inside, and the inmates of the place had gone to bed.

"Old Gates," Paul smiled, "must be upstairs. They don't expect visitors at this hour."

He hammered loudly. "Gates!" he called out. "Henry Gates!"

A long interval passed, and presently a *scuff-scuff* of footsteps was audible inside. But the door did not open immediately. A face was suddenly framed in the window at the right, and a groping glare of lamplight illuminated the veranda. Then the face and the light vanished, and the bolt rattled. The door opened cautiously.

"Ye're lookin' for me, sir?"

"You're Gates?" Paul said, knowing that he was.

"Yes, sir. I am that."

"Good. We're staying here a day or two, Gates. You've two good rooms vacant?"

"Ye're stayin' here, sir? Here?"

"Yes. Why not? Full up, are you?"

"No, no, sir. I've got rooms. Sure I've got 'em. Only the likes of you, with an automobile like that un, don't generally—"

Paul forced a laugh. He knew what Gates was thinking.

"That's all right," he shrugged. "Quite all right. We want to do a bit of looking around. Might even decide to set up a hunting camp around here somewhere. Just show us the rooms and never mind about the car."

Old Gates was willing enough, once his fears were allayed. He held the door wide. Paul and Jeremy passed inside casually and gazed about them.

There was nothing inspiring. Bare, cracked walls leered down as if resenting the intrusion. A musty lounge, long unused, leaned on

scarred legs. A squat table, bearing the flickering oil lamp which
Gates had first held, stood in the middle of the floor. Beyond, a
flight of stairs angled up into darkness.

"D'ye mind tellin' me your names, sir?" Gates said hesitantly.
"I'll show ye to your rooms, and then I'll be makin' out the register."

"Mr James Potter will do," Paul nodded. "James Potter and
chauffeur. And by the way, Gates, have you a typewriter?"

"Typewriter, sir?" Gates hobbled behind the desk and took
down a key. "Afraid not, sir. I used to have, but you see business
ain't what it used to be." He wheezed up the stairs with Paul and
Jeremy following him. "Rehobeth be such an out-of-the-way place,
sir, and nobody comes this way very often lately, and. . . ."

The rooms were at the end of the upper corridor, adjoining each
other and connected by an open door. Paul inspected them quietly
and smiled, and pressed a bill into the old man's hand. And presently, alone in Paul's chamber with the hall door shut, the two
newcomers stared at each other and nodded grimly. That much
was over with.

"Didn't recognize me," Paul said evenly.

"Recognize you, sir?" Jeremy frowned.

"This is the place, Jeremy, where Miss Ruth and I stopped that
night. You don't know the details. You were in Florida with Mr
LeGeurn."

"Oh. I see, sir. And you thought he might—"

"Remember me? Yes. But seven months is a long time. The
madhouse can change a man in less time than that. Open the bag,
Jeremy, will you?"

Jeremy did so, putting his knee to the leather and jerking the
straps loose. Lifting the suit-case to the bed, Paul fumbled a moment with the contents, then stepped to the old-fashioned desk
and sat down with paper and fountain pen in hand.

And he wrote two letters, one to Doctor Anton Kermeff, the
other to Doctor Franklin Allenby, addressing both to the State
Hospital in the city he had just left. The letter to Kermeff read:

My dear Kermeff:
You will, I am sure, consider this note most carefully and act upon it
as soon as possible. Mr Paul Hill, the young man whom you and
Allenby declared insane some seven months ago, and who escaped only

*very recently from confinement, is now at the Rehobeth Hotel in a
state of most complete and mystifying coma. Fortunately I am on my
vacation and was passing through Rehobeth at the time of his attack,
and I am now attending him.*

*The case, I assure you, is worth your gravest attention. It is the
most unusual condition I have ever had the fortune to stumble upon.
Of course, I am remaining here incognito. The name is James Potter. I
suggest that you come at once, saying nothing to arouse undue
attention to yourselves or to me. Later, of course, the patient must be
returned to confinement; but meanwhile I believe I have something
worthy of your esteemed consideration.*

*A copy of this letter I am also sending to Allenby, since you are
both equally interested in the case.*

Yours in haste,
Hendrick Von Heller, M.D.

The letter to Allenby was an exact duplicate. Paul sat very still,
staring at what he had created. He was gambling, of course. Only
one thing he was sure of: that Von Heller, the very noted specialist,
was actually somewhere in this part of the state, on vacation. Von
Heller had discussed that with the doctors at the asylum, on one of
his regular visits.

As for the rest, Von Heller was known, by reputation at least, to
both Kermeff and Allenby. But would the handwriting of the letters prove fatal? That was the risk. It might; it might not. Possibly
Kermeff and Allenby had never seen, or never particularly noticed, Von Heller's script. Perhaps—and it was very likely, considering the man's importance and prestige—he had employed a secretary. At any rate, the element of chance was there. A typewriter
would have lessened it, and could easily have been purchased on
the way here. But old Gates had none, and it was too late now.

"We'll have to face it," Paul shrugged. "We can't be sure."

"If it means a scrap, sir. . . ."

"It might, Jeremy. Part of it might. But we'll need minds, as
well. *Wills.*"

"Well now—"

"Never mind," Paul said. "It's getting late. Come."

He shoved the door open. Henry Gates had lighted the oil burners in the corridor, filling the upper part of the inn with a furtive,
uneasy, yellowish glare. Probably those burners had not been ig-

nited in months past. Perhaps not for seven months. And the lower lobby, illuminated only by the oil lamp on the desk, was deep with moving shadows, gaunt and repelling.

Gates was writing in the register when Paul and Jeremy descended. He looked up and grunted, obviously startled. Holding his pen at an awkward angle, he said hurriedly:

"Just puttin' your names down, sir, I was. Be ye goin' out?"

"For a short drive," Paul nodded.

"M-m-m. It be a dark night, sir. Not a star in the sky when I looked out the window just now. And no moon at all to speak of. These be lonely roads about here."

Paul smiled bitterly. Lord, what mockery! Gates, huddled here, mumbling to him—to *him*—about the loneliness of the surrounding roads! As if he didn't know! As if he hadn't learned every conceivable horror there was to learn, seven months ago!

"You've a mail box here?" he questioned curtly.

"I'll take it, sir," Gates replied, eyeing the white oblongs in Paul's hand. "Two of 'em, hey? Ain't often the postman gets anythin' here, sir. He'll be comin' by in the mornin', on his route."

"They'll get to the city before night?"

"Well, sir, the postman takes 'em to Marssen in his tin lizzie."

"That's quite all right, then. Come, Jeremy."

"Be ye goin' anywheres in particular, sir?" Gates blinked, raising his eyebrows.

"I thought we might turn down the old road that cuts in a mile or so below here. Looked rather interesting when we came through. Leads to Marssen, doesn't it?"

"It does that."

"Hm-m. I think I've been over it before. Vaguely familiar, somehow. If I'm right, there ought to be an old inn about two miles down. The Gray Goose, or the Gray Gull, or—"

"Ye mean the Gray Toad?"

"That's it, I guess. Closed up, is it?"

"No, sir," Gates' voice was a whisper as he came out from behind his barlike desk and scuffed forward ominously. "It ain't closed, sir. And if I was you—"

"Who runs the place, I wonder? Do you know?"

"I know, sir. Yus, I know. It's a queer cripple as runs it, sir. A queer foreigner what never goes nowhere nor comes into the village, nor ever does anythin' but limp around inside his own dwellin'. Murgunstrumm is his name, sir. Murgunstrumm."

"Strange name," Paul mused, keeping his voice level with an effort. "And what's so wrong about the place, Gates?"

"I dunno, sir. Only I've heard noises which ain't the kind I like to hear. I've seen automobiles stop there, sir—fine automobiles, too—and ladies and gentlemen go inside, all dressed up in fine clothes. But I ain't never seen 'em again. They don't come out, sir. And I know one thing, as I'm certain of."

"Yes?"

"About seven months ago it happened, sir. I'm sittin' here behind my desk one night along about evenin', and a young couple comes walkin' down the road from the woods. A pretty girl she was, if ever there was one; and the young man was about your height and looks, only not—excusin' me, sir—so kind of pale-lookin' and thin. They said as how their car was broke down about a mile up the road, and could they use my telephone to call a garage feller in Marssen. And then—"

Gates peered furtively about him and came a step nearer. He was rubbing his hands together with an unpleasant sucking sound, as if he feared the consequences of saying too much.

"They had supper here, sir, the two of them, and then they went out for a walk. Said they might walk down the valley, seein' as how it was such a fine night. But they didn't get there, sir. No, sir, they didn't ever get there."

"They got lost?" Jeremy said curtly.

"I'm not knowin'. All I know is, I'm sittin' here about one o'clock in the mornin', havin' a bite to eat with the garage man after he'd got their automobile fixed up and waitin' for them to come back for it—and we sudden hear footsteps stumblin' up the steps. There's a shout, and we run out. And it's the young man, sir, walkin' like one in a dream and white as a ghost. And he's carryin' the girl in his arms, like she's dead; only she ain't dead, sir, because she's moanin' and mumblin' like she's gone clean mad. . . ."

Gates' voice choked off to a faltering hiss, leaving only a feeble echo to chase fretfully around the room. Jeremy was staring at him with wide eyes. Paul stood very stiff, white and silent.

"And what happened then?" Jeremy whispered.

"Well, the young man fell down on the floor here like a dead one for sure, and he never moved a muscle when me and the garage feller bent over him. The girl, she lay here twitchin' and sobbin' and talkin' a lot of words which didn't make sense. Then the garage man and me, we got both of 'em into the young man's car, and the garage feller he drove 'em as quick as he could to Marssen, to the hospital there. They called up the city for some real good doctors, and"—Gates shuddered violently and peered around him again—"and both the young man and his lady friend was put away in the insane-house," he finished fearfully.

There was silence for an instant. An unnatural, ugly silence, broken only by the sound of men breathing and the *pft-pft-pft* of the oil lamp on the desk. Then Paul laughed softly, queerly.

"The insane-house, eh?" he shrugged. "A good story, Gates. Not bad at all. And they're still there?"

"It's the God's honest truth, sir. I swear it is. And the young people are still locked up, they are. I'm tellin' ye, sir, I think of it even now on dark nights, sir, and I fair get the horrors from it!"

"Thanks. I guess we'll be moving along, Gates. We'll have a look at your ghastly inn."

"But nobody goes along that road no more, sir. Not after nightfall!"

"All right, old man," Paul shrugged, knowing that his voice faltered slightly and his assumed indifference lacked the sincerity he strove to stuff into it. "Don't sit up and worry about us. We won't come back the way the others did. I'd have a hard job carrying you, eh, Jeremy?"

Jeremy's laugh, too, was vaguely harsh. But he turned and followed to the door. And an instant later, leaving Gates stiff-legged and staring in the middle of the unclean floor, with the sputtering oil lamp casting spider-shadows on the wall behind him, Paul and Jeremy stepped over the threshold. The door creaked shut behind them. They descended the wooden steps slowly.

Murgunstrumm
V

The lonely untraveled road between Rehobeth and the buried little town of Marssen, twelve miles distant, was particularly black and abandoned that night. Leaving the main dirt highway a mile or so below the last of Rehobeth's straggling houses, it

plunged immediately into sullen unbroken woods, where all
sounds died to nothingness and the light was a dim, uneven, flickering gloom.

The mud-crusted black roadster, with Jeremy at the wheel,
careened recklessly down the main road, boring its way with twin
beams of bright light. At the intersection, it slowed to a crawl, and
Jeremy swung the wheel. Then, more slowly, the car proceeded
down the Marssen road; and presently it was moving at snail-
speed, groping along a snake track of deep ruts and loose, damp
sand.

"It ain't," Jeremy said laconically, "what you'd want to call a
pleasure drive, sir. Fair gives me the creeps, it does, after the old
guy's talk."

Paul nodded. He said nothing. He was thinking again, and remembering, in spite of himself. What Gates had narrated back at
the hotel was true, and the old man's words had awakened memories which were better a thousand times dead.

Paul's face was strained, colorless now. His hands were
clenched defensively. He stared straight ahead of him through the
dirty windshield, watching every sudden twist of the way, every
looming shadow. Once he touched the revolver in his pocket and
felt suddenly relieved. But he remembered again, and knew that
the weapon would mean nothing. And presently, after ten minutes
of slow, cautious progress, he said quietly:

"Stop the car here, Jeremy."

"Here, sir?"

"We'll walk the rest. It isn't far. They mustn't see us."

Jeremy grunted. The roadster turned to the side of the road,
scraped noisily against the thick bushes, and came to a jerky stop.

"Will I lock it, sir?"

"Yes. And keep the key in your hand. We may need it quickly."

Jeremy glanced at him quizzically. Then, with a shrug, he
turned the ignition key, removed it, and slid out of his seat. In a
moment Paul was beside him, gripping his arm.

"Sure you want to come, Jeremy?"

"Why not, sir? I'm pretty handy with my fists, ain't I?"

"That won't help, Jeremy. Nothing will help, if we're seen."

"Well then, we won't be seen. You're shiverin', sir!"

"Am I?" Paul's laugh was harsh, toneless. "That's bad. I

shouldn't be. Not after what happened before. Shivering won't help, either. Come on."

They passed down the narrow road, leaving the roadster half hidden, black and silent, behind them. Paul, thinking again, peered furtively on either side, fighting back his fear of the darkness. Shadows leaped at him from matted walls of gloom. Faint whispers sucked down from above as the night breeze whimpered and muttered through rustling leaves. The horrors of the madhouse came back, vivid and close. Supernatural voices laughed hideously and screamed, and everywhere ahead, in the gloom, a limping shape seemed to be waiting and leering and pointing triumphantly.

Jeremy, more or less indifferent to intangible terror, plodded along with a set frown on his square features. Shadows and whispers did not trouble him. He did not know. And Paul, pressing close to him, found relief in the man's presence, and courage in his stolidness.

So they walked on and on, until presently out of the darkness ahead of them, on the right, a gray mass took form with maddening slowness. Paul stood quite still, drawing his companion close.

"That's the place," he said almost inaudibly.

"There's a light, sir," Jeremy observed.

Yes, there was a light. But it was a feeble thing, a mere oblong slit of illumination, visible faintly through a cracked shutter. And the house itself, upstairs and down, was sinister with darkness. Like an enormous humpbacked toad it squatted just off the road, isolated in its own desolate clearing, hemmed in on three sides by unbroken walls of gloom and silence.

Not a lovely place, the Gray Toad Inn. Not any more. At one time, Paul reflected, it had been a roadhouse of gay repute, situated pleasantly on an out-of-the-way road between semi-dead villages, with desirable seclusion a strong point in its favor. Here, night after night, had come revelers from the nearby city and even nearer towns, to laugh and drink and fill the big house with youthful clamor.

But not any more. All that had changed. The inn had grown cold and lonely. The road itself had fallen more and more into disuse and obscurity. That very isolation which had made the place a popular resort had now buried it in abject solitude and left it dark and dismal, hoary with interred memories, sinking into slow rot.

Yet a light glowed now in the lower level, winking out into the darkness. A wan yellow light, filtered through a cracked blind, clutching outward like a thin bony finger, as if pleading for old times to return. And Paul and Jeremy, staring at it, crept slowly, noiselessly, through the deep grass of the overgrown clearing toward it.

And there was something else, which the inn had never known in its days of laughter and gaiety—something which even Jeremy, who lacked imagination and feared no foe but of flesh and form, noticed furtively.

"There's somethin'," he whispered, reaching out to grasp Paul's coat, "there's somethin' awful queer here, sir. The air. . . ."

Paul stiffened. Fifty yards before him, the humpbacked structure bulged sullenly against the crawling sky above. Deep grass rustled against his legs. He stared suddenly into Jeremy's set face.

"What do you mean?" he said thickly. But to himself, in his mind, he muttered triumphantly: "He's noticed it too! He's noticed it too! Ruth wouldn't believe me when we came here before, but it's true, it's true!"

"The air has a funny smell, sir," Jeremy said slowly. "Like—like earth, or dirt. Like a mushroom cellar or somethin'. I must be crazy, sir, but it seems to hang all around here, heavy-like."

Crazy? Paul choked out a jangling laugh, full of triumph. No, not crazy. Not yet. Jeremy was right. This place—this ancient abode of infernal silence and monstrous horror—was alive within itself. It breathed and felt. It was no part of the woods around it.

But Jeremy wouldn't understand. The explanation was far too intricate and vague and impossible for him. Yet it was true. The atmosphere surrounding this structure before them, the air that clung tenaciously to the entire clearing, was a living entity, a dull leaden *thing*, visible to eyes that dared seek it out. It was a part of the inn itself, having no connection, no acquaintance, with the air about it. It reeked up out of the very earth, and from the decaying walls of the building, and from the bodies of the dead-alive creatures who inhabited the place.

But to Jeremy it was simply a creepy sensation, vaguely inexplicable and unpleasant. And so Paul moved on, more and more slowly, cautioning his companion to complete silence.

Thus they reached the side of the inn itself, and Paul crouched there in utter darkness, with the great structure hunched over him, mastodonic and gaunt, enveloped in its pall of dull, moving, viscous exhalation.

For an instant Paul clung there, unable to put down his deepening dread. All the ancient horrors rushed upon him viciously, striving to shatter the walls of his mind and send him back, back down the road, reeling and laughing and screaming in madness, as they had done on that other night seven months ago. And then, slowly, he stood erect until he could peer through the cracked shutter. And hung there, rigid and flat-pressed against the window-ledge, staring.

Only a vague semicircle of illumination was visible inside through the filthy window glass. There at a small square table against the farther wall, unaware of Paul's presence, sat a long figure. The oil lamp on the table, peculiarly shaded with an agate cup-shaped globe, cast a restless, unreal glow into the man's face.

An ugly face it was, in the full horrible significance of the word. A sunken savage gargoyle, frog-like in shape, with narrow close-set eyes blinking continually beneath beetled brows that crawled together, like thick hairy fingers, in the center. The broad nose, twisted hookwise, seemed stuck on, like a squatting toad with bunched legs. And the mouth was wide, thick, sensuous, half leering as if it could assume no other expression.

The man made no movement. Apparently in a state of semi-stupor, he leaned on the table in the near gloom. Beyond him the feeble light played up and down the cream-colored wall and over the worn green carpet, revealing shadowed shapes of other tables and other chairs and objects without definite form.

Paul stared, utterly fascinated and terrified, clutching the window-sill with white hands, standing stiff and unalive in the darkness. He might have clung there indefinitely, remembering every separate fear of his last visit here, had not Jeremy's guarded voice hissed suddenly behind him:

"Somethin's comin', sir! A car!"

Paul turned. A faint purring sound came to his ears from somewhere down the road. He stepped forward violently and seized Jeremy's arm.

"Down!" he cried sharply. "Get down, man!" And then he was flat in the deep grass, heaving, breathing heavily, with Jeremy prone beside him, so close that their bodies fused together.

"What is it, sir?" Jeremy whispered.

"Be still!"

In the road, the purring became an audible drone, as of a motor. Nearer and nearer it came, and then, just once, a muted horn shrilled out, sending a muffled blast through the night. Twin headlights took form and grew into glaring, accusing orbs.

At that moment the door of the inn opened creaking back softly. A lantern swung in the aperture, dangling from an uplifted hand; and the man with the toad face scuffed slowly over the threshold, muttering to himself and blinking his eyes. Bent, twisted grotesquely, he limped down the stone flagging a dozen paces and stood still, holding the lantern high.

The headlights of the oncoming car became brilliant bowls of fire, cutting slantwise through the unearthly mist of the grounds. They slowed and stopped, and the drone of the engine became suddenly still. The lights were extinguished. The car door clicked and swung open. A voice—a girl's voice, vaguely timid and afraid and fantastically out of place in such sordid surroundings—said:

"This—this is the place you are bringing me?"

And the voice that answered her was somehow packed with subtlety, gloating and possessive in spite of its quiet smoothness.

"Certainly, my dear. You will enjoy yourself."

Two shapes materialized. Shadows in the gloom, nothing more, they moved down the path to where the lantern swayed before them. Then the outer rays of the light encompassed them, and Paul stared mutely with every ounce of color ebbed from his face.

A man and a girl. Man-and-a-girl. It surged over and over in his brain. God! After seven months, the horror was still going on, still happening! The man—the man was like all the others, tall, straight, smiling, attired in immaculate evening clothes. The girl was young and lovely and radiant in a trailing white gown and flame-colored velvet wrap. But she was not happy; she was not a willing guest. She was afraid and helpless, and her oval face was pathetically pale in the lantern glow—pale as alabaster; the face of one who was very close to death, and knew it, and had no resistance left in body or soul to fight against it.

She walked mechanically, staring straight ahead of her. And then the glare of the lantern swept full over her, revealing a mark —but no one would have seen it who did not look closely. Jeremy did not notice it, certainly. Only Paul discerned it—Paul, who was praying that the mark would not be there.

A mere patch of whiteness, where the girl had tried in vain to cover, with powder, a pair of ghastly crimson incisions, fiendishly significant. And the marks themselves were faintly visible as she came closer in the accusing halo of the uplifted lantern.

She stopped very abruptly then, and peered at the hideous face behind the upraised arm. She trembled and shrank away from it, and a subdued frightened whisper came involuntarily from her lips. Her companion put his arm about her and laughed, glanced indifferently at the man with the lantern, and laughed again, mockingly.

"It's only Murgunstrumm, my dear. He wouldn't harm a fly. He wouldn't know how, really. Come."

The girl paced on, walking like one already dead, like one who had been so long in the clutch of fear that nothing more mattered. The lantern cast a long gaunt shadow on the walk as she stepped in front of it. One long shadow—only one. The man in evening clothes, pacing just behind his lovely comrade, left nothing. Nothing but empty glaring whiteness. . . .

They went inside; and Murgunstrumm, scuffing over the sill behind them, reached out an abnormally long arm to swing the heavy door shut. The last thing Paul saw, as the lantern light died behind the closing barrier, was the unholy grin which transfigured that toadlike face. Then—then something possessed him.

He was on his feet blindly, fists clenched until the palms of his hands stabbed with pain.

"Great God, don't let them do it! Don't—"

He stumbled forward, thrashing through the deep grass, retching with the sudden turmoil which roared within him. Frantically he staggered toward the door of the inn; mad, unreasoning, knowing only that he could not stand still and let the horror continue.

He would have rushed to the door, then, and hammered upon it, screaming to the heavens above him; would have slashed his way into the house and fought—fought with hands and teeth and feet in a mad attempt to drag the girl from that foul embrace; would have continued until they overwhelmed him, killed him. All to no purpose!

But luck saved him. His blundering foot twisted beneath him as it cracked against an immovable something in the grass. Agony welled up through his leg, letting him down. He pitched violently forward and plunged headlong.

And the madness left him as he lay there, gasping. Ahead of him he heard the door of the inn creak open. A probing shaft of lantern light swept the clearing, and Murgunstrumm stood there on the threshold, peering out. Then the innkeeper muttered something inaudible, and the door closed again. The light vanished. The clearing was very dark and still.

What a fool he was! In the fury of a moment's insanity he had come within an inch of condemning Ruth forever to the asylum. He had come within an instant of awful death, when life was the most necessary possession in the world.

The girl in the flame-colored wrap was beyond his power to save. Beyond any power, except of a merciful God. The mark of the vampire was already imprinted in her throat. She was a slave of the demon who had stolen her soul. Nothing could help her now.

Paul's hands dug savagely into his face. A snarl came from his throat as he lay there in the deep grass. And then another sound, behind him, took his attention as something wriggled close. Jeremy's voice said in a thick whisper:

"You—you're all right, sir?"

"Yes, I'm all right."

"You ain't hurt, sir?"

"No. Not—hurt."

"Will we try to break into the place? That girl, she looked as if they might mean to do some damage—"

"No. It's too late."

Paul reached out and gripped the big man's arm. He lay still for a moment then, waiting for strength to return. Then, with a warning whisper, he began to crawl backward through the grass. Not once did he take his gaze from that closed barrier. Inch by inch he retreated until at last the deep grass gave way to underbrush and crackling bushes, and sheltering black trees loomed over him. Rising, he stood in the darkness until Jeremy joined him. Then together they crept silently back to the road.

"Listen," Jeremy cautioned him suddenly.

They stood quite still. A burst of laughter—feminine laughter, wild and shrill and vaguely mad—pursued them. Paul shuddered, took a step forward. Then, with an effort, he turned and hurried on again. He said nothing until the roadhouse, with its pall of evanescent vapor, was buried again in the gloom behind them. Then he muttered grimly:

"Did you see, clearly, the man in evening clothes?"

Jeremy's big body twitched as if something had jostled him. He turned a white, frightened face.

"That feller, sir," he whispered huskily, "there was somethin' creepy about him. When he stepped in front of the lantern back there—"

"You saw it too?"

"I don't know what it was, sir, but he didn't seem natural."

"I know," Paul said.

"Who is he, sir?"

"I don't know. I only know what he is."

"And the cripple, sir. He's the same Murgunstrumm feller the hotel man was tellin' us about?"

"The cripple," Paul replied, and his voice was low and vibrant and full of hate, "is Murgunstrumm."

They paced on in silence after that. Reaching the car, they got in quickly. Jeremy stuck the key in the slot and turned it. The motor coughed, purred softly. The black roadster jerked backward, swung fretfully about, reversed again, and straightened with a lunge.

"Back to the hotel, sir?" Jeremy said sharply.

Paul answered, almost inaudibly: "Yes. Back to the hotel."

Kermeff and Allenby
VI

At seven o'clock the following evening a large gray touring car, smeared and panting from sixty miles of fast travel, crunched to a stop before the Rehobeth Hotel. Twilight had already swooped down on the little community. A murky gloom welled up from the valley below. Lights blinked in the shadows, and the village lay silent and peaceful in the lassitude of coming night.

The car door clicked open. A gray-coated figure slid from the chauffeur's seat and moved quietly to the rear, glancing queerly, frowningly at the hotel. Mechanically he pulled open the rear door.

The two men who descended after him were, it was evident, somehow ill at ease and vaguely apprehensive. For an instant they clung close to the car, scowling unpleasantly and impatiently. They exchanged glances and comments. Then, with a word to the driver, they advanced to the steps.

Old Gates, aroused by the sound of the machine's arrival, met them in the doorway. Squinting at them, he asked hesitantly:

"Be ye lookin' for someone, sirs?"

"For Mr James Potter," the larger of the two said distinctly. "He expects us. We should like to go directly to his rooms, if you please."

"To be sure, sir," Gates grimaced. "I'll take ye right up now, I will. Come this way, sir."

"Er—it will perhaps be better if we go up alone. Will you direct us?"

Gates blinked, and stared more intently then, as if distrustful. But he turned with a shrug and said, rather stiffly:

"Of course, sir. Walk right through the lobby here and up the stairs, and turn right and go straight down the hall to the last door."

"Thank you."

Kermeff and Allenby ascended the stairs slowly, with Kermeff in the lead. They were strange companions, these two. Of different nationalities, they differed also in face and form, and obviously in temperament. Kermeff, the larger, was a bull-shouldered, aggressive man with huge hands that gripped the railing viciously. He possessed a sensitive mouth and keen eyes that declared him fiery, alert, possibly headstrong, and as stubborn as stone.

Allenby, trailing behind him, was smaller, wiry in stature, stern and deliberate of movement. Sullen, aloof, he climbed without a word and without a backward glance.

Together they strode along the upper landing to the door of James Potter's room. Kermeff knocked sharply. The door opened, framing Matt Jeremy on the threshold.

"Mr Potter?" Kermeff said gutturally.

"Yes, sir," Jeremy nodded. "Come right in."

Kermeff stepped over the sill. Allenby, hesitating an instant, peered up and down the corridor, shrugged and followed him closely. Very quietly, unobtrusively, Jeremy closed the door as he had been told to do.

A single lamp, not too efficient, burned on the desk in the corner. Beside it Paul Hill leaned silently against the wall, waiting.

Kermeff and Allenby, pacing into the room, saw him each at the same moment.

The big man stiffened as if a wire had been drawn taut within him. He flung up his head and stared. He wet his lips and sucked a long noisy breath into them. Allenby took a sudden step forward, stopped abruptly and stood quite still.

"You!" Kermeff rasped violently. "Where is Doctor Von Heller?"

"Sit down, gentlemen," Paul said evenly.

"Where is Von Heller?"

"Von Heller is not here."

"What? What are you saying? Are you . . . ?"

"I wrote the letters myself, gentlemen," Paul shrugged, "to bring you here."

Kermeff realized the truth. He had been trapped. He had gulped the bait completely. His one desire now was to spit it out again, to leave before the madman before him became violent. Kermeff swung about with a lurid growl.

But the exit was barred, and the physician stiffened again. The door was closed; Jeremy leaned against it. Kermeff stood on braced legs, swaying. He gathered himself. With a great oath he flung himself forward.

He stopped almost in the same movement. Jeremy's hand, sliding out of a bulging pocket, gripped a leveled revolver. Kermeff glared at it with animal hate. Turning again, very slowly and deliberately, he faced Paul.

"Sit down," Paul ordered.

"You are mad!"

"Sit down, I said."

Kermeff sank into a chair. He was trembling not with fear, but with rage. He sat like a coiled spring, ready to leap erect. He glared sullenly at his colleague, as if expecting Allenby to work the impossible.

Instead, Allenby glanced furtively from the rigid revolver to Paul's set face, and sat down also. Not until then did Paul move away from the wall. He, too, drew a revolver from his pocket.

"It is your car outside, I suppose?" he said quietly, addressing Kermeff. "Yes?"

"Yes."

"Come with me, then. At once, please."

Kermeff stood up, watching every move with smoldering eyes that threatened to blaze any moment into flame. He said harshly, gutturally:

"Why did you summon us here?"

"You will see, in time."

"It is an outrage! I demand—"

"Demanding will do you no good," Paul said crisply. "You are here and you will stay here. There will be no argument."

"I will have you arrested for forgery!"

"You are going downstairs with me and instruct your driver to return to town. You will tell him, very simply, that you have no further need for him. And you will make no false move, Kermeff. I didn't bring you here for pleasure or for any petty hate. If you attempt in any way to trick me, I will kill you."

Kermeff faltered. For an instant it seemed that he would give way to his violent anger and rush forward blindly, despite the twin revolvers that covered him. Then, trembling from head to foot, he turned to the door.

Jeremy held the door open as the physician strode into the hall. Paul followed silently, close enough behind to keep his protruding coat pocket, with his revolver buried in it, on a direct unwavering line with the man's back.

And Kermeff tried no tricks. Obviously he realized the grim severity of his position. He walked deliberately down the corridor, descended the stairs, and strode across the lobby. Gates, glancing at him from behind the desk, mumbled an inaudible greeting. Kermeff, without replying, went directly to the door and stepped out on the veranda, with Paul only inches behind him.

The chauffeur stood there, leaning indifferently against the rail. Kermeff looked squarely at him and said distinctly:

"We are staying here, Peter. You may go back to the city. We shall not need you."

"You won't want me, sir?"

"When we do, I will send for you."

The chauffeur touched his hand to his cap and turned to the steps. Kermeff, swinging on his heel, re-entered the hotel. He climbed the stairs with methodical precision. He said nothing. With Paul still behind him, very close and silent, he returned to the room he had just left.

And there, with the door closed again, Paul said evenly:

"That is all, gentlemen. I must ask you to remain here quietly until it is dark. Then. . . ." He shrugged his shoulders.

Allenby, peering at him sharply, said in a thick voice: "Then what?"

"I don't know. Perhaps we shall go mad."

Paul sat down, toying with the revolver. Kermeff and Allenby glared at him, then glanced significantly at each other. Jeremy, stolid and silent, remained standing at the door.

This occured at seven-thirty. At nine, Paul glanced at his watch, stirred impatiently in his chair, and stood up. Crossing quickly to the window, he drew the shade and peered out. It was very dark outside. The village was a thing of brooding silence and blackness. The sky held no twinkling points of light, no visible moon. There was no need to wait longer.

He stepped to the bed and drew back the covers, exposing the white sheets beneath. Methodically he pulled the top sheet free and tore it into inch-wide strips and ripped the strips into sections. Jeremy was watching queerly. Kermeff and Allenby stared and said nothing. Perhaps they thought he was mad.

And perhaps he was! Certainly it was a mad thing he was doing —a crazy, fantastic idea which had crept into his mind while he sat there in the chair, thinking of what the night might hold. And now, as he pulled his suit-case from the corner and rummaged through it in search of the needle and thread which Armand LeGeurn had stowed there, a thin smile played on his lips. Without a doubt they would think him mad in another moment.

He found what he sought. Crossing quietly to the door, he put his revolver into Jeremy's hand and said simply: "Be careful." To do what he intended, he would have to bend over within reach of Kermeff's thick arms and then within reach of Allenby's. It would not do to leave the gun unguarded in his pocket, for a groping hand to seize.

He turned and gathered up the strips of white cloth. To Kermeff he said evenly:

"Put your hands behind you."

"What are you going to do?"

"Nothing to hurt you. Perhaps something that may save you from harm later. Put them behind you."

With a shrug, as if to imply that insane men must be humored, the big man complied.

Paul bent over him. Across the front of the man's vest he stretched a twelve-inch strip of cloth and sewed it quickly into place. A second strip, somewhat shorter, he sewed across the first, forming a large gleaming cross. The stitching was crude and clumsy, but it would hold. Unless clutching fingers or teeth tore the sheeting loose, the thing would remain in place.

Kermeff, meanwhile, was watching with hostile eyes. When the operation was finished he relaxed and held his coat open, studying the cross as if he could not quite believe. Then he scowled unpleasantly and peered again into Paul's face.

"In God's name, what is this for?"

"For your protection," Paul said grimly. "And you are right. Protection in God's name."

Kermeff laughed—a strained unnatural laugh that was more animal than human. But Paul was already at work upon Allenby, and presently he was attaching a third cross to his own body, in such a position that a single outward fling of his coat would reveal it to anyone who stood before him. Finally, pacing to the door, he took the two revolvers from Jeremy's hand and said quietly:

"Do the same to yourself, Jeremy. I'll stand guard. As soon as you've finished, we'll be leaving."

The Innkeeper
VII

The Gray Toad Inn was half a mile ahead. Paul, huddled over the wheel of the roadster, glanced quickly into the face of the man beside him and wondered if Anton Kermeff were afraid. But there was no trace of fear in the big man's features. They were fixed and tense; the thick brows were knitted together in a set frown, the eyes focused straight ahead, unblinking. If anything, Kermeff was violently angry.

But he was also helpless. He was unarmed, and the door-pocket under his right hand contained nothing which might serve as a weapon. Paul has seen to that before leaving the hotel. And Paul's own hand, resting carelessly on the rim of the wheel, hovered only a few inches above the revolver in his coat pocket. If Kermeff made a single treacherous move, that hand could sweep down in a scant second and lash up again.

Moreover, the roadster's convertible top was down; and Matt

Jeremy, in the spacious rumble-seat beside the huddled form of
Franklin Allenby, commanded a view of the front. If Kermeff
moved, Jeremy had orders to strike first. As for Allenby, the very
presence of the powerful Jeremy beside him seemed to have
driven all thought of resistance from his mind.

The car purred on, eating its way with twin shafts of light drilling the uncanny darkness. The Gray Toad Inn was just ahead.

This time Paul did not stop the car. Approaching on foot, under
cover, would avail nothing to-night. The car was part of the plan.
Paul clung to the wheel and drove steadily along the unused road,
until at last the massive grotesquery of the inn materialized in the
gloom on the right.

As before, a light glowed on the lower floor, struggling feebly to
grope through the atmosphere of abomination that hung over the
entire building. The car slowed to a groping pace, approaching
almost noiselessly. Kermeff was staring. Paul looked at him,
smiled thinly, and said in a low voice:

"The Gray Toad, Kermeff. You've heard of it before?"

The physician said nothing. He sat very stiff, his hands clenching and unclenching nervously. Obviously he was beginning to
realize the peril of his position, the danger of being hauled blindly
through the night, on a strange mission, by a madman who presumably sought revenge.

Ahead, the light winked suddenly as if an obstruction inside the
grim walls had stepped momentarily in front of it. Then it glowed
again. The door of the inn swung back.

Instinctively Paul's foot touched the brake. The car stopped
with a tremor. With sudden dread Paul waited for whatever
would emerge.

At first he saw nothing. He was looking for the wrong thing. He
expected a human shape—the hunched body of Murgunstrumm
or perhaps one of the immaculate evening-attired inhabitants. But
it was no human form that slunk over the threshold into the night.
It was an indistinct creature of low-slung belly and short legs. It
crept forth, hugging the ground, and broke into a loping run
straight for the road. A long thin howl rose on the still air. The
howl of a wolf.

Paul shuddered, still staring. Wolves, here in Murgunstrumm's
house, meant only one thing! They were not flesh and blood, but—

Kermeff cried aloud. The loping thing ahead had reached the

road and stopped quite still. Crouching, it swung about to face the car, as if seeing the machine for the first time. The twin lights fell full upon it as it bellied forward, revealing a sleek black body and glittering eyes of fire.

There was an instant of emptiness, of stiffening inaction, while the thing's eyes glared balefully. Then, all at once, it rushed forward with amazing speed, hurtling through the intervening space so quickly that it seemed to lose form as it came.

And it had no form! Even as it swept the last few yards it became a shapeless blur and vanished utterly; and in its place, swooping up before the headlight, came a flapping winged thing which drove straight at Paul's face.

Just once it struck. An unearthly stench invaded Paul's nostrils. The smell of the grave enveloped him, choking him. Then the creature was high above, hanging like a painted shape against the sky, with wings swaying slowly. And Kermeff was laughing in a peculiarly cracked shrill voice:

"It's a bat! It's only a bat!"

Paul's foot hit the accelerator sharply. The car jerked forward, careening down the road. But even as it groaned to a stop again before the driveway of the inn, Paul looked up again apprehensively, muttering to himself. And the bat still hovered near, seeming to eye the occupants of the car with a malicious hungry glare of hate.

"Come," Paul said sharply, climbing out. "Hurry!"

He strode toward the door. Somehow the thought that Kermeff and Allenby might choose this moment to chance an attack, or to attempt escape, seemed insignificant. The other peril was so much greater and closer that he could consider nothing else.

He was a fool—that was it! No sane man would be deliberately walking into the horrors of this diabolical place after once having had the luck to escape. Yet he was doing precisely that. He was risking something more than life, more than the lives of his three companions—for Ruth.

Still he advanced, not daring to hesitate or look above him. He knew, without looking, that the same significant shape hovered there—the thing which had once been a wolf and now was a bat, and in reality was neither. And it was there for a reason. Pangs of hunger had driven it out into the night, to prowl the countryside or perhaps to pay a visit to one of the nearby villages. And here—

here at hand was a means of satiating that hunger, in the shape of four unwary visitors to the abode of evil. Four humans of flesh and blood. Flesh which meant nothing; blood which meant everything!

But it was too late to turn back. The door creaked open in Paul's face. A glare of light blinded him. A lantern swung before him, and behind it gleamed a pair of penetrating, searching eyes. Paul gazed fearfully into the eyes, into the contorted frowning mask of features in which they were set at incredible depth. With an effort he smothered his increasing fear and said in an uneven voice:

"You—you're still open, my good man?"

The repulsive face shook sideways. The thick lips parted soundlessly, mouthing an unspoken negative.

"Oh, come," Paul insisted, forcing something like a careless laugh. "We're hungry. We've come a long way and have even farther to go. Can't you stretch it a bit and scrape up something for us to eat and drink?"

Again Murgunstrumm shook his head without answering. The lantern swayed directly in front of Paul's face, vivid and repelling.

"We'll make it worth your while," Paul argued desperately. "We'll pay you—"

He did not finish. That same nauseating stench assailed him abruptly and a distorted black thing flopped past his head to careen against the lantern and lurch sideways into Murgunstrumm's face. Paul recoiled with an involuntary cry. But the thing had no evil intentions; it merely circled Murgunstrumm's shoulders erratically, uttering queer whispering sounds. And then all at once it darted away.

"We'll pay you double," Paul said again, recovering himself and stepping forward crisply. "We'll—" He stopped. Murgunstrumm was no longer scowling. The twisted face was fixed in a hungry grin. The sunken eyes were riveted, like the eyes of a starved animal, squarely in Paul's face. Murgunstrumm lifted the lantern higher and said thickly:

"You come in."

Paul stepped forward, knowing only that he felt suddenly weak and very afraid. Mechanically he crossed the sill. Kermeff followed him, and Allenby, and Jeremy entered last. Then the door swung shut and Murgunstrumm was leaning against it, the lantern dangling in his hand. His lips were spread in a huge idiotic grin. His eyes were twin sloes of fire, fixed and unmoving.

It was a queer room. The only two sources of light, the lantern and the slender-necked oil lamp on the table, were feeble and flickering, filling the entire chamber with a faltering, dancing yellow glow and uncouth crawling shadows. A bare floor, evidently once a polished dance surface, but now merely a layer of blackened boards, extended away into unlimited gloom. The walls were mere suggestions of shapes in the semidark, visible only when the fitful lamps were generous enough to spurt into restive brilliance.

There were tables—three, four of them. Round squat tables of dark color, holding candle stumps with black dejected wicks set in green glass holders, which threw out tiny jeweled facets of light.

And it was the light—lamplight and lanternlight—which put the room in motion and lent it that restless, quivering sensation of being furtively alive. First the lamp flare, sputtering and winking, fighting against stray drafts which came out of cracked walls and loose windows. And then, more particularly, the glare of the lantern in Murgunstrumm's hanging fist, jerking slowly into the center of the room as the cripple limped forward.

"Sit down, sirs," Murgunstrumm leered. "We be all alone here to-night."

He scuffed past, seeming to sink into the floor each time his twisted right foot came in contact. His guests stared at him, fascinated utterly, as he hobbled to the farther wall. There, grinning at them indifferently, he raised the lantern face high and clawed up its globe with crooked fingers, and peered fixedly at the burning wick as if it were a thing of evil significance.

And his face was full in the realm of it—a gargoyle of malicious expectation. A contorted mass of shapeless features, assembled by some unholy chance or perhaps developed by some unholy habit. And then the lips protruded, the cheeks bloated for an instant. The thick tongue licked out, directing a gust of air into the lantern. The flame expired.

After that, Paul and his companions retreated to an out-of-the-way table, as near the door as possible, and sat very close together, in silence.

Murgunstrumm vanished, to reappear a moment later with a cloth, ghastly white in the contrasting gloom, slung over his stiffened arm. Grinning, he bent over the table, lifted the lamp, and spread the cloth in place. Lowering the lamp again, he said gutturally:

"Ye'll be wantin' food, huh?"

"Anything," Paul said, cringing from the hovering face. "Anything will do."

"Uh-uh. I'll find somethin', I will."

"And—er—"

"Yus?"

"Can't we have a bit more light here? It's—it's ghastly."

The innkeeper hesitated. It seemed to Paul for an instant that the man's lips tightened almost imperceptibly and the dull sheen of his eyes brightened as if some nerve, buried in that venomous head, had been short-circuited. Then with a shrug the fellow nodded and said:

"Yus, sir. We don't generally have much light here. I'll touch up the candles, I will."

He groped to the other tables and bent over them, one after another, scratching matches and holding his deformed, cupped hands over the cold candle wicks. And presently four tiny flames burned in the thick gloom, like tiny moving eyes, animal eyes glowing through fog.

"Who"—it was Anton Kermeff speaking for the first time—"who is that man?"

"Murgunstrumm," Paul said dully.

"He is horrible. Horrible!"

"He is more than that," Paul replied bitterly.

"I refuse to remain here. I shall go—"

"No." Paul bent over the table, gazing straight into the physician's face. "You will not leave so easily, Kermeff."

"You have no right!"

"I have nothing to do with it."

Kermeff's mouth tightened in the midst of a guttural exclamation. He said very sharply: "What?"

"You would never leave here alive. Wait, and watch."

Kermeff's face whitened. Allenby, sitting just opposite him, looked sharply, furtively, at Paul and trembled visibly. He licked his lips. He said falteringly, in a whisper:

"Why did we come here?"

"To wait—and watch."

"But it is madness! That man—"

"That man is all you imagine," Paul said, "and more. You will see, before the night is over."

His voice choked off. He was aware of no sound behind him, no scuff of feet or suck of breath; only of a ghastly sensation that something, someone, was very close and gloating over him. He could feel eyes, boring through and through, with the awful penetrating power of acid.

Abruptly he swung in his chair. He found himself staring straight into Murgunstrumm's prognathous countenance, and the man's mouth was lengthened in a mocking grin. Not of humor, but of mocking hate. And the eyes were boring, unblinking, unmoving.

An instant passed while Paul returned the glare. Then Allenby cracked under the strain. Half rising, he said in a sharp, childishly shrill voice:

"What do you want? Don't glare like that, man!"

The grinning lips opened. Murgunstrumm laughed. It seemed no laugh at all; it was soundless, merely a trembling of the man's breath.

"I bring wine now, or later? Huh?"

Allenby relaxed, white, trembling. Paul turned, released from the binding clutch of that unholy stare, and looked mechanically, mutely, at his companions. Kermeff nodded slowly. Jeremy, with fists clenched on the table, said raspingly:

"Tell him to bring some wine, sir. We need it."

Murgunstrumm, without a word, limped back into the gloom. His boots scraped ominously, accenting every second beat as his crooked leg thumped under him. There was no other sound.

And the silence persisted for many maddening minutes. The massive structure seemed to have stopped breathing. Paul's voice, when he spoke at last, was a sibilant hiss, whispering into the shadows and back again like a thing of separate being.

"Your watch, Kermeff. What time is it?"

"Eleven," Kermeff said lifelessly.

"Seven hours," Paul muttered. "Seven hours until daylight. They will soon be returning."

"They?"

"The others. The inhabitants. The awful—"

Paul's voice died. He twitched convulsively, as if a hand had been clapped across his mouth. But it was no hand; it was a sound

—a sound that jangled down from far above, from the blackness beyond the cracked ceiling, seemingly from the very depths of the night; a mocking, muffled laugh that hung endlessly in the still air, like the vibrating twang of a loose violin string. Then silence, dead, stifling. And then, very suddenly, a thin scream of utter terror.

There was nothing else. The sound lived and died and was not reborn. Silence, as of the grave, possessed the room. Then, violently, Kermeff flung back his chair and lurched to his feet.

"What was that?"

No one answered him. Jeremy was without motion, gripping the table with huge hands. Allenby sat like a man dead, stark white, eyes horribly wide and ivory-hued. The lamp's flame gutted the dark. Paul said mechanically:

"Sit down."

"What was it?"

"I was wrong," Paul mumbled. "The inhabitants have not all left. One—at least one—is here still."

"That scream! It was a girl! A girl!"

"A girl," Paul said in a monotone. "A girl in a flame-colored wrap. But we can do nothing. It is too late. It was too late last night, when she came here. It is always too late, here."

"What do you mean?"

"Sit down, Kermeff."

Kermeff floundered into his chair and hunched there, quivering. Muttering aloud, he clawed at his throat and loosened his shirt collar. His hands slid down jerkily, fumbling with the buttons of his coat.

But Paul's hand, darting forward with incredible swiftness, closed over the man's wrists, holding them rigid.

"No, Kermeff."

"What?"

"Keep your coat buttoned, if you love life. Have you forgotten what we did at the hotel?"

Kermeff faced him without understanding. His hands unclenched and fell away.

"It is hot in here," he choked. "Too hot. I was going to—"

But another voice, soft and persuasive, interrupted him. Something scraped against the back of his chair. A long, deformed arm reached over his shoulder to place a tray with four glasses—thick greenish glasses, filled with brilliant carmine liquid—on the white cloth before him. And the voice, Murgunstrumm's voice, announced quietly:

"It be good wine. Very good wine. The meat'll be near ready, sirs."

Something snapped in Kermeff's brain. Perhaps it was the shock of that naked arm, gliding so unexpected before his face. Perhaps it was the sight of the red liquid, thick and sweet smelling and deep with color. Whatever it was, he swung about savagely and seized the cripple's arm in both hands.

"That scream!" he shouted luridly. "You heard it! What was it?"

"Scream?"

"You heard it! Don't deny it!"

The innkeeper's mouth writhed slowly into a smile, a significant, guarded smile. And his lips were wet and crimson—crimson with a liquid which had only recently passed through them.

"It was the night, sir," he said, bending forward a little. "Only the night, outside. These be lonely roads. No one comes or goes."

"You are lying! That sound came from upstairs!"

But Murgunstrumm released his arm from the clutching fingers and slid backward. He was grinning hideously. Without a word he retreated into the shadows of the doorway and vanished.

And Kermeff, turning again in his chair, sat quite without motion for more than a minute. He gazed at the glasses of red wine before him. Then, as if remembering something, he lifted both his hands, palms up, stared fixedly at them, and mumbled slowly, almost inaudibly:

"His arm—his arm was cold and flabby—cold like dead tissue. . . ."

The Winged Thing
VIII

Murgunstrumm did not return. The four guests sat alone at their table, waiting. The room, with its pin points of groping, wavering, uncertain candle-light, was otherwise empty and very still. Paul, bending forward quietly, abnormally calm and self-contained now that the moment of action had arrived, said in a low voice:

"It is time to do what we came here to do."

Kermeff studied him intently, as if remembering all at once that they had come here for a reason. Allenby remained motionless, remembering other things more close at hand and more Tartarean. Matt Jeremy's fists knotted, eager to take something in their powerful grip and crush it.

"What do you mean?" Kermeff said warily.

"We must overpower him."

"But—"

"If I once get that filthy neck in my fingers," Jeremy flared, "I'll break it!"

"There are four of us," Paul said evenly. "We can handle him. Then, before the others return, we can explore this house from top to bottom."

"It won't take four, sir," Jeremy growled. "I'm just itchin' to show that dirty toad what two good human hands can do to him."

"Human hands?" It was Allenby interrupting in a cracked mumble. "Do you mean . . . ?"

"I mean he ain't human, that's what! But when he comes back here, I'll—" Jeremy gulped a mouthful of red wine and laughed ominously in his throat—"I'll strangle him until he thinks he is!"

"Not when he first returns," Paul commanded sharply. "He suspects us already. He'll be on guard."

"Well, then—"

"Let him bring food. Then I'll ask him for—"

A sudden hissing sound came from Allenby's tight lips. Paul turned quickly. The door of the inner room had opened, and Murgunstrumm stood there, watching wolfishly, listening. He glared a moment, then vanished again. And presently, carrying a tray in his malformed hands, he limped into view again.

He said nothing as he lowered the tray to the table and slid the dishes onto the white cloth. Methodically he reached out with his long arms and placed four cracked plates in their proper positions. Knives and forks and spoons, black and lustreless, as if removed from some dark drawer for the first time in years, clinked dully as he pushed them before each of his guests. Then he stood back, his fists flat and bony on the cloth.

"It ain't often we have visitors here no more," he said curtly, looking from one face to another with intent eyes. "But the meat's fresh. Good and fresh. And I'll be askin' you to hurry with it. Near midnight it is, and I'm wantin' to be closin' up for the night."

Kermeff lifted his knife and touched the stuff on his plate. It was steak of some sort, red and rare in brown gravy. The vegetables piled about it were thick and sodden and obviously very old.

Paul said abruptly: "You're expecting visitors?"

"Huh?"

"You're expecting someone to come here?"

The innkeeper glared. His eyes seemed to draw together and become a single penetrating shaft of ochre-hued luminosity.

"No one comes here, I told you."

"Oh, I see. Well, we'll hurry and let you go to bed. Fetch some bread, will you?"

Murgunstrumm swept the table with his eyes. Mumbling, he limped away; and as he reached the doorway leading to the other room he turned and looked sharply back. Then he disappeared, and Paul said viciously, crowding over his plate:

"This time, Jeremy. As soon as he returns. If we fail—"

"Listen!"

There was a sound outside. The sound of a motor. It seeped into the room with a dull vibrant hum, growing louder. Out there in the road a car was approaching. Paul's hands clenched. If it were coming here—

He heard something else then. The shrill blast of a horn, just once. And then, from the inner room, Murgunstrumm came limping, one-two, one-two, one-two, with quick steps. He seized the lantern from its hook on the wall. He lit it and proceeded to the door, without a glance at the table.

Jeremy clutched the cloth spasmodically, ready to rise.

"No!" Paul cried in a whisper. "No! Not now!"

The door creaked open. Murgunstrumm scraped over the threshold. A breath of cold sweet air swept into the room, rustling the table cloth. The four men at the table sat quite still, silent, waiting.

There were voices outside, and the drone of the car's engine was suddenly still. Then footsteps crunched on the gravel walk and clicked on the stone flagging as they neared the door. An accusing, resentful voice, low yet audible, said thickly:

"That other car, Murgunstrumm? You have visitors?"

The innkeeper's reply was a whisper. Then, in a shrill feminine voice, lifted in mock horror, so typical of character that Paul could almost see the dainty eyebrows go up in assumed consternation:

"Goodness, what an odd hangout! I shan't stay here long. Why, I'd be thoroughly frightened to death."

Laughter—and then the door opened wider, revealing two figures very close together, and behind them the restive halo of Murgunstrumm's bobbing lantern.

The man was in evening clothes, straight, smiling, surveying the room with slightly narrowed eyes. Certainly he seemed out of place here, where every separate thing reeked of age and decay. Yet something about him was not so incongruous. His eyes glittered queerly, with a phosphorescent force that suggested ancient lust and wisdom. And his lips were thick, too thick, curled back in a sinister scowl as he peered suddenly at the four men at the table, and nodded. Then, whispering something to his companion, he moved toward the flickering candle-points in the misty gloom.

The woman was younger, perhaps twenty, perhaps less. A mere girl, Paul decided, watching her covertly. The sort of girl who would go anywhere in the spirit of reckless adventure, who ridiculed conventions and sought everlasting excitement, fearing nothing and conquering all doubts with ready laughter.

And she was lovely. Her gown was of deep restless black, trailing the crude floor as she moved into the shadows. Her white wrap—ermine, it must be—was a blob of dazzling brilliance in the well of semidarkness which leaped out to engulf her.

To a remote table near the wall they went together, and their conversation was merely a murmur, containing no audible words. They leaned there close to each other, their hands meeting between them. And Murgunstrumm, flat against the closed door with the lantern fuming in his dangling hand, followed their movements with eyes of abhorrent anticipation—sloe eyes that seemed to be no part of the man himself but separate twin orbs of malice.

Then it was that Jeremy, bending close over the table, said almost inaudibly:

"Shall I go for him, sir? Them others won't interfere."

"No," Paul said quickly. "Wait."

Jeremy subsided, muttering. His hands knotted and unclenched significantly. Then he stiffened, for Murgunstrumm was groping over the floor toward them, swinging the lantern. Stopping just behind Paul's chair, the proprietor blinked sullenly into each man's face, and said harshly, nervously:

"Ye'll have to go."

"But we've only just been served. We haven't had time to—"

"Ye'll have to go. Now."

"Look here," Paul said impatiently. "We're not bothering your guests. We're. . . ."

He stopped. Gazing at Murgunstrumm, he saw something in the far part of the room that caused the words to die on his lips and made him recoil involuntarily. His hands gripped the table. Murgunstrumm, seeing the sudden intentness of his gaze, turned slowly and peered in the same direction.

There in the near darkness a door had opened noiselessly. It hung open now, and the threshold was filled with a silent, erect human figure. Even as the four men at the table watched it fearfully, the figure moved out of the aperture and advanced with slow, mechanical steps.

The man was in black and white, the contrasting black and white of evening attire. But there was nothing immaculate about him. His hair was rumpled, crawling crudely about his flat forehead. His chalk-colored face was a mask, fixed and expressionless. He walked with the exaggerated stride of a man seeped, saturated with liquor. His eyes were wide open, gleaming. His lips were wet and red.

And there was something else, visible in ghastly detail as the lantern light fell upon it. A stain marred the crumpled whiteness of his stiff shirt-front—a fresh glistening stain of bright scarlet, which was blood.

He stood quite still, staring. For an instant there was no other movement in the room. Then, mumbling throaty words, Murgunstrumm placed the lantern on the table and cautiously advanced to meet him.

And then Paul and the others heard words—guarded, strangely vague words that for all their lack of meaning were nevertheless hideously suggestive, significant and, to Paul, who alone understood them, the ultimate of horror.

"You have finished?" Murgunstrumm demanded eagerly.

The other nodded heavily, searching the cripple's face with his eyes.

"I am finished. It is your turn now."

Trembling violently, Murgunstrumm reached out an unsteady hand to claw the man's arm.

"Now?" he cried hungrily, sucking his lips. "I can go now?"

"In a moment. First I would talk to you. These strangers here. . . ."

But Paul heard no more. The table quivered under his hands and lurched suddenly into him, hurling him backward. A harsh, growling cry came from the other side of it; and then, all at once, someone was racing to the door. It was Allenby, utterly unnerved by what he had just seen, and seeking desperately to escape.

And he was quick, amazingly quick. The door clattered back on its hinges before any other inmate of the room moved. Arms out-flung, Allenby clawed his way through the aperture, shouting incoherently. And then Paul was on his feet, lurching forward.

"Stay here!" he cried to Jeremy, who would have followed him. "Hold Kermeff!"

The threshold was empty when he reached it. He stopped, bewildered by the vast darkness before him. Vaguely he saw that Murgunstrumm and the creature in black and white, standing in the middle of the room, were quite motionless, watching every move. Then he stumbled over the sill, into the gloom of the path.

Nothing moved. The clearing was a silent black expanse of shadow, flat and empty under its pall of decayed atmosphere. The air was cold, pungent, sweeping into Paul's face as he swayed there. High above, feeble stars were visible.

Blindly Paul ran down the driveway, staring on either side. He stopped again, muttering. There was no movement anywhere, no sign of the man who had fled. Nothing but night and cold darkness. And a low-hanging winding-sheet of shallow vapor, swirling lazily between earth and heaven.

But Allenby had to be found. If he escaped and got back to the Rehobeth Hotel, he would use Henry Gates' phone to summon help. He would call the police at Marssen. He would lead a searching party here. And then everything that mattered would be over. The madhouse again. And Ruth would never be released from the asylum at Morrisdale.

Savagely Paul slashed on through the deep grass, moving farther and farther from the open door of the inn. Allenby had not reached the road; that was certain. He was hiding, waiting for an opportunity to creep away unobserved.

Paul's lips whitened. He glanced toward the car. The car—that was it. The key was still in the lock. Allenby knew it was. Paul stood stock still, watching. Then, smiling grimly, he deliberately turned his back and moved in the opposite direction.

Without hesitating, he blundered on, as if searching the reeds for a prone figure which might be lying there. A long moment dragged by, and another. There was no sound.

And then it came. A scurrying of feet on the gravel walk, as a crouching figure darted from the shadows under the very wall of the house. An instant of scraping, scuttling desperation, as the man flung himself across that narrow stretch of intervening space. Then a sharp thud, as the car door was flung back.

Paul whirled. Like a hound he leaped forward, racing toward the road. The motor roared violently, just ahead of him. The car door was still open. Allenby was hunched over the wheel, struggling with the unfamiliar instruments.

And he was fiendishly quick, even then. Too quick. The car jerked forward, bounding over the uneven surface. Like a great black beast it swept past the man who ran toward it, even as he reached the edge of the road. Then, with a triumphant roar, it was clear.

Clear! Paul stumbled to a stop. A dry moan came from his lips as his prey screamed beyond reach. He stood helpless—for a fraction of an instant.

Then, out of his pocket, his revolver leaped into his fist. He spun about. Twin spurts of flame burned toward the fleeing shape which was already careening from side to side in wild sweeps. There was an explosion, sharp and bellowing. The car lurched drunkenly, whirled sideways. Brakes screeched. Like a blundering mastodon the machine shot into the deep grass as the bursting tire threw it out of Allenby's feeble control.

And Paul was running again. He was beside the groaning shape before the driver could get out from behind the wheel. The revolver dug viciously into Allenby's ribs.

"Get out!"

Allenby hesitated, then obeyed, trembling.

"I—I won't go back there!"

The gun pressed deeper. Allenby stared suddenly into Paul's face. What he saw there made him shudder. He stood quite still. Then, pushing the revolver away nervously, he mumbled.

"You—you are not as mad as I thought."

"You should have known that before you tried to get away."

"Perhaps I should have."

"You're going back with me."

Allenby's voice trembled. "I have no alternative?"

"None."

With a shrug of defeat, the physician walked very quietly, very slowly, back toward the house.

The Gray Toad Inn had not changed. At one table Kermeff sat stiff and silent, under Jeremy's cold scrutiny. In the corner, among the shadows, sat the girl of the ermine wrap with her escort, only vaguely interested in what had happened.

Murgunstrumm still stood in the center of the floor, staring. The creature who had come, only a few moments before, from the bowels of the house, now sat alone at a nearby table. He glanced up as the door closed behind Paul and the physician. Then he looked down again, indifferently. And then, eagerly, Murgunstrumm approached him.

"Can I go now?" the cripple demanded.

"Yes. Get out."

Murgunstrumm rubbed thick hands together in anticipation. Breathing harshly, noisily, he wheeled about and limped quickly back to the table where his four guests were once again sitting quietly. His mouth was moving as he swept the lantern away and turned again.

He had forgotten, now, the presence of his undesirable guests. He did not look at them. His eyes, stark with want, were visioning something else—something he had waited for for hours. And he was trembling, as if in the grip of fever, as he started toward the door where the strange gentleman had first appeared.

But he did not reach it. Before he had covered half the intervening distance he stopped very abruptly and wheeled with a snarl of impatience, glaring at one of the covered windows. He stood rigid, listening.

Whatever he heard, it was a sound so inaudible and slight that only his own ears, attuned to it by long habit, caught its vibrations. The men at the table, turning jerkily to peer in the same direction, at the same window, saw nothing, heard nothing. But Murgunstrumm was scraping hurriedly toward the aperture, swinging his lantern resentfully.

He twisted the shade noisily. As it careened up, exposing the bleak oblong of unclean glass, the lantern light fell squarely upon the opening, revealing a fluttering shape outside. More than that the watching men did not discover, for the innkeeper's hands clawed at the window latch and heaved the barrier up quickly.

It was a winged thing that swooped through the opening into the room. The same hairy obscene creature that had whispered to Murgunstrumm, more than an hour ago, to admit the four unsuspecting guests! Rushing through the aperture now, it flopped erratically about the lantern, then darted to the ceiling and momentarily hung there, as if eyeing the occupants of the inn with satisfaction. Murgunstrumm closed the window hurriedly and drew the shade again. And the bat—for bat it was—dropped suddenly, plummet-like, to the table where sat the man who had recently come from the inner rooms.

It happened very quickly. At one moment, as Paul and his companions gazed in sudden dread, the winged thing was fluttering blindly about the ghastly white face of the man who sat there. Next moment there was no winged thing. It had vanished utterly, disintegrated into nothingness; and there at the table, instead of a solitary red-lipped man in evening clothes, sat two men. Two men strangely alike, similarly dressed, with the same colorless masks of faces.

They spoke in whispers for a moment, then turned, both of them, to glance at the four men near them. And one—the one who had appeared from the mysterious internals of the inn—said casually:

"We have visitors to-night, eh, Costillan?"

The answer was a triumphant gloating voice, obviously meant to be overheard.

"Ay, and why not? They were coming here as I was leaving. Our fool of an innkeeper would have refused them admission."

"So? But he was afraid. He is always afraid that he will one day be discovered. We must cure that, Costillan. Even now he has told your guests to leave."

The man called Costillan—he who had an instant before been something more than a man—turned sharply in his chair. Paul, staring at him mutely, saw a face suddenly distorted with passion. And the man's voice, flung suddenly into the silence, was vibrant with anger.

"Murgunstrumm!"

Hesitantly, furtively, the cripple limped toward him.

"What—what is it, sir?"

"You would have allowed our guests to depart, my pretty?"

"I—I was—"

"Afraid they would learn things, eh?" The man's fingers closed savagely over Murgunstrumm's wrist. He made no attempt to guard his voice. Obviously he held only contempt for the men who were listening. "Have we not promised you protection?"

"Yes, but—"

"But you would have let them leave! Did I not order you to keep them here? Did I not whisper to you that I might return—hungry?"

Murgunstrumm licked his lips, cringing. And suddenly, with a snarl, the creature flung him back.

"Go down to your foul den and stay there!"

At that Murgunstrumm scuttled away.

No sound came from Paul's lips. He sat without stirring, fascinated and afraid. And then a hand closed over his arm, and Jeremy's voice said thickly, harshly:

"I'm goin' to get out of here. This place ain't human!"

Paul clutched at the fingers and held them. Escape was impossible; he knew that. It meant death, now. But he had only two hands: he could not also hold Kermeff and the physician's terrified companion. Lurching to his feet, Kermeff snarled viciously:

"If we stay here another instant, those fiends will—"

"You cannot leave," Paul countered dully.

"We shall see!" And Kermeff kicked back his chair violently as he reeled away from the table. Allenby, rising after him, clung very close.

A revolver lay in Paul's pocket. His hand slid down and closed over it, then relaxed. Jeremy, frowning into his face, muttered thickly. The two physicians stumbled toward the door.

Sensing what was coming, Paul sat quite still and peered at the nearby table. The two men in evening attire had stopped talking. They were watching with hungry, triumphant eyes. They followed every movement as Kermeff and Allenby groped to the door. And then, silent as shadows, they rose from the table.

The two fleeing men saw them each at the same instant. Both stood suddenly still. Kermeff's face lost every trace of color, even in the yellow hue of the lamp. Allenby cried aloud and trembled violently. The two creatures advanced with slow, deliberate steps, gliding steps, from such an angle that retreat to the door was cut off.

And then, abruptly, Paul saw something else, something infinitely more horrible.

The remaining two inhabitants of this place of evil—the man and woman who had entered together but a short time ago—were rising silently from their table near the wall. The man's face, swathed in the glow of the candlelight beneath it, was a thing of triumph, smiling hideously. The girl—the girl in the white ermine wrap—stood facing him like one in the grip of deep sleep. No expression marred her features; no light glowed in her eyes.

The candle flame flickered on the table between them. The man spoke. Spoke softly, persuasively, as one speaks to a mindless hypnotic. And then, taking her arm, he led her very quietly toward the door through which Murgunstrumm had vanished.

And, as on that other occasion when he had lain in the deep grass of the clearing outside, Paul's mind broke with sudden madness.

"No, no!" he shrieked. "Don't go with him!"

He rushed forward blindly, tumbling a chair out of his path. At the other end of the room, the creature turned to look at him, and laughed softly. And then the man and the girl were gone. The door swung silently shut. A lock clicked. Even as Paul's hands seized the knob, a vibrant laugh echoed through the heavy panels. And the door was fast.

Savagely Paul turned.

"Jeremy! Jeremy, help me! We can't let her go—"

The cry choked on his lips. Across the room, Jeremy was standing transfixed, staring. Kermeff and Allenby huddled together, rigid with fear. And the two macabre demons in evening clothes were advancing with arms outthrust.

A Strange Procession
IX

They were no longer men. Like twin vultures they slunk forward, an unholy metamorphosis already taking place in their appearance. A misty bluish haze enveloped them, originating it seemed from the very pores of their obscene bodies, growing thicker and deeper until it was in itself a thing of motion, writhing about them like heavy opaque fog moved by an unseen breeze. More and more pungent it grew, until only a single feature of those original loathsome forms was visible—until only *eyes* glowed through it.

Kermeff and Allenby retreated before those eyes in stark terror. They were stabbing pits of swirling green flame, deep beyond human knowledge of depth, ghastly wide, hungry. They came on relentlessly, two separate awful pairs of them, glittering through dimly human shapes of sluggish, evil-smelling vapor.

As they came, those twin shapes of abomination, uncouth hands extended before them. Misty, distorted fingers curled forth to grope toward the two cringing victims. Allenby and Kermeff fell away from them like men already dead: Kermeff stiff, mechanical, frozen to a fear-wracked carcass of robotlike motion; Allenby mumbling, ghastly gray with terror.

Back, step by step, the two physicians retreated, until at last the wall pressed into their bodies, ending their flight. And still the twin forms of malevolence came on, vibrant with evil.

Not until then did reason return to the remaining two men in the room. Jeremy flung himself forward so violently that his careening hips sent the table skidding sideways with a clink of jumping china. Paul, rushing past him, flung out a rasping command.

"The cross! The cross under your coats!"

Perhaps it was the stark torment of the words, perhaps the very sound of his voice, as shrill as cutting steel. Something, at any rate, penetrated the fear that held Kermeff and Allenby helpless. Something drove into Kermeff's brain and gave him life, movement, power of thought. The physician's big hands clawed up and ripped down again. And there, gleaming white and livid on his chest hung the cross-shaped strips of cloth which Paul had sewn there.

Its effect was instantaneous. The advancing shapes of repugnance became suddenly quite still, then recoiled as if the cross were a thing of flame searing into them. Kermeff shouted luridly, madly. He stumbled a step forward, ripping his coat still farther apart. The shapes retreated with uncanny quickness, avoiding him.

But the eyes were pools of absolute hate. They drilled deep into Kermeff's soul, stopping him. He could not face them. And as he stood there, flat-pressed against the wall, the uncouth fiends be-

fore him began once again to assume their former shape. The
bluish haze thinned. Outlines of black, blurred with the white of
shirt-fronts, glowed through the swirling vapor. When Paul
looked again the shapes were men: and the men stood close together, eyeing Kermeff and Allenby—and the cross—with desperate diabolical eyes.

Suddenly one of them, the one called Costillan, moved away.
Swiftly he walked across the floor—was it walking or floating or
some unearthly condition halfway between?—and vanished
through the doorway which led to the mysterious rear rooms. The
other, retreating slowly to the outside door, flattened there with
both arms outflung, batlike, and waited, glaring with bottomless
green orbs at the four men who confronted him.

And then Paul moved. Shrill words leaped to his lips: "That girl
—we've got to get to her before—"

But the cry was drowned in another voice, Jeremy's. Stumbling
erect, Jeremy said hoarsely:

"Come on. I'm gettin' out of here."

"Look out! You can't—"

But Jeremy was already across the intervening space, confronting the creature who barred the barrier.

"Get out of the way!" he bellowed. "I've had enough of this."

There was no answer. The vulture simply stood there, smiling a
little in anticipation. And suddenly, viciously, a revolver leaped
into Jeremy's fist.

"Get out of the way!"

The creature laughed. His boring eyes fixed themselves in Jeremy's face. They deepened in color, became luminous, virulent,
flaming again. And Jeremy, staggering from the force of them,
reeled backward.

"I'll kill you!" he screeched. "I'll—"

He lost control. Panic-stricken, he flung up the revolver and
pulled the trigger again and again. The room trembled with the
roar of the reports. And then the gun hung limp in Jeremy's fingers. He stood quite still, licking his lips, staring. Amazed, he
stepped backward into the table, upsetting a glass of red liquid
over the white cloth.

For the man in evening clothes, despite the bullets which had
burned through him, still stood motionless against the closed

door, and still laughed with that leering, abhorrent expression of triumph.

There was silence after that for many minutes, broken finally by the familiar *shf-shf-shf* of limping feet. Into the room, glaring from one still form to another, came Murgunstrumm, and behind him the companion of the undead fiend at the door.

Costillan pointed with a long thin arm at Kermeff, and at the white cross which hung on the physician's breast.

"Remove it," he said simply.

Murgunstrumm's lips curled. His huge hands lifted, as if only too eager to make contact with the cross and the human flesh beneath it. Slowly, malignantly, he advanced upon Kermeff's still form, arms outstretched, mouth twisted back over protruding teeth. And the mouth was fresh with blood—blood which had not come from the cripple's own lips.

But Paul was before him, and a revolver lay in Paul's fingers. The muzzle of the gun pointed squarely into the innkeeper's face.

"Stand back," Paul ordered curtly.

Murgunstrumm hesitated. He took another step forward.

"Back! Do you want to die?"

Fear showed in the cripple's features. He came no closer. And a thin breath of relief sobbed from Paul's lips as he realized the truth. He had not known, had not been sure, whether Murgunstrumm was a member of the ghoulish clan that inhabited this place, or was a mere servant, a mere confederate.

"Jeremy," Paul's voice was level again with resolution.

"What—what do you want, sir?"

"Lock every window and door in this room except the one behind me."

"But, sir—"

"Do as I say! We've got to find that girl before any harm comes to her—if it's not already too late. When you've locked the exits, take—You have a pencil?"

Jeremy groped in his pockets, frowning. Fumbling with what he drew out, he said falteringly:

"I've a square of chalk, sir. It's only cue chalk, from the master's billiard room."

"Good. When you've locked the doors and windows, make a cross on each one as clear and sharp as you can. Quickly!"

Jeremy stared, then moved away. The other occupants of the

room watched him furtively. Only one moved—Costillan. And Costillan, snarling with sudden vehemence, stepped furtively to the door and flattened there.

One by one Jeremy secured the windows and marked them with a greenish cross, including the locked door in the farther shadows, through which the girl in the white wrap had vanished. When he turned at last to the final barrier, which led to the gravel walk outside, his way was blocked by the threatening shape which clung there, glowering at him, waiting for him to come within reach.

"One side," Jeremy blurted. "One side or I'll—"

"Not that way!" Paul cried sharply. "The cross on your chest, man. Show it."

Jeremy faltered, then laughed grimly. Deliberately he unbuttoned his jacket and advanced. The creature's eyes widened, glowing most strangely. Unflinching, Jeremy strode straight toward them.

Just once, as if fighting back an unconquerable dread, Costillan lifted his arms to strike. Then, cringing, he slunk sideways. And at the same moment, seeing the barrier unguarded, Kermeff lurched forward.

"I'm getting out of here!"

"You're staying, Kermeff."

The physician jerked around, glaring. Paul's revolver shifted very slightly away from Murgunstrumm's tense body to include Kermeff in its range of control. Kermeff's forehead contracted with hate.

"I tell you I won't stay!"

But he made no attempt to reach the door, and Paul said evenly to Jeremy:

"Lock it."

Jeremy locked it and made the sign of the cross. And then Paul's finger curled tighter on the trigger of the gun. The muzzle was still on a line with Murgunstrumm's cowering carcass. Paul said roughly:

"Allenby!"

"Yes?"

"You are remaining here, to make sure nothing attempts to enter from outside. Do you understand? And if the girl in the white wrap comes back through that door"—Paul pointed quickly to the

locked barrier which had baffled him only an instant before—"or
if that fiend comes back alone, lock the door on this side and keep
the key!"

"I can't stay here alone!"

"Nothing will harm you, man. Keep your coat open, or strip it
off. They can't come near the cross. Sit at the table and don't move.
We're going."

"You're going? Where?" Allenby croaked.

"To find that girl, you fool! And you"—Paul glared into
Murgunstrumm's bloated face—"are going to lead us."

A bestial growl issued from the innkeeper's lips. He fell back,
rumbling. But the revolver followed him and menaced him with
dire meaning, and he thought better of his refusal. Silently he
scuffed backward toward the inner door.

"For your life, Allenby," Paul snapped, "don't lose your head
and try to escape." He took the chalk from Jeremy's hand and
dropped it on the table. "As soon as we've passed through this
door, mark it with the sign of the cross, then stay here on pain of
death. You're safe here, and with the door sanctified, and locked
on the outside, these—these blood-hungry ghouls cannot escape.
Do you hear?"

"I'll stay," Allenby muttered. "For the love of Heaven, come
back soon. And—and give me a gun!"

"A gun is no good to you."

"But if I've got to stay here alone, I—"

Paul glared at the man suspiciously. But there was no sign of
treachery in Allenby's white face. No sign that he perhaps wanted
the revolver for another reason, to use on the men who had
brought him here. And a gun might really prove valuable. It
would give the man courage, at any rate.

But Paul took no chances. "Put your revolver on the table, Jeremy," he said curtly. "If you touch it before we're out of this room,
Allenby, I'll shoot you. Do you understand?"

"I—I only want it for protection, I tell you!"

Jeremy slid the weapon within reach of the man's hand. Allenby
stood stiff, staring at it. And then Paul's revolver pressed again
into the thick flabbiness of Murgunstrumm's shrunken body, forcing the cripple over the threshold.

"Take the lantern, Jeremy."

The door closed then, shutting out the last view of the chamber

—the last view of two thwarted demons in evening clothes, standing motionless, staring; and Allenby, close to the table, reaching for the revolver and flinging back his coat at the same time, to expose the stern white mark of protection on his chest.

The lantern sputtered eerily in Jeremy's hand. He turned, locked the door carefully, removed the key. Murgunstrumm watched silently.

"Now." Paul's weapon dug viciously into the cripple's abdomen. "Where is she? Quickly!"

"I—I ain't sure where they went. Maybe—"

"You know!"

"I tell you they might've gone anywhere. I ain't never sure."

"Then you'll show us every last room and corner of this devilish house until we find her. Cellar and all."

"Cellar?" The repeated word was a quick, passionate whisper. "No, no, there be no cellar here!"

"And if you try any tricks, I'll kill you."

It was a strange procession filing silently through the musty rooms and corridors of the ancient structure. Murgunstrumm, a contorted, malformed monkey swathed in dancing lantern light, led the way with limping steps, scraping resentfully over the bare floors. Very close behind him strode Paul, leveled revolver ready to cut short any move the man might make to escape or turn on his captors. Jeremy came next, huge and silent; and last of all, Kermeff, in whom all thought of rebellion had seemingly been replaced by deepening dread and his acute realization that here were things beyond the minds of men.

Room after room they hurried through—empty, dead rooms, with all windows locked and curtained, and every shutter closed. In one, obviously the kitchen, an oil stove was still warm and a large platter of fresh meat lay on the unclean table.

Room after room. Empty, all of them, of life and laughter. In some stood beds, stripped to bare springs; bare tables; chairs coated with dust. Like cells of a sunken dungeon the chambers extended deeper and deeper into the bowels of the house. From one to another the strange procession moved, eating its anxious way with the clutching glare of the lantern.

"There is nothing here," Kermeff said at last, scowling impatiently. "We are fools to go farther."

"There is something, somewhere."

Murgunstrumm, leering crookedly, said:

"They might've gone outdoors. I ain't never sure where."

"We have not yet explored upstairs."

"Huh?"

"Or down."

"Down? No, no! There be no downstairs! I told you—"

"We'll see. Here; here's something." Paul stopped as the advancing lantern rays touched a flight of black stairs winding up into complete darkness. "Lead on, Murgunstrumm. No tricks."

Murgunstrumm scuffed to the bottom of the steps and moved up with maddening slowness, gripping the rail. And suddenly, then, the man behind him hesitated. A single word, "Listen!" whispered softly through Paul's lips.

"What is it?" Kermeff said thickly.

"I heard—"

"No, no!" Murgunstrumm's cry was vibrant with fear. "There be no one up here!"

"Be still!"

The cracked voice subsided gutturally. Another sound was audible above it. A strange nameless sound, vaguely akin to the noise of sucking lips or the hiss of gusty air through a narrow tube. A grotesque sound, half human, half bestial.

"An animal," Kermeff declared in a low voice. "An animal of some sort, feeding—"

But Paul's shrill voice interrupted.

"Up, Murgunstrumm! Up quickly!"

"There be nothin', I tell you!"

"Be quiet!"

The cripple advanced again, moving reluctantly, as if some inner bonds held him back. His face was convulsed. He climbed morosely, slowly hesitatingly before each step. And his move, when it came, was utterly unexpected.

He whirled abruptly, confronting his captors. Luridly he cried out, so that his voice carried into every corner of the landing above:

"I tell you there be no one! I tell you—"

Paul's hand clapped savagely over his mouth, crushing the outcry into a gurgling hiss. Jeremy and Kermeff stood taut, dismayed. Then Paul's gun rammed into the cripple's back, prodding him on.

No mistaking the meaning of that grim muzzle. One more sound would bring a bullet.

Groping again, Murgunstrumm at last reached the end of the climb, where the railing twisted sharply back on itself and the upper landing lay straight and level and empty before him. The sucking sounds had ceased. The corridor lay in absolute uncanny silence, nerve-wracking and repelling.

"That noise," Paul said curtly, "came from one of these rooms. We've got to locate it."

"What—what was it?"

There was no answer. The reply in Paul's mind could not be uttered aloud. Kermeff did not know, and the truth would make a gibbering idiot of him. Kermeff, for all his medical knowledge, was an ignorant blind fool in matters macabre.

And another array of gloomy rooms extended before them, waiting to be examined. With Murgunstrumm probing the way, the four men stole forward and visited each chamber, one after another. There was nothing. These rooms were like those below, abandoned, sinister with memories of long-dead laughter, dust-choked, broodingly still.

"Something," Kermeff gasped suddenly, "is watching us. I can feel it!"

The others glanced at him, and Jeremy forced a dry laugh. Half the corridor lay behind them; the remaining doors stretched ahead beyond the restless circle of light. Paul muttered fretfully and pushed the innkeeper before him over the next threshold. His companions blundered close behind. The lantern light flooded the chamber, disclosing a blackened window and yellowish time-scarred walls. A four-poster bed stood against the wall, covered with mattress and crumpled blanket.

And Paul, too, as he bent over the bed examining the peculiar brownish stains there, felt eyes upon him. He whirled about bitterly, facing the doorway—and stood as if a hand of ice had suddenly gripped his throat, forcing a frosty breath from his open mouth.

A man stood there, garbed meticulously in black evening clothes, smiling vindictively. He was the same creature who earlier in the evening had escorted the girl in the white ermine wrap into the inn. The same, but somehow different; for the man's eyes were glowing now with that hellish green light, and his lips were full, thick and very red.

He said nothing. His gaze passed from Paul's colorless face to Murgunstrumm's, and the cripple answered it with a triumphant step forward. Kermeff shrank back until the bed post crushed into his back and held him rigid. Jeremy crouched, waiting. The creature stirred slightly and advanced.

But Paul did not wait. He dared not. In one move he wrenched his coat open, baring the white sign beneath, and staggered forward. The intruder hesitated. The green eyes contracted desperately to slits of fire. The face writhed into a mask of hate. Violently the man spun back, recoiling with arms upflung. And the doorway, all at once, was empty.

For an instant Paul was limp, overcome. Then he was across the threshold, lurching into the hall in time to see a shape—a tawny, four-legged shape, wolfish in contour—race down the corridor and bound into darkness, to land soundlessly upon the stairs and vanish into lower gloom.

There was nothing else. Nothing but Kermeff, dragging at his arm and saying violently:

"He'll overpower Allenby downstairs!"

"Allenby's safe," Paul said dully, mechanically. "He has the cross."

He remembered the revolver in his hand and raised it quickly, swinging back to face Murgunstrumm. But the cripple was helpless, held in Jeremy's big hands, in the doorway.

And so they continued their investigation, and at the end of the long passageway, in the final room of all, found what Paul in the bottom of his heart had expected. There, on the white sheets of an enameled bed, lay the lady of the ermine wrap, arms outflung, head lolling over the side, lifeless hair trailing the floor.

Murgunstrumm, seeing her there, rushed forward to stand above her, glaring down, working his lips, muttering incoherent words. He would have dropped to his knees beside her, clawing at her fiendishly, had not Jeremy flung him back.

For she was dead. Kermeff, bending above her, announced that without hesitation. Her gown had been torn at the breast, exposing soft flesh as delicately white as fine-grained gypsum. An ethereal smile of bewilderment marred her lips. And upon her throat, vivid in the ochre glare of the lantern, were two blots of blood, two cruel incisions in the jugular vein.

Paul stepped back mutely, turning away. He waited at the door until Kermeff, examining the marks, stood up at last and came to him.

"I don't understand," the physician was saying stiffly. "Such marks—I have never encountered them before."

"The marks of the vampire," Paul muttered.

"What?"

"You wouldn't understand, Kermeff." And then Paul seized the man's arm abruptly, jerking him around. "Listen to me, Kermeff. I didn't force you to come to this horrible place for revenge. I only wanted to prove to you that I'm not mad. But we've got to destroy these fiends. It doesn't matter why we came here. We've got to make sure no one else ever comes. Do you understand?"

Kermeff hesitated, biting his lips nervously. Then he stiffened. "Whatever you say," he said thickly, "I will do."

Paul swung about then, and called quickly to Jeremy. And Jeremy, looking up from the limp figure on the bed, had to drag Murgunstrumm with him in order to make the innkeeper move away. A fantastic hunger gleamed in Murgunstrumm's sunken eyes. His hands twitched convulsively. He peered back and continued to peer back until Jeremy shoved him roughly over the threshold and kicked the door shut.

"Lead the way, Murgunstrumm," Paul snapped. "We have not yet seen the cellars."

The cripple's lips twisted open.

"No, no! There be no cellars. I have told you—"

"Lead the way!"

A Girl's Voice
X

The cellars of the Gray Toad Inn were sunken pits of gloom and silence, deep below the last level of rotted timbers and plastered walls. From the obscurity of the lower corridor a flight of wooden steps plunged sharply into nothingness; and Murgunstrumm, groping down them, was forced to bend almost double lest a low-hanging beam crush his great malformed head.

No amount of prodding or whispered threats could induce the

captured innkeeper to hurry. He probed each step with his club-like feet before descending. And there was that in his eyes, in the whole convulsed mask of his features, which spoke of virulent dread. The revolver in Paul's hand did not for an instant relax its vigil.

Like a trapped beast, lips moving soundlessly and huge hands twisting at his sides, the cripple reached the bottom and crouched, there against the damp wall, while his captors crowded about him, peering into surrounding darkness.

"Well," Paul said curtly, "what are you waiting for?"

A mutter was Murgunstrumm's only response. Sluggishly he felt his way; and the lantern light, hovering over him, revealed erratic lines of footprints, old and new, in the thick dust of the stone floor. Footprints, all of them, which harmonized with the shape and size of the cripple's own feet. He alone had visited these pits, or else the other visitors had left no marks! And the signs in the dust led deeper and deeper into a labyrinth of impossible gloom, luring the intruders onward.

And here, presently, as in the central square of some medieval, subterranean city, the floor was crossed and recrossed with many lines of footprints, and chambers gaped on all sides, chambers small and square, with irregular walls of stone and high ceilings of beams and plaster.

Broken chairs, tables, choked every corner, for these rooms had been used, in the years when the house above had been a place of merrymaking and laughter, as storage vaults. Now they were vaults of decay and impregnable gloom. Spiderwebs dangled in every dark corner; and the spiders themselves, brown and bloated and asleep, were the only living inhabitants.

And with each successive chamber Murgunstrumm's features contracted more noticeably to a mask of animal fear. Not fear of the revolver, but the dread of a caged beast that something dear to him—food, perhaps, or some object upon which he loved to feast his eyes—would be taken from him. As he approached a certain doorway, at last, he drew back, muttering.

"There be nothing more. I have told you there be nothing here."

Only the pressure of the revolver forced him on, and he seemed to shrivel into himself with apprehension as he clawed through the aperture and the lantern light revealed the chamber's contents. There was a reason for his reluctance. The room was large enough to have been at one time two separate enclosures, made into a whole by the removal of the partition. And it was a display gallery of horrible possessions. The three men who entered behind Murgunstrumm, keeping close together, stood as if transfixed, while utter awe and abhorrence welled over them.

It was a vault, choked with things white and gleaming. Things moldy with the death that clung to them. And there was no sound, no intruding breeze to rustle the huge shapeless heap. It was death and mockery flung together in horror. And the men who looked upon it were for an interminable moment stricken mute with the fiendishness of it.

Then at last Kermeff stepped forward and cried involuntarily: "Horrible! It is too horrible!"

Jeremy, turning in a slow circle, began to mumble to himself, as if clutching eagerly at something sane, something ordinary, to kill the throbbing of his heart.

"Bones! God, sir, it looks like a slaughterhouse!"

The lantern in Paul's hand was trembling violently, casting jiggling shadows over the array, throwing laughter and hate and passion into gaping faces which would never again, in reality, assume any expression other than the sunken empty glare of death. And Murgunstrumm was in the center of the floor, huddled into himself like a thing without shape. And Kermeff was pacing slowly about, inspecting the stack of disjointed things around him, poking at them professionally and scowling to himself.

"Women, all of them," he announced gutturally. "Young women. Impossible to estimate the number—"

"Let's get out of here!" Jeremy snarled.

Kermeff turned, nodded. And so, jerking Murgunstrumm's shoulder, Paul forced the cripple once again to lead the way. And the inspection continued.

Other chambers revealed nothing. The horror was not repeated. As the procession moved from doorway to doorway, Jeremy said bitterly, touching Paul's arm:

"Why don't you ask him what those things are, sir? He knows."

"I know, too," Paul said heavily.

Jeremy stared at him. The big man fell back, then, as Murgunstrumm, taking advantage of their lack of attention, attempted to scuff past a certain doorway without entering. Fresh footprints led into that particular aperture. And Kermeff was alert. Ignoring the cripple, Kermeff strode into the chamber alone, and suddenly cried aloud in a cracked voice.

There, upon a table, lay a thing infinitely more horrible than any heap of decayed human bones. Murgunstrumm, forced into the room by Paul, strove with a sharp cry to fall back from it, until he was caught up in Jeremy's arms and hurled forward again. And the three intruders stood mute, staring.

A sheet of canvas, ancient and very dirty, partly covered what lay there. A long, bone-handled knife was stuck upright beside it, in the table.

The operation, if such a fiendish process could be so termed, was half completed. Kermeff, faltering to the table, lifted the blanket halfway and let it drop again with a convulsive twitch. Jeremy looked only once. Then, twisting with insane rage, he seized Murgunstrumm's throat in his big hands.

"You did this!" he thundered. "You came down here when that rat came up and told you—told you he was finished. You came down here and—"

"Jeremy." Paul's voice was mechanical, lifeless. "Do you recognize her?"

Jeremy stiffened and looked again. And then a glint of mingled rage and horror and pity came into his eyes. He released the cripple abruptly and stood quite still.

"It's—it's the girl who came in here last night, sir!" he whispered hoarsely. "When you and I was outside alone, in the grass, watchin'—"

"God in Heaven!" Kermeff cried suddenly, reached up with both hands.

Paul had had enough. He swung about to grope to the door, and froze like a paralytic in his tracks.

There in the doorway a revolver was leveled at him in the hands of a leering creature in evening clothes. The revolver was Allenby's; and the man behind it, Costillan, was standing very still, very straight, with parted lips and penetrating eyes that were hypnotic.

Paul acted blindly, desperately, without thinking. Flinging up his own gun, he fired. An answering burst of flame roared in his face. Something razor-sharp and hot lashed into his shoulder, tearing the flesh. He stumbled back, falling across the table where lay that mutilated body. The gun slipped from his fingers; and the creature in the doorway was still there, still smiling, unharmed.

It was Jeremy who leaped for the fallen gun, and Murgunstrumm who fell upon it with the agility of a snake. The man in evening clothes, advancing very slowly, pointed his own weapon squarely at Jeremy's threatening face and said distinctly:

"Back, or you will taste death."

Then Murgunstrumm was up, to his knees, to his feet, clutching the retrieved gun in quivering fingers. Like an ape he stood there, peering first into the stark white faces of Paul's companions, then into the drilling eyes of his master. And Paul, at the same instant, staggered erect and stood swaying, clutching at his shoulder where blood was beginning to seep through the coat.

At sight of the blood, the creature's eyes widened hungrily. He glided forward, lips wide. Then he stopped, as if realizing what he had forgotten. To Murgunstrumm he said harshly:

"Remove that—that abomination! Tear down the cross and rip it to shreds!"

And Murgunstrumm did so. Protected by the menacing revolver in Costillan's hand, and the gun in his own fist, he tore the white cross from Paul's chest and ripped it apart. To Kermeff and Jeremy he did the same. And when he had finished, when the rags lay limp at his feet, the creature in black and white said, smiling:

"Upstairs it will be more pleasant. Come, my friends. This is Murgunstrumm's abbatoir, unfit for the business of fastidious men. Come."

Outside, two more of the macabre demons were waiting. They came close as the three victims filed out of the chamber. One of them was the man who had fled from the upper room where lay that other half-naked body with twin punctures in its crushed throat. The other was the companion of the smiling Costillan—the second of the two who had been left in the central room under Allenby's guard.

In grim silence the three horribles led their victims out of the pits, with Murgunstrumm limping triumphantly behind.

Cold dread clawed at Paul's soul during that short journey out of one world of horror into another; dread combined with a hopelessness that left him weak, shuddering. Somehow, now, the resistance had been drawn out of him. Further agony of mind and spirit could drag no more response from flesh and muscle.

He had been so close to success! He had learned every secret of this grim house of hell, and had shown Kermeff the same.

But the truth would avail nothing now. Paul, climbing the stairs slowly, mutely, glanced at Kermeff and moaned inwardly. Kermeff was convinced. Kermeff would have freed Ruth, signed a statement that the girl, after escaping from this house of evil seven months ago, had been not mad but horrified and delirious. But now Kermeff himself would never leave; there would be no statement. Ruth would remain indefinitely in the asylum.

A sound rose above the scrape of footsteps—a sudden hammering on some distant door, and the muffled vibration of a man's voice demanding entrance. The creatures beside Paul glanced at each other quickly. One said, in a low voice:

"It is Maronaine, returning from the city."

"With good fortune, probably. Trust Maronaine."

"Murgunstrumm, go and open the door to him. Wait. One of these fools has the key."

"This one has it," the cripple growled, prodding Jeremy.

"Then take it."

Jeremy stood stiff as the innkeeper's hands groped in his pockets. For an instant it seemed that he would clutch that thick neck in his grip and twist it, despite the danger that threatened. But he held himself rigid. Murgunstrumm, key in hand, stepped back and turned quickly into the dark, swinging the lantern as he limped away.

The revolver pressed again into Paul's back. His captor said quietly, in a voice soft with subtlety:

"And we go in the same direction, my friend, to pay a visit to your friend Allenby."

Allenby! What had happened to him? How had the vampires escaped from the prison chamber where he had been left to guard them? Pacing through the gloom, Paul found the problem almost a relief from the dread of what was coming. In some way the monsters had overcome Allenby. Somehow they had forced him to open one of the doors, or the windows. . . .

"Did you hear that, my friend?"

Paul stopped and peered into the colorless features of his persecutor. Kermeff and Jeremy were standing quite still.

"Hear what?"

"Listen."

It came again, the sound that had at first been so soft and muffled that Paul had not heard it. A girl's voice, pleading, uttering
broken words. And as he heard it, a slow, terrible fear crept into
Paul's face. The muscles of his body tightened to the breaking
point. That voice, it was—

The gun touched him. Mechanically he moved forward again.
Darkness hung all about him. Once, turning covertly, he saw that
the gloom was so opaque that the moving shapes behind him were
invisible. Only the sound of men breathing, and the scrape of feet;
only the sight of three pairs of greenish eyes, like glowing balls of
phosphorus. There was nothing else.

But resistance was madness. The demons behind him were
ghouls born of darkness, vampires of the night, with the eyes of
cats.

And so, presently, with deepening dread, he stumbled through
the last black room and arrived at the threshold of the central
chamber. And there, as his eyes became accustomed again to the
glare of the lantern which stood on the table, he saw Allenby lying
lifeless on the floor, just beyond the sill. The door closed behind
him and he was forced forward; and suddenly the room seemed
choked with moving forms. Kermeff and Jeremy were close beside
him. The three macabre demons hovered near. Allenby lay there,
silent and prone. Murgunstrumm—

Murgunstrumm was standing, bat-like, against the opposite
barrier which led to the night outside, glaring, peering invidiously
at two people who were visible at a nearby table. These were the
guests whom the innkeeper had just admitted. Man and woman.
The man, like all the others, was standing now beside the table
with arms folded on his chest, lips curled in a hungry smile. The
girl stared in mute horror straight into Paul's frozen face.

The girl was Ruth LeGeurn.

Compelling Eyes. . . .
XI

You see, your friend possessed a weakling's mind."
The man with the gun kicked Allenby's dead body dispassionately, grinning.

"He had no courage. He was bound with fear and unable to
combat the force of two pairs of eyes upon him. He became—

hypnotized, shall we say? And obedient, very obedient. Soon you will understand how it was done."

Paul hardly heard the words. He still stared at the girl, and she at him. For seven mad months he had longed for that face, moaned for it at night, screamed for it. Now his prayers were answered, and he would have given his very soul, his life, to have them recalled. Yet she was lovely, even in such surroundings, lovely despite the ghastly whiteness of her skin and the awful fear in her wide eyes.

And her companion, gloating over her, was telling triumphantly how he had obtained her.

"There were three of them," he leered, "in a machine, moving slowly along the road just below here. I met them and I was hungry, for nothing had come to me this night. There in the road I became human for their benefit, and held up my hand as befitting one who wishes to ask directions. They stopped. And then—then it was over very quickly, eh, my lovely bride? The boy, he lies beside the road even now. When he awakes, he will wonder and be very sad. Oh, so sad! The older man hangs over the door of the car, dead or alive I know not. And here—here is what I have brought home with me!"

"And look at her, Maronaine!"

"Look at her? Have I not looked?"

"Fool!" It was another of the vampires who spoke. "Look closely, and then examine this one!"

Eyes, frowning, penetrating eyes which seemed bottomless, examined Paul's features intently and turned to inspect the girl.

"What mean you, Francisco?"

"These are the two who came here before, so long ago, and escaped. Look at them, together!"

"Ah!" The exclamation was vibrant with understanding.

"These are the two, Maronaine."

A white hand gripped Paul's shoulder savagely. The face that came close to his was no longer leering with patient anticipation of satisfaction to come, but choked with hate and bestial fury.

"You will learn what it means to escape this house. You have come back to find out, eh? You and she, both. No others have ever departed from here, or ever will."

"They should be shown together, Francisco. No?"

"Together? Ah, because they are lovers and should be alone, eh?" The laugh was satanic.

"Up there"—an angry arm flung toward the ceiling—"where it is very quiet. You, Maronaine, and you, Costillan, it is your privilege. Francisco and I will amuse ourselves here with these other guests of ours."

A grunt of agreement muttered from Maronaine's lips. His fingers clasped the girl's arm, lifting her from the chair where she cringed in terror. Ugly hands dragged her forward.

"Paul—Paul! Oh, help!"

But Paul himself was helpless, caught in a savage grip from which there was no escape. His captor swung him toward the door. Struggling vainly, he was hauled over the threshold into the darkness beyond, and the girl was dragged after him.

The door rasped shut. The last Paul saw, as it closed, was a blurred vision of Jeremy and Kermeff flattened desperately against the wall, staring at the two remaining vampires; and Murgunstrumm, crouching against the opposite barrier, cutting off any possibility of retreat.

Then a voice growled curtly:

"Go back to your feast, Murgunstrumm. We have no use for you here. Go!"

And as the two victims were prodded up the twisting stairs to the upper reaches of the inn, the door below them opened and closed again. And Murgunstrumm scurried along the lower corridor, mumbling to himself, clawing his way fretfully toward the stairway that led down into the buried pits.

It was a cruel room into which they were thrust. Situated on the upper landing, directly across the hall from where that pitiful feminine figure lay on the musty bed, it was no larger than a dungeon cell, and illuminated only by a stump of candle which lay in a pool of its own gray wax on the window sill.

Here, forced into separate chairs by their captors, Paul and Ruth stared at each other—Ruth sobbing, with horror-filled eyes wide open; Paul sitting with unnatural stiffness, waiting.

Powerful hands groped over Paul's shoulder and held him motionless, as if knowing that he would soon be straining in torment. At the same time, the door clicked shut. The candlelight wavered and became smooth again. The second vampire advanced slowly toward Ruth.

A scream started from the girl's lips as she saw that face. The eyes were green again. The features were voluptuous, bloated beyond belief.

"We will show them what it means to escape this house. Her blood will be warm, Costillan. Warm and sweet. I will share it with you."

The girl struggled up, staring horribly, throwing out her hands to ward off the arms she expected to crush her. But those arms did not move. It was the eyes that changed, even as she cringed back half erect against the wall. The eyes followed her, boring, drilling, eating into her soul. She stood quite still. Then, moaning softly, she took a step forward, and another, faltering, and slumped again into the chair.

The creature bent over her triumphantly. Fingers caressed her hair, her cheeks, her mouth—the fingers of a slave buyer, appraising a prospective purchase. Very slowly, gently, they thrust the girl's limp head back, exposing the white, tender, lovely throat. And then the creature's lips came lower. His eyes were points of vivid fire. His mouth parted, his tongue curled over a protruding lower lip. Teeth gleamed.

Paul's voice pierced the room with a roar of animal fury. Violently he wrenched himself forward, only to be dragged back again by the amazingly powerful hands on his shoulders. But the demon beside Ruth straightened quickly, angrily, and glared.

"Can you not keep that fool still? Am I to be disturbed with his discordant voice while—"

"Listen, Maronaine."

The room was deathly still. Suddenly the man called Costillan strode to the door and whipped it open. Standing there, he was motionless, alert. And there was no sound anywhere, no sound audible to human ears.

But those ears were not human. Costillan said curtly:

"Someone is outside the house, prowling. Come!"

"But these two here . . . ?"

"The door, Maronaine, locks on the outside. They will be here when we return, and all the sweeter for having thought of us."

The chamber was suddenly empty of those macabre forms, and the door closed. A key turned in the slot outside. And then Paul was out of his chair with a bound. Out of it, and clawing frantically at the barrier.

A mocking laugh from the end of the corridor was the only answer.

No amount of straining would break that lock. An eternity passed while Paul struggled there. Time and again he flung himself against the panels. But one shoulder was already a limp, bleeding thing from that bullet wound, and the other could not work alone. And presently came the voice of Ruth LeGeurn behind him, very faint and far away.

"They said . . . someone outside, Paul. If it is Martin and Von Heller. . . ."

"Who?"

"I escaped from Morrisdale last night, Paul. Martin told me how to do it. He met me outside the walls. We drove straight to the city, to find you. You were gone."

Paul was leaning against the door, gasping. Wildly he stared about the room, seeking something to use as a bludgeon.

"Martin went to the hospital, to plead with Kermeff and Allenby for both of us, Paul. Your letters were there. He knew the handwriting. We traced you to Rehobeth to-night and—and we were on our way here when that horrible man in the road—"

"But Von Heller!" Paul raved. "Where does he come into it?"

"He was at the Rehobeth Hotel. He—he read the account of your escape and said he knew you would return there."

"He'll be no help now," Paul said bitterly, fighting again at the door. "I can't open this."

Ruth was suddenly beside him, tugging at him.

"If we can find some kind of protection from them, Paul, even for a little while, to hold them off until Martin and Von Heller find a way to help us! Von Heller will know a way!"

Protection! Paul stared about him with smoldering eyes. What protection could there be? The vampires had torn away his cross. There was nothing left.

Suddenly he swept past Ruth and fell on his knees beside the bed. The bed had blankets, sheets, covers! White sheets! Feverishly he tore at them, ripping them to shreds. When he turned again his eyes were aglow with fanatical light. He thrust a gleaming thing into Ruth's hands—a crudely fashioned cross, formed of two strips knotted in the center.

"Back to your chair!" he cried. "Quickly!"

Footsteps were audible in the corridor, outside the door. And muffled voices:

"You were hearing sounds which did not exist, Costillan."

"I tell you I heard—"

"Hold the cross before you," Paul ordered tersely, dragging his own chair close beside Ruth's. "Sit very still. For your life don't drop it from fear of anything you may see. Have courage, beloved."

The door was opening. Whether it was Costillan or Maronaine who entered first it was impossible to say. Those ghastly colorless faces, undead and abhorrent, contained no differentiating points strong enough to be so suddenly discernible in flickering candlelight. But whichever it was, the creature advanced quickly, hungrily, straight toward Ruth. And, close enough to see the white bars which she thrust out abruptly, he recoiled with sibilant hiss, to lurch into his companion behind him.

"The cross! They have found the cross! Ah!"

Nightmare came then. The door was shut. The candle glow revealed two crouching creeping figures; two gaunt, haggard, vicious faces; two pairs of glittering eyes. Like savage beasts fascinated by a feared and hated object, yet afraid to make contact, the vampires advanced with rigid arms outthrust, fingers curled.

"Back!" Paul cried. "Back!"

He was on his feet with the cross clutched before him. Ruth, trembling against him, did as he did. The two horribles retreated abruptly, snarling.

And then the transformation came. The twin bodies lost their definite outline and became blurred. Bluish vapor emanated from them, misty and swirling, becoming thicker and thicker with the passing seconds. And presently nothing remained but lurking shapes of phosphorescence, punctured by four glaring unblinking eyes of awful green.

Eyes!

Paul realized with a shudder what they were striving to do. He fought against them.

"Don't look at them," he muttered. "Don't!"

But he had to look at them. Despite the horror in his heart, his own gaze returned to those advancing bottomless pits of vivid green as if they possessed the power of lodestone. He found himself peering into them, and knew that Ruth too was staring.

Ages went by, then, while he fought against the subtle numbness that crept into his brain. He knew then what Allenby had gone through before merciful death. Another will was fighting his, crushing and smothering him. Other thoughts than his own were finding a way into his mind, no matter how he struggled to shut them out. And a voice—his own voice, coming from his own lips —was saying heavily, dully:

"Nothing will harm us. These are our friends. There is no need to hold the cross any longer. Throw down the cross. . . ."

Somehow, in desperation, he realized what he was doing, what he was saying. He lurched to his feet, shouting hoarsely:

"No, no, don't let them do it! Ruth, they are fiends, vampires! They are the undead, living on blood!"

His careening body struck the window ledge, crushing the last remnant of candle that clung there. The room was all at once in darkness, and the two mad shapes of bluish light were a thousand times more real and horrible and close. Completely unnerved, Paul flung out his hand and clawed at the window shade. It rattled up with the report of an explosion. His fingers clutched at the glass. He saw that the darkness outside had become a sodden gray murk.

Then he laughed madly, harshly, because he knew that escape was impossible. Death was the only way out of this chamber of torment. The window was high above the ground, overlooking the stone flagging of the walk. And the eyes were coming nearer. And Ruth was screeching luridly as two shapeless hands hovered over her throat.

Somewhere in the bowels of the house, under the floor, a revolver roared twice in quick succession. A voice—Jeremy's voice —bellowed in triumph. A long shrill scream vibrated high above everything else. There was a splintering crash as of a door breaking from its hinges—and footsteps on the stairs, running.

Paul hurled himself upon the bluish monstrosity which hung over Ruth's limp body. Wildly, desperately, he leaped forward, thrusting the cross straight into those boring eyes.

Something foul and fetid assailed his nostrils as he tripped and fell to the floor. He rolled over frantically, groping for the bits of white rag which had been torn from his hands on the bedpost as he fell. He knew that Ruth was flat against the wall, holding out both arms to embrace the earth-born fiend which advanced toward her. Her hands were empty. She had let the cross fall. She was no longer a woman, but a human without a will, utterly hypnotized by the eyes.

Paul's fingers found the bit of white rag. Instinctively he twisted backward over the floor, avoiding the uncouth hands that sought his throat. Then he was on his feet, leaping to Ruth's side. Even as that ghoulish mouth lowered to fasten on the girl's throat, the cross intervened. The mouth recoiled with a snarl of awful rage.

"Back!" Paul screamed. "Look, it is daylight!"

The snarling shape stiffened abruptly, as if unseen fingers had snatched at it.

"Daylight!" The word was a thin frightened whisper, lashing through the room and echoing sibilantly. The green eyes filled with apprehension. Suddenly, where the distorted shapes of swirling mist had stood, appeared men—the same men, Costillan and Maronaine, with faces of utter hate. The candlelight was not needed to reveal them now. The room was dim and cold with a thin gray glare from the window.

"Daylight," Costillan muttered, staring fixedly at the aperture. "We have only a moment, Maronaine. Come quickly."

His companion was standing with clenched hands, confronting the two prisoners.

"You have not won," he was saying harshly. "You will never escape. To the ends of hell we will follow you for what you have done this night."

"Come, Maronaine. Quickly!"

"Yours will be the most horrible of all deaths. I warn you—"

A mighty crash shook the door, and another. With sharp cries the two undead creatures whirled about. Triumphantly, Paul knew the thoughts in their malignant minds. They were demons of the night, these fiends. Their hours of existence endured only from sunset to sunrise. If they were not back in their graves. . . .

And now they were trapped, as the barrier clattered inward, torn and splintered from its hinges. A battering ram of human flesh—Jeremy—hurtled over the threshold. Other figures crowded in the doorway.

And suddenly the two vampires were gone. Even as the men in the corridor rushed forward, the twin shapes of black and white vanished. And only Paul saw the method of it. Only Paul saw the black-winged things that swirled with lightning speed through the aperture, into the gloom of the corridor beyond.

The Vault
XII

Strong hands held Paul up then. Jeremy and Martin LeGeurn stood beside him, supporting him. Kermeff was on his knees beside the limp unconscious form on the floor. And a stranger, a huge man with bearded face and great thick shoulders, was standing like a mastodon in the center of the room, glaring about him—Von Heller, the mightiest brain in medical circles; the man who understood what other men merely feared.

"Where are they?" he roared, whirling upon Paul. "Stand up, man. You're not hurt. Where did they go?"

"It was daylight," Paul whispered weakly. "They—"

"Daylight?" Von Heller swung savagely to face the window. "My God, what a fool I—Where are the cellars? Hurry. Take me to the cellars."

To Paul it was a blurred dream. He knew that strong hands gripped him and led him rapidly to the door. He heard Von Heller's booming voice commanding Kermeff to remain with the girl. Then moving shapes were all about him. Jeremy was close on one side. Martin LeGeurn was supporting him on the other, talking to him in a low voice of encouragement. Von Heller was striding furiously down the corridor.

The darkness here was as opaque as before, as thick and deep as the gloom of sunken dungeons. But there was no sound in the house; no sound anywhere, except Paul's own voice, muttering jerkily:

"Thank God, Martin, you came in time. If those demons had hurt Ruth or killed Jeremy and Kermeff. . . ."

The answer was a guttural laugh from Jeremy. And in the dark Paul saw on Jeremy's breast a gleaming green cross, glittering with its own fire. He stared mutely at it, then turned and looked back toward the room they had just left, as if visualizing the same on Kermeff's kneeling body. And he knew, then, why his companions were still alive; why they were not now lying lifeless and bloodless on the floor of the downstairs chamber.

One of them—Jeremy, probably—had rushed to Allenby's dead

body and seized the square of chalk in the pocket of the corpse. And the pantomime of the upper room had been reenacted in the lower room, the same way, until Martin LeGeurn and Von Heller had battered down the outside door.

The revolver shots—Martin had fired them, more than likely. Martin did not know that bullets were useless.

"Thank God," Paul muttered again. And then he was descending the stairs to the lower floor, and descending more stairs, black and creaking, to the pits.

"Which way?" Von Heller demanded harshly. "We must find the coffins."

"Coffins?" It was Jeremy frowning. "There ain't no coffins down here, sir. We looked in every single room. Besides"—viciously—"them two fiends upstairs won't never need coffins any more. When you leaped on 'em, sir, and made that cross mark over their filthy hearts with the chalk, they just folded up. Shriveled away to dust, they did. Lord, what a stench! I'll never forget—"

"Never mind that. Where is the burial vault?"

"But there ain't any burial vault. We were just—"

Jeremy's words ended abruptly. He stood still, one hand gripping the lower end of the railing, the other uplifted.

"Listen to that!"

There was a sound, emanating from somewhere deep in the gloom of the cellar—a sucking, grinding sound, utterly revolting, mingled with the mumbling and gurgling of a man's voice.

"An animal, eating," Von Heller said in a whisper.

"It ain't an animal, sir."

"My God! Murgunstrumm. Well, he'll be able to show us where the coffins are."

Von Heller groped forward, eyes burning with terrible eagerness. He was a man no longer, but a hound on a hot scent which meant to him more than life and death. Crouching, he advanced noiselessly through the pits, staring straight ahead, ignoring the chambers on all sides of him as he went deeper and deeper into the maze. And the others followed right at his heels in a group.

And the sight that met the eyes of the intruders, when they reached at last the threshold of the slaughter room, soured the blood in their veins and made them rigid. The lantern flared there, on the floor against the wall. The sodden canvas sheet had been torn from its former position and lay now in an ugly gray heap on the floor.

Murgunstrumm crouched there, unaware of the eyes that watched him.

Von Heller was upon him before he knew it. With awful rage the physician hurled him back from the table. Like a madman Von Heller stood over him, hurling frightful words upon the cripple's malformed head.

And the result was electrifying. Murgunstrumm's face whipped up. His sunken eyes, now completely mad with mingled fear and venom, glared into Von Heller's writhing countenance and into the masks of the men in the doorway. Then, with a great suck of breath, Murgunstrumm stiffened.

The jangling words which spewed from his lips were not English. They were guttural, thick Serbian. And even as they echoed and re-echoed through the chamber, through the entire cellar, the cripple sprang forward.

There was no stopping him. His move was too sudden and savage. Hurling Von Heller aside, he lunged to the table, grabbed the huge knife, then was at the threshold, tearing and slashing his way clear. And with a last violent scream he vanished into the outer dark.

A moment passed. No man moved. Then Von Heller seized the lantern and rushed forward.

"After him!"

"What did he say?"

"He thinks his masters betrayed him. Thinks they sent us here. He will destroy them, and I want them alive for research. After him, I say!"

Footprints led the way—footprints in the dust, twisting along the wall where other prints were not intermingled. With the lantern swaying crazily in his outflung hand, Von Heller ran forward. Straight to the smallest of the cell-like chambers the trail led him; and when the others reached his side he was standing in the center of the stone vault, glaring hungrily at a tall, rectangular opening in the wall.

Seeing it, Paul gasped. Jeremy said hoarsely:

"We looked in here before. There wasn't no—"

"You were blind!"

And Von Heller was striding forward again, through the aper-

ture. It was a narrow doorway; the barrier hung open, fashioned of
stone, on concealed hinges. Little wonder that in the gloom Paul
and Jeremy and Kermeff had not discovered it before. Every chamber had been alike then.

But not now. Now they were pacing onward through a blind
tunnel. The stone walls were no longer stone, but thick boards on
both sides and above and below, to hold out the earth behind
them. This was not the cellar of the inn, but a cunningly contrived
extension, leading into subterranean gloom.

Strange realizations came into Paul's mind. The Gray Toad had
not always been an inn of death. At one time it had prospered with
gaiety and life. Then the decay had come. Murgunstrumm had
come here to live. And these creatures of the night had discovered
the place and come here, too, and made Murgunstrumm their
slave, promising him the remains of their grim feasts. They had
brought their grave earth here. . . .

For twenty yards the passage continued, penetrating deeper and
deeper at a sharp incline. And then it came to an end, and the
lantern light revealed a buried chamber where every sound, every
shred of light, was withheld by walls of unbroken earth. A tomb,
sunk deep beneath the surface of the clearing above.

And the lantern disclosed other things. Long wooden boxes lay
side by side in the center of the vault. Seven of them. Seven gaunt
ancient coffins.

They were open, all but one. The lids were flung back. The
corpses had been hauled out savagely, madly, and hurled upon
the floor. They lay there now like sodden heaps of flesh in a
slaughterhouse, covered with strips and shreds of evening clothes.
Great pools of blood welled beneath them. The lantern glare revealed sunken shriveled faces, hideous in decay, already beginning to disintegrate. Gaunt bones protruded from rotting flesh.

And Murgunstrumm was there. He was no longer human, but a
grave robber, a resurrection man with hideous intentions, as he
crouched over the lid of the last oblong box, tearing it loose. Even
as the men watched him, stricken motionless by the fiendishness
of it, he leaped catlike upon the enclosed body and dragged it into
the open. The man was Maronaine. And there, with inarticulate
cries of hate, Murgunstrumm fell upon it, driving his knife again
and again into the creature's heart, laughing horribly. Then he
stumbled erect, and a discordant cackle jangled from his thick lips.

"Betrayed me! Betrayed me, did yer! Turned on old Murgunstrumm, which served yer for 'most twenty-eight years! Yer won't never betray no one else! I'll tear every limb of yer rotten bodies—"

He looked up then, and saw that he was not alone. His rasping voice stopped abruptly. He lurched back with uncanny quickness. His hands jerked up like claws. His convulsed face glared, masklike, between curled fingers. A screech of madness burned through his lips. For an instant he crouched there, twisting back into the wall. Then, with a cry tearing upward through his throat, he hurled himself forward.

In his madness he saw only Von Heller. Von Heller was the central object of his hate. Von Heller was the first to step forward to meet him.

It was horror, then. It was a shambles, executed in the gloom of a sunken burial vault with only the sputtering, dancing glow of the lantern to reveal it. Four men fought to overpower a mad beast gone amuck. Four lunging desperate shapes blundered about in the treacherous semidark, clawing, slashing, striking at the horribly swift creature in their midst.

For Murgunstrumm was human no longer. Madness made a bestial mask of his features. His thick, flailing arms possessed the strength of twenty men. His heaving, leaping body was a thing of unbound fury. His eyes were wells of gleaming white, pupil-less. His drooling mouth, curled back over protruding teeth, whined and whimpered and screamed sounds which had no human significance.

He had flung the knife away in that first vicious rush. Always, as he battled, his attention was centered on Von Heller. The others did not matter. They were only objects of interference to be hurled aside. And hurl them aside he did, at last, with the sheer savagery of his attack.

For a split second, alone in the center of the chamber, he crouched with arms and head outthrust, fingers writhing. He glared straight into Von Heller's face, as the physician flattened against the wall. And then, oblivious of the revolver which came into Von Heller's hand, the cripple leaped.

Von Heller's revolver belched flame directly in his path, again and again.

In mid-air, Murgunstrumm stiffened. His twisted foot struck the edge of the open coffin before him. He tripped, lunged forward. His writhing body sprawled in a shapeless mass.

A long rattling moan welled through his parted lips. He struggled again to his knees and swayed there, shrieking. His hands flailed empty air, clawed at nothingness. And then, with a great shudder, he collapsed.

His broken body crashed across the coffin lid. His head snapped down, burying itself in Maronaine's upturned features. And then he lay quite still, staring with wide dead eyes at the ceiling.

It was Von Heller who spoke first, after many minutes of complete silence. With a last glance at the scene, the physician turned very quietly and motioned to the doorway.

"Come."

Thus, with the lantern finding the way, the four men left the cellar of horror and returned to the upstairs room where Kermeff and Ruth LeGeurn awaited them. Kermeff, standing quickly erect, said in a husky voice:

"You found them?"

"It is over," Von Heller shrugged. "Quite over. As soon as Miss LeGeurn is better, we shall leave here and return—"

"To Morrisdale?" Paul cried, seizing the man's arm.

"To Miss LeGeurn's home, where Doctor Kermeff will sign the necessary papers. Kermeff made a very natural mistake, my boy. But he will rectify it."

"I was ignorant," Kermeff muttered. "I did not know."

"There was only one way to know, to learn the truth. Paul has shown you. Now we shall leave and. . . ."

But Paul was not listening. He was sitting on the edge of the bed, holding the girl's hands. The room was sweet and clean with daylight, and he was whispering words which he wished no one but Ruth to hear.

And later, as the big car droned through sun-streaked country roads toward the distant city, Ruth LeGeurn lay in the back seat, with her head in Paul's arms, and listened to the same whispered words over again. And she smiled, for the first time in months.

The Hills of the Dead

ROBERT E. HOWARD

Voodoo
I

The twigs which N'Longa flung on the fire broke and crack-led. The up-leaping flames lighted the countenances of the two men. N'Longa, voodoo man of the Slave Coast, was very old. His wizened and gnarled frame was stooped and brittle, his face creased by hundreds of wrinkles. The red firelight glinted on the human finger-bones which composed his necklace.

The other was a white man and his name was Solomon Kane. He was tall and broad-shouldered, clad in black close garments, the garb of the Puritan. His featherless slouch hat was drawn low over his heavy brows, shadowing his darkly pallid face. His cold deep eyes brooded in the firelight.

"You come again, brother," droned the fetish-man, speaking in the jargon which passed for a common language of black man and white on the West Coast. "Many moons burn and die since we make blood-palaver. You go to the setting sun, but you come back!"

"Aye." Kane's voice was deep and almost ghostly. "Yours is a grim land, N'Longa, a red land barred with the black darkness of horror and the bloody shadows of death. Yet I have returned—"

N'Longa stirred the fire, saying nothing, and after a pause Kane continued.

"Yonder in the unknown vastness"—his long finger stabbed at the black silent jungle which brooded beyond the firelight—"yonder lie mystery and adventure and nameless terror. Once I dared the jungle—once she nearly claimed my bones. Something entered into my blood, something stole into my soul like a whisper of unnamed sin. The jungle! Dark and brooding—over leagues of the blue salt sea she has drawn me and with the dawn I go to seek the heart of her. Mayhap I shall find curious adventure—mayhap my doom awaits me. But better death than the ceaseless and everlasting urge, the fire that has burned my veins with bitter longing."

"She call," muttered N'Longa. "At night she coil like serpent about my hut and whisper strange things to me. *Ai ya!* The jungle call. We be blood-brothers, you and I. Me, N'Longa, mighty worker of nameless magic. You go to the jungle as all men go who hear her call. Maybe you live, more like you die. You believe in my fetish work?"

"I understand it not," said Kane grimly, "but I have seen you send your soul forth from your body to animate a lifeless corpse."

"Aye! Me N'Longa, priest of the Black God! Now watch, I make magic."

Kane gazed at the black man who bent over the fire, making even motions with his hands and mumbling incantations. Kane watched and he seemed to grow sleepy. A mist wavered in front of him, through which he saw dimly the form of N'Longa, etched black against the flames. Then all faded out.

Kane awoke with a start, hand shooting to the pistol in his belt. N'Longa grinned at him across the flame and there was a scent of early dawn in the air. The fetish-man held a long stave of curious black wood in his hands. This stave was carved in a strange manner, and one end tapered to a sharp point.

"This voodoo staff," said N'Longa, putting it in the Englishman's hand. "Where your guns and long knife fail, this save you. When you want me, lay this on your breast, fold your hand on it and sleep. I come to you in your dreams."

Kane weighed the thing in his hand, highly suspicious of witchcraft. It was not heavy, but seemed hard as iron. A good weapon at least, he decided. Dawn was just beginning to steal over the jungle and the river.

Red Eyes
II

Solomon Kane shifted his musket from his shoulder and let the stock fall to the earth. Silence lay about him like a fog. Kane's lined face and tattered garments showed the effect of long bush travel. He looked about him.

Some distance behind him loomed the green, rank jungle, thinning out to low shrubs, stunted trees and tall grass. Some distance in front of him rose the first of a chain of bare, somber hills, littered with boulders, shimmering in the merciless heat of the sun. Between the hills and the jungle lay a broad expanse of rough, uneven grasslands, dotted here and there by clumps of thorntrees.

An utter silence hung over the country. The only sign of life was a few vultures flapping heavily across the distant hills. For the last few days Kane had noticed the increasing number of these unsavory birds. The sun was rocking westward but its heat was in no way abated.

Trailing his musket he started forward slowly. He had no objective in view. This was all unknown country and one direction was as good as another. Many weeks ago he had plunged into the jungle with the assurance born of courage and ignorance. Having by some miracle survived the first few weeks, he was becoming hard and toughened, able to hold his own with any of the grim denizens of the fastness he dared.

As he progressed he noted an occasional lion spoor but there seemed to be no animals in the grasslands—none that left tracks, at any rate. Vultures sat like black, brooding images in some of the stunted trees, and suddenly he saw an activity among them some distance beyond. Several of the dusky birds circled about a clump of high grass, dipping, then rising again. Some beast of prey was defending his kill against them, Kane decided, and wondered at the lack of snarling and roaring which usually accompanied such scenes. His curiosity was roused and he turned his steps in that direction.

At last, pushing through the grass which rose about his shoulders, he saw, as through a corridor walled with the rank waving blades, a ghastly sight. The corpse of a black man lay, face down, and as the Englishman looked, a great dark snake rose and slid away into the grass, moving so quickly that Kane was unable to decide its nature. But it had a weird human-like suggestion about it.

Kane stood over the body, noting that while the limbs lay awry as if broken, the flesh was not torn as a lion or leopard would have torn it. He glanced up at the whirling vultures and was amazed to see several of them skimming along close to the earth, following a waving of the grass which marked the flight of the thing which had presumably slain the black man. Kane wondered what thing the carrion birds, which eat only the dead, were hunting through the grasslands. But Africa is full of never-explained mysteries.

Kane shrugged his shoulders and lifted his musket again. Adventures he had had in plenty since he parted from N'Longa some moons agone, but still that nameless paranoid urge had driven him on and on, deeper and deeper into those trackless ways. Kane could not have analyzed this call; he would have attributed it to Satan, who lures men to their destruction. But it was but the restless turbulent spirit of the adventurer, the wanderer—the same urge which sends the gipsy caravans about the world, which drove the Viking galleys over unknown seas and which guides the flights of the wild geese.

Kane sighed. Here in this barren land seemed neither food nor water, but he had wearied unto death of the dank, rank venom of the thick jungle. Even a wilderness of bare hills was preferable, for a time at least. He glanced at them, where they lay brooding in the sun, and started forward again.

He held N'Longa's fetish stave in his left hand, and though his conscience still troubled him for keeping a thing so apparently diabolic in nature, he had never been able to bring himself to throw it away.

Now as he went toward the hills, a sudden commotion broke out in the tall grass in front of him, which was, in places, taller than a man. A thin, high-pitched scream sounded and on its heels an earth-shaking roar. The grass parted and a slim figure came flying toward him like a wisp of straw blown on the wind—a brown-skinned girl, clad only in a skirt-like garment. Behind her, some yards away but gaining swiftly, came a huge lion.

The girl fell at Kane's feet with a wail and a sob, and lay clutching at his ankles. The Englishman dropped the voodoo stave, raised his musket to his shoulder and sighted coolly at the ferocious feline face which neared him every instant. Crash! The girl screamed once and slumped on her face. The huge cat leaped high and wildly, to fall and lie motionless.

Kane reloaded hastily before he spared a glance at the form at his feet. The girl lay as still as the lion he had just slain, but a quick examination showed that she had only fainted.

He bathed her face with water from his canteen and presently she opened her eyes and sat up. Fear flooded her face as she looked at her rescuer and she made to rise.

Kane held out a restraining hand and she cowered down, trembling. The roar of his heavy musket was enough to frighten any native who had never before seen a white man, Kane reflected.

The girl was a much higher type than the thick-lipped, bestial West Coast Negroes to whom Kane had been used. She was slim and finely formed, of a deep brown hue rather than ebony; her nose was straight and thin-bridged, her lips were not too thick. Somewhere in her blood there was a strong Berber strain.

Kane spoke to her in a river dialect, a simple language he had learned during his wandering, and she replied haltingly. The inland tribes traded slaves and ivory to the river people and were familiar with their jargon.

"My village is there," she answered Kane's question, pointing to the southern jungle with a slim, rounded arm. "My name is Zunna. My mother whipped me for breaking a cooking-kettle and I ran away because I was angry. I am afraid; let me go back to my mother!"

"You may go," said Kane, "but I will take you, child. Suppose another lion came along? You were very foolish to run away."

She whimpered a little. "Are you not a god?"

"No, Zunna. I am only a man, though the color of my skin is not as yours. Lead me now to your village."

She rose hesitantly, eyeing him apprehensively through the wild tangle of her hair. To Kane she seemed like some frightened young animal. She led the way and Kane followed. She indicated that her village lay to the southeast, and their route brought them nearer to the hills. The sun began to sink and the roaring of lions reverberated over the grasslands. Kane glanced at the western sky; this open country was no place in which to be caught by night. He glanced toward the hills and saw that they were within a few hundred yards of the nearest. He saw what seemed to be a cave.

"Zunna," said he haltingly, "we can never reach your village

before nightfall and if we bide here the lions will take us. Yonder is
a cavern where we may spend the night—"

She shrank and trembled.

"Not in the hills, master!" she whimpered. "Better the lions!"

"Nonsense!" His tone was impatient; he had had enough of
native superstition, "We will spend the night in yonder cave."

She argued no further, but followed him. They went up a short
slope and stood at the mouth of the cavern, a small affair, with
sides of solid rock and a floor of deep sand.

"Gather some dry grass, Zunna," commanded Kane, standing
his musket against the wall at the mouth of the cave, "but go not
far away, and listen for lions. I will build here a fire which shall
keep us safe from beasts tonight. Bring some grass and any twigs
you may find, like a good child, and we will sup. I have dried meat
in my pouch and water also."

She gave him a strange, long glance, then turned away without
a word. Kane tore up grass near at hand, noting how it was seared
and crisp from the sun, and heaping it up, struck flint and steel.
Flame leaped up and devoured the heap in an instant. He was
wondering how he could gather enough grass to keep a fire going
all night, when he was aware that he had visitors.

Kane was used to grotesque sights, but at first glance he started
and a slight coldness traveled down his spine. Two black men
stood before him in silence. They were tall and gaunt and entirely
naked. Their skins were a dusty black, ringed with a gray, ashy
hue, as of death. Their faces were different from any Negroes he
had seen. The brows were high and narrow, the noses huge and
snout-like; the eyes were inhumanly large and inhumanly red. As
the two stood there it seemed to Kane that only their burning eyes
lived.

He spoke to them, but they did not answer. He invited them to
eat with a motion of his hand, and they silently squatted down
near the cave mouth, as far from the dying embers of the fire as
they could get.

Kane turned to his pouch and began taking out the strips of
dried meat which he carried. Once he glanced at his silent guests;
it seemed to him that they were watching the glowing ashes of his
fire, rather than him.

The sun was about to sink behind the western horizon. A red,
fierce glow spread over the grasslands, so that all seemed like a

waving sea of blood. Kane knelt over his pouch, and glancing up, saw Zunna come around the shoulder of the hill with her arms full of grass and dry branches.

As he looked, her eyes flared wide; the branches dropped from her arms and her scream knifed the silence, fraught with terrible warning. Kane whirled on his knee. Two great black forms loomed over him as he came up with the lithe motion of a springing leopard. The fetish stave was in his hand and he drove it through the body of the nearest foe with a force which sent its sharp point out between the negro's shoulders. Then the long, lean arms of the other locked about him, and white man and black man went down together.

The talon-like nails of the black were tearing at his face, the hideous red eyes staring into his with a terrible threat, as Kane writhed about and, fending off the clawing hands with one arm, drew a pistol. He pressed the muzzle close against the black's side and pulled the trigger. At the muffled report, the Negro's body jerked to the concussion of the bullet, but the thick lips merely gaped in a horrid grin.

One long arm slid under Kane's shoulders, the other hand gripped his hair. The Englishman felt his head being forced back irresistibly. He clutched at the other's wrist with both hands, but the flesh under his frantic fingers was as hard as wood. Kane's brain was reeling; his neck seemed ready to break with a little more pressure. He threw his body backward with one volcanic effort, breaking the deathly hold. The black was on him and the talons were clutching again. Kane found and raised the empty pistol, and he felt the black man's skull cave in like a shell as he brought down the long barrel with all his strength. And once again the writhing lips parted in fearful mockery.

And now a near panic clutched Kane. What sort of man was this, who still menaced his life with tearing fingers, after having been shot and mortally bludgeoned? No man, surely, but one of the sons of Satan! At the thought Kane wrenched and heaved explosively, and the close-locked combatants tumbled across the earth to come to a rest in the smoldering ashes before the cave mouth. Kane barely felt the heat, but the mouth of his foe gaped, this time in seeming agony. The frightful fingers loosened their hold and Kane sprang clear.

The black man with his shattered skull was rising on one hand

and one knee when Kane struck, returning to the attack as a gaunt wolf returns to a wounded bison. From the side he leaped, landing full on the black giant's back, his steely arms seeking and finding a deadly wrestling hold; and as they went to the earth together he broke the Negro's neck, so that the hideous dead face looked back over one shoulder. The black man lay still but to Kane it seemed that he was not dead even then, for the red eyes still burned with their grisly light.

The Englishman turned to see the girl crouching against the cave wall. He looked for his stave; it lay in a heap of dust, among which were a few moldering bones. He stared, his brain reeling. Then with one stride he caught up the voodoo staff and turned to the fallen negro. His face set in grim lines as he raised it; then he drove it through the black breast. And before his eyes, the giant body crumbled, dissolving to dust as he watched horror-struck, even as had crumbled he through whom Kane had first thrust the stave.

Dream Magic
III

reat God!" whispered Kane; "these men were dead! Vampires! This is Satan's handiwork manifested."

Zunna crawled to his knees and clung there.

"These be walking dead men, master," she whimpered. "I should have warned you."

"Why did they not leap on my back when they first came?" asked he.

"They feared the fire. They were waiting for the embers to die entirely."

"Whence came they?"

"From the hills. Hundreds of their kind swarm among the boulders and caverns of these hills, and they live on human life, for a man they will slay, devouring his ghost as it leaves his quivering body. Aye, they are suckers of souls!

"Master, among the greater of these hills there is a silent city of stone, and in the old times, in the days of my ancestors, these people lived there. They were human, but they were not as we, for they had ruled this land for ages and ages. The ancestors of my people made war on them and slew many, and their magicians made all the dead men as these were. At last all died.

"And for ages have they preyed on the tribes of the jungle, stalking down from the hills at midnight and at sunset to haunt the jungle-ways and slay and slay. Men and beasts flee them and only fire will destroy them."

"Here is that which will destroy them," said Kane grimly, raising the voodoo stave. "Black magic must fight black magic, and I know not what spell N'Longa put hereon, but—"

"You are a god," said Zunna decidedly. "No man could overcome two of the walking dead men. Master, can you not lift this curse from my tribe? There is nowhere for us to flee and the monsters slay us at will, catching wayfarers outside the village wall. Death is on this land and we die helpless!"

Deep in Kane stirred the spirit of the crusader, the fire of the zealot—the fanatic who devotes his life to battling the powers of darkness.

"Let us eat," said he; "then we will build a great fire at the cave mouth. The fire which keeps away beasts shall also keep away fiends."

Later Kane sat just inside the cave, chin rested on clenched fist, eyes gazing unseeingly into the fire. Behind in the shadows, Zunna watched him, awed.

"God of Hosts," Kane muttered, "grant me aid! My hand it is which must lift the ancient curse from this dark land. How am I to fight these dead fiends, who yield not to mortal weapons? Fire will destroy them—a broken neck renders them helpless—the voodoo stave thrust through them crumbles them to dust—but of what avail? How may I prevail against the hundreds who haunt these hills, and to whom human life-essence is Life? Have not—as Zunna says—warriors come against them in the past, only to find them fled to their high-walled city where no man can come against them?"

The night wore on. Zunna slept, her cheek pillowed on her round, girlish arm. The roaring of the lions shook the hills and still Kane sat and gazed broodingly into the fire. Outside, the night was alive with whispers and rustlings and stealthily soft footfalls. And at times Kane, glancing up from his meditations, seemed to catch the gleam of great red eyes beyond the flickering light of the fire.

Gray dawn was stealing over the grasslands when Kane shook Zunna into wakefulness.

"God have mercy on my soul for delving in barbaric magic," said he, "but demonry must be fought with demonry, mayhap. Tend ye the fire and awake me if aught untoward occur."

Kane lay down on his back on the sand floor and laid the voodoo staff on his breast, folding his hands upon it. He fell asleep instantly. And sleeping, he dreamed. To his slumbering self it seemed that he walked through a thick fog and in this fog he met N'Longa, true to life. N'Longa spoke, and the words were clear and vivid, impressing themselves on his consciousness so deeply as to span the gap between sleeping and waking.

"Send this girl to her village soon after sun-up when the lions have gone to their lairs," said N'Longa, "and bid her bring her lover to you at this cave. There make him lie down as if to slumber, holding the voodoo stave."

The dream faded and Kane awoke suddenly, wondering. How strange and vivid had been the vision, and how strange to hear N'Longa talking in English, without the jargon! Kane shrugged his shoulders. He knew that N'Longa claimed to possess the power of sending his spirit through space, and he himself had seen the voodoo man animate a dead man's body. Still—

"Zunna," said Kane, giving the problem up, "I will go with you as far as the edge of the jungle and you must go on to your village and return here to this cave with your lover."

"Kran?" she asked naïvely.

"Whatever his name is. Eat and we will go."

Again the sun slanted toward the west. Kane sat in the cave, waiting. He had seen the girl safely to the place where the jungle thinned to the grasslands, and though his conscience stung him at the thought of the dangers which might confront her, he sent her on alone and returned to the cave. He sat now, wondering if he would not be damned to everlasting flames for tinkering with the magic of a black sorcerer, blood-brother or not.

Light footfalls sounded, and as Kane reached for his musket, Zunna entered, accompanied by a tall, splendidly proportioned youth whose brown skin showed that he was of the same race as the girl. His soft dreamy eyes were fixed on Kane in a sort of awesome worship. Evidently the girl had not minimized the white god's glory in her telling.

He bade the youth lie down as he directed and placed the voodoo stave in his hands. Zunna crouched at one side, wide-eyed. Kane stepped back, half ashamed of this mummery and wondering what, if anything, would come of it. Then to his horror, the youth gave one gasp and stiffened!

Zunna screamed, bounding erect.

"You have killed Kran!" she shrieked, flying at the Englishman who stood struck speechless.

Then she halted suddenly, wavered, drew a hand languidly across her brow—she slid down to lie with her arms about the motionless body of her lover.

And this body moved suddenly, made aimless motions with hands and feet, then sat up, disengaging itself from the clinging arms of the still senseless girl.

Kran looked up at Kane and grinned, a sly, knowing grin which seemed out of place on his face somehow. Kane started. Those soft eyes had changed in expression and were now hard and glittering and snaky—N'Longa's eyes!

"*Ai ya*," said Kran in a grotesquely familiar voice. "Blood-brother, you got no greeting for N'Longa?"

Kane was silent. His flesh crawled in spite of himself. Kran rose and stretched his arms in an unfamiliar sort of way, as if his limbs were new to him. He slapped his breast approvingly.

"Me N'Longa!" said he in the old boastful manner. "Mighty ju-ju man! Blood-brother, not you know me, eh?"

"You are Satan," said Kane sincerely. "Are you Kran or are you N'Longa?"

"Me N'Longa," assured the other. "My body sleep in ju-ju hut on Coast many treks from here. I borrow Kran's body for while. My ghost travel ten days' march in one breath; twenty days' march in same time. My ghost go out from my body and drive out Kran's."

"And Kran is dead?"

"No, he no dead. I send his ghost to shadowland for a while—send the girl's ghost too, to keep him company; bimeby come back."

"This is the work of the Devil," said Kane frankly, "but I have seen you do even fouler magic—shall I call you N'Longa or Kran?"

"Kran—*kah!* Me N'Longa—bodies like clothes! Me N'Longa, in

here now!'' he rapped his breast. ''Bimeby Kran live along here—
then he be Kran and I be N'Longa, same like before. Kran no live
along now; N'Longa live along this one fellow body. Blood-
brother, I am N'Longa!''

Kane nodded. This was in truth a land of horror and enchantment; anything was possible, even that the thin voice of N'Longa
should speak to him from the great chest of Kran, and the snaky
eyes of N'Longa should blink at him from the handsome young
face of Kran.

''This land I know long time,'' said N'Longa, getting down to
business. ''Mighty ju-ju, these dead people! No, no need to waste
one fellow time—I know—I talk to you in sleep. My blood-brother
want to kill out these dead black fellows, eh?''

'''Tis a thing opposed to nature,'' said Kane somberly. ''They are
known in my land as vampires—I never expected to come upon a
whole nation of them.''

The Silent City
IV

Now we find this stone city,'' said N'Longa.
       ''Yes? Why not send your ghost out to kill these vampires?''
Kane asked idly.

''Ghost got to have one fellow body to work in,'' N'Longa answered. ''Sleep now. Tomorrow we start.''

The sun had set; the fire glowed and flickered in the cave
mouth. Kane glanced at the still form of the girl, who lay where
she had fallen, and prepared himself for slumber.

''Awake me at midnight,'' he admonished, ''and I will watch
from then until dawn.''

But when N'Longa finally shook his arm, Kane awoke to see the
first light of dawn reddening the land.

''Time we start,'' said the fetish-man.

''But the girl—are you sure she lives?''

''She live, blood-brother.''

''Then in God's name, we can not leave her here at the mercy of
any prowling fiend who might chance upon her. Or some lion
might—''

''No lion come. Vampire scent still linger, mixed with man scent.
One fellow lion he no like man scent and he fear the walking dead

men. No beast come; and"—lifting the voodoo stave and laying it across the cave entrance—"no dead man come now."

Kane watched him soberly and without enthusiasm.

"How will that rod safeguard her?"

"That mighty ju-ju," said N'Longa. "You see how one fellow vampire go along dust alongside that stave! No vampire dare touch or come near it. I gave it to you, because outside Vampire Hills one fellow man sometimes meet a corpse walking in jungle when shadows be black. Not all walking dead man be here. And all must suck Life from men—if not, they rot like dead wood."

"Then make many of these rods and arm the people with them."

"No can do!" N'Longa's skull shook violently. "That ju-ju rod be mighty magic! Old, old! No man live today can tell how old that fellow ju-ju stave be. I make my blood-brother sleep and do magic with it to guard him, that time we make palaver in Coast village. Today we scout and run; no need it. Leave it here to guard girl."

Kane shrugged his shoulders and followed the fetish-man, after glancing back at the still shape which lay in the cave. He would never have agreed to leave her so casually, had he not believed in his heart that she was dead. He had touched her, and her flesh was cold.

They went up among the barren hills as the sun was rising. Higher they climbed, up steep clay slopes, winding their way through ravines and between great boulders. The hills were honeycombed with dark, forbidding caves, and these they passed warily, and Kane's flesh crawled as he thought of the grisly occupants therein. For N'Longa said:

"Them vampires, he sleep in caves most all day till sunset. Them caves, he be full of one fellow dead man."

The sun rose higher, baking down on the bare slopes with an intolerable heat. Silence brooded like an evil monster over the land. They had seen nothing, but Kane could have sworn at times that a black shadow drifted behind a boulder at their approach.

"Them vampires, they stay hid in daytime," N'Longa with a low laugh. "They be afraid of one fellow vulture! No fool vulture! He know death when he see it! He pounce on one fellow dead man and tear and eat if he be lying or walking!"

A strong shudder shook his companion.

"Great God," Kane cried, striking his thigh with his hat; "is there no end to the horror of this hideous land? Truly this land is dedicated to the powers of darkness!"

Kane's eyes burned with a dangerous light. The terrible heat, the solitude and the knowledge of the horrors lurking on either hand were shaking even his steely nerves.

"Keep on one fellow hat, blood-brother," admonished N'Longa with a low gurgle of amusement. "That fellow sun, he knock you dead, suppose you no look out."

Kane shifted the musket he had insisted on bringing and made no reply. They mounted an eminence at last and looked down on a sort of plateau. And in the center of this plateau was a silent city of gray and crumbling stone. Kane was smitten by a sense of incredible age as he looked. The walls and houses were of great stone blocks, yet they were falling into ruin. Grass grew on the plateau, and high in the streets of that dead city. Kane saw no movement among the ruins.

"That is their city—why do they choose to sleep in caves?"

"Maybe-so one fellow stone fall on them from roof and crush. Them stone huts, he fall down bimeby. Maybe-so they no like to stay together—maybe-so they eat each other, too."

"Silence!" whispered Kane; "how it hangs over all!"

"Them vampires no talk nor yell; they dead. They sleep in caves, wander at sunset and at night. Maybe-so them black fellow bush tribes come with spears, them vampires go to stone kraal and fight behind walls."

Kane nodded. The crumbling walls which surrounded that dead city were still high and solid enough to resist the attack of spearmen—especially when defended by these snout-nosed fiends.

"Blood-brother," said N'Longa solemnly, "I have mighty magic thought! Be silent a little while."

Kane seated himself on a boulder and gazed broodingly at the bare crags and slopes which surrounded them. Far away to the south he saw the leafy green ocean that was the jungle. Distance lent a certain enchantment to the scene. Closer at hand loomed the dark blotches that were the mouths of the caves of horror.

N'Longa was squatting, tracing some strange pattern in the clay with a dagger point. Kane watched him, thinking how easily they might fall victim to the vampires if even three or four of the fiends should come out of their caverns. And even as he thought it, a black and horrific shadow fell across the crouching fetish-man.

Kane acted without conscious thought. He shot from the boulder where he sat like a stone hurled from a catapult, and his musket stock shattered the face of the hideous black thing who had stolen upon them. Back and back Kane drove his inhuman foe staggering, never giving him time to halt or launch an offensive, battering him with the onslaught of a frenzied tiger.

At the very edge of the cliff the vampire wavered, then pitched back over, to fall for a hundred feet and lie writhing on the rocks of the plateau below. N'Longa was on his feet pointing; the hills were giving up their dead.

Out of the caves they were swarming, the terrible black silent shapes; up the slopes they came charging and over the boulders they came clambering, and their red eyes all turned toward the two humans who stood above the silent city. The caves belched them forth in an unholy judgment day.

N'Longa pointed to a crag some distance away and with a shout started running fleetly toward it. Kane followed. From behind boulders black-taloned hands clawed at them, tearing their garments. They raced past caves, and mummied monsters came lurching out of the dark, gibbering silently, to join in the pursuit.

The dead hands were close at their back when they scrambled up the last slope and stood on a ledge which was the top of the crag. The fiends halted silently a moment, then came clambering after them. Kane clubbed his musket and smashed down into the red-eyed faces, knocking aside the upleaping hands. They surged up like a black wave; he swung his musket in a silent fury that matched theirs. The black wave broke and wavered back; came on again.

He—could—not—kill—them! These words beat on his brain like a sledge on an anvil as he shattered wood-like flesh and dead bone with his smashing swings. He knocked them down, hurled them back, but they rose and came on again. This could not last— what in God's name was N'Longa doing? Kane spared one swift, tortured glance over his shoulder. The fetish-man stood on the highest part of the ledge, head thrown back, arms lifted as if in invocation.

Kane's vision blurred to the sweep of hideous black faces with red, staring eyes. Those in front were horrible to see now, for their skulls were shattered, their faces caved in and their limbs broken. But still they came on and those behind reached across their shoulders to clutch at the man who defied them.

Kane was red but the blood was all his. From the long-withered veins of those monsters no single drop of warm red blood trickled. Suddenly from behind him came a long piercing wail—N'Longa! Over the crash of the flying musket-stock and the shattering of bones it sounded high and clear—the only voice lifted in that hideous fight.

The black wave washed about Kane's feet, dragging him down. Keen talons tore at him, flaccid lips sucked at his wounds. He reeled up again, disheveled and bloody, clearing a space with a shattering sweep of his splintered musket. Then they closed in again and he went down.

"This is the end!" he thought, but even at that instant the press slackened and the sky was suddenly filled with the beat of great wings.

Then he was free and staggered up, blindly and dizzily, ready to renew the strife. He halted, frozen. Down the slope the black horde was fleeing and over their heads and close at their shoulders flew huge vultures, tearing and rending avidly, sinking their beaks in the dead black flesh, devouring the vampires as they fled.

Kane laughed, almost insanely.

"Defy man and God, but you may not deceive the vultures, sons of Satan! They know whether a man be alive or dead!

N'Longa stood like a prophet on the pinnacle and the great black birds soared and wheeled about him. His arms still waved and his voice still wailed out across the hills. And over the skylines they came, hordes on endless hordes—vultures, vultures, vultures! come to the feast so long denied them. They blackened the sky with their numbers, blotted out the sun; a strange darkness fell on the land. They settled in long dusky lines, diving into the caverns with a whir of wings and a clash of beaks. Their talons tore at the black horrors which these caves disgorged.

Now all the vampires were fleeing to their city. The vengeance held back for ages had come down on them and their last hope was the heavy walls which had kept back the desperate human foes. Under those crumbling roofs they might find shelter. And N'Longa watched them stream into the city, and he laughed until the crags re-echoed.

Now all were in and the birds settled like a cloud over the doomed city, perching in solid rows along the walls, sharpening their beaks and claws on the towers.

And N'Longa struck flint and steel to a bundle of dry leaves he had brought with him. The bundle leaped into instant flame and he straightened and flung the blazing thing far out over the cliffs. It fell like a meteor to the plateau beneath, showering sparks. The tall grass of the plateau leaped aflame.

From the silent city beneath them Fear flowed in unseen waves, like a white fog. Kane smiled grimly.

"The grass is sere and brittle from the drouth," he said; "there has been even less rain than usual this season; it will burn swiftly."

Like a crimson serpent the fire ran through the high dead grass. It spread and it spread and Kane, standing high above, yet felt the fearful intensity of the hundreds of red eyes which watched from the stone city.

Now the scarlet snake had reached the walls and was rearing as if to coil and writhe over them. The vultures rose on heavily flapping wings and soared reluctantly. A vagrant gust of wind whipped the blaze about and drove it in a long red sheet around the wall. Now the city was hemmed in on all sides by a solid barricade of flame. The roar came up to the two men on the high crag.

Sparks flew across the wall, lighting in the high grass in the streets. A score of flames leaped up and grew with terrifying speed. A veil of red cloaked streets and buildings, and through this crimson, whirling mist Kane and N'Longa saw hundreds of black shapes scamper and writhe, to vanish suddenly in red bursts of flame. There rose an intolerable scent of decaying flesh burning.

Kane gazed, awed. This was truly a hell on earth. As in a nightmare he looked into the roaring red cauldron where black insects fought against their doom and perished. The flames leaped a hundred feet in air, and suddenly above their roar sounded one bestial, inhuman scream like a shriek from across nameless gulfs of cosmic space, as one vampire, dying, broke the chains of silence which had held him for untold centuries. High and haunting it rose, the death cry of a vanishing race.

Then the flames dropped suddenly. The conflagration had been a typical grass fire, short and fierce. Now the plateau showed a blackened expanse and the city a charred and smoking mass of crumbling stone. Not one corpse lay in view, not even a charred bone. Above all whirled the dark swarms of the vultures, but they, too, were beginning to scatter.

Kane gazed hungrily at the clean blue sky. Like a strong sea wind clearing a fog of horror was the sight to him. From some-where sounded the faint and far-off roaring of a distant lion. The vultures were flapping away in black, straggling lines.

Palaver Set!
V

Kane sat in the mouth of the cave where Zunna lay, submitting to the fetish-man's bandaging.

The Puritan's garments hung in tatters about his frame; his limbs and breast were deeply gashed and darkly bruised, but he had had no mortal wound in that deathly fight on the cliff.

"Mighty men, we be!" declared N'Longa with deep approval. "Vampire city be silent now, sure 'nough! No walking dead man live along these hills."

"I do not understand," said Kane, resting chin on hand. "Tell me, N'Longa, how have you done things? How talked you with me in my dreams; how came you into the body of Kran; and how summoned you the vultures?"

"My blood-brother," said N'Longa, discarding his pride in his pidgin English, to drop into the river language understood by Kane, "I am so old that you would call me a liar if I told you my age. All my life I have worked magic, sitting first at the feet of mighty ju-ju men of the south and the east; then I was a slave to the Buckra—the white man—and learned more. My brother, shall I span all these years in a moment and make you understand with a word, what has taken me so long to learn? I could not even make you understand how these vampires have kept their bodies from decay by drinking the lives of men.

"I sleep and my spirit goes out over the jungle and the rivers to talk with the sleeping spirits of my friends. There is a mighty magic on the voodoo staff I gave you—a magic out of the Old Land which draws my ghost to it as a white man's magnet draws metal."

Kane listened unspeaking, seeing for the first time in N'Longa's glittering eyes something stronger and deeper than the avid gleam of the worker in black magic. To Kane it seemed almost as if he looked into the far-seeing and mystic eyes of a prophet of old.

"I spoke to you in dreams," N'Longa went on, "and I made a deep sleep come over the souls of Kran and of Zunna, and removed them to a far dim land, whence they shall soon return, unremembering. All things bow to magic, blood-brother, and beasts and birds obey the master words. I worked strong voodoo, vulture-magic, and the flying people of the air gathered at my call.

"These things I know and am a part of, but how shall I tell you of them? Blood-brother, you are a mighty warrior, but in the ways of magic you are as a little child lost. And what has taken me long dark years to know, I may not divulge to you so you would understand. My friend, you think only of bad spirits, but were my magic always bad, should I not take this fine young body in place of my old wrinkled one and keep it? But Kran shall have his body back safely.

"Keep the voodoo staff, blood-brother. It has mighty power against all sorcerers and serpents and evil things. Now I return to the village on the Coast where my true body sleeps. And what of you, my blood-brother?"

Kane pointed silently eastward.

"The call grows no weaker. I go."

N'Longa nodded, held out his hand. Kane grasped it. The mystical expression had gone from the dusky face and the eyes twinkled snakily with a sort of reptilian mirth.

"Me go now, blood-brother," said the fetish-man, returning to his beloved jargon, of which knowledge he was prouder than all his conjuring tricks. "You take care—that one fellow jungle, she pluck your bones yet! Remember that voodoo stave, brother. Ai ya, palaver set!"

He fell back on the sand, and Kane saw the keen sly expression of N'Longa fading from the face of Kran. His flesh crawled again. Somewhere back on the Slave Coast, the body of N'Longa, withered and wrinkled, was stirring in the ju-ju hut, was rising as if from a deep sleep. Kane shuddered.

Kran sat up, yawned, stretched and smiled. Beside him the girl Zunna rose, rubbing her eyes.

"Master," said Kran apologetically, "we must have slumbered."

Black Thirst

❦

C. L. MOORE

northwest Smith leant his head back against the warehouse
wall and stared up into the black night-sky of Venus. The
waterfront street was very quiet tonight, very dangerous.
He could hear no sound save the eternal slap-slap of water against
the piles, but he knew how much of danger and sudden death
dwelt here voiceless in the breathing dark, and he may have been a
little homesick as he stared up into the clouds that masked a green
star hanging lovely on the horizon—Earth and home. And if he
thought of that he must have grinned wryly to himself in the dark,
for Northwest Smith had no home, and Earth would not have
welcomed him very kindly just then.

He sat quietly in the dark. Above him in the warehouse wall a
faintly lighted window threw a square of pallor upon the wet
street. Smith drew back into his angle of darkness under the slanting shaft, hugging one knee. And presently he heard footsteps
softly on the street.

He may have been expecting footsteps, for he turned his head
alertly and listened, but it was not a man's feet that came so lightly
over the wooden quay, and Smith's brow furrowed. A woman,
here, on this black waterfront by night? Not even the lowest class
of Venusian street-walker dared come along the waterfronts of

Ednes on the nights when the space-liners were not in. Yet across the pavement came clearly now the light tapping of a woman's feet.

Smith drew farther back into the shadows and waited. And presently she came, a darkness in the dark save for the triangular patch of pallor that was her face. As she passed under the light falling dimly from the window overhead he understood suddenly how she dared walk here and who she was. A long black cloak hid her, but the light fell upon her face, heart-shaped under the little three-cornered velvet cap that Venusian women wear, fell on ripples of half-hidden bronze hair; and by that sweet triangular face and shining hair he knew her for one of the Minga maids—those beauties that from the beginning of history have been bred in the Minga stronghold for loveliness and grace, as race-horses are bred on Earth, and reared from earliest infancy in the art of charming men. Scarcely a court on the three planets lacks at least one of these exquisite creatures, long-limbed, milk-white, with their bronze hair and lovely brazen faces—if the lord of that court has the wealth to buy them. Kings from many nations and races have poured their riches into the Minga gateway, and girls like pure gold and ivory have gone forth to grace a thousand palaces, and this has been so since Ednes first rose on the shore of the Greater Sea.

This girl walked here unafraid and unharmed because she wore the beauty that marked her for what she was. The heavy hand of the Minga stretched out protectingly over her bronze head, and not a man along the wharf-fronts but knew what dreadful penalties would overtake him if he dared so much as to lay a finger on the milk-whiteness of a Minga maid—terrible penalties, such as men whisper of fearfully over *segir*-whisky mugs in the waterfront dives of many nations—mysterious, unnamable penalties more dreadful than any knife or gun-flash could inflict.

And these dangers, too, guarded the gates of the Minga castle. The chastity of the Minga girls was proverbial, a trade boast. This girl walked in peace and safety more sure than that attending the steps of a nun through slum streets by night on Earth.

But even so, the girls went forth very rarely from the gates of the castle, never unattended. Smith had never seen one before, save at a distance. He shifted a little now, to catch a better glimpse as she went by, to look for the escort that must surely walk a pace or two behind, though he heard no footsteps save her own. The slight motion caught her eye. She stopped. She peered closer into the dark, and said in a voice as sweet and smooth as cream,

"How would you like to earn a goldpiece, my man?"

A flash of perversity twisted Smith's reply out of its usual slovenly dialect, and he said in his most cultured voice, in his most perfect High Venusian,

"Thank you, no."

For a moment the woman stood quite still, peering through the darkness in a vain effort to reach his face. He could see her own, a pale oval in the window light, intent, surprized. Then she flung back her cloak and the dim light glinted on the case of a pocket flash as she flicked the catch. A beam of white radiance fell blindingly upon his face.

For an instant the light held him—lounging against the wall in his spaceman's leather, the burns upon it, the tatters, ray-gun in its holster low on his thigh, and the brown scarred face turned to hers, eyes the colorless color of pale steel narrowed to the glare. It was a typical face. It belonged here, on the waterfront, in these dark and dangerous streets. It belonged to the type that frequents such places, those lawless men who ride the spaceways and live by the rule of the ray-gun, recklessly, warily outside the Patrol's jurisdiction. But there was more than that in the scarred brown face turned to the light. She must have seen it as she held the flash unwavering, some deep-buried trace of breeding and birth that made the cultured accents of the High Venusian not incongruous. And the colorless eyes derided her.

"No," she said, flicking off the light. "Not one gold-piece, but a hundred. And for another task than I meant."

"Thank you," said Smith, not rising. "You must excuse me."

"Five hundred," she said without a flicker of emotion in her creamy voice.

In the dark Smith's brows knit. There was something fantastic in the situation. Why—?

She must have sensed his reaction almost as he realized it himself, for she said,

"Yes, I know. It sounds insane. You see—I knew you in the light just now. Will you?—can you?—I can't explain here on the street. . . ."

* * *

Smith held the silence unbroken for thirty seconds, while a lightning debate flashed through the recesses of his wary mind. Then he grinned to himself in the dark and said,

"I'll come." Belatedly he got to his feet. "Where?"

"The Palace Road on the edge of the Minga. Third door from the central gate, to the left. Say to the door-warden—'Vaudir'."

"That is—?"

"Yes, my name. You will come, in half an hour?"

An instant longer Smith's mind hovered on the verge of refusal. Then he shrugged.

"Yes."

"At the third bell, then." She made the little Venusian gesture of parting and wrapped her cloak about her. The blackness of it, and the softness of her footfalls, made her seem to melt into the darkness without a sound, but Smith's trained ears heard her footsteps very softly on the pavement as she went on into the dark.

He sat there until he could no longer detect any faintest sound of feet on the wharf. He waited patiently, but his mind was a little dizzy with surprise. Was the traditional inviolability of the Minga a fraud? Were the close-guarded girls actually allowed sometimes to walk unattended by night, making assignations as they pleased? Or was it some elaborate hoax? Tradition for countless centuries had declared the gates in the Minga wall to be guarded so relentlessly by strange dangers that not even a mouse could slip through without the knowledge of the Alendar, the Minga's lord. Was it then by order of the Alendar that the door would open to him when he whispered "Vaudir" to the warden? Or would it open? Was the girl perhaps the property of some Endes lord, deceiving him for obscure purposes of her own? He shook his head a little and grinned to himself. After all, time would tell.

He waited a while longer in the dark. Little waves lapped the piles with sucking sounds, and once the sky lit up with the long, blinding roar of a space-ship splitting the dark.

At last he rose and stretched his long body as if he had been sitting there for a good while. Then he settled the gun on his leg and set off down the black street. He walked very lightly in his spaceman's boots.

A twenty-minute walk through dark byways, still and deserted, brought him to the outskirts of that vast city-within-a-city called the Minga. The dark, rough walls of it towered over him, green with the lichen-like growths of the Hot Planet. On the Palace Road one deeply-sunk central gateway opened upon the mysteries within. A tiny blue light burned over the arch. Smith went softly through the dimness to the left of it, counting two tiny doors half hidden in deep recesses. At the third he paused. It was painted a rusty green, and a green vine spilling down the wall half veiled it, so that if he had not been searching he would have passed it by.

Smith stood for a long minute, motionless, staring at the green panels deep-sunk in rock. He listened. He even sniffed the heavy air. Warily as a wild beast he hesitated in the dark. But at last he lifted his hand and tapped very lightly with his fingertips on the green door.

It swung open without a sound. Pitch-blackness confronted him, an archway of blank dark in the dimly seen stone wall. And a voice queried softly, "Qu'a lo'val?"

"Vaudir," murmured Smith, and grinned to himself involuntarily. How many romantic youths must have stood at these doors in nights gone by, breathing hopefully the names of bronze beauties to doormen in dark archways! But unless tradition lied, no man before had ever passed. He must be the first in many years to stand here invited at a little doorway in the Minga wall and hear the watchman murmur, "Come."

Smith loosened the gun at his side and bent his tall head under the arch. He stepped into blackness that closed about him like water as the door swung shut. He stood there with quickened heart-beats, hand on his gun, listening. A blue light, dim and ghostly, flooded the place without warning and he saw that the doorman had crossed to a switch at the far side of the tiny chamber wherein he stood. The man was one of the Minga eunuchs, a flabby creature, splendid in crimson velvet. He carried a cloak of purple over his arm, and made a splash of royal colors in the dimness. His sidelong eyes regarded Smith from under lifted brows, with a look that the Earthman could not fathom. There was amusement in it, and a touch of terror and a certain reluctant admiration.

Smith looked about him in frank curiosity. The little entry was apparently hollowed out of the enormously thick wall itself. The only thing that broke its bareness was the ornate bronze door set in the far wall. His eyes sought the eunuch's in mute inquiry.

The creature came forward obsequiously, murmuring, "Permit

me—" and flung the purple cloak he carried over Smith's shoulders. Its luxurious folds, faintly fragrant, swept about him like a caress. It covered him, tall as he was, to the very boot-soles. He drew back in faint distaste as the eunuch lifted his hands to fasten the jeweled clasp at his throat. "Please to draw up the hood also," murmured the creature without apparent resentment, as Smith snapped the fastening himself. The hood covered his sun-bleached hair and fell in thick folds about his face, casting it into deep shadow.

The eunuch opened the bronze inner door and Smith stared down a long hallway curving almost imperceptibly to the right. The paradox of elaborately decorated simplicity was illustrated in every broad polished panel of the wall, so intricately and exquisitely carved that it gave at first the impression of a strange, rich plainness.

His booted feet sank sensuously into the deep pile of the carpet at every step as he followed the eunuch down the hall. Twice he heard voices murmuring behind lighted doors, and his hand lay on the butt of the ray-gun under the folds of his robe, but no door opened and the hall lay empty and dim before them. So far it had been amazingly easy. Either tradition lied about the impregnability of the Minga, or the girl Vaudir had bribed with incredible lavishness or—that thought again, uneasily—it was with the Alendar's consent that he walked here unchallenged. But why?

They came to a door of silver grille at the end of the curved corridor, and passed through it into another hallway slanting up, as exquisitely voluptuous as the first. A flight of stairs wrought from dully gleaming bronze curved at the end of it. Then came another hall lighted with rosy lanterns that swung from the arched ceiling, and beyond another stairway, this time of silvery metal fretwork, spiraling down again.

And in all that distance they met no living creature. Voices hummed behind closed doors, and once or twice strains of music drifted faintly to Smith's ears, but either the corridors had been cleared by a special order, or incredible luck was attending them. And he had the uncomfortable sensation of eyes upon his back more than once. They passed dark hallways and open, unlighted doors, and sometimes the hair on his neck bristled with the feeling of human nearness, inimical, watching.

For all of twenty minutes they walked through curved corridors and up and down spiral stairs until even Smith's keen senses were confused and he could not have said at what height above the ground he was, or in what direction the corridor led into which they at last emerged. At the end of that time his nerves were tense as steel wire and he restrained himself only by force from nervous, over-the-shoulder glances each time they passed an open door. An air of languorous menace brooded almost visibly over the place, he thought. The sound of soft voices behind doors, the feel of eyes, of whispers in the air, the memory of tales half heard in waterfront dives about the secrets of the Minga, the nameless dangers of the Minga. . . .

Smith gripped his gun as he walked through the splendor and the dimness, every sense assailed by voluptuous appeals, but his nerves strained to wire and his flesh crawled as he passed un-lighted doors. This was too easy. For so many centuries the tradition of the Minga had been upheld, a byword of impregnability, a stronghold guarded by more than swords, by greater dangers than the ray-gun—and yet here he walked, unquestioned, into the deepest heart of the place, his only disguise a velvet cloak, his only weapon a holstered gun, and no one challenged him, no guards, no slaves, not even a passer-by to note that a man taller than any dweller here should be strode unquestioned through the inner-most corridors of the inviolable Minga. He loosened the ray-gun in its sheath.

The eunuch in his scarlet velvet went on confidently ahead. Only once did he falter. They had reached a dark passageway, and just as they came opposite its mouth the sound of a soft, slithering scrape, as of something over stones, draggingly, reached their ears. He saw the eunuch start and half glance back, and then hurry on at a quicker pace, nor did he slacken until they had put two gates and a length of lighted corridor between them and that dark pas-sage.

So they went on, through halls half lighted, through scented air and empty dimness where the doorways closed upon mumurous mysteries within or opened to dark and the feel of watching eyes. And they came at last, after endless, winding progress, into a hallway low-ceiled and paneled in mother-of-pearl, pierced and filigreed with carving, and all the doors were of silver grille. And as the eunuch pushed open the silver gate that led into this corridor the thing happened that his taut nerves had been expecting ever since the start of the fantastic journey. One of the doors opened and a figure stepped out and faced them.

Under the robe Smith's gun slid soundlessly from its holster. He thought he saw the eunuch's back stiffen a little, and his step falter, but only for an instant. It was a girl who had come out, a slave-girl in a single white garment, and at the first glimpse of the tall, purple-robed figure with hooded face, towering over her, she gave a little gasp and slumped to her knees as if under a blow. It was obeisance, but so shocked and terrified that it might have been a faint. She laid her face to the very carpet, and Smith, looking down in amazement on the prostrate figure, saw that she was trembling violently.

The gun slid back into its sheath and he paused for a moment over her shuddering homage. The eunuch twisted round to beckon with soundless violence, and Smith caught a glimpse of his face for the first time since their journey began. It was glistening with sweat, and the sidelong eyes were bright and shifting, like a hunted animal's. Smith was oddly reassured by the sight of the eunuch's obvious panic. There was danger then—danger of discovery, the sort of peril he knew and could fight. It was that creeping sensation of eyes watching, of unseen things slithering down dark passages, that had strained his nerves so painfully. And yet, even so, it had been too easy. . . .

The eunuch had paused at a silver door half-way down the hall and was murmuring something very softly, his mouth against the grille. A panel of green brocade was stretched across the silver door on the inside, so they could see nothing within the room, but after a moment a voice said, "Good!" in a breathing whisper, and the door quivered a little and swung open six inches. The eunuch genuflected in a swirl of scarlet robes, and Smith caught his eye swiftly, the look of terror not yet faded, but amusement there too, and a certain respect. And then the door opened wider and he stepped inside.

He stepped into a room green as a seacave. The walls were paneled in green brocade, low green couches circled the room, and, in the center, the blazing bronze beauty of the girl Vaudir. She wore a robe of green velvet cut in the startling Venusian fashion to loop over one shoulder and swathe her body in tight, molten folds, and the skirt of it was slit up one side so that at every other motion the long white leg flashed bare.

He saw her for the first time in a full light, and she was lovely beyond belief with her bronze hair cloudy on her shoulders and the pale, lazy face smiling. Under deep lashes the sidelong black eyes of her race met his.

He jerked impatiently at the hampering hood of the cloak. "May I take this off?" he said. "Are we safe here?"

She laughed with a short, metallic sound. "Safe!" she said ironically. "But take it off if you must. I've gone too far now to stop at trifles."

And as the rich folds parted and slid away from his leather brownness she in turn stared in quickened interest at what she had seen only in a half-light before. He was almost laughably incongruous in this jewel-box room, all leather and sunburn and his scarred face keen and wary in the light of the lantern swinging from its silver chain. She looked a second time at that face, its lean, leathery keenness and the scars that ray-guns had left, and the mark of knife and talon, and the tracks of wild years along the spaceways. Wariness and resolution were instinct in that face, there was ruthlessness in every line of it, and when she met his eyes a little shock went over her. Pale, pale as bare steel, colorless in the sunburnt face. Steady and clear and no-colored, expressionless as water. Killer's eyes.

And she knew that this was the man she needed. The name and fame of Northwest Smith had penetrated even into these mother-of-pearl Minga halls. In its way it had spread into stranger places than this, by strange and devious paths and for strange, devious reasons. But even had she never heard the name (nor the deed she connected it with, which does not matter here), she would have known from this scarred face, these cold and steady eyes, that here stood the man she wanted, the man who could help her if any man alive could.

And with that thought, others akin to it flashed through her mind like blades crossing, and she dropped her milk-white lids over the sword-play to hide its deadliness, and said, "Northwest . . . Smith," in a musing murmur.

"To be commanded," said Smith in the idiom of her own tongue, but a spark of derision burned behind the courtly words.

Still she said nothing, but looked him up and down with slow eyes. He said at last,

"Your desire—?" and shifted impatiently.

"I had need of a wharfman's services," she said, still in that breathing whisper. "I had not seen you, then. . . . There are many wharfmen along the seafront, but only one of you, oh man of Earth—" and she lifted her arms and swayed toward him exactly as a reed sways to a lake breeze, and her arms lay lightly on his shoulders and her mouth was very near. . . .

Smith looked down into the veiled eyes. He knew enough of the breed of Venus to guess the deadly sword-flash of motive behind anything a Venusian does, and he had caught a glimpse of that particular sword-flash before she lowered her lids. And if her thoughts were sword-play, his burnt like heat-beams straight to their purpose. In the winking of an eye he knew a part of her motive—the most obvious part. And he stood there unanswering in the circle of her arms.

She looked up at him, half incredulous not to feel a leather embrace tighten about her.

"*Qu'a lo'val?*" she murmured whimsically. "So cold, then, Earthman? Am I not desirable?"

Wordlessly he looked down at her, and despite himself the blood quickened in him. Minga girls for too many centuries had been born and bred to the art of charming men for Northwest Smith to stand here in the warm arms of one and feel no answer to the invitation in her eyes. A subtle fragrance rose from her brazen hair, and the velvet molded a body whose whiteness he could guess from the flash of the long bare thigh her slashed skirt showed. He grinned a little crookedly and stepped away, breaking the clasp of her hands behind his neck.

"No," he said. "You know your art well, my dear, but your motive does not flatter me."

She stood back and regarded him with a wry, half-appreciative smile.

"What do you mean?"

"I'll have to know much more about all this before I commit myself as far as—that."

"You fool," she smiled. "You're in over your head now, as

deeply as you could ever be. You were the moment you crossed the door-sill at the outer wall. There is no drawing back."

"Yet it was so easy—so very easy, to come in," murmured Smith.

She came forward a step and looked up at him with narrowed eyes, the pretense of seduction dropped like a cloak.

"You saw that, too?" she queried in a half-whisper. "It seemed so—to you? Great Shar, if I could be *sure.* . . ." And there was terror in her face.

"Suppose we sit down and you tell me about it," suggested Smith practically.

She laid a hand—white as cream, soft as satin—on his arm and drew him to the low divan that circled the room. There was inbred, generations-old coquetry in the touch, but the white hand shook a little.

"What is it you fear so?" queried Smith curiously as they sank to the green velvet. "Death comes only once, you know."

She shook her bronze head contemptuously.

"Not that," she said. "At least—no, I wish I knew just what it is I do fear—and that is the most dreadful part of it. But I wish—I wish it had not been so easy to get you here."

"The place was deserted," he said thoughtfully. "Not a soul along the halls. Not a guard anywhere. Only once did we see any other creature, and that was a slave-girl in the hall just outside your door."

"What did she—do?" Vaudir's voice was breathless.

"Dropped to her knees as if she'd been shot. You might have thought me the devil himself by the way she acted."

The girl's breath escaped in a sigh.

"Safe, then," she said thankfully. "She must have thought you the—the Alendar." Her voice faltered a little over the name, as if she half feared to pronounce it. "He wears a cloak like that you wore when he comes through the halls. But he comes so very seldom. . . ."

"I've never seen him," said Smith, "but, good Lord, is he such a monster? The girl dropped as if she'd been hamstrung."

"Oh, hush, hush!" Vaudir agonized. "You mustn't speak of him so. He's—he's—of course she knelt and hid her face. I wish to heaven I had. . . ."

Smith faced her squarely and searched the veiled dark eyes with a gaze as bleak as empty seas. And he saw very clearly behind the veils the stark, nameless terror at their depths.

"What is it?" he demanded.

She drew her shoulders together and shivered a little, and her eyes were furtive as she glanced around the room.

"Don't you feel it?" she asked in that half-whisper to which her voice sank so caressingly. And he smiled to himself to see how instinctively eloquent was the courtezan in her—alluring gestures though her hands trembled, soft voice huskily seductive even in its terror. "—always, always!" she was saying. "The soft, hushed, hovering menace! It haunts the whole place. Didn't you feel it as you came in?"

"I think I did," Smith answered slowly. "Yes—that feel of something just out of sight, hiding in dark doorways . . . a sort of tensity in the air. . . ."

"Danger," she whispered, "terrible, nameless danger . . . oh, I feel it wherever I go . . . it's soaked into me and through me until it's a part of me, body and soul. . . ."

Smith heard the note of rising hysteria in her voice, and said quickly,

"Why did you come to me?"

"I didn't, consciously." She conquered the hysteria with an effort and took up her tale a little more calmly. "I was really looking for a wharfman, as I said, and for quite another reason than this. It doesn't matter, now. But when you spoke, when I flashed my light and saw your face, I knew you. I'd heard of you, you see, and about the—the Lakkmanda affair, and I knew in a moment that if anyone alive could help me, it would be you."

"But what is it? Help you in what?"

"It's a long story," she said, "and too strange, almost, to believe, and too vague for you to take seriously. And yet I *know*. . . . Have you heard the history of the Minga?"

"A little of it. It goes back very far."

"Back into the beginning—and farther. I wonder if you can understand. You see, we on Venus are closer to our beginnings than you. Life here developed faster, of course, and along lines more different than Earthmen realize. On Earth civilization rose slowly enough for the—the elementals—to sink back into darkness. On Venus—oh, it's bad, *bad* for men to develop too swiftly!

Life rises out of dark and mystery and things too strange and terrible to be looked upon. Earth's civilization grew slowly, and by the time men were civilized enough to look back they were sufficiently far from their origins not to see, not to know. But we here who look back see too clearly, sometimes, too nearly and vividly the black beginning. . . . Great Shar defend me, what I have seen!"

White hands flashed up to hide sudden terror in her eyes, and hair in a brazen cloud fell fragrantly over her fingers. And even in that terror was an inbred allure as natural as breathing.

In the little silence that followed, Smith caught himself glancing furtively over his shoulder. The room was ominously still. . . .

Vaudir lifted her face from her hands, shaking back her hair. The hands trembled. She clasped them on her velvet knee and went on.

"The Minga," she said, and her voice was resolutely steady, "began too long ago for anyone to name the date. It began before dates. When Far-thursa came out of the sea-fog with his men and founded this city at the mountain's foot he built it around the walls of a castle already here. The Minga castle. And the Alendar sold Minga girls to the sailors and the city began. All that is myth, but the Minga had always been here.

"The Alendar dwelt in his stronghold and bred his golden girls and trained them in the arts of charming men, and guarded them with—with strange weapons—and sold them to kings at royal prices. There has always been an Alendar. I have seen him, once. . . .

"He walks the halls on rare occasions, and it is best to kneel and hide one's face when he comes by. Yes, it is best. . . . But I passed him one day, and—and—he is tall, tall as you, Earthman, and his eyes are like—the space between the worlds. I looked into his eyes under the hood he wore—I was not afraid of devil or man, then. I looked him in the eyes before I made obeisance, and I—I shall never be free of fear again. I looked into evil as one looks into a pool. Blackness and blankness and raw evil. Impersonal, not malevolent. Elemental . . . the elemental dreadfulness that life rose from. And I know very surely, now, that the first Alendar sprang from no mortal seed. There were races before man. . . . Life goes back very dreadfully through many forms and evils, before it reaches the well-spring of its beginning. And the Alendar had not the eyes of a human creature, and I met them—and I am damned!"

Her voice trailed softly away and she sat quiet for a space, staring before her with remembering eyes.

"I am doomed and damned to a blacker hell than any of Shar's priests threaten," she resumed. "No, wait—this is not hysteria. I haven't told you the worst part. You'll find it hard to believe, but it's truth—truth—Great Shar, if I could hope it were not!

"The origin of it is lost in legend. But why, in the beginning, did the first Alendar dwell in the misty sea-edge castle, alone and unknown, breeding his bronze girls?—not for sale, then. Where did he get the secret of producing the invariable type? And the castle, legend says, was age-old when Far-thursa found it. The girls had a perfected, consistent beauty that could be attained only by generations of effort. How long had the Minga been built, and by whom? Above all, why? What possible reason could there be for dwelling there absolutely unknown, breeding civilized beauties in a world half-savage? Sometimes I think I have guessed the reason. . . ."

Her voice faded into a resonant silence, and for a while she sat staring blindly at the brocaded wall. When she spoke again it was with a startling shift of topic.

"Am I beautiful, do you think?"

"More so than any I have ever seen before," answered Smith without flattery.

Her mouth twisted.

"There are girls here now, in this building, so much lovelier than I that I am humbled to think of them. No mortal man has ever seen them, except the Alendar, and he—is not wholly mortal. No mortal man will ever see them. They are not for sale. Eventually they will disappear. . . .

"One might think that feminine beauty must reach an apex beyond which it can not rise, but this is not true. It can increase and intensify until—I have no words. And I truly believe that there is no limit to the heights it can reach, in the hands of the Alendar. And for every beauty we know and hear of, through the slaves that tend them, gossip says there are as many more, too immortally lovely for mortal eyes to see. Have you ever considered that beauty might be refined and intensified until one could scarcely bear to look upon it? We have tales here of such beauty, hidden in some of the secret rooms of the Minga.

"But the world never knows of these mysteries. No monarch on any planet known is rich enough to buy the loveliness hidden in the Minga's innermost rooms. It is not for sale. For countless centuries the Alendars of the Minga have been breeding beauty, in higher and higher degrees, at infinite labor and cost—beauty to be locked in secret chambers, guarded most terribly, so that not even a whisper of it passes the outer walls, beauty that vanishes, suddenly, in a breath—like that! Where? Why? How? No one knows.

"And it is that I fear. I have not a fraction of the beauty I speak of, yet a fate like that is written for me—somehow I know. I have looked into the eyes of the Alendar, and—I know. And I am sure that I must look again into those blank black eyes, more deeply, more dreadfully. . . . I know—and I am sick with terror of what more I shall know, soon. . . .

"Something dreadful is waiting for me, drawing nearer and nearer. Tomorrow, or the next day, or a little while after, I shall vanish, and the girls will wonder and whisper a little, and then forget. It has happened before. Great Shar, what shall I do?"

She wailed it, musically and hopelessly, and sank into a little silence. And then her look changed and she said reluctantly,

"And I have dragged you in with me. I have broken every tradition of the Minga in bringing you here, and there has been no hindrance—it has been too easy, too easy. I think I have sealed your death. When you first came I was minded to trick you into committing yourself so deeply that perforce you must do as I asked to win free again. But I know now that through the simple act of asking you here I have dragged you in deeper than I dreamed. It is a knowledge that has come to me somehow, out of the air tonight. I can feel knowledge beating upon me—compelling me. For in my terror to get help I think I have precipitated damnation upon us both. I know now—I have known in my soul since you entered so easily, that you will not go out alive—that—*it* —will come for me and drag you down too. . . . Shar, Shar, what have I done!"

"But what, what?" Smith struck his knee impatiently. "What is it we face? Poison? Guards? Traps? Hypnotism? Can't you give me even a guess at what will happen?"

He leaned forward to search her face commandingly, and saw her brows knit in an effort to find words that would cloak the mysteries she had to tell. Her lips parted irresolutely.

"The Guardians," she said. "The—Guardians. . . ."

And then over her hesitant face swept a look of such horror that his hand clenched on his knee and he felt the hairs rise along his neck. It was not horror of any material thing, but an inner dreadfulness, a terrible awareness. The eyes that had met his glazed and escaped his commanding stare without shifting their focus. It was as if they ceased to be eyes and became dark windows—vacant. The beauty of her face set like a mask, and behind the blank windows, behind the lovely set mask, he could sense dimly the dark command flowing in. . . .

She put out her hands stiffly and rose. Smith found himself on his feet, gun in hand, while his hackles lifted shudderingly and sometimes pulsed in the air as tangibly as the beat of wings. Three times that nameless shudder stirred the air, and then Vaudir stepped forward like an automaton and faced the door. She walked in her dream of masked dreadfulness, stiffly, through the portal. As she passed him he put out a hesitant hand and laid it on her arm, and a little stab of pain shot through him at the contact, and once more he thought he felt the pulse of wings in the air. Then she passed by without hesitation, and his hand fell.

He made no further effort to arouse her, but followed after on cat-feet, delicately as if he walked on eggs. He was crouching a little, unconsciously, and his gun-hand held a tense finger on the trigger.

They went down the corridor in a breathing silence, an empty corridor where no lights showed beyond closed doors, where no murmur of voices broke the live stillness. But little shudders seemed to shake in the air somehow, and his heart was pounding suffocatingly.

Vaudir walked like a mechanical doll, tense in a dream of horror. When they reached the end of the hall he saw that the silver grille stood open, and they passed through without pausing. But Smith noted with a little qualm that a gateway opening to the right was closed and locked, and the bars across it were sunk firmly into wall-sockets. There was no choice but to follow her.

The corridor slanted downward. They passed others branching to right and left, but the silver gateways were closed and barred across each. A coil of silver stairs ended the passage, and the girl went stiffly down without touching the rails. It was a long spiral, past many floors, and as they descended, the rich, dim light lessened and darkened and a subtle smell of moisture and salt invaded the scented air. At each turn where the stairs opened on successive floors, gates were barred across the outlets; and they passed so many of these that Smith knew, as they went down and down, that however high the green jewel-box room had been, by now they were descending deep into the earth. And still the stair wound downward. The stories that opened beyond the bars like honeycomb layers became darker and less luxurious, and at last ceased altogether and the silver steps wound down through a well of rock, lighted so dimly at wide intervals that he could scarcely see the black polished walls circling them in. Drops of moisture began to appear on the dark surface, and the smell was of black salt seas and dank underground.

And just as he was beginning to believe that the stairs went on and on into the very black, salt heart of the planet, they came abruptly to the bottom. A flourish of slim, shining rails ended the stairs, at the head of a hallway, and the girl's feet turned unhesitatingly to follow its dark length. Smith's pale eyes, searching the dimness, found no trace of other life than themselves; yet eyes were upon him—he knew it surely.

They came down the black corridor to a gateway of wrought metal set in bars whose ends sank deep into the stone walls. She went through, Smith at her heels raking the dark with swift, unresting eyes like a wild animal's, wary in a strange jungle. And beyond the great gates a door hung with sweeping curtains of black ended the hall. Somehow Smith felt that they had reached their destination. And nowhere along the whole journey had he had any choice but to follow Vaudir's unerring, unseeing footsteps. Grilles had been locked across every possible outlet. But he had his gun. . . .

Her hands were white against the velvet as she pushed aside the folds. Very bright she stood for an instant—all green and gold and white—against the blackness. Then she passed through and the folds swept to behind her—candle-flame extinguished in dark velvet. Smith hesitated the barest instant before he parted the curtains and peered within.

He was looking into a room hung in black velvet that absorbed the light almost hungrily. That light radiated from a single lamp swinging from the ceiling directly over an ebony table. It shone softly on a man—a very tall man.

He stood darkly under it, very dark in the room's darkness, his head bent, staring up from under level black brows. His eyes in the half-hidden face were pits of blackness, and under the lowered brows two pinpoint gleams stabbed straight—not at the girl—but at Smith hidden behind the curtains. It held his eyes as a magnet holds steel. He felt the narrow glitter plunging blade-like into his very brain, and from the keen, burning stab something within him shuddered away involuntarily. He thrust his gun through the curtains, stepped through quietly, and stood meeting the sword-gaze with pale, unwavering eyes.

Vaudir moved forward with a mechanical stiffness that somehow could not hide her grace—it was as if no power existing could ever evoke from that lovely body less than loveliness. She came to the man's feet and stopped there. Then a long shudder swept her from head to foot and she dropped to her knees and laid her forehead to the floor.

Across the golden loveliness of her the man's eyes met Smith's, and the man's voice, deep, deep, like black waters flowing smoothly, said,

"I am the Alendar."

"Then you know me," said Smith, his voice harsh as iron in the velvet dimness.

"You are Northwest Smith," said the smooth, deep voice dispassionately. "An outlaw from the planet Earth. You have broken your last law, Northwest Smith. Men do not come here uninvited —and live. You perhaps have heard tales. . . ."

His voice melted into silence, lingeringly.

Smith's mouth curled into a wolfish grin, without mirth, and his gun hand swung up. Murder flashed bleakly from his steel-pale eyes. And then with stunning abruptness the world dissolved about him. A burst of coruscations flamed through his head, danced and wheeled and drew slowly together in a whirling darkness until they were two pinpoint sparks of light—a dagger stare under level brows. . . .

When the room steadied about him he was standing with slack arms, the gun hanging from his fingers, an apathetic numbness slowly withdrawing from his body. A dark smile curved smoothly on the Alendar's mouth.

The stabbing gaze slid casually away, leaving him dizzy in sudden vertigo, and touched the girl prostrate on the floor. Against the black carpet her burnished bronze curls sprayed out exquisitely. The green robe folded softly back from the roundness of her body, and nothing in the universe could have been so lovely as the creamy whiteness of her on the dark floor. The pit-black eyes brooded over her impassively. And then, in his smooth, deep voice the Alendar asked, amazingly, matter-of-factly,

"Tell me, do you have such girls on Earth?"

Smith shook his head to clear it. When he managed an answer his voice had steadied, and in the receding of that dizziness even the sudden drop into casual conversation seemed not unreasonable.

"I have never seen such a girl anywhere," he said calmly.

The sword gaze flashed up and pierced him.

"She has told you," said the Alendar. "You know I have beauties here that outshine her as the sun does a candle. And yet . . . she has more than beauty, this Vaudir. You have felt it, perhaps?"

Smith met the questioning gaze, searching for mockery, but finding none. Not understanding—a moment before the man had threatened his life—he took up the conversation.

"They all have more than beauty. For what other reason do kings buy the Minga girls?"

"No—not that charm. She has it too, but something more subtle than fascination, much more desirable than loveliness. She has courage, this girl. She has intelligence. Where she got it I do not understand. I do not breed my girls for such things. But I looked into her eyes once, in the hallway, as she told you—and saw there more arousing things than beauty. I summoned her—and you come at her heels. Do you know why? Do you know why you did not die at the outer gate or anywhere along the hallways on your way in?"

Smith's pale stare met the dark one questioningly. The voice flowed on.

"Because there are—interesting things in your eyes too. Courage and ruthlessness and a certain—power, I think. Intensity is in you. And I believe I can find a use for it, Earthman."

Smith's eyes narrowed a little. So calm, so matter-of fact, this talk. But death was coming. He felt it in the air—he knew that feel of old. Death—and worse things than that, perhaps. He remembered the whispers he had heard.

On the floor the girl moaned a little, and stirred. The Alendar's quiet, pinpoint eyes flicked her, and he said softly, "Rise." And she rose, stumbling, and stood before him with bent head. The stiffness was gone from her. On an impulse Smith said suddenly, "Vaudir!" She lifted her face and met his gaze, and a thrill of horror rippled over him. She had regained consciousness, but she would never be the same frightened girl he had known. Black knowledge looked out of her eyes, and her face was a strained mask that covered horror barely—barely! It was the face of one who has walked through a blacker hell than any of humanity's understanding, and gained knowledge there that no human soul could endure knowing and live.

She looked him full in the face for a long moment, silently, and then turned away to the Alendar again. And Smith thought, just before her eyes left his, he had seen in them one wild flash of hopeless, desperate appeal. . . .

"Come," said the Alendar.

He turned his back—Smith's gun-hand trembled up and then fell again. No, better wait. There was always a bare hope, until he saw death closing in all around.

He stepped out over the yielding carpet at the Alendar's heels. The girl came after with slow steps and eyes downcast in a horrible parody of meditation, as if she brooded over the knowledge that dwelt so terribly behind her eyes.

The dark archway at the opposite end of the room swallowed them up. Light failed for an instant—a breath-stopping instant while Smith's gun leaped up involuntarily, like a live thing in his hand, futilely against invisible evil, and his brain rocked at the utter blackness that enfolded him. It was over in the wink of an eye, and he wondered if it had ever been as his gun-hand fell again. But the Alendar said across one shoulder,

"A barrier I have placed to guard my—beauties. A mental barrier that would have been impassable had you not been with me, yet which—but you understand now, do you not, my Vaudir?" And there was an indescribable leer in the query that injected a note of monstrous humanity into the inhuman voice.

"I understand," echoed the girl in a voice as lovely and toneless as a sustained musical note. And the sound of those two inhuman voices proceeding from the human lips of his companions sent a shudder thrilling along Smith's nerves.

They went down the long corridor thereafter in silence, Smith treading soundlessly in his spaceman's boots, every fiber of him tense to painfulness. He found himself wondering, even in the midst of his strained watchfulness, if any other creature with a living human soul had ever gone down this corridor before—if frightened golden girls had followed the Alendar thus into blackness, or if they too had been drained of humanity and steeped in that nameless horror before their feet followed their master through the black barrier.

The hallway led downward, and the salt smell became clearer and the light sank to a glimmer in the air, and in a silence that was not human they went on.

Presently the Alendar said—and his deep, liquid voice did nothing to break the stillness, blending with it softly so that not even an echo roused,

"I am taking you into a place where no other man than the Alendar has ever set foot before. It pleases me to wonder just how your unaccustomed senses will react to the things you are about to see. I am reaching an—an age"—he laughed softly—"where experiment interests me. Look!"

Smith's eyes blinked shut before an intolerable blaze of sudden light. In the streaked darkness of that instant while the glare flamed through his lids he thought he felt everything shift unaccountably about him, as if the very structure of the atoms that built the walls were altered. When he opened his eyes he stood at the head of a long gallery blazing with a soft, delicious brilliance. How he had got there he made no effort even to guess.

Very beautifully it stretched before him. The walls and floor and ceiling were of sheeny stone. There were low couches along the walls at intervals, and a blue pool broke the floor, and the air sparkled unaccountably with golden light. And figures were moving through that champagne sparkle. . . .

Smith stood very still, looking down the gallery. The Alendar watched him with a subtle anticipation upon his face, the pinpoint glitter of his eyes sharp enough to pierce the Earthman's very brain. Vaudir with bent head brooded over the black knowledge behind her drooping lids. Only Smith of the three looked down the gallery and saw what moved through the golden glimmer of the air.

They were girls. They might have been goddesses—angels haloed with bronze curls, moving leisurely through a golden heaven where the air sparkled like wine. There must have been a score of them strolling up and down the gallery in twos and threes, lolling on the couches, bathing in the pool. They wore the infinitely graceful Venusian robe with its looped shoulder and slit skirt, in soft, muted shades of violet and blue and jewel-green, and the beauty of them was breath-stopping as a blow. Music was in every gesture they made, a flowing, singing grace that made the heart ache with its sheer loveliness.

He had thought Vaudir lovely, but here was beauty so exquisite that it verged on pain. Their sweet, light voices were pitched to send little velvety burrs along his nerves, and from a distance the soft sounds blended so musically that they might have been singing together. The loveliness of their motion made his heart contract suddenly, and the blood pounded in his ears. . . .

"You find them beautiful?" The Alendar's voice blended into the humming lilt of voices as perfectly as it had blended with silence. His dagger-glitter of eyes was fixed piercingly on Smith's pale gaze, and he smiled a little, faintly. "Beautiful? Wait!"

He moved down the gallery, tall and very dark in the rainbow light. Smith, following after, walked in a haze of wonder. It is not given to every man to walk through heaven. He felt the air tingle like wine, and a delicious perfume caressed him and the haloed girls drew back with wide, amazed eyes fixed on him in his stained leather and heavy boots as he passed. Vaudir paced quietly after, her head bent, and from her the girls turned away their eyes, shuddering a little.

He saw now that their faces were as lovely as their bodies, languorously, colorfully. They were contented faces, unconscious of beauty, unconscious of any other existence than their own— soulless. He felt that instinctively. Here was beauty incarnate, physically, tangibly; but he had seen in Vaudir's face—before—a sparkle of daring, a tenderness of remorse at having brought him here, that gave her an indefinable superiority over even this incredible beauty, soulless.

They went down the gallery in a sudden hush as the musical

voices fell silent from very amazement. Apparently the Alendar was a familiar figure here, for they scarcely glanced at him, and from Vaudir they turned away in a shuddering revulsion that preferred not to recognize her existence. But Smith was the first man other than the Alendar whom they had ever seen, and the surprize of it struck them dumb.

They went on through the dancing air, and the last lovely, staring girls fell behind, and an ivory gateway opened before them, without a touch. They went downstairs from there, and along another hallway, while the tingle died in the air and a hum of musical voices sprang up behind them. They passed beyond the sound. The hallway darkened until they were moving again through dimness.

Presently the Alendar paused and turned.

"My more costly jewels," he said, "I keep in separate settings. As here—"

He stretched out his arm, and Smith saw that a curtain hung against the wall. There were others, farther on, dark blots against the dimness. The Alendar drew back black folds, and light from beyond flowed softly through a pattern of bars to cast flowery shadows on the opposite wall. Smith stepped forward and stared.

He was looking through a grille window down into a room lined with dark velvet. It was quite plain. There was a low couch against the wall opposite the window, and on it—Smith's heart gave a stagger and paused—a woman lay. And if the girls in the gallery had been like goddesses, this woman was lovelier than men have ever dared to imagine even in legends. She was beyond divinity—long limbs white against the velvet, sweet curves and planes of her rounding under the robe, bronze hair spilling like lava over one white shoulder, and her face calm as death with closed eyes. It was a passive beauty, like alabaster shaped perfectly. And charm, a fascination all but tangible, reached out from her like a magic spell. A sleeping charm, magnetic, powerful. He could not wrench his eyes away. He was like a wasp caught in honey. . . .

The Alendar said something across Smith's shoulder, in a vibrant voice that thrilled the air. The closed lids rose. Life and loveliness flowed into the calm face like a tide, lighting it unbearably. That heady charm wakened and brightened to a dangerous liveness—tugging, pulling. . . . She rose in one long glide like a wave over rocks; she smiled (Smith's senses reeled to the beauty of that smile) and then sank in a deep salaam, slowly, to the velvet floor, her hair rippling and falling all about her, until she lay abased in a blaze of loveliness under the window.

The Alendar let the curtain fall, and turned to Smith as the dazzling sight was blotted out. Again the pinpoint glitter stabbed into Smith's brain. The Alendar smiled again.

"Come," he said, and moved down the hall.

They passed three curtains, and paused at a fourth. Afterward Smith remembered that the curtain must have been drawn back and he must have bent forward to stare through the window bars, but the sight he saw blasted every memory of it from his mind. The girl who dwelt in this velvet-lined room was stretching on tiptoe just as the drawn curtain caught her, and the beauty and grace of her from head to foot stopped Smith's breath as a ray-stab to the heart would have done. And the irresistible, wrenching charm of her drew him forward until he was clasping the bars with white-knuckled hands, unaware of anything but her compelling, soul-destroying desirability. . . .

She moved, and the dazzle of grace that ran like a song through every motion made his senses ache with its pure, unattainable loveliness. He knew, even in his daze of rapture, that he might hold the sweet, curved body in his arms for ever, yet hunger still for the fulfillment which the flesh could never wring from her. Her loveliness aroused a hunger in the soul more maddening than the body's hunger could ever be. His brain rocked with the desire to possess that intangible, irresistible loveliness that he knew he could never possess, never reach with any sense that was in him. That bodiless desire raged like madness through him, so violently that the room reeled and the white outlines of the beauty unattainable as the stars wavered before him. He caught his breath and choked and drew back from the intolerable, exquisite sight.

The Alendar laughed and dropped the curtain.

"Come," he said again, the subtle amusement clear in his voice, and Smith in a daze moved after him down the hall.

They went a long way, past curtains hanging at regular intervals along the wall. When they paused at last, the curtain before which they stopped was faintly luminous about the edges, as if something dazzling dwelt within. The Alendar drew back the folds.

"We are approaching," he said, "a pure clarity of beauty, hampered only a little by the bonds of flesh. Look."

One glance only Smith snatched of the dweller within. And the exquisite shock of that sight went thrilling like torture through every nerve of him. For a mad instant his reason staggered before the terrible fascination beating out from that dweller in waves that wrenched at his very soul—incarnate loveliness tugging with strong fingers at every sense and every nerve and intangibly, irresistibly, at deeper things than these, groping among the roots of his being, dragging his soul out. . . .

Only one glance he took, and in the glance he felt his soul answer that dragging, and the terrible desire tore futilely through him. Then he flung up an arm to shield his eyes and reeled back into the dark, and a wordless sob rose to his lips and the darkness reeled about him.

The curtain fell. Smith pressed the wall and breathed in long, shuddering gasps, while his heart-beats slowed gradually and the unholy fascination ebbed from about him. The Alendar's eyes were glittering with a green fire as he turned from the window, and a nameless hunger lay shadowily on his face. He said,

"I might show you others, Earthman. But it could only drive you mad, in the end—you were very near the brink for a moment just now—and I have another use for you. . . . I wonder if you begin to understand, now, the purpose of all this?"

The green glow was fading from that dagger-sharp gaze as the Alendar's eyes stabbed into Smith's. The Earthman gave his head a little shake to clear away the vestiges of that devouring desire, and took a fresh grip on the butt of his gun. The familiar smoothness of it brought him a measure of reassurance, and with it a reawakening to the peril all around. He knew now that there could be no conceivable mercy for him, to whom the innermost secrets of the Minga had been unaccountably revealed. Death was waiting— strange death, as soon as the Alendar wearied of talking—but if he kept his ears open and his eyes alert it might not—please God— catch him so quickly that he died alone. One sweep of that blade-blue flame was all he asked, now. His eyes, keen and hostile, met the dagger-gaze squarely. The Alendar smiled and said,

"Death in your eyes, Earthman. Nothing in your mind but murder. Can that brain of yours comprehend nothing but battle? Is there no curiosity there? Have you no wonder of why I brought you here? Death awaits you, yes. But a not unpleasant death, and it awaits all, in one form or another. Listen, let me tell you—I have reason for desiring to break through that animal shell of self-defense that seals in your mind. Let me look deeper—if there are depths. Your death will be—useful, and in a way, pleasant. Otherwise—well, the black beasts hunger. And flesh must feed them, as a sweeter drink feeds me. . . . Listen."

Smith's eyes narrowed. A sweeter drink. . . . Danger, danger —the smell of it in the air—instinctively he felt the peril of opening his mind to the plunging gaze of the Alendar, the force of those compelling eyes beating like strong lights into his brain. . . .

"Come," said the Alendar softly, and moved off soundlessly through the gloom. They followed, Smith painfully alert, the girl walking with lowered, brooding eyes, her mind and soul afar in some wallowing darkness whose shadow showed so hideously beneath her lashes.

The hallway widened to an arch, and abruptly, on the other side, one wall dropped away into infinity and they stood on the dizzy brink of a gallery opening on a black, heaving sea. Smith bit back a startled oath. One moment before the way had led through low-roofed tunnels deep underground; the next instant they stood on the shore of a vast body of rolling darkness, a tiny wind touching their faces with the breath of unnamable things.

Very far below, the dark waters rolled. Phosphorescence lighted them uncertainly, and he was not even sure it was water that surged there in the dark. A heavy thickness seemed to be inherent in the rollers, like black slime surging.

The Alendar looked out over the fire-tinged waves. He waited for an instant without speaking, and then, far out in the slimy surges, something broke the surface with an oily splash, something mercifully veiled in the dark, then dived again, leaving a wake of spreading ripples over the surface.

"Listen," said the Alendar, without turning his head. "Life is very old. There are older races than man. Mine is one. Life rose out of the black slime of the sea-bottoms and grew toward the light along many diverging lines. Some reached maturity and deep wisdom when man was still swinging through the jungle trees.

"For many centuries, as mankind counts time, the Alendar has dwelt here, breeding beauty. In later years he has sold some of his lesser beauties, perhaps to explain to mankind's satisfaction what it could never understand were it told the truth. Do you begin to see? My race is very remotely akin to those races which suck blood from man, less remotely to those which drink his life-forces for nourishment. I am more refined even than that. I drink—beauty. I live on beauty. Yes, literally.

"Beauty is as tangible as blood, in a way. It is a separate, distinct force that inhabits the bodies of men and women. You must have noticed the vacuity that accompanies perfect beauty in so many women . . . the force so strong that it drives out all other forces and lives vampirishly at the expense of intelligence and goodness and conscience and all else.

"In the beginning, here—for our race was old when this world began, spawned on another planet, and wise and ancient—we woke from slumber in the slime, to feed on the beauty force inherent in mankind even in cave-dwelling days. But it was meager fare, and we studied the race to determine where the greatest prospects lay, then selected specimens for breeding, built this stronghold and settled down to the business of evolving mankind up to its limit of loveliness. In time we weeded out all but the present type. For the race of man we have developed the ultimate type of loveliness. It is interesting to see what we have accomplished on other worlds, with utterly different races. . . .

"Well, there you have it. Women, bred as a spawning-ground for the devouring force of beauty on which we live.

"But—the fare grows monotonous, as all food must without change. Vaudir I took because I saw in her a sparkle of something that except in very rare instances has been bred out of the Minga girls. For beauty, as I have said, eats up all other qualities but beauty. Yet somehow intelligence and courage survived latently in Vaudir. It decreases her beauty, but the tang of it should be a change from the eternal sameness of the rest. And so I thought until I saw you.

"I realized then how long it had been since I tasted the beauty of man. It is so rare, so different from female beauty, that I had all but forgotten it existed. And you have it, very subtly, in a raw, harsh way. . . .

"I have told you all this to test the quality of that—that harsh beauty in you. Had I been wrong about the deeps of your mind, you would have gone to feed the black beasts, but I see that I was not wrong. Behind your animal shell of self-preservation are depths of that force and strength which nourish the roots of male beauty. I think I shall give you a while to let it grow, under the forcing methods I know, before I—drink. It will be delightful. . . ."

The voice trailed away in a murmurous silence, the pinpoint glitter sought Smith's eyes. And he tried half-heartedly to avoid it, but his eyes turned involuntarily to the stabbing gaze, and the alertness died out of him, gradually, and the compelling pull of those glittering points in the pits of darkness held him very still.

And as he stared into the diamond glitter he saw its brilliance slowly melt and darken, until the pinpoints of light had changed to pools that dimmed, and he was looking into black evil as elemental and vast as the space between the worlds, a dizzying blankness wherein dwelt unnamable horror . . . deep, deep . . . all about him the darkness was clouding. And thoughts that were not his own seeped into his mind out of that vast, elemental dark . . . crawling, writhing thoughts . . . until he had a glimpse of that dark place where Vaudir's soul wallowed, and something sucked him down and down into a waking nightmare he could not fight. . . .

Then somehow the pull broke for an instant. For just that instant he stood again on the shore of the heaving sea and gripped a gun with nerveless fingers—then the darkness closed about him again, but a different, uneasy dark that had not quite the all-compelling power of that other nightmare—it left him strength enough to fight.

And he fought, a desperate, moveless, soundless struggle in a black sea of horror, while worm-thoughts coiled through his straining mind and the clouds rolled and broke and rolled again about him. Sometimes, in the instants when the pull slackened, he had time to feel a third force struggling here between that black, blind downward suck that dragged at him and his own sick, frantic effort to fight clear, a third force that was weakening the black drag so that he had moments of lucidity when he stood free on the brink of the ocean and felt the sweat roll down his face and was aware of his laboring heart and how gaspingly breath tortured his lungs, and he knew he was fighting with every atom of himself, body and mind and soul, against the intangible blackness sucking him down.

And then he felt the force against him gather itself in a final effort—he sensed desperation in that effort—and come rolling over him like a tide. Bowled over, blinded and dumb and deaf, drowning in utter blackness, he floundered in the deeps of that nameless hell where thoughts that were alien and slimy squirmed through his brain. Bodiless he was, and unstable, and as he wallowed there in the ooze more hideous than any earthly ooze, because it came from black, inhuman souls and out of ages before man, he became aware that the worm-thoughts a-squirm in his brain were forming slowly into monstrous meanings—knowledge like a formless flow was pouring through his bodiless brain, knowledge so dreadful that consciously he could not comprehend it, though subconsciously every atom of his mind and soul sickened and writhed futilely away. It was flooding over him, drenching him, permeating him through and through with the very essence of dreadfulness—he felt his mind melting away under the solvent power of it, melting and running fluidly into new channels and fresh molds—horrible molds. . . .

And just at that instant, while madness folded around him and his mind rocked on the verge of annihilation, something snapped, and like a curtain the dark rolled away, and he stood sick and dizzy on the gallery above the black sea. Everything was reeling about him, but they were stable things that shimmered and steadied before his eyes, blessed black rock and tangible surges that had form and body—his feet pressed firmness and his mind shook itself and was clean and his own again.

And then through the haze of weakness that still shrouded him a voice was shrieking wildly, "Kill! . . . kill!" and he saw the Alendar staggering against the rail, all his outlines unaccountably blurred and uncertain, and behind him Vaudir with blazing eyes and face wrenched hideously into life again, screaming "Kill!" in a voice scarcely human.

Like an independent creature his gun-hand leaped up—he had gripped that gun through everything that happened—and he was dimly aware of the hardness of it kicking back against his hand with the recoil, and of the blue flash flaming from its muzzle. It struck the Alendar's dark figure full, and there was a hiss and a dazzle. . . .

Smith closed his eyes tight and opened them again, and stared with a sick incredulity; for unless that struggle had unhinged his brain after all, and the worm-thoughts still dwelt slimily in his mind, tingeing all he saw with unearthly horror—unless this was true, he was looking not at a man just rayed through the lungs, and who should be dropping now in a bleeding, collapsed heap to the floor, but at—at—God, what *was* it? The dark figure had slumped against the rail, and instead of blood gushing, a hideous, nameless, formless black poured sluggishly forth—a slime like the heaving sea below. The whole dark figure of the man was melting, slumping farther down into the pool of blackness forming at his feet on the stone floor.

Smith gripped his gun and watched in numb incredulity, and the whole body sank slowly down and melted and lost all form—hideously, gruesomely—until where the Alendar had stood a heap of slime lay viscidly on the gallery floor, hideously alive, heaving and rippling and striving to lift itself into a semblance of humanity again. And as he watched, it lost even that form, and the edges melted revoltingly and the mass flattened and slid down into a pool of utter horror, and he became aware that it was pouring slowly through the rails into the sea. He stood watching while the whole rolling, shimmering mound melted and thinned and trickled through the bars, until the floor was clear again, and not even a stain marred the stone.

A painful constriction of his lungs roused him, and he realized he had been holding his breath, scarcely daring to realize. Vaudir had collapsed against the wall, and he saw her knees give limply, and staggered forward on uncertain feet to catch her as she fell.

"Vaudir, Vaudir!" he shook her gently. "Vaudir, what's happened? Am I dreaming? Are we safe now? Are you—awake again?"

Very slowly her white lids lifted, and the black eyes met his. And he saw shadowily there the knowledge of that wallowing void he had dimly known, the shadow that could never be cleared away. She was steeped and foul with it. And the look of her eyes was such that involuntarily he released her and stepped away. She staggered a little and then regained her balance and regarded him from under bent brows. The level inhumanity of her gaze struck into his soul, and yet he thought he saw a spark of the girl she had been, dwelling in torture amid the blackness. He knew he was right when she said, in a far-away, toneless voice,

"Awake? . . . No, not ever now, Earthman. I have been down too deeply into hell . . . he had dealt me a worse torture than he knew, for there is just enough humanity left within me to realize what I have become, and to suffer. . . .

"Yes, he is gone, back into the slime that bred him. I have been a part of him, one with him in the blackness of his soul, and I know. I have spent eons since the blackness came upon me, dwelt for eternities in the dark, rolling seas of his mind, sucking in knowledge . . . and as I was one with him, and he now gone, so shall I die; yet I will see you safely out of here if it is in my power, for it was I who dragged you in. If I can remember—if I can find the way. . . ."

She turned uncertainly and staggered a step back along the way they had come. Smith sprang forward and slid his free arm about her, but she shuddered away from the contact.

"No, no—unbearable—the touch of clean human flesh—and it breaks the chord of my remembering. . . . I can not look back into his mind as it was when I dwelt there, and I must, I must. . . ."

She shook him off and reeled on, and he cast one last look at the billowing sea, and then followed. She staggered along the stone floor on stumbling feet, one hand to the wall to support herself, and her voice was whispering gustily, so that he had to follow close to hear, and then almost wished he had not heard,

"—black slime—darkness feeding on light—everything wavers so—slime, slime and a rolling sea—he rose out of it, you know, before civilization began here—he is age-old—there never has been but one Alendar. . . . And somehow—I could not see just how, or remember why—he rose from the rest, as some of his race on other planets had done, and took the man-form and stocked his breeding-pens. . . ."

They went on up the dark hallway, past curtains hiding incarnate loveliness, and the girl's stumbling footsteps kept time to her stumbling, half-incoherent words.

"—has lived all these ages here, breeding and devouring beauty —vampire-thirst, a hideous delight in drinking in that beauty-force—I felt it and remembered it when I was one with him— wrapping black layers of primal slime about—quenching human loveliness in ooze, sucking—blind black thirst. . . . And his wisdom was ancient and dreadful and full of power—so he could draw a soul out through the eyes and sink it in hell, and drown it there, as he would have done mine if I had not had, somehow, a difference from the rest. Great Shar, I wish I had not! I wish I were drowned in it and did not feel in every atom of me the horrible uncleanness of—what I know. But by virtue of that hidden strength I did not surrender wholly, and when he had turned his power to subduing you I was able to struggle, there in the very heart of his mind, making a disturbance that shook him as he fought us both—making it possible to free you long enough for you to destroy the human flesh he was clothed in—so that he lapsed into the ooze again. I do not quite understand why that happened—only that his weakness, with you assailing him from without and me struggling strongly in the very center of his soul, was such that he was forced to draw on the power he had built up to maintain himself in the man form, and weakened it enough so that he collapsed when the man-form was assailed. And he fell back into the slime again—whence he rose—black slime—heaving —oozing. . . .''

Her voice trailed away in murmurs, and she stumbled, all but falling. When she regained her balance she went on ahead of him at a greater distance, as if his very nearness were repugnant to her, and the soft babble of her voice drifted back in broken phrases without meaning.

Presently the air began to tingle again, and they passed the silver gate and entered that gallery where the air sparkled like champagne. The blue pool lay jewel-clear in its golden setting. Of the girls there was no sign.

When they reached the head of the gallery the girl paused, turning to him a face twisted with the effort at memory.

"Here is the trial," she said urgently. "If I can remember—" She seized her head in clutching hands, shaking it savagely. "I haven't the strength, now—can't—can't—" the piteous little murmur reached his ears incoherently. Then she straightened resolutely, swaying a little, and faced him, holding out her hands. He clasped them hesitantly, and saw a shiver go through her at the contact, and her face contort painfully, and then a shudder communicated itself through that clasp and he too winced in revolt. He saw her

eyes go blank and her face strain in lines of tensity, and a fine dew
broke out on her forehead. For a long moment she stood so, her
face like death, and strong shudders went over her body and her
eyes were blank as the void between the planets.

And as each shudder swept her it went unbroken through the
clasping of their hands to him, and they were black waves of
dreadfulness, and again he saw the heaving sea and wallowed in
the hell he had fought out of on the gallery, and he knew for the
first time what torture she must be enduring who dwelt in the very
deeps of that uneasy dark. The pulses came faster, and for moments together he went down into the blind blackness and the
slime, and felt the first wriggling of the worm-thoughts tickling
the roots of his brain. . . .

And then suddenly a clean darkness closed round them and
again everything shifted unaccountably, as if the atoms of the
gallery were changing, and when Smith opened his eyes he was
standing once more in the dark, slanting corridor with the smell of
salt and antiquity heavy in the air.

Vaudir moaned softly beside him, and he turned to see her
reeling against the wall and trembling so from head to foot that he
looked to see her fall the next moment.

"Better—in a moment," she gasped. "It took—nearly all my
strength to—to get us through—wait. . . ."

So they halted there in the darkness and the dead salt air, until
the trembling abated a little and she said, "Come," in her little
whimpering voice. And again the journey began. It was only a
short way, now, to the barrier of black blankness that guarded the
door into the room where they had first seen the Alendar. When
they reached the place she shivered a little and paused, then resolutely held out her hands. And as he took them he felt once more
the hideous slimy waves course through him, and plunged again
into the heaving hell. And as before the clean darkness flashed
over them in a breath, and then she dropped his hands and they
were standing in the archway looking into the velvet-hung room
they had left—it seemed eons ago.

He watched as waves of blinding weakness flooded over her
from that supreme effort. Death was visible in her face as she
turned to him at last.

"Come—oh, come quickly," she whispered, and staggered forward.

At her heels he followed, across the room, past the great iron gateway, down the hall to the foot of the silver stairs. And here his heart sank, for he felt sure she could never climb the long spiral distances to the top. But she set her foot on the step and went upward resolutely, and as he followed he heard her murmuring to herself,

"Wait—oh, wait—let me reach the end—let me undo this much —and then—no, no! Please Shar, not the black slime again. . . . Earthman, Earthman!"

She paused on the stair and turned to face him, and her haggard face was frantic with desperation and despair.

"Earthman, promise—do not let me die like this! When we reach the end, ray me! Burn me clean, or I shall go down for eternity into the black sinks from which I dragged you free. Oh, promise!"

"I will," Smith's voice said quietly. "I will."

And they went on. Endlessly the stairs spiraled upward and endlessly they climbed. Smith's legs began to ache intolerably, and his heart was pounding like a wild thing, but Vaudir seemed not to notice weariness. She climbed steadily and no more unsurely than she had come along the halls. And after eternities they reached the top.

And there the girl fell. She dropped like a dead woman at the head of the silver spiral. Smith thought for a sick instant that he had failed her and let her die uncleansed, but in a moment or two she stirred and lifted her head and very slowly dragged herself to her feet.

"I will go on—I will, I will," she whispered to herself. "—come this far—must finish—" and she reeled off down the lovely, rosily-lit hallway paneled in pearl.

He could see how perilously near she was to her strength's end, and he marveled at the tenacity with which she clung to life though it ebbed away with every breath and the pulse of darkness flowed in after it. So with bulldog stubbornness she made her wavering way past door after door of carven shell, under rosy lights that flushed her face with a ghastly mockery of health, until they reached the silver gateway at the end. The lock had been removed from it by now, and the bar drawn.

She tugged open the gate and stumbled through.

And the nightmare journey went on. It must be very near morn-

ing, Smith thought, for the halls were deserted, but did he not
sense a breath of danger in the still air? . . .

The girl's gasping voice answered that half-formed query as if,
like the Alendar, she held the secret of reading men's minds.

"The—Guardians—still rove the halls, and unleashed now—so
keep your ray-gun ready, Earthman. . . ."

After that he kept his eyes alert as they retraced, stumbling and
slow, the steps he had taken on his way in. And once he heard
distinctly the soft slither of—something—scraping over the marble
pavement, and twice he smelt with shocking suddenness in this
scented air a whiff of salt, and his mind flashed back to a rolling
black sea. . . . But nothing molested them.

Step by faltering step the hallways fell behind them, and he
began to recognize landmarks, and the girl's footsteps staggered
and hesitated and went on gallantly, incredibly, beating back
oblivion, fighting the dark surges rolling over her, clinging with
tenacious fingers to the tiny spark of life that drove her on.

And at long last, after what seemed hours of desperate effort,
they reached the blue-lit hallway at whose end the outer door
opened. Vaudir's progress down it was a series of dizzy staggers,
interspersed with pauses while she hung to the carven doors with
tense fingers and drove her teeth into a bloodless lip and gripped
that last flicker of life. He saw the shudders sweep over her, and
knew what waves of washing dark must be rising all about her,
and how the worm-thoughts writhed through her brain. . . . But
she went on. Every step now was a little tripping, as if she fell
from one foot to the other, and at each step he expected that knee
to give way and pitch her down into the black deeps that yawned
for her. But she went on.

She reached the bronze door, and with a last spurt of effort she
lifted the bar and swung it open. Then that tiny spark flickered out
like a lamp. Smith caught one flash of the rock room within—and
something horrible on the floor—before he saw her pitch forward
as the rising tide of slimy oblivion closed at last over her head. She
was dying as she fell, and he whipped the ray-gun up and felt the
recoil against his palm as a blue blaze flashed forth and transfixed
her in mid-air. And he could have sworn her eyes lighted for a
flickering instant and the gallant girl he had known looked forth,
cleansed and whole, before death—clean death—glazed them.

She slumped down in a huddle at his feet, and he felt a sting of tears beneath his eyelids as he looked down on her, a huddle of white and bronze on the rug. And as he watched, a film of defilement veiled the shining whiteness of her—decay set in before his eyes and progressed with horrible swiftness, and in less time than it takes to tell he was staring with horrified eyes at a pool of black slime across which green velvet lay bedraggled.

Northwest Smith closed his pale eyes, and for a moment struggled with memory, striving to wrest from it the long-forgotten words of a prayer learned a score of years ago on another planet. Then he stepped over the pitiful, horrible heap on the carpet and went on.

In the little rock room of the outer wall he saw what he had glimpsed when Vaudir opened the door. Retribution had overtaken the eunuch. The body must have been his, for tatters of scarlet velvet lay about the floor, but there was no way to recognize what its original form had been. Smith's ray-gun had blasted the eunuch through the partly opened door as he flashed the death-ray on Vaudir. The smell of salt was heavy in the air, and a trail of black slime snaked across the floor toward the wall. The wall was solid, but it ended there. . . .

Smith laid his hand on the outer door, drew the bar, swung it open. He stepped out under the hanging vines and filled his lungs with pure air, free, clear, untainted with scent or salt. A pearly dawn was breaking over Ednes.

The Shunned House

∗∋)⊩(∈∗

H. P. LOVECRAFT

I

From even the greatest of horrors irony is seldom absent. Sometimes it enters directly into the composition of the events, while sometimes it relates only to their fortuitous position among persons and places. The latter sort is splendidly exemplified by a case in the ancient city of Providence, where in the late forties Edgar Allan Poe used to sojourn often during his unsuccessful wooing of the gifted poetess, Mrs. Whitman. Poe generally stopped at the Mansion House in Benefit Street—the renamed Golden Ball Inn whose roof has sheltered Washington, Jefferson, and Lafayette—and his favourite walk led northward along the same street to Mrs. Whitman's home and the neighbouring hillside churchyard of St. John's, whose hidden expanse of eighteenth-century gravestones had for him a peculiar fascination.

Now the irony is this. In this walk, so many times repeated, the world's greatest master of the terrible and the bizarre was obliged to pass a particular house on the eastern side of the street; a dingy, antiquated structure perched on the abruptly rising side-hill, with a great unkempt yard dating from a time when the region was partly open country. It does not appear that he ever wrote or spoke of it, nor is there any evidence that he even noticed it. And yet that house, to the two persons in possession of certain information, equals or outranks in horror the wildest phantasy of the genius who so often passed it unknowingly, and stands starkly leering as a symbol of all that is unutterably hideous.

The house was—and for that matter still is—of a kind to attract the attention of the curious. Originally a farm or semi-farm building, it followed the average New England colonial lines of the middle eighteenth century—the prosperous peaked-roof sort, with two stories and dormerless attic, and with the Georgian doorway and interior panelling dictated by the progress of taste at that time. It faced south, with one gable end buried to the lower windows in the eastward rising hill, and the other exposed to the foundations toward the street. Its construction, over a century and a half ago, had followed the grading and straightening of the road in that especial vicinity; for Benefit Street—at first called Back Street—was laid out as a lane winding amongst the graveyards of the first settlers, and straightened only when the removal of the bodies to the North Burial Ground made it decently possible to cut through the old family plots.

At the start, the western wall had lain some twenty feet up a precipitous lawn from the roadway; but a widening of the street at about the time of the Revolution sheared off most of the intervening space, exposing the foundations so that a brick basement wall had to be made, giving the deep cellar a street frontage with door and two windows above ground, close to the new line of public travel. When the sidewalk was laid out a century ago the last of the intervening space was removed; and Poe in his walks must have seen only a sheer ascent of dull grey brick flush with the sidewalk and surmounted at a height of ten feet by the antique shingled bulk of the house proper.

The farm-like grounds extended back very deeply up the hill, almost to Wheaton Street. The space south of the house, abutting on Benefit Street, was of course greatly above the existing sidewalk level, forming a terrace bounded by a high bank wall of damp, mossy stone pierced by a steep flight of narrow steps which led inward between canyon-like surfaces to the upper region of mangy lawn, rheumy brick walls, and neglected gardens whose dismantled cement urns, rusted kettles fallen from tripods of knotty sticks, and similar paraphernalia set off the weather-beaten front door with its broken fanlight, rotting Ionic pilasters, and wormy triangular pediment.

What I heard in my youth about the shunned house was merely that people died there in alarmingly great numbers. That, I was told, was why the original owners had moved out some twenty years after building the place. It was plainly unhealthy, perhaps because of the dampness and fungous growth in the cellar, the general sickish smell, the draughts of the hallways, or the quality of the well and pump water. These things were bad enough, and these were all that gained belief among the persons whom I knew. Only the notebooks of my antiquarian uncle, Dr. Elihu Whipple, revealed to me at length the darker, vaguer surmises which formed an undercurrent of folklore among old-time servants and humble folk; surmises which never travelled far, and which were largely forgotten when Providence grew to be a metropolis with a shifting modern population.

The general fact is, that the house was never regarded by the solid part of the community as in any real sense "haunted". There were no widespread tales of rattling chains, cold currents of air, extinguished lights, or faces at the window. Extremists sometimes said the house was "unlucky", but that is as far as even they went. What was really beyond dispute is that a frightful proportion of persons died there; or more accurately, *had* died there, since after some peculiar happenings over sixty years ago the building had become deserted through the sheer impossibility of renting it. These persons were not all cut off suddenly by any one cause; rather did it seem that their vitality was insidiously sapped, so that each one died the sooner from whatever tendency to weakness he may have naturally had. And those who did not die displayed in varying degree a type of anaemia or consumption, and sometimes a decline of the mental faculties, which spoke ill for the salubriousness of the building. Neighbouring houses, it must be added, seemed entirely free from the noxious quality.

This much I knew before my insistent questioning led my uncle to shew me the notes which finally embarked us both on our hideous investigation. In my childhood the shunned house was vacant, with barren, gnarled, and terrible old trees, long, queerly pale grass, and nightmarishly misshapen weeds in the high terraced yard where birds never lingered. We boys used to overrun the place, and I can still recall my youthful terror not only at the morbid strangeness of this sinister vegetation, but at the eldritch atmosphere and odour of the dilapidated house, whose unlocked front door was often entered in quest of shudders. The small-paned windows were largely broken, and a nameless air of desolation hung round the precarious panelling, shaky interior shutters, peeling wall-paper, falling plaster, rickety staircases, and such fragments of battered furniture as still remained. The dust and cobwebs added their touch of the fearful; and brave indeed was the boy who would voluntarily ascend the ladder to the attic, a vast raftered length lighted only by small blinking windows in the gable ends, and filled with a massed wreckage of chests, chairs, and spinning-wheels which infinite years of deposit had shrouded and festooned into monstrous and hellish shapes.

But after all, the attic was not the most terrible part of the house. It was the dank, humid cellar which somehow exerted the strongest repulsion on us, even though it was wholly above ground on the street side, with only a thin door and window-pierced brick wall to separate it from the busy sidewalk. We scarcely knew whether to haunt it in spectral fascination, or to shun it for the sake of our souls and our sanity. For one thing, the bad odour of the house was strongest there; and for another thing, we did not like the white fungous growths which occasionally sprang up in rainy summer weather from the hard earth floor. Those fungi, grotesquely like the vegetation in the yard outside, were truly horrible in their outlines; detestable parodies of toadstools and Indian pipes, whose like we had never seen in any other situation. They rotted quickly, and at one stage became slightly phosphorescent; so that nocturnal passers-by sometimes spoke of witch-fires glowing behind the broken panes of the foetor-spreading windows.

We never—even in our wildest Hallowe'en moods—visited this cellar by night, but in some of our daytime visits could detect the phosphorescence, especially when the day was dark and wet. There was also a subtler thing we often thought we detected—a very strange thing which was, however, merely suggestive at most. I refer to a sort of cloudy whitish pattern on the dirt floor—a vague, shifting deposit of mould or nitre which we sometimes thought we could trace amidst the sparse fungous growths near the huge fireplace of the basement kitchen. Once in a while it struck us that this patch bore an uncanny resemblance to a doubled-up human figure, though generally no such kinship existed, and often there was no whitish deposit whatever. On a certain rainy afternoon when this illusion seemed phenomenally strong, and when, in addition, I had fancied I glimpsed a kind of thin, yellowish, shimmering exhalation rising from the nitrous pattern toward the yawning fireplace, I spoke to my uncle about the matter. He smiled at this odd conceit, but it seemed that his smile was tinged with reminiscence. Later I heard that a similar notion entered into some of the wild ancient tales of the common folk—a notion likewise alluding to ghoulish, wolfish shapes taken by smoke from the great chimney, and queer contours assumed by certain of the sinuous tree-roots that thrust their way into the cellar through the loose foundation-stones.

II

Not till my adult years did my uncle set before me the notes and data which he had collected concerning the shunned house. Dr. Whipple was a sane, conservative physician of the old school, and for all his interest in the place was not eager to encourage young thoughts toward the abnormal. His own view, postulating simply a building and location of markedly unsanitary qualities, had nothing to do with abnormality; but he realised that the very picturesqueness which aroused his own interest would in a boy's fanciful mind take on all manner of gruesome imaginative associations.

The doctor was a bachelor; a white-haired, clean-shaven, old-fashioned gentleman, and a local historian of note, who had often broken a lance with such controversial guardians of tradition as Sidney S. Rider and Thomas W. Bicknell. He lived with one man-servant in a Georgian homestead with knocker and iron-railed steps, balanced eerily on a steep ascent of North Court Street beside the ancient brick court and colony house where his grandfather—a cousin of that celebrated privateersman, Capt. Whipple, who burnt His Majesty's armed schooner *Gaspee* in 1772—had voted in the legislature on May 4, 1776, for the independence of the Rhode-Island Colony. Around him in the damp, low-ceiled library with the musty white panelling, heavy carved overmantel, and small-paned, vine-shaded windows, were the relics and records of his ancient family, among which were many dubious allusions to the shunned house in Benefit Street. That pest spot lies not far distant—for Benefit runs ledgewise just above the courthouse along the precipitous hill up which the first settlement climbed.

When, in the end, my insistent pestering and maturing years evoked from my uncle the hoarded lore I sought, there lay before me a strange enough chronicle. Long-winded, statistical, and drearily genealogical as some of the matter was, there ran through it a continuous thread of brooding, tenacious horror and preternatural malevolence which impressed me even more than it had impressed the good doctor. Separate events fitted together uncannily, and seemingly irrelevant details held mines of hideous possibilities. A new and burning curiosity grew in me, compared to which my boyish curiosity was feeble and inchoate. The first revelation led to an exhaustive research, and finally to that shuddering quest which proved so disastrous to myself and mine. For at last my uncle insisted on joining the search I had commenced, and after a certain night in that house he did not come away with me. I am lonely without that gentle soul whose long years were filled only with honour, virtue, good taste, benevolence, and learning. I have reared a marble urn to his memory in St. John's churchyard— the place that Poe loved—the hidden grove of giant willows on the hill, where tombs and headstones huddle quietly between the hoary bulk of the church and the houses and bank walls of Benefit Street.

The history of the house, opening amidst a maze of dates, revealed no trace of the sinister either about its construction or about the prosperous and honourable family who built it. Yet from the first a taint of calamity, soon increased to boding significance, was apparent. My uncle's carefully compiled record began with the building of the structure in 1763, and followed the theme with an unusual amount of detail. The shunned house, it seems, was first inhabited by William Harris and his wife Rhoby Dexter, with their children, Elkanah, born in 1755, Abigail, born in 1757, William, Jr., born in 1759, and Ruth, born in 1761. Harris was a substantial merchant and seaman in the West India trade, connected with the firm of Obadiah Brown and his nephews. After Brown's death in 1761, the new firm of Nicholas Brown & Co. made him master of the brig *Prudence*, Providence-built, of 120 tons, thus enabling him to erect the new homestead he had desired ever since his marriage.

The site he had chosen—a recently straightened part of the new and fashionable Back Street, which ran along the side of the hill above crowded Cheapside—was all that could be wished, and the building did justice to the location. It was the best that moderate means could afford, and Harris hastened to move in before the birth of a fifth child which the family expected. That child, a boy, came in December; but was still-born. Nor was any child to be born alive in that house for a century and a half.

The next April sickness occurred among the children, and Abigail and Ruth died before the month was over. Dr. Job Ives diagnosed the trouble as some infantile fever, though others declared it was more of a mere wasting-away or decline. It seemed, in any event, to be contagious; for Hannah Bowen, one of the two servants, died of it in the following June. Eli Liddeason, the other servant, constantly complained of weakness; and would have returned to his father's farm in Rehoboth but for a sudden attachment for Mehitabel Pierce, who was hired to succeed Hannah. He died the next year—a sad year indeed, since it marked the death of William Harris himself, enfeebled as he was by the climate of Martinique, where his occupation had kept him for considerable periods during the preceding decade.

The widowed Rhoby Harris never recovered from the shock of her husband's death, and the passing of her first-born Elkanah two years later was the final blow to her reason. In 1768 she fell victim to a mild form of insanity, and was thereafter confined to the upper part of the house; her elder maiden sister, Mercy Dexter, having moved in to take charge of the family. Mercy was a plain, raw-boned woman of great strength; but her health visibly declined from the time of her advent. She was greatly devoted to her unfortunate sister, and had an especial affection for her only surviving nephew William, who from a sturdy infant had become a sickly, spindling lad. In this year the servant Mehitabel died, and the other servant, Preserved Smith, left without coherent explanation—or at least, with only some wild tales and a complaint that he disliked the smell of the place. For a time Mercy could secure no more help, since the seven deaths and case of madness, all occurring within five years' space, had begun to set in motion the body of fireside rumour which later became so bizarre. Ultimately, however, she obtained new servants from out of town; Ann White, a morose woman from that part of North Kingstown now set off as the township of Exeter, and a capable Boston man named Zenas Low.

It was Ann White who first gave definite shape to the sinister idle talk. Mercy should have known better than to hire anyone from the Nooseneck Hill country, for that remote bit of backwoods was then, as now, a seat of the most uncomfortable superstitions. As lately as 1892 an Exeter community exhumed a dead body and ceremoniously burnt its heart in order to prevent certain alleged visitations injurious to the public health and peace, and one may imagine the point of view of the same section in 1768. Ann's tongue was perniciously active, and within a few months Mercy discharged her, filling her place with a faithful and amiable Amazon from Newport, Maria Robbins.

Meanwhile poor Rhoby Harris, in her madness, gave voice to dreams and imaginings of the most hideous sort. At times her screams became insupportable, and for long periods she would utter shrieking horrors which necessitated her son's temporary residence with his cousin, Peleg Harris, in Presbyterian-Lane near the new college building. The boy would seem to improve after these visits, and had Mercy been as wise as she was well-meaning, she would have let him live permanently with Peleg. Just what Mrs. Harris cried out in her fits of violence, tradition hesitates to say; or rather, presents such extravagant accounts that they nullify themselves through sheer absurdity. Certainly it sounds absurd to hear that a woman educated only in the rudiments of French often shouted for hours in a coarse and idiomatic form of that language, or that the same person, alone and guarded, complained wildly of a staring thing which bit and chewed at her. In 1772 the servant Zenas died, and when Mrs. Harris heard of it she laughed with a shocking delight utterly foreign to her. The next year she herself died, and was laid to rest in the North Burial Ground beside her husband.

Upon the outbreak of trouble with Great Britain in 1775, William Harris, despite his scant sixteen years and feeble constitution, managed to enlist in the Army of Observation under General Greene; and from that time on enjoyed a steady rise in health and prestige. In 1780, as a Captain in Rhode Island forces in New Jersey under Colonel Angell, he met and married Phebe Hetfield of Elizabethtown, whom he brought to Providence upon his honourable discharge in the following year.

The young soldier's return was not a thing of unmitigated happiness. The house, it is true, was still in good condition; and the street had been widened and changed in name from Back Street to Benefit Street. But Mercy Dexter's once robust frame had undergone a sad and curious decay, so that she was now a stooped and pathetic figure with hollow voice and disconcerting pallor—qualities shared to a singular degree by the one remaining servant Maria. In the autumn of 1782 Phebe Harris gave birth to a stillborn daughter, and on the fifteenth of the next May Mercy Dexter took leave of a useful, austere, and virtuous life.

William Harris, at last thoroughly convinced of the radically unhealthful nature of his abode, now took steps toward quitting it and closing it forever. Securing temporary quarters for himself and his wife at the newly opened Golden Ball Inn, he arranged for the building of a new and finer house in Westminster Street, in the growing part of the town across the Great Bridge. There, in 1785, his son Dutee was born; and there the family dwelt till the encroachments of commerce drove them back across the river and over the hill to Angell Street, in the newer East Side residence district, where the late Archer Harris built his sumptuous but hideous French-roofed mansion in 1876. William and Phebe both succumbed to the yellow fever epidemic of 1797, but Dutee was brought up by his cousin Rathbone Harris, Peleg's son.

Rathbone was a practical man, and rented the Benefit Street house despite William's wish to keep it vacant. He considered it an obligation to his ward to make the most of all the boy's property, nor did he concern himself with the deaths and illnesses which caused so many changes of tenants, or the steadily growing aversion with which the house was generally regarded. It is likely that he felt only vexation when, in 1804, the town council ordered him to fumigate the place with sulphur, tar, and gum camphor on account of the much-discussed deaths of four persons, presumably caused by the then diminishing fever epidemic. They said the place had a febrile smell.

Dutee himself thought little of the house, for he grew up to be a privateersman, and served with distinction on the *Vigilant* under Capt. Cahoone in the War of 1812. He returned unharmed, married in 1814, and became a father on that memorable night of September 23, 1815, when a great gale drove the waters of the bay over half the town, and floated a tall sloop well up Westminster Street so that its masts almost tapped the Harris windows in symbolic affirmation that the new boy, Welcome, was a seaman's son.

Welcome did not survive his father, but lived to perish gloriously at Fredericksburg in 1862. Neither he nor his son Archer knew of the shunned house as other than a nuisance almost impossible to rent—perhaps on account of the mustiness and sickly odour of unkempt old age. Indeed, it never was rented after a series of deaths culminating in 1861, which the excitement of the war tended to throw into obscurity. Carrington Harris, last of the male line, knew it only as a deserted and somewhat picturesque centre of legend until I told him my experience. He had meant to tear it down and build an apartment house on the site, but after my account decided to let it stand, install plumbing, and rent it. Nor has he yet had any difficulty in obtaining tenants. The horror has gone.

III

It may well be imagined how powerfully I was affected by the annals of the Harrises. In this continuous record there seemed to me to brood a persistent evil beyond anything in Nature as I had known it; an evil clearly connected with the house and not with the family. This impression was confirmed by my uncle's less systematic array of miscellaneous data—legends transcribed from servant gossip, cuttings from the papers, copies of death-certificates by fellow-physicians, and the like. All of this material I cannot hope to give, for my uncle was a tireless antiquarian and very deeply interested in the shunned house; but I may refer to several dominant points which earn notice by their recurrence through many reports from diverse sources. For example, the servant gossip was practically unanimous in attributing to the fungous and malodorous *cellar* of the house a vast supremacy in evil influence. There had been servants—Ann White especially—who would not use the cellar kitchen, and at least three well-defined legends bore upon the queer quasi-human or diabolic outlines assumed by tree-roots and patches of mould in that region. These latter narratives interested me profoundly, on account of what I had seen in my boyhood, but I felt that most of the significance had in each case been largely obscured by additions from the common stock of local ghost lore.

Ann White, with her Exeter superstition, had promulgated the most extravagant and at the same time most consistent tale; alleg-

ing that there must lie buried beneath the house one of those
vampires—the dead who retain their bodily form and live on the
blood or breath of the living—whose hideous legions send their
preying shapes or spirits abroad by night. To destroy a vampire
one must, the grandmothers say, exhume it and burn its heart, or
at least drive a stake through that organ; and Ann's dogged insistence on a search under the cellar had been prominent in bringing
about her discharge.

Her tales, however, commanded a wide audience, and were the
more readily accepted because the house indeed stood on land
once used for burial purposes. To me their interest depended less
on this circumstance than on the peculiarly appropriate way in
which they dovetailed with certain other things—the complaint of
the departing servant Preserved Smith, who had preceded Ann
and never heard of her, that something "sucked his breath" at
night; the death-certificates of fever victims of 1804, issued by Dr.
Chad Hopkins, and shewing the four deceased persons all unaccountably lacking in blood; and the obscure passages of poor
Rhoby Harris's ravings, where she complained of the sharp teeth
of a glassy-eyed, half-visible presence.

Free from unwarranted superstition though I am, these things
produced in me an odd sensation, which was intensified by a pair
of widely separated newspaper cuttings relating to deaths in the
shunned house—one from the *Providence Gazette and Country-Jour-
nal* of April 12, 1815, and the other from the *Daily Transcript and
Chronicle* of October 27, 1845—each of which detailed an appall-
ingly grisly circumstance whose duplication was remarkable. It
seems that in both instances the dying person, in 1815 a gentle old
lady named Stafford and in 1845 a school-teacher of middle age
named Eleazar Durfee, became transfigured in a horrible way;
glaring glassily and attempting to bite the throat of the attending
physician. Even more puzzling, though, was the final case which
put an end to the renting of the house—a series of anaemia deaths
preceded by progressive madnesses wherein the patient would
craftily attempt the lives of his relatives by incisions in the neck or
wrist.

This was in 1860 and 1861, when my uncle had just begun his
medical practice; and before leaving for the front he heard much of
it from his elder professional colleagues. The really inexplicable
thing was the way in which the victims—ignorant people, for the

ill-smelling and widely shunned house could now be rented to no others—would babble maledictions in French, a language they could not possibly have studied to any extent. It made one think of poor Rhoby Harris nearly a century before, and so moved my uncle that he commenced collecting historical data on the house after listening, some time subsequent to his return from the war, to the first-hand account of Drs. Chase and Whitmarsh. Indeed, I could see that my uncle had thought deeply on the subject, and that he was glad of my own interest—an open-minded and sympathetic interest which enabled him to discuss with me matters at which others would merely have laughed. His fancy had not gone so far as mine, but he felt that the place was rare in its imaginative potentialities, and worthy of note as an inspiration in the field of the grotesque and macabre.

For my part, I was disposed to take the whole subject with profound seriousness, and began at once not only to review the evidence, but to accumulate as much more as I could. I talked with the elderly Archer Harris, then owner of the house, many times before his death in 1916; and obtained from him and his still surviving maiden sister Alice an authentic corroboration of all the family data my uncle had collected. When, however, I asked them what connexion with France or its language the house could have, they confessed themselves as frankly baffled and ignorant as I. Archer knew nothing, and all that Miss Harris could say was that an old allusion her grandfather, Dutee Harris, had heard of might have shed a little light. The old seaman, who had survived his son Welcome's death in battle by two years, had not himself known the legend; but recalled that his earliest nurse, the ancient Maria Robbins, seemed darkly aware of something that might have lent a weird significance to the French ravings of Rhoby Harris, which she had so often heard during the last days of that hapless woman. Maria had been at the shunned house from 1769 till the removal of the family in 1783, and had seen Mercy Dexter die. Once she hinted to the child Dutee of a somewhat peculiar circumstance in Mercy's last moments, but he had soon forgotten all about it save that it was something peculiar. The granddaughter, moreover, recalled even this much with difficulty. She and her brother were not so much interested in the house as was Archer's son Carrington, the present owner, with whom I talked after my experience.

Having exhausted the Harris family of all the information it

could furnish, I turned my attention to early town records and
deeds with a zeal more penetrating than that which my uncle had
occasionally shewn in the same work. What I wished was a com-
prehensive history of the site from its very settlement in 1636—or
even before, if any Narragansett Indian legend could be unearthed
to supply the data. I found, at the start, that the land had been part
of the long strip of home lot granted originally to John Throckmorton; one of many similar strips beginning at the Town Street beside
the river and extending up over the hill to a line roughly corresponding with the modern Hope Street. The Throckmorton lot had
later, of course, been much subdivided; and I became very assidu-
ous in tracing that section through which Back or Benefit Street
was later run. It had, a rumour indeed said, been the Throckmorton graveyard; but as I examined the records more carefully, I
found that the graves had all been transferred at an early date to
the North Burial Ground on the Pawtucket West Road.

Then suddenly I came—by a rare piece of chance, since it was
not in the main body of records and might easily have been missed
—upon something which aroused my keenest eagerness, fitting in
as it did with several of the queerest phases of the affair. It was the
record of a lease, in 1697, of a small tract of ground to an Etienne
Roulet and wife. At last the French element had appeared—that,
and another deeper element of horror which the name conjured up
from the darkest recesses of my weird and heterogeneous reading
—and I feverishly studied the platting of the locality as it had been
before the cutting through and partial straightening of Back Street
between 1747 and 1758. I found what I had half expected, that
where the shunned house now stood the Roulets had laid out their
graveyard behind a one-story and attic cottage, and that no record
of any transfer of graves existed. The document, indeed, ended in
much confusion; and I was forced to ransack both the Rhode Island Historical Society and Shepley Library before I could find a
local door which the name Etienne Roulet would unlock. In the
end I did find something; something of such vague but monstrous
import that I set about at once to examine the cellar of the shunned
house itself with a new and excited minuteness.

The Roulets, it seemed, had come in 1696 from East Greenwich,
down the west shore of Narragansett Bay. They were Huguenots
from Caude, and had encountered much opposition before the
Providence selectmen allowed them to settle in the town. Unpopu-

larity had dogged them in East Greenwich, whither they had come in 1686, after the revocation of the Edict of Nantes, and rumour said that the cause of dislike extended beyond mere racial and national prejudice, or the land disputes which involved other French settlers with the English in rivalries which not even Governor Andros could quell. But their ardent Protestantism—too ardent, some whispered—and their evident distress when virtually driven from the village down the bay, had moved the sympathy of the town fathers. Here the strangers had been granted a haven; and the swarthy Etienne Roulet, less apt at agriculture than at reading queer books and drawing queer diagrams, was given a clerical post in the warehouse at Pardon Tillinghast's wharf, far south in Town Street. There had, however, been a riot of some sort later on—perhaps forty years later, after old Roulet's death—and no one seemed to hear of the family after that.

For a century and more, it appeared, the Roulets had been well remembered and frequently discussed as vivid incidents in the quiet life of a New England seaport. Etienne's son Paul, a surly fellow whose erratic conduct had probably provoked the riot which wiped out the family, was particularly a source of speculation; and though Providence never shared the witchcraft panics of her Puritan neighbours, it was freely intimated by old wives that his prayers were neither uttered at the proper time nor directed toward the proper object. All this had undoubtedly formed the basis of the legend known by old Maria Robbins. What relation it had to the French ravings of Rhoby Harris and other inhabitants of the shunned house, imagination or future discovery alone could determine. I wondered how many of those who had known the legends realised that additional link with the terrible which my wider reading had given me; that ominous item in the annals of morbid horror which tells of the creature *Jacques Roulet, of Caude,* who in 1598 was condemned to death as a daemoniac but afterward saved from the stake by the Paris parliament and shut in a madhouse. He had been found covered with blood and shreds of flesh in a wood, shortly after the killing and rending of a boy by a pair of wolves. One wolf was seen to lope away unhurt. Surely a pretty hearthside tale, with a queer significance as to name and place; but I decided that the Providence gossips could not have generally known of it. Had they known, the coincidence of names would have brought some drastic and frightened action—indeed,

might not its limited whispering have precipitated the final riot
which erased the Roulets from the town?

I now visited the accursed place with increased frequency;
studying the unwholesome vegetation of the garden, examining
all the walls of the building, and poring over every inch of the
earthen cellar floor. Finally, with Carrington Harris's permission, I
fitted a key to the disused door opening from the cellar directly
upon Benefit Street, preferring to have a more immediate access to
the outside world than the dark stairs, ground floor hall, and front
door could give. There, where morbidity lurked most thickly, I
searched and poked during long afternoons when the sunlight
filtered in through the cobwebbed above-ground windows, and a
sense of security glowed from the unlocked door which placed me
only a few feet from the placid sidewalk outside. Nothing new
rewarded my efforts—only the same depressing mustiness and
faint suggestions of noxious odours and nitrous outlines on the
floor—and I fancy that many pedestrians must have watched me
curiously through the broken panes.

At length, upon a suggestion of my uncle's, I decided to try the
spot nocturnally; and one stormy midnight ran the beams of an
electric torch over the mouldy floor with its uncanny shapes and
distorted, half-phosphorescent fungi. The place had dispirited me
curiously that evening, and I was almost prepared when I saw—or
thought I saw—amidst the whitish deposits a particularly sharp
definition of the "huddled form" I had suspected from boyhood.
Its clearness was astonishing and unprecedented—and as I
watched I seemed to see again the thin, yellowish, shimmering
exhalation which had startled me on that rainy afternoon so many
years before.

Above the anthropomorphic patch of mould by the fireplace it
rose; a subtle, sickish, almost luminous vapour which as it hung
trembling in the dampness seemed to develop vague and shocking
suggestions of form, gradually trailing off into nebulous decay
and passing up into the blackness of the great chimney with a
foetor in its wake. It was truly horrible, and the more so to me
because of what I knew of the spot. Refusing to flee, I watched it
fade—and as I watched I felt that it was in turn watching me
greedily with eyes more imaginable than visible. When I told my
uncle about it he was greatly aroused; and after a tense hour of
reflection, arrived at a definite and drastic decision. Weighing in

his mind the importance of the matter, and the significance of our relation to it, he insisted that we both test—and if possible destroy—the horror of the house by a joint night or nights of aggressive vigil in that musty and fungus-cursed cellar.

IV

On Wednesday, June 25, 1919, after a proper notification of Carrington Harris which did not include surmises as to what we expected to find, my uncle and I conveyed to the shunned house two camp chairs and a folding camp cot, together with some scientific mechanism of greater weight and intricacy. These we placed in the cellar during the day, screening the windows with paper and planning to return in the evening for our first vigil. We had locked the door from the cellar to the ground floor; and having a key to the outside cellar door, we were prepared to leave our expensive and delicate apparatus—which we had obtained secretly and at great cost—as many days as our vigils might need to be protracted. It was our design to sit up together till very late, and then watch singly till dawn in two-hour stretches, myself first and then my companion; the inactive member resting on the cot.

The natural leadership with which my uncle procured the instruments from the laboratories of Brown University and the Cranston Street Armoury, and instinctively assumed direction of our venture, was a marvellous commentary on the potential vitality and resilience of a man of eighty-one. Elihu Whipple had lived according to the hygienic laws he had preached as a physician, and but for what happened later would be here in full vigour today. Only two persons suspect what did happen—Carrington Harris and myself. I had to tell Harris because he owned the house and deserved to know what had gone out of it. Then too, we had spoken to him in advance of our quest; and I felt after my uncle's going that he would understand and assist me in some vitally necessary public explanations. He turned very pale, but agreed to help me, and decided that it would now be safe to rent the house.

To declare that we were not nervous on that rainy night of watching would be an exaggeration both gross and ridiculous. We were not, as I have said, in any sense childishly superstitious, but scientific study and reflection had taught us that the known universe of three dimensions embraces the merest fraction of the whole cosmos of substance and energy. In this case an overwhelming preponderance of evidence from numerous authentic sources pointed to the tenacious existence of certain forces of great power and, so far as the human point of view is concerned, exceptional malignancy. To say that we actually believed in vampires or werewolves would be a carelessly inclusive statement. Rather must it be said that we were not prepared to deny the possibility of certain unfamiliar and unclassified modifications of vital force and attenuated matter; existing very infrequently in three-dimensional space because of its more intimate connexion with other spatial units, yet close enough to the boundary of our own to furnish us occasional manifestations which we, for lack of a proper vantage-point, may never hope to understand.

In short, it seemed to my uncle and me that an incontrovertible array of facts pointed to some lingering influence in the shunned house; traceable to one or another of the ill-favoured French settlers of two centuries before, and still operative through rare and unknown laws of atomic and electronic motion. That the family of Roulet had possessed an abnormal affinity for outer circles of entity—dark spheres which for normal folk hold only repulsion and terror—their recorded history seemed to prove. Had not, then, the riots of those bygone seventeen-thirties set moving certain kinetic patterns in the morbid brain of one or more of them—notably the sinister Paul Roulet—which obscurely survived the bodies murdered and buried by the mob, and continued to function in some multiple-dimensioned space along the original lines of force determined by a frantic hatred of the encroaching community?

Such a thing was surely not a physical or biochemical impossibility in the light of a newer science which includes the theories of relativity and intra-atomic action. One might easily imagine an alien nucleus of substance or energy, formless or otherwise, kept alive by imperceptible or immaterial subtractions from the life-force or bodily tissues and fluids of other and more palpably living things into which it penetrates and with whose fabric it sometimes completely merges itself. It might be actively hostile, or it might be dictated merely by blind motives of self-preservation. In any case such a monster must of necessity be in our scheme of things an anomaly and an intruder, whose extirpation forms a primary duty with every man not an enemy to the world's life, health, and sanity.

What baffled us was our utter ignorance of the aspect in which we might encounter the thing. No sane person had even seen it, and few had ever felt it definitely. It might be pure energy—a form ethereal and outside the realm of substance—or it might be partly material; some unknown and equivocal mass of plasticity, capable of changing at will to nebulous approximations of the solid, liquid, gaseous, or tenuously unparticled states. The anthropomorphic patch of mould on the floor, the form of the yellowish vapour, and the curvature of the tree-roots in some of the old tales, all argued at least a remote and reminiscent connexion with the human shape; but how representative or permanent that similarity might be, none could say with any kind of certainty.

We had devised two weapons to fight it; a large and specially fitted Crookes tube operated by powerful storage batteries and provided with peculiar screens and reflectors, in case it proved intangible and opposable only by vigorously destructive ether radiations, and a pair of military flame-throwers of the sort used in the world-war, in case it proved partly material and susceptible of mechanical destruction—for like the superstitious Exeter rustics, we were prepared to burn the thing's heart out if heart existed to burn. All this aggressive mechanism we set in the cellar in positions carefully arranged with reference to the cot and chairs, and to the spot before the fireplace where the mould had taken strange shapes. That suggestive patch, by the way, was only faintly visible when we placed our furniture and instruments, and when we returned that evening for the actual vigil. For a moment I half doubted that I had ever seen it in the more definitely limned form —but then I thought of the legends.

Our cellar vigil began at 10 P.M., daylight saving time, and as it continued we found no promise of pertinent developments. A weak, filtered glow from the rain-harassed street-lamps outside, and a feeble phosphorescence from the detestable fungi within, shewed the dripping stone of the walls, from which all traces of whitewash had vanished; the dank, foetid, and mildew-tainted hard earth floor with its obscene fungi; the rotting remains of what had been stools, chairs, and tables, and other more shapeless furniture; the heavy planks and massive beams of the ground floor overhead; the decrepit plank door leading to bins and chambers beneath other parts of the house; the crumbling stone staircase with ruined wooden hand-rail; and the crude and cavernous fireplace of blackened brick where rusted iron fragments revealed the past presence of hooks, andirons, spit, crane, and a door to the Dutch oven—these things, and our austere cot and camp chairs, and the heavy and intricate destructive machinery we had brought.

We had, as in my own former explorations, left the door to the street unlocked; so that a direct and practical path of escape might lie open in case of manifestations beyond our power to deal with. It was our idea that our continued nocturnal presence would call forth whatever malign entity lurked there; and that being prepared, we could dispose of the thing with one or the other of our provided means as soon as we had recognised and observed it sufficiently. How long it might require to evoke and extinguish the thing, we had no notion. It occurred to us, too, that our venture was far from safe; for in what strength the thing might appear no one could tell. But we deemed the game worth the hazard, and embarked on it alone and unhesitatingly; conscious that the seeking of outside aid would only expose us to ridicule and perhaps defeat our entire purpose. Such was our frame of mind as we talked—far into the night, till my uncle's growing drowsiness made me remind him to lie down for his two-hour sleep.

Something like fear chilled me as I sat there in the small hours alone—I say alone, for one who sits by a sleeper is indeed alone; perhaps more alone than he can realise. My uncle breathed heavily, his deep inhalations and exhalations accompanied by the rain outside, and punctuated by another nerve-racking sound of distant dripping water within—for the house was repulsively damp even in dry weather, and in this storm positively swamp-like. I studied the loose, antique masonry of the walls in the fungus-light and the feeble rays which stole in from the street through the screened windows; and once, when the noisome atmosphere of the place seemed about to sicken me, I opened the door and looked up and down the street, feasting my eyes on familiar sights and my nostrils on the wholesome air. Still nothing occurred to reward my watching; and I yawned repeatedly, fatigue getting the better of apprehension.

Then the stirring of my uncle in his sleep attracted my notice. He had turned restlessly on the cot several times during the latter half of the first hour, but now he was breathing with unusual irregularity, occasionally heaving a sigh which held more than a few of the qualities of a choking moan. I turned my electric flashlight on him and found his face averted, so rising and crossing to the other side of the cot, I again flashed the light to see if he seemed in any pain. What I saw unnerved me most surprisingly, considering its relative triviality. It must have been merely the association of any odd circumstance with the sinister nature of our location and mission, for surely the circumstance was not in itself frightful or unnatural. It was merely that my uncle's facial expression, disturbed no doubt by the strange dreams which our situation prompted, betrayed considerable agitation, and seemed not at all characteristic of him. His habitual expression was one of kindly and well-bred calm, whereas now a variety of emotions seemed struggling within him. I think, on the whole, that it was this *variety* which chiefly disturbed me. My uncle, as he gasped and tossed in increasing perturbation and with eyes that had now started open, seemed not one but many men, and suggested a curious quality of alienage from himself.

All at once he commenced to mutter, and I did not like the look of his mouth and teeth as he spoke. The words were at first indistinguishable, and then—with a tremendous start—I recognised something about them which filled me with icy fear till I recalled the breadth of my uncle's education and the interminable translations he had made from anthropological and antiquarian articles in the *Revue des Deux Mondes.* For the venerable Elihu Whipple was muttering *in French,* and the few phrases I could distinguish seemed connected with the darkest myths he had ever adapted from the famous Paris magazine.

Suddenly a perspiration broke out on the sleeper's forehead, and he leaped abruptly up, half awake. The jumble of French changed to a cry in English, and the hoarse voice shouted excitedly, "My breath, my breath!" Then the awakening became complete, and with a subsidence of facial expression to the normal state my uncle seized my hand and began to relate a dream whose nucleus of significance I could only surmise with a kind of awe.

He had, he said, floated off from a very ordinary series of dream-pictures into a scene whose strangeness was related to nothing he had ever read. It was of this world, and yet not of it—a shadowy geometrical confusion in which could be seen elements of familiar things in most unfamiliar and perturbing combinations. There was a suggestion of queerly disordered pictures superimposed one upon another; an arrangement in which the essentials of time as well as of space seemed dissolved and mixed in the most illogical fashion. In this kaleidoscopic vortex of phantasmal images were occasional snapshots, if one might use the term, of singular clearness but unaccountable heterogeneity.

Once my uncle thought he lay in a carelessly dug open pit, with a crowd of angry faces framed by straggling locks and three-cornered hats frowning down on him. Again he seemed to be in the interior of a house—an old house, apparently—but the details and inhabitants were constantly changing, and he could never be certain of the faces or the furniture, or even of the room itself, since doors and windows seemed in just as great a state of flux as the more presumably mobile objects. It was queer—damnably queer—and my uncle spoke almost sheepishly, as if half expecting not to be believed, when he declared that of the strange faces many had unmistakably borne the features of the Harris family. And all the while there was a personal sensation of choking, as if some pervasive presence had spread itself through his body and sought to possess itself of his vital processes. I shuddered at the thought of those vital processes, worn as they were by eighty-one years of continuous functioning, in conflict with unknown forces of which the youngest and strongest system might well be afraid; but in another moment reflected that dreams are only dreams, and that these uncomfortable visions could be, at most, no more than my uncle's reaction to the investigations and expectations which had lately filled our minds to the exclusion of all else.

Conversation, also, soon tended to dispel my sense of strangeness; and in time I yielded to my yawns and took my turn at slumber. My uncle seemed now very wakeful, and welcomed his period of watching even though the nightmare had aroused him far ahead of his allotted two hours. Sleep seized me quickly, and I was at once haunted with dreams of the most disturbing kind. I felt, in my visions, a cosmic and abysmal loneness; with hostility surging from all sides upon some prison where I lay confined. I seemed bound and gagged, and taunted by the echoing yells of distant multitudes who thirsted for my blood. My uncle's face came to me with less pleasant associations than in waking hours, and I recall many futile struggles and attempts to scream. It was not a pleasant sleep, and for a second I was not sorry for the echoing shriek which clove through the barriers of dream and flung me to a sharp and startled awakeness in which every actual object before my eyes stood out with more than natural clearness and reality.

V

I had been lying with my face away from my uncle's chair, so that in this sudden flash of awakening I saw only the door to the street, the more northerly window, and the wall and floor and ceiling toward the north of the room, all photographed with morbid vividness on my brain in a light brighter than the glow of the fungi or the rays from the street outside. It was not a strong or even a fairly strong light; certainly not nearly strong enough to read an average book by. But it cast a shadow of myself and the cot on the floor, and had a yellowish, penetrating force that hinted at things more potent than luminosity. This I perceived with unhealthy sharpness despite the fact that two of my other senses were violently assailed. For on my ears rang the reverberations of that shocking scream, while my nostrils revolted at the stench which filled the place. My mind, as alert as my senses, recognised the gravely unusual; and almost automatically I leaped up and turned about to grasp the destructive instruments which we had left trained on the mouldy spot before the fireplace. As I turned, I dreaded what I was to see; for the scream had been in my uncle's voice, and I knew not against what menace I should have to defend him and myself.

Yet after all, the sight was worse than I had dreaded. There are horrors beyond horrors, and this was one of those nuclei of all dreamable hideousness which the cosmos saves to blast an accursed and unhappy few. Out of the fungus-ridden earth steamed up a vaporous corpse-light, yellow and diseased, which bubbled and lapped to a gigantic height in vague outlines half-human and half-monstrous, through which I could see the chimney and fireplace beyond. It was all eyes—wolfish and mocking—and the rugose insect-like head dissolved at the top to a thin stream of mist which curled putridly about and finally vanished up the chimney. I say that I saw this thing, but it is only in conscious retrospection that I ever definitely traced its damnable approach to form. At the time it was to me only a seething, dimly phosphorescent cloud of fungous loathsomeness, enveloping and dissolving to an abhor-

rent plasticity the one object to which all my attention was focussed. That object was my uncle—the venerable Elihu Whipple—
who with blackening and decaying features leered and gibbered at
me, and reached out dripping claws to rend me in the fury which
this horror had brought.

It was a sense of routine which kept me from going mad. I had
drilled myself in preparation for the crucial moment, and blind
training saved me. Recognising the bubbling evil as no substance
reachable by matter or material chemistry, and therefore ignoring
the flame-thrower which loomed on my left, I threw on the current
of the Crookes tube apparatus, and focussed toward that scene of
immortal blasphemousness the strongest ether radiations which
man's art can arouse from the spaces and fluids of Nature. There
was a bluish haze and a frenzied sputtering, and the yellowish
phosphorescence grew dimmer to my eyes. But I saw the dimness
was only that of contrast, and that the waves from the machine
had no effect whatever.

Then, in the midst of that daemoniac spectacle, I saw a fresh
horror which brought cries to my lips and sent me fumbling and
staggering toward that unlocked door to the quiet street, careless
of what abnormal terrors I loosed upon the world, or what
thoughts or judgments of men I brought down upon my head. In
that dim blend of blue and yellow the form of my uncle had
commenced a nauseous liquefaction whose essence eludes all description, and in which there played across his vanishing face such
changes of identity as only madness can conceive. He was at once
a devil and a multitude, a charnel-house and a pageant. Lit by the
mixed and uncertain beams, that gelatinous face assumed a dozen
—a score—a hundred—aspects; grinning, as it sank to the ground
on a body that melted like tallow, in the caricatured likeness of
legions strange and yet not strange.

I saw the features of the Harris line, masculine and feminine,
adult and infantile, and other features old and young, coarse and
refined, familiar and unfamiliar. For a second there flashed a de-
graded counterfeit of a miniature of poor mad Rhoby Harris that I
had seen in the School of Design Museum, and another time I
thought I caught the raw-boned image of Mercy Dexter as I recalled her from a painting in Carrington Harris's house. It was
frightful beyond conception; toward the last, when a curious blend
of servant and baby visages flickered close to the fungous floor

where a pool of greenish grease was spreading, it seemed as though the shifting features fought against themselves, and strove to form contours like those of my uncle's kindly face. I like to think that he existed at that moment, and that he tried to bid me farewell. It seems to me I hiccoughed a farewell from my own parched throat as I lurched out into the street; a thin stream of grease following me through the door to the rain-drenched sidewalk.

The rest is shadowy and monstrous. There was no one in the soaking street, and in all the world there was no one I dared tell. I walked aimlessly south past College Hill and the Athenaeum, down Hopkins Street, and over the bridge to the business section where tall buildings seemed to guard me as modern material things guard the world from ancient and unwholesome wonder. Then grey dawn unfolded wetly from the east, silhouetting the archaic hill and its venerable steeples, and beckoning me to the place where my terrible work was still unfinished. And in the end I went, wet, hatless, and dazed in the morning light, and entered that awful door in Benefit Street which I had left ajar, and which still swung cryptically in full sight of the early householders to whom I dared not speak.

The grease was gone, for the mouldy floor was porous. And in front of the fireplace was no vestige of the giant doubled-up form in nitre. I looked at the cot, the chairs, the instruments, my neglected hat, and the yellowed straw hat of my uncle. Dazedness was uppermost, and I could scarcely recall what was dream and what was reality. Then thought trickled back, and I knew that I had witnessed things more horrible than I had dreamed. Sitting down, I tried to conjecture as nearly as sanity would let me just what had happened, and how I might end the horror, if indeed it had been real. Matter it seemed not to be, nor ether, nor anything else conceivable by mortal mind. What, then, but some exotic *emanation;* some vampirish vapour such as Exeter rustics tell of as lurking over certain churchyards? This I felt was the clue, and again I looked at the floor before the fireplace where the mould and nitre had taken strange forms. In ten minutes my mind was made up, and taking my hat I set out for home, where I bathed, ate, and gave by telephone an order for a pickaxe, a spade, a military gas-mask, and six carboys of sulphuric acid, all to be delivered the next morning at the cellar door of the shunned house in Benefit Street. After that I tried to sleep; and failing, passed the hours in reading and in the composition of inane verses to counteract my mood.

At 11 A.M. the next day I commenced digging. It was sunny weather, and I was glad of that. I was still alone, for as much as I feared the unknown horror I sought, there was more fear in the thought of telling anybody. Later I told Harris only through sheer necessity, and because he had heard odd tales from old people which disposed him ever so little toward belief. As I turned up the stinking black earth in front of the fireplace, my spade causing a viscous yellow ichor to ooze from the white fungi which it severed, I trembled at the dubious thoughts of what I might uncover. Some secrets of inner earth are not good for mankind, and this seemed to me one of them.

My hand shook perceptibly, but still I delved; after a while standing in the large hole I had made. With the deepening of the hole, which was about six feet square, the evil smell increased; and I lost all doubt of my imminent contact with the hellish thing whose emanations had cursed the house for over a century and a half. I wondered what it would look like—what its form and substance would be, and how big it might have waxed through long ages of life-sucking. At length I climbed out of the hole and dispersed the heaped-up dirt, then arranging the great carboys of acid around and near two sides, so that when necessary I might empty them all down the aperture in quick succession. After that I dumped earth only along the other two sides; working more slowly and donning my gas-mask as the smell grew. I was nearly unnerved at my proximity to a nameless thing at the bottom of a pit.

Suddenly my spade struck something softer than earth. I shuddered, and made a motion as if to climb out of the hole, which was now as deep as my neck. Then courage returned, and I scraped away more dirt in the light of the electric torch I had provided. The surface I uncovered was fishy and glassy—a kind of semi-putrid congealed jelly with suggestions of translucency. I scraped further, and saw that it had form. There was a rift where a part of the substance was folded over. The exposed area was huge and roughly cylindrical; like a mammoth soft blue-white stovepipe doubled in two, its largest part some two feet in diameter. Still more I scraped, and then abruptly I leaped out of the hole and away from the filthy thing; frantically unstopping and tilting the heavy carboys, and precipitating their corrosive contents one after another down that charnel gulf and upon the unthinkable abnormality whose titan *elbow* I had seen.

The blinding maelstrom of greenish-yellow vapour which surged tempestuously up from that hole as the floods of acid descended, will never leave my memory. All along the hill people tell of the yellow day, when virulent and horrible fumes arose from the factory waste dumped in the Providence River, but I know how mistaken they are as to the source. They tell, too, of the hideous roar which at the same time came from some disordered water-pipe or gas main underground—but again I could correct them if I dared. It was unspeakably shocking, and I do not see how I lived through it. I did faint after emptying the fourth carboy, which I had to handle after the fumes had begun to penetrate my mask; but when I recovered I saw that the hole was emitting no fresh vapours.

The two remaining carboys I emptied down without particular result, and after a time I felt it safe to shovel the earth back into the pit. It was twilight before I was done, but fear had gone out of the place. The dampness was less foetid, and all the strange fungi had withered to a kind of harmless greyish powder which blew ash-like along the floor. One of earth's nethermost terrors had perished forever; and if there be a hell, it had received at last the daemon soul of an unhallowed thing. And as I patted down the last spadeful of mould, I shed the first of the many tears with which I have paid unaffected tribute to my beloved uncle's memory.

The next spring no more pale grass and strange weeds came up in the shunned house's terraced garden, and shortly afterward Carrington Harris rented the place. It is still spectral, but its strangeness fascinates me, and I shall find mixed with my relief a queer regret when it is torn down to make way for a tawdry shop or vulgar apartment building. The barren old trees in the yard have begun to bear small, sweet apples, and last year the birds nested in their gnarled boughs.

The Feasting Dead

※※※

JOHN METCALFE

I

Our boy, Denis, had at no time been very strong, and when his mother, whom he had adored, died suddenly, I fetched him from his boarding school by Edinburgh and let him stop for a while at home.

Poor little fellow! I had tended previously perhaps to be a trifle stern with him, but we needed each other now, and I did all I could to make up to him for anything of harshness in the past and soften, for his tender sensibilities, the blow I myself felt so sorely.

No doubt, I had become a thoroughly "indulgent" father and would not, I think, have rued it but for that train of circumstances to be narrated. We were living, then, in the big pleasant old place "Ashtoft", near Winchester, which I had bought on my retirement from the army, and when Denis asked still to stay from school for one more term and 'keep me company' I was secretly flattered I expect as well as comforted. The milder southern air, and his daily rides over the downs, would do him good and he would take no harm from missing a few months of Greek and Algebra.

There was, that May and June, a French family—or rather, a father with his young son and daughter—spending part of the summer in the neighbourhood, and that Denis should like them and they him I found altogether fortunate. Cécile, my wife, had been half French, and when it transpired that our new acquaintances were not only residents of her native province but must actually (as we compared notes and worked it out together) be some sort of distant cousins, this chance encountering seemed more than ordinarily felicitous. Cécile had never tired of talking to Denis of Auvergne—its history, scenery, and above all its legends, some of them she admitted rather shocking—and we had frequently regretted that, as yet, he had not seen it for himself. He could however, read and speak French very tolerably—putting me to a total shame—and now, in a variety of loyalty, I fancy, to his mother's memory, was doubly prejudiced in favour of anything or anyone of Gallic origin.

As for these Vaignons, the father, who cultivated us with considerable assiduity, was, I believed, a landowner of consequence, with a château not far from Issoire. He was a lean, somewhat nervous yet taciturn man, with sunken cheeks and an unhappy brooding manner which I set down to his recent bereavement. The fact that he, too, had lost his wife last year was an added, if unspoken, reason for sympathy amongst us, and I was wholly glad that Denis had the orphaned Augustine and Marcel for his playmates. Truth compels me to confess that they weren't very prepossessing little scamps—being undernourished-looking, swarthy, narrow-eyed and quarrelsome!—but for Denis their society evidently had charm.

"This shall be *au revoir* and not good-bye, M. le Colonel," said M. Vaignon upon leaving. "For Denis, at the least. Denis shall come to see me in Auvergne, if you can spare him, in his holidays, while, to be quits, my own Marcel and Augustine might visit you."

Here was a new idea! But, when I questioned him, Denis, it seemed, knew all about it.

"And would you care to go?" I asked, surprised.

"Oh, yes . . . I may, mayn't I?"

"We'll see . . . Yes, I daresay," I temporised. "Wait and we'll see."

The notion had been rather sprung upon me, yet such holiday exchanges were constantly advertised in the Press, and in the present instance there was an already-existing acquaintance between the families, to say nothing of a degree, if slender, of relationship. As for "holidays"—Denis had had plenty of *them*, lately, but he *would* be off to school again, nearer home, before so long. He had been falling behind, inevitably, in his studies, and now, I thought, he had a golden opportunity of picking up his French.

Next August I went over with him to Foant, saw him installed in M. Vaignon's château, where I stopped one night, and returned placidly enough to Hampshire with Marcel and Augustine the following day.

This arrangement remained in force for well over a year till Denis was thirteen, through several successive holidays, or parts of them. My boy's persistence and perseverance with the business, I must say, somewhat astonished me. What kind of fun could he have there, I wondered, that so attracted him? Marcel and Augustine, when they came to me as they usually did, could largely amuse each other, but Denis had no one of his own age to play with. Cécile had had a young nephew, Willi, her brother's child, but he had died two years ago, or else, I thought regretfully, my Denis might have looked *him* up and found him, possibly, congenial company. Now, even Willi's parents, who had lived within easy drive of the château, had moved to Dijon, and Denis was reduced, as I have said, to M. Vaignon for the supply of entertainment. I was perplexed and, maybe, a shade jealous.

Thus far, I had had but that one glimpse of the château, since it was either M. Vaignon or his major domo Flébard who, on the next few occasions, took the children to and fro; and now, still wondering, I tried to recall the place more clearly.

The château was old, and generally in somewhat poor repair, though its interior was pleasing. Its exterior, and the immediate approaches, had been dusk-shrouded when we arrived, but before that I had had to hire a taxi, at an exorbitant fare, from the nearest station, a dozen miles away, and had had some chance of viewing the countryside between. It was austere, and grimly forbidding, with a burnt-out, cindery quality I found depressing. However, that didn't matter particularly, and our effusive welcome from M. Vaignon, coupled with repeated apologies for the breakdown of the car that should have met us, had reassured me, if I needed it. After Denis was in bed, my host and I had chatted till midnight, over some superlative brandy. There had been, from him, some laughing allusion to a "haunted" turret room, but the story attached to it seemed confused and I could not subsequently recollect it.

"Do you still want to go to Foant *every* holiday?" I had asked Denis once. "Why don't you give a trial to Uncle Michel and Aunt Bette instead? They'd love to have you there with them, at Dijon."

"Oh *no* . . . I like it so at Foant, yes I *do* . . .' A quick anxiety in his tone surprised me.

Till then, I had acquiesced in the arrangement somewhat luke-warmly, though certainly without misgiving; and even now it would be an exaggeration to say I was at all uneasy. Simply, I felt that, from such slight and casual beginnings, the thing had some-how become too important or endured too long.

"But surely, you must be terribly dull there sometimes. What do you do with yourself all day?"

"Oh . . . there's a lot to do. We—' He faltered, embarrassedly, and I experienced a faint, disquiet qualm. His delicacy had always caused his mother and myself concern, and at her death I had feared seriously the effect upon his health. But he had borne his share of grief for her manfully enough and, for a while, had seemed to benefit from exercise and a respite from lessons. At the moment, however, he was nervously flushed—maybe dreading my vetoing his further visits—and his eyes had an odd strained look, as if, the idea curiously struck me, he were carrying some sort of burden.

No more was said, at that time, on the subject, and the appear-ance, the next week, of escort Flébard—a decent, sober fellow who seemed propriety incarnate—temporarily allayed my doubts.

Yet after Denis was gone they naggingly revived. What *was* it, at the château, I could not stop wondering, that held this strong continuing attraction for my boy? Without, exactly, scenting any-thing amiss, I recognised that here was an affair or situation which I had been to blame in not exploring thoroughly, and which, at least, would bear more careful scrutiny.

I resolved that, on Denis's next trip, if there should be one, I would again accompany him, or perhaps bring him back, myself, and possibly, in either case, remain with him at Foant for a day or so before returning.

That visit I remember very well. I remember, at its close, conclud-ing that no, there was really nothing after all to worry about, and then, as a wave of unaccountable depression over-came me, feel-ing as vaguely puzzled and undecided in my mind as ever.

M. Vaignon, pressing me to stop longer than the three days I did, had been almost too attentive a host, scarcely indeed permitting me out of his sight. With his own children (of whom, next year he would see less, one being entered for a lycée at Bourges, the other for a convent school in the same town) he seemed stricter than in Hampshire, and I reflected wryly that, while it lasted, this exchange-system certainly gave him the better of the bargain, for there could be no comparison between my handsome, graceful Denis and his two "replacements"—queer, cryptic little monkeys that they were.

For my sojourn at the château it had turned out more convenient to choose not the beginning but the end of a stay there, by Denis, of four weeks. The hours passed, not disagreeably and till my final night quite unremarkably, in talking, eating, card-playing, sheer loafing, and a short series of amiably conducted tours of the estate. Upon these rambles Denis would go with us, not ill-pleased to assist M. Vaignon in the part of showman, and yet, I thought, a trifle distrait and subdued, his bright head glinting on before us in the sun. It was extremely sultry, the middle of August, and the scorched country frowned quivering around us through a heathaze. Towards Foant, the turmoiled landscape was a gross tumble of smirched rocks, like something caught in the act of an explosion or—a more fanciful comparison occurred to me—as if these riven slabs, seared spires and pinnacles and blackened ingots of fused earth had been the "men" which sportive devils had hurled down upon the gaming-table of the puys in some infernal tourney, and then left in disarray. I told myself I would be very thankful when my boy and I were home.

But what had chiefly struck me during my three days at the château was a peculiar faint change—for all his courtesy—in M. Vaignon. Once, when I referred casually to Denis's next visit, a strange hesitating and constrained look crossed his face.

"Yes," he replied, without conviction. "Ah well, we all grow up, and the best of things come to an end . . ."

That night—the eve of our return to England—I was restless. My feather-bed stifled me, and I remembered that a winding stair outside my room, adjoining Denis's, led to a small garden. To snatch a breath of fresher air I began, in my dressing-gown, to descend the stairway, but stopped short at the sound of voices.

It was M. Vaignon, talking, I rather guessed, to Flébard.

"No, no," the disturbed half-whisper reached me. "We can't
. . . I tell you *hélas*, it has *come again* . . ."

Hastily but softly I retreated. M. Vaignon's last words had been
spoken with a curious emphasis—of fear or of a kind of despairing
disgust—and for an instant I regretted not having waited for a
sentence or two more. Undecidedly I regained the landing, and
saw a crack of light under Denis's door. I gently opened it, and
entered.

"Hello," I said, "so you can't get to sleep either."

"No . . . It's so hot . . ."

He was sitting up in bed, a candle burning in a wall-sconce
beside him. In some way he seemed apprehensive and excited.

"It's not as quiet as you'd suppose, out here in the country," I
remarked, less from an interest in the fact than to conceal my own
continuing agitation. "I thought just now I could hear those old
cows moving in the barn—or it may have been the horses in the
stable . . ."

"—Or the ghost," said Denis, "in the tower room."

I smiled, as I presumed he expected me to smile. "Oh, does the
ghost make noises?" I inquired, preoccupiedly, and with my mind
still running upon M. Vaignon.

"Yes . . ." Denis paused, smiling, too, then added, oracularly:
"Rinking noises. I—I make it make them."

' "*Rinking*" noises?' I came out of my brown study, startled,
somehow, both by this odd description and by a peculiar intonation in his voice.

"Like roller-skating," he exclaimed. "Ever so funny. We—"

He had checked himself abruptly; though the smile lingered on
his lips. It was a smile, I had the unpleasant intuition, that saw
musingly beyond what *I* could see—a smile of some superior intimacy and acquaintance, real or fancied. But I considered it wiser
not, at this time, to pursue the subject. "Good night," I said presently, and went back to my room.

After all this, I had reckoned gloomily on further wakefulness,
yet, actually, fell very soon asleep, arousing with my spirits lightened and refreshed. If it were nothing worse, I remember thinking,
than some absurd superstition that was afflicting M. Vaignon, then
most of my anxiety was groundless. Merely, I was now tired of the
business. Just one more visit, possibly, and then this holiday-ex-
change arrangement must begin to die a natural death.

However, as we were leaving, I had a mild resurgence of my previous qualms. M. Vaignon's looks were wan and the hand that shook mine trembled. Suddenly, a word to characterise his altered manner—the word I had been seeking, unsuccessfully three days —flashed disconcertingly into my brain. "Guilty." But how preposterous . . . ! What had he to feel *guilty* over? And yet . . . A shadow seemed to darken round me and round Denis too as we entered the car and waved our farewells through its windows.

But in the train and on the boat I managed temporarily to re-dismiss my bothersome forebodings. Perhaps M. Vaignon had privately decided that he had seen enough of us, had resolved gradually to drop us, and yet found it hard frankly to tell us so. Well, *I* had felt for my part that the Vaignons latterly were bulking too oppressively and largely on our own Habgood horizon, and if the break did come eventually from their side rather than from mine, so much the better and the easier for me! I was in cheerful mood as we returned to "Ashtoft".

Two days had passed when the postman delivered to me a registered envelope, postmarked Foant. The enclosed letter from M. Vaignon read:

> *Dear Colonel Habgood,*
> *It is with infinite distress that I am driven to inform*
> *you that it has become advisable for the hitherto so*
> *pleasant intimacy between our families to cease; nor can*
> *I, I am afraid, give any explanation of this deplorable*
> *necessity that could satisfy you. I am the victim, it*
> *appears, of a fantastic persecution or visitation with*
> *which it would not be fair that you should any longer*
> *be remotely and even unknowingly associated. This is*
> *the most that I am able to tell you in condonation of a*
> *gesture that must seem so brutal; but, in effect, I have*
> *to draw a* cordon sanitaire *around myself—not for my*
> *own protection but for that of those outside it! I can*
> *only hope, with my most extreme regrets that one*
> *whom I esteem so highly may accept this fact as it*
> *unfortunately stands, and grant me, henceforwards, the*
> *privilege of silence.*
> 　　　　　　　　　*Yours,*
> 　　　　　　　　　　　*V. de la F. Vaignon*

I replaced this amazing missive in its envelope. A little while ago I had been meditating just such a development—but not in this style, no indeed! Was the man mad? Oddly, my predominant emotion was not of hurt, or any anger with him. It was, rather, of bewildered consternation, and even a sort of fear, as if, instead of ending, as it seemed, the real trouble were just beginning.

Somehow, the thing hit me in the face. I did not immediately tell Denis of M. Vaignon's letter, and for over a week I was considerably exercised as to how I could best and most wisely do so. Finally, I let him know of it, saying that the Vaignons were going through some kind of private domestic crisis which would probably prevent his staying again at the château, for some while at least.

Admittedly, this was putting a mighty gloss on the affair, yet how else was I to phrase it? Probably, as I had surmised, M. Vaignon had been brooding this step for several months, and failed to muster courage to declare it verbally—but now its absurd written, black and white, announcement was, in all conscience, blunt to crudity (whatever its excuses, and whatever the dickens "persecution" and "visitation" might be held to mean!)—and I could hardly show Denis *that*.

He received the news quietly, though I felt it a false and deceptive quiet. It must have been a serious matter to him, and, as I see it now, he was inwardly and desperately trying to measure its gravity and to decide how far this set-back might be neutralised or remedied and still accommodated to his own desires. I was extremely sorry for him, and cast about in my mind for anything that would render the blow less wounding, and leave him a little happier.

Oddly and soon enough he himself sought to help me out of this difficulty, but in a fashion I by no means relished.

"I think it'll be Raoul I'll miss most," he said as if reflectively, yet with a certain patness that did not escape me. "I told you about him, didn't I?"

' "Raoul"? No, you didn't.'

"*Didn't* I? Not Raoul Privache? Surely I—"

"No, you never spoke of him. Who is he?"

"Why, he was my greatest friend over there, in a way. I *must* have told you . . . We caught moles and bats together, and went up the puy. He's—well, he's a sort of odd-job man I suppose you'd

call him. He gardens, and fells trees, and looks after horses, and—
Oh, I know!" Denis paused, as though struck by a sudden inspiration. "He could come *here*. He could work for *you*. You need someone like that! Oh, if we had Raoul here I wouldn't mind not going
to the château . . ."

"Nonsense!" I answered brusquely. "Now, *really* . . . How
many licences d'you think I'd have to get for importing an article
like *that* from France?"

What made my tone momentarily bitter had not been the bizarre character of the suggestion so much as the recognition, in my
own boy, of a species of duplicity. For he had never mentioned
this Raoul previously, and must have known it.

While most emphatically I wanted no more Vaignon echoes, of
any sort, size or description.

Denis's brows had contracted in a kind of secret defiance.

"Oh, well," he said glumly, "I expect we'll see him here anyhow
. . . I expect he'll turn up, one day, just the same."

And, the devil of it was, he did. We had finished breakfast, and I
was lighting my pipe in the morning room when I heard a light
tap at the window. Glancing up, I saw a man outside. He was
short and rather shabby, but his face I could not then properly
discern. In an instant, heart-sinkingly, I realised who it must be.
The fellow was gesturing, and I, in turn, found myself echoing his
signals, and pointing sidewise towards the front door, which I
opened for him.

He stood there, in the porch, and again, with vague non-plus-
ment, I had the incidentally worried feeling that, somehow, I
could not make out his features as plainly as I should. But at that
moment there was a scamper of footsteps behind me, and Denis all
but flung himself into the figure's arms. "Raoul! Raoul!" he exclaimed ecstatically. "Oh, I *knew* you'd come!"

"*Bonjour, m'sieu.*" Our visitant had put out a hand, which I
mechanically shook. The hand wore a mitten leaving only the
fingers exposed, and in clasping them I experienced a strange
repugnance. They were cold, and lifeless as a dummy's.

But the man could speak, it soon appeared, and volubly. Denis
had led him to a back room giving on to the lawn, and there the
creature began to chatter, presumably in French of sorts, though
too quickly for my comprehension. Denis translated sketchily.

"Raoul", it seemed, was offering me his services as general handy-
man. He had always wanted to live in England, and to have my
son for his young master would be bliss indeed. His manner, as he
waited while Denis was interpreting, was an odd mixture of defer-
ence and sly assurance.

"But, good heavens!" I protested. "*I* can't employ him. What
about his labour-permit? He can't just plant himself on us like this
and—"

The man sat there, impassive, his shadowed face averted. Denis
was talking with him again, conveying, I supposed, the substance
of my objections.

"He's staying here, in the village anyhow," Denis announced,
"though it would be nicer if he could use our loft over the old
coachhouse while he was looking around . . ."

"He shall *not* use our loft . . . !" I remember almost spluttering
in my dumbfounded indignation.

But, in the end, he did.

Whether a greater, and a prompter, firmness on my part would
have prevented or, later on, ejected him I do not know. I believe
now that it would not, and, in a sense, that what was had to be.

Since Cécile's death I had denied the child nothing, and if such
"pampering" were weakness it had at least been, hitherto, a natural and perhaps pardonable weakness. But my acceptance, or tol-
eration, of this creature, this object, this ambiguous knot-in-a-
board, with whom Denis's infatuation seemed quite in-explicable,
was a capitulation to my boy's half tearful and half sullen impor-
tunities surpassing any previous indulgence.

Be that as it might, "Raoul" took up his abode in the loft, and,
thus confronted with the *fait accompli*, I realised gloomily that it
would mean, now, a lot of unpleasantness and fuss to shift him.
So, for the time being, and the time being only (as I tried to make it
plain), he stayed.

There were nearly three weeks still to run of Denis's summer
holidays, and he spent their waking hours, to my chagrin, almost
entirely in his idol's company. I felt bewildered. Why, actually,
had the man come here, and had there been a prior secret understanding between him and his admirer in the matter? Was his
passport in order (though I presume it must be, for him to have

arrived at all), and what would the neighbours, and my own servants, think?

However, superficially and for a while, there was less trouble than I had anticipated. The fellow, to grant him his due, was unobtrusive to the point of self-effacement and indeed appeared anxious to keep out of people's way. He insisted on some pretence of working for me and occasionally was to be seen polishing boots and harness, clearing dead wood from the shrubbery, and the like. His meals he ate, usually, apart, fetching them from the kitchen, and consuming them in his loft. How he got on with my cook, Jenny, or with my maid Clara I was at first unable to find out. Probably they decided that the curious importation represented merely one more whim of the young master's and for the present let it go at that. As for my regular groom and gardener, Dobbs, he, as it happened, was in hospital, so his reactions were not yet available.

Just the same, the position was bizarre. Denis would shortly be returning to school, and then of course there could be no excuse for Raoul's remaining. I half thought, once or twice, and despite the "silence" so mysteriously enjoined on me, of writing to "sound" M. Vaignon on the subject, but, as may be imagined, I was pretty much on my dignity in that quarter, and had, besides, no right whatever to assume that *he* was implicated or involved in any way with Raoul.

I was on edge and out of sorts, living it seemed unreally in a kind of semi-dream. More and more I became sensible of this man Raoul's presence, irking me in a manner I could not describe. And one small item in particular still teased me. The fellow had been here, now, close on two weeks, and yet for some reason, I had never formed a clear idea of his appearance. Either his features struck me differently at different times or had a queer indefiniteness that amounted, as it were, to nullity. It was not till later that I discovered that this little difficulty of his facelessness had bothered other people too.

One day, less than a week before the end of his holidays, Denis had started a slight cold. It seemed nothing much—and hadn't stopped his going out all morning, as was now his rule, with his obnoxious playmate on the down—but was enough, in view of the nearness of his return to school, to worry me. I remembered telling

him to take it easy indoors for the rest of the afternoon and then
retiring myself, to my study with the intention, I also recall, of
settling, finally, my future course of action in this whole exasperating *"affaire Raoul"*.

But my deliberations had not got very far when they were interrupted by a visit from a Mr Walstron, a local farmer to whom I was
arranging to lease a meadow. Terms having been agreed to mutual
satisfaction, the old man went on to gossip amiably of other
things.

"Your boy misses his mother, sure-*ly*. Up there on the Winacre I
met him this morning, looking right poorly, and chattering away
like that, all to himself . . ."

"To himself? Why he—" I faltered, confused and apprehensive.

"Well, yes . . . Talking, or it might have been singing, you
know, and—funny thing—my two dogs, they—oh, you should 'a
seen 'em. Such a snarling and a snapping . . . ! Never seen 'em
act that way with *your* young lad before . . ."

Presently Mr Walstron wished me good day, leaving me, certainly, with plenty to think over.

It was extremely strange. Denis, I knew, had gone out, not alone
but with Raoul. And then—those dogs . . . For, oddly, it had
been with dogs that Raoul had achieved, as yet, his summit of
unpopularity. My own setter, Trixie, could not abide him, shivering and growling quite dementedly whenever he was by, and
evidently undecided whether to fly from him or at him.

I was still trying to digest the implications of Mr Walstron's
story when the form of Raoul himself darkened the panes. Out-
wardly and otherwise well conducted, he had an annoying habit
of coming round to the windows and tapping to attract attention.
This time, perceiving I had already observed him, he did not tap
but simply held up a hand. To my disgusted consternation I saw
that the wrist and forearm were bloody.

Hurrying out, I examined his hurt. The flesh was badly lacer-
ated. *"Chiens,"* I understood him to mutter. *"Chiens . . ."*

Here was a further complication! Dog bites can be mischievous
and I would not risk attempting to treat such wounds myself. So
far, I had shirked bringing the man's residence to any official or
even semi-official cognisance, but now, if the doctor were called,
my precious piece of contraband must be declared and I foresaw

all sorts of tiresome queries as to the fellow's position under the Health Insurance Act and any amount of stupid fuss . . .

In the event, I summoned my old friend and adviser, Goderich, who had attended Cécile during her last illness. He dressed Raoul's arm and, while on the spot, looked at my boy as well. Denis's cold had got worse. He was running a temperature, and Goderich promised to come again next day.

Reports, then, on the two patients were discouraging. As for Raoul, he had had to be moved to a small attic bedroom. His wound was an ugly one, and I somehow gathered an impression that Goderich was puzzled by the case.

Denis, it seemed probable, would not be fit to return punctually to school and for a time I half suspected him of shamming in order to postpone the parting with his friend. He, Denis, had been told of Raoul's misadventure and pleaded, vainly, to be allowed to see him. The pair were upon different floors, and in different wings, the farther from each other, I had thought, the better.

Raoul's accident (and he could or would not state which dog or dogs it was that had attacked him) had been upon a Thursday, and by the Sunday his arm still showed no improvement. The following morning, Goderich rather surprised me by asking me to "see of myself", and I watched him unwrap the bandages. I caught, I fancied, an expression of something approaching astonishment on his face when the torn flesh was bared. The entire limb below the elbow was swollen and had a repulsive livid hue. Goderich motioned me to go. "I'll see you afterwards," he murmured.

"Well," he said, rejoining me downstairs. "I'll confess I'm a bit foxed. The latest wonder-drug's proved a flop and—it's—it's quite extraordinary, but the whole forearm seems—"

"Yes, what?" I pressed impatiently.

"Why, to have mortified. But it—it *couldn't* have, to that extent, without other associated symptoms, gross symptoms, which just aren't there. Yet—well-pah . . . ! Well, the damn thing almost stinks . . . !"

I stared at him, and he went on. "I'm speaking unprofessionally, Habgood, and not merely being nosey. Precisely how you came by this odd customer I'm not inquiring, but—"

Our talk was interrupted by a scurrying commotion in the passage. The door burst open and Clara entered with scarcely a preliminary knock. "Oh . . . excuse me, sir, but—Master Denis—"

Behind her, at that instant, Denis himself appeared, tearfully distraught.

"What is it?" I said, pushing Clara aside and catching him up in my arms. "What's happened?"

But for a while, after I had carried him back to bed, he refused to tell us. It was only, at first, from Clara that we discovered that Raoul must have stealthily crept from his room, traversed the intervening corridors, and visited the boy. Clara had heard a cry from within the bedroom and seen Raoul emerging just as she arrived upon the scene.

Furious, I was starting off there and then for Raoul's attic, but Goderich restrained me. "Let me," he said. "I'll go."

He was away a long time, and when he returned his words further amazed me.

"Well . . . I give up. I'm not a doctor. Doctors don't see such things . . . Call me a bald-headed Belgian and be done with it . . . I give it up!"

"What do you mean?"

'Why, when I got there, the fellow was smiling—by the way, has he a face to smile with? I'm never sure . . . was sort of smiling and holding out his arm and saying "guéri, guéri", like a cheshire cat . . . if they do . . . I—I'm a bit overcome . . .'

"You mean—?"

"I mean that it *was* cured, *is* cured. A little swelling, and he's a normal slight fever. Here, gimme a tot of your Glenlivet . . . I tell you, I give up."

This episode, itself grotesque, marked the beginning of a fresh, more ominous phase in my relationship with Raoul, and brought into my mind's open a host of doubts and until then but dimly realised fears. Just as the startled eye may all at once perceive the latent shapes of horror in the far, nobly drifting clouds and summer leaves, or as the meek familiar pattern of a wallpaper may spring into a sudden tracery of hell, so now the course of these events revealed a darker trend. The unaccountable affair of Raoul's arm had left me quite uncertain what to believe or disbelieve or what might happen next.

Circumstances had forced me to admit Goderich to my confidence, yet for a while we each fought shy of a direct discussion.

What had occurred was so fantastically out of line with ordinary experience that we had, I suppose, to try somehow to deny and to discredit it a little even to ourselves.

Raoul made a complete recovery, and my determination to evict him was renewed. Denis however remained by no means well and I still shrank from distressing him. As if guessing what I meditated he had grown louder than usual in his companion's praises.

"You don't like him," he accused, reproachfully yet with a suppressed tight smile that had about it—how shall I express it?—a sort of odd repugnant coyness.

"I—well, I just don't see anything much in him . . . He can't stay here forever."

"Why, what harm does he do? I *wish* you liked him . . ."

I did not answer and we turned presently to other topics, but I continued baffled and, in some deeper sense, dismayed. It might be, as Denis said, that Raoul appeared to do no active harm, but it was this very negativity that partly was the trouble and made his evident attraction for my boy so utterly incomprehensible. The fellow, in his coarse labourer's clothes and ridiculous mittens, was an incongruity and an excrescence on the English countryside— and yet his most outstanding characteristic, to be paradoxical, was his characterlessness. He seemed as sinisterly unresponsive and empty of emotion as a robot.

The date when Denis should have returned to school was passed. He had got better, then had a relapse, developing a variety of low undulant fever. An X-ray of his chest reassured me as to the state of his lungs, but the symptoms did not abate.

I was disappointed also in finding it, now, the harder to give Raoul his *congé*, and I could not but connect the two things in my mind. Raoul, I was certain, was somehow the cause of Denis's poor appetite, his wan and wasted look, and alternating fits of nervous stimulation and depression. Denis slept in a room close to mine, and once or twice I fancied I heard noises of bumping and what I could then only describe as a kind of dull sustained metallic humming coming from it. A dark suspicion visited me. Could Raoul be there? But on softly opening the door I found Denis alone and apparently asleep. The noises, if there had been any, had entirely ceased.

However, and recalling the anomaly—or prodigy—of the instantaneously healed arm, I remained still convinced that Raoul must be, ultimately, their author.

This instinct or persuasion—that Raoul was the source of some pernicious influence destructive of my boy—gained steady strength. Denis's manner to me had changed, and his constant terror that I should part him from his strange playmate was obvious. While, more specifically, the noises I had heard *were* noises, I would swear it. They increased towards midnight but for a time, whenever I approached, died down.

Goderich, up to a point, did what he could, but was, I felt, as well aware as I that tonics and cough mixtures did not touch the matter's root. At last, after I had told him of the odd sounds, he remarked, mildly: "If I were you, Habgood, I *would* consider getting rid of that chap "Raoul", you know . . . I really would."

The restraint of this recommendation was almost comical, but I did not smile.

"Do you know anything *about* him? I was just wondering if, by any chance, he had ever had anything to do with your wife's family—worked for them once maybe, and used that as an introduction to you? I'm only guessing . . ."

"Oh, no," I replied confidently enough. "Denis chummed up with the beauty in the Vaignon's village in Auvergne, that's all."

"These noises—is there ever anything broken or disarranged as well, after you hear them?"

"No, I've—wait a bit though . . ." Yes, I remembered, I *had* found a vase smashed once, and more than once had noticed drawers pulled out, and a general air of untidiness or confusion. I told Goderich so.

"Well, pass the word if that sort of thing hots up. And, seriously, I *should* give that chap the boot. It'll upset the lad, but—I should risk it."

When Goderich had gone I pondered his indubitably sound advice lugubriously. I could readily guess what had been at the back of his mind in asking, as to the noises, whether anything had been broken or moved about, yet the notion of poltergeist activities, while certainly sufficiently unpleasant, did not appear, entirely, to fit the case. They might, for all I knew, be present but, even so, would fall short of providing a complete explanation.

For, possibly, the hundredth time I vowed that Raoul *must* go;

and indeed, quite apart from my own resolutions, matters were coming to a head. The commotions in Denis's room increased, being heard now by the servants, and were at last admitted by Denis himself. He denied all responsibility for them—in which I fully believed him—but did not seem afraid of, or disturbed by, them.

"But don't they wake you up and spoil your rest?"

"Oh . . . sometimes. But I don't care. I go to sleep again."

He looked restive under my interrogation. Nowadays, he was dressed and intermittently able to stroll out of doors if it were sunny, but spent much of his time in a *chaise-longue*, either in his room or, latterly, with Raoul, on a glass-roofed veranda. The pair would sit there, conversing softly, the man whittling sticks which he would fashion into a variety of uncouth dolls, and my boy watching him, fascinatedly, as if the world's fate hung upon these operations.

Denis glanced up at me appealingly. "Promise me something."

"What?" But I guessed what it would be.

"That—that you won't send Raoul away."

"Well, as I've said already, he can't stay forever. Why do you think I shouldn't send him away?"

Denis's eyes, wide in some secret conjuring of disaster, met mine squarely. "It would kill me," he said simply.

As well as I might, although, I felt, evasively and with some sacrifice of honesty, I pacified him, and then left him. What *could* I do? Denis, of course, had been exaggerating and distraught, but such words, from a child . . . !

Of late, he had grown appreciably thinner, and I had only to contrast these waxen cheeks and pallid lips with his comparatively vigorous appearance a short month ago to realise the alarming swiftness of the change. To say I could not *prove* this to Raoul was idle. It was from Raoul's arrival that the symptoms dated, and it was from him, I was certain, that they sprang. This lay-figure—this *fantôche*, this hollow puppet—was the unhallowed instrument of a vile infestation that had assaulted Denis's whole physical and moral organism . . . Watching the two together (as I was often able from a window overlooking the veranda) I would be driven into a kind of agony of speculation as to the nature of the bond between them. My boy's face, raptly brooding or wearing that charmed smile I loathed even more, was usually averted, but I caught on it, sometimes, an enthralled abandon or absorption that would chill my blood. The creature Raoul, meanwhile, in his adorer's presence, would seem re-animated, made less neuter and less negative, as if his very being was enhanced and—how to put it?—as if it were at Denis's expense, by Denis's depletion of vitality, that he existed or that his actuality was heightened, as if, as the one waxed, the other shrank and waned . . . Scarcely troubling to hide my agitation as such ideas possessed me, I had tried, once or twice, to break in upon the pair in these ambiguous intimacies, but, I soon recognised, to no avail. The two would fall momentarily silent, Denis looking half guilty and half angry; then, as I knew, the instant that my back was turned their curious *tête-à-tête* would recommence.

Nevertheless, despite its accumulating worry and distraction, my life had still preserved a surface ordinariness and normality. Friends would occasionally drop in on me, or I on them, as heretofore, and I do not think, now, that they noticed much amiss. To be sure, they commented upon Denis's exhausted, drooping air and sympathised with my anxiety about him, but they can have seen little of Raoul, and probably the "gossip" I had tended to imagine rife was confined chiefly to my own household.

There, certainly, there must have been some. Clara and old Jenny, even while not appreciating its significance, could not be blind (and deaf) to a good deal of what was happening under their noses, and their refusal to spread tales or "fuss" was testimony to their loyalty and long-suffering discretion.

As for Raoul's outward or official status, this had been regularised with less ado than I expected. A week or so after his arrival, on the insistence as I learned surprisedly of Denis, he had gone into Winchester and, Denis acting as interpreter, registered at the police station as an alien.

"What did he put himself down as?" I had asked disturbedly. "Not as my employee, I hope." And "Oh, no," Denis reassured me. "Just as a visitor. Just as your guest." That sounded well enough and I had grudgingly had to give Denis credit for his enterprise, but to confirm it I went in myself next day to Winchester. Yes, everything, I was told, was quite in order; oh yes, perfectly . . . I would have been interested to see the passport which must have been produced by Raoul, but had not pressed the matter.

I was recalling this piece of compliance with legalities—comfortingly factual and satisfactory-seeming so far as it went—to Goderich.

"'M . . .'" he mused dubiously. "The blighter's an infernal incubus whatever else he is or ain't, and I wish you could just show him the door. As I've confessed, I'm a finger or so out of my depth . . . The case is fairer game I fancy for a psychical researching bloke, or a psychiatrist. You're prejudiced, I realise, against *them*, and I'm not insisting, but—I'm worried about *you*, as well as Denis. I'll have two patients here, instead of one, directly . . ."

It was true that the business was wrecking me. Each day, I felt that I could stand no more and that, to end it, I should be driven to some act of violence.

When I, eventually, *was* so driven it appeared, for a short time, almost a relief.

The situation had continued to deteriorate. Denis, after a session with his dear, would wear an aspect veritably of the grave, and the idea which had been shaping in my mind before beseiged me now with an increasing force. He is losing something, giving something, I thought, but he would not *want* to do that, do it deliberately, more or less voluntarily, for nothing. He must get something, be tempted by something, in return—but what—ah, what?

I lived in a waking nightmare, and the idea's hold on me grew stronger. That Denis's delicately nurtured boyhood should fall prey to the appetites of an amorphous doll and become the meat of this uncanny zany seemed of all things the most abominable. The details and precise technique of such infernal commerce were beyond my fathoming, but that the ghastly trade existed and that Denis was its dedicated victim I felt positive. *Who* was this "Raoul"? When he had first arrived I had attempted, if simply in grudging "common courtesy", to engage him in conversation, but his thick Auvergnat dialect (as I presumed it) had defeated me, and nowadays I did not try to talk with him. As I watched him through the window, whittling his sticks and looking rather like a well-fed scarecrow, a speechless rage possessed me. Was the man knave or loon? For hours on end, complacently yet dully and only his hands moving, he would squat there, with the bland corpulence and mindless sedentary persistence of some gigantic blowfly and my own hands would writhe in fury. "If I could catch him at it," I thought chokingly, "—if I could catch him at it I would strangle him . . ."

"If I could catch him . . ." Yes . . . I had, emotionally, a very vague and general notion or suspicion of what might be going on, but that was all. While, as for "evidence" . . . If this dumb, gangrened oaf were a variety of psychic leech as I surmised, able to tap and suck away my boy's vitality, his health and spiritual stamina, how was it done? It was probably, I realised, a vain or at least not ordinarily answerable question, yet the business, I argued, must have some sort of "rationale", some sort of place and time. During a good part of the day the pair were under—or liable, if I chose, to come under—my observation, and I hardly believed Denis received his consort in his bedroom, or vice versa. Latterly, Raoul had returned to his old sleeping-quarters in the loft, and in any case I had taken, I considered, adequate precautions against a nocturnal meeting. It was, however, then—between dusk and midnight—that the "noises" and other disturbances were most troublesome; and this too, I reflected, fitted in with my "theory" to some extent. Poltergeists, I had heard, were regarded as the prankish play of a surplus vital force or energy; and it was just after this force's flow, from Denis, had been stimulated but yet deprived, temporarily, of its accustomed receptacle in Raoul that the impish manifestations, centring round my boy, were commonest. As to the poltergeists themselves, if poltergeists they were, I was not primarily concerned about or bothered by them, and it was commentary enough upon the situation, as I saw it, that such a matter should be reckoned a mere minor and subsidiary nuisance.

Could it be only—how long?—barely five weeks today, since "Raoul" appeared . . . ?

At this time, my nights were as a rule dark stretches of tormented wakefulness, and when—not, often, till towards early morning—I did fall asleep, my rest would usually be broken, and haunted by appalling dreams.

One of these I especially remember.

I was in France, and Cécile was still with me. She had been recounting, it seemed, a legend of her native province and, with an unexplained urgency, was directing my attention to a particular passage in a book. We were both standing by a wide window, and the diabolically piled Silurian landscape of Auvergne stretched from us, for many leagues, under a breathless summer heat. But the odd thing was that Cécile was holding the book up in front of her face, and expecting me to read it *through* its covers and all the intervening pages! This, in some miraculous manner, I was able, in my dream, to do, though with difficulty and a sense of growing apprehension and oppression. Of one sentence, which she was extraordinarily anxious I should read, I could make out four words only: ". . . shall feast upon thee . . ." I was on the point, I thought, of deciphering the rest when suddenly the book slipped from my wife's hands, revealing, not her face, but—empty air. With a cry of terror, I awoke.

The dream *was* only a dream, and probably, just before I fell asleep, my mind had again been running on Goderich's query, once, as to a possible connection between Raoul and Cécile's family; yet its tense, loaded flavour clung to me, and had the quality, somehow, of a presentiment.

I felt I had no need to ask of what. For a good while now I had been scarcely capable of keeping up the pretence of normal living, and a crisis would not be long delayed. "If I could catch him at it," I found myself always repeating, "If I could catch him . . ."

And then, one day, I did.

It was an afternoon in October and Denis had been sitting, with his inseparable companion, on the sun-porch. Occasionally, he would desist from his talking and take up a book. It was a child's book from the shelves of his old nursery, and I was mildly surprised that he should still be interested in what I thought he had outgrown.

The veranda, as I have said, was glass-topped, and there was a glass-paned wind-break at one end too. Branches of a wisteria tree at the side had been persuaded to straggle irregularly over part of the roof, and there were pots of hydrangeas along the front. The blooms, now, were past their best, but the place retained a faded greenness and a, to me, pleasantly shabby, half-neglected air which I should have been sorry to see give way to greater trimness.

A window, as I have also said, commanded a restricted view of this semi-enclosed space, and it was through this window (the high french window of a small spare parlour) that I had often, with an uneasiness that had mounted, as the weeks dragged by, to anguish, watched my boy and his companion. Yet what was the

good of that, I asked myself? They must realise, by this, my bursting suspicions and antagonism, and, to them, my harrowed
glances would be merely "spying". Denis was alienated from me
—from his own father—and there was nothing I could do.

On this afternoon I quickly abandoned such entirely fruitless
surveillance. I must find something to occupy my thoughts and
hands or else go mad, and I had remembered a broken fence by the
apple orchard that needed mending. But, having collected hammer and nails, I had scarcely started on my job before a fearful
premonition of disaster gathered in my brain. I was aware, as if by
a direct insight, of something enormously, incredibly evil. I must
go back . . . This recognition of sheer calamity was so overpowering that I instantly dropped my tools and actually started running towards the house.

However, an instinct of discretion slowed my steps and I approached more cautiously. I could not, where I was, be seen from
the veranda but, to make doubly sure, I took a devious route
around a hedge of macracarpa. Mingled with my apprehension
was a swelling rage. How could I have been so blind, I remember
thinking, to what was going on under my nose? For that was what
it had amounted to. Why had I fancied that this infernal traffic
necessarily required a set "rendezvous", or any physical propin-
quity? "I will strangle him," I heard myself saying. "He deserves it
and I shall do it." It was as if my fingers were upon the creature's
neck, as if time were foreshortened or in some fashion telescoped,
as if what was to happen had already happened and I was already
there . . .

The October day was waning as, very quietly, I re-entered the
parlour, tip-toed across the room, and looked.

Raoul, from where I stood, was invisible, but I could see Denis
plainly, still sitting, as I had left him, in a battered old wicker chair,
reading his book. Or rather, he was not so much "sitting" as
crouching, hunched forward in an odd stiff posture on the edge of
the chair-seat. A last shift of reddening light drew frail fire from
his blond hair, but his face was hidden by the book.

An intimation of horror and of an unnameable corruption filled
my heart. Something in Denis's queer locked attitude, in his whole
appearance, utterly dismayed and sickened me.

Hardly breathing, I stole nearer. My movement was very soft, but Denis must have caught or have divined it, for he started violently. The book slipped from his hands.

Upon his suddenly revealed face was an expression I will not describe. It was open before me, like a dreadful flower. Evil, we know, exacts its dues of ruin from the tenderest transgressors, but the reverse side of the matter is less willingly admitted and more shocking; and now the swift unveiling for me of sin's fleeting wage to my unhappy boy was beyond words appalling.

I would, if I could, have shut my eyes on what I had surprised. Denis's features, fixed in their long enchantment, wore a look that was a travesty of boyhood and a blasphemy of all my memories of him. The face, in its ecstasy, was laced and hemmed, and old, with an oldness that had nothing to do with years. Watching him, while the running sands of his being received their frightful recompense, I too was a prisoner to an unreal eternity, though in my case of anguish.

Then, instantaneously, the spell was broken, as Denis gave a low despairing cry. I flung apart the french windows and dashed on to the veranda.

Where was Raoul? Denis, I must subconsciously have told myself, would recover presently from his half-swoon and my first business was with his despoiler. Had the thing vanished? Not altogether. Below the veranda, in the direction of the shrubbery, I indistinctly glimpsed it, already in lumbering flight.

I caught it up beside the hedge of macracarpa, making for the coach-house. The figure, shadowy in the fading light, had turned at my approach and in an odd ineffective way put up a fumbling arm to keep me off.

My hands closed round its throat and for a while we struggled, swaying. Some seconds passed, and as yet the loathsome ninny had remained quite silent, but, all at once, I heard a little noise. It is said that certain creatures, ordinarily voiceless, may in extremity, find feeble tongue—that, in the agony of boiling, wretched lobsters compass a last faint unexampled squeak—and it was, now, of such a puny cry that I was put in mind. The sound filled me with revulsion.

My fingers pressed more strongly, Raoul, as we grappled, was being forced slowly backwards towards a tree-trunk, against which it was my idea to pin him and . . .

Either he had managed to trip me, or I had slipped and stumbled. The two of us crashed heavily, I uppermost. For some seconds longer I was still aware of him beneath me, writhing and battling, yet, somehow, eluding me; but the next moment, he had gone.

Dazedly, I picked myself up and gazed round me in search of the thing that had melted into vacancy from my grasp; and there was no sign of it, anywhere at all.

II

They were black days that followed—I cannot convey *how* black. Though, with the exit of Denis's sinister playfellow, the worst seemed over, I felt in my heart, chilly, that this was only an uneasy breathing-space and that the story, yet, was far from done.

"Breathing-space"—no, it was not really even that. Raoul, I hoped, was banished, but his work remained. Denis was ill. Staring at me with horror and aversion, as if *I* were the sole author of his misery, he could scarcely bear that I should speak to him or go near his bed. The loss, I recognised with anguish, of his frightful parasite and paramour had virtually prostrated him, and he had ceased to be the boy Cécile and I had loved.

As to the eerie lummox who had plagued us, I concluded that he had succeeded, somehow, in wriggling free from me and fleeing, that he would probably make his way back to France, and that, at least in person (if he *were* a person) he would trouble us no more. Or rather, this was what I tried to tell myself I had concluded. Truth is not necessarily or always "sober", and there was something here, I realised inwardly, of which all ordinary "sane" explanations and conjectures failed to take account.

Denis, when I had re-entered the house after Raoul's flight, had been in a half-faint. The servants, roused by my running footsteps along the veranda, had found him lying by the chair, and carried him to his room. Reviving, he had set up a low continuous moaning which did not abate till Goderich, whom I had at once rung up, had given him a sedative. That had secured him a night's sleep; but next day, as I have said, he would hardly suffer my approach, and once had even barricaded his door against me. I was at my wit's end, and terrified less he should do himself an injury.

Goderich shared my anxiety.

"Have you discovered any more about this unholy creature, now he's gone?" he asked.

' "Any more?" Why, how—'

"I mean that, now he *has* gone, tongues might wag a bit more freely. Your servants', for instance . . ."

"Oh yes," I agreed. "yes . . . plenty of that!"

It was a fact that Jenny and Clara had unbosomed themselves to me of a good deal as to Raoul and their sentiments towards him which they had hitherto repressed—though without adding materially to my actual information. I told Goderich so.

"How did you explain the fellow's sudden disappearance to them?"

"I didn't. In any detail. They must have guessed that I—well, chased him off. I don't think they cared how he went, as long *as* he went."

"M . . . well, honestly, I feel I can't do much. I wish you *would* try a psychiatrist . . ."

But I was not ready for that, yet. And was there, possibly, an ever so slightly hurt or reproachful tone in my friend's voice? If so, it must have been because he could divine that with him too, in my description of the final scene, I had been reticent of what I had called "details" . . .

Denis recovered to the extent of leaving his bed and room and occasionally loitering, alone, about the orchard and the meadow; but we were strangers to each other. My acquaintance, or partial acquaintance, with his dreadful secret made me a terror to him, and there seemed something pathetically horrible in the evident efforts of this child to wrest the situation to his own partisan, extenuating view of it—to digest, modify or soften it so as to render it more tolerable to him, and to see me, not Raoul, as his enemy.

It could not, I would think, go on like this. How, if I lived to be a hundred, could I forget—or *he* forget that I must still remember? I would remind him always. As he grew up, if not already, in a sham so poignantly embarrassed, he would wish my death . . .

Thus, for a week or so, matters continued. My uncertainty as to what had really happened to Raoul prevented my finding much consolation even in his absence, and soon after his disappearance I had a visit from the Winchester City police. "Privache," they said

(at first I barely recalled the fellow's surname) had failed to report
at the expiration of one month's residence—and was he with me
still? I could only reply, with a modicum of truth, that he had run
off suddenly, I had no notion where. "Run off?" "Yes." I explained
that the defaulter was a friend of my boy's of whom I had practically no knowledge; and I could see that my worthy—and, to me,
very respectful—constable was dissatisfied and puzzled. "He
should 'a checked out properly,' he grumbled. "If'e went back to
France, now, there'd be trouble and an 'itch, you see, o' some kind,
at the port."

Meanwhile the improvement in Denis's condition had been, at
least superficially, maintained. That was, he looked a shade less
pale and had a better appetite. The nightly thumpings, hummings
and (a new ingredient) derisive hootings had, however, increased,
the racket finally attaining such proportions that, out of consider-
ations for my domestics' rest, I had his bedroom changed to one as
far from theirs as possible.

To me, his manner remained stubbornly hostile. I had plead-
ingly attempted to get him to speak openly, frankly and give me
his own version of affairs, but quite in vain. It seemed but too
apparent that he had suffered a veritable bereavement and was
still pining for his vanished mate. Reluctantly, I was beginning to
resign myself to taking Goderich's advice and trying a psychiatrist. This course would pretty evidently expose me, as well as the
patient proper, to a good deal of awkwardness and incredulous
silly catechisings, but I must shirk no measure that might restore
my boy.

The leaves were falling and the October days growing colder
when I happened to receive a note reminding me of the approaching anniversary dinner of my old regiment. I had never missed
attending it, and the formal invitation card was enclosed, but now
I had no heart to go, and besides it would be out of the question.
On the other hand, it was from Winchester, barely six miles away,
that Mayfield, who had been my adjutant and was organising the
affair this year, had written me. He chanced, he told me, to be
spending the inside of a week there on business—and he was
probably expecting, I surmised, that I should ask him to stay with
me instead of at his hotel, at any rate for Saturday and Sunday.

This too, as matters were, was scarcely practicable, but the least
I could do, I thought, was to run over to Winchester and see him. I

decided to risk leaving Denis in Jenny's and Clara's care, and drove off after lunch.

My chat with Mayfield, to whom I explained the position so far as necessary, was as pleasant as anything could be in my state of worry about Denis, but I hurried home from it so as to arrive by tea-time.

Clara and Jenny, to my dismay, were both waiting for me at the porch, and their first words, as I jumped out of the car, told me the worst.

Denis had gone.

Self-reproach was as useless as unavoidable. I had to act.

"When did you miss him?" I asked.

It had been only twenty minutes ago. He had been on the veranda, and then, no longer seeing him there and wishing to reassure themselves, they had looked for him. His room was empty, and fairly tidy, but a small suit-case was undiscoverable, likewise some socks and a shirt. The most conclusive piece of evidence, however, which seemed to rule out hope that he had merely set off for a walk and might return, was the fact that Jenny's room also had been entered, and her money stolen.

"How much?"

"Four pounds ten, sir. I—I had it in a little china box and was going to bank it Tuesday."

Expecting me at any moment, they had not as yet given an alarm to the police, and I decided, rather than telephone, to drive back again myself to Winchester. Meanwhile, Jenny could ring me at the police station if my poor truant did, after all, return.

The desk sergeant knew me well and listened attentively to my story. "It's early yet,' he encouraged, "and he *may* be just—just larking. But of course we'll notify it and alert other stations round about. Five-fifteen now . . . He can't be very far."

"And watch the ports too," I reminded him. My first thought, naturally, had been of Raoul, and my first fear that Denis was rejoining him.

"Oh, yes, we'll do that, as routine—although he couldn't get across, you know, without a passport."

As to that I had, privately, my doubts. Given sufficient determination, there *were* ways of doing it, as a recent instance happened to have shown.

After a further consultation—this time with the local superin-
tendent in his adjoining sanctum—I drove home.

"No news, I suppose, Jenny?"

"No, sir."

With what fortitude we could we resigned ourselves, as re-
morseful empty hours passed, to the wretched, and in my case
almost sleepless, night.

Feeling that the emergency had more than justified my breaking
any rule of silence, I sent a wire of inquiry to M. Vaignon. An
answer arrived, fairly promptly: "Not here yet."

This left me more "up in the air" than ever, and in vain did I
strive to supply, as it were, the real and un-telegraphable intonation of the word "yet". It sounded as if M. Vaignon rather expected that Denis *might* come, later—but I could not be sure.

I returned to the question of the passport. Denis *had* had a passport—an individual one, to allow of his escort sometimes by
Flébard and sometimes by myself. But I had locked it up after his
last trip, and had it locked up still. In any case, I thought, he must
have realised that, before he could possibly reach the coast, the
dock police would have been warned, so that the document would
be useless to him.

The Winchester district, I was told, had been combed thoroughly without result and, as time passed, it surprised me that a
boy could elude the police net for so long. It argued, certainly,
either a degree of ineptitude on the one side or considerable
adroitness and resource upon the other. Perhaps, whatever official
incredulity might say, Denis had succeeded, by walking only at
night and spending each day up a tree (in a manner I had read of)
in striking a place where French fishing-boats put in, and then
bribed some sailor into smuggling him across . . .

This notion was if anything strengthened by a discovery made
by Clara when the hunt was six days old. She ran excitedly to me
in my study one morning, crying: "Oh, we've found something!"

It transpired that, in cleaning out the loft, she had come upon
two loaves, two tins of sardines and a can-opener, a jar of marma-
lade *and* the suit-case, which was empty—a veritable *cache!*

These objects, which I went with her to inspect, had been hidden under sacking near a back door giving on to a short outer stair
by which access could be gained to the loft without first passing

through the coach-house below. Close by, I noticed with aversion, was a collection of the grotesque wooden dolls, something like ninepins, which Raoul had been used to whittle and—most significantly—an empty opened tin and scattered crumbs showed that one meal at least had been consumed up there already.

However illogically, this find, and particularly the abandoned suitcase, established as an emotional certainty in my mind the belief that Denis had managed to reach France, or was upon his way there. He had been clever enough, I told myself, to lie hidden in the immediate vicinity while the search was most intensive, and then to slip off by night as I had supposed. Yes, that was it—that must be it! I came to a prompt decision.

That very afternoon, having rung Goderich to tell him what I contemplated, I set off for Southampton, calling in at the Winchester police station *en route*. I could see that my plan to "pursue" (they would not admit that it *was* that) my boy to France had met with official scepticism and disfavour, but—though I did concur in the suggestion that a watch be set, if all too tardily, around the loft —I would not allow the cold water thrown on it to weaken my resolve.

And, as it happened, while I was not to know it then, I had only as it were anticipated matters by a single night. A second wire from M. Vaignon, I learned later, "Denis here", arrived for me the morning after I had left.

Once more, the prosaic and accustomed train, my gentle heaving bunk upon the almost accustomed channel packet, and the familiar harbour of Le Havre at misty dawn. The same, yes all the same, and yet how different! Many times had I made this crossing, but with a heart unracked, as now, by care.

Eating my *petit déjeuner* in the station buffet when I had passed through the customs, I brought a newspaper and a further supply of brioches and again boarded the train.

Paris and lunch, then southwards—on to what?? As we begun to breast the gradual ascent towards the *massif* a vague but dreadful apprehension grew upon me. I had dashed off from England, I realised, largely because inaction had become intolerable—yet here, in France, I quailed. It was as if, while I approached that black and tortured landscape of Auvergne, I were adventuring foolhardy into some citadel of evil powers, pitting my puny strength against a host of devils.

I took up my newspaper and tried to read—in vain. Denis, I thought, where are you? What are you doing now—and why?

With an effort, I forced myself to re-examine, as critically and calmly as I might, the chain of circumstances that had led to my being where I was, and upon such a quest.

Vaignon—and Raoul . . . The whole business of the holiday exchanges had been so casual, so casual, so benign, and yet—yes, . . . There must be some connection, beyond mere coincidence, between the two.

I recalled M. Vaignon's brooding and half-guilty looks—and that peculiar scrap of conversation I had overheard. "It has *come again*,' he had said then to Flébard. What had "come again"? Could it . . .

Suddenly my mind snapped on something, and deliberately, for a second, I made it blank, as if afraid of the light that threatened all at once to flood it. I even grabbed my paper and feigned a furious engrossment in its long columns of advertisements. Next moment, however, I gave up the pretence, and a sigh escaped me—a sort of cold sigh of recognition and admission. "Could it . . . ?" Why yes, of course it could. The "It" of M. Vaignon's terrified lament was—Raoul.

How this lurking while fairly obvious conjecture had managed to get itself hushed up in the recesses of my brain (as I am sure it had) for such a time before issuing forth at last to startle me I did not know. But I found it, now, a highly disturbing one. Without, as yet, being able to appreciate all its implications I felt, dimly, a kind of spreading illumination, as though the contours of some formidable truth would presently emerge.

To reach Foant I had, directly, to change to a slower train, with a number of stops. The countryside remained, on the whole, placidly pastoral, but I fancied I began to detect in it, here and there, faint earnests or intimations of that sinister quality which the Auvergne whither I travelled had always held for me. M. Vaignon would be prepared for my coming, since I had telegraphed him from Le Havre, but what sort of welcome he would accord me I had no idea. I had not, it must be remembered, received the wire from him that would arrive at "Ashtoft" the next morning, and I had nothing, at the moment, but my impulsive intuition to lead me to suppose Denis at the château.

The sun was westering as we slackened speed for Foant, and before that, of course, the scenery had assumed the intimidating gigantism and catalclysmic look of violence which, every time I visited the place, had sent a shiver up my spine.

Alighting, I stared round me but could see no one, on my own island platform or on either of the other two except the ticket collector and a couple of peasant women. Perhaps M. Vaignon was so indignant at my flat defiance of his previous virtual prohibition that he was not sending anyone to meet me! Owing to his strange imposition of silence I had felt unable to write to him—or question him maybe concerning Raoul—and though I now suspected him of knowing more about it than he might confess, his official state was one of ignorance, and he might not appreciate the seriousness of the case.

For a quarter of an hour I waited impatiently in the little *selle d'attente.* Had M. Vaignon actually resolved to deny me his hospitality? But no; he *had* answered my first wire, and surely, in common humanity, he couldn't be such a bear—and such a brute!

I was however on the point either of telephoning the château or, without doing so, of hiring, if I could, a taxi, when a car hurtled furiously into the station yard. It hurtled in *so* furiously that I experienced a curious start of anticlimax at sight of the form that crawled feebly out from the driving-seat.

The figure advanced immediately, with a sort of frenzied impetuous hobble, towards me.

Yes, it was M. Vaignon.

III

Question and answer between us tumbled over each other, standing on no ceremony of greeting. "Is he with you?"

"Yes . . . but you could not have my telegram so soon."

"Is he—all right?"

"He—you will see . . ."

We got into the car. "Flébard", M. Vaignon explained interjectorily, "has left, and it is I who am chauffeur. I fear I am late."

I mumbled something, to which he paid no attention. We had shot out of the station yard into the gathering dusk of the highway, M. Vaignon still driving like a maniac. His manner, notwithstanding, had a kind of distrait, debonair moroseness, and the conditions generally, as we careered wildly onwards, were unfavourable to conversation. Yet I did, once, attempt it. "Denis has been terribly ill," I said. "He is not himself, or he would not have run away, and I would not have had to trouble you. How does he seem, now?"

M. Vaignon's nearer shoulder gave me an absent shrug. "I cannot tell you . . . We are all bedevilled, n'est-ce pas, and the evil days are on us. They are on your boy, who does not know you are here, but won't, I bet you, let you talk to him, or get within ten feet of him . . ."

My heart sank, but despair goaded me to a flare of anger too. "We shall see about that!" I said.

The château, when we entered it at nightfall, was a place of dark, uneasy stillness. A man whose face was unfamiliar had admitted us and he immediately retreated again from us.

"Where is Denis?" I asked M. Vaignon. "Where is he?"

We had passed, from the hall, into a small salon to the left, wherein, I remembered, it had once been promised that Denis should devote a daily hour to the study of De Musset, the Dumas and Victor Hugo. Whether he had ever done so I doubted, but two walls of the room were book-lined.

"Where is he?" I repeated, but at this very instant, hearing a step along the hall, I glanced up towards the door, and there, staring back frozenly at me, was—Denis.

It was a glimpse only that I had of him for with a kind of indignantly affrighted "Ah . . ." he vanished. I rushed out after him into the hall, calling his name.

A man—it was he who had let us in—stood there. "Dinner will be—" he was beginning.

"Where is my boy, le jeune garçon?" I interrupted him. "Which way did he go just now? Which is his room?"

The fellow regarded me consideringly as he replied, slowly: "The same . . . but—" He stopped, then, with a quick and as if guilty or surreptitious movement, crossed himself.

Denis's old room was on the first floor, by the stairhead. Having run up to it, I tried the door, but it was locked and there was no answer to my knocks. "Denis!" I cried. "Denis, are you there?"

Not a sound. It was just possible though most unlikely that the door had been locked from the outside. I knocked and called again, in vain.

Descending to the *salon*, I debated, wretchedly. It appeared but too evident that M. Vaignon had spoken truly and that Denis had not ceased to regard me as his enemy. I recalled, in misery, the intonation of his *"Ah . . . !"* when he caught sight of me some moments since. It had been an "Ah!" not merely of disconcertment and dismay but, I realised, of actual execration.

M. Vaignon had come out into the hall. "You see," he murmured drily, "I was right . . ."

At dinner, no place was laid for Denis, and M. Vaignon must have noticed my disappointedly inquiring glances. In the presence, however, of the ever-attendant Dorlot (as, I gathered, was his name) nothing of any importance could be said, and our talk was of trivialities.

Meanwhile, my mind ran feverishly on what I had so far discovered. It had already seen, alas, enough to recognise that matters could not be adjusted offhand, or hurried, and that the home-bringing of my poor prodigal would prove no simple and probably no brief procedure. There would be difficulties, especially in a foreign country, about compelling him, forcibly, to go with me, and, in consulting with M. Vaignon and striving to come at the inner truth of the whole business, I must do what I could to practise greater patience and restraint.

After the meal I again followed M. Vaignon into the *salon*, where he motioned me to a seat by the fire.

"As you will doubtless have observed," he began immediately, anticipating one, though certainly not the most pressing, of the questions that burned upon my tongue, "Marcel and Augustine are gone. They were in all benevolence snatched from me by an aunt, my sister-in-law, who considered the atmosphere here not—not altogether sympathetic to young children . . . *Mon dieu*, ha, ha . . . how very right she was . . . !"

My good resolutions, at such words, broke down, and I burst out: "And *my* child, *Monsieur*, what about *him*? He wasn't at dinner with us. Where is he *now*? Is he safe *now*, this minute . . . ? When did he come here, and why? You have told me nothing yet. There is a person, a creature, "Raoul", who—"

"Ah, ça . . . !" M. Vaignon had raised a nervously, or it may

only have been contemptuously, deprecating hand to check me.
"Let us not speak that name too loudly! It is a name, to me, of
ridicule and of annoyance; to others, many people, whose suscep-
tibilities one must regard, of—well, of something infinitely worse.
It—"

He paused, continuing presently: "You are bound, now that you
are here, to hear of this—this nonsense—anyhow, and I may just
as well prepare you and forewarn you . . . *Enfin*—it was of that,
in fact, I wrote to you, or anyhow of that that I was thinking when
I advised you in my letter not to send me your boy again. When I
told you I was the victim of a persecution, as, in a mood of some
exasperation, I recall I did, I was hardly exaggerating, and—"

"But," I broke in, "I don't understand how—" I hesitated, for
my most urgent question would not be repressed. "Is he—is it—
here now?"

M. Vaignon considered me warily. "It—if we are to call this
damnable old wives" tale an "it"—is not here, or active, now. That
is to say—*enfin*, it is not here now . . ."

After a moment he went on, morosely: "As for "understanding"
. . . There are things of which one can perceive the effect, upon
oneself and others, but which one may not altogether "understand", and may indeed, in a sense, entirely repudiate. As I have
just told you, this—this nuisance, this most supreme and consum-
mate nuisance—is not with us, *actuellement*, but your boy—your
boy arrived here late last night, in—in search of it. He is trying—he
will do his best, to get it back . . ."

It would be hard to describe the unhappy confusion into which
these words had thrown me. What was I to believe? M. Vaignon
had alluded almost scoffingly to Raoul as if to a sort of troublesome but relatively minor notifiable disease or garden pest—much
as he might have spoken of some curiously periodic scarlatina or
potato-blight!—yet underneath his shrugging air I could divine a
genuine and continuing apprehension.

He rose abruptly, with an access of agitation. "This thing—this
kind of molestation, or superstition of a molestation—is not entirely unexampled if one may credit certain authors, certain
bogeymongers, of—oh, of at least two centuries and more
ago . . ." He had moved to the bookshelves, ran a finger along
the tops of a few heavy-looking tomes, and half pulled one out.

"No matter . . ." he said, pushing the volume into place again. "It is there . . . and duly catalogued, though under an evasive appellation. They called these—these preposterousnesses, or the cast of mind that fostered and engendered them, "sans noms"— simply that. The "nameless" . . ."

Undecidedly, he resumed his seat. "I—I give you my word of honour that, when I first met you and until recently, this particular —"nameless" had not, to my recognition, bothered us, or at all events . . . I do not deny that it, or the—the rumour of it, was supposed to have bothered us in the past, but it was presumed to be gone. Tant même, there was a technical, an academic risk of which I might no doubt have warned you earlier . . ."

A tide of bewildered anger swelled in me. "Yes," I said bitterly, " 'rumour" or not, whatever the thing was, and whether we are mad or sane, you might indeed! You certainly should have warned me!"

"Yet you would have laughed, and rightly or au moins most excusably, at such a history. You would have derided it and me."

"And what would that have mattered if I had?" I almost shouted, unable longer to contain the explosion of impatience. I had had to wait, on tenterhooks, all through the drive from Foant and then through dinner to ask anything of what I had been bursting desperately to ask—and now, when I could at least demand straightforward answers, I was treated to nothing but sidesteppings and prevarications.

M. Vaignon was silent, his head bowed. I was entirely convinced that he knew very well he had not told me the whole story and was still keeping something back.

'This—this "nameless",' I insisted. "What is it? I mean this particular specimen . . . We are just beating round the bush about it all and I can't in the least follow what it really is you think you are telling me—if you are telling me. What is it? That's what I've got to know! But whatever it is you surely could have stopped my boy from—from meeting it. He told me it was someone he—chummed up with in the village. A kind of semi-vagrant, it sounded, but . . ."

My words trailed away. M. Vaignon, his face white under my accusation, twirled his brandy of which a glass was before me too, untasted.

He raised his own glass all at once and drained it. His expression showed an almost morbid exaltation.

"Ah, bah!" "It", you say, *"it"* . . . *! Eh bien* . . . *"It"* is something, if you please, that ebbs and flows and that refuses to be satisfactorily dead, something that crops up and comes and goes, and is reputed to have plagued my family through three generations; something that has nourished itself, at intervals, so the tale runs, at our expense and owes its very being and persistence to its victims. All that—ha, ha!—is in the text book . . . Oh, we are not unique in this affliction. "The So-and-so's," you will hear, "—ah yes, a fine old family, *but*—they have a *sans-nom* . . ." As for this —this particular example, as you say, it has a human shape, which you have seen. It eats, drinks, sleeps as other men, while it exists. *Mon dieu* . . . "it" has even mended my hedges, and bought soap or tea or salt and the *épicerie*, before I suspected it and till it was recognised . . . And then, when it *was* recognised—oh what a how-d'ye-do . . . ! But, *to* exist, it must, they say, have an—an attachment. And—its attachment must be young. If and when its victim, its *petit ami*, dies, the pest transfers its—its attentions, we are to believe, to the children of another, and the nearest branch. The thing is amorous and—and rapacious. *Ah, nom d'un nom, quelle histoire! Quel fumisterie! Quelle imbécilité! C'est ridicule, fantastique, incroyable . . . !"*

His voice had risen wildly on a note, it might be equally of scorn or terror as a knock, at first soft, then louder, was repeated on the door. The man Dorlot entered, wearing a look of remonstrance.

"Monsieur should know that such excitement, of which the noise has penetrated to the kitchen, is very bad for him. Go to bed, *Monsieur*, I advise it. Go to bed, where you may forget our troubles possibly in sleep."

Meekly accepting the rebuke—and, I imagined, rather welcoming the excuse to escape further questioning—M. Vaignon said, to me: "Dorlot is right, and, if you will forgive me, I shall leave you now. My health, latterly, is precarious . . . Dorlot will give you anything you require. But first"—he turned to the man—"where is the young *monsieur*? Is he in his room, and—and quiet?"

"Yes; he is in his room, as is to be inferred from the very fact that his room is *not* entirely quiet. The noises are there again, while not, as yet, excessive."

My heart sank at these words; though they conveyed nothing

new. The "poltergeist" disturbances, however, were connected in
my mind with Raoul, and their continuance depressed me.

"Good-night . . ." said M. Vaignon.

I was desperately tired, but lingered a little longer in the "library".

What, honestly, could I believe, and what try, still, to disbelieve?
Ordinarily, of course, the recital which my host had just concluded
would be dismissible as a farrago of lurid and unpleasant nonsense—but I had had experience, alas, myself, of what too plainly
contradicted this consoling view.

As I was going over what M. Vaignon had said, and sipping my
brandy at last, my eye fell on the volume he had started to pull out
from the shelves. It protruded slightly still, and I got up and took it
to my seat.

Légendes d'Autrefois the tome was entitled, tritely, but I had
scarcely flicked over a haphazard page or two before I read, as if
my glance had been directed to the spot: '. . . *et, c'est à dire, les
morts se régaleront des vivants* . . .''

I experienced a cold grue of that sort of surprise which is not
surprise at all, but eerier confirmation, and immediately restored
the volume. "The dead shall feast upon the living" . . . There it
was, and I did not want, at present, to read more. It was the
completion of the passage in that dream that I had had, some
weeks ago, about my wife, holding the book before her non-exis-
tent face . . .

I don't know what had made me so optimistic, in leaving England,
as to the prospect of an early return there with my boy. No doubt I
had the legal right to compel him to come home, but if he still
repulsed me and offered physical resistance the practical difficulties would be, to put it mildly, formidable. On the morning after
my arrival and throughout that day and the next I had tried again
to speak with him, but either his room would be locked and silent
or, if I caught sight of him at all upon the stairs or in the grounds,
he would take literally to his heels.

"Where does he eat?" I asked—for he continued absent from
our meals—and it appeared that sometimes he would raid the
larder and carry off his plunder to the fields. Neither M. Vaignon
nor his domestics had any control over him, and, even if they had,
I could not have relied on them to exercise it upon my behalf. As to

the servants, they were in all respects so unco-operative as to be almost obstructionist, while, in particular, their extraordinary reticence caused me to think that they had probably been forbidden to "gossip" with me, upon this or any other subject.

How fervently I wished that Goderich were here! But of course he could not desert his patients at short notice, nor, obviously, was M. Vaignon's hospitality in my gift.

Denis, I found, had done as I had thought and managed to stow away upon a fishing-boat at Brixham. It had been evidently useless for him to pretend that his visit had my sanction and he must have known I would eventually pursue him—but, beyond his infatuated determination to be reunited with Raoul at any cost, I doubted whether he could have had much of a settled plan of action and campaign. He had steered as clear as possible, it seemed, of M. Vaignon and so far as I could gather had confided the manner of his crossing only—half inadvertently—to Dorlot, who had retailed the story subsequently to his master.

Well it was a beautiful kettle of fish all round. I sent a wire to the police at Winchester, reflecting what slight satisfaction it brought me thus to have proved them wrong.

In my anxiety, I had little or no help from M. Vaignon. Either he was genuinely ill, or feigned it to avoid my "badgering". Never joining me at breakfast, he would retire, though with excuses, immediately after lunch and dinner; and, since our talk on the first evening, had said nothing to me of the least seriousness, sincerity or moment as to what should have been our common problem.

Left to my own devices, I would wander wretchedly around the estate and nearer villages, exchanging a *"bonjour"* occasionally with some peasant, but often meeting no one, as I chose the less frequented paths. The autumn days were dull, but now and then a brighter spell invited me to extend my rambles towards a puy that topped a line of rocky hillocks to the north.

One afternoon—it was the fourth or fifth since my arrival—I had set out thither at about three o'clock. I paid no particular heed to where I was going, and walked on. I suppose, with my head bent in gloomy thought, for which I certainly had food enough.

Yes, the position was fantastic, and a description of it, given badly, would provoke only pitying disbelief. And yet the history was *true*. That was, I knew that as much of it as I had seen with my own eyes was true. As for the rest—for M. Vaignon's wild while half-contemptuous elaborations on the theme—I reserved judgement. He was a sick man, whatever the cause, and his troubles seemed reflected in the unprosperous, depleted and decayed condition generally of his estate and household. The château was in disrepair and its staff, whether by flight or by dismissal, reduced to an uneasy remnant. Why, for example, had the trusted Flébard left? My heart was leaden with misgiving. Could M. Vaignon—a diabolic suspicion flashed into my brain—could he, initially, have asked Denis to the château, or anyhow have gone on having him there, in order to—to safeguard *his* children? Could he, at one time, to protect *them,* to divert something from them and fasten it on Denis, have actually been tempted to promote and foster the disastrous intimacy between Raoul and my boy . . . ? But I rejected such a vile hypothesis as altogether too far-fetched. *My* mind, as well, must be infected to have harboured it, and . . .

Suddenly, rousing from my reverie, I looked about me. The country was unfamiliar and very lonely, and small half-ruined—church or chapel, with a graveyard attached, added to its general air of desolation. In that indifference of purpose which is born of mental exhaustion rather than of any, even "idle", curiosity. I entered the graveyard and wandered aimlessly among its tombs. Some distance off, I noticed, a man was wending towards me down the road ahead.

I loitered absently round the inside of the boundary wall. The burial-ground was evidently disused and the graves were untended, many overgrown with bramble or rank grass. Now and then a date caught my eye—1830, 1813, 1770 . . . Possibly the—all at once I stopped, transfixed, as in the silence, a name stole, staring back at me. It was inscribed upon a headstone slightly taller than the rest, though lichen-coated, tilted, cracked and weather-worn as they. "Privache" . . . And, just decipherable below—yes. **"Raoul. Mourut 1873."**

A footfall made me start. It was the man I had seen on the road and whose approach, over the grass, had been noiseless. He seemed a respectable, decent fellow of the sturdy "bon-homme" type, probably a small tradesman or petty farmer—but he was regarding me, and the grave, with a frown of sombre disapproval.

He gave a significant upward jerk of the head and pointed to the tomb. "*Monsieur* knows perhaps of whom that is the grave?"

In a double disconcertment I stammered, faintly: "Yes, I—I know the—no, I cannot, I—I mean it is the name, the same name as somebody's I know."

The man took a step backward, crossed himself, and said coldly: "Enough . . . then it is to be hoped that *Monsieur* knows also that it is a bad name . . . *Alors, bonjour, Monsieur.*"

He was going slowly away from me but, on an impulse, I detained him.

"Why, who—who was he?" I asked. "Was he a—a criminal, or—"

My tongue faltered, and, as the man's glance met mine searchingly, it was as if a thousand things had passed wordlessly between us.

"No, *Monsieur*, in life he was not a criminal but—" He paused, then, stooping, traced with a forefinger the date, 1873. "That, *Monsieur*, was when he died. It is there, cut in the stone, and is, so far as it goes, correct. My father was *maire* of the *commune* and could remember all about it. I have even, myself, seen the burial record, which was in the register of the parish before the amalgamation. I can tell you no more than that, if you please, *Monsieur*—that he died almost eighty years ago, in 1873 . . ."

Again he crossed himself, and this time, as he withdrew, I did not stay him. I was thrown, momentarily, into a kind of panic. In a sense, my talk several evenings since with M. Vaignon should have prepared me for this further shock, yet I still tended then, I think, to discount a good deal of his discourse as crazy ranting—which he had not repeated and, probably, repented. But now the story, borne out in another mouth, had gained fresh substance and solidarity. Something—a mortuary breath of evil—had addressed me, subverting reason and defeating sanity. "Raoul"—if it were he . . . dead eighty years ago . . . Or what would lead this steady countryman and sober citizen thus to accost me so suspiciously and reprehendingly?

Waiting only until he disappeared across a field, I walked quickly back to the château.

That same evening I got M. Vaignon's consent to my begging Goderich, if he could possibly arrange it, to join me at the earliest opportunity. I had spent six days here, quite uselessly. My boy remained obdurate in avoiding me, keeping out of doors as much as he could and eating his meals I knew not when nor precisely where. This could not go on indefinitely, and he must be removed somehow, but I did not feel confident of my ability to hale him home single-handed, or wish, either, to invoke police assistance, French or British. I worded my letter to Goderich very strongly and, having posted it, was slightly easier in mind.

Otherwise, I was more tortured by anxiety than ever, and my discovery of the lonely grave had had a horrible effect on me. Coupled with the queer manner of the honest fellow who had spoken to me beside it—his doubting, fearful looks and his ambiguous reticence—it left me prey to a complete bewilderment and cold dismay.

Of Denis, meanwhile, as I have just said, I caught only fleeting glimpses. M. Vaignon, who had warned me that he, Denis, would "try to get it back", pretended to have interceded with him, but on this I placed no least reliance. I had little real idea of what my boy did with himself all day, of whether he still slept in the same room (though I was assured this was so) or of when he fed, or bathed, or changed his clothes. As to this last point, I had brought with me for him some clean shirts, socks and underwear, which I had handed to Dorlot and were now, I was informed, in use. But, generally, it seemed to me, his condition was one almost of semi-vagabondage, the château being for him not much more than a base or headquarters from which to "forage" in the countryside.

However, the next morning I did have news of him which, while unreassuring, was somewhat more detailed than previous accounts. Denis, Dorlot remarked, had latterly been spending a good deal of his time in the east wing "near the tower". But on my asking what my boy was doing there the man had shrugged *"Qui sait, Monsieur?* I have seen him reading, or carving wood with his knife . . ."

"Is he there now?"

"Non, Monsieur. It was yesterday and the day before. This morning he has gone out."

This conversation had been at my *petit déjeuner,* which I always had alone, my host preferring his brought to his bed. After the meal I busied myself in writing a short note to my faithful Jenny, from whom I had heard two days ago. She had reported all well at home, and that she and Clara were hoping, poor things, to welcome us *both* back very soon.

I went out to post my reply to her, struck, as I passed beneath the *porte-cochère*, by the château's latterday appearance of neglect. It was as if it lay under a spell—as if some blight, of doom and galloping decay, attacked it. Yes—and assailed its inmates too, I thought—one Colonel Walter Habgood not excepted! *I*, to be sure, was only a temporary occupant of the place, a guest yet I was conscious, whenever I walked abroad, that something of its ill-repute attached to me. With the local peasantry I, too, was in bad odour, the carrier of an aura, an aroma, of the dimly sinister and menacing. And when I had mailed my letter to Goderich yesterday at the little office three kilos up the road to Foant whither I now and again was on my way, the postmistress had eyed me balefully, touching her scapula as I was leaving. Go where I might, a species of anxious hostility attended me, expressed in covert stares, in sullen glances, crossing and avoidances. Even the children scattered from my path.

What *was* the truth, I demanded for the hundredth time, about this whole fantastic business? These yokels (*and* M. Vaignon, I suspected) were abjectly superstition-ridden. You might suppose a recent world-war would have knocked such nonsense out of them, but—suddenly, and wryly, I laughed at myself—though it wasn't at all funny. Yes, that was rich! Talk of the pot and kettle . . . ! For *I* was equally in thrall to a grotesque myth with any of the folk I was deriding.

It was exasperating not to know quite what I did believe or disbelieve. Everything and everybody seemed to be conspiring to throw dust in my eyes and keep me ignominiously in the dark. Here was I, Denis's own father, thankful when I could pick up, as just now, a few crumbs of second-hand intelligence about him from a conceited surly menial like Dorlot! More than once, latterly, I had been tempted to question the fellow bluntly, about many things, but hitherto my pride had not allowed me to interrogate the man behind his master's back. As for the master aforesaid, M. Vaignon, since his first outburst, had retired completely into his shell and been as cordially informative as any oyster.

I felt I could endure this mystifying and maddening secretiveness no longer. I must request from someone—anyone—a forthright explanation of the whole engima and see, at least, what sort of answer was provoked. Accordingly, when I had posted my letter to Jenny, I asked the postmistress to direct me to some person of responsibility—the *maire*, perhaps, or school-master—with whom I could discuss a private matter.

The woman regarded me dirtily enough, replying only after a suspicious pause. "The *maire* is ill," she said, "but there is M. Boidilleule the *garde champêtre, qui était de la résistance* and is ill likewise, or M. Tanvy the *pharmacien*. M. Tanvy", she added more amiably, "is very clever, and of a great discretion, having been a quartermaster in the army . . . Then there is too, of course, Père Puindison, the *curé* . . ."

Rejecting the belauded M. Tanvy, I decided on the *curé*—an obvious choice which it was strange had not occurred to me before. There was no difficulty in locating him. He had just returned from Mass and welcomed me into his *vicairie* politely.

Somewhat haltingly I outlined as much as necessary of my story, including particularly, my discovery of the grave. Was, I inquired, the "Raoul" from whom my boy had this unfortunate infatuation a grandson, possibly, of the deceased?

The *curé's* face had darkened and at my final question wore a look of, as it were, a scandalised discomfiture. I was quite sure he had known all about me in advance.

"*Franchement, Monsieur*, it is not easy to reply. This is a district *assez superstitieux* and . . . *Enfin*, the individual whose grave you saw up there at Saint Orvin had no descendants. He was, it would appear, a butler at the château Vaignon, where, actually, he died. But that was eighty years ago, and . . ."

"Yes, yes," I said. "But—but this other fellow, that my boy met . . . Who is *he*?"

The good father blinked at me morosely. He was an elderly, florid-visaged man, with eyes that were worldly but, at the moment, troubled and unsubtle.

"*Monsieur*," he said, reproachfully, "you come to me, like this, and ask me—what? To confirm and to endorse a doubt that has, beforehand, been implanted in your mind—or maybe to deny it. I can state to you only that the Privache we *know* of died in 1873. The rest is—is merely superstition."

"And the superstition is—?"

He shrugged weakly, uncomfortable and disdainfully apologetic under my pressure. "*Evidemment*, the superstition you insist that I enunciate so clearly is that the Privache who died in 1873 and he for whom, you say, your boy had this *engouement* are one and the same . . . *C'est ridicule! Alors* . . . And I have told you, *absolument*, all I can . . ."

His manner, while still courteous, showed the beginning of a self-protective frostiness, and again, marvelling, I felt defeated. All these folk, when you tried to tackle them and pin them down upon the subject of this preposterous myth, affected superiorly to scoff at it—yet all of them, in their hearts, were really scared of it!

Thanking the *curé*, I took my dissatisfied and disappointed leave.

I have been at the château just a week—an utterly, completely useless week!

Each day, I had sought every chance of pleading with my boy, so far quite unavailingly. Must I then drag him home a literal captive and so make him hate me worse than ever? Possibly, if need be, but not till I had tried every other, more persuasive measure. Denis was like a wild thing, a wild thing piteously spellbound and enchanted, and it would profit little, I thought, to trap and pinion the poor body if the spirit still eluded me. I wished to snare him—yes—but to snare the whole of him, and lovingly; and bonds and handcuffs seemed an unhappy way of doing this.

Yet if he would not voluntarily come with me there was nothing for it but a degree of force, and it had been with this necessity in closer prospect that I appealed to Goderich, whose sympathetically auxiliary convoy, at the pinch, would certainly be less humiliating than that of a police escort!

In this pass, M. Vaignon was a broken reed, his nerve-racked manition now, indeed, almost amounting to a kind of passive, undeclared resistance. And why, after exploding as violently as he had about his blessed *"sans-noms"*, had he stopped short there? The *curé* had grudgingly enlightened me to the limit that his scruples or timidity allowed—but why couldn't M. Vaignon have told me all this, and more, himself?

I walked to the window of my breakfast room and surveyed the autumn fields. From here, they were visible, in brown or sallow squares, stretching irregularly up a saucer's rim to misty hillocks, and in one of them, far off, I fancied, with a start, that I saw Denis. But no, the figure was motionless, and I remembered now that it was only a scarecrow, lingering purposelessly in the stubble.

My letter should reach Goderich today, and, if and when he

came, we could hold some sort of council of war. How glad I
would be of his refreshing sanity and clearer judgement! My own
ideas had become quite chaotic and my affronted reason hurled
itself hour by hour against brick walls of contradiction. It was a
veritable antinomy. On the one hand, here was the mid-twentieth
century, with (even in this backwater) the trains, post, newspaper
and radio (should M. Vaignon but elect to buy a set) and an occasional *avion* droning overhead; while, on the other, equally com-
pulsive of assent, there lay—sheer medievalism, rank mythology,
a weird anachronism of fantastic horror. The two worlds, though
interpenetrating, were irreconcilable—and each was true.

I went undecidedly towards my room and then, passing it,
along a series of corridors. I had often roamed unchallenged up
and down the château's twisting stairs, beneath its faded tapestries and seigneurial banners and across its echoing halls; and
now, uneasily while unpremeditatedly enough, my steps trended
in the direction of the east wing and its tower.

Nothing in particular rewarded my reconnoitre, if it were one,
though in a chamber just below the so-called "haunted" room I
did find a few chips and shavings of the sticks, presumably that as
Dorlot informed me, Denis had been whittling. It was not till I had
redescended that a speculation springing from my recent conversation with the *curé* crossed my mind. "Raoul," Père Puindison
had stated, had died in the château—and Denis, long ago, as I
could now also remember, had said, in speaking of the turret
room, that "someone died there".

Was the "someone" Raoul, and was it actually in the tower that
he had died? It seemed more than probable.

I spent the rest of the morning and most of the afternoon in desul-
tory "mooching", too anxious and distracted, till at least I had
Goderich's reply, to settle definitely to anything.

My visit to the east wing and my ensuing conjecture about
Raoul had, admittedly, disturbed me, but, beyond that, I seemed
dimly conscious of some other cause of a vague apprehension or
dissatisfaction. It was something—I had the feeling—that had happened, or that I had briefly noticed, during the course of the day,
but which I could not quite lay finger on—something of which the
impact had been oblique and that now tapped irritatingly, with an

obscure persistent warning, at my mind. For a time, I tried vainly to recall it, whatever it had been, then gave it up.

I wandered, restively, into the "library" again and took out the volume of "Legends", despite a kind of contemptuous repugnance, to consider, more attentively, what it might have to say.

Presently I found the passage I wanted. It was in a long section entitled, simply, *Auvergne*, and its immediate context was rather mystifying—too occult or too rhapsodical in diction for me to follow clearly. Regretting the inadequacy of my French, I read on, puzzled. ". . . exceptional tenacity of life . . . enabling the said nameless to withdraw vital force . . ." (a line or two here that I could not make head nor tail of) ". . . so to rebuild itself around the mammet as around a nucleus of focus and . . ." (again a string of unfamiliar words defeated me) ". . . or other homely object, so be it have the semblance of a man. But woe to all who do adventure thus, and whether child or woman, if the right fixative be not supplied . . ." And then some sentences of what appeared to be a sort of general description: ". . . their chief weakness being in the wrists and wattles. Yellow above all they joy in, and a certain tint of bluish grey they do defy, wherefore, in extirpating them . . ."

Disappointed at my stumbling translation, I rested the volume, open, on my knee, and pondered. In a sense, what I *had* managed to translate relieved me, because it seemed such arrant, puerile nonsense. Why yes, I thought, in a delighted welling of, as it were, half-hesitant astonished thankfulness, it *was* all nonsense. Sheer, utter nonsense, and I *could* laugh at it. How had I ever—my fleeting elation ebbed. But Denis—I remembered . . . Yes Denis . . . That was the trouble. "Nonsense" or no, my boy's plight was actual enough, and . . .

My host entered—suddenly and brusquely. Owing, ostensibly, to his continued indisposition, we had scarcely encountered for the last several days, and his face now wore a slight frown. "*Bonjour*," he greeted, peevishly. "I—I regret to see you so poorly entertained. You will hardly derive much profit, or even amusement I should think, from *that* . . ." To my amazement he swooped upon the volume and replaced it smartly in the shelves.

Really, M. Vaignon was very trying; and it was now, all in an instant, that, as the result of this comparatively trivial incident, I found myself having an outright, first-class row with him. No doubt, on each side, nerves were frayed to breaking point, and it had needed but this spark to set our tempers in a blaze.

I had stood up. "You might, *Monsieur*, at least have had the courtesy not to *snatch* from my very knees a book that I was actually reading . . . !"

He glared at me, out of eyes swimming with tears. "It is my book. It is *my* book," he repeated childishly, "and I shall do, as I believe you say, what I bloody well like with it! I am going to bloody-burn it. There *Monsieur!* Can you advance any argument against my bloody-burning my own property, including the entire château, if I see fit? And should anybody still insist on lingering—on *lingering* I say—in this so-charming château of mine *when* I burn it, he will be burnt too, neck and crop, along with it, unless . . ."

Staggering, he had clapped a hand to his breast. "Forgive me . . . I am desolated to have made such an exhibition of myself and caused you to think me like—like a stage-Frenchman, *n'est-ce pas*, but—but certain things in this establishment are not quite as they should be . . . A large—an infinitely large—bluebottle has got loose in my bedroom and kept me awake all night, and I, too, am as your *sans-noms*—weak in the wrist and wattles . . . !"

Was he going mad? Or shamming mad? *"My"* sans-noms! I was really completely disgusted with him, the more so perhaps because he had somehow succeeded, in this ridiculous fashion, in taking the wind out of my sails.

"This creature of yours, whatever it is," I was startled to hear myself shouting, "this precious *sans-nom* of *yours*, I say, that has attacked my boy and that for some reason you'll tell me nothing more about—he died here, didn't he? Up in the tower room, or under it . . ."

M. Vaignon regarded me, at first uncomprehendingly and then almost as if pityingly. "My poor friend," he said slowly. "My poor friend—all this had been too much for you and—and, ha, ha, you are going crazy. *Mon dieu, c'est le comble, ça!"* He approached nearer, with a curious dancing step and, to my utter dumbfounding, snapped a finger and thumb beneath my nose. "I repeat it, *Monsieur*. I repeat, with inexpressible regret, that you are quite demented!"

I had backed from him, far too bewildered to feel insulted by the taunting words and gesture, and it was at this instant that, as at a previous, somewhat similar, crisis, the tall form of Dorlot filled the doorway.

"*Calmez-vous, mon maître*," he remonstrated. "*Calmez-vous!* It is this heavy weather that surcharges the nerves, but to yield to your temperament in this manner and with these antics is unseemly. *Calmez-vous!* Thank heaven," he added in a lower tone, "it cannot last much longer now."

M. Vaignon looked at us wildly. "Forgive me," he murmured again, "forgive me . . ." A strange expression, a sort of leering, still half-impudent despair, flickered over his features as, turning, he let Dorlot lead him unsteadily away.

I stayed motionless where I was a full minute. The whole scene had been incredible, and bedlam had flowered, unashamed, before my eyes.

At length, dazedly, I walked from the house.

Outside, I recovered. That was, my immediate emotional disturbance gradually died down, but I felt exhausted, as if I had been through a fight or in a mêlée, and my fundamental apprehension and confusion were increased.

It is a nightmare, I thought, a nightmare. That is why everyone appears mad and why you yourself behave like a madman. All at once you will wake up—perhaps when Goderich comes . . .

The air, as Dorlot had observed, was close and muggy. It was mild, but with a treacherous intimation of tenseness—of I did not quite know what. The fields stretched round me passively—too passively I fancied oddly, as if conspiring, or abandoned, to a gathering sly enchantment. They rolled, in their meek rectangles of ochre, dun and beige, up to unstirring foothills, dreaming a guileful dream. Crossing one of them, I remarked, idly, that the scarecrow I had noticed earlier from the *salon* window seemed to have altered its position slightly.

M. Vaignon . . . Good heavens! "*Sans-noms*" . . . His, if you please, not mine! I wished him joy of them! "*Sans-noms*"! Ye gods . . . ! Who would invent such bogeys such farcically loathsome things, unless . . . I raised my eyes to the grey bated sky, and shivered. No, I was not, to word it temperately, much enamoured of this devil's nook, this baleful twelfth- or thirteenth-century pocket of provincial France, where superstitions and obscene mythologies, instead of just remaining paintly decorative, had the unpleasant trick of springing suddenly alive and driving mad all those who brooded on them overlong. If only . . .

My disjointed ruminations petered out. Once more I raised my eyes, with a faint shudder. All about me, as I walked, the hills, the waiting fields, kept quiet pace with me. I was aware—how shall I put it?—of a bland banking-up, of a demure stealth, a kind of tiptoe ripening of something . . . My head ached and I had an indescribably oppressive feeling. The château, from the spot where I had now come rather giddily to a halt, was visible, maybe a kilo off, but partially obscured by a dip and by a thin belt of trees. I would get back to it as quickly as I could in case my disagreeable symptoms should increase.

Slowly, I proceeded, conscious, upon my mental palate, of some recrudescent flavour that was dimly nauseous and half-familiar. I had covered perhaps a third of the distance to the château when a dog ran up behind me, whining. It was one of the three or four dogs of the house, an amiable enough little creature, mainly poodle, called Zizi. Denis had been fond of it, and I supposed it still companioned him in his present, gipsyish style of life. But now it appeared distressed or frightened and slunk whimpering and cringing at my heels.

We went on together, skirting a field of stubble. It was the field containing the useless scarecrow, and again, puzzled, I had the impression that the object had moved slightly, in the direction of the château. Hang it! I thought querulously in a sort of mildly annoyed perplexity, this was preposterous, and I must previously have misjudged the confounded thing's position. Zizi, beside me, cowered closer and gave, very low, a series of curious suppressed yelps.

The day had grown overcast and my headache was no better. I had a sense of something brewing, something "making"—a kind of dumbly guarded watchfulness and wakefulness—in the dull air, the trees, the hilltops and the whelming sky, as if they too were, like myself, alerted and upon some strange and semi-animate *qui-vive*. The dog, while we passed opposite the middle of the field, darted for a moment from me and through the hedge, venting two stiff little barks, of actual terror or of a variety of canine scandal.

Gradually, as we neared the house, my head ached less, yet a conviction of uneasy imminence, a presentiment of swiftly gathering evil, knocked still at my mind's door, and again, more fervently, I longed for Goderich.

I entered the château, and there, on a tray in the hall, lay an answer to my prayer. Yes, said the telegraph, he could come on Tuesday, that was, in three days' time.

IV

This heartening news was confirmed in a letter from him the next morning, explaining that he would have joined me instantly had not his partner been somewhat indisposed and hardly capable, till the promised Tuesday, of shouldering the extra work. Well, it was more than I had had the right to hope that my friend should have been able to arrange to get away at all, and, heaven knew, I blessed him.

During the week-end, however, my feeling of tension increased, and was appreciably heightened, as it happened, by my host's ill-humour. M. Vaignon, after our recent row, had offered me a somewhat grudging apology for his rudeness—but now he was exasperated again upon a different score. While *I* had had, from Goderich, a cheering and reassuring letter, *he* had received, it seemed, a violently upsetting one. The aunt, he told me, with whom *les petits* had been staying had written saying she was compelled to visit Tunisie on business, it might be for several months, and must accordingly send her brother-in-law's children home.

"It is an excuse!" he fumed. "Business" . . . Pah! They *cannot* come here yet—not yet!"

My sympathy for him, when I remembered the plight of my own boy, was not excessive, and privily I blamed no aunt for getting sick of young Marcel and Augustine, but the matter set my mind running, with a revival of curiosity, on the connection (or in the case of Denis actual relationship) between our respective families, for it was through the sister of this same discredited and disobliging lady that it existed. She had been, before her marriage to M. Vaignon, a Mlle Drouard, and, by a common ancestor three generations back, a cousin (though I do not think they knew each other) of my wife's.

This train of thought led naturally to a reconsideration of the whole question of M. Vaignon's conduct and attitude throughout; and here I was as far as ever from a satisfactory conclusion. He had blown hot and cold and been, by turns, solicitous and callous, courteous and grossly impolite. He had been contrite enough (if it were that) to break off the "holiday exchange" arrangement, yet insufficiently honest to warn me, plainly, about Raoul. He had had the grace, later, to wire me twice after Denis had run away to France, but then, when I arrived for the retrieval of my truant, had given me no help. There was no making the man out . . .

I had been puzzling, alone, upon the Saturday evening, over these and allied problems when I heard a confused noise of angry shouting. The sounds seemed to come from the direction of the stables, suggesting by their volume and persistence that several persons, possibly a dozen or so, were engaged in a violent fracas. But by the time I had gone out to look, just as the hubbub had rather suddenly subsided, the disputants must evidently have stopped their fight, and scattered. Crossing the *basse cour*, however, I saw a man, limping painfully and holding a bloodstained rag to his face. I recognised him as a fellow I had noticed driving one of the wagons that carried hay, or milk and butter from the *laiterie*, and might have asked him what the trouble was had I not at that moment caught, from somewhere within, the shrilly furious tones of M. Vaignon.

As to this incident it was again from Dorlot that I received enlightenment, incomplete though it was. His master (who made no allusion to the matter) having retired immediately after dinner, he, Dorlot, brought me my customary glass of lonely brandy in the library and said: "That parcel of rascals from Saint Orvin were after Batiste and your boy this afternoon, and nearly had them too . . . !"

"What!" I exclaimed, alarmed. "After my boy? What for? Is he all right?"

The man replied, coldly, addressing the ceiling, it appeared, rather than me.

"The young *monsieur* is entirely unharmed since they were unable to catch him, but Batiste—that one, he certainly got a scratch or two . . ."

"But why—why should they be attacked?"

Dorlot shrugged, spreading his hands. People here, *Monsieur*, are superstitious. They are believers in all kinds of nonsense, and possibly the young *monsieur* had been doing something, quite inadvertently, which caused them to suspect him, *sans dire* most wrongfully, of dealing in—in such matters. I cannot tell . . . *Enfin*, the two of them, he and Batiste, were pursued by this band of ignoramuses and ruffians into our very yard, where they found refuge. It is unfortunate", he added as if meditatively, "that certain, even, of our own servants, too, should take sides with this rabble . . . Enough—it is no longer my affair or properly my concern. I leave this place tomorrow . . ."

I was exceedingly disturbed, not only by Dorlot's story and its implications but also, if to a less degree, by his announcement of departure. It would have been foolish to regard him as an ally, yet he had not been actively hostile and latterly had constituted almost my only source of news concerning Denis.

As to the tale itself—more lay behind it, obviously, than Dorlot would disclose, but of this I could guess at a good deal. Amongst the peasantry Denis would not too naturally be a prime object of suspicion, and it was really a wonder he had evaded molestation (if he had) till now. The man Batiste, surmisably, had been his friend or his associate and fallen, consequently, under the same stigma . . . Evidently, the business had attained the proportions of a feud, and M. Vaignon's ranks, within the château, had been split. Dorlot, I fancied, would not lack company upon the train tomorrow . . .

While I was counting the hours to Goderich's arrival with a fresh sense of urgency I renewed, vainly, my efforts to lessen Denis's hostility. I no longer hoped, now, for a full reconciliation so speedily, but, short of that, I would have liked, before Goderich lent me what help he could, to be at all events on speaking terms with my own child.

Twice I tried to talk with him through his locked door, receiving on the first occasion no reply and on the second the response: "Oh, go away! I *hate* you!" And twice, also, I got within undignified hailing distance of him in the grounds, only to be humiliated by his almost offhandedly contemptuous flight. Obviously, at any time, I might probably have rallied M. Vaignon's odds and ends of still faithful retainers (a further couple had left with Dorlot in the morning!) to round up my quarry, and then forced him, as my prisoner, to parley—but such trappings or waylayings would have been very much against the grain and, as I saw it then, have done more harm than good.

What, I would wonder could be his view of the position? How, in his own opinion, was he faring? Pretty evidently he had expected, or at least hoped, to find his odious playmate here—and had not M. Vaignon told me that he, Denis, would do his best to get Raoul back? In that, however, so far as I could judge, he had been disappointed. What had become of the physical "Raoul"—of the physical "aspect" of him—I had no idea. Presumably, after my half-throttling of him, he had returned somehow to France, but had not yet (I trusted) reappeared in his old haunts. Upon this point I could have, to be sure, no certainty, but, whoever or whatever the creature was, its headquarters seemed to lie on this side of the Channel, and the next step of minimum precaution was to transport Denis to the other.

Monday—and tomorrow Goderich would be here. Indeed, a letter for him, *aux soins de* M. Vaignon, had rather surprisingly preceded him already, arriving together with one for me from Jenny. The weather was still gloomy, rainless but boding, and again I strolled dejectedly around the nearer fields.

The landscape, as before, was sere and sullen, but its mood, to my imagining, had subtly changed. The sense of stealthy ferment and evil quickening had departed, and the drab acres had an empty look, as if delivered or relieved of something. Loth to accuse myself of being over-fanciful, I stared about me, seeking for anything that might account, more factually, for this impression, but could find nothing. Merely, the scarecrow I had noticed formerly had gone, having been removed and set up for whatever none too obvious reason, as I subsequently discovered, in another field considerably closer to the house.

I wandered slowly back to the château. Help was at last at hand—for Goderich should be here tomorrow evening—yet my heart was curiously unlightened. The countryside, louring and secret, with that discharged and voided aspect of an ominous fulfilment, seemed to wear a mien of hidden ridicule, of some kind of deceptive somnolence and inward mockery, as though it were laughing at me up its sleeve. Nonsense! I tried to think. What utter nonsense . . . ! With a derisive apt theatricality a trio of stage-property bats, encouraged by the dusk, skimmed past me as I turned by the corner of a barn.

And then, suddenly, I had a shock.

"Hello, Daddy . . ." said Denis.

He was there, in front of me, shyly smiling and addressing me in this form he had discarded for some years, as "babyish". His clothes were stained and torn and his cheeks wan under their grime. I did not believe he had washed properly for days.

But it was far less his ragamuffin air that horrified me than his manner. It was flat and almost bored, yet confident; casual and unconstrained in some utterly wrong way, as though he were so tired out with whatever he had been up to that he had forgotten, even, what it was. How could he, else, have carried it off with this weary, this to me actually hideous, aplomb? He stood, gazing at me in a sort of forlorn and rather vacant friendliness, as if nothing had happened, as if he were completely unconscious of my misery, or his own.

"Come in," I think I said to him. "And—and talk things over, shall we . . . ?"

"Yes . . ." he replied absently. "All right. I'm hungry too." He paused, then added, reconsideringly and as a careful qualification, "That is, you know, not really *very* . . ."

We had begun to walk on, from the barn and the fading light shone, briefly, on his face, discovering there a look that sickened me but is not easy to describe. It was at once wily and exhausted, an expression so to speak of supreme irrelevance or imperviousness to the situation, of a precocious unconcern and hard frivolity or falsity—a falsity all the worse for being undeliberate and still childish. My gorge rose as at something odious. Rage filled me and, to my dismay, I found my fist clenched to strike him. It was with the greatest effort that I controlled the impulse.

"Denis . . ." I heard myself saying *"Denis . . . !"* My anger had turned suddenly to yearning and I had him, unresisting, in my arms. He was light as a feather, limply yielding, and weighing nothing, almost nothing. I felt, while I strained him to me, as if he were liable at any instant to melt away from my embrace into thin air.

At the château, when he entered, M. Vaignon had just come into the hall, gaping at us as though quite confounded.

I do not really know how the next few hours passed, what words were said or what was done in them. I do know and remember that they were not happy or triumphant hours—alas, far from that. A deep emotional conviction of impending sorrow or calamity persisted and I could not banish it. Superficially, it was to

the good that the pursuits, the trappings and lassoings I had envis-
aged were dispensed with—yet what had I instead! *Not* Denis.
That was the trouble. It was only the curious shell of him I had. He
was a wanling, almost a changeling—something that most horribly denied each trait and feature of the Denis I recalled, and of
which the contemplation could but be agonising.

None the less, as I say, this unexpected turn of events was a
practical simplification. Presumably, Denis would "come quietly"
and not have to be dragged home a prisoner. Goderich, when he
arrived, would have nothing to do but go back with us again. And
then . . . ?"

"Are you tired?" I believe I asked once, "after all the—the
camping-out . . . ?"

He regarded me queerly, head cocked, with the suspicious,
quasi-intelligent incomprehension, the notion visited me dreadfully, of a parrot. "A—a little. Yes, a little . . ."

That was all; but the manner if not the matter of the reply had
remained vaguely hostile—and violently unsatisfactory. His tone
held a deplorable sort of cunning, or a fancied cunning—as if,
despite his sudden yielding, he still had an ace hidden somewhere
in the pack, or thought he had.

What had prompted his surrender? Had he merely wearied of
roughing it and craved the ordinary home comforts he had
missed, now, for three weeks? Had his designs, whatever was
their nature, been frustrated, or miscarried, so that at last he had
had to give them up? Or had he, possibly, decided that my rein-
forcement by Goderich (of whose coming, apart from servants'
gossip, he could have got wind in any case from the letter in the
hall) would be too much for him and that he might as well cave in
to me right away?

I must wait to find out all that, for the time was not propitious
yet, I felt, for direct catechisings. Fortunately, perhaps, for that
evening at any rate this question did not arise, as Denis professed
himself so drowsy that, as soon as he had had his tea, and then a
bath, he went to bed.

Of M. Vaignon, save for his startled apparition in the hall, I had
seen nothing since lunch. I dined alone and, after a couple of pipes
in the *petit salon*, was glad to get up to my room.

Denis and I, I reflected, had forgotten, or at least—perhaps on
both sides semi-deliberately—omitted to say good night to each

other. I wondered whether he was yet awake, or (if his sleep were half as troubled as I feared like in his father's case) what dreams would visit him.

Next day, I was in two minds about taking Denis with me to the station to meet Goderich, deciding finally against it. I did not think he would slip off again, and if he did it would only prove his capitulation no real capitulation after all. As to that, indeed, I still felt something disquietingly planned or spurious in it; but my misgivings did not include, now, any apprehensions of his renewed and literal bolting.

Nothing much had happened during the morning. M. Vaignon, encountering me just before lunch, congratulated me, with a deathly simper, on my improved *entente* with Denis and made no difficulties over lending me the car, which I was mightily relieved he did not propose to drive, this time, himself. Goderich would stay one night at the château, and tomorrow the three of us would return to England.

I pictured my friend's surprise when he learned of the fresh development. In a sense he would have had his journey for nothing, but I didn't think he would mind that. A wire yesterday evening might just have caught and stopped him, but, actually, Denis's unexpected "surrender" had put everything else out of my head, and I was selfishly glad, now, that it had.

At the station, I had still ten minutes to wait, and outside the yard entrance to the baggage-office I noticed a wagon drawn up, and a long box being unloaded from it and then carried in to the clerk. The wagon I could recognise as from the château, and the fellow awkwardly shouldering the box was, I was pretty sure, that same "Batiste" I had seen limping, with the blood-stained kerchief to his face, in the *basse cour* two days ago. As he climbed again into his seat, the *chef de gare* himself came out to confer for a few moments with him in an under-tone.

But here at last was Goderich's train. It had scarcely clanked puffing to a standstill before he leaped out and clasped my hand in his.

"Well," he was saying, "it's rather like one's toothache fleeing on the dentist's doorstep. If I hadn't "Come for nothing", as you are so kind as to suggest, you and your young jackanapes would probably still be at loggerheads."

We were approaching the château, and I wondered. Goderich's hearty vigour, his very tone of cheerful lightness, was a gust of health and hope from another world—and yet, I doubted, and was even, somehow, shocked.

"If we're *not* still at loggerheads, as it is," I remember answering. "You'll see for yourself presently."

We drove under the *porte-cochère,* and alighted. M. Vaignon was there to greet us, all politeness. A small, dim figure hung back, hugging the shadows.

"Hello, scallywag!" called Goderich. "Hi, come out of that!"

Denis moved forwards undecidedly. His face, again, horrified me by its hollow wanness.

"'M . . .'" Goderich commented. "Not altogether a walking advertisement of anything I must say. That's the deserts of being A.W.O.L. . . . Nineteen days adrift, eh? But we won't clap him in the glass-house this time, sergeant-major . . ."

Once more, I gave a mental gasp. I did not know whether to admire or be scared out of my wits by Goderich's breeziness. Wasn't it, I misdoubted, a trifle overdone? It jolted me, I think, not so much through a fear of its effect on Denis as by appearing almost *too* temerarious a defiance of the evil gods.

But Denis did not seem to mind this "joshing". He even smiled faintly, as Goderich persevered with his hardy badinage, and ate, under the friendly bombardment, a reasonably good tea.

None the less, I could divine, beneath his fun-poking, that Goderich was concerned. When Denis had gone off, "to see the horses fed" he said, with Zizi, my friend's expression became grave.

"What do you make of this, Habgood?" he surprised me by inquiring.

"I . . . ? Why, I—I want *you* to tell *me!*"

"Of course. But first I'd be interested in your opinions, so far as you have any. Do you, for instance, really—" He broke off: "Wait a bit. Are we likely to be disturbed here? Our perfect host isn't liable to butt in, is he?"

"I shouldn't think so. He's completely haywire these days, and we probably won't see him again this evening."

"Suits me . . . And if—"

But at this moment, to falsify my prophecy, M. Vaignon *did* "butt in", insisting upon "entertaining" us, with the most oddly vapid small talk, until and throughout dinner; and it was only when he had at length proffered his excuses and retired that I and Goderich could continue our discussion. Denis himself, as on the previous night, had gone early to his bed.

"Well," Goderich resumed, "what *is* your feeling, about the whole thing now? For example—and putting a conceivable crackbrained "impersonation" out of it, as I think we may—do you actually believe that the pernicious loon we both knew down in Hampshire is the same Privache whose grave, you've said, you saw near here last week?"

"It—it certainly *sounds* nonsense," I replied.

" 'Nonsense'—yes, naturally it does. But even nonsense can be dynamic. In its proper realm, where its writ runs and it holds sway, it *isn't* nonsense. And it can, often, effectually intrude into a sphere beyond its own. It has become at least *mentally* real for Denis, and also, up to a point, for you. I just wanted to know how real.'

"I tell you, I don't know. It simply doesn't add up."

"All right. It doesn't. If it *did*, for instance, this damned sallydore could eventually be traced, and be run-in for something. But for what, exactly? In what terms could you prefer a charge? I'd hate to see you trying! The notion would be quite absurd—which just shows you that it *can't* "add up" for us in any ordinary way. But the next obvious practical step anyhow is to get your boy as clear of it all as we can and pray that later he'll—well, respond to treatment."

"But what do *you* think, honestly? Is . . . ?" I faltered.

"I know what you're going to ask. Well, *is* it? Or again, *is* it? How can *I* tell? It was *there*, that precious gaby was, and it appeared to be more or less passably a man—and, for some revolting reason, it wore mittens. Also, it had an arm which acted up pretty unorthodoxly . . . What I *don't* see is how a mere throttling, a semi-throttling, could have snuffed it out and kiboshed it, at all events temporarily, as it seems to have done . . . No doubt, that rubbed in the fact that it wasn't too popular, and would be a deterrent to some extent, but . . ."

Goderich, too, hesitated; then went on: "I don't fancy we can get much forrarder along those lines. It's easy enough to say the whole

thing's farcical—and if you could *feel* that as well as say it, it would
be fine. What about the "poltergeist" noises? Do they still go on?''

''I was told so. I've not heard them here myself.''

'And the "haunted" room, where you're persuaded the original
fee-faw-fum demised. How does that come into it? Did our host
admit definitely that Privache No. 1 *had* died there?'

'' 'Definitely' . . . ! No indeed. He's never said anything definite or straightforward. When I did as it were challenge him to
deny that the—the first Privache had died where I felt he had, he
just behaved quite weirdly, was abominably rude, and accused *me*
of going mad . . .''

For some while longer our talk continued without leading us to
any more concrete conclusion than we had reached already—that
our sole hope for Denis lay in getting him away immediately and
that, when this was done, it would be only in the nick of time.

We had thought, Goderich and I, that we were bringing Denis
home, and that morning we treated our precious freight as if no
precaution for its safety could be excessive. Denis was, actually
and in literal truth so worn and wasted that such an attitude
would have been natural in any case, and I think we both felt that,
unless the greatest care were exercised, he might as it were collapse in our hands or be blown away by a puff. His eyes were
lustreless and his skin dry, and his manner held some ingredient I
could not define, at once apathetic and expectant, or perhaps apprehensive.

The day had broken cloudily after, for me, a restless night. I had
had dreams, but could not recall them clearly. Mostly, they had
been of absurdities—of M. Vaignon addressing a meeting of pup-
pets in the library, of Dorlot roller-skating somewhere overhead,
and even of the ridiculous scarecrow, shifting from field to field in
a continued march towards the house—but their persisting savour
was oppressive, and I had woken from them with nerves jangled.

Our train was to leave Foant at about ten-thirty, and we had
risen, we realised, rather unnecessarily early. Denis, glancing at us
distraitly from under lowered brows, ate an extremely sketchy
breakfast. Once, he appeared lost in a kind of reverie, and then,
arousing from it with a start, upset his chocolate bowl. The slight
mishap caused him to open his mouth, aghastly, in an unuttered
scream.

This time, we wouldn't need our host's car. I had arranged,

yesterday, for a taxi to come out for us from Foant, and now I prayed it might be punctual. Our luggage was stacked in the hall; I had tipped the servants, and M. Vaignon, dressing-gowned, had made a grisly mountebank descent to say goodbye. Bowing, and stiffly shaking hands, he muttered something else that sounded like: ". . . if it will let you . . ."

At last the three of us drove off. For a while, my spirits lightened and I breathed more freely.

"Are you all right?" I asked Denis.

"Oh yes . . ."

He was next me and facing Goderich, gazing dreamily—or raptly—out of the window. His expression was remote, as though he were attending to something we could not see, or not appreciate. His hair, I noticed, had grown long and wanted cutting.

Suddenly, from under his seat, issued a low bark. Zizi! How he had managed it I did not know, but the little creature must have leaped in after Denis, and we should now have to ask the stationmaster to restore him to his owner.

This, on alighting from the taxi, we did, and presently the train drew in. Denis, for a second or two as Goderich and I were about to board it, was not to be found, and my heart froze. But next moment he came scurrying from the direction of the *consigne* and clambered in with us just in time.

I was so thankful at retrieving him! A passion of yearning sympathy for my poor darling rose in me, and I pressed his arm. The train gathered speed and I remember sighing in relief and thinking that every mile now was a mile further towards his safety. Actually, I had hardly expected or quite dared to hope we *would* ever do it—ever get away. I had feared, all the while, that something—though I couldn't guess how or what—would happen or put out a hand to halt us or detain us—some sort of accident or hitch—and . . .

But my satisfaction ebbed, and died. Denis's manner suddenly alarmed me. He was distressed, I could not tell why. "The—the scare—" He seemed to be trying, unsuccessfully, to say something; then, changing to French, at length got out: ". . . l' épouvantail, c'est dans . . ." He paused, and added, with an urgency I could not understand, the one word: "Zizi . . ."

Sure enough, to my annoyed confusion, the dog was there, and with us still, whether or not with Denis's abetting I did not know.

But it was not the dog's presence I was bothered over: it was the curious looks and bearing of my boy.

Another train, which must be an express, was overtaking us, coming up rapidly upon a parallel track. Our own train, as if inspired to a race, increased its speed, and the express gained on us less swiftly. Zizi had burst in upon us, at first delightedly, from the corridor, wagging his tail, but now appeared strangely subdued. With a short bark of half-hearted challenge he slunk cowering under the seat, by Denis.

"What *is* it, Denis? What's the matter?" I implored.

Goderich had pulled out a brandy flask and held it to Denis's lips. They moved slowly and bewilderedly. "*l'épouvantail* . . . The—the scarecrow . . . *c'est* . . ."

Suddenly he broke from us, moaning, and dashed into the corridor. Both I and Goderich had grabbed at him, ineffectually. The dog, as though torn between its fear and a kind of loyalty, had emerged from under the seat and stood whimpering in the doorway.

Thrusting it aside with my boot, I followed Denis. The express was quickly overhauling us. I could just see, at the moment, the front of its locomotive showing level with the corridor's end, then creeping foot by foot along our windows.

"Denis, Denis!" I repeated. "What *is* it? What are you *doing?*"

He was hunched oddly, staring out at the other train with a quite indescribable look of terror on his face. His eyes were round with fright and his body was pressed desperately against the corridor's inner wall as if, despite his fascinated interest, he were trying to get as far from the pursuing coaches as he could.

What followed has an *outré* horror and grotesqueness which puts such a strain on ordinary credence that even I who witnessed it still find it hard if not impossible at times to reconcile with, or accept as, "literal" truth. I cannot, in any way, explain it, but I believe, now, that something, then, went hideously wrong—went wrong from Denis's and Raoul's point of view, I mean—and that whatever sort of ghastly schemes and machinations may have been afoot were, at the last moment, bungled. What I did see, or what at all events I seemed to see, was the result, I feel, of some bizarre and odious miscarriage . . .

I had caught Denis's arm, and shook it, but he paid no attention to me. Two men, on the farther side of him, stuck curious heads out of their compartment, and gaped foolishly at us. Behind me, squeezed up in the narrow passage, Goderich was shouting over my shoulder, above the uproar of the trains: "Come on, young man, snap out of it! Come back!" His voice was cool, but he added, in my ear: "For heaven's sake get hold of him somehow!"

Denis had wedged himself against the jamb of a half-open door, and it was now, as I was struggling, in the cramped space, to wrest him from it, that our own pace abruptly slackened, so that the express began to flash by our windows at a rush. I learned later that it was then that Goderich had pulled the communication cord. Meanwhile I still could not drag Denis free. I was aware that he was in some awful danger but tugged at him in vain. As in a nightmare, I strained till the sweat stood on my forehead, praying that the dream would break.

It never did, or has. For an instant I had looked out of the window. The guard's van of the express was just passing us. Something, a long box like a coffin, cocked lewdly up and protruded slowly from it, flew out of it towards us. The corridor was littered with shivered glass.

The train had stopped with a violent jolt. People were running along the track, and already I caught, from somewhere, amazed exclamations: *"Un épouvantail . . . !* It was, in that box there, solely a scarecrow . . . !"

I turned again to Denis, thinking I heard his call. "Zizi . . ." I fancied he had said. But what had happened to the dog I did not, then or later, know or care.

My boy's face was seamed and wizened as that of an old man, and the starkest terror was graven on it. His body now was quite limp in my hands.

Goderich and I carried him back to the compartment and laid him on a seat, and it was then I saw that, before his last cry, his hair, which had changed to elf-locks, had gone white.

Pages from a Young Girl's Journal

Robert Aickman

3 October. Padua—Ferrara—Ravenna. We've reached Ravenna only four days after leaving that horrid Venice. And all in a hired carriage! I feel sore and badly bitten too. It was the same yesterday, and the day before, and the day before that. I wish I had someone to talk to. This evening, Mamma did not appear for dinner at all. Papa just sat there saying nothing and looking at least 200 years old instead of only 100, as he usually does. I wonder how old he *really* is? But it's no good wondering. We shall never know, or at least I shan't. I often think Mamma *does* know, or very nearly. I wish Mamma were someone I could talk to, like Caroline's Mamma. I often used to think that Caroline and her Mamma were more like sisters together, though of course I could never say such a thing. But then Caroline is pretty and gay, whereas I am pale and quiet. When I came up here to my room after dinner, I just sat in front of the long glass and stared and stared. I must have done it for half an hour or perhaps an hour. I only rose to my feet when it had become quite dark outside.

I don't like my room. It's much too big and there are only two wooden chairs, painted in greeny-blue with gold lines, or once painted like that. I hate having to lie on my bed when I should prefer to sit and everyone knows how bad it is for the back. Besides, this bed, though it's enormous, seems to be as hard as when the earth's dried up in summer. Not that the earth's like that here. Far from it. The rain has never stopped since we left Venice. Never once. Quite unlike what Miss Gisborne said before we set out from my dear, dear Derbyshire. This bed really is *huge*. It would take at least eight people my size. I don't like to think about it. I've just remembered: it's the third of the month so that we've been gone exactly half a year. What a lot of places I have been to in that time —or been through! Already I've quite forgotten some of them. I never properly saw them in any case. Papa has his own ideas and one thing I'm sure of is that they are quite unlike other people's ideas. To me the whole of Padua is just a man on a horse—stone or bronze, I suppose, but I don't even know which. The whole of Ferrara is a huge palace—castle—fortress that simply frightened me, so that I didn't *want* to look. It was as big as this bed—in its own way, of course. And those were two large, famous towns I have visited this very week. Let alone where I was perhaps two months ago! What a farce! as Caroline's Mamma always says. I wish she were here now and Caroline too. No one ever hugged and kissed me and made things happy as they do.

The contessa has at least provided me with no fewer than twelve candles. I found them in one of the drawers. I suppose there's nothing else to do but read—except perhaps to say one's prayers. Unfortunately, I finished all the books I brought with me long ago, and it's so difficult to buy any new ones, especially in English. However, I managed to purchase two very long ones by Mrs Radcliffe before we left Venice. Unfortunately, though there are twelve candles, there are only two candlesticks, both broken, like everything else. Two candles *should* be enough, but all they seem to do is make the room look even larger and darker. Perhaps they are not-very-good foreign candles. I noticed that they seemed very dirty and discoloured in the drawer. In fact, one of them looked quite black. That one must have lain in the drawer a very long time. By the way, there is a framework hanging from the ceiling in the middle of the room. I cannot truthfully describe it as a chandelier: perhaps as the ghost of a chandelier. In any case, it is a long way from even the foot of the bed. They do have the most *enormous* rooms in these foreign houses where we stay. Just as if it were very warm the whole time, which it certainly is not. What a farce!

As a matter of fact, I'm feeling quite cold at this moment, even though I'm wearing my dark-green woollen dress that in Derbyshire saw me through the whole of last winter. I wonder if I should be any warmer *in* bed? It is something I can never make up my mind about. Miss Gisborne always calls me "such a chilly mortal". I see I have used the present tense. I wonder if that is appropriate in the case of Miss Gisborne? Shall I ever see Miss Gisborne again? I mean in *this* life, of course.

Now that six days have passed since I have made an entry in this journal, I find that I am putting down *everything*, as I always do once I make a start. It is almost as if nothing horrid could happen to me as long as I keep on writing. That is simply silly, but I sometimes wonder whether the silliest things are not often the truest.

I write down words on the page, but what do I say? Before we started, everyone told me that, whatever else I did, I *must* keep a journal, a travel journal. I do not think this a travel journal at all. I find that when I am travelling with Papa and Mamma, I seem hardly to look at the outside world. Either we are lumbering along, with Papa and Mamma naturally in the places from which something can be seen, or at least from which things can be best seen; or I find that I am alone in some great vault of a bedroom for hours and hours and hours, usually quite unable to go to sleep, sometimes for the whole night. I should see so much more if I could sometimes walk about the different cities on my own—naturally, I do not mean at night. I wish that were possible. Sometimes I really hate being a girl. Even Papa cannot hate my being a girl more than I do sometimes.

And then when there *is* something to put down, it always seems to be the same thing! For example, here we are in still another of these households to which Papa always seems to have an entrée. Plainly it is very wicked of me, but I sometimes wonder *why* so many people should want to know Papa, who is usually so silent and disagreeable, and always so old! Perhaps the answer is simple enough: it is that they never meet him—or Mamma—or me. We drive up, Papa gives us all over to the major-domo or someone, and the family never sets eyes on us, because the family is never at home. These foreign families seem to have terribly many houses and always to be living in another of them. And when one of the family *does* appear, he or she usually seems to be almost as old as

Papa and hardly able to speak a word of English. I think I have a pretty voice, though it's difficult to be quite sure, but I deeply wish I had worked harder at learning foreign languages. At least—the trouble is that Miss Gisborne is so bad at teaching them. I must say *that* in my own defence, but it doesn't help much now. I wonder how Miss Gisborne would be faring if she were in this room with me? Not much better than I am, if you ask me.

I have forgotten to say, though, that this is one of the times when we *are* supposed to be meeting the precious family; though, apparently, it consists only of two people, the contessa and her daughter. Sometimes I feel that I have already seen enough women without particularly wanting to meet any new ones, whatever their ages. There's something rather monotonous about women—unless, of course, they're like Caroline and her Mamma, which none of them are, or could be. So far the contessa and her daughter have not appeared. I don't know why not, though no doubt Papa knows. I am told that we are to meet them both tomorrow. I expect very little. I wonder if it will be warm enough for me to wear my green satin dress instead of my green woollen dress? Probably not.

And this is the town where the great, the immortal Lord Byron lives in sin and wildness! Even Mamma has spoken of it several times. Not that this melancholy house is actually *in* the town. It is a villa at some little distance away from it, though I do not know in which direction, and I am sure that Mamma neither knows nor cares. It seemed to me that after we passed through the town this afternoon, we travelled on for fifteen or twenty minutes. Still, to be even in the same *region* as Lord Byron must somewhat move even the hardest heart; and my heart, I am very sure, is not hard in the least.

I find that I have been scribbling away for nearly an hour. Miss Gisborne keeps on saying that I am too prone to the insertion of unnecessary hyphens, and that it is a weakness. If a weakness it is, I intend to cherish it.

I know that an hour has passed because there is a huge clock somewhere that sounds every quarter. It must be a *huge* clock because of the noise it makes, and because everything abroad *is* huge.

I am colder than ever and my arms are quite stiff. But I must drag off my clothes somehow, blow out the candles, and insinuate

my tiny self into this enormous, frightening bed. I do hate the
lumps you get all over your body when you travel abroad, and so
much hope I don't get many more during the night. Also I hope I
don't start feeling thirsty, as there's no water of any kind, let alone
water safe to drink.

Ah, Lord Byron, living out there in riot and wickedness! It is
impossible to forget him. I wonder what he would think of *me?* I
do hope there are not too many biting things in this room.

4 October. What a surprise! The contessa has said it will be quite in
order for me to go for short walks in the town, provided I have my
maid with me; and when Mamma at once pointed out that I had
no maid, offered the services of her own! To think of this happening the very day after I wrote down in this very journal that it
could never happen! I am now quite certain that it would have
been perfectly correct for me to walk about the other towns too. I
daresay that Papa and Mamma suggested otherwise only because
of the difficulty about the maid. Of course I *should* have a maid,
just as Mamma should have a maid too and Papa a man, and just
as we should all have a proper carriage of our own, with our crest
on the doors! If it was that we were too poor, it would be humiliating. As we are not too poor (I am sure we are not), it is farcical. In
any case, Papa and Mamma went on making a fuss, but the contessa said we had now entered the States of the Church, and were,
therefore, all living under the special beneficence of God. The contessa speaks English very well and even knows the English *idioms*,
as Miss Gisborne calls them.

Papa screwed up his face when the contessa mentioned the
States of the Church, as I knew he would. Papa remarked several
times while we were on the way here, that the Papal States, as he
calls them, are the most misgoverned in Europe and that it was not
only as a Protestant that he said so. I wonder. When Papa expresses opinions of that kind, they often seem to me to be just
notions of his own, like his notions of the best way to travel. After
the contessa had spoken as she did, I felt—very strongly—that it
must be rather beautiful to be ruled directly by the Pope and his
cardinals. Of course, the cardinals and even the Pope are subject to
error, as are our own bishops and rectors, all being but men, as Mr
Biggs-Hartley continually emphasizes at home; but, all the same,
they simply *must* be nearer to God than the sort of people who rule

us in England. I do not think Papa can be depended upon to judge such a question.

I am determined to act upon the contessa's kind offer. Miss Gisborne says that though I am a pale little thing, I have very much a will of my own. Here will be an opportunity to prove it. There may be certain difficulties because the contessa's maid can only speak Italian; but when the two of us shall be alone together, it is I who shall be mistress and she who will be maid, and nothing can change that. I have seen the girl. She is a pretty creature, apart from the size of her nose.

Today it has been wet, as usual. This afternoon we drove round Ravenna in the contessa's carriage: a proper carriage for once, with arms on the doors and a footman as well as the coachman. Papa has paid off our hired coach. I suppose it has lumbered away back to Fusina, opposite to Venice. I expect I can count upon our remaining in Ravenna for a week. That seems to be Papa's usual sojourn in one of our major stopping places. It is not very long, but often it is quite long enough, the way we live.

This afternoon we saw Dante's Tomb, which is simply by the side of the street, and went into a big church with the Throne of Neptune in it, and then into the Tomb of Galla Placidia, which is blue inside, and very beautiful. I was on the alert for any hint of where Lord Byron might reside, but it was quite unnecessary to speculate, because the contessa almost shouted it out as we rumbled along one of the streets: "The Palazzo Guiccioli. See the netting across the bottom of the door to prevent Lord Byron's animals from straying." "Indeed, indeed," said Papa, looking out more keenly than he had at Dante's Tomb. No more was said, because, though both Papa and Mamma had more than once alluded to Lord Byron's present way of life so that I should be able to understand things that might come up in conversation, yet neither the contessa nor Papa and Mamma knew how much I might really understand. Moreover, the little contessina was in the carriage, sitting upon a cushion on the floor at her Mamma's feet, making five of us in all, foreign carriages being as large as everything else foreign; and I daresay *she* knew nothing at all, sweet little innocent.

"Contessina" is only a kind of nickname or *sobriquet*, used by the family and the servants. The contessina is really a contessa: in foreign noble families, if one person is a duke, then all the other

men seem to be dukes also, and all the women duchesses. It is very
confusing and nothing like such a good arrangement as ours,
where there is only one duke and one duchess to each family. I do
not know the little contessina's age. Most foreign girls look far
older than they really are, whereas most of our girls look younger.
The contessa is *very* slender, a veritable sylph. She has an olive
complexion, with no blemish of any kind. People often write about
"olive complexions": the contessina really has one. She has absolutely enormous eyes, the shape of broad beans, and not far off
that in colour; but she never uses them to look at anyone. She
speaks so little and often has such an empty, lost expression that
one might think her more than slightly simple; but I do not think
she is. Foreign girls are raised quite differently from the way our
girls are raised. Mamma frequently refers to this, pursing her lips.
I must admit that I cannot see myself finding in the contessina a
friend, pretty though she is in her own way, with feet about half
the size of mine or Caroline's.

When foreign girls grow up to become women, they usually
continue, poor things, to look older than they are. I am sure this
applies to the contessa. The contessa has been very kind to me—in
the few hours that I have so far known her—and even seems to be
a little sorry for me—as, indeed, I am for her. But I do not understand the contessa. Where was she last night? Is the little contessina her only child? What has become of her husband? Is it because he is dead that she seems—and looks—so sad? Why does
she want to live in such a big house—it is called a villa, but one
might think it a palazzo—when it is all falling to bits, and much of
it barely even furnished? I should like to ask Mamma these questions, but I doubt whether she would have the right answers, or
perhaps any answers.

The contessa did appear for dinner this evening, and even the
little contessina. Mamma was there too: in that frock I dislike. It
really is the wrong kind of red—especially for Italy, where *dark*
colours seem to be so much worn. The evening was better than last
evening; but then it could hardly have been worse. (Mr Biggs-
Hartley says we should never say that: things can *always* be
worse.) It was not a *good* evening. The contessa was trying to be
quite gay, despite her own obvious trouble, whatever that is; but
neither Papa nor Mamma know how to respond and I know all too
well that I myself am better at thinking about things than at cast-

ing a spell in company. What I like most is just a few friends I know really well and whom I can truly trust and love. Alas, it is long since I have had even one such to clasp by the hand. Even letters seem mostly to lose themselves en route, and I can hardly wonder; supposing people are still bothering to write them in the first place, needless to say, which it is difficult to see why they should be after all this time. When dinner was over, Papa and Mamma and the contessa played an Italian game with both playing cards and dice. The servants had lighted a fire in the salone and the contessina sat by it doing nothing and saying nothing. If given a chance, Mamma would have remarked that "the child should have been in bed long ago", and I am sure she should. The contessa wanted to teach me the game, but Papa said at once that I was too young, which is absolutely farcical. Later in the evening, the contessa, after playing a quite long time with Papa and Mamma, said that tomorrow she would put her foot down (the contessa knows so many such expressions that one would swear she must have *lived* in England) and would *insist* on my learning. Papa screwed his face up and Mamma pursed her lips in the usual way. I had been doing needlework, which I shall never like nor see any point in when servants can always do it for us; and I found that I was thinking many deep thoughts. And then I noticed that a small tear was slowly falling down the contessa's face. Without thinking, I sprang up; but then the contessa smiled, and I sat down. One of my deep thoughts was that it is not so much particular disasters that make people cry, but something always there in life itself, something that a light falls on when we are trying to enjoy ourselves in the company of others.

I must admit that the horrid lumps are going down. I certainly do not seem to have acquired any more, which is an advantage when compared with what happened every night in Dijon, that smelly place. But I wish I had a more cheerful room, with better furniture, though tonight I have succeeded in bringing to bed one of our bottles of mineral water and even a glass from which to drink it. It is only the Italian mineral water, of course, which Mamma says may be very little safer than the ordinary water; but as all the ordinary water seems to come from the dirty wells one sees down the side streets, I think that Mamma exaggerates. I admit, however, that it is not like the bottled water one buys in France. How farcical to have to buy water in a bottle, anyway! All the same, there are some things that I have grown to *like* about foreign countries; perhaps even to prefer. It would never do to let Papa and Mamma hear me talk in such a way. I often wish I were not so sensitive, so that the rooms I am given and things of that kind, did not matter so much. And yet Mamma is more sensitive about the water than I am! I am sure it is not so *important*. It can't be. To me it is *obvious* that Mamma is *less* sensitive than I am, where *important* things are concerned. My entire life is based on that obvious fact; my real life, that is.

I rather wish the contessina would invite me to share *her* room, because I think she is sensitive in the same way that I am. But perhaps the little girl sleeps in the contessa's room. I should not really mind that. I do not *hate* or even dislike the little contessina. I expect she already has troubles herself. But Papa and Mamma would never agree to it anyway, and now I have written all there is to write about this perfectly ordinary, but somehow rather odd, day. In this big cold room, I can hardly move with chilliness.

5 October. When I went in to greet Mamma this morning, Mamma had the most singular news. She told me to sit down (Mamma and Papa have more chairs in their rooms than I have, and more of other things too), and then said that there was to be a party! Mamma spoke as though it would be a dreadful ordeal, which it was impossible for us to avoid; and she seemed to take it for granted that I should receive the announcement in the same way. I do not know what I really thought about it. It is true that I have never enjoyed a party yet (not that I have been present at many of them); but all day I have been aware of feeling different inside myself, lighter and swifter in some way, and by this evening I cannot but think it is owing to the knowledge that a party lies before me. After all, foreign parties may be different from parties at home, and probably are. I keep pointing that out to myself. This particular party will be given by the contessa, who, I feel sure, knows more about it than does Mamma. If she does, it will not be the only thing that the contessa knows more about than Mamma.

The party is to be the day after tomorrow. While we were drinking our coffee and eating our panini (always very flaky and powdery in Italy), Mamma asked the contessa whether she was sure there would be time enough for the preparations. But the contessa only smiled—in a very polite way, of course. It is probably easier to do things quickly in Italy (when one really wants to, that is), because everyone has so many servants. It is hard to believe that the contessa has much money, but she seems to keep more servants than we do, and, what is more, they behave more like slaves than like servants, quite unlike our Derbyshire keel-the-pots. Perhaps it is simply that everyone is so fond of the contessa. That I should entirely understand. Anyway, preparations for the party have been at a high pitch all day, with people hanging up banners, and funny smells from the kitchen quarters. Even the Bath House at the far end of the formal garden (it is said to have been built by the Byzantines) has had the spiders swept out and been populated with cooks, perpetrating I know not what. The transformation is quite bewildering. I wonder when Mamma first knew of what lay ahead? Surely it must at least have been before we went to bed last night?

I feel I should be vexed that a new dress is so impracticable. A train of seamstresses would have to work day and night for 48 hours, as in the fairy tales. I should like that (who would not?), but I am not at all sure that *I* should be provided with a new dress even if whole weeks were available in which to make it. Papa and Mamma would probably still agree that I had quite enough dresses already even if it were the Pope and his cardinals who were going to entertain me. All the same, I am not really vexed. I sometimes think that I am deficient in a proper interest in clothes, as Caroline's Mamma calls it. Anyway, I have learned from experience that new dresses are more often than not thoroughly disappointing. I keep reminding myself of that.

The other important thing today is that I have been out for my first walk in the town with the contessa's maid, Emilia. I just swept through what Papa had to say on the subject, as I had promised myself. Mamma was lying down at the time, and the contessa simply smiled her sweet smile and sent for Emilia to accompany me.

I must admit that the walk was not a *complete* success. I took with me our copy of Mr Grubb's *Handbook to Ravenna and Its Antiquities* (Papa could hardly say No, lest I do something far worse), and began looking places up on the map with a view to visiting them. I felt that this was the best way to start, and that, once started, I could wait to see what life would lay before me. I am often quite resolute when there is some specific situation to be confronted. The first difficulty was the quite long walk into Ravenna itself. Though it was nothing at all to me, and though it was not raining, Emilia soon made it clear that she was unaccustomed to walking a step. This could only have been an affectation, or rather pretention, because everyone knows that girls of that kind come from peasant families, where I am quite sure they have to walk about all day, and much more than merely walk about. Therefore, I took no notice at all, which was made easier by my hardly understanding a word that Emilia actually said. I simply pushed and dragged her forward. Sure enough, she soon gave up all her pretences, and made the best of the situation. There were some rough carters on the road and large numbers of horrid children, but for the most part they stopped annoying us as soon as they saw who we were, and in any case it was as nothing to the roads into Derby, where they have lately taken to throwing stones at the passing carriages.

The next trouble was that Emilia was not in the least accustomed to what I had in mind when we reached Ravenna. Of course people do not go again and again to look at their own local antiquities, however old they may be; and least of all, I suspect, Italian people. When she was not accompanying her mistress, Emilia was used to going to town only for some precise purpose: to buy something, to sell something, or to deliver a letter. There was that in her attitude which made me think of the saucy girls in the old comedies: whose only work is to fetch and carry billets-doux, and sometimes to take the places of their mistresses, with their mistresses' knowledge or otherwise. I did succeed in visiting another of these Bath Houses, this one a public spectacle and called the Baptistry of the Orthodox, because it fell into Christian hands after the last days of the Romans, who built it. It was, of course, far larger than the Bath House in the contessa's garden, but in the interior rather dark and with a floor so uneven that it was difficult not to fall. There was also a horrible dead animal inside. Emilia began laughing, and it was quite plain what she was laughing at. She was striding about as if she were back on her mountains and the kind of thing she seemed to be suggesting was that if I proposed to walk all the way to the very heel or toe of Italy she was quite prepared to walk with me, and perhaps to walk ahead of me. As an English girl, I did not care for this, nor for the complete reversal of Emilia's original attitude, almost suggesting that she has a deliberate and impertinent policy of keeping the situation between us under her own control. So, as I have said, the walk was not a complete success. All the same, I have made a start. It is obvious that the world has more to offer than would be likely to come my way if I were to spend my whole life creeping about with Papa at one side of me and Mamma at the other. I shall think about how best to deal with Emilia now that I better understand her ways. I was not in the least tired when we had walked back to the villa. I despise girls who get tired, quite as much as Caroline despises them.

Believe it or not, Mamma was still lying down. When I went in, she said that she was resting in preparation for the party. But the party is not until the day after tomorrow. Poor dear Mamma might have done better not to have left England in the first place! I must take great care that I am not like that when I reach the same time of life and am married, as I suppose I shall be. Looking at Mamma in repose, it struck me that she would still be quite pretty if she did not always look so tired and worried. Of course she was once far prettier than I am now. I know that well. I, alas, am not really pretty at all. I have to cultivate other graces, as Miss Gisborne puts it.

I saw something unexpected when I was going upstairs to bed. The little contessina had left the salone before the rest of us and, as usual, without a word. Possibly it was only I who saw her slip out, she went so quietly. I noticed that she did not return and supposed that, at her age, she was quite worn out. Assuredly, Mamma would have said so. But then when I myself was going upstairs, holding my candle, I saw for myself what had really happened. At the landing, as we in England should call it, there is in one of the corners an odd little closet or cabinet, from which two doors lead off, both locked, as I know because I have cautiously turned the handles for myself. In this corner, by the light of my candle, I saw the contessina, and she was being hugged by a man. I think it could only have been one of the servants, though I was not really able to tell. Perhaps I am wrong about that, but I am not wrong about it being the contessina. They had been there in complete darkness, and, what is more, they never moved a muscle as I came up the stairs and walked calmly along the passage in the opposite direction. I suppose they hoped I should fail to see them in the dimness. They must have supposed that no one would be coming to bed just yet. Or perhaps they were lost to all sense of time, as Mrs Radcliffe expresses it. I have very little notion of the contessina's age, but she often looks about twelve or even less. Of course I shall say nothing to anybody.

6 October. I have been thinking on and off all day about the differences between the ways we are supposed to behave and the ways we actually do behave. And both are different from the ways in which God calls upon us to behave, and which we can never achieve whatever we do and however hard we apply ourselves, as Mr Biggs-Hartley always emphasizes. We seem, every one of us, to be at least three different people. And that's just to start with.

I am disappointed by the results of my little excursion yesterday with Emilia. I had thought that there was so much of which I was deprived by being a girl and so being unable to go about on my own, but now I am not sure that I have been missing anything. It is almost as if the nearer one approaches to a thing, the less it proves to be there, to exist at all. Apart, of course, from the bad smells and bad words and horrid rough creatures from which and from whom we women are supposed to be "shielded". But I am waxing metaphysical; against which Mr Biggs-Hartley regularly cautions us. I wish Caroline were with us. I believe I might feel quite differently about things if she were here to go about with me, just the two of us. Though, needless to say, it would make no difference to what the things truly were—or were not. It is curious that things should seem not to exist when visited with one person, and then to exist after all if visited with another person. Of course it is all just fancy, but what (I think at moments like this) is not?

I am so friendless and alone in this alien land. It occurs to me that I must have great inner strength to bear up as I do and to fulfil my duties with so little complaint. The contessa has very kindly given me a book of Dante's verses, with the Italian on one side and an English translation on the page opposite. She remarked that it would aid me to learn more of her language. I am not sure that it will. I have dutifully read through several pages of the book, and there is nothing in this world that I like more than reading, but Dante's ideas are so gloomy and complicated that I suspect he is no writer for a woman, certainly not for an English woman. Also his face frightens me, so critical and severe. After looking at his portrait, beautifully engraved at the beginning of the book, I begin to fear that I shall see that face looking over my shoulder as I sit gazing into the looking glass. No wonder Beatrice would have nothing to do with him. I feel that he was quite deficient in the graces that appeal to our sex. Of course one must not even hint such a thing to an Italian, such as the contessa, for to all Italians Dante is as sacred as Shakespeare or Dr Johnson is to us.

For once I am writing this during the afternoon. I suspect that I am suffering from ennui and, as that is a sin (even though only a minor one), I am occupying myself in order to drive it off. I know by now that I am much more prone to such lesser shortcomings as ennui and indolence than to such vulgarities as letting myself be embraced and kissed by a servant. And yet it is not that I feel myself wanting in either energy or passion. It is merely that I lack for anything or anyone worthy of such feelings, and refuse to spend them upon what is unworthy. But what a "merely" is that! How well I understand the universal ennui that possesses our neighbour, Lord Byron! I, a tiny slip of a girl, feel, at least in this particular, at one with the great poet! There might be consolation in the thought, were I capable of consolation. In any case, I am sure that there will be nothing more that is worth record before my eyes close tonight in slumber.

Later. I was wrong! After dinner tonight, it struck me simply to ask the contessa whether she had ever *met* Lord Byron. I suppose it might not be a thing she would proclaim unsolicited, either when Papa and Mamma were present, or, for reasons of delicacy, on one of the too rare occasions when she and I were alone; but I thought that I might now be sufficiently simpatica to venture a discreet enquiry.

I fear that I managed it very crudely. When Papa and Mamma had become involved in one of their arguments together, I walked across the room and sat down at the end of the sofa on which the contessa was reclining; and when she smiled at me and said something agreeable, I simply blurted out my question, quite directly. "Yes, *mia cara*," she replied, "I have met him, but we cannot invite him to our party because he is too political, and many people do not agree with his politics. Indeed, they have already led to several deaths; which some are reluctant to accept at the hands of a straniero, however eminent." And of course it *was* the wonderful possibility of Lord Byron attending the contessa's party that *had been* at the back of my thoughts. Not for the first time, the contessa showed her fascinating insight into the minds of others—or assuredly into my mind.

7 October. The day of the party! It is quite early in the morning and the sun is shining as I have not seen it shine for some time. Perhaps it regularly shines at this time of the day, when I am still asleep? "What you girls miss by not getting up!" as Caroline's Mamma always exclaims, though she is the most indulgent of parents. The trouble is that one *always* awakens early just when it is most desirable that one should slumber longest; as today, with the party before us. I am writing this now because I am *quite certain* that I shall be nothing but a tangle of nerves all day and, after everything is over, utterly spent and exhausted. So, for me, it always is with parties! I am glad that the day after tomorrow will be Sunday.

8 October. I met a man at the party who, I must confess, interested me very much; and, beside that, what matters, as Mrs Fremlinson enquires in *The Hopeful and the Despairing Heart, almost* my favourite of all books, as I truly declare?

Who could believe it? Just now, while I was still asleep, there was a knocking at my door, just loud enough to awaken me, but otherwise so soft and discreet, and there was the contessa *herself*, in the most beautiful negligée, half-rose-coloured and half-mauve, with a tray on which were things to eat and drink, a complete foreign breakfast, in fact! I must acknowledge that at that moment I could well have devoured a complete English breakfast, but what could have been kinder or more thoughtful on the part of the charming contessa? Her dark hair (but not so dark as with the majority of the Italians) had not yet been dressed, and hung about her beautiful, though sad, face, but I noticed that all her rings were on her fingers, flashing and sparkling in the sunshine. "Alas, *mia cara*," she said, looking round the room, with its many deficiencies; "the times that were and the times that are." Then she actually bent over my face, rested her hand lightly on the top of my night-gown, and kissed me. "But how pale you look!" she continued. "You are white as a lily on the altar." I smiled. "I am English," I said, "and I lack strong colouring." But the contessa went on staring at me. Then she said: "The party has quite fatigued you?" She seemed to express it as a question, so I replied, with vigour: "Not in the least, I assure you, Contessa. It was the most beautiful evening of my life" (which was unquestionably the truth and no more than the truth). I sat up in the big bed and, so doing, saw myself in the glass. It was true that I *did* look pale, unusually pale. I was about to remark upon the earliness of the hour, when the contessa suddenly seemed to draw herself together with a gasp and turn remarkably pale herself, considering the native hue of her skin. She stretched out her hand and pointed. She seemed to be pointing at the pillow behind me. I looked round, disconcerted by her demeanour; and I saw an irregular red mark upon the pillow, not a very large mark, but undoubtedly a mark of blood. I raised my hands to my throat. "*Dio Illustrissimo!*" cried out the contessa. "*Ell' e stregata!*" I know enough Italian, from Dante and from elsewhere, to be informed of what that means: "She is bewitched." I leapt out of bed and threw my arms round the contessa before she could flee, as she seemed disposed to do. I besought her to say more, but I was all the time fairly sure that she would not. Italians, even educated ones, still take the idea of "witchcraft" with a seriousness that to us seems unbelievable; and regularly fear even to speak of it. Here I knew by instinct that Emilia and her mistress would be at one. Indeed, the contessa seemed most uneasy at my mere embrace, but she soon calmed herself, and left the room saying, quite pleasantly, that she must have a word with my parents about me. She even managed to wish me "*Buon appetito*" of my little breakfast.

I examined my face and throat in the looking-glass and there, sure enough, was a small scar on my neck which explained everything—except, indeed, how I had come by such a mark, but for that the novelties, the rigours, and the excitements of last night's party would *entirely* suffice. One cannot expect to enter the tournament of love and emerge unscratched: and it is into the tournament that, as I thrill to think, I verily have made my way. I fear it is perfectly typical of the Italian manner of seeing things that a perfectly natural, and very tiny, mishap should have such a disproportionate effect upon the contessa. For myself, an English girl, the mark upon my pillow does not even disturb me. We must hope that it does not cast into screaming hysterics the girl whose duty it will be to change the linen.

If I look especially pale, it is partly because the very bright sunlight makes a contrast. I returned at once to bed and rapidly consumed every scrap and drop that the contessa had brought to me. I seemed quite weak from lack of sustenance, and indeed I have but the slenderest recollection of last night's fare, except that, naturally, I drank far more than on most previous days of my short life, probably more than on *any*.

And now I lie here in my pretty night-gown and nothing else, with my pen in my hand and the sun on my face, and think about *him!* I did not believe such people existed in the real world. I thought that such writers as Mrs Fremlinson and Mrs Radcliffe *improved* men, in order to reconcile their female readers to their lot, and to put their less numerous male readers in a good conceit of themselves. Caroline's Mamma and Miss Gisborne, in their quite different ways, have both indicated as much most clearly; and my own observation hitherto of the opposite sex has confirmed the opinion. But now I have actually met a man at whom even Mrs Fremlinson's finest creation does but hint! He is an Adonis! an Apollo! assuredly a god! Where he treads, sprouts asphodel!

The first romantic thing was that he was not properly presented to me—indeed, he was not presented at all. I know this was very incorrect, but it cannot be denied that it was very exciting. Most of the guests were dancing an old-fashioned *minuetto*, but as I did not know the steps, I was sitting at the end of the room with Mamma, when Mamma was suddenly overcome in some way and had to leave. She emphasized that she would be back in only a minute or two, but almost as soon as she had gone, *he* was standing there, quite as if he had emerged from between the faded tapestries that covered the wall or even from the tapestries themselves, except that he looked very far from faded, though later, when more candles were brought in for supper, I saw that he was older than I had at first supposed, with such a wise and experienced look as I have never seen on any other face.

Of course he had not only to speak to me at once, or I should have risen and moved away, but to *compel* me, with his eyes and words, to remain. He said something pleasant about my being the only rosebud in a garden otherwise autumnal, but I am not such a goose as never to have heard speeches like that before, and it was what he said next that made me fatally hesitate. He said (and never, *never* shall I forget his words): "As we are both visitants from a world that is not this one, we should know one another". It was so exactly what I always feel about myself, as this journal (I fancy) makes clear, that I could not but yield a trifle to his apperceptiveness in finding words for my deepest conviction, extremely irregular and dangerous though I well knew my position to be. *And* he spoke in beautiful English; his accent (not, I think, an Italian one) only making his words the more choice-sounding and delightful!

I should remark here that it was not true that *all* the contessa's guests were "autumnal", even though most of them certainly were. Sweet creature that she is, she had invited several *cavalieri* from the local nobility *expressly* for my sake, and several of them had duly been presented to me, but with small conversation resulting, partly because there was so little available of a common tongue, but more because each single *cavaliero* seemed to me very much what in Derbyshire we call a peg-Jack. It was typical of the contessa's sympathetic nature that she perceived the unsuccess of these *rencontres*, and made no attempt to fan flames that were never so much as faint sparks. How unlike the matrons of Derbyshire, who, when they have set their minds to the task, will work the bellows in such cases not merely for a whole single evening, but for weeks, months, or, on occasion, years! But then it would be unthinkable to apply the word "matron" to the lovely contessa! As it was, the four *cavalieri* were left to make what they could of the young contessina and such other *bambine* as were on parade.

I pause for a moment seeking words in which to describe him. He is above the average tall, and, while slender and elegant, conveys a wondrous impression of force and strength. His skin is somewhat pallid, his nose aquiline and commanding (though with quivering, sensitive nostrils), his mouth scarlet and (I must apply the word) passionate. Just to look at his mouth made me think of great poetry and wide seas. His fingers are very long and fine, but powerful in their grip: as I learned for myself before the end of the evening. His hair I at first thought quite black, but I saw later that it was delicately laced with grey, perhaps even white. His brow is high, broad, and noble. Am I describing a god or a man? I find it hard to be sure.

As for his conversation I can only say that, indeed, it was not of this world. He proffered none of the empty chatter expected at social gatherings; which, in so far as it has any meaning at all, has a meaning quite different from that which the words of themselves convey—a meaning often odious to me. Everything he said (at least after that first conventional compliment) spoke to something deep within me, and everything I said in reply was what I really wanted to say. I have been able to talk in that way before with no man of any kind, from Papa downwards; and with very few women. And yet I find it difficult to recall what subjects we discussed. I think that may be a *consequence* of the feeling with which we spoke. The feeling I not merely recollect but feel still—all over and through me—deep and warm—transfiguring. The subjects, no. They were life, and beauty, and art, and nature, and myself: in fact, *everything*. Everything, that is, except the very different and very silly things that almost everyone else talks about all the time, chatter and chump without stopping this side of the churchyard. He did once observe that "Words are what prevail with women", and I could only smile, it was so true.

Fortunately, Mamma *never* re-appeared. As for the rest of them, I daresay they were more relieved than otherwise to find the gauche little English girl off their hands, so to speak, and apparently provided for. With Mamma indisposed, the obligation to watch over me would descend upon the contessa, but her I saw only in the distance. Perhaps she was resolved not to intrude where *I* should not wish it. If so, it would be what I should expect of her. I do not know.

Then came supper. Much to my surprise (and chagrin), my friend, if so I may call him, excused himself from participating. His explanation, lack of appetite, could hardly be accepted as sufficient or courteous, but the words he employed, succeeded (as always, I feel, with him) in purging the offence. He affirmed most earnestly that I must sustain myself even though he were unable to escort me, and that he would await my return. As he spoke, he gazed at me so movingly that I could but accept the situation, though I daresay I had as little appetite (for the coarse foods of this world) as he. I perceive that I have so far omitted to refer to the beauty and power of his eyes; which are so dark as to be almost black—at least by the light of candles. Glancing back at him, perhaps a little keenly, it occurred to me that he might be bashful about showing himself in his full years by the bright lights of the supper tables. It is a vanity *by no means* confined to my own sex. Indeed he seemed almost to be shrinking away from the augmented brightness even at this far end of the room. And this for all the impression of strength which was the most marked thing about him. Tactfully I made to move off. "You will return?" he asked, so anxiously and compellingly. I remained calm. I merely smiled.

And then Papa caught hold of me. He said that Mamma, having gone upstairs, had succumbed totally, as I might have known in advance she would do, and in fact *did* know; and that, when I had supped, I had "better come upstairs also". At that Papa elbowed me through to the tables and started trying to stuff me like a turkey, but, as I have said, I had little gusto for it, so little that I cannot now name a single thing that I ate, or that Papa ate either. Whatever it was, I "washed it down" (as we say in Derbyshire) with an unusual quantity (for me) of the local wine, which people, including Papa, always say is so "light", but which always seems to me no "lighter" than any other, but noticeably "heavier" than some I could name. What is more, I had already consumed a certain amount of it earlier in the evening when I was supposed to be flirting with the local peg-Jacks. One curious thing is that Papa, who never fails to demur at my doing almost anything else, seems to have no objection to my drinking wine quite heavily. I do not think I have ever known him even try to impose a limit. That is material, of course, only in the rare absence of Mamma, to whom this observation does not apply. But Mamma herself is frequently unwell after only two or three glasses. At supper last night, I was in a state of "trance": eating food was well-nigh-impossible, but drinking wine almost fatally facile. Then Papa started trying to push me off to bed again—or perhaps to hold Mamma's head. After all that wine, and with my new friend patiently waiting for me, it was farcical. But I had to dispose of Papa somehow, so I promised him faithfully, and forgot my promise (whatever it was) immediately. Mercifully, I have not so far set eyes upon Papa since that moment.

Or, in reality, upon *anyone* until the contessa waked me this morning: on anyone but *one*.

There he was quietly awaiting me among the shadows cast by the slightly swaying tapestries and by the flapping bannerets ranged round the walls above us. This time he actually clutched my hand in his eagerness. It was only for a moment, of course, but I felt the firmness of his grip. He said he hoped he was not keeping me from the dance floor, but I replied No, oh No. In truth, I was barely even capable of dancing at that moment; and I fancy that

316 Robert Aickman

the measures trod by the musty relics around us were, at the best
of times, not for me. Then he said, with a slight smile, that once he
had been a great dancer. Oh, I said idly and under the power of
the wine; where was that? At Versailles, he replied; and in Peters-
burg. I must say that, wine or no wine, this surprised me; because
surely, as everyone knows, Versailles was burned down by the
incendiaries in 1789, a good thirty years ago? I must have glanced
at him significantly, because he then said, smiling once more,
though faintly: "Yes, I am very, *very* old." He said it with such
curious emphasis that he did not seem to demand some kind of
denial, as such words normally do. In fact, I could find nothing
immediate to say at all. And yet it was nonsense, and denial
would have been sincere. I do not know his age, and find even an
approximation difficult, but "very, very old" he most certainly is
not, but in all important ways one of the truly youngest people
that can be imagined, and one of the most truly ardent. He was
wearing the most beautiful black clothes, with a tiny Order of
some kind, I am sure *most* distinguished, because so unobtrusive.
Papa has often remarked that the flashy display of Honours is no
longer correct.

In some ways the most romantic thing of all is that I do not even
know his name. As people were beginning to leave the party, not
so very late, I suppose, as most of the people were, after all, quite
old, he took my hand and this time held it, nor did I even affect to
resist. "We shall meet again," he said, "many times;" looking so
deeply and steadily into my eyes that I felt he had penetrated my
inmost heart and soul. Indeed, there was something so powerful
and mysterious about my own feelings at that moment that I could
only murmur "Yes," in a voice so weak that he could hardly have
heard me, and then cover my eyes with my hands, those eyes into
which he had been gazing so piercingly. For a moment (it cannot
have been longer, or my discomposure would have been observed
by others), I sank down into a chair with all about me black and
swimming, and when I had recovered myself, he was no longer
there, and there was nothing to do but be kissed by the contessa,
who said "You're looking tired, child," and be hastened to my big
bed, immediately.

And though new emotions are said to deprive us of rest (as I
have myself been able to confirm on one or two occasions), I seem
to have *slept* immediately too, and very deeply, and for a very long

time. I know, too, that I dreamed remarkably, but I cannot at all recollect of what. Perhaps I do not need the aid of memory, for surely I can surmise?

On the first occasion since I have been in Italy, the sun is truly very hot. I do not think I shall write any more today. I have already covered pages in my small, clear handwriting, which owes so much to Miss Gisborne's patience and severity, and to her high standards in all matters touching young girlhood. I am rather surprised that I have been left alone for so long. Though Papa and Mamma do not seem to me to accomplish very much in proportion to the effort they expend, yet they are very inimical to "lying about and doing nothing", especially in my case, but in their own cases also, as I must acknowledge. I wonder how Mamma is faring after the excitement of last night? I am sure I should arise, dress, and ascertain; but instead I whisper to myself that once more I feel powerfully drawn towards the embrace of Morpheus.

9 October. Yesterday morning I decided that I had already recorded enough for one single day (though for what wonderful events I had to try, however vainly, to find words!), but there are few private occupations in this world about which I care more than inscribing the thoughts and impressions of my heart in this small, secret journal, which no one else shall ever in this world see (I shall take good care of that), so that I am sure I should again have taken up my pen in the evening, had there been any occurrence sufficiently definite to write about. *That*, I fear, is what Miss Gisborne would call one of my overloaded sentences, but overloaded sentences can be the reflection, I am sure, of overloaded spirits, and even be their only relief and outlet! How well at this moment do I recall Miss Gisborne's moving counsel: Only find the right words for your troubles, and your troubles become half-joys. Alas, for me at this hour there can be no right words: in some strange way that I can by no means grasp hold of, I find myself fire and ice in equal parts. I have never before felt so greatly alive and yet I catch in myself an eerie conviction that my days are now closely numbered. It does not frighten me, as one would expect it to do. Indeed, it is very nearly a relief. I have never moved at my ease in this world, despite all the care that has been lavished on me; and if I had never known Caroline, I can only speculate what would have become of me. And now! What is Caroline, hitherto

my dearest friend (and sometimes her Mamma too), by comparison with . . . Oh, there *are* no words. Also I have not completely recovered from the demands which last night made upon me. This is something I am rather ashamed of and shall admit to no one. But it is true. As well as being torn by emotion, I am worn to a silken thread.

The contessa, having appeared in my room yesterday morning, then disappeared and was not seen again all day, as on the day we arrived. All the same she seemed to have spoken to Mamma about me, as she had said she would be doing. This soon became clear.

It was already afternoon before I finally rose from my bed and ventured from my sunny room. I was feeling very hungry once more, and I felt that I really must find out whether Mamma was fully recovered. So I went first and knocked at the door of Mamma and Papa's rooms. As there was no answer, I went downstairs, and, though there was no one else around (when it is at all sunny, most Italians simply lie down in the shade), there was Mamma, in full and blooming health, on the terrace overlooking the garden. She had her workbox with her and was sitting in the full sun trying to do two jobs at once, perhaps three, in her usual manner. When Mamma is feeling quite well, she always fidgets terribly. I fear that she lacks what the gentleman we met in Lausanne called "the gift of repose". (I have never forgotten that expression.)

Mamma set about me at once. "Why didn't you dance with even one of those nice young men whom the contessa had gone to the trouble of inviting simply for your sake? The contessa is very upset about it. Besides, what have you been doing all the morning? This lovely, sunny day? And what is all this other rubbish the contessa has been trying to tell me about you? I cannot understand a word of it. Perhaps you can enlighten me? I suppose it is something I ought to know about. No doubt it is a consequence of your father and mother agreeing to your going into the town on your own?"

Needless to say, I know by this time how to reply to Mamma when she rants on in terms such as these.

"The contessa is very upset about it all," Mamma exclaimed again after I had spoken; as if a band of knaves had stolen all the spoons, and I had been privy to the crime. "She is plainly hinting at something which courtesy prevents her putting into words, and it is something to do with you. I should be obliged if you would tell me what it is. Tell me at once," Mamma commanded very fiercely.

Of course I was aware that something had taken place between the contessa and me that morning, and by now I knew very well what lay behind it: in one way or another the contessa had divined my *rencontre* of the evening before and had realized something (though how far from the whole!) of the effect it had made upon me. Even to me she had expressed herself in what English people would regard as an overwrought, Italianate way. It was clear that she had said something to Mamma on the subject, but of a veiled character, as she did not wish actually to betray me. She had, indeed, informed me that she was going to do this, and I now wished that I had attempted to dissuade her. The fact is that I had been so somnolent as to be half without my wits.

"Mamma," I said, with the dignity I have learned to display at these times, "if the contessa has anything to complain of in my conduct, I am sure she will complain only when I am present." And, indeed, I *was* sure of that; though doubtful whether the contessa would ever consider complaining about me at all. Her addressing herself to Mamma in the present matter was, I could be certain, an attempt to aid me in some way, even though possibly misdirected, as was almost inevitable with someone who did not know Mamma very well.

"You are defying me, child," Mamma almost screamed. "You are defying your own mother." She had so worked herself up (surely about nothing? Even less than usual?) that she managed to prick herself. Mamma is constantly pricking herself when she attempts needlework, mainly, I always think, because she *will* not concentrate upon any one particular task; and she keeps a wad of lint in her box against the next time it occurs. This time, however, the lint seemed to be missing, and she appeared to have inflicted quite a gash. Poor Mamma flapped about like a bird beneath a net, while the blood was beginning to flow quite freely. I bent forward and sucked it away with my tongue. It was really strange to have Mamma's blood in my mouth. The strangest part was that it tasted delightful; almost like an exceptionally delicious sweetmeat! I feel my own blood mantling to my cheek as I write the words now.

Mamma then managed to staunch the miniature wound with her pocket handkerchief: one of the pretty ones she had purchased in Besançon. She was looking at me in her usual critical way, but all she said was: "It is perhaps fortunate that we are leaving here on Monday."

Though it was our usual routine, nothing had been said on the present occasion, and I was aghast. (Here, I suppose, *was* something definite to record yesterday evening!)

"What!" I cried. "Leave the sweet contessa so soon! Leave, within only a week, the town where Dante walked and wrote!" I smile a little as I perceive how, without thinking, I am beginning to follow the flamboyant, Italian way of putting things. I am not really sure that Dante did *write* anything much in Ravenna, but to Italians such objections have little influence upon the choice of words. I realize that it is a habit I must guard against taking to an extreme.

"Where Dante walked may be not at all a suitable place for you to walk," rejoined Mamma, uncharitably, but with more sharpness of phrase and thought than is customary with her. She was fondling her injured thumb the while, and had nothing to mollify her acerbity towards me. The blood was beginning to redden the impromptu bandage, and I turned away with what writers call "very mixed feelings".

All the same, I did manage to see some more of the wide world before we left Ravenna; and on the very next day, this day, Sunday, and even though it is a Sunday. Apparently, there is no English church in Ravenna, so that all we could compass was for Papa to read a few prayers this morning and go through the Litany, with Mamma and me making the responses. The major-domo showed the three of us to a special room for the purpose. It had nothing in it but an old table with shaky legs and a line of wooden chairs: all dustier and more decrepit even than other things I have seen in the villa. Of course all this has happened in previous places when it was a Sunday, but never before under such dispiriting conditions—even, as I felt, *unhealthy* conditions. I was *most* disagreeably affected by the entire experience and *entirely* unable to imbibe the Word of God, as I should have done. I have never felt like that before even at the least uplifting of Family Prayers. Positively *irreverent* thoughts raced uncontrolledly through my little head: for example, I found myself wondering how efficacious God's Word could be for Salvation when droned and stumbled over by a mere uncanonized layman such as Papa—no, I mean, of course, *unordained*, but I have let the first word stand because it is so comic when applied to Papa, who is always denouncing "the Roman Saints" and all they represent, such as frequent days of public devotion in their honour. English people speak so unkindly of the Roman Catholic priests, but at least they have all, including the most unworthy of them, been touched by hands that go back and back and back to Saint Peter and so to the Spurting Fountain of Grace itself. You can hardly say the same for Papa, and I believe that even Mr Biggs-Hartley's consecrationary position is a matter of dispute. I feel very strongly that the Blood of the Lamb cannot be mediated unless by the Elect or washed in by hands that are not strong and white.

Oh, how can he fulfil his promise that "We shall meet again", if Papa and Mamma drag me, protesting, from the place where we met first? Let alone meet "Many times"? These thoughts distract me, as I need not say; and yet I am quite sure that they distract me less than one might expect. For that the reason is simple enough: deep within me I *know* that some wondrous thing, some special election, has passed between him and me, and that meet again we shall in consequence, and no doubt "Many times". Distracted about it all though I am, I am simultaneously so sure as to be almost at peace: fire and ice, as I have said. I find I can still sometimes think about other things, which was by no means the case when I fancied, long, long ago, that I was "in love" (perish the thought!) with Mr Franklin Stobart. Yes, yes, my wondrous friend has brought to my wild soul a measure of peace at last! I only wish I did not feel so tired. Doubtless it will pass when the events of the night before last are more distant (what sadness, though, when they are! What sadness, happen what may!), and, I suppose, this afternoon's tiring walk also. No, *not* "tiring". I refuse to admit the word, and that malapert Emilia returned home "fresh as a daisy", to use the expression her kind of person uses where I come from.

But what a walk it proved to be, none the less! We wandered through the *Pineta di Classe:* a perfectly enormous forest between Ravenna and the sea, with pine trees like very thick, dark, bushy umbrellas, and, so they say, either a brigand or a bear hiding behind each one of them! I have never seen such pine trees before; not in France or Switzerland or the Low Countries, let alone in England. They are more like trees in the *Thousand Nights and a Night* (not that I have read that work), dense enough at the top and stout-trunked enough for rocs to nest in! And such countless numbers of them, all so old! Left without a guide, I should easily have found myself lost within only a few minutes, so many and so vague are the different tracks among the huge conifers but I have to admit that Emilia, quite shed now of her *bien élevée* finicking, strode out almost like a boy, and showed a knowledge of the best routes that I could only wonder at and take advantage of. There is now almost an understanding between me and Emilia, and it is mainly from her that I am learning an amount of Italian that is beginning quite to surprise me. All the time I recall, however, that it is a very simple language: the great poet of *Paradise Lost* (not that I have read that work either) remarked that it was unnecessary to set aside special periods for instruction in Italian, because one could simply pick it up as one went along. So it is proving between me and Emilia.

The forest routes are truly best suited to gentlemen on horseback, and at one place two such emerged from one of the many tracks going off to our left. "*Guardi!*" cried out Emilia and clutched my arm as if she were my intimate. "Milord Byron and Signor Shelley!" (I do not attempt to indicate Emilia's funny approximation to the English names.) What a moment in my life—or in anyone's life! To see at the same time two persons both so great and famous and both so irrevocably doomed! There was not, of course, time enough for any degree of close observation, though Mr Shelley seemed slightly to acknowledge with his crop our standing back a little to allow him and his friend free passage, but I fear that my main impression was of both *giaours* looking considerably older than I had expected and Lord Byron considerably more corpulent (as well as being quite grey-headed, though I believe only at the start of his life's fourth decade). Mr Shelley was remarkably untidy in his dress and Lord Byron most comical: in that respect at least, the reality was in accord with the report. Both were without hats or caps. They cantered away down the track up which we had walked. They were talking in loud voices (Mr Shelley's noticeably high in pitch), both together, above the thudding of their horse's hoofs. Neither of them really stopped talking even when slowing in order to wheel, so to speak, round the spot where we stood.

And so I have at length set eyes upon the fabled Lord Byron! A wondrous moment indeed; but how much more wondrous for me if it had occurred before that recent most wondrous of all possible moments! But it would be very wrong of me to complain because the red and risen moon has quite dimmed my universal nightlight! Lord Byron, that child of destiny, is for the whole world and, no doubt, for all time, or at least for a great deal of it! My fate is a different one and I draw it to my breast with a young girl's eager arms!

"Come gentili!" exclaimed Emilia, gazing after our two horse-men. It was not perhaps the most appropriate comment upon Lord Byron, or even upon Mr Shelley, but there was nothing for me to reply (even if I could have found the Italian words), so on went our walk, with Emilia now venturing so far as to sing, in a quite pretty voice, and me lacking heart to chide her, until in the end the pine-trees parted and I got my first glimpse of the Adriatic Sea, and, within a few more paces, a whole wide prospect of it. (The Venetian Lagoon I refuse to take seriously.) The Adriatic Sea is linked with the Mediterranean Sea, indeed quite properly a part or portion of it, so that I can now say to myself that I have "seen the Mediterranean"; which good old Doctor Johnson defined as the true object of all travel. It was almost as if at long last my own eyes had seen the Holy Grail, with the Redemptive Blood streaming forth in golden splendour; and I stood for whole moments quite lost in my own deep thoughts. The world falls from me once more in a moment as I muse upon that luminous, rapturous flood.

But I can write no more. So unwontedly weary do I feel that the vividness of my vision notwithstanding is something to be mar-velled at. It is as if my hand were guided as was Isabella's by the distant Traffio in Mrs Fremlinson's wonderful book; so that Isa-bella was enabled to leave a record of the strange events that preceded her death—without which record, as it now occurs to me, the book, fiction though it be, could hardly with sense have been written at all. The old moon is drenching my sheets and my night-gown in brightest crimson. In Italy, the moon is always full and always so red.

Oh, when next shall I see my friend, my paragon, my genius!

10 October. I have experienced so sweet and great a dream that I must write down the fact before it is forgotten, and even though I find that already there is almost nothing left that *can* be written. I have dreamed that he was with me; that he indued my neck and breast with kisses that were at once the softest and the sharpest in

the world; that he filled my ears with thoughts so strange that they could have come only from a world afar.

And now the Italian dawn is breaking: all the sky is red and purple. The rains have gone, as if for ever. The crimson sun calls to me to take flight before it is once more autumn and then winter. Take flight! Today we are leaving for Rimini! Yes, it is but to Rimini that I am to repair. It is farcical.

And in my dawn-red room there is once again blood upon my person. But this time I know. It is at his embrace that my being springs forth, in joy and welcome; his embrace that is at once the softest and the sharpest in the world. How strange that I could ever have failed to recall such bliss!

I rose from my bed to look for water, there being, once more, none in my room. I found that I was so weak with happiness that I all but fainted. But after sinking for a moment upon my bed, I somewhat recovered myself and succeeded in gently opening the door. And what should I find there? Or, rather, whom? In the faintly lighted corridor, at some distance, stood silently none other than the little contessina, whom I cannot recollect having previously beheld since her Mamma's *soirée à danse*. She was dressed in some kind of loose dark wrapper, and I may only leave between her and her conscience what she can have been doing. No doubt for some good reason allied therewith, she seemed turned to stone by the sight of *me*. Of course I was in *déshabillé* even more complete than her own. I had omitted even to cover my night-gown. And upon that there was blood—as if I had suffered an injury. When I walked towards her reassuringly (after all, we are but two young girls and I am not her judge—nor anyone's), she gave a low croaking scream and fled from me as if I had been the Erl Queen herself, but still almost silently, no doubt for her same good reasons. It was foolish of the little contessina, because all I had in mind to do was to take her in my arms, and then to kiss her in token of our common humanity and the strangeness of our encounter at such an hour.

I was disconcerted by the contessina's childishness (these Italians manage to be shrinking *bambine* and hardened women of the world at one and the same time), and, again feeling faint, leaned against the passage wall. When I stood full on my feet once more, I saw by the crimson light coming through one of the dusty windows that I had reached out to stop myself falling and left a scarlet impression of my hand on the painted plaster. It is difficult to excuse and impossible to remove. How I weary of these *règles* and conventionalities by which I have hitherto been bound! How I long for the measureless liberty that has been promised me and of which I feel so complete a future assurance!

But I managed to find some water (the contessa's villa is no longer of the kind that has servitors alert—or supposedly alert—all night in the larger halls), and with this water I did what I could, at least in my own room. Unfortunately I had neither enough water nor enough strength to do all. Besides, I begin to grow reckless.

11 October. No dear dream last night!

Considerable crafty unpleasantness, however, attended our departure yesterday from Ravenna. Mamma disclosed that the contessa was actually lending us her own carriage. "It's because she wants to see the last of us," said Mamma to me, looking at the cornice. "How can that be, Mamma?" I asked. "Surely, she's hardly seen us at all? She was invisible when we arrived, and now she's been almost invisible again for days." "There's no connection between those two things," Mamma replied. "At the time we arrived, the contessa was feeling unwell, as we mothers often do, you'll learn that for yourself soon. But for the last few days, she's been very upset by your behaviour, and now she wants us to go." As Mamma was still looking at the wall instead of at me, I put out the tip of my tongue, only the merest scrap of it, but *that* Mamma did manage to see, and had lifted her hand several inches before she recollected that I was now as good as an adult and so not to be corrected by a simple cuff.

And then when we were all about to enter the draggled old carriage, lo and behold the contessa did manage to haul herself into the light, and I caught her actually crossing herself behind my back, or what she no doubt thought was behind my back. I had to clench my hands to stop myself spitting at her. I have since begun to speculate whether she did not really *intend* me to see what she did. I was once so fond of the contessa, so drawn to her—I can still *remember* that quite well—but *all* is now changed. A week, I find, can sometimes surpass a lifetime; and so, for that matter, can one single indelible night. The contessa took great care to prevent her eyes once meeting mine, though, as soon as I perceived this, I never for a moment ceased glaring at her like a little basilisk. She apologised to Papa and Mamma for the absence of the contessina whom she described as being in bed with screaming megrims or the black cramp or some other malady (I truly cared not what! nor care now!) no doubt incident to girlish immaturity in Italy! And Papa and Mamma made response as if they really minded about the silly little child! Another way of expressing their disapproval of *me*, needless to observe. My considered opinion is that the contessina and her Mamma are simply two of a kind, but that the contessa has had time to become more skilled in concealment and duplicity. I am sure that all Italian females are alike, when one really knows them. The contessa had made me dig my finger-nails so far into my palms that my hands hurt all the rest of the day and still look as if I had caught a dagger in each of them, as in Sir Walter Scott's tale.

We had a coachman and a footman on the box, neither of them at all young, but more like two old wiseacres; and, when we reached Classe, we stopped in order that Papa, Mamma, and I could go inside the church, which is famous for its mosaics, going back, as usual to the Byzantines. The big doors at the western end were open in the quite hot sunshine and indeed the scene inside did look very pretty, all pale azure, the colour of Heaven, and shining gold; but I saw no more of it than that, because as I was about to cross the threshold, I was again overcome by my faintness, and sitting down on a bench, bade Papa and Mamma go in without me, which they immediately did, in the sensible English way, instead of trying to make an ado over me, in the silly Italian way. The bench was of marble, with arms in the shape of lions, and though the marble was worn, and cut, and pock-marked, it was a splendid, heavy object, carved, if I mistake not, by the Romans themselves. Seated on it, I soon felt better once more, but then I noticed the two fat old men on the coach doing something or other to the doors and windows. I supposed they were greasing them, which I am sure would have been very much in order, as would have been a considerable application of paint to the entire vehicle. But when Papa and Mamma at last came out of the church, and we all resumed our places, Mamma soon began to complain of a smell, which she said was, or at least resembled, that of the herb, garlic. Of course when one is abroad, the smell of garlic is *everywhere*, so that I quite understood when Papa merely told Mamma not to be fanciful; but then I found that I myself was more and more affected, so that we completed the journey in almost total silence, none of us, except Papa, having much appetite for the very crude meal set before us en route at Cesenatico. "You're looking white," said Papa to me, as we stepped from the coach. Then he added to Mamma, but hardly attempting to prevent my hearing, "I can see why the contessa spoke to you as she did". Mamma merely shrugged her shoulders: something she would never have thought of doing before we came abroad, but which now she does frequently. I nearly said something spiteful. At the end, the contessa, when she condescended to appear at all, was constantly disparaging my appearance, and indeed I am pale, paler than I once was, though always I have been pale enough, pale as a little phantom; but only I know the reason for the change in me, and no one else shall know it ever, because no one else ever can. It is not so much a "secret". Rather is it a revelation.

In Rimini we are but stopping at the inn; and we are almost the only persons to be doing so. I cannot wonder at this: the inn is a gaunt, forbidding place; the *padrona* has what in Derbyshire we call a "hare-lip"; and the attendance is of the worst. Indeed, no one has so far ventured to come near me. All the rooms, including mine, are very large; and all lead into one another, in the style of 200 years ago. The building resembles a palazzo that has fallen upon hard times, and perhaps that is what it is. At first I feared that my dear Papa and Mamma were to be ensconced in the apartment adjoining my own, which would have suited me not at all, but, for some reason, it has not happened, so that between my room and the staircase are two dark and empty chambers, which would once have caused me alarm, but which now I welcome. Everything is poor and dusty. Shall I ever repose abroad in such ease and *bien-être* as one takes for granted in Derbyshire? Why No, I shall not: and a chill runs down my back as I inscribe the words; but a chill more of excitement than of fear. Very soon now shall I be entirely elsewhere and entirely above such trivia.

I have opened a pair of the big windows, a grimy and, I fear, a noisy task. I flitted out in the moonlight on to the stone balcony, and gazed down into the *piazza*. Rimini seems now to be a very poor town, and there is nothing of the nocturnal uproar and riot which are such usual features of Italian existence. At this hour, all is completely silent—even strangely so. It is still very warm, but there is a mist between the earth and the moon.

I have crept into another of these enormous Italian beds. He is winging towards me. There is no further need for words. I have but to slumber, and that will be simple, so exhausted I am.

12 13 14 October. Nothing to relate but him, and of him nothing that can be related.

I am very tired, but it is tiredness that follows exaltation, not the vulgar tiredness of common life. I noticed today that I no longer have either shadow or reflection. Fortunately Mamma was quite destroyed (as the Irish simpletons express it) by the journey from Ravenna, and has not been seen since. How many, many hours one's elders pass in retirement! How glad I am never to have to experience such bondage! How I rejoice when I think about the new life which spreads before me into infinity, the new ocean which already laps at my feet, the new vessel with the purple sail and the red oars upon which I shall at any moment embark! When one is confronting so tremendous a transformation, how foolish seem words, but the habit of them lingers even when I have hardly strength to hold the pen! Soon, soon, new force will be mine, fire that is inconceivable; and the power to assume any night-shape that I may wish, or to fly through the darkness with none. What love is his! How chosen among all women am I; and I am just a little English girl! It is a miracle, and I shall enter the halls of Those Other Women with pride.

Papa is so beset by Mamma that he has failed to notice that I am eating nothing and drinking only water; that at our horrid, odious meals I am but feigning.

Believe it or not, yesterday we visited, Papa and I, the Tempio Malatestiano. Papa went as an English Visitor: I (at least by comparison with Papa) as a Pythoness. It is a beautiful edifice, among the most beautiful in the world, they say. But for me a special splendour lay in the noble and amorous dead it houses, and in the control over them which I feel increase within me. I was so rent and torn with new power that Papa had to help me back to the inn. Poor Papa, burdened, as he supposes, by *two* weak invalid women! I could almost pity him.

I wish I had reached the pretty little contessina and kissed her throat.

15 October. Last night I opened my pair of windows (the other pair resists me, weak—in terms of this world—as I am), and, without quite venturing forth, stood there in nakedness and raised both my arms. Soon a soft wind began to rustle, where all had previously been still as death. The rustling steadily rose to roaring, and the faint chill of the night turned to heat as when an oven door is opened. A great crying out and weeping, a buzzing and screaming and scratching, swept in turmoil past the open window, as if invisible (or almost invisible) bodies were turning around and around in the air outside, always lamenting and accusing. My head was split apart by the sad sounds and my body as moist as if I were an Ottoman. Then, on an instant, all had passed by. *He* stood there before me in the dim embrasure of the window. "That," he said, "is Love as the elect of this world know it." "The *elect?*" I besought him, in a voice so low that it was hardly a voice at all (but what matter?). "Why yes," he seemed to reaffirm. "Of this world, the elect."

16 October. The weather in Italy changes constantly. Today once more it is cold and wet.

They have begun to suppose me ill. Mamma, back on her legs for a spell, is fussing like a blowfly round a dying lamb. They even called in a *medico*, after discussing at length in my presence whether an Italian physician could be regarded as of any utility. With what voice I have left, I joined in vigorously that he could not. All the same, a creature made his appearance: wearing fusty black, and, believe it or not, a grey *wig*—in all, a veritable Pantalone. What a farce! With my ever sharper fangs, I had him soon despatched, and yelling like the Old Comedy he belonged to. Then I spat forth his enfeebled, senile lymph, cleaning my lips of his skin and smell, and returned, hugging myself, to my couch.

Janua mortis vita, as Mr Biggs-Hartley says in his funny dog latin. And to think that today is Sunday! I wonder why no one has troubled to pray over me?

17 October. I have been left alone all day. Not that it matters.

Last night came the strangest and most beautiful event of my life, a seal laid upon my future.

I was lying here with my double window open, when I noticed that mist was coming in. I opened my arms to it, but my blood began to trickle down my bosom from the wound in my neck, which of course no longer heals—though I seem to have no particular trouble in concealing the mark from the entire human race, not forgetting learned men with certificates from the University of Sciozza.

Outside in the *piazza* was a sound of shuffling and nuzzling, as of sheep being folded on one of the farms at home. I climbed out of bed, walked across, and stepped on to the balcony.

The mist was filtering the moonlight into a silver-grey that I have never seen elsewhere.

The entire *piazza*, a very big one, was filled with huge, grizzled wolves, all perfectly silent, except for the small sounds I have mentioned, all with their tongues flopping and lolling, black in the silvery light, and all gazing up at my window.

Rimini is near to the Appennine Mountains, where wolves notoriously abound, and commonly devour babies and small children. I suppose that the coming cold is drawing them into the towns.

I smiled at the wolves. Then I crossed my hands on my little bosom and curtsied. They will be prominent among my new people. My blood will be theirs, and theirs mine.

I forgot to say that I have contrived to lock my door. Now, I am assisted in such affairs.

Somehow I have found my way back to bed. It has become exceedingly cold, almost icy. For some reason I think of all the empty rooms in this battered old palazzo (as I am sure it once was), so fallen from their former stateliness. I doubt if I shall write any more. I do not think I shall have any more to say.

Beyond Any Measure

✖

KARL EDWARD WAGNER

I

In the dream I find myself alone in a room. I hear musical
chimes—a sort of music-box tune—and I look around to see
where the sound is coming from.

"I'm in a bedroom. Heavy curtains close off the windows, and
it's quite dark, but I can sense that the furnishings are entirely
antique—late Victorian, I think. There's a large four-poster bed,
with its curtains drawn. Beside the bed is a small night table upon
which a candle is burning. It is from here that the music seems to
be coming.

"I walk across the room toward the bed, and as I stand beside it
I see a gold watch resting on the night table next to the candlestick.
The music-box tune is coming from the watch, I realize. It's one of
those old pocket-watch affairs with a case that opens. The case is
open now, and I see that the watch's hands are almost at midnight.
I sense that on the inside of the watchcase there will be a picture,
and I pick up the watch to see whose picture it is.

"The picture is obscured with a red smear. It's fresh blood.

"I look up in sudden fear. From the bed, a hand is pulling aside
the curtain.

"That's when I wake up."

* * *

"Bravo!" applauded someone.

Lisette frowned momentarily, then realized that the comment was directed toward another of the chattering groups crowded into the gallery. She sipped her champagne; she must be a bit tight, or she'd never have started talking about the dreams.

"What do you think, Dr. Magnus?"

It was the gala reopening of Covent Garden. The venerable fruit, flower and vegetable market, preserved from the demolition crew, had been renovated into an airy mall of expensive shops and galleries: "London's new shopping experience." Lisette thought it an unhappy hybrid of born-again Victorian exhibition hall and trendy "shoppes." Let the dead past bury its dead. She wondered what they might make of the old Billingsgate fish market, should SAVE win its fight to preserve that landmark, as now seemed unlikely.

"Is this dream, then, a recurrent one, Miss Seyrig?"

She tried to read interest or skepticism in Dr. Magnus' pale blue eyes. They told her nothing.

"Recurrent enough."

To make me mention it to Danielle, she finished in her thoughts. Danielle Borland shared a flat—she'd stopped terming it an apartment even in her mind—with her in a row of terrace houses in Bloomsbury, within an easy walk of London University. The gallery was Maitland Reddin's project; Danielle was another. Whether Maitland really thought to make a business of it, or only intended to showcase his many friends' not always evident talents was not open to discussion. His gallery in Knightsbridge was certainly successful, if that meant anything.

"How often is that?" Dr. Magnus touched his glass to his blonde-bearded lips. He was drinking only Perrier water, and, at that, was using his glass for little more than to gesture.

"I don't know. Maybe half a dozen times since I can remember. And then, that many again since I came to London."

"You're a student at London University, I believe Danielle said?"

"That's right. In art. I'm over here on fellowship."

Danielle had modelled for an occasional session—Lisette now was certain it was solely from a desire to display her body rather than due to any financial need—and when a muttered profanity at a dropped brush disclosed a common American heritage, the two *émigrés* had rallied at a pub afterward to exchange news and views. Lisette's bed-sit near the Museum was impossible, and Danielle's roommate had just skipped to the Continent with two months' owing. By closing time it was settled.

"How's your glass?"

Danielle, finding them in the crowd, shook her head in mock dismay and refilled Lisette's glass before she could cover it with her hand.

"And you, Dr. Magnus?"

"Quite well, thank you."

"Danielle, let me give you a hand?" Maitland had charmed the two of them into acting as hostesses for his opening.

"Nonsense, darling. When you see me starting to pant with the heat, then call up the reserves. Until then, do keep Dr. Magnus from straying away to the other parties."

Danielle swirled off with her champagne bottle and her smile. The gallery, christened "Such Things May Be" after Richard Burton (*not* Liz Taylor's ex, Danielle kept explaining, and got laughs each time), was ajostle with friends and well-wishers—as were most of the shops tonight: private parties with evening dress and champagne, only a scattering of displaced tourists, gaping and photographing. She and Danielle were both wearing slit-to-thigh crepe de Chine evening gowns and could have passed for sisters: Lisette blonde, green-eyed, with a dust of freckles; Danielle light brunette, hazel-eyed, acclimated to the extensive facial makeup London women favored; both tall without seeming coltish, and close enough of a size to wear each other's clothes.

"It must be distressing to have the same nightmare over and again," Dr. Magnus prompted her.

"There have been others as well. Some recurrent, some not. Similar in that I wake up feeling like I've been through the sets of some old Hammer film."

"I gather you were not actually troubled with such nightmares until recently?"

"Not really. Being in London seems to have triggered them. I suppose it's repressed anxieties over being in a strange city." It was bad enough that she'd been taking some of Danielle's pills in order to seek dreamless sleep.

"Is this, then, your first time in London, Miss Seyrig?"

"It is." She added, to seem less the typical American student: "Although my family was English."

"Your parents?"

"My mother's parents were both from London. They emigrated to the States just after World War I."

"Then this must have been rather a bit like coming home for you."

"Not really. I'm the first of our family to go overseas. And I have no memory of Mother's parents. Grandmother Keswicke died the morning I was born." Something Mother never was able to work through emotionally, Lisette added to herself.

"And have you consulted a physician concerning these nightmares?"

"I'm afraid your National Health Service is a bit more than I can cope with." Lisette grimaced at the memory of the night she had tried to explain to a Pakistani intern why she wanted sleeping medications.

She suddenly hoped her words hadn't offended Dr. Magnus, but then, he scarcely looked the type who would approve of socialized medicine. Urbane, perfectly at ease in formal evening attire, he reminded her somewhat of a blonde-bearded Peter Cushing. Enter Christopher Lee, in black cape, she mused, glancing toward the door. For that matter, she wasn't at all certain just what sort of doctor Dr. Magnus might be. Danielle had insisted she talk with him, very likely had insisted that Maitland invite him to the private opening: "The man has such *insight!* And he's written a number of books on dreams and the subconscious—and not just rehashes of Freudian silliness!"

"Are you going to be staying in London for some time, Miss Seyrig?"

"At least until the end of the year."

"Too long a time to wait to see whether these bad dreams will go away once you're back home in San Francisco, don't you agree? It can't be very pleasant for you, and you really should look after yourself."

Lisette made no answer. *She* hadn't told Dr. Magnus she was from San Francisco. So then, Danielle had already talked to him about her.

Dr. Magnus smoothly produced his card, discreetly offered it to her. "I should be most happy to explore this further with you on a professional level, should you so wish."

"I don't really think it's worth . . ."

"Of course it is, my dear. Why otherwise would we be talking? Perhaps next Tuesday afternoon? Is there a convenient time?"

Lisette slipped his card into her handbag. If nothing else, perhaps he could supply her with some barbs or something. "Three?"

"Three it is, then."

II

The passageway was poorly lighted, and Lisette felt a vague sense of dread as she hurried along it, holding the hem of her nightgown away from the gritty filth beneath her bare feet. Peeling scabs of wallpaper blotched the leprous plaster, and, when she held the candle close, the gouges and scratches that patterned the walls with insane graffiti seemed disquietingly nonrandom. Against the mottled plaster, her figure threw a double shadow: distorted, one crouching forward, the other following.

A full-length mirror panelled one segment of the passageway, and Lisette paused to study her reflection. Her face appeared frightened, her blonde hair in disorder. She wondered at her nightgown—pale, silken, billowing, of an antique mode—not remembering how she came to be wearing it. Nor could she think how it was that she had come to this place.

Her reflection puzzled her. Her hair seemed longer than it should be, trailing down across her breasts. Her finely chiselled features, prominent jawline, straight nose—her face, except the expression, was not hers: lips fuller, more sensual, redder than her lip-gloss, glinted; teeth fine and white. Her green eyes, intense beneath level brows, cat-cruel, yearning.

Lisette released the hem of her gown, raised her fingers to her reflection in wonder. Her fingers passed through the glass, touched the face beyond.

Not a mirror. A doorway. Of a crypt.

The mirror-image fingers that rose to her face twisted in her hair, pulled her face forward. Glass-cold lips bruised her own. The dank breath of the tomb flowed into her mouth.

Dragging herself from the embrace, Lisette felt a scream rip from her throat . . .

. . . And Danielle was shaking her awake.

III

The business card read *Dr. Ingmar Magnus*, followed simply by *Consultations* and a Kensington address. Not Harley Street, at any rate. Lisette considered it for the hundredth time, watching for street names on the corners of buildings as she walked down Kensington Church Street from the Notting Hill Gate station. No clue as to what type of doctor, nor what sort of consultations; wonderfully vague, and just the thing to circumvent licensing laws, no doubt.

Danielle had lent her one of his books to read: *The Self Reborn*, put out by one of those miniscule scholarly publishers clustered about the British Museum. Lisette found it a bewildering mélange of occult philosophy and lunatic-fringe theory—all evidently having something to do with reincarnation—and gave it up after the first chapter. She had decided not to keep the appointment, until her nightmare Sunday night had given force to Danielle's insistence.

Lisette wore a loose silk blouse above French designer jeans and ankle-strap sandal-toe high heels. The early summer heat wave now threatened rain, and she would have to run for it if the grey skies made good. She turned into Holland Street, passed the recently closed Equinox bookshop, where Danielle had purchased various works by Aleister Crowley. A series of back streets—she consulted her map of Central London—brought her to a modestly respectable row of nineteenth-century brick houses, now done over into offices and flats. She checked the number on the brass plaque with her card, sucked in her breath and entered.

Lisette hadn't known what to expect. She wouldn't have been surprised, knowing some of Danielle's friends, to have been greeted with clouds of incense, Eastern music, robed initiates. Instead she found a disappointingly mundane waiting room, rather small but expensively furnished, where a pretty Eurasian receptionist took her name and spoke into an intercom. Lisette noted that there was no one else—patients? clients?—in the waiting room. She glanced at her watch and noticed she was several minutes late.

"Please do come in, Miss Seyrig." Dr. Magnus stepped out of his office and ushered her inside. Lisette had seen a psychiatrist briefly a few years before, at her parents' demand, and Dr.

Magnus's office suggested the same—from the tasteful, relaxed decor, the shelves of scholarly books, down to the traditional psychoanalyst's couch. She took a chair beside the modern, rather carefully arranged desk, and Dr. Magnus seated himself comfortably in the leather swivel chair behind it.

"I almost didn't come," Lisette began, somewhat aggressively.

"I'm very pleased that you did decide to come." Dr. Magnus smiled reassuringly. "It doesn't require a trained eye to see that something is troubling you. When the unconscious tries to speak to us, it is foolhardy to attempt to ignore its message."

"Meaning that I may be cracking up?"

"I'm sure that must concern you, my dear. However, very often dreams such as yours are evidence of the emergencce of a new level of self-awareness—sort of growing pains of the psyche, if you will—and not to be considered a negative experience by any means. They distress you only because you do not understand them—even as a child kept in ignorance through sexual repression is frightened by the changes of puberty. With your cooperation, I hope to help you come to understand the changes of your growing self-awareness, for it is only through a complete realization of one's self that one can achieve personal fulfillment and thereby true inner peace."

"I'm afraid I can't afford to undergo analysis just now."

"Let me begin by emphasizing to you that I am not suggesting psychoanalysis; I do not in the least consider you to be neurotic, Miss Seyrig. What I strongly urge is an *exploration* of your unconsciousness—a discovery of your whole self. My task is only to guide you along the course of your self-discovery, and for this privilege I charge no fee."

"I hadn't realized the National Health Service was this inclusive."

Dr. Magnus laughed easily. "It isn't, of course. My work is supported by a private foundation. There are many others who wish to learn certain truths of our existence, to seek answers where mundane science has not yet so much as realized there are questions. In that regard I am simply another paid researcher, and the results of my investigations are made available to those who share with us this yearning to see beyond the stultifying boundaries of modern science."

He indicated the book-lined wall behind his desk. Much of one shelf appeared to contain books with his own name prominent upon their spines.

"Do you intend to write a book about me?" Lisette meant to put more of a note of protest in her voice.

"It is possible that I may wish to record some of what we discover together, my dear. But only with scupulous discretion, and, needless to say, only with your complete permission."

"My dreams." Lisette remembered the book of his that she had tried to read. "Do you consider them to be evidence of some previous incarnation?"

"Perhaps. We can't be certain until we explore them further. Does the idea of reincarnation smack too much of the occult to your liking, Miss Seyrig? Perhaps we should speak in more fashionable terms of Jungian archetypes, genetic memory or mental telepathy. The fact that the phenomenon has so many designations is ample proof that dreams of a previous existence are a very real part of the unconscious mind. It is undeniable that many people have experienced, in dreams or under hypnosis, memories that cannot possibly arise from their personal experience. Whether you believe that the immortal soul leaves the physical body at death to be reborn in the living embryo, or prefer to attribute it to inherited memories engraved upon DNA, or whatever explanation—this is a very real phenomenon and has been observed throughout history.

"As a rule, these memories of past existence are entirely buried within the unconscious. Almost everyone has experienced *déjà vu*. Subjects under hypnosis have spoken in languages and archaic dialects of which their conscious mind has no knowledge, have recounted in detail memories of previous lives. In some cases these submerged memories burst forth as dreams; in these instances, the memory is usually one of some emotionally laden experience, something too potent to remain buried. I believe that this is the case with your nightmares—the fact that they are recurrent being evidence of some profound significance in the events they recall."

Lisette wished for a cigarette; she'd all but stopped buying cigarettes with British prices, and from the absence of ashtrays here, Dr. Magnus was a nonsmoker.

"But why have these nightmares only lately become a problem?"

"I think I can explain that easily enough. Your forebears were from London. The dreams became a problem after you arrived in London. While it is usually difficult to define any relationship between the subject and the remembered existence, the timing and the force of your dream regressions would seem to indicate that you may be the reincarnation of someone—an ancestress, perhaps —who lived here in London during this past century."

"In that case, the nightmares should go away when I return to the States."

"Not necessarily. Once a doorway to the unconscious is opened, it is not so easily closed again. Moreover, you say that you had experienced these dreams on rare occasions prior to your coming here. I would suggest that what you are experiencing is a natural process—a submerged part of your self is seeking expression, and it would be unwise to deny this shadow-stranger within you. I might further argue that your presence here in London is hardly coincidence—that your decision to study here was determined by that part of you who emerges in these dreams."

Lisette decided she wasn't ready to accept such implications just now. "What do you propose?"

Dr. Magnus folded his hands as neatly as a bishop at prayer. "Have you ever undergone hypnosis?"

"No." She wished she hadn't made that sound like two syllables.

"It has proved to be extraordinarily efficacious in a great number of cases such as your own, my dear. Please do try to put from your mind the ridiculous trappings and absurd mumbo-jumbo with which the popular imagination connotes hypnotism. Hypnosis is no more than a technique through which we may release the entirety of the unconscious mind to free expression, unrestricted by the countless artificial barriers that make us strangers to ourselves."

"You want to hypnotize me?" The British inflection came to her, turning her statement into both question and protest.

"With your fullest cooperation, of course. I think it best. Through regressive hypnosis we can explore the significance of these dreams that trouble you, discover the shadow stranger within your self. Remember—this is a part of *you* that cries out for conscious expression. It is only through the full realization of one's identify, of one's total self, that true inner tranquillity may be achieved. Know thyself, and you will find peace."

"Know myself?"

"Precisely. You must put aside this false sense of guilt, Miss Seyrig. You are not possessed by some alien and hostile force. These dreams, these memories of another existence—this is *you*."

IV

S ome bloody weirdo made a pass at me this afternoon," Lisette confided.

"On the tube, was it?" Danielle stood on her toes, groping along the top of their bookshelf. Freshly showered, she was wearing only a lace-trimmed teddy—cami-knickers, they called them in the shops here—and her straining thigh muscles shaped her buttocks nicely.

"In Kensington, actually. After I had left Dr. Magnus's office." Lisette was lounging in an old satin slip she'd found at a stall in Church Street. They were drinking Bristol Cream out of brandy snifters. It was an intimate sort of evening they loved to share together, when not in the company of Danielle's various friends.

"I was walking down Holland Street, and there was this seedy-looking creep all dressed out in punk regalia, pressing his face against the door where that Equinox bookshop used to be. I made the mistake of glancing at him as I passed, and he must have seen my reflection in the glass, because he spun right around, looked straight at me, and said: 'Darling! What a lovely surprise to see you!'"

Lisette sipped her sherry. "Well, I gave him my hardest stare, and would you believe the creep just stood there smiling like he knew me, and so I yelled, 'Piss off!' in my loudest American accent, and he just froze there with his mouth hanging open."

"Here it is," Danielle announced. "I'd shelved it beside Roland Franklyn's *We Pass from View*—that's another you ought to read. I must remember someday to return it to that cute Liverpool writer who lent it to me."

She settled cozily beside Lisette on the couch, handed her a somewhat smudged paperback, and resumed her glass of sherry. The book was entitled *More Stately Mansions: Evidences of the Infinite* by Dr. Ingmar Magnus, and bore an affectionate inscription from the author to Danielle. "This is the first. The later printings had two of his studies deleted; I can't imagine why. But these are the sort of sessions he was describing to you."

"He wants to put *me* in one of his books," Lisette told her with an extravagant leer. "Can a woman trust a man who writes such ardent inscriptions to place her under hypnosis?"

"Dr. Magnus is a perfect gentleman," Danielle assured her, somewhat huffily. "He's a distinguished scholar and is thoroughly dedicated to his research. And besides, I've let him hypnotize me on a few occasions."

"I didn't know that. Whatever for?"

"Dr. Magnus is always seeking suitable subjects. I was fascinated by his work, and when I met him at a party I offered to undergo hypnosis."

"What happened?"

Danielle seemed envious. "Nothing worth writing about, I'm afraid. He said I was either too thoroughly integrated, or that my previous lives were too deeply buried. That's often the case, he says, which is why absolute proof of reincarnation is so difficult to demonstrate. After a few sessions I decided I couldn't spare the time to try further."

"But what was it like?"

"As adventurous as taking a nap. No caped Svengali staring into my eyes. No lambent girasol ring. No swirling lights. Quite dull, actually. Dr. Magnus simply lulls you to sleep."

"Sounds safe enough. So long as I don't get molested walking back from his office."

Playfully, Danielle stroked her hair. "You hardly look the punk rock type. You haven't chopped off your hair with garden shears and dyed the stubble green. And not a single safety pin through your cheek."

"Actually I suppose he may not have been a punk rocker. Seemed a bit too old, and he wasn't garish enough. It's just that he was wearing a lot of black leather, and he had gold earrings and some sort of medallion."

"In front of the Equinox, did you say? How curious."

"Well, I think I gave him a good start. I glanced in a window to see whether he was trying to follow me, but he was just standing there looking stunned."

"*Might* have been an honest mistake. Remember the old fellow at Midge and Fiona's party who kept insisting he knew you?"

"And who was pissed out of his skull. Otherwise he might have been able to come up with a more original line."

Lisette paged through *More Stately Mansions* while Danielle selected a Tangerine Dream album from the stack and placed it on her stereo at low volume. The music seemed in keeping with the grey drizzle of the night outside and the coziness within their sitting room. Seeing she was busy reading, Danielle poured sherry for them both and stood studying the bookshelves—a hodgepodge of occult and metaphysical topics stuffed together with art books and recent paperbacks in no particular order. Wedged between Aleister Crowley's *Magick in Theory and Practice* and *How I Discovered My Infinite Self* by "An Initiate," was Dr. Magnus's most recent book, *The Shadow Stranger*. She pulled it down, and Dr. Magnus stared thoughtfully from the back of the dust jacket.

"Do you believe in reincarnation?" Lisette asked her.

"I do. Or rather, I do some of the time." Danielle stood behind the couch and bent over Lisette's shoulder to see where she was reading. "Midge Vaughn assures me that in a previous incarnation I was hanged for witchcraft."

"Midge should be grateful she's living in the twentieth century."

"Oh, Midge says we were sisters in the same coven and were hanged together; that's the reason for our close affinity."

"I'll bet Midge says that to all the girls."

"Oh, I like Midge." Danielle sipped her sherry and considered the rows of spines. "Did you say that man was wearing a medallion? Was it a swastika or that sort of thing?"

"No. It was something like a star in a circle. And he wore rings on every finger."

"Wait! Kind of greasy black hair slicked back from a widow's peak to straight over his collar in back? Eyebrows curled up into points like they've been waxed?"

"That's it."

"Ah, Mephisto!"

"Do you know him, then?"

"Not really. I've just seen him a time or two at the Equinox and a few other places. He reminds me of some ham actor playing Mephistopheles. Midge spoke to him once when we were by there, but I gather he's not part of her particular coven. Probably hadn't heard that the Equinox had closed. Never impressed me as a masher; very likely he actually did mistake you for someone."

"Well, they do say that everyone has a double. I wonder if mine is walking somewhere about London, being mistaken for me?"

"And no doubt giving some unsuspecting classmate of yours a resounding slap on the face."

"What if I met her suddenly?"

"Met your double—your *Doppelgänger*? Remember William Wilson? Disaster, darling—*disaster!*"

ʋ

There really wasn't much to it; no production at all. Lisette felt nervous, a bit silly and perhaps a touch cheated.

"I want you to relax," Dr. Magnus told her. "All you have to do is just relax."

That's what her gynecologist always said, too, Lisette thought with a sudden tenseness. She lay on her back on Dr. Magnus's analyst's couch: her head on a comfortable cushion, legs stretched primly out on the leather upholstery (she'd deliberately worn jeans again), fingers clenched damply over her tummy. A white gown instead of jeans, and I'll be ready for my coffin, she mused uncomfortably.

"Fine. That's it. You're doing fine, Lisette. Very fine. Just relax. Yes, just relax, just like that. Fine, that's it. Relax."

Dr. Magnus's voice was a quiet monotone, monotonously repeating soothing encouragements. He spoke to her tirelessly, patiently, slowly dissolving her anxiety.

"You feel sleepy, Lisette. Relaxed and sleepy. Your breathing is slow and relaxed, slow and relaxed. Think about your breathing now, Lisette. Think how slow and sleepy and deep each breath comes. You're breathing deeper, and you're feeling sleepier. Relax and sleep, Lisette, breathe and sleep. Breathe and sleep . . ."

She *was* thinking about her breathing. She counted the breaths; the slow monotonous syllables of Dr. Magnus' voice seemed to blend into her breathing like a quiet, tuneless lullaby. She *was* sleepy, for that matter, and it was very pleasant to relax here, listening to that dim, droning murmur while he talked on and on. How much longer until the end of the lecture . . .

"You are asleep now, Lisette. You are asleep, yet you can still

hear my voice. Now you are falling deeper, deeper, deeper into a
pleasant, relaxed sleep, Lisette. Deeper and deeper asleep. Can
you still hear my voice?"

"Yes."

"You are asleep, Lisette. In a deep, deep sleep. You will remain
in this deep sleep until I shall count to three. As I count to three,
you will slowly arise from your sleep until you are fully awake
once again. Do you understand?"

"Yes."

"But when you hear me say the word *amber*, you will again fall
into a deep, deep sleep, Lisette, just as you are asleep now. Do you
understand?"

"Yes."

"Listen to me as I count, Lisette. One. Two. Three."

Lisette opened her eyes. For a moment her expression was
blank, then a sudden confusion. She looked at Dr. Magnus seated
beside her, then smiled ruefully. "I was asleep, I'm afraid. Or was
I . . . ?"

"You did splendidly, Miss Seyrig." Dr. Magnus beamed reassurance. "You passed into a simple hypnotic state, and as you can
see now, there was no more cause for concern than in catching an
afternoon nap."

"But I'm sure I just dropped off." Lisette glanced at her watch.
Her appointment had been for three, and it was now almost four
o'clock.

"Why not just settle back and rest some more, Miss Seyrig.
That's it, relax again. All you need is to rest a bit, just a pleasant
rest."

Her wrist fell back onto the cushions, as her eyes fell shut.

"Amber."

Dr. Magnus studied her calm features for a moment. "You are
asleep now, Lisette. Can you hear me?"

"Yes."

"I want you to relax, Lisette. I want you to fall deeper, deeper,
deeper into sleep. Deep, deep sleep. Far, far, far into sleep."

He listened to her breathing, then suggested: "You are thinking
of your childhood now, Lisette. You are a little girl, not even in
school yet. Something is making you very happy. You remember
how happy you are. Why are you so happy?"

Lisette made a childish giggle. "It's my birthday party, and Ollie the Clown came to play with us."

"And how old are you today?"

"I'm five." Her right hand twitched, extended fingers and thumb.

"Go deeper now, Lisette. I want you to reach farther back. Far, far back into your memories. Go back to a time before you were a child in San Francisco. Far, farther back, Lisette. I want you to go back to the time of your dreams."

He studied her face. She remained in a deep hypnotic trance, but her expression registered sudden anxiousness. It was as if she lay in normal sleep—reacting to some intense nightmare. She moaned.

"Deeper, Lisette. Don't be afraid to remember. Let your mind flow back to another time."

Her features still showed distress, but she seemed less agitated as his voice urged her deeper.

"Where are you?"

"I'm . . . I'm not certain." Her voice came in a well-bred English accent. "It's quite dark. Only a few candles are burning. I'm frightened."

"Go back to a happy moment," Dr. Magnus urged her, as her tone grew sharp with fear. "You are happy now. Something very pleasant and wonderful is happening to you."

Anxiety drained from her features. Her cheeks flushed; she smiled pleasurably.

"Where are you now?"

"I'm dancing. It's a grand ball to celebrate Her Majesty's Diamond Jubilee, and I've never seen such a throng. I'm certain Charles means to propose to me tonight, but he's ever so shy, and now he's simply fuming that Captain Stapledon has the next two dances. He's so dashing in his uniform. Everyone is watching us together."

"What is your name?"

"Elisabeth Beresford."

"Where do you live, Miss Beresford?"

"We have a house in Chelsea. . . ."

Her expression abruptly changed. "It's dark again. I'm all alone. I can't see myself, although surely the candles shed sufficient light. There's something there in the candlelight. I'm moving closer."

"One."

"It's an open coffin." Fear edged her voice.

"Two."

"God in Heaven!"

"Three."

VI

We," Danielle announced grandly, "are invited to a party."
She produced an engraved card from her bag, presented it
to Lisette, then went to hang up her damp raincoat.

"Bloody English summer weather!" Lisette heard her from the
kitchen. "Is there any more coffee made? Oh, fantastic!"

She reappeared with a cup of coffee and an opened box of cook-
ies—Lisette couldn't get used to calling them biscuits. "Want
some?"

"No, thanks. Bad for my figure."

"And coffee on an empty tummy is bad for the nerves," Danielle said pointedly.

"Who is Beth Garrington?" Lisette studied the invitation.

"Um." Danielle tried to wash down a mouthful of crumbs with
too-hot coffee. "Some friend of Midge's. Midge dropped by the
gallery this afternoon and gave me the invitation. A costume revel.
Rock stars to royalty among the guests. Midge promises that it will
be super fun; said the last party Beth threw was unbridled debauchery—there was cocaine being passed around in an antique
snuff box for the guests. Can you imagine that much coke!"

"And how did Midge manage the invitation?"

"I gather the discerning Ms. Garrington had admired several of
my drawings that Maitland has on display—yea, even unto so far
as to purchase one. Midge told her that she knew me and that we
two were ornaments for any debauchery."

"The invitation is in both our names."

"Midge *likes* you."

"Midge despises me. She's jealous as a cat."

"Then she must have told our depraved hostess what a lovely
couple we make. Besides, Midge is jealous of everyone—even dear
Maitland, whose interest in me very obviously is not of the flesh.
But don't fret about Midge—English women are naturally bitchy
toward 'foreign' women. They're oh-so proper and fashionable,

but they never shave their legs. That's why I love mah fellow Americans."

Danielle kissed her chastely on top of her head, powdering Lisette's hair with biscuit crumbs. "And I'm cold and wet and dying for a shower. How about you?"

"A masquerade?" Lisette wondered. "What sort of costume? Not something that we'll have to trot off to one of those rental places for, surely?"

"From what Midge suggests, anything goes so long as it's wild. Just create something divinely decadent, and we're sure to knock them dead." Danielle had seen *Cabaret* half a dozen times. "It's to be in some back alley stately old home in Maida Vale, so there's no danger that the tenants downstairs will call the cops."

When Lisette remained silent, Danielle gave her a playful nudge. "Darling, it's a party we're invited to, not a funeral. What is it—didn't your session with Dr. Magnus go well?"

"I suppose it did." Lisette smiled without conviction. "I really can't say; all I did was doze off. Dr. Magnus seemed quite excited about it, though. I found it all . . . well, just a little bit scary."

"I thought you said you just dropped off. *What* was scary?"

"It's hard to put into words. It's like when you're starting to have a bad trip on acid: there's nothing wrong that you can explain, but somehow your mind is telling you to be afraid."

Danielle sat down beside her and squeezed her arm about her shoulders. "That sounds to me like Dr. Magnus is getting somewhere. I felt just the same sort of free anxiety the first time I underwent analysis. It's a good sign, darling. It means you're beginning to understand all those troubled secrets the ego keeps locked away."

"Perhaps the ego keeps them locked away for some perfectly good reason."

"Meaning hidden sexual conflicts, I suppose." Danielle's fingers gently massaged Lisette's shoulders and neck. "Oh, Lisette. You musn't be shy about getting to know yourself. *I* think it's exciting."

Lisette curled up against her, resting her cheek against Danielle's breast while the other girl's fingers soothed the tension from her muscles. She supposed she was overreacting. After all, the nightmares were what distressed her so; Dr. Magnus seemed completely confident that he could free her from them.

"Which of your drawings did our prospective hostess buy?" Lisette asked, changing the subject.

"Oh, didn't I tell you?" Danielle lifted up her chin. "It was that charcoal study I did of you."

Lisette closed the shower curtains as she stepped into the tub. It was one of those long, narrow, deep tubs beloved of English bathrooms that always made her think of a coffin for two. A Rube Goldberg plumbing arrangement connected the hot and cold faucets, and from the common spout was affixed a rubber hose with a shower head which one might either hang from a hook on the wall or hold in hand. Danielle had replaced the ordinary shower head with a shower massager when she moved in, but she left the previous tenant's shaving mirror—a bevelled glass oval in a heavily enameled antique frame—hanging on the wall above the hook.

Lisette glanced at her face in the steamed-over mirror. "I shouldn't have let you display that at the gallery."

"But why not?" Danielle was shampooing, and lather blinded her as she turned about. "Maitland thinks it's one of my best."

Lisette reached around her for the shower attachment. "It seems a bit personal somehow. All those people looking at me. It's an invasion of privacy."

"But it's thoroughly modest, darling. Not like some topless billboard in Soho."

The drawing was a charcoal and pencil study of Lisette, done in what Danielle described as her David Hamilton phase. In sitting for it, Lisette had piled her hair in a high chignon and dressed in an antique cotton camisole and drawers with lace insertions that she'd found at a shop in Westbourne Grove. Danielle called it *Dark Rose*. Lisette had thought it made her look fat.

Danielle grasped blindly for the shower massage, and Lisette placed it in her hand. "It just seems a bit too personal to have some total stranger owning my picture." Shampoo coursed like seafoam over Danielle's breasts. Lisette kissed the foam.

"Ah, but soon she won't be a total stranger," Danielle reminded her, her voice muffled by the pulsing shower spray.

Lisette felt Danielle's nipples harden beneath her lips. The brunette still pressed her eyes tightly shut against the force of the shower, but the other hand cupped Lisette's head encouragingly. Lisette gently moved her kisses downward along the other girl's slippery belly, kneeling as she did so. Danielle murmured, and when Lisette's tongue probed her drenched curls, she shifted her legs to let her knees rest beneath the blonde girl's shoulders. The shower massage dropped from her fingers.

Lisette made love to her with a passion that surprised her—spontaneous, suddenly fierce, unlike their usual tenderness together. Her lips and tongue pressed into Danielle almost ravenously, her own ecstasy even more intense than that which she was drawing from Danielle. Danielle gasped and clung to the shower rail with one hand, her other fist clenched upon the curtain, sobbing as a long orgasm shuddered through her.

"Please, darling!" Danielle finally managed to beg. "My legs are too wobbly to hold me up any longer!"

She drew away. Lisette raised her face.

"Oh!"

Lisette rose to her feet with drugged movements. Her wide eyes at last registered Danielle's startled expression. She touched her lips and turned to look in the bathroom mirror.

"I'm sorry," Danielle put her arm about her shoulder. "I must have started my period. I didn't realize . . ."

Lisette stared at the blood-smeared face in the fogged shaving mirror.

Danielle caught her as she started to slump.

VII

She was conscious of the cold rain that pelted her face, washing from her nostrils the too-sweet smell of decaying flowers. Slowly she opened her eyes onto darkness and mist. Rain fell steadily, spiritlessly, glueing her white gown to her drenched flesh. She had been walking in her sleep again.

Wakefulness seemed forever in coming to her, so that only by slow degrees did she become aware of herself, of her surroundings. For a moment she felt as if she were a chess piece arrayed upon a board in a darkened room. All about her, stone monuments crowded together, their weathered surfaces streaming with moisture. She felt neither fear nor surprise that she stood in a cemetery.

She pressed her bare arms together across her breasts. Water ran over her pale skin as smoothly as upon the marble tombstones, and though her flesh felt as cold as the drenched marble, she did not feel chilled. She stood barefoot, her hair clinging to her shoulders above the low-necked cotton gown that was all she wore.

Automatically, her steps carried her through the darkness, as if following a familiar path through the maze of glistening stone. She knew where she was: this was Highgate Cemetery. She could not recall how she knew that, since she had no memory of ever having been to this place before. No more could she think how she knew her steps were taking her deeper into the cemetery instead of toward the gate.

A splash of color trickled onto her breast, staining its paleness as the rain dissolved it into a red rose above her heart.

She opened her mouth to scream, and a great bubble of unswallowed blood spewed from her lips.

"Elisabeth! Elisabeth!"
"Lisette! Lisette!"
Whose voice called her?
"Lisette! You can wake up now, Lisette."
Dr. Magnus' face peered into her own. Was there sudden concern behind that urbane mask?
"You're awake now, Miss Seyrig. Everything is all right."
Lisette stared back at him for a moment, uncertain of her reality, as if suddenly awakened from some profound nightmare.
"I . . . I thought I was dead." Her eyes still held her fear.
Dr. Magnus smiled to reassure her. "Somnambulism, my dear. You remembered an episode of sleepwalking from a former life. Tell me, have you yourself ever walked in your sleep?"
Lisette pressed her hands to her face, abruptly examined her fingers. "I don't know. I mean, I don't think so."
She sat up, searched in her bag for her compact. She paused for a moment before opening the mirror.
"Dr. Magnus, I don't think I care to continue these sessions." She stared at her reflection in fascination, not touching her makeup, and when she snapped the case shut, the frightened strain began to relax from her face. She wished she had a cigarette.
Dr. Magnus sighed and pressed his fingertips together, leaning back in his chair; watched her fidget with her clothing as she sat nervously on the edge of the couch.
"Do you really wish to terminate our exploration? We have, after all, made excellent progress during these last few sessions."

"Have we?"

"We have, indeed. You have consistently remembered incidents from the life of one Elisabeth Beresford, a young English lady living in London at the close of the last century. To the best of your knowledge of your family history, she is not an ancestress."

Dr. Magnus leaned forward, seeking to impart his enthusiasm. "Don't you see how important this is? If Elisabeth Beresford was not your ancestress, then there can be no question of genetic memory being involved. The only explanation must therefore be reincarnation—proof of the immortality of the soul. To establish this I must first confirm the existence of Elisabeth Beresford, and from that demonstrate that no familial bond exists between the two of you. We simply must explore this further."

"Must we? I meant, what progress have we made toward helping me, Dr. Magnus? It's all very good for you to be able to confirm your theories of reincarnation, but that doesn't do anything for me. If anything, the nightmares have grown more disturbing since we began these sessions."

"Then perhaps we dare not stop."

"What do you mean?" Lisette wondered what he might do if she suddenly bolted from the room.

"I mean that the nightmares will grow worse regardless of whether you decide to terminate our sessions. Your unconscious self is struggling to tell you some significant message from a previous existence. It will continue to do so no matter how stubbornly you will yourself not to listen. My task is to help you listen to this voice, to understand the message it must impart to you—and with this understanding and self-awareness, you will experience inner peace. Without my help . . . Well, to be perfectly frank, Miss Seyrig, you are in some danger of a complete emotional breakdown."

Lisette slumped back against the couch. She felt on the edge of panic and wished Danielle were here to support her.

"Why are my memories always nightmares?" Her voice shook, and she spoke slowly to control it.

"But they aren't always frightening memories, my dear. It's just that the memory of some extremely traumatic experience often seeks to come to the fore. You would expect some tremendously emotional laden memory to be a potent one."

"Is Elisabeth Beresford . . . dead?"

"Assuming she was approximately twenty years of age at the time of Queen Victoria's Diamond Jubilee, she would have been past one hundred today. Besides, Miss Seyrig, her soul has been born again as your own. It must therefore follow . . ."

"Dr. Magnus. I don't *want* to know how Elisabeth Beresford died."

"Of course," Dr. Magnus told her gently. "Isn't that quite obvious?"

VIII

For a wonder, it's forgot to rain tonight."

"Thank god for small favors," Lisette commented, thinking July in London had far more to do with monsoons than the romantic city of fogs celebrated in song. "All we need is to get these rained on."

She and Danielle bounced about on the back seat of the black Austin taxi, as their driver democratically seemed as willing to challenge lorries as pedestrians for right-of-way on the Edgeware Road. Feeling a bit self-conscious, Lisette tugged at the hem of her patent leather trench coat. They had decided to wear brightly embroidered Chinese silk lounging pyjamas that they'd found at one of the vintage clothing shops off the Portobello Road—gauzy enough for stares, but only a demure trouser-leg showing beneath their coats. "We're going to a masquerade party," Lisette had felt obliged to explain to the driver. Her concern was needless, as he hadn't given them a second glance. Either he was used to the current Chinese look in fashion, or else a few seasons of picking up couples at discos and punk rock clubs had inured him to any sort of costume.

The taxi turned into a series of side streets off Maida Vale and eventually made a neat U-turn that seemed almost an automotive pirouette. The frenetic beat of a new wave rock group clattered past the gate of an enclosed courtyard: something Mews—the iron plaque on the brick wall was too rusted to decipher in the dark—but from the lights and noise it must be the right address. A number of expensive-looking cars—Lisette recognized a Rolls or two and at least one Ferrari—were among those crowded against the curb. They squeezed their way past them and made for the source

of the revelry, a brick-fronted townhouse of three or more storeys
set at the back of the courtyard.

The door was opened by a girl in an abbreviated maid's costume. She checked their invitation while a similarly clad girl took
their coats, and a third invited them to select from an assortment
of masks and indicated where they might change. Lisette and Danielle chose sequined domino masks that matched the dangling
scarves they wore tied low across their brows.

Danielle withdrew an ebony cigarette holder from her bag and
considered their reflections with approval. "Divinely decadent,"
she drawled, gesturing with her black-lacquered nails. "All that
time for my eyes, and just to cover them with a mask. Perhaps
later—when it's cock's-crow and all unmask . . . Forward, darling."

Lisette kept at her side, feeling a bit lost and out of place. When
they passed before a light, it was evident that they wore nothing
beneath the silk pyjamas, and Lisette was grateful for the strategic
brocade. As they came upon others of the newly arriving guests,
she decided there was no danger of outraging anyone's modesty
here. As Midge had promised, anything goes so long as it's wild,
and while their costumes might pass for street wear, many of the
guests needed avail themselves of the changing rooms upstairs.

A muscular young man clad only in a leather loincloth and a
sword belt with broadsword descended the stairs leading a buxom
girl by a chain affixed to her wrists; aside from her manacles, she
wore a few scraps of leather. A couple in punk rock gear spat at
them in passing; the girl was wearing a set of panties with dangling razor blades for tassels and a pair of black latex tights that
might have been spray paint. Two girls in vintage Christian Dior
New Look evening gowns ogled the seminude swordsman from
the landing above; Lisette noted their pronounced shoulders and
Adam's apples and felt a twinge of jealousy that hormones and
surgery could let them show a better cleavage than she could.

A new wave group called the Needle was performing in a large
first-floor room—Lisette supposed it was an actual ballroom, although the house's original tenants would have considered tonight's ball a *danse macabre*. Despite the fact that the decibel level
was well past the threshold of pain, most of the guests were con-
gregated here, with smaller, quieter parties gravitating into other
rooms. Here, about half were dancing, the rest standing about

trying to talk. Marijuana smoke was barely discernible within the harsh haze of British cigarettes.

"There's Midge and Fiona," Danielle shouted in Lisette's ear. She waved energetically and steered a course through the dancers.

Midge was wearing an elaborate medieval gown—a heavily brocaded affair that ran from the floor to midway across her nipples. Her blonde hair was piled high in some sort of conical headpiece, complete with flowing scarf. Fiona waited upon her in a page boy's costume.

"Are you just getting here?" Midge asked, running a deprecative glance down Lisette's costume. "There's champagne over on the sideboard. Wait, I'll summon one of the cute little French maids."

Lisette caught two glasses from a passing tray and presented one to Danielle. It was impossible to converse, but then she hadn't anything to talk about with Midge, and Fiona was no more than a shadow.

"Where's our hostess?" Danielle asked.

"Not down yet," Midge managed to shout. "Beth always waits to make a grand entrance at her little dos. You won't miss her."

"Speaking of entrances . . ." Lisette commented, nodding toward the couple who were just coming onto the dance floor. The woman wore a Nazi SS officer's hat, jackboots, black trousers and braces across her bare chest. She was astride the back of her male companion, who wore a saddle and bridle in addition to a few other bits of leather harness.

"I can't decide whether that's kinky or just tacky," Lisette said.

"Not like your little sorority teas back home, is it?" Midge smiled.

"Is there any coke about?" Danielle interposed quickly.

"There was a short while ago. Try the library—that's the room just down from where everyone's changing."

Lisette downed her champagne and grabbed a refill before following Danielle upstairs. A man in fish-net tights, motorcycle boots and a vest comprised mostly of chain and bits of Nazi medals caught at her arm and seemed to want to dance. Instead of a mask, he wore about a pound of eye shadow and black lipstick. She shouted an inaudible excuse, held a finger to her nostril and sniffed, and darted after Danielle.

"That was Eddie Teeth, lead singer for the Trepans, whom you just cut," Danielle told her. "Why didn't he grab *me!*"

"You'll get your chance," Lisette told her. "I think he's following us."

Danielle dragged her to a halt halfway up the stairs.

"Got toot right here, loves." Eddie Teeth flipped the silver spoon and phial that dangled amidst the chains on his vest.

"Couldn't take the noise in there any longer," Lisette explained.

"Needle's shit." Eddie Teeth wrapped an arm about either waist and propelled them up the stairs. "You gashes sisters? I can dig incest."

The library was pleasantly crowded—Lisette decided she didn't want to be cornered with Eddie Teeth. A dozen or more guests stood about, sniffing and conversing energetically. Seated at a table, two of the ubiquitous maids busily cut lines onto mirrors and set them out for the guests, whose number remained more or less constant as people wandered in and left. A cigarette box offered tightly rolled joints.

"That's Thai." Eddie Teeth groped for a handful of the joints, stuck one in each girl's mouth, the rest inside his vest. Danielle giggled and fitted hers to her cigarette holder. Unfastening a silver tube from his vest, he snorted two thick lines from one of the mirrors. "Toot your eyeballs out, loves," he invited them.

One of the maids collected the mirror when they had finished and replaced it with another—a dozen lines of cocaine neatly arranged across its surface. Industriously she began to work a chunk of rock through a sifter to replenish the empty mirror. Lisette watched in fascination. This finally brought home to her the wealth this party represented: all the rest simply seemed to her like something out of a movie, but dealing out coke to more than a hundred guests was an extravagance she could relate to.

"Danielle Borland, isn't it?"

A man dressed as Mephistopheles bowed before them. "Adrian Tregannet. We've met at one of Midge Vaughn's parties, you may recall."

Danielle stared at the face below the domino mask. "Oh, yes. Lisette, it's Mephisto himself."

"Then this is Miss Seyrig, the subject of your charcoal drawing that Beth so admires." Mephisto caught Lisette's hand and bent his lips to it. "Beth is so much looking forward to meeting you both."

Lisette retrieved her hand. "Aren't you the . . ."

"The rude fellow who accosted you in Kensington some days ago," Tregannet finished apologetically. "Yes, I'm afraid so. But you really must forgive me for my forwardness. I actually did mistake you for a very dear friend of mine, you see. Won't you let me make amends over a glass of champagne?"

"Certainly." Lisette decided that she had had quite enough of Eddie Teeth, and Danielle was quite capable of fending for herself if she grew tired of having her breasts squeezed by a famous pop star.

Tregannet quickly returned with two glasses of champagne. Lisette finished another two lines and smiled appreciatively as she accepted a glass. Danielle was trying to shotgun Eddie Teeth through her cigarette holder, and Lisette thought it a good chance to slip away.

"Your roommate is tremendously talented," Tregannet suggested. "Of course, she chose so charming a subject for her drawing."

Slick as snake oil, Lisette thought, letting him take her arm. "How very nice of you to say so. However, I really feel a bit embarrassed to think that some stranger owns a portrait of me in my underwear."

"Utterly chaste, my dear—as chaste as the *Dark Rose* of its title. Beth chose to hang it in her boudoir, so I hardly think it is on public display. I suspect from your garments in the drawing that you must share Beth's appreciation for the dress and manners of this past century."

Which is something I'd never suspect of our hostess, judging from this party, Lisette considered. "I'm quite looking forward to meeting her. I assume then that Ms. is a bit too modern for one of such quiet tastes. Is it Miss or Mrs. Garrington?"

"Ah, I hadn't meant to suggest an impression of a genteel dowager. Beth is entirely of your generation—a few years older than yourself, perhaps. Although I find Ms. too suggestive of American slang, I'm sure Beth would not object. However, there's no occasion for such formality here."

"You seem to know her well, Mr. Tregannet."

"It is an old family. I know her aunt, Julia Weatherford, quite well through our mutual interest in the occult. Perhaps you, too . . . ?''

"Not really; Danielle is the one you should chat with about that. My field is art. I'm over here on fellowship at London University." She watched Danielle and Eddie Teeth toddle off for the ballroom and jealously decided that Danielle's taste in her acquaintances left much to be desired. "Could I have some more champagne?"

"To be sure. I won't be a moment."

Lisette snorted a few more lines while she waited. A young man dressed as an Edwardian dandy offered her his snuff box and gravely demonstrated its use. Lisette was struggling with a sneezing fit when Tregannet returned.

"You needn't have gone to all the bother," she told him. "These little French maids are dashing about with trays of champagne."

"But those glasses have lost the proper chill," Tregannet explained. "To your very good health."

"Cheers." Lisette felt lightheaded, and promised herself to go easy for a while. "Does Beth live here with her aunt, then?"

"Her aunt lives on the Continent; I don't believe she's visited London for several years. Beth moved in about ten years ago. Theirs is not a large family, but they are not without wealth, as you can observe. They travel a great deal as well, and it's fortunate that Beth happened to be in London during your stay here. Incidently, just how long will you be staying in London?"

"About a year is all." Lisette finished her champagne. "Then it's back to my dear, dull family in San Francisco."

"Then there's no one here in London . . . ?"

"Decidedly not, Mr. Tregannet. And now if you'll excuse me, I think I'll find the ladies'."

Cocaine might well be the champagne of drugs, but cocaine and champagne didn't seem to mix well, Lisette mused, turning the bathroom over to the next frantic guest. Her head felt really buzzy, and she thought she might do better if she found a bedroom somewhere and lay down for a moment. But then she'd most likely wake up and find some man on top of her, judging from this lot. She decided she'd lay off the champagne and have just a line or two to shake off the feeling of having been sandbagged.

The crowd in the study had changed during her absence. Just now it was dominated by a group of guests dressed in costumes from *The Rocky Horror Show*, now closing out its long run at the

Comedy Theatre in Piccadilly. Lisette had grown bored with the
fad the film version had generated in the States, and pushed her
way past the group as they vigorously danced the Time Warp and
bellowed out songs from the show.

" 'Give yourself over to absolute pleasure,' " someone sang in
her ear as she industriously snorted a line from the mirror.
" 'Erotic nightmares beyond any measure,' " the song continued.

Lisette finished a second line, and decided she had had enough.
She straightened from the table and broke for the doorway. The
tall transvestite dressed as Frankie barred her way with a dramatic
gesture, singing ardently: " 'Don't dream it—be it!' "

Lisette blew him a kiss and ducked around him. She wished she
could find a quiet place to collect her thoughts. Maybe she should
find Danielle first—if she could handle the ballroom that long.

The dance floor was far more crowded than when they'd come
in. At least all these jostling bodies seemed to absorb some of the
decibels from the blaring banks of amplifiers and speakers. Lisette
looked in vain for Danielle amidst the dancers, succeeding only in
getting champagne sloshed on her back. She caught sight of
Midge, recognizable above the mob by her conical medieval head-
dress, and pushed her way toward her.

Midge was being fed caviar on bits of toast by Fiona while she
talked with an older woman who looked like the pictures Lisette
had seen of Marlene Dietrich dressed in men's formal evening
wear.

"Have you seen Danielle?" Lisette asked her.

"Why, not recently, darling," Midge smiled, licking caviar from
her lips with the tip of her tongue. "I believe she and that rock
singer were headed upstairs for a bit more privacy. I'm sure she'll
come collect you once they're finished."

"Midge, you're a cunt," Lisette told her through her sweetest
smile. She turned away and made for the doorway, trying not to
ruin her exit by staggering. Screw Danielle—she needed to have
some fresh air.

A crowd had gathered at the foot of the stairway, and she had to
push through the doorway to escape the ballroom. Behind her, the
Needle mercifully took a break. "She's coming down!" Lisette
heard someone whisper breathlessly. The inchoate babel of the
party fell to a sudden lull that made Lisette shiver.

At the top of the stairway stood a tall woman, enveloped in a black velvet cloak from her throat to her ankles. Her blonde hair was piled high in a complex variation of the once-fashionable French twist. Strings of garnets entwined in her hair and edged the close-fitting black mask that covered the upper half of her face. For a hushed interval she stood there, gazing imperiously down upon her guests.

Adrian Tregannet leapt to the foot of the stairway. He signed to a pair of maids, who stepped forward to either side of their mistress.

"Milords and miladies!" he announced with a sweeping bow. "Let us pay honor to our bewitching mistress whose feast we celebrate tonight! I give you the lamia who haunted Adam's dreams—Lilith!"

The maids smoothly swept the cloak from their mistress' shoulders. From the multitude at her feet came an audible intake of breath. Beth Garrington was attired in a strapless corselette of gleaming black leather, laced tightly about her waist. The rest of her costume consisted only of knee-length, stiletto-heeled tight boots, above-the-elbow gloves, and a spiked collar around her throat—all of black leather that contrasted starkly against her white skin and blonde hair. At first Lisette thought she wore a bull-whip coiled about her body as well, but then the coils moved, and she realized that it was an enormous black snake.

"Lilith!" came the shout, chanted in a tone of awe. "Lilith!"

Acknowledging their worship with a sinuous gesture, Beth Garrington descended the staircase. The serpent coiled from gloved arm to gloved arm, entwining her cinched waist, its eyes considered the revellers imperturbably. Champagne glasses lifted in a toast to Lilith, and the chattering voice of the party once more began to fill the house.

Tregannet touched Beth's elbow as she greeted her guests at the foot of the stairway. He whispered into her ear, and she smiled graciously and moved away with him.

Lisette clung to the staircase newel, watching them approach. Her head was spinning, and she desperately needed to lie down in some fresh air, but she couldn't trust her legs to carry her outside. She stared into the eyes of the serpent, hypnotized by its flickering tongue.

The room seemed to surge in and out of focus. The masks of the guests seemed to leer and gloat with the awareness of some secret jest; the dancers in their fantastic costumes became a grotesque horde of satyrs and wanton demons, writhing about the ballroom in some witches' sabbat of obscene mass copulation. As in a nightmare, Lisette willed her legs to turn and run, realized that her body was no longer obedient to her will.

"Beth, here's someone you've been dying to meet," Lisette heard Tregannet say. "Beth Garrington, allow me to present Lisette Seyrig."

The lips beneath the black mask curved in a pleasurable smile. Lisette gazed into the eyes behind the mask, and discovered that she could no longer feel her body. She thought she heard Danielle cry out her name.

The eyes remained in her vision long after she slid down the newel and collapsed upon the floor.

IX

The Catherine Wheel was a pub on Kensington Church Street. They served good pub lunches there, and Lisette liked to stop in before walking down Holland Street for her sessions with Dr. Magnus. Since today was her final such session, it seemed appropriate that they should end the evening here.

"While I dislike repeating myself," Dr. Magnus spoke earnestly, "I really do think we should continue."

Lisette drew on a cigarette and shook her head decisively. "No way, Dr. Magnus. My nerves are shot to hell. I mean, look—when I freak out at a costume party and have to be carted home to bed by my roommate! It was like when I was a kid and got hold of some bad acid: the whole world was some bizarre and sinister freak show for weeks. Once I got my head back on, I said: No more acid."

"That was rather a notorious circle you were travelling in. Further, you were, if I understand you correctly, overindulging a bit that evening."

"A few glasses of champagne and a little toot never did anything before but make me a bit giggly and talkative." Lisette sipped her half of lager; she'd never developed a taste for English bitter, and at least the lager was chilled. They sat across from each other at a table the size of a hubcap; she in the corner of a padded bench against the wall, he at a chair set out into the room, pressed in by a wall of standing bodies. A foot away from her on the padded bench, three young men huddled about a similar table, talking animatedly. For all that, she and Dr. Magnus might have been all alone in the room. Lisette wondered if the psychologist who had coined the faddish concept of "space" had been inspired in a crowded English pub.

"It isn't just that I fainted at the party. It isn't just the nightmares." She paused to find words. "It's just that everything somehow seems to be drifting out of focus, out of control. It's . . . well, it's frightening."

"Precisely why we must continue."

"Precisely why we must not." Lisette sighed. They'd covered this ground already. It had been a moment of weakness when she agreed to allow Dr. Magnus to buy her a drink afterward instead of heading back to the flat. Still, he had been so distressed when she told him she was terminating their sessions.

"I've tried to cooperate with you as best I could, and I'm certain you are entirely sincere in your desire to help me." Well, she wasn't all *that* certain, but no point in going into that. "However, the fact remains that since we began these sessions, my nerves have gone to hell. You say they'd be worse without the sessions, I say the sessions have made them worse, and maybe there's no connection at all—it's just that my nerves have gotten worse, so now I'm going to trust my intuition and try life without these sessions. Fair enough?"

Dr. Magnus gazed uncomfortably at his barely tasted glass of sherry. "While I fully understand your rationale, I must in all conscience beg you to reconsider, Lisette. You are running risks that . . ."

"Look. If the nightmares go away, then terrific. If they don't, I can always pack up and head back to San Francisco. That way I'll be clear of whatever it is about London that disagrees with me, and if not, I'll see my psychiatrist back home."

"Very well, then." Dr. Magnus squeezed her hand. "However, please bear in mind that I remain eager to continue our sessions at any time, should you change your mind."

"That's fair enough, too. And very kind of you."

Dr. Magnus lifted his glass of sherry to the light. Pensively, he remarked: "Amber."

X

Lisette?"

Danielle locked the front door behind her and hung up her inadequate umbrella in the hallway. She considered her face in the mirror and grimaced at the mess of her hair. "Lisette? Are you here?"

No answer, and her rain things were not in the hallway. Either she was having a late session with Dr. Magnus, or else she'd wisely decided to duck under cover until this bloody rain let up. After she'd had to carry Lisette home in a taxi when she passed out at the party, Danielle was starting to feel real concern over her state of health.

Danielle kicked off her damp shoes as she entered the living room. The curtains were drawn against the greyness outside, and she switched on a lamp to brighten the flat a bit. Her dress clung to her like a clammy fish-skin; she shivered, and thought about a cup of coffee. If Lisette hadn't returned yet, there wouldn't be any brewed. She'd have a warm shower instead, and after that she'd see to the coffee—if Lisette hadn't returned to set a pot going in the meantime.

"Lisette?" Their bedroom was empty. Danielle turned on the overhead light. Christ, it was gloomy! So much for long English summer evenings—with all the rain, she couldn't remember when she'd last seen the sun. She struggled out of her damp dress, spread it flat across her bed with the vague hope that it might not wrinkle too badly, then tossed her bra and tights onto a chair.

Slipping into her bathrobe, Danielle padded back into the living room. Still no sign of Lisette, and it was past nine. Perhaps she'd stopped off at a pub. Crossing to the stereo, Danielle placed the new Blondie album on the turntable and turned up the volume. Let the neighbors complain—at least this would help dispel the evening's gloom.

She cursed the delay needed to adjust the shower temperature to satisfaction, then climbed into the tub. The hot spray felt good, and she stood under it contentedly for several minutes—initially revitalized, then lulled into a delicious sense of relaxation. Through the rush of the spray, she could hear the muffled beat of the stereo. As she reached for the shampoo, she began to move her body with the rhythm.

The shower curtain billowed as the bathroom door opened. Danielle risked a soapy squint around the curtain—she knew the flat was securely locked, but after seeing *Psycho* . . . It was only Lisette, already undressed, her long blonde hair falling over her breasts.

"Didn't hear you come in with the stereo going," Danielle greeted her. "Come on in before you catch cold."

Danielle resumed lathering her hair as the shower curtain parted and the other girl stepped into the tub behind her. Her eyes squeezed shut against the soap, she felt Lisette's breasts thrust against her back, her flat belly press against her buttocks. Lisette's hands came around her to cup her breasts gently.

At least Lisette had gotten over her silly tiff about Eddie Teeth. She'd explained to Lisette that she'd ditched that greasy slob when he'd tried to dry hump her on the dance floor, but how do you reason with a silly thing who faints at the sight of a snake?

"Jesus, you're chilled to the bone!" Danielle complained with a shiver. "Better stand under the shower and get warm. Did you get caught in the rain?"

The other girl's fingers continued to caress her breasts, and instead of answering, her lips teased the nape of Danielle's neck. Danielle made a delighted sound deep in her throat, letting the spray rinse the lather from her hair and over their embraced bodies. Languidly she turned about to face her lover, closing her arms about Lisette's shoulders for support.

Lisette's kisses held each taut nipple for a moment, teasing them almost painfully. Danielle pressed the other girl's face to her breasts, sighed as her kisses nibbled upward to her throat. She felt weak with arousal, and only Lisette's strength held her upright in the tub. Her lover's lips upon her throat tormented her beyond enduring; Danielle gasped and lifted Lisette's face to meet her own.

Her mouth was open to receive Lisette's red-lipped kiss, and it opened wider as Danielle stared into the eyes of her lover. Her first emotion was one of wonder.

"You're not Lisette!"

It was nearly midnight when Lisette unlocked the door to their flat and quietly let herself in. Only a few lights were on, and there was no sign of Danielle—either she had gone out, or, more likely, had gone to bed.

Lisette hung up her raincoat and wearily pulled off her shoes. She'd barely caught the last train. She must have been crazy to let Dr. Magnus talk her into returning to his office for another session that late, but then he was quite right: as serious as her problems were, she really did need all the help he could give her. She felt a warm sense of gratitude to Dr. Magnus for being there when she so needed his help.

The turntable had stopped, but a light on the amplifier indicated that the power was still on. Lisette cut it off and closed the lid over the turntable. She felt too tired to listen to an album just now.

She became aware that the shower was running. In that case, Danielle hadn't gone to bed. She supposed she really ought to apologize to her for letting Midge's bitchy lies get under her skin. After all, she had ruined the party for Danielle; poor Danielle had had to get her to bed and had left the party without ever getting to meet Beth Garrington, and she was the one Beth had invited in the first place.

"Danielle? I'm back." Lisette called through the bathroom door. "Do you want anything?"

No answer. Lisette looked into their bedroom, just in case Danielle had invited a friend over. No, the beds were still made up; Danielle's clothes were spread out by themselves.

"Danielle?" Lisette raised her voice. Perhaps she couldn't hear over the noise of the shower. "Danielle?" Surely she was all right.

Lisette's feet felt damp. She looked down. A puddle of water was seeping beneath the door. Danielle must not have the shower curtains closed properly.

"Danielle! You're flooding us!"

Lisette opened the door and peered cautiously within. The curtain was closed, right enough. A thin spray still reached through a gap, and the shower had been running long enough for the puddle to spread. It occurred to Lisette that she should see Danielle's silhouette against the translucent shower curtain.

"Danielle!" She began to grow alarmed. "Danielle! Are you all right?"

She pattered across the wet tiles and drew aside the curtain. Danielle lay in the bottom of the tub, the spray falling on her upturned smile, her flesh paler than the porcelain of the tub.

I t was early afternoon when they finally allowed her to return to the flat. Had she been able to think of another place to go, she probably would have gone there. Instead, Lisette wearily slumped onto the couch, too spent to pour herself the drink she desperately wanted.

Somehow she had managed to phone the police, through her hysteria make them understand where she was. Once the squad car arrived, she had no further need to act out of her own initiative; she simply was carried along in the rush of police investigation. It wasn't until they were questioning her at New Scotland Yard that she realized she herself was not entirely free from suspicion.

The victim had bled to death, the medical examiner ruled, her blood washed down the tub drain. A safety razor used for shaving legs had been opened, its blade removed. There were razor incisions along both wrists, directed lengthwise, into the radial artery, as opposed to the shallow, crosswise cuts utilized by suicides unfamiliar with human anatomy. There was, in addition, an incision in the left side of the throat. It was either a very determined suicide, or a skillfully concealed murder. In view of the absence of any signs of forced entry or of a struggle, more likely the former. The victim's roommate did admit to a recent quarrel. Laboratory tests would indicate whether the victim might have been drugged or rendered unconscious through a blow. After that, the inquest would decide.

Lisette had explained that she had spent the evening with Dr. Magnus. The fact that she was receiving emotional therapy, as they interpreted it, caused several mental notes to be made. Efforts to reach Dr. Magnus by telephone proved unsuccessful, but his secretary did confirm that Miss Seyrig had shown up for her appointment the previous afternoon. Dr. Magnus would get in touch with them as soon as he returned to his office. No, she did not know why he had cancelled today's appointments, but it was not unusual for Dr. Magnus to dash off suddenly when essential research demanded immediate attention.

After a while they let Lisette make phone calls. She phoned her parents, then wished she hadn't. It was still the night before in California, and it was like turning back the hands of time to no avail. They urged her to take the next flight home, but of course it wasn't all that simple, and it just wasn't feasible for either of them to fly over on a second's notice, since after all there really was nothing they could do. She phoned Maitland Reddin, who was stunned at the news and offered to help in any way he could, but Lisette couldn't think of any way. She phoned Midge Vaughn, who hung up on her. She phoned Dr. Magnus, who still couldn't be reached. Mercifully, the police took care of phoning Danielle's next of kin.

A physician at New Scotland Yard had spoken with her briefly and had given her some pills—a sedative to ease her into sleep after her ordeal. They had driven her back to the flat after impressing upon her the need to be present at the inquest. She must not be concerned should any hypothetical assailant yet be lurking about, inasmuch as the flat would be under surveillance.

Lisette stared dully about the flat, still unable to comprehend what had happened. The police had been thorough—measuring, dusting for fingerprints, leaving things in a mess. Bleakly, Lisette tried to convince herself that this was only another nightmare, that in a moment Danielle would pop in and find her asleep on the couch. Christ, what was she going to do with all of Danielle's things? Danielle's mother was remarried and living in Colorado; her father was an executive in a New York investment corporation. Evidently he had made arrangements to have the body shipped back to the States.

"Oh, Danielle." Lisette was too stunned for tears. Perhaps she should check into a hotel for now. No, she couldn't bear being all alone with her thoughts in a strange place. How strange to realize now that she really had no close friends in London other than Danielle—and what friends she did have were mostly people she'd met through Danielle.

She'd left word with Dr. Magnus's secretary for him to call her once he came in. Perhaps she should call there once again, just in case Dr. Magnus had missed her message. Lisette couldn't think what good Dr. Magnus could do, but he was such an understanding person, and she felt much better whenever she spoke with him.

She considered the bottle of pills in her bag. Perhaps it would be best to take a couple of them and sleep around the clock. She felt too drained just now to have energy enough to think.

The phone began to ring. Lisette stared at it for a moment without comprehension, then lunged up from the couch to answer it.

"Is this Lisette Seyrig?"

It was a woman's voice—one Lisette didn't recognize. "Yes. Who's calling, please?"

"This is Beth Garrington, Lisette. I hope I'm not disturbing you."

"That's quite all right."

"You poor dear! Maitland Reddin phoned to tell me of the tragedy. I can't tell you how shocked I am. Danielle seemed such a dear from our brief contact, and she had such a great talent."

"Thank you. I'm sorry you weren't able to know her better." Lisette sensed guilt and embarrassment at the memory of that brief contact.

"Darling, you can't be thinking about staying in that flat alone. Is there someone there with you?"

"No, there isn't. That's all right. I'll be fine."

"Don't be silly. Listen, I have enough empty bedrooms in this old barn to open a hotel. Why don't you just pack a few things and come straight over?"

"That's very kind of you, but I really couldn't."

"Nonsense! It's no good for you to be there all by yourself. Strange as this may sound, but when I'm not throwing one of these invitational riots, this is a quiet little backwater and things are dull as church. I'd love the company, and it will do you a world of good to get away."

"You're really very kind to invite me, but I . . ."

"Please, Lisette—be reasonable. I have guest rooms here already made up, and I'll send the car around to pick you up. All you need do is say yes and toss a few things into your bag. After a good night's sleep, you'll feel much more like coping with things tomorrow."

When Lisette didn't immediately reply, Beth added carefully: "Besides, Lisette. I understand the police haven't ruled out the possibility of murder. In that event, unless poor Danielle simply forgot to lock up, there is a chance that whoever did this has a key to your flat."

"The police said they'd watch the house."

"He might also be someone you both know and trust, someone Danielle invited in."

Lisette stared wildly at the sinister shadows that lengthened about the flat. Her refuge had been violated. Even familiar objects seemed tainted and alien. She fought back tears. "I don't know what to think." She realized she'd been clutching the receiver for a long, silent interval.

"Poor dear! There's nothing you need think about! Now listen. I'm at my solicitor's tidying up some property matters for Aunt Julia. I'll phone right now to have my car sent around for you. It'll be there by the time you pack your toothbrush and pyjamas, and whisk you straight off to bucolic Maida Vale. The maids will plump up your pillows for you, and you can have a nice nap before I get home for dinner. Poor darling, I'll bet you haven't eaten a thing. Now, say you'll come."

"Thank you. It's awfully good of you. Of course I will."

"Then it's done. Don't worry about a thing, Lisette. I'll see you this evening."

XII

Dr. Magnus hunched forward on the narrow seat of the taxi, wearily massaging his forehead and temples. It might not help his mental fatigue, but maybe the reduced muscle tension would ease his headache. He glanced at his watch. Getting on past ten. He'd had no sleep last night, and it didn't look as if he'd be getting much tonight. If only those girls would answer their phone!

It didn't help matters that his conscience plagued him. He had broken a sacred trust. He should never have made use of posthypnotic suggestion last night to persuade Lisette to return for a further session. It went against all principles, but there had been no other course: the girl was adamant, and he had to know—he was so close to establishing final proof. If only for one final session of regressive hypnosis . . .

Afterward he had spent a sleepless night, too excited for rest, at work in his study trying to reconcile the conflicting elements of Lisette's released memories with the historical data his research had so far compiled. By morning he had been able to pull together just enough facts to deepen the mystery. He had phoned his secretary at home to cancel all his appointments, and had spent the day at the tedious labor of delving through dusty municipal records and newspaper files, working feverishly as the past reluctantly yielded one bewildering clue after another.

By now Dr. Magnus was exhausted, hungry and none too clean, but he had managed to establish proof of his theories. He was not elated. In doing so he had uncovered another secret, something undreamt of in his philosophies. He began to hope that his life work was in error.

"Here's the address, sir."

"Thank you, driver." Dr. Magnus awoke from his grim revery and saw that he had reached his destination. Quickly, he paid the driver and hurried up the walk to Lisette's flat. Only a few lights were on, and he rang the bell urgently—a helpless sense of foreboding making his movements clumsy.

"Just one moment, sir!"

Dr. Magnus jerked about at the voice. Two men in plain clothes approached him briskly from the pavement.

"Stand easy! We're police."

"Is something the matter, officers?" Obviously, something was.

"Might we ask what your business here is, sir?"

"Certainly. I'm a friend of Miss Borland and Miss Seyrig. I haven't been able to reach them by phone, and as I have some rather urgent matters to discuss with Miss Seyrig, I thought perhaps I might try reaching her here at her flat." He realized he was far too nervous.

"Might we see some identification, sir?"

"Is there anything wrong, officers?" Magnus repeated, producing his wallet.

"Dr. Ingmar Magnus." The taller of the pair regarded him quizzically. "I take it you don't keep up with the news, Dr. Magnus."

"Just what is this about!"

"I'm Inspector Bradley, Dr. Magnus, and this is Detective Sergeant Wharton. CID. We've been wanting to ask you a few questions, sir, if you'll just come with us."

It was totally dark when Lisette awoke from troubled sleep. She stared wide-eyed into the darkness for a moment, wondering where she was. Slowly memory supplanted the vague images of her dream. Switching on a lamp beside her bed, Lisette frowned at her watch. It was close to midnight. She had overslept.

Beth's Rolls had come for her almost before she had had time hastily to pack her overnight bag. Once at the house in Maida Vale, a maid—wearing a more conventional uniform than those at her last visit—had shown her to a spacious guest room on the top floor. Lisette had taken a sedative pill and gratefully collapsed onto the bed. She'd planned to catch a short nap, then meet her hostess for dinner. Instead she had slept for almost ten solid hours. Beth must be convinced she was a hopeless twit after this.

As so often happens after an overextended nap, Lisette now felt restless. She wished she'd thought to bring a book. The house was completely silent. Surely it was too late to ring for a maid. No doubt Beth had meant to let her sleep through until morning, and by now would have retired herself. Perhaps she should take another pill and go back to sleep herself.

On the other hand, Beth Garrington hardly seemed the type to make it an early night. She might well still be awake, perhaps watching television where the noise wouldn't disturb her guest. In any event, Lisette didn't want to go back to sleep just yet.

She climbed out of bed, realizing that she'd only half undressed before falling asleep. Pulling off bra and panties, Lisette slipped into the antique nightdress of ribbons and lace she'd brought along. She hadn't thought to pack slippers or a robe, but it was a warm night, and the white cotton gown was modest enough for a peek into the hall.

There was a ribbon of light edging the door of the room at the far end of the hall. The rest of the hallway lay in darkness. Lisette stepped quietly from her room. Since Beth hadn't mentioned other guests, and the servants' quarters were elsewhere, presumably the light was coming from her hostess' bedroom and indicated she might still be awake. Lisette decided she really should make the effort to meet her hostess while in a conscious state.

She heard a faint sound of music as she tiptoed down the hallway. The door to the room was ajar, and the music came from within. She was in luck; Beth must still be up. At the doorway she knocked softly.

"Beth? Are you awake? It's Lisette."

There was no answer, but the door swung open at her touch.

Lisette started to call out again, but her voice froze in her throat. She recognized the tune she heard, and she knew this room. When she entered the bedroom, she could no more alter her actions than she could control the course of her dreams.

It was a large bedroom, entirely furnished in the mode of the late Victorian period. The windows were curtained, and the room's only light came from a candle upon a night table beside the huge four-poster bed. An antique gold pocket watch lay upon the night table also, and the watch was chiming an old music-box tune.

Lisette crossed the room, praying that this was no more than another vivid recurrence of her nightmare. She reached the night table and saw that the watch's hands pointed toward midnight. The chimes stopped. She picked up the watch and examined the picture that she knew would be inside the watchcase.

The picture was a photograph of herself.

Lisette let the watch clatter onto the table, stared in terror at the four-poster bed.

From within, a hand drew back the bed curtains.

Lisette wished she could scream, could awaken.

Sweeping aside the curtains, the occupant of the bed sat up and gazed at her.

And Lisette stared back at herself.

"Can't you drive a bit faster than this?"

Inspector Bradley resisted the urge to wink at Detective Sergeant Wharton. "Sit back, Dr. Magnus. We'll be there in good time. I trust you'll have rehearsed some apologies for when we disrupt a peaceful household in the middle of the night."

"I only pray such apologies will be necessary," Dr. Magnus said, continuing to sit forward as if that would inspire the driver to go faster.

It hadn't been easy, Dr. Magnus reflected. He dare not tell them the truth. He suspected that Bradley had agreed to making a late night call on Beth Garrington more to check out his alibi than from any credence he gave to Magnus's improvised tale.

Buried all day in frenzied research, Dr. Magnus hadn't listened to the news, had ignored the tawdry London tabloids with their lurid headlines: "Naked Beauty Slashed in Tub" "Nude Model Slain in Bath" "Party Girl Suicide or Ripper's Victim?" The shock of learning of Danielle's death was seconded by the shock of discovering that he was one of the "important leads" police were following.

It had taken all his powers of persuasion to convince them to

release him—or, at least, to accompany him to the house in Maida
Vale. Ironically, he and Lisette were the only ones who could account for each other's presence elsewhere at the time of Danielle's
death. While the CID might have been sceptical as to the nature of
their late night session at Dr. Magnus's office, there were a few
corroborating details. A barman at the Catherine Wheel had remembered the distinguished gent with the beard leaving after his
lady friend had dropped off of a sudden. The cleaning lady had
heard voices and left his office undisturbed. This much they'd
already checked, in verifying Lisette's whereabouts that night.
Half a dozen harassed records clerks could testify as to Dr.
Magnus's presence for today.

Dr. Magnus grimly reviewed the results of his research. There
was an Elisabeth Beresford, born in London in 1879, of a well-to-
do family who lived in Cheyne Row on the Chelsea Embankment.
Elisabeth Beresford married a Captain Donald Stapledon in 1899
and moved to India with her husband. She returned to London,
evidently suffering from consumption contracted while abroad,
and died in 1900. She was buried in Highgate Cemetery. That
much Dr. Magnus had initially learned with some difficulty. From
that basis he had pressed on for additional corroborating details,
both from Lisette's released memories and from research into
records of the period.

It had been particularly difficult to trace the subsequent
branches of the family—something he must do in order to establish that Elisabeth Beresford could not have been an ancestress of
Lisette Seyrig. And it disturbed him that he had been unable to
locate Elisabeth Stapledon nee Beresford's tomb in Highgate Cemetery.

Last night he had pushed Lisette as relentlessly as he dared. Out
of her resurfacing visions of horror he finally found a clue. These
were not images from nightmare, not symbolic representations of
buried fears. They were literal memories.

Because of the sensation involved and the considerable station
of the families concerned, public records had discreetly avoided
reference to the tragedy, as had the better newspapers. The yellow
journals were less reticent, and here Dr. Magnus began to know
fear.

Elisabeth Stapledon had been buried alive.

At her final wishes, the body had not been embalmed. The papers suggested that this was a clear premonition of her fate, and quoted passages from Edgar Allan Poe. Captain Stapledon paid an evening visit to his wife's tomb and discovered her wandering in a dazed condition about the graves. This was more than a month after her entombment.

The newspapers were full of pseudo-scientific theories, spiritualist explanations and long accounts of Indian mystics who had remained in a state of suspended animation for weeks on end. No one seems to have explained exactly how Elisabeth Stapledon escaped from both coffin and crypt, but it was supposed that desperate strength had wrenched loose the screws, while providentially the crypt had not been properly locked after a previous visit.

Husband and wife understandably went abroad immediately afterward, in order to escape publicity and for Elisabeth Stapledon to recover from her ordeal. This she very quickly did, but evidently the shock was more than Captain Stapledon could endure. He died in 1902, and his wife returned to London soon after, inheriting his extensive fortune and properties, including their house in Maida Vale. When she later inherited her own family's estate—her sole brother fell in the Boer War—she was a lady of great wealth.

Elisabeth Stapledon became one of the most notorious hostesses of the Edwardian era and on until the close of the First World War. Her beauty was considered remarkable, and men marvelled while her rivals bemoaned that she scarcely seemed to age with the passing years. After the War she left London to travel about the exotic East. In 1924 news came of her death in India.

Her estate passed to her daughter, Jane Stapledon, born abroad in 1901. While Elisabeth Stapledon made occasional references to her daughter, Jane was raised and educated in Europe and never seemed to have come to London until her arrival in 1925. Some had suggested that the mother had wished to keep her daughter pure from her own Bohemian life style, but when Jane Stapledon appeared, it seemed more likely that her mother's motives for her seclusion had been born of jealousy. Jane Stapledon had all her mother's beauty—indeed, her older admirers vowed she was the very image of Elisabeth in her youth. She also had inherited her mother's taste for wild living; with a new circle of friends from her own age group, she took up where her mother had left off. The newspapers were particularly scandalized by her association with

Aleister Crowley and others of his circle. Although her dissipations bridged the years of Flaming Youth to the Lost Generation, even her enemies had to admit she carried her years extremely well. In 1943 Jane Stapledon was missing and presumed dead after an air raid levelled and burned a section of London where she had gone to dine with friends.

Papers in the hands of her solicitor left her estate to a daughter living in America, Julia Weatherford, born in Miami in 1934. Evidently her mother had enjoyed a typical whirlwind resort romance with an American millionaire while wintering in Florida. Their marriage was a secret one, annulled following Julia's birth, and her daughter had been left with her former husband. Julia Weatherford arrived from the States early in 1946. Any doubts as to the authenticity of her claim were instantly banished, for she was the very picture of her mother in her younger days. Julia again seemed to have the family's wild streak, and she carried on the tradition of wild parties and bizarre acquaintances through the Beat Generation to the Flower Children. Her older friends thought it amazing that Julia in a minidress might easily be mistaken as being of the same age group as her young, pot-smoking, hippie friends. But it may have been that at last her youth began to fade, because since 1967 Julia Weatherford had been living more or less in seclusion in Europe, occasionally visited by her niece.

Her niece, Beth Garrington, born in 1950, was the orphaned daughter of Julia's American half-sister and a wealthy young Englishman from Julia's collection. After her parents' death in a plane crash in 1970, Beth had become her aunt's protegée, and carried on the mad life in London. It was apparent that Beth Garrington would inherit her aunt's property as well. It was also apparent that she was the spitting image of her Aunt Julia when the latter was her age. It would be most interesting to see the two of them together. And that, of course, no one had ever done.

At first Dr. Magnus had been unwilling to accept the truth of the dread secret he had uncovered. And yet, with the knowledge of Lisette's released memories, he knew there could be no other conclusion.

It was astonishing how thoroughly a woman who thrived on notoriety could avoid having her photographs published. After all, changing fashions and new hair styles, careful adjustments with cosmetics, could only do so much, and while the mind's eye had an inaccurate memory, a camera lens did not. Dr. Magnus did succeed in finding a few photographs through persistent research. Given a good theatrical costume and makeup crew, they all might have been taken of the same woman on the same day.

They might also all have been taken of Lisette Seyrig.

However, Dr. Magnus knew that it *would* be possible to see Beth Garrington and Lisette Seyrig together.

And he prayed he would be in time to prevent this.

With this knowledge tormenting his thoughts, it was a miracle that Dr. Magnus had held onto sanity well enough to persuade New Scotland Yard to make this late night drive to Maida Vale— desperate, in view of what he knew to be true. He had suffered a shock as severe as any that night when they told him at last where Lisette had gone.

"She's quite all right. She's staying with a friend."

"Might I ask where?"

"A chauffered Rolls picked her up. We checked registration, and it belongs to a Miss Elisabeth Garrington in Maida Vale."

Dr. Magnus had been frantic then, had demanded that they take him there instantly. A telephone call informed them that Miss Seyrig was sleeping under sedation and could not be disturbed; she would return his call in the morning.

Controlling his panic, Dr. Magnus had managed to contrive a disjointed tangle of half-truths and plausible lies—anything to convince them to get over to the Garrington house as quickly as possible. They already knew he was one of those occult kooks. Very well, he assured them that Beth Garrington was involved in a secret society of drug fiends and satanists (all true enough), that Danielle and Lisette had been lured to their most recent orgy for unspeakable purposes. Lisette had been secretly drugged, but Danielle had escaped to carry her roommate home before they could be used for whatever depraved rites awaited them—perhaps ritual sacrifice. Danielle had been murdered—either to shut her up or as part of the ritual—and now they had Lisette in their clutches as well.

All very melodramatic, but enough of it was true. Inspector Bradley knew of the sex and drugs orgies that took place there, but there was firm pressure from higher up to look the other way. Further, he knew enough about some of the more bizarre cult groups in London to consider that ritual murder was quite feasi-

ble, given the proper combination of sick minds and illegal drugs.
And while it hadn't been made public, the medical examiner was
of the opinion that the slashes to the Borland girl's throat and
wrists had been an attempt to disguise the fact that she had already bled to death from two deep punctures through the jugular
vein.

A demented killer, obviously. A ritual murder? You couldn't
discount it just yet. Inspector Bradley had ordered a car.

"Who are you, Lisette Seyrig, that you wear my face?"

Beth Garrington rose sinuously from her bed. She was dressed
in an off-the-shoulder nightgown of antique lace, much the same
as that which Lisette wore. Her green eyes—the eyes behind the
mask that had so shaken Lisette when last they'd met—held her in
their spell.

"When first faithful Adrian swore he'd seen my double, I
thought his brain had begun to reel with final madness. But after
he followed you to your little gallery and brought me there to see
your portrait, I knew I had encountered something beyond even
my experience."

Lisette stood frozen with dread fascination as her nightmare
came to life. Her twin paced about her, appraising her coolly as a
serpent considers its hypnotized victim.

"Who are you, Lisette Seyrig, that yours is the face I have seen
in my dreams, the face that haunted my nightmares as I lay dying,
the face that I thought was my own?"

Lisette forced her lips to speak. "*Who* are you?"

"My name? I change that whenever it becomes prudent for me
to do so. Tonight I am Beth Garrington. Long ago I was Elisabeth
Beresford."

"How can this be possible?" Lisette hoped she was dealing with
a madwoman, but knew her hope was false.

"A spirit came to me in my dreams and slowly stole away my
mortal life, in return giving me eternal life. You understand what I
say, even though your reason insists that such things cannot be."

She unfastened Lisette's gown and let it fall to the floor, then did
the same with her own. Standing face to face, their nude bodies
seemed one a reflection of the other.

Elisabeth took Lisette's face in her hands and kissed her full on
the lips. The kiss was a long one; her breath was cold in Lisette's

mouth. When Elisabeth released her lips and gazed longingly into her eyes, Lisette saw the pointed fangs that now curved downward from her upper jaw.

"Will you cry out, I wonder? If so, let it be in ecstasy and not in fear. I shan't drain you and discard you as I did your silly friend. No, Lisette, my new-found sister. I shall take your life in tiny kisses from night to night—kisses that you will long for with your entire being. And in the end you shall pass over to serve me as my willing chattel—as have the few others I have chosen over the years."

Lisette trembled beneath her touch, powerless to break away. From the buried depths of her unconscious mind, understanding slowly emerged. She did not resist when Elisabeth led her to the bed and lay down beside her on the silken sheets. Lisette was past knowing fear.

Elisabeth stretched her naked body upon Lisette's warmer flesh, lying between her thighs as would a lover. Her cool fingers caressed Lisette; her kisses teased a path from her belly across her breasts and to the hollow of her throat.

Elisabeth paused and gazed into Lisette's eyes. Her fangs gleamed with a reflection of the inhuman lust in her expression.

"And now I give you a kiss sweeter than any passion your mortal brain dare imagine, Lisette Seyrig—even as once I first received such a kiss from a dream-spirit whose eyes stared into mine from my own face. Why have you haunted my dreams, Lisette Seyrig?"

Lisette returned her gaze silently, without emotion. Nor did she flinch when Elisabeth's lips closed tightly against her throat, and the only sound was a barely perceptible tearing, like the bursting of a maidenhead, and the soft movement of suctioning lips.

Elisabeth suddenly broke away with an inarticulate cry of pain. Her lips smeared with scarlet, she stared down at Lisette in bewildered fear. Lisette, blood streaming from the wound on her throat, stared back at her with a smile of unholy hatred.

"*What* are you, Lisette Seyrig?"

"I am Elisabeth Beresford." Lisette's tone was implacable. "In another lifetime you drove my soul from my body and stole my flesh for your own. Now I have come back to reclaim that which once was mine."

Elisabeth sought to leap away, but Lisette's arms embraced her

with sudden, terrible strength—pulling their naked bodies together in a horrid imitation of two lovers at the moment of ecstasy.
The scream that echoed into the night was not one of ecstasy.

At the sound of the scream—afterward they never agreed
whether it was two voices together or only one—Inspector Bradley
ceased listening to the maid's outraged protests and burst past her
into the house.

"Upstairs! On the double!" He ordered needlessly. Already Dr.
Magnus had lunged past him and was sprinting up the stairway.

"I think it came from the next floor up! Check inside all the
rooms!" Later he cursed himself for not posting a man at the door,
for by the time he was again able to think rationally, there was no
trace of the servants.

In the master bedroom at the end of the third-floor hallway, they
found two bodies behind the curtains of the big four-poster bed.
One had only just been murdered; her nude body was drenched in
the blood from her torn throat—seemingly far too much blood for
one body. The other body was a desiccated corpse, obviously dead
for a great many years. The dead girl's limbs obscenely embraced
the mouldering cadaver that lay atop her, and her teeth, in final
spasm, were locked in the lich's throat. As they gaped in horror,
clumps of hair and bits of dried skin could be seen to drop away.

Detective Sergeant Wharton looked away and vomited on the
floor.

"I owe you a sincere apology, Dr. Magnus." Inspector Bradley's
face was grim. "You were right. Ritual murder by a gang of sick
degenerates. Detective Sergeant! Leave off that, and put out an all-
points bulletin for Beth Garrington. And round up anyone else
you find here! Move, man!"

"If only I'd understood in time," Dr. Magnus muttered. He was
obviously to the point of collapse.

"No, I should have listened to you sooner," Bradley growled.
"We might have been in time to prevent this. The devils must have
fled down some servants' stairway when they heard us burst in. I
confess I've bungled this badly."

"She was a vampire, you see," Dr. Magnus told him dully,
groping to explain. "A vampire loses its soul when it becomes one
of the undead. But the soul is deathless; it lives on even when its
previous incarnation has become a soulless demon. Elisabeth

Beresford's soul lived on, until Elisabeth Beresford found reincarnation in Lisette Seyrig. Don't you see? Elisabeth Beresford met her own reincarnation, and that meant destruction for them both."

Inspector Bradley had been only half listening. "Dr. Magnus, you've done all you can. I think you should go down to the car with Detective Sergeant Wharton now and rest until the ambulance arrives."

"But you must see that I was right!" Dr. Magnus pleaded. Madness danced in his eyes. "If the soul is immortal and infinite, then time has no meaning for the soul. Elisabeth Beresford was haunting herself."

Carrion Comfort

❦❖❦

Dan Simmons

ina was going to take credit for the death of the Beatle, John.
I thought that was in very bad taste. She had her scrapbook
laid out on my mahogany coffee table, newspaper clippings
neatly arranged in chronological order, the bald statements of
death recording all of her Feedings. Nina Drayton's smile was
radiant, but her pale-blue eyes showed no hint of warmth.

"We should wait for Willi," I said.

"Of course, Melanie. You're right, as always. How silly of me. I
know the rules." Nina stood and began walking around the room,
idly touching the furnishings or exclaiming softly over a ceramic
statuette or piece of needlepoint. This part of the house had once
been the conservatory, but now I used it as my sewing room.
Green plants still caught the morning light. The light made it a
warm, cozy place in the daytime, but now that winter had come
the room was too chilly to use at night. Nor did I like the sense of
darkness closing in against all those panes of glass.

"I love this house," said Nina.

She turned and smiled at me. "I can't tell you how much I look
forward to coming back to Charleston. We should hold all of our
reunions here."

I knew how much Nina loathed this city and this house.

"Willi would be hurt," I said. "You know how he likes to show off his place in Beverly Hills—and his new girlfriends."

"And boyfriends," Nina said, laughing. Of all the changes and darkenings in Nina, her laugh has been least affected. It was still the husky but childish laugh that I had first heard so long ago. It had drawn me to her then—one lonely, adolescent girl responding to the warmth of another as a moth to a flame. Now it served only to chill me and put me even more on guard. Enough moths had been drawn to Nina's flame over the many decades.

"I'll send for tea," I said.

Mr. Thorne brought the tea in my best Wedgwood china. Nina and I sat in the slowly moving squares of sunlight and spoke softly of nothing important: mutually ignorant comments on the economy, references to books that the other had not gotten around to reading, and sympathetic murmurs about the low class of persons one meets while flying these days. Someone peering in from the garden might have thought he was seeing an aging but attractive niece visiting her favorite aunt. (I drew the line at suggesting that anyone would mistake us for mother and daughter.) People usually consider me a well-dressed if not stylish person. Heaven knows I have paid enough to have the wool skirts and silk blouses mailed from Scotland and France. But next to Nina I've always felt dowdy.

This day she wore an elegant, light-blue dress that must have cost several thousand dollars. The color made her complexion seem even more perfect than usual and brought out the blue of her eyes. Her hair had gone as gray as mine, but somehow she managed to get away with wearing it long and tied back with a single barrette. It looked youthful and chic on Nina and made me feel that my short artificial curls were glowing with a blue rinse.

Few would suspect that I was four years younger than Nina. Time had been kind to her. And she had Fed more often.

She set down her cup and saucer and moved aimlessly around the room again. It was not like Nina to show such signs of nervousness. She stopped in front of the glass display case. Her gaze passed over the Hummels and the pewter pieces and then stopped in surprise.

"Good heavens, Melanie. A pistol! What an odd place to put an old pistol."

"It's an heirloom," I said. "A Colt Peacemaker from right after the War Between the States. Quite expensive. And you're right, it *is* a silly place to keep it. But it's the only case I have in the house with a lock on it and Mrs. Hodges often brings her grandchildren when she visits—"

"You mean it's *loaded?*"

"No, of course not," I lied. "But children should not play with such things . . ." I trailed off lamely. Nina nodded but did not bother to conceal the condescension in her smile. She went to look out the south window into the garden.

Damn her. It said volumes about Nina that she did not recognize that pistol.

On the day he was killed, Charles Edgar Larchmont had been my beau for precisely five months and two days. There had been no formal announcement, but we were to be married. Those five months had been a microcosm of the era itself—naive, flirtatious, formal to the point of preciosity, and romantic. Most of all, romantic. Romantic in the worst sense of the word: dedicated to saccharine or insipid ideals that only an adolescent—or an adolescent society—would strive to maintain. We were children playing with loaded weapons.

Nina, she was Nina Hawkins then, had her own beau—a tall, awkward, but well-meaning Englishman named Roger Harrison. Mr. Harrison had met Nina in London a year earlier, during the first stages of the Hawkinses' Grand Tour. Declaring himself smitten—another absurdity of those times—the tall Englishman had followed her from one European capital to another until, after being firmly reprimanded by Nina's father (an unimaginative little milliner who was constantly on the defensive about his doubtful social status), Harrison returned to London to "settle his affairs." Some months later he showed up in New York just as Nina was being packed off to her aunt's home in Charleston in order to terminate yet another flirtation. Still undaunted, the clumsy Englishman followed her south, ever mindful of the protocols and restrictions of the day.

We were a gay group. The day after I met Nina at Cousin Celia's June ball, the four of us were taking a hired boat up the Cooper River for a picnic on Daniel Island. Roger Harrison, serious and solemn on every topic, was a perfect foil for Charles's irreverent sense of humor. Nor did Roger seem to mind the good-natured jesting, since he was soon joining in the laughter with his peculiar *haw-haw-haw*.

Nina loved it all. Both gentlemen showered attention on her, and although Charles never failed to show the primacy of his affection for me, it was understood by all that Nina Hawkins was one of those young women who invariably becomes the center of male gallantry and attention in any gathering. Nor were the social strata of Charleston blind to the combined charm of our foursome. For two months of that now-distant summer, no party was complete, no excursion adequately planned, and no occasion considered a success unless we four were invited and had chosen to attend. Our happy dominance of the youthful social scene was so pronounced that Cousins Celia and Loraine wheedled their parents into leaving two weeks early for their annual August sojourn in Maine.

I am not sure when Nina and I came up with the idea of the duel. Perhaps it was during one of the long, hot nights when the other "slept over"—creeping into the other's bed, whispering and giggling, stifling our laughter when the rustling of starched uniforms betrayed the presence of our colored maids moving through the darkened halls. In any case, the idea was the natural outgrowth of the romantic pretensions of the time. The picture of Charles and Roger actually dueling over some abstract point of honor relating to *us* thrilled both of us in a physical way that I recognize now as a simple form of sexual titilation.

It would have been harmless except for the Ability. We had been so successful in our manipulation of male behavior—a manipulation that was both expected and encouraged in those days—that neither of us had yet suspected that there was anything beyond the ordinary in the way we could translate our whims into other people's actions. The field of parapsychology did not exist then; or rather, it existed only in the rappings and knockings of parlor-game séances. At any rate, we amused ourselves for several weeks with whispered fantasies, and then one of us—or perhaps both of us—used the Ability to translate the fantasy into reality.

In a sense, it was our first Feeding.

I do not remember the purported cause of the quarrel, perhaps some deliberate misinterpretation of one of Charles's jokes. I cannot recall who Charles and Roger arranged to have serve as seconds on that illegal outing. I do remember the hurt and confused

expression on Roger Harrison's face during those few days. It was
a caricature of ponderous dullness, the confusion of a man who
finds himself in a situation not of his making and from which he
cannot escape. I remember Charles and his mercurial swings of
mood—the bouts of humor, periods of black anger, and the tears
and kisses the night before the duel.

I remember with great clarity the beauty of that morning. Mists
were floating up from the river and diffusing the rays of the rising
sun as we rode out to the dueling field. I remember Nina reaching
over and squeezing my hand with an impetuous excitement that
was communicated through my body like an electric shock.

Much of the rest of that morning is missing. Perhaps in the
intensity of that first, subconscious Feeding, I literally lost consciousness as I was engulfed in the waves of fear, excitement,
pride—of *maleness*—emanating from our two beaus as they faced
death on that lovely morning. I remember experiencing the shock
of realizing, *this is really happening*, as I shared the tread of high
boots through the grass. Someone was calling off the paces. I
dimly recall the weight of the pistol in my hand—Charles's hand, I
think; I will never know for sure—and a second of cold clarity
before an explosion broke the connection, and the acrid smell of
gunpowder brought me back to myself.

It was Charles who died. I have never been able to forget the
incredible quantities of blood that poured from the small, round
hole in his breast. His white shirt was crimson by the time I
reached him. There had been no blood in our fantasies. Nor had
there been the sight of Charles with his head lolling, mouth drib-
bling saliva onto his bloodied chest while his eyes rolled back to
show the whites like two eggs embedded in his skull.

Roger Harrison was sobbing as Charles breathed his final, shuddering gasps on that field of innocence.

I remember nothing at all about the confused hours that followed. The next morning I opened my cloth bag to find Charles's
pistol lying with my things. Why would I have kept that revolver?
If I had wished to take something from my fallen lover as a sign of
remembrance, why that alien piece of metal? Why pry from his
dead fingers the symbol of our thoughtless sin?

It said volumes about Nina that she did not recognize
that pistol.

* * *

"Willi's here," announced Nina's amanuensis, the loathsome Miss Barrett Kramer. Kramer's appearance was as unisex as her name: short-cropped, black hair, powerful shoulders, and a blank, aggressive gaze that I associated with lesbians and criminals. She looked to be in her mid-thirties.

"Thank you, Barrett dear," said Nina.

Both of us went out to greet Willi, but Mr. Thorne had already let him in, and we met in the hallway.

"Melanie! You look marvelous! You grow younger each time I see you. Nina!" The change in Willi's voice was evident. Men continued to be overpowered by their first sight of Nina after an absence. There were hugs and kisses. Willi himself looked more dissolute than ever. His alpaca sport coat was exquisitely tailored, his turtleneck sweater successfully concealed the eroded lines of his wattled neck, but when he swept off his jaunty sports-car cap the long strands of white hair he had brushed forward to hide his encroaching baldness were knocked into disarray. Willi's face was flushed with excitement, but there was also the telltale capillary redness about the nose and cheeks that spoke of too much liquor, too many drugs.

"Ladies, I think you've met my associates, Tom Luhar and Jenson Reynolds?" The two men added to the crowd in my narrow hall. Mr. Luhar was thin and blond, smiling with perfectly capped teeth. Mr. Reynolds was a gigantic Negro, hulking forward with a sullen, bruised look on his coarse face. I was sure that neither Nina nor I had encountered these specific cat's-paws of Willi's before. It did not matter.

"Why don't we go into the parlor?" I suggested. It was an awkward procession ending with the three of us seated on the heavily upholstered chairs surrounding the Georgian tea table that had been my grandmother's. "More tea, please, Mr. Thorne." Miss Kramer took that as her cue to leave, but Willi's two pawns stood uncertainly by the door, shifting from foot to foot and glancing at the crystal on display as if their mere proximity could break something. I would not have been surprised if that had proved to be the case.

"Jense!" Willi snapped his fingers. The Negro hesitated and then brought forward an expensive leather attaché case. Willi set it on the tea table and clicked the catches open with his short, broad fingers. "Why don't you two see Mrs. Fuller's man about getting something to drink?"

When they were gone Willi shook his head and smiled apologetically at Nina. "Sorry about that, Love."

Nina put her hand on Willi's sleeve. She leaned forward with an air of expectancy. "Melanie wouldn't let me begin the Game without you. Wasn't that *awful* of me to want to start without you, Willi dear?"

Willi frowned. After fifty years he still bridled at being called Willi. In Los Angeles he was Big Bill Borden. When he returned to his native Germany—which was not often because of the dangers involved—he was once again Wilhelm von Borchert, lord of dark manor, forest, and hunt. But Nina had called him Willi when they had first met in 1931 in Vienna, and Willi he had remained.

"You begin, Willi dear," said Nina. "You go first."

I could remember the time when we would have spent the first few days of our reunion in conversation and catching up with one another's lives. Now there was not even time for small talk.

Willi showed his teeth and removed news clippings, notebooks, and a stack of cassettes from his briefcase. No sooner had he covered the small table with his material than Mr. Thorne arrived with the tea and Nina's scrapbook from the sewing room. Willi brusquely cleared a small space.

At first glance one might see certain similarities between Willi Borchert and Mr. Thorne. One would be mistaken. Both men tended to the florid, but Willi's complexion was the result of excess and emotion; Mr. Thorne had known neither of these for many years. Willi's balding was a patchy, self-consciously concealed thing—a weasel with mange; Mr. Thorne's bare head was smooth and unwrinkled. One could not imagine Mr. Thorne ever having *had* hair. Both men had gray eyes—what a novelist would call cold, gray eyes—but Mr. Thorne's eyes were cold with indifference, cold with a clarity coming from an absolute absence of troublesome emotion or thought. Willi's eyes were the cold of a blustery North Sea winter and were often clouded with shifting curtains of the emotions that controlled him—pride, hatred, love of pain, the pleasures of destruction.

Willi never referred to his use of the Ability as *Feedings*—I was evidently the only one who thought in those terms—but Willi sometimes talked of The Hunt. Perhaps it was the dark forests of his homeland that he thought of as he stalked his human quarry through the sterile streets of Los Angeles. Did Willi dream of the forest, I wondered. Did he look back to green wool hunting jackets, the applause of retainers, the gouts of blood from the dying boar? Or did Willi remember the slam of jack-boots on cobblestones and the pounding of his lieutenants' fists on doors? Perhaps Willi still associated his Hunt with the dark European night of the ovens that he had helped to oversee.

I called it Feeding. Willi called it The Hunt. I had never heard Nina call it anything.

"Where is your VCR?" Willi asked. "I have put them all on tape."

"Oh, Willi," said Nina in an exasperated tone. "You know Melanie. She's *so* old-fashioned. You know she wouldn't have a video player."

"I don't even have a television," I said. Nina laughed.

"Goddamn it," muttered Willi. "It doesn't matter. I have other records here." He snapped rubber bands from around the small, black notebooks. "It just would have been better on tape. The Los Angeles stations gave much coverage to the Hollywood Strangler, and I edited in the . . . Ach! Never mind."

He tossed the videocassettes into his briefcase and slammed the lid shut.

"Twenty-three," he said. "Twenty-three since we met twelve months ago. It doesn't seem that long, does it?"

"Show us," said Nina. She was leaning forward, and her blue eyes seemed very bright. "I've been wondering since I saw the Strangler interviewed on *Sixty Minutes*. He *was* yours, Willi? He seemed so—"

"*Ja, ja*, he was mine. A nobody. A timid little man. He was the gardener of a neighbor of mine. I left him alive so that the police could question him, erase any doubts. He will hang himself in his cell next month after the press loses interest. But this is more interesting. Look at this." Willi slid across several glossy black-and-white photographs. The NBC executive had murdered the five members of his family and drowned a visiting soap-opera actress in his pool. He had then stabbed himself repeatedly and written 50 SHARE in blood on the wall of the bathhouse.

"Reliving old glories, Willi?" asked Nina. "DEATH TO THE PIGS and all that?"

"No, goddamn it. I think it should receive points for irony. The girl had been scheduled to drown on the program. It was already in the script outline."

"Was he hard to Use?" It was my question. I was curious despite myself.

Willi lifted one eyebrow. "Not really. He was an alcoholic and heavily into cocaine. There was not much left. And he hated his family. Most people do."

"Most people in California, perhaps," said Nina primly. It was an odd comment from Nina. Years ago her father had committed suicide by throwing himself in front of a trolley car.

"Where did you make contact?" I asked.

"A party. The usual place. He bought the coke from a director who had ruined one of my—"

"Did you have to repeat the contact?"

Willi frowned at me. He kept his anger under control, but his face grew redder. "*Ja, ja.* I saw him twice more. Once I just watched from my car as he played tennis."

"Points for irony," said Nina. "But you lose points for repeated contact. If he were as empty as you say, you should have been able to Use him after only one touch. What else do you have?"

He had his usual assortment. Pathetic skid-row murders. Two domestic slayings. A highway collision that turned into a fatal shooting. "I was in the crowd," said Willi. "I made contact. He had a gun in the glove compartment."

"Two points," said Nina.

Willi had saved a good one for last. A once-famous child star had suffered a bizarre accident. He had left his Bel Air apartment while it filled with gas and then returned to light a match. Two others had died in the ensuing fire.

"You get credit only for him," said Nina.

"*Ja, ja.*"

"Are you absolutely sure about this one? It *could* have been an accident."

"Don't be ridiculous," snapped Willi. He turned toward me. "*This* one was very hard to Use. Very strong. I blocked his memory of turning on the gas. Had to hold it away for two hours. Then forced him into the room. He struggled not to strike the match."

"You should have had him use his lighter," said Nina.

"He didn't smoke," growled Willi. "He gave it up last year."

"Yes," smiled Nina. "I seem to remember him saying that to Johnny Carson." I could not tell whether Nina was jesting.

The three of us went through the ritual of assigning points. Nina did most of the talking. Willi went from being sullen to expansive to sullen again. At one point he reached over and patted my knee as he laughingly asked for my support. I said nothing. Finally he gave up, crossed the parlor to the liquor cabinet, and poured himself a tall glass of bourbon from father's decanter. The evening light was sending its final, horizontal rays through the stained-glass panels of the bay windows, and it cast a red hue on Willi as he stood next to the oak cupboard. His eyes were small, red embers in a bloody mask.

"Forty-one," said Nina at last.

She looked up brightly and showed the calculator as if it verified some objective fact. "I count forty-one points. What do you have, Melanie?"

"Ja," interrupted Willi. "That is fine. Now let us see your claims, Nina." His voice was flat and empty. Even Willi had lost some interest in the Game.

Before Nina could begin, Mr. Thorne entered and motioned that dinner was served. We adjourned to the dining room—Willi pouring himself another glass of bourbon and Nina fluttering her hands in mock frustration at the interruption of the Game. Once seated at the long, mahogany table, I worked at being a hostess. From decades of tradition, talk of the Game was banned from the dinner table. Over soup we discussed Willi's new movie and the purchase of another store for Nina's line of boutiques. It seemed that Nina's monthly column in *Vogue* was to be discontinued but that a newspaper syndicate was interested in picking it up.

Both of my guests exclaimed over the perfection of the baked ham, but I thought that Mr. Thorne had made the gravy a trifle too sweet. Darkness had filled the windows before we finished our chocolate mousse. The refracted light from the chandelier made Nina's hair dance with highlights while I feared that mine glowed more bluely than ever.

Suddenly there was a sound from the kitchen. The huge Negro's face appeared at the swinging door. His shoulder was hunched against white hands and his expression was that of a querulous child.

". . . the hell you think we are sittin' here like goddamned—"
The white hands pulled him out of sight.

"Excuse me, ladies." Willi dabbed linen at his lips and stood up.
He still moved gracefully for all of his years.

Nina poked at her chocolate. There was one sharp, barked command from the kitchen and the sound of a slap. It was the slap of a
man's hand—hard and flat as a small-caliber-rifle shot. I looked up
and Mr. Thorne was at my elbow, clearing away the dessert
dishes.

"Coffee, please, Mr. Thorne. For all of us." He nodded and his
smile was gentle.

Franz Anton Mesmer had known of it even if he had not understood it. I suspect that Mesmer must have had some small touch of
the Ability. Modern pseudosciences have studied it and renamed
it, removed most of its power, confused its uses and origins, but it
remains the shadow of what Mesmer discovered. They have no
idea of what it is like to Feed.

I despair at the rise of modern violence. I truly give in to despair
at times, that deep, futureless pit of despair that poet Gerard Man-
ley Hopkins called carrion comfort. I watch the American slaughterhouse, the casual attacks on popes, presidents, and uncounted
others, and I wonder whether there are many more out there with
the Ability or whether butchery has simply become the modern
way of life.

All humans feed on violence, on the small exercises of power
over another. But few have tasted—as we have—the ultimate
power. And without the Ability, few know the unequaled pleasure
of taking a human life. Without the Ability, even those who do
feed on life cannot savor the flow of emotions in stalker and victim, the total exhilaration of the attacker who has moved beyond
all rules and punishments, the strange, almost sexual submission
of the victim in that final second of truth when all options are
canceled, all futures denied, all possibilities erased in an exercise
of absolute power over another.

I despair at modern violence. I despair at the impersonal nature
of it and the casual quality that has made it accessible to so many. I
had a television set until I sold it at the height of the Vietnam War.
Those sanitized snippets of death—made distant by the camera's
lens—meant nothing to me. But I believe it meant something to

these cattle that surround me. When the war and the nightly tele-
vised body counts ended, they demanded more, *more,* and the
movie screens and streets of this sweet and dying nation have
provided it in mediocre, mob abundance. It is an addiction I know
well.

They miss the point. Merely observed, violent death is a sad and
sullied tapestry of confusion. But to those of us who have Fed,
death can be a *sacrament.*

"My turn! My turn!" Nina's voice still resembled that of the
visiting belle who had just filled her dance card at Cousin Celia's
June ball.

We had returned to the parlor. Willi had finished his coffee and
requested a brandy from Mr. Thorne. I was embarrassed for Willi.
To have one's closest associates show any hint of unplanned behavior was certainly a sign of weakening Ability. Nina did not
appear to have noticed.

"I have them all in order," said Nina. She opened the scrapbook
on the now-empty tea table. Willi went through them carefully,
sometimes asking a question, more often grunting assent. I murmured occasional agreement although I had heard of none of
them. Except for the Beatle, of course. Nina saved that for near the
end.

"Good God, Nina, that was you?" Willi seemed near anger.
Nina's Feedings had always run to Park Avenue suicides and mat-
rimonial disagreements ending in shots fired from expensive,
small-caliber ladies' guns. This type of thing was more in Willi's
crude style. Perhaps he felt that his territory was being invaded. "I
mean . . . you were risking a lot, weren't you? It's so . . . damn
it . . . so *public.*"

Nina laughed and set down the calculator. "Willi *dear,* that's
what the Game is *about,* is it not?"

Willi strode to the liquor cabinet and refilled his brandy snifter.
The wind tossed bare branches against the leaded glass of the bay
window. I do not like winter. Even in the South it takes its toll on
the spirit.

"Didn't this guy . . . what's his name . . . buy the gun in
Hawaii or someplace?" asked Willi from across the room. "That
sounds like his initiative to me. I mean, if he was *already* stalking
the fellow—"

"Willie dear." Nina's voice had gone as cold as the wind that raked the branches. "No one said he was *stable*. How many of yours are stable, Willi? But I made it *happen*, darling. I chose the place and the time. Don't you see the irony of the *place*, Willi? After that little prank on the director of that witchcraft movie a few years ago? It was straight from the script—"

"I don't know," said Willi. He sat heavily on the divan, spilling brandy on his expensive sport coat. He did not notice. The lamplight reflected from his balding skull. The mottles of age were more visible at night, and his neck, where it disappeared into his turtleneck, was all ropes and tendons. "I don't know." He looked up at me and smiled suddenly, as if we shared a conspiracy. "It could be like that writer fellow, eh, Melanie? It could be like that."

Nina looked down at the hands in her lap. They were clenched and the well-manicured fingers were white at the tips.

The Mind Vampires. That's what the writer was going to call his book.

I sometimes wonder if he really would have written anything. What was his name? Something Russian.

Willi and I received telegrams from Nina: COME QUICKLY YOU ARE NEEDED. That was enough. I was on the next morning's flight to New York. The plane was a noisy, propeller-driven Constellation, and I spent much of the flight assuring the overly solicitous stewardess that I needed nothing, that, indeed, I felt fine. She obviously had decided that I was someone's grandmother, who was flying for the first time.

Willi managed to arrive twenty minutes before me. Nina was distraught and as close to hysteria as I had ever seen her. She had been at a party in lower Manhattan two days before—she was not so distraught that she forgot to tell us what important names had been there—when she found herself sharing a corner, a fondue pot, and confidences with a young writer. Or rather, the writer was sharing confidences. Nina described him as a scruffy sort with a wispy little beard, thick glasses, a corduroy sport coat worn over an old plaid shirt—one of the type invariably sprinkled around successful parties of that era, according to Nina. She knew enough not to call him a beatnik, for that term had just become passé, but no one had yet heard the term *hippie*, and it wouldn't have applied to him anyway. He was a writer of the sort that barely ekes out a living, these days at least, by selling blood and doing novelizations of television series. Alexander something.

His idea for a book—he told Nina that he had been working on it for some time—was that many of the murders then being committed were actually the result of a small group of psychic killers, he called them *mind vampires*, who used others to carry out their grisly deeds.

He said that a paperback publisher had already shown interest in his outline and would offer him a contract tomorrow if he would change the title to *The Zombie Factor* and put in more sex.

"So what?" Willi had said to Nina in disgust. "You have me fly across the continent for this? I might buy the idea myself."

That turned out to be the excuse we used to interrogate this Alexander somebody during an impromptu party given by Nina the next evening. I did not attend. The party was not overly successful according to Nina but it gave Willi the chance to have a long chat with the young would-be novelist. In the writer's almost pitiable eagerness to do business with Bill Borden, producer of *Paris Memories, Three on a Swing,* and at least two other completely forgettable Technicolor features touring the drive-ins that summer, he revealed that the book consisted of a well-worn outline and a dozen pages of notes.

He was sure, however, that he could do a treatment for Mr. Borden in five weeks, perhaps even as fast as three weeks if he were flown out to Hollywood to get the proper creative stimulation.

Later that evening we discussed the possibility of Willi simply buying an option on the treatment, but Willi was short on cash at the time and Nina was insistent. In the end the young writer opened his femoral artery with a Gillette blade and ran screaming into a narrow Greenwich Village side street to die. I don't believe that anyone ever bothered to sort through the clutter and debris of his remaining notes.

"It could be like that writer, *ja*, Melanie?" Willi patted my knee. I nodded. "He was mine," continued Willi, "and Nina tried to take credit. Remember?"

Again I nodded. Actually he had been neither Nina's nor Willi's. I had avoided the party so that I could make contact later without the young man noticing he was being followed. I did so easily. I

remember sitting in an overheated little delicatessen across the
street from the apartment building. It was over so quickly that
there was almost no sense of Feeding. Then I was aware once
again of the sputtering radiators and the smell of salami as people
rushed to the door to see what the screaming was about. I remember finishing my tea slowly so that I did not have to leave before
the ambulance was gone.

"Nonsense," said Nina. She busied herself with her little calculator. "How many points?" She looked at me. I looked at Willi.

"Six," he said with a shrug. Nina made a small show of totaling
the numbers.

"Thirty-eight," she said and sighed theatrically. "You win
again, Willi. Or rather, you beat *me* again. We must hear from
Melanie. You've been so quiet, dear. You must have some surprise
for us."

"Yes," said Willi, "it is your turn to win. It has been several
years."

"None," I said. I had expected an explosion of questions, but the
silence was broken only by the ticking of the clock on the mantelpiece. Nina was looking away from me, at something hidden by
the shadows in the corner.

"None?" echoed Willi.

"There was . . . one," I said at last. "But it was by accident. I
came across them robbing an old man behind . . . but it was
completely by accident."

Willi was agitated. He stood up, walked to the window, turned
an old straight-back chair around and straddled it, arms folded.
"What does this mean?"

"You're quitting the Game?" Nina asked as she turned to look at
me. I let the question serve as the answer.

"Why?" snapped Willi. In his excitement it came out with a
hard *v*.

If I had been raised in an era when young ladies were allowed to
shrug, I would have done so. As it was, I contented myself with
running my fingers along an imaginary seam on my skirt. Willi
had asked the question, but I stared straight into Nina's eyes when
I finally answered, "I'm tired. It's been too long. I guess I'm getting
old."

"You'll get a lot *older* if you do not Hunt," said Willi. His body,
his voice, the red mask of his face, everything signaled great anger

just kept in check. "My God, Melanie, you *already* look older! You look terrible. This is *why* we hunt, woman. Look at yourself in the mirror! Do you want to die an old woman just because you're tired of using *them?*" Willi stood and turned his back.

"Nonsense!" Nina's voice was strong, confident, in command once more. "Melanie's *tired*, Willi. Be nice. We all have times like that. I remember how *you* were after the war. Like a whipped puppy. You wouldn't even go outside your miserable little flat in Baden. Even after we helped you get to New Jersey you just sulked around feeling sorry for yourself. Melanie *made up* the Game to help you feel better. So quiet! *Never* tell a lady who feels tired and depressed that she looks terrible. Honestly, Willi, you're such a *Schwachsinniger* sometimes. And a crashing boor to boot."

I had anticipated many reactions to my announcement, but this was the one I feared most. It meant that Nina had also tired of the game. It meant that she was ready to move to another level of play.

It had to mean that.

"Thank you, Nina darling," I said. "I knew you would understand."

She reached across and touched my knee reassuringly. Even through my wool skirt, I could feel the cold of her fingers.

My guests would not stay the night. I implored. I remonstrated. I pointed out that their rooms were ready, that Mr. Thorne had already turned down the quilts.

"Next time," said Willi. "Next time, Melanie, my little love. We'll make a weekend of it as we used to. A week!" Willi was in a much better mood since he had been paid his thousand-dollar prize by each of us. He had sulked, but I had insisted. It soothed his ego when Mr. Thorne brought in a check already made out to WILLIAM D. BORDEN.

Again I asked him to stay, but he protested that he had a midnight flight to Chicago. He had to see a prizewinning author about a screenplay. Then he was hugging me good-bye, his companions were in the hall behind me and I had a brief moment of terror.

But they left. The blond young man showed his white smile, and the Negro bobbed his head in what I took as a farewell. Then we were alone.

Nina and I were alone.

Not quite alone. Miss Kramer was standing next to Nina at the
end of the hall. Mr. Thorne was out of sight behind the swinging
door to the kitchen. I left him there.

Miss Kramer took three steps forward. I felt my breath stop for
an instant. Mr. Thorne put his hand on the swinging door. Then
the husky little brunette opened the door to the hall closet, removed Nina's coat, and stepped back to help her into it.

"Are you sure you won't stay?"

"No, thank you, darling. I've promised Barrett that we would
drive to Hilton Head tonight."

"But it's late—"

"We have reservations. Thank you anyway, Melanie. I *will* be in
touch."

"Yes."

"I mean it, dear. We must talk. I understand *exactly* how you
feel, but you have to remember that the Game is still important to
Willi. We'll have to find a way to end it without hurting his feelings. Perhaps we could visit him next spring in Karinhall or whatever he calls that gloomy old Bavarian place of his. A trip to the
Continent would do wonders for you, dear."

"Yes."

"I *will* be in touch. After this deal with the new store is settled.
We need to spend some time together, Melanie . . . just the two
of us . . . like old times." Her lips kissed the air next to my cheek.
She held my forearms tightly. "Good-bye, darling."

"Good-bye, Nina."

I carried the brandy glass to the kitchen. Mr. Thorne took it in
silence.

"Make sure the house is secure," I said. He nodded and went to
check the locks and alarm system. It was only nine forty-five, but I
was very tired. *Age*, I thought. I went up the wide staircase, perhaps the finest feature of the house, and dressed for bed. It had
begun to storm, and the sound of the cold raindrops on the window carried a sad rhythm to it.

Mr. Thorne looked in as I was brushing my hair and wishing it
were longer. I turned to him. He reached into the pocket of his
dark vest. When his hand emerged a slim blade flicked out. I
nodded. He palmed the blade shut and closed the door behind

him. I listened to his footsteps recede down the stairs to the chair in the front hall, where he would spend the night.

I believe I dreamed of vampires that night. Or perhaps I was thinking about them just prior to falling asleep, and a fragment had stayed with me until morning. Of all mankind's self-inflicted terrors, of all its pathetic little monsters, only the myth of the vampire had any vestige of dignity. Like the humans it feeds on, the vampire must respond to its own dark compulsions. But unlike its petty human prey, the vampire carries out its sordid means to the only possible ends that could justify such actions—the goal of literal immortality. There is a nobility there. And a sadness.

Before sleeping I thought of that summer long ago in Vienna. I saw Willi young again—blond, flushed with youth, and filled with pride at escorting two such independent American ladies.

I remembered Willi's high, stiff collars and the short dresses that Nina helped to bring into style that summer. I remembered the friendly sounds of crowded *Biergartens* and the shadowy dance of leaves in front of gas lamps.

I remembered the footsteps on wet cobblestones, the shouts, the distant whistles, and the silences.

Willi was right; I had aged. The past year had taken a greater toll than the preceding decade. But I had not Fed. Despite the hunger, despite the aging reflection in the mirror, *I had not Fed*.

I fell asleep trying to think of that writer's last name. I fell asleep hungry.

Morning. Bright sunlight through bare branches. It was one of those crystalline, warming winter days that make living in the South so much less depressing than merely surviving a Yankee winter. I had Mr. Thorne open the window a crack when he brought in my breakfast tray. As I sipped my coffee I could hear children playing in the courtyard. Once Mr. Thorne would have brought the morning paper with the tray, but I had long since learned that to read about the follies and scandals of the world was to desecrate the morning. I was growing less and less interested in the affairs of men. I had done without a newspaper, telephone, or television for twelve years and had suffered no ill effects unless one were to count a growing self-contentment as an ill thing. I smiled as I remembered Willi's disappointment at not being able to play his video cassettes. He was such a child.

"It is Saturday, is it not, Mr. Thorne?" At his nod I gestured for the tray to be taken away. "We will go out today," I said. "A walk. Perhaps a trip to the fort. Then dinner at Henry's and home. I have arrangements to make."

Mr. Thorne hesitated and half-stumbled as he was leaving the room. I paused in the act of belting my robe. It was not like Mr. Thorne to commit an ungraceful movement. I realized that he too was getting old. He straightened the tray and dishes, nodded his head, and left for the kitchen.

I would not let thoughts of aging disturb me on such a beautiful morning. I felt charged with a new energy and resolve. The reunion the night before had not gone well but neither had it gone as badly as it might have. I had been honest with Nina and Willi about my intention of quitting the Game. In the weeks and months to come, they—or at least Nina—would begin to brood over the ramifications of that, but by the time they chose to react, separately or together, I would be long gone. Already I had new (and old) identities waiting for me in Florida, Michigan, London, southern France, and even in New Delhi. Michigan was out for the time being. I had grown unused to the harsh climate. New Delhi was no longer the hospitable place for foreigners it had been when I resided there briefly before the war.

Nina had been right about one thing—a return to Europe would be good for me. Already I longed for the rich light and cordial *savoir vivre* of the villagers near my old summer house outside of Toulon.

The air outside was bracing. I wore a simple print dress and my spring coat. The trace of arthritis in my right leg had bothered me coming down the stairs, but I used my father's old walking stick as a cane. A young Negro servant had cut it for father the summer we moved from Greenville to Charleston. I smiled as we emerged into the warm air of the courtyard.

Mrs. Hodges came out of her doorway into the light. It was her grandchildren and their friends who were playing around the dry fountain. For two centuries the courtyard had been shared by the three brick buildings. Only my home had not been parceled into expensive town houses or fancy apartments.

"Good morning, Miz Fuller."

"Good morning, Mrs. Hodges. A beautiful day, isn't it?"

"It is that. Are you off shopping?"

"Just for a walk, Mrs. Hodges. I'm surprised that Mr. Hodges isn't out today. He always seems to be working in the yard on Saturdays."

Mrs. Hodges frowned as one of the little girls ran between us. Her friend came squealing after her, sweater flying. "Oh, George is at the marina already."

"In the daytime?" I had often been amused by Mr. Hodges's departure for work in the evening, his security-guard uniform neatly pressed, gray hair jutting out from under his cap, black lunch pail gripped firmly under his arm.

Mr. Hodges was as leathery and bowlegged as an aged cowboy. He was one of those men who were always on the verge of retiring but who probably realized that to be suddenly inactive would be a form of death sentence.

"Oh, yes. One of those colored men on the day shift down at the storage building quit, and they asked George to fill in. I told him that he was too old to work four nights a week and then go back on the weekend, but you know George. He'll never retire."

"Well, give him my best," I said.

The girls running around the fountain made me nervous.

Mrs. Hodges followed me to the wrought-iron gate. "Will you be going away for the holidays, Miz Fuller?"

"Probably, Mrs. Hodges. Most probably." Then Mr. Thorne and I were out on the sidewalk and strolling toward the Battery. A few cars drove slowly down the narrow streets, some tourists stared at the houses of our Old Section, but the day was serene and quiet.

I saw the masts of the yachts and sailboats before we came in sight of the water as we emerged onto Broad Street.

"Please acquire tickets for us, Mr. Thorne," I said. "I believe I would like to see the fort."

As is typical of most people who live in close proximity to a popular tourist attraction, I had not taken notice of it for many years. It was an act of sentimentality to visit the fort now. An act brought on by my increasing acceptance of the fact that I would have to leave these parts forever. It is one thing to plan a move; it is something altogether different to be faced with the imperative reality of it.

There were few tourists. The ferry moved away from the marina and into the placid waters of the harbor. The combination of warm sunlight and the steady throb of the diesel caused me to doze briefly. I awoke as we were putting in at the dark hulk of the island fort.

For a while I moved with the tour group, enjoying the catacomb silences of the lower levels and the mindless singsong of the young woman from the Park Service. But as we came back to the museum, with its dusty dioramas and tawdry little trays of slides, I climbed the stairs back to the outer walls. I motioned for Mr. Thorne to stay at the top of the stairs and moved out onto the ramparts.

Only one other couple—a young pair with a cheap camera and a baby in an uncomfortable-looking papoose carrier—were in sight along the wall.

It was a pleasant moment. A midday storm was approaching from the west and it set a dark backdrop to the still-sunlit church spires, brick towers, and bare branches of the city.

Even from two miles away I could see the movement of people strolling along the Battery walkway. The wind was blowing in ahead of the dark clouds and tossing whitecaps against the rocking ferry and wooden dock. The air smelled of river and winter and rain by nightfall.

It was not hard to imagine that day long ago. The shells had dropped onto the fort until the upper layers were little more than protective piles of rubble. People had cheered from the rooftops behind the Battery. The bright colors of dresses and silk parasols must have been maddening to the Yankee gunners. Finally one had fired a shot above the crowded rooftops. The ensuing confusion must have been amusing from this vantage point.

A movement down below caught my attention. Something dark was sliding through the gray water—something dark and shark silent. I was jolted out of thoughts of the past as I recognized it as a Polaris submarine, old but obviously still operational, slipping through the dark water without a sound. Waves curled and rippled over the porpoise-smooth hull, sliding to either side in a white wake. There were several men on the tower. They were muffled in heavy coats, their hats pulled low. An improbably large pair of binoculars hung from the neck of one man, whom I assumed to be the captain. He pointed at something beyond Sullivan's Island. I stared. The periphery of my vision began to fade as I made contact. Sounds and sensations came to me as from a distance.

Tension. The pleasure of salt spray, breeze from the north, northwest. Anxiety of the sealed orders below. Awareness of the sandy shallows just coming into sight on the port side.

I was startled as someone came up behind me. The dots flickering at the edge of my vision fled as I turned.

Mr. Thorne was there. At my elbow. Unbidden. I had opened my mouth to command him back to the top of the stairs when I saw the cause of his approach. The youth who had been taking pictures of his pale wife was now walking toward me. Mr. Thorne moved to intercept him.

"Hey, excuse me, ma'am. Would you or your husband mind taking our picture?"

I nodded and Mr. Thorne took the proffered camera. It looked minuscule in his long-fingered hands. Two snaps and the couple were satisfied that their presence there was documented for posterity. The young man grinned idiotically and bobbed his head. Their baby began to cry as the cold wind blew in.

I looked back to the submarine, but already it had passed on, its gray tower a thin stripe connecting the sea and sky.

We were almost back to town, the ferry was swinging in toward the ship, when a stranger told me of Willi's death.

"It's awful, isn't it?" The garrulous old woman had followed me out onto the exposed section of deck. Even though the wind had grown chilly and I had moved twice to escape her mindless chatter, the woman had obviously chosen me as her conversational target for the final stages of the tour. Neither my reticence nor Mr. Thorne's glowering presence had discouraged her. "It must have been terrible," she continued. "In the dark and all."

"What was that?" A dark premonition prompted my question.

"Why, the airplane crash. Haven't you heard about it? It must have been awful, falling into the swamp and all. I told my daughter this morning—"

"What airplane crash? When?" The old woman cringed a bit at the sharpness of my tone, but the vacuous smile stayed on her face.

"Why last night. This morning I told my daughter—"

"Where? What aircraft are you talking about?" Mr. Thorne came closer as he heard the tone of my voice.

"The one last night," she quavered. "The one from Charleston.

The paper in the lounge told all about it. Isn't it terrible? Eighty-five people. I told my daughter—"

I left her standing there by the railing. There was a crumpled newspaper near the snack bar, and under the four-word headline were the sparse details of Willi's death. Flight 417, bound for Chicago, had left Charleston International Airport at twelve-eighteen A.M. Twenty minutes later the aircraft had exploded in midair not far from the city of Columbia. Fragments of fuselage and parts of bodies had fallen into Congaree Swamp, where fishermen had found them. There had been no survivors. The FAA and FBI were investigating.

There was a loud rushing in my ears, and I had to sit down or faint. My hands were clammy against the green-vinyl upholstery. People moved past me on their way to the exits.

Willi was dead. Murdered. Nina had killed him. For a few dizzy seconds I considered the possibility of a conspiracy—an elaborate ploy by Nina and Willi to confuse me into thinking that only one threat remained. But no. There would be no reason. If Nina had included Willi in her plans, there would be no need for such absurd machinations.

Willi was dead. His remains were spread over a smelly, obscure marshland. I could imagine his last moments. He would have been leaning back in first-class comfort, a drink in his hand, perhaps whispering to one of his loutish companions.

Then the explosion. Screams. Sudden darkness. A brutal tilting and the final fall to oblivion. I shuddered and gripped the metal arm of the chair.

How had Nina done it? Almost certainly not one of Willi's entourage. It was not beyond Nina's powers to Use Willi's own cat's-paws, especially in light of his failing Ability, but there would have been no reason to do so. She could have Used anyone on that flight. It *would* have been difficult. The elaborate step of preparing the bomb. The supreme effort of blocking all memory of it, and the almost unbelievable feat of Using someone even as we sat together drinking coffee and brandy.

But Nina could have done it. Yes, she *could* have. And the timing. The timing could mean only one thing.

The last of the tourists had filed out of the cabin. I felt the slight bump that meant we had tied up to the dock. Mr. Thorne stood by the door.

Nina's timing meant that she was attempting to deal with both of us at once. She obviously had planned it long before the reunion and my timorous announcement of withdrawal. How amused Nina must have been. No wonder she had reacted so generously! Yet, she had made one great mistake. By dealing with Willi first, Nina had banked everything on my not hearing the news before she could turn on me. She knew that I had no access to daily news and only rarely left the house anymore. Still, it was unlike Nina to leave anything to chance. Was it possible that she thought I had lost the Ability completely and that Willi was the greater threat?

I shook my head as we emerged from the cabin into the gray afternoon light. The wind sliced at me through my thin coat. The view of the gangplank was blurry, and I realized that tears had filled my eyes. For Willi? He had been a pompous, weak old fool. For Nina's betrayal? Perhaps it was only the cold wind.

The streets of the Old Section were almost empty of pedestrians. Bare branches clicked together in front of the windows of fine homes. Mr. Thorne stayed by my side. The cold air sent needles of arthritic pain up my right leg to my hip. I leaned more heavily upon father's walking stick.

What would her next move be? I stopped. A fragment of newspaper, caught by the wind, wrapped itself around my ankle and then blew on.

How would she come at me? Not from a distance. She was somewhere in town. I knew that. While it is possible to Use someone from a great distance, it would involve great rapport, an almost intimate knowledge of that person. And if contact were lost, it would be difficult if not impossible to reestablish at a distance. None of us had known why this was so. It did not matter now. But the thought of Nina still here, nearby, made my heart begin to race.

Not from a distance. I would see my assailant. If I knew Nina at all, I knew that. Certainly Willi's death had been the least personal Feeding imaginable, but that had been a mere technical operation. Nina obviously had decided to settle old scores with *me*, and Willi had become an obstacle to her, a minor but measurable threat that had to be eliminated before she could proceed. I could easily imagine that in Nina's own mind her choice of death for Willi would be interpreted as an act of compassion, almost a sign of affection. Not so with me. I felt that Nina would want me to know, however briefly, that she was behind the attack. In a sense, her own vanity would be my warning. Or so I hoped.

I was tempted to leave immediately. I could have Mr. Thorne get the Audi out of storage, and we could be beyond Nina's influence in an hour—away to a new life within a few more hours. There were important items in the house, of course, but the funds that I had stored elsewhere would replace most of them. It would be almost welcome to leave everything behind with the discarded identity that had accumulated them.

No. I could not leave. Not yet.

From across the street the house looked dark and malevolent. Had *I* closed those blinds on the second floor? There was a shadowy movement in the courtyard, and I saw Mrs. Hodges's granddaughter and a friend scamper from one doorway to another. I stood irresolutely on the curb and tapped father's stick against the black-barked tree. It was foolish to dither so—I knew it was—but it had been a long time since I had been forced to make a decision under stress.

"Mr. Thorne, please check the house. Look in each room. Return quickly."

A cold wind came up as I watched Mr. Thorne's black coat blend into the gloom of the courtyard. I felt terribly exposed standing there alone. I found myself glancing up and down the street, looking for Miss Kramer's dark hair, but the only sign of movement was a young woman pushing a perambulator far down the street.

The blinds on the second floor shot up, and Mr. Thorne's face stared out whitely for a minute. Then he turned away, and I remained staring at the dark rectangle of window. A shout from the courtyard startled me, but it was only the little girl—what was her name?—calling to her friend. Kathleen, that was it. The two sat on the edge of the fountain and opened a box of animal crackers. I stared intently at them and then relaxed. I even managed to smile a little at the extent of my paranoia. For a second I considered using Mr. Thorne directly, but the thought of being helpless on the street dissuaded me. When one is in complete contact, the senses still function but are a distant thing at best.

Hurry. The thought was sent almost without volition. Two bearded men were walking down the sidewalk on my side of the street. I crossed to stand in front of my own gate. The men were laughing and gesturing at each other. One looked over at me. *Hurry.*

Mr. Thorne came out of the house, locked the door behind him, and crossed the courtyard toward me. One of the girls said something to him and held out the box of crackers, but he ignored her. Across the street the two men continued walking. Mr. Thorne handed me the large front-door key. I dropped it in my coat pocket and looked sharply at him. He nodded. His placid smile unconsciously mocked my consternation.

"You're sure?" I asked. Again the nod. "You checked all of the rooms?" Nod. "The alarms?" Nod. "You looked in the basement?" Nod. "No sign of disturbance?" Mr. Thorne shook his head.

My hand went to the metal of the gate, but I hesitated. Anxiety filled my throat like bile. I was a silly old woman, tired and aching from the chill, but I could not bring myself to open that gate.

"Come." I crossed the street and walked briskly away from the house. "We will have dinner at Henry's and return later." Only I was not walking toward the old restaurant. I was heading away from the house in what I knew was a blind, directionless panic. It was not until we reached the waterfront and were walking along the Battery wall that I began to calm down.

No one else was in sight. A few cars moved along the street, but to approach us someone would have to cross a wide, empty space. The gray clouds were quite low and blended with the choppy, white-crested waves in the bay.

The open air and fading evening light served to revive me, and I began to think more clearly. Whatever Nina's plans had been, they certainly had been thrown into disarray by my day-long absence. I doubted that Nina would stay if there were the slightest risk to herself. No, she would be returning to New York by plane even as I stood shivering on the Battery walk. In the morning I would receive a telegram, I could see it. MELANIE ISN'T IT TERRIBLE ABOUT WILLI? TERRIBLY SAD. CAN YOU TRAVEL WITH ME TO THE FUNERAL? LOVE, NINA.

I began to realize that my reluctance to leave immediately had come from a desire to return to the warmth and comfort of my home. I simply had been afraid to shuck off this old cocoon. I could do so now. I would wait in a safe place while Mr. Thorne returned to the house to pick up the one thing I could not leave behind. Then he would get the car out of storage, and by the time

Nina's telegram arrived I would be far away. It would be *Nina* who would be starting at shadows in the months and years to come. I smiled and began to frame the necessary commands.

"Melanie."

My head snapped around. Mr. Thorne had not spoken in twenty-eight years. He spoke now.

"Melanie." His face was distorted in a rictus that showed his back teeth. The knife was in his right hand. The blade flicked out as I stared. I looked into his empty, gray eyes, and I knew.

"Melanie."

The long blade came around in a powerful arc. I could do nothing to stop it. It cut through the fabric of my coat sleeve and continued into my side. But in the act of turning, my purse had swung with me. The knife tore through the leather, ripped through the jumbled contents, pierced my coat, and drew blood above my lowest left rib. The purse had saved my life.

I raised father's heavy walking stick and struck Mr. Thorne squarely in his left eye. He reeled but did not make a sound. Again he swept the air with the knife, but I had taken two steps back and his vision was clouded. I took a two-handed grip on the cane and swung sideways again, bringing the stick around in an awkward chop. Incredibly, it again found the eye socket. I took three more steps back.

Blood streamed down the left side of Mr. Thorne's face, and the damaged eye protruded onto his cheek. The rictal grin remained. His head came up, he raised his left hand slowly, plucked out the eye with a soft snapping of a gray cord, and threw it into the water of the bay. He came toward me. I turned and ran.

I *tried* to run. The ache in my right leg slowed me to a walk after twenty paces. Fifteen more hurried steps and my lungs were out of air, my heart threatening to burst. I could feel a wetness seeping down my left side and there was a tingling—like an ice cube held against the skin—where the knife blade had touched me. One glance back showed me that Mr. Thorne was striding toward me faster than I was moving. Normally he could have overtaken me in four strides. But it is hard to make someone run when you are Using him. Especially when that person's body is reacting to shock and trauma. I glanced back again, almost slipping on the slick pavement. Mr. Thorne was grinning widely. Blood poured from the empty socket and stained his teeth. No one else was in sight.

Down the stairs, clutching at the rail so as not to fall. Down the twisting walk and up the asphalt path to the street. Pole lamps flickered and went on as I passed. Behind me Mr. Thorne took the steps in two jumps. As I hurried up the path, I thanked God that I had worn low-heel shoes for the boat ride. What would an observer think seeing this bizarre, slow-motion chase between two old people? There were no observers.

I turned onto a side street. Closed shops, empty warehouses. Going left would take me to Broad Street, but to the right, half a block away, a lone figure had emerged from a dark storefront. I moved that way, no longer able to run, close to fainting. The arthritic cramps in my leg hurt more than I could ever have imagined and threatened to collapse me on the sidewalk. Mr. Thorne was twenty paces behind me and quickly closing the distance.

The man I was approaching was a tall, thin Negro wearing a brown nylon jacket. He was carrying a box of what looked like framed sepia photographs.

He glanced at me as I approached and then looked over my shoulder at the apparition ten steps behind.

"Hey!" The man had time to shout the single syllable and then I reached out with my mind and *shoved.* He twitched like a poorly handled marionette. His jaw dropped, and his eyes glazed over, and he lurched past me just as Mr. Thorne reached for the back of my coat.

The box flew into the air, and glass shattered on the brick sidewalk. Long, brown fingers reached for a white throat. Mr. Thorne backhanded him away, but the Negro clung tenaciously, and the two swung around like awkward dance partners. I reached the opening to an alley and leaned my face against the cold brick to revive myself. The effort of concentration while Using this stranger did not afford me the luxury of resting even for a second.

I watched the clumsy stumblings of the two tall men for a while and resisted an absurd impulse to laugh.

Mr. Thorne plunged the knife into the other's stomach, withdrew it, plunged it in again. The Negro's fingernails were clawing at Mr. Thorne's good eye now. Strong teeth were snapping in search of the blade for a third time, but the heart was still beating and he was still usable. The man jumped, scissoring his legs around Mr. Thorne's middle while his jaws closed on the muscular

throat. Fingernails raked bloody streaks across white skin. The two
went down in a tumble.

Kill him. Fingers groped for an eye, but Mr. Thorne reached up
with his left hand and snapped the thin wrist. Limp fingers continued to flail. With a tremendous exertion, Mr. Thorne lodged his
forearm against the other's chest and lifted him bodily as a reclining father tosses a child above him. Teeth tore away a piece of
flesh, but there was no vital damage. Mr. Thorne brought the knife
between them, up, left, then right. He severed half the Negro's
throat with the second swing, and blood fountained over both of
them. The smaller man's legs spasmed twice, Mr. Thorne threw
him to one side, and I turned and walked quickly down the alley.

Out into the light again, the fading evening light, and I realized
that I had run myself into a dead end. Backs of warehouses and
the windowless, metal side of the Battery Marina pushed right up
against the waters of the bay. A street wound away to the left, but
it was dark, deserted, and far too long to try.

I looked back in time to see the black silhouette enter the alley
behind me.

I tried to make contact, but there was nothing there. Nothing.
Mr. Thorne might as well have been a hole in the air. I would
worry later how Nina had done this thing.

The side door to the marina was locked. The main door was
almost a hundred yards away and would also be locked. Mr.
Thorne emerged from the alley and swung his head left and right
in search of me. In the dim light his heavily streaked face looked
almost black. He began lurching toward me.

I raised father's walking stick, broke the lower pane of the window, and reached in through the jagged shards. If there was a
bottom or top bolt I was dead. There was a simple doorknob lock
and crossbolt. My fingers slipped on the cold metal, but the bolt
slid back as Mr. Thorne stepped up on the walk behind me. Then I
was inside and throwing the bolt.

It was very dark. Cold seeped up from the concrete floor and
there was a sound of many small boats rising and falling at their
moorings. Fifty yards away light spilled out of the office windows.
I had hoped there would be an alarm system, but the building was
too old and the marina too cheap to have one. I walked toward the
light as Mr. Thorne's forearm shattered the remaining glass in the
door behind me. The arm withdrew. A great kick broke off the top

hinge and splintered wood around the bolt. I glanced at the office, but only the sound of a radio talk show came out of the impossibly distant door. Another kick.

I turned to my right and stepped to the bow of a bobbing inboard cruiser. Five steps and I was in the small, covered space that passed for a forward cabin. I closed the flimsy access panel behind me and peered out through the Plexiglas.

Mr. Thorne's third kick sent the door flying inward, dangling from long strips of splintered wood. His dark form filled the doorway. Light from a distant streetlight glinted off the blade in his right hand.

Please. Please hear the noise. But there was no movement from the office, only the metallic voices from the radio. Mr. Thorne took four paces, paused, and stepped down onto the first boat in line. It was an open outboard, and he was back up on the concrete in six seconds. The second boat had a small cabin. There was a ripping sound as Mr. Thorne kicked open the tiny hatch door, and then he was back up on the walkway. My boat was the eighth in line. I wondered why he couldn't just hear the wild hammering of my heart.

I shifted position and looked through the starboard port. The murky Plexiglas threw the light into streaks and patterns. I caught a brief glimpse of white hair through the window, and the radio was switched to another station. Loud music echoed in the long room. I slid back to the other porthole. Mr. Thorne was stepping off the fourth boat.

I closed my eyes, forced my ragged breathing to slow, and tried to remember countless evenings watching a bowlegged old figure shuffle down the street. Mr. Thorne finished his inspection of the fifth boat, a longer cabin cruiser with several dark recesses, and pulled himself back onto the walkway.

Forget the coffee in the thermos. Forget the crossword puzzle. Go look!

The sixth boat was a small outboard. Mr. Thorne glanced at it but did not step onto it. The seventh was a low sailboat, mast folded down, canvas stretched across the cockpit. Mr. Thorne's knife slashed through the thick material. Blood-streaked hands pulled back the canvas like a shroud being torn away. He jumped back to the walkway.

Forget the coffee. Go look! Now!

Mr. Thorne stepped onto the bow of my boat. I felt it rock to his weight. There was nowhere to hide, only a tiny storage locker under the seat, much too small to squeeze into. I untied the canvas strips that held the seat cushion to the bench. The sound of my ragged breathing seemed to echo in the little space. I curled into a fetal position behind the cushion as Mr. Thorne's leg moved past the starboard port. *Now.* Suddenly his face filled the Plexiglas strip not a foot from my head. His impossibly wide grimace grew even wider. *Now.* He stepped into the cockpit.

Now. Now. Now.

Mr. Thorne crouched at the cabin door. I tried to brace the tiny louvered door with my legs, but my right leg would not obey. Mr. Thorne fist slammed through the thin wooden strips and grabbed my ankle.

"Hey there!"

It was Mr. Hodges's shaky voice. His flashlight bobbed in our direction.

Mr. Thorne shoved against the door. My left leg folded painfully. Mr. Thorne's left hand firmly held my ankle through the shattered slats while the hand with the knife blade came through the opening hatch.

"Hey—" My mind shoved. Very hard. The old man stopped. He dropped the flashlight and unstrapped the buckle over the grip of his revolver.

Mr. Thorne slashed the knife back and forth. The cushion was almost knocked out of my hands as shreds of foam filled the cabin. The blade caught the tip of my little finger as the knife swung back again.

Do it. Now. Do it. Mr. Hodges gripped the revolver in both hands and fired. The shot went wide in the dark as the sound echoed off concrete and water. *Closer, you fool. Move!* Mr. Thorne shoved again and his body squeezed into the open hatch. He released my ankle to free his left arm, but almost instantly his hand was back in the cabin, grasping for me. I reached up and turned on the overhead light. Darkness stared at me from his empty eye socket. Light through the broken shutters spilled yellow strips across his ruined face. I slid to the left, but Mr. Thorne's hand, which had my coat, was pulling me off the bench. He was on his knees, freeing his right hand for the knife thrust.

Now! Mr. Hodges's second shot caught Mr. Thorne in the right hip. He grunted as the impact shoved him backward into a sitting position. My coat ripped, and buttons rattled on the deck.

The knife slashed the bulkhead near my ear before it pulled away.

Mr. Hodges stepped shakily onto the bow, almost fell, and inched his way around the starboard side. I pushed the hatch against Mr. Thorne's arm, but he continued to grip my coat and drag me toward him. I fell to my knees. The blade swung back, ripped through foam, and slashed at my coat. What was left of the cushion flew out of my hands. I had Mr. Hodges stop four feet away and brace the gun on the roof of the cabin.

Mr. Thorne pulled the blade back and poised it like a matador's sword. I could sense the silent scream of triumph that poured out over the stained teeth like a noxious vapor. The light of Nina's madness burned behind the single, staring eye.

Mr. Hodges fired. The bullet severed Mr. Thorne's spine and continued on into the port scupper. Mr. Thorne arched backward, splayed out his arms, and flopped onto the deck like a great fish that had just been landed. The knife fell to the floor of the cabin, while stiff, white fingers continued to slap nervelessly against the deck. I had Mr. Hodges step forward, brace the muzzle against Mr. Thorne's temple just above the remaining eye, and fire again. The sound was muted and hollow.

There was a first-aid kit in the office bathroom. I had the old man stand by the door while I bandaged my little finger and took three aspirin.

My coat was ruined, and blood had stained my print dress. I had never cared very much for the dress—I thought it made me look dowdy—but the coat had been a favorite of mine. My hair was a mess. Small, moist bits of gray matter flecked it. I splashed water on my face and brushed my hair as best I could. Incredibly, my tattered purse had stayed with me although many of the contents had spilled out. I transferred keys, billfold, reading glasses, and Kleenex to my large coat pocket and dropped the purse behind the toilet. I no longer had father's walking stick, but I could not remember where I had dropped it.

Gingerly I removed the heavy revolver from Mr. Hodges's grip. The old man's arm remained extended, fingers curled around air. After fumbling for a few seconds I managed to click open the cylinder. Two cartridges remained unfired. The old fool had been walking around with all six chambers loaded! *Always leave an empty chamber under the hammer.* That is what Charles had taught me that gay and distant summer so long ago when such weapons were merely excuses for trips to the island for target practice punctuated by the shrill shrieks of our nervous laughter as Nina and I allowed ourselves to be held, arms supported, bodies shrinking back into the firm support of our so-serious tutors' arms. *One must always count the cartridges*, lectured Charles, as I half-swooned against him, smelling the sweet, masculine shaving soap and tobacco smell rising from him on that warm, bright day.

Mr. Hodges stirred slightly as my attention wandered. His mouth gaped, and his dentures hung loosely. I glanced at the worn leather belt, but there were no extra bullets there, and I had no idea where he kept any. I probed, but there was little left in the old man's jumble of thoughts except for a swirling tape-loop replay of the muzzle being laid against Mr. Thorne's temple, the explosion, the—

"Come," I said. I adjusted the glasses on Mr. Hodges's vacant face, returned the revolver to the holster, and let him lead me out of the building.

It was very dark out. We had gone six blocks before the old man's violent shivering reminded me that I had forgotten to have him put on his coat. I tightened my mental vise, and he stopped shaking.

The house looked just as it had . . . my God . . . only forty-five minutes earlier. There were no lights. I let us into the courtyard and searched my overstuffed coat pocket for the key. My coat hung loose and the cold night air nipped at me. From behind lighted windows across the courtyard came the laughter of little girls, and I hurried so that Kathleen would not see her grandfather entering my house.

Mr. Hodges went in first, with the revolver extended. I had him switch on the light before I entered.

The parlor was empty, undisturbed. The light from the chandelier in the dining room reflected off polished surfaces. I sat down for a minute on the Williamsburg reproduction chair in the hall to let my heart rate return to normal. I did not have Mr. Hodges lower the hammer on the still-raised pistol. His arm began to shake from the strain of holding it. Finally, I rose and we moved down the hall toward the conservatory.

Miss Kramer exploded out of the swinging door from the kitchen with the heavy iron poker already coming down in an arc. The gun fired harmlessly into the polished floor as the old man's arm snapped from the impact. The gun fell from limp fingers as Miss Kramer raised the poker for a second blow.

I turned and ran back down the hallway. Behind me I heard the crushed-melon sound of the poker contacting Mr. Hodges's skull. Rather than run into the courtyard I went up the stairway. A mistake. Miss Kramer bounded up the stairs and reached the bedroom door only a few seconds after me. I caught one glimpse of her widened, maddened eyes and of the upraised poker before I slammed and locked the heavy door. The latch clicked just as the brunette on the other side began to throw herself against the wood. The thick oak did not budge. Then I heard the concussion of metal against the door and frame. Again.

Cursing my stupidity, I turned to the familiar room, but there was nothing there to help me. There was not as much as a closet to hide in, only the antique wardrobe. I moved quickly to the window and threw up the sash. My screams would attract attention but not before that monstrosity had gained access. She was prying at the edges of the door now. I looked out, saw the shadows in the window across the way, and did what I had to do.

Two minutes later I was barely conscious of the wood giving away around the latch. I heard the distant grating of the poker as it pried at the recalcitrant metal plate. The door swung inward.

Miss Kramer was covered with sweat. Her mouth hung slack, and drool slid from her chin. Her eyes were not human. Neither she nor I heard the soft tread of sneakers on the stairs behind her.

Keep moving. Lift it. Pull it back—all the way back. Use both hands. Aim it.

Something warned Miss Kramer. Warned Nina, I should say; there was no more Miss Kramer. The brunette turned to see little Kathleen standing on the top stair, her grandfather's heavy weapon aimed and cocked. The other girl was in the courtyard shouting for her friend.

This time Nina knew she had to deal with the threat. Miss Kramer hefted the poker and turned into the hall just as the pistol fired. The recoil tumbled Kathleen backward down the stairs as a red corsage blossomed above Miss Kramer's left breast. She spun but grasped the railing with her left hand and lurched down the stairs after the child. I released the ten-year-old just as the poker fell, rose, fell again. I moved to the head of the stairway. I had to see.

Miss Kramer looked up from her grim work. Only the whites of her eyes were visible in her spattered face. Her masculine shirt was soaked with her own blood, but still she moved, functioned. She picked up the gun in her left hand. Her mouth opened wider, and a sound emerged like steam leaking from an old radiator.

"Melanie . . ." I closed my eyes as the thing started up the stairs for me.

Kathleen's friend came in through the open door, her small legs pumping. She took the stairs in six jumps and wrapped her thin, white arms around Miss Kramer's neck in a tight embrace.

The two went over backward, across Kathleen, all the way down the wide stairs to the polished wood below.

The girl appeared to be little more than bruised. I went down and moved her to one side. A blue stain was spreading along one cheekbone, and there were cuts on her arms and forehead. Her blue eyes blinked uncomprehendingly.

Miss Kramer's neck was broken. I picked up the pistol on the way to her and kicked the poker to one side. Her head was at an impossible angle, but she was still alive. Her body was paralyzed, urine already stained the wood, but her eyes still blinked and her teeth clicked together obscenely. I had to hurry. There were adult voices calling from the Hodgeses' town house. The door to the courtyard was wide open. I turned to the girl. "Get up." She blinked once and rose painfully to her feet.

I shut the door and lifted a tan raincoat from the coatrack.

It took only a minute to transfer the contents of my pockets to the raincoat and to discard my ruined spring coat. Voices were calling in the courtyard now.

I kneeled down next to Miss Kramer and seized her face in my hands, exerting pressure to keep the jaws still. Her eyes had rolled upward again, but I shook her head until the irises were visible. I leaned forward until our cheeks were touching. My whisper was louder than a shout.

"I'm coming for you, Nina."

I dropped her head onto the wood and walked quickly to the

conservatory, my sewing room. I did not have time to get the key from upstairs; so I raised a Windsor side chair and smashed the glass of the cabinet. My coat pocket was barely large enough.

The girl remained standing in the hall. I handed her Mr. Hodges's pistol. Her left arm hung at a strange angle and I wondered if she had broken something after all. There was a knock at the door, and someone tried the knob.

"This way," I whispered, and led the girl into the dining room.

We stepped across Miss Kramer on the way, walked through the dark kitchen as the pounding grew louder, and then were out, into the alley, into the night.

There were three hotels in this part of the Old Section. One was a modern, expensive motor hotel some ten blocks away, comfortable but commercial. I rejected it immediately. The second was a small, homey lodging house only a block from my home. It was a pleasant but nonexclusive little place, exactly the type I would choose when visiting another town. I rejected it also. The third was two and a half blocks farther, an old Broad Street mansion done over into a small hotel, expensive antiques in every room, absurdly overpriced. I hurried there. The girl moved quickly at my side. The pistol was still in her hand, but I had her remove her sweater and carry it over the weapon. My leg ached, and I frequently leaned on the girl as we hurried down the street.

The manager of the Mansard House recognized me. His eyebrows went up a fraction of an inch as he noticed my disheveled appearance. The girl stood ten feet away in the foyer, half-hidden in the shadows.

"I'm looking for a friend of mine," I said brightly. "A Mrs. Drayton."

The manager started to speak, paused, frowned without being aware of it, and tried again. "I'm sorry. No one under that name is registered here."

"Perhaps she registered under her maiden name," I said. "Nina Hawkins. She's an older woman but very attractive. A few years younger than I. Long, gray hair. Her friend may have registered for her . . . an attractive, young, dark-haired lady named Barrett Kramer—"

"No, I'm sorry," said the manager in a strangely flat tone. "No one under that name has registered. Would you like to leave a message in case your party arrives later?''

"No," I said. "No message."

I brought the girl into the lobby, and we turned down a corridor leading to the restrooms and side stairs. "Excuse me, please," I said to a passing porter. "Perhaps you can help me."

"Yes, ma'am." He stopped, annoyed, and brushed back his long hair. It would be tricky. If I was not to lose the girl, I would have to act quickly.

"I'm looking for a friend," I said. "She's an older lady but quite attractive. Blue eyes. Long, gray hair. She travels with a young woman who has dark, curly hair."

"No, ma'am. No one like that is registered here."

I reached out and grabbed hold of his forearm tightly. I released the girl and focused on the boy. "Are you sure?"

"Mrs. Harrison," he said. His eyes looked past me. "Room 207. North front."

I smiled. *Mrs. Harrison.* Good God, what a fool Nina was. Suddenly the girl let out a small whimper and slumped against the wall. I made a quick decision. I like to think that it was compassion, but I sometimes remember that her left arm was useless.

"What's your name?" I asked the child, gently stroking her bangs. Her eyes moved left and right in confusion. "Your name!"

"Alicia." It was only a whisper.

"All right, Alicia. I want you to go home now. Hurry, but don't run."

"My *arm* hurts," she said. Her lips began to quiver. I touched her forehead again and *pushed*.

"You're going home," I said. "Your arm does not hurt. You won't remember anything. This is like a dream that you will forget. Go home. Hurry, but do not run." I took the pistol from her but left it wrapped in the sweater. "Bye-bye, Alicia."

She blinked and crossed the lobby to the doors. I handed the gun to the bellhop. "Put it under your vest," I said.

"Who is it?" Nina's voice was light.

"Albert, ma'am. The porter. Your car's out front, and I'll take your bags down."

There was the sound of a lock clicking and the door opened the width of a still-secured chain. Albert blinked in the glare, smiled shyly, and brushed his hair back. I pressed against the wall.

"Very well." She undid the chain and moved back. She had already turned and was latching her suitcase when I stepped into the room.

"Hello, Nina," I said softly. Her back straightened, but even that move was graceful. I could see the imprint on the bedspread where she had been lying. She turned slowly. She was wearing a pink dress I had never seen before.

"Hello, Melanie." She smiled. Her eyes were the softest, purest blue I had ever seen. I had the porter take Mr. Hodges's gun out and aim it. His arm was steady. He pulled back the hammer and held it with his thumb. Nina folded her hands in front of her. Her eyes never left mine.

"Why?" I asked.

Nina shrugged ever so slightly. For a second I thought she was going to laugh. I could not have borne it if she had laughed—that husky, childlike laugh that had touched me so many times. Instead she closed her eyes. Her smile remained.

"Why Mrs. Harrison?" I asked.

"Why, darling, I felt I owed him *something*. I mean, poor Roger. Did I ever tell you how he died? No, of course I didn't. And you never asked." Her eyes opened. I glanced at the porter, but his aim was steady. It only remained for him to exert a little more pressure on the trigger.

"He *drowned*, darling," said Nina. "Poor Roger threw himself from that steamship—what was its name?—the one that was taking him back to England. So strange. And he had just written me a letter promising marriage. Isn't that a *terribly* sad story, Melanie? Why do you think he did a thing like that? I guess we'll never know, will we?"

"I guess we never will," I said. I silently ordered the porter to pull the trigger.

Nothing.

I looked quickly to my right. The young man's head was turning toward me. *I had not made him do that.* The stiffly extended arm began to swing in my direction. The pistol moved smoothly like the tip of a weather vane swinging in the wind.

No! I strained until the cords in my neck stood out. The turning slowed but did not stop until the muzzle was pointing at my face. Nina laughed now. The sound was very loud in the little room.

"Good-bye, Melanie *dear*," Nina said, and laughed again. She laughed and nodded at the porter. I stared into the black hole as the hammer fell. On an empty chamber. And another. And another.

"Good-bye, Nina," I said as I pulled Charles's long pistol from the raincoat pocket. The explosion jarred my wrist and filled the room with blue smoke. A small hole, smaller than a dime but as perfectly round, appeared in the precise center of Nina's forehead. For the briefest second she remained standing as if nothing had happened. Then she fell backward, recoiled from the high bed, and dropped face forward onto the floor.

I turned to the porter and replaced his useless weapon with the ancient but well-maintained revolver. For the first time I noticed that the boy was not much younger than Charles had been. His hair was almost exactly the same color. I leaned forward and kissed him lightly on the lips.

"Albert," I whispered, "there are four cartridges left. One must always count the cartridges, mustn't one? Go to the lobby. Kill the manager. Shoot one other person, the nearest. Put the barrel in your mouth and pull the trigger. If it misfires, pull it again. Keep the gun concealed until you are in the lobby."

We emerged into general confusion in the hallway.

"Call for an ambulance!" I cried. "There's been an accident. Someone call for an ambulance!" Several people rushed to comply. I swooned and leaned against a white-haired gentleman. People milled around, some peering into the room and exclaiming. Suddenly there was the sound of three gunshots from the lobby. In the renewed confusion I slipped down the back stairs, out the fire door, into the night.

Time has passed. I am very happy here. I live in southern France now, between Cannes and Toulon, but not, I am happy to say, too near St. Tropez.

I rarely go out. Henri and Claude do my shopping in the village. I never go to the beach. Occasionally I go to the townhouse in Paris or to my pensione in Italy, south of Pescara, on the Adriatic. But even those trips have become less and less frequent.

There is an abandoned abbey in the hills, and I often go there to sit and think among the stones and wild flowers. I think about isolation and abstinence and how each is so cruelly dependent upon the other.

I feel younger these days. I tell myself that this is because of the climate and my freedom and not as a result of that final Feeding. But sometimes I dream about the familiar streets of Charleston and the people there. They are dreams of hunger.

On some days I rise to the sound of singing as girls from the village cycle by our place on their way to the dairy. On those days the sun is marvelously warm as it shines on the small white flowers growing between the tumbled stones of the abbey, and I am content simply to be there and to share the sunlight and silence with them.

But on other days—cold, dark days when the clouds move in from the north—I remember the shark-silent shape of a submarine moving through the dark waters of the bay, and I wonder whether my self-imposed abstinence will be for nothing. I wonder whether those I dream of in my isolation will indulge in their own gigantic, final Feeding.

It is warm today. I am happy. But I am also alone. And I am very, very hungry.

The Yougoslaves

✻✣❧

ROBERT BLOCH

I didn't come to Paris for adventure.

Long experience has taught me there are no Phantoms in the Opera, no bearded artists hobbling through Montmartre on stunted legs, no straw-hatted *boulevardiers* singing the praises of a funny little honey of a Mimi.

The Paris of story and song, if it ever existed, is no more. Times have changed, and even the term "Gay Paree" now evokes what in theatrical parlance is called a bad laugh.

A visitor learns to change habits accordingly, and my hotel choice was a case in point. On previous trips I'd stayed at the Crillon or the Ritz; now, after a lengthy absence, I put up at the George V.

Let me repeat, I wasn't seeking adventure. That first evening I left the hotel for a short stroll merely to satisfy my curiosity about the city.

I had already discovered that some aspects of Paris remain immutable; the French still don't seem to understand how to communicate by telephone, and they can't make a good cup of coffee. But I had no need to use the phone and no craving for coffee, so these matters didn't concern me.

Nor was I greatly surprised to discover that April in Paris—

Paris in the spring, tra-la-la-la—is apt to be cold and damp. Warmly-dressed for my little outing, I directed my footsteps to the arch-ways of the Rue de Rivoli.

At first glance Paris by night upheld its traditions. All of the tourist attractions remained in place; the steel skeleton of the Eiffel Tower, the gaping maw of the Arch of Triumph, the spurting fountains achieving their miraculous transubstantiation of water into blood with the aid of crimson light.

But there were changes in the air—quite literally—the acrid odor of traffic fumes emanating from the exhausts of snarling sports cars and growling motor bikes racing along to the counterpoint of police and ambulance sirens. Gershwin's tinny taxi-horns would be lost in such din; I doubt if he'd approve, and I most certainly did not.

My disapproval extended to the clothing of local pedestrians. Young Parisian males now mimicked the youths of other cities; bare-headed, leather-jacketed, and blue-jeaned, they would look equally at home in Times Square or on Hollywood Boulevard. As for their female companions, this seemed to be the year when every girl in France decided to don atrociously-wrinkled patent leather boots which turned shapely lower limbs into the legs of elephantiasis victims. The *chic* Parisienne had vanished, and above the traffic's tumult I fancied I could detect a sound of rumbling dismay as Napoleon turned over in his tomb.

I moved along under the arches, eyeing the lighted window displays of expensive jewelry mingled with cheap gimcracks. At least the Paris of tourism hadn't altered; there would still be sex shops in the Pigalle, and somewhere in the deep darkness of the Louvre the Mona Lisa smiled enigmatically at the antics of those who came to the city searching for adventure.

Again I say this was not my intention. Nonetheless, adventure sought me.

Adventure came on the run, darting out of a dark and deserted portion of the arcade just ahead, charging straight at me on a dozen legs.

It happened quickly. One moment I was alone; then suddenly and without warning, the children came. There were six of them, surrounding me like a small army—six dark-haired, swarthy-skinned urchins in dirty, disheveled garments, screeching and jabbering at me in a foreign tongue. Some of them clutched at my clothing, others jabbed me in the ribs. Encircling me they clamored for a beggar's bounty, and as I fumbled for loose change one of them thrust a folded newspaper against my chest, another grabbed and kissed my free hand, yet another grasped my shoulder and whirled me around. Deafened by the din, dazed by their instant attack, I broke free.

In seconds, they scattered swiftly and silently, scampering into the shadows. As they disappeared I stood alone again, stunned and shaken. Then, as my hand rose instinctively to press against my inner breast pocket, I realized that my wallet had disappeared too.

My first reaction was shock. To think that I, a grown man, had been robbed on the public street by a band of little ragamuffins, less than ten years old!

It was an outrage, and now I met it with rage of my own. The sheer audacity of their attack provoked anger, and the thought of the consequences fueled my fury. Losing the money in the wallet wasn't important; he who steals my purse steals trash.

But there was something else I cherished; something secret and irreplaceable. I carried it in a billfold compartment for a purpose; after completing my sightseeing jaunt I'd intended to seek another destination and make use of the other item my wallet contained.

Now it was gone, and hope vanished with it.

But not entirely. The sound of distant sirens in the night served as a strident reminder that I still had a chance. There was, I remembered, a police station near the Place Vendome. The inconspicuous office was not easy to locate on the darkened street beyond an open courtyard, but I managed.

Once inside, I anticipated a conversation with an *Inspecteur*, a return to the scene of the affair in the company of sympathetic *gendarmes* who were knowledgeable concerning such offenses and alert in ferreting out the hiding place of my assailants.

The young lady seated behind the window in the dingy outer office listened to my story without comment or a change of expression. Inserting forms and carbons in her typewriter, she took down a few vital statistics—my name, date of birth, place of origin, hotel address, and a short inventory of the stolen wallet's contents.

For reasons of my own I neglected to mention the one item that really mattered to me. I could be excused for omitting it in my excited state, and hoped to avoid the necessity of doing so unless the *Inspecteur* questioned me more closely.

But there was no interview with an *Inspecteur*, and no uniformed officer appeared. Instead I was merely handed a carbon copy of the *Recepisse de Declaration;* if anything could be learned about the fate of my wallet I would be notified at my hotel.

Scarcely ten minutes after entering the station I found myself back on the street with nothing to show for my trouble but a buff-colored copy of the report. Down at the very bottom, on a line identified in print as *Mode Operatoire—Precisons Complementaires,* was a typed sentence reading *"Vol commis dans la Rue par de jeunes enfant yougoslaves."*

"Yougoslaves?"

Back at the hotel I addressed the question to an elderly night-clerk. Sleepy eyes blinking into nervousness, he nodded knowingly.

"Ah!" he said. "The gypsies!"

"Gypsies? But these were only children—"

He nodded again. "Exactly so." And then he told me the story.

Pickpockets and purse-snatchers had always been a common nuisance here, but within the past few years their presence had escalated.

They came out of Eastern Europe, their exact origin unknown, but "yougoslaves" or "gypsies" served as a convenient label.

Apparently they were smuggled in by skillful and enterprising adult criminals who specialized in educating children in the art of thievery, very much as Fagin trained his youngsters in the London of Dickens' *Oliver Twist.*

But Fagin was an amateur compared to today's professors of pilfering. Their pupils—orphans, products of broken homes, or no homes at all—were recruited in foreign city streets, or even purchased outright from greedy, uncaring parents. These little ones could be quite valuable; an innocent at the age of four or five became a seasoned veteran after a few years of experience, capable of bringing in as much as a hundred thousand American dollars over the course of a single year.

When I described the circumstances of my own encounter the clerk shrugged.

"Of course. That is how they work, my friend—in gangs." Gangs, expertly adept in spotting potential victims, artfully in-

structed how to operate. Their seemingly spontaneous outcries
were actually the product of long and exacting rehearsal, their
apparently impromptu movements perfected in advance. They
danced around me because they had been choreographed to do so.
It was a bandits' ballet in which each one played an assigned role
—to nudge, to gesture, to jab and jabber and create confusion.
Even the hand-kissing was part of a master plan, and when one
ragged waif thrust his folded newspaper against my chest it concealed another who ducked below and lifted my wallet. The entire
performance was programmed down to the last detail.

I listened and shook my head. "Why don't the police tell me
these things? Surely they must know."

"*Oui, M'sieur.*" The clerk permitted himself a confidential wink.
"But perhaps they do not care." He leaned across the desk, his
voice sinking to a murmur. "Some say an arrangement has been
made. The yougoslaves are skilled in identifying tourists by their
dress and manner. They can recognize a foreign visitor merely by
the kind of shoes he wears. One supposes a bargain has been
struck because it is only the tourists who are attacked, while ordinary citizens are spared."

I frowned. "Surely others like myself must lodge complaints.
One would think the police would be forced to take action."

The clerk's gesture was as eloquent as his words. "But what can
they do? These yougoslaves strike quickly, without warning. They
vanish before you realize what has happened, and no one knows
where they go. And even if you managed to lay hands on one of
them, what then? You bring this youngster to the police and tell
your story, but the little ruffian has no wallet—you can be sure it
was passed along immediately to another who ran off with the
evidence. Also, your prisoner cannot speak or understand French,
or at least pretends not to."

"So the gendarmes have nothing to go by but your words, and
what can they do with the kid if they did have proof, when the law
prohibits the arrest and jailing of children under thirteen?"

"It's all part of the scheme. And if you permit me, it is a beautiful scheme, this one."

My frown told him I lacked appreciation of beauty, and he
quickly leaned back to a position of safety behind the desk, his
voice and manner sobering. "Missing credit cards can be reported
in the morning, though I think it unlikely anyone would be foolish

enough to attempt using them with a forged signature. It's the money they were after."

"I have other funds in your safe," I said.

"*Tres bien*. In that case I advise you to make the best of things. Now that you know what to expect, I doubt if you will be victimized again. Just keep away from the tourist traps and avoid using the Metro." He offered me the solace of a smile which all desk clerks reserve for complaints about stalled elevators, lost luggage, faulty electrical fixtures, or clogged plumbing.

Then, when my frown remained fixed, his smile vanished. "Please, my friend! I understand this has been a most distressing occurrence, but I trust you will chalk it up to experience. Believe me, there is no point in pursuing the matter further."

I shook my head. "If the police won't go after these children—"

"Children?" Again his voice descended to a murmur. "Perhaps I did not make myself clear. The yougoslaves are not ordinary kids. As I say, they have been trained by masters. The kind of man who is capable of buying or stealing a child and corrupting it for a life of crime is not likely to stop there. I have heard certain rumors, *M'sieur*, rumors which make a dreadful sort of sense. These kids, they are hooked on drugs. They know every manner of vice but nothing of morals, and many carry knives, even guns. Some have been taught to break and enter into homes, and if discovered, to kill. Their masters, of course, are even more dangerous when crossed. I implore you, for your own safety—forget what has happened tonight and go on your way."

"Thank you for your advice." I managed a smile and went on my way. But I did not forget.

I did not forget what had happened, nor did I forget I'd been robbed of what was most precious to me.

Retiring to my room, I placed the *Do Not Disturb* sign on the outer doorknob and after certain makeshift arrangements I sank eventually into fitful slumber.

By the following evening I was ready; ready and waiting. Paris by night is the City of Light, but it is also the city of shadows. And it was in the shadows that I waited, the shadows under the archways of the Rue de Rivoli. My dark clothing was deliberately donned to blend inconspicuously with the background; I would be unnoticed if the predators returned to seek fresh prey.

Somehow I felt convinced that they would do so. As I stood

Robert Bloch

against a pillar, scanning the occasional passerby who wandered past, I challenged myself to see the hunted through the eyes of the hunters.

Who would be the next victim? That party of Japanese deserved no more than a glance of dismissal; it wasn't wise to confront a group. By the same token, those who traveled in pairs or couples would be spared. And even the lone pedestrians were safe if they were able-bodied or dressed in garments which identified them as local citizens.

What the hunters sought was someone like myself, someone wearing clothing of foreign cut, preferably elderly and obviously alone. Someone like the gray-headed old gentleman who was approaching now, shuffling past a cluster of shops already closed for the night. He was short, slight of build, and his uncertain gait hinted at either a physical impairment or mild intoxication. A lone traveler on an otherwise-deserted stretch of street—he was the perfect target for attack.

And the attack came.

Out of the deep dark doorway to an arcade the yougoslaves danced forth, squealing and gesticulating, to suddenly surround their startled victim.

They ringed him, hands outstretched, their cries confusing, their fingers darting forth to prod and pry in rhythm with the outbursts.

I saw the pattern now, recognized the roles they played. Here was the hand-kisser, begging for bounty, here the duo tugging at each arm from the rear, here the biggest of the boys, brandishing the folded paper to thrust it against the oldster's chest while an accomplice burrowed into the gaping front of the jacket below. Just behind him the sixth and smallest of the band stood poised. The instant the wallet was snatched it would be passed to him, and while the others continued their distraction for a few moments more before scattering, he'd run off in safety.

The whole charade was brilliant in its sheer simplicity, cleverly contrived so that the poor old gentleman would never notice his loss until too late.

But I noticed—and I acted.

As the thieves closed in I stepped forward, quickly and quietly. Intent on their quarry, they were unaware of my approach. Moving up behind the youngster who waited to receive the wallet, I grasped his upraised arm in a tight grip, bending it back against his shoulderblade as I yanked him away into the shadows. He looked up and my free hand clamped across his oval mouth before he could cry out.

He tried to bite, but my fingers pressed his lips together. He tried to kick, but I twisted his bent arm and tugged him along offbalance, his feet dragging over the pavement as we moved past the shadowy archway to the curb beyond.

My rental car was waiting there. Opening the door, I hurled him down onto the seat face-forward. Before he could turn I pulled the handcuffs from my pocket and snapped them shut over his wrists.

Locking the passenger door, I hastened around to the other side of the car and entered, sliding behind the wheel. Seconds later we were moving out into the traffic.

Hands confined behind him, my captive threshed helplessly beside me. He could scream now, and he did.

"Stop that!" I commanded. "No one can hear you with the windows closed."

After a moment he obeyed. As we turned off onto a side street he glared up at me, panting.

"*Merde!*" he gasped.

I smiled. "So you speak French, do you?"

There was no reply. But when the car turned again, entering one of the narrow alleyways off the Rue St. Roch, his eyes grew wary.

"Where are we going?"

"That is a question for you to answer."

"What do you mean?"

"You will be good enough to direct me to the place where I can find your friends."

"Go to hell!"

"*Au contraire.*" I smiled again. "If you do not cooperate, and quickly, I'll knock you over the head and dump your body in the Seine."

"You old bastard—you can't scare me!"

Releasing my right hand from the steering wheel I gave him a clout across the mouth, knocking him back against the seat.

"That's a sample," I told him. "Next time I won't be so gentle." Clenching my fist, I raised my arm again, and he cringed.

"Tell me!" I said.

And he did.

The blow across the mouth seemed to have loosened his tongue,

for he began to answer my questions as I reversed our course and
crossed over a bridge which brought us to the Left Bank.

When he told me our destination and described it, I must confess I was surprised. The distance was much greater than I anticipated, and finding the place would not be easy, but I followed his
directions on a mental map. Meanwhile I encouraged Bobo to
speak.

That was his name—Bobo. If he had another he claimed he did
not know it, and I believed him. He was nine years old but he'd
been with the gang for three of them, ever since their leader spirited him off the streets of Dubrovnik and brought him here to Paris ·
on a long and illegal route while hidden in the back of a truck.

"Dubrovnik?" I nodded. "Then you really are a yougoslave.
What about the others?"

"I don't know. They come from everywhere. Where ever he
finds them."

"Your leader? What's his name?"

"We call him Le Boss."

"He taught you how to steal like this?"

"He taught us many things," Bobo gave me a sidelong glance.
"Listen to me, old man—if you find him there will be big trouble.
Better to let me go."

"Not until I have my wallet."

"Wallet?" His eyed widened, then narrowed, and I realized that
for the first time he'd recognized me as last night's victim. "If you
think Le Boss will give you back your money, then you really are a
fool."

"I'm not a fool. And I don't care about the money."

"Credit cards? Don't worry, Le Boss won't try to use them. Too
risky."

"It's not the cards. There was something else. Didn't you see it?"

"I never touched your wallet. It was Pepe who took it to the van
last night."

The van, I learned, was always parked just around the corner
from the spot where the gang set up operations. And it was there
that they fled after a robbery. Le Boss waited behind the wheel
with the motor running; the stolen property was turned over to
him immediately as they drove off to safer surroundings.

"So Le Boss has the wallet now," I said.

"Perhaps. Sometimes he takes the money out and throws the

billfold away. But if there was more than money and cards inside as you say—" Bobo hesitated, peering up at me. "What is this thing you're looking for?"

"That is a matter I will discuss with Le Boss when I see him."

"Diamonds, maybe? You a smuggler?"

"No."

His eyes brightened and he nodded quickly. "Cocaine? Don't worry, I get some for you, no problem—good stuff, not the junk they cut for street trade. All you want, and cheap, too."

I shook my head. "Stop guessing. I talk only to Le Boss."

But Bobo continued to eye me as I guided the car out of the suburban residential and industrial areas, through a stretch of barren countryside, and into an unpaved side road bordering the empty lower reaches of the river. There were no lights here, no dwellings, no signs of life—only shadows, silence, and swaying trees.

Bobo was getting nervous, but now he forced a smile.

"Hey, old man—you like girls? Le Boss got one the other day."

"Not interested."

"I mean *little* girls. Fresh meat, only five, six maybe—"

I shook my head again and he sidled closer on the seat. "What about boys? I'm good, you'll see. Even Le Boss says so—"

He rubbed against me; his clothes were filthy and he smelled of sweat and garlic. "Never mind," I said quickly, pushing him away.

"Okay," he murmured. "I figured if we did a deal you'd give up trying to see Le Boss. It's just going to make things bad for you, and there's no sense getting yourself hurt."

"I appreciate your concern." I smiled. "But it's not me you're really worried about. You'll be the one who gets hurt for bringing me, is that not so?"

He stared at me without replying but I read the answer in his fear-filled eyes.

"What will he do to you?" I said.

The fear spilled over into his voice. "Please, *M'sieu*—don't tell him how you got here! I will do anything you want, anything—"

"You'll do exactly what I say," I told him.

He glanced ahead, and again I read his eyes.

"Are we here?" I asked. "Is this the place?"

"*Oui*. But—"

"Be silent." I shut off the motor and headlights, but not before the beam betrayed a glimpse of the river bank beyond the rutted side road. Through the tangle of trees and rampant underbrush I could see the parked van hidden from sight amidst the sheltering shadows ahead. Beyond it, spanning the river, was a crude and ancient wooden foot bridge, the narrow and rotting relic of a bygone era.

I slipped out of the car, circling to the other side, then opened the passenger door and collared my captive.

"Where are they?" I whispered.

"On the other side." Bobo's voice was faint but the apprehension it held was strong. "Please don't make me take you there!"

"Shut up and come with me." I jerked him forward toward the trees, then halted as I stared across the rickety old makeshift bridge. The purpose it served in the past was long forgotten, and so was the huge oval on the far bank which opened close to the water's edge.

But Le Boss had not forgotten. Once this great circular conduit was part of the earliest Paris sewer-system. Deep within its depths, dozens of connecting branches converged into a gigantic single outlet and spewed their waste into the water below. Now the interior channels had been sealed off, leaving the main tunnel dry but not deserted. For it was here, within a circle of metal perhaps twenty feet in diameter, that Le Boss found shelter from prying eyes, past the unused dirt road and the abandoned bridge.

The huge opening gaped like the mouth of Hell, and from within the fires of Hell blazed forth.

Actually the fires were merely the product of candle light flickering from tapers set in niches around the base of the tunnel. I sensed that their value was not only practical but precautionary, for they would be quickly extinguished in the event of an alarm.

Alarm?

I tugged at Bobo's soiled collar. "The lookout," I murmured. "Where is he?"

Reluctantly the boy stabbed a finger in the direction of a tall and tangled weed bordering the side of the bridge. In the shadows I made out a small shape huddled amid surrounding clumps of vegetation.

"Sandor." My captive nodded. "He's asleep."

I glanced up. "What about Le Boss and the others?"

"Inside the sewer. Farther back, where nobody can see them."

"Good. You will go in now."

"Alone?"

"Yes, alone." As I spoke I took out my key and unlocked the handcuffs, but my grip on Bobo's neck did not loosen.

He rubbed his chafed wrists. "What am I supposed to do?"

"Tell Le Boss that I grabbed you on the street, but you broke free and ran."

"How do I say I got here?"

"Perhaps you hitched a ride."

"And then—"

"You didn't know I was following you, not until I caught you here again. Tell him I'm waiting on this side of the river until you bring me my key. Once I get it I will go away—no questions asked, no harm done."

Bobo frowned. "Suppose he doesn't have the key?"

"He will," I said. "You see, it's just an old brass gate-key, but the handle is shaped into my family crest. Mounted in the crest is a large ruby."

Bobo's frown persisted. "What if he just pried it loose and threw the key away?"

"That's possible." I shrugged. "But you had better pray he didn't." My fingers dug into his neck. "I want that key, understand? And I want it now."

"He's not going to give it to you, not Le Boss! Why should he?"

For answer I dragged him toward the sleeping sentry in the weeds. Reaching into my jacket I produced a knife. As Bobo gaped in surprise, I aimed a kick at the slumbering lookout. He blinked and sat up quickly, then froze as I pressed the tip of the broad blade against his neck.

"Tell him that if you don't bring me back the key in five minutes I'll cut Sandor's throat."

Sandor believed me, I know, because he started to whimper. And Bobo believed me too, for when I released my grip on his collar he started running toward the bridge.

Now there was only one question. Would Le Boss believe me?

I sincerely hoped so. But for the moment all I could do was be patient. Yanking the sniveling Sandor to his feet, I tugged him along to position myself at the edge of the bridge, staring across it as Bobo reached the mouth of the sewer on the other side. The mouth swallowed him; I stood waiting.

Except for the rasp of Sandor's hoarse breathing, the night was still. No sound emanated from the great oval of the sewer across the river, and my vision could not penetrate the flashing of flame from within.

But the reflection of the light served me as I studied my prisoner. Like Bobo, he had the body of a child, but the face peering up at me was incongruously aged—not by wrinkles but by the grim set of his cracked lips, the gaunt hollows beneath protruding cheekbones, and the sunken circles outlining the eyes above. The eyes were old, those deep dark eyes that had witnessed far more than any child should see. In them I read a present submissiveness, but that was merely surface reaction. Beyond it lay a cold cunning, a cruel craftiness governed not by intelligence but by animal instinct, fully developed, ready for release. And he was an animal, I told myself; a predator, dwelling in a cave, issuing forth to satisfy ageless atavistic hungers.

He hadn't been born that way, of course. It was Le Boss who transformed the innocence of childhood into amoral impulse, who eradicated humanity and brought forth the beast beneath.

Le Boss. What was he doing now? Surely Bobo had reached him by this time, told his tale. What was happening? I held Sandor close at knife-point, my eyes searching the swirl of firelight and shadow deep in the tunnel's iron maw.

Then, suddenly and shockingly, the metal mouth screamed.

The high, piercing echo rose only for an instant before fading into silence, but I knew its source.

Tightening my grip on Sandor's ragged collar and pressing the knife blade close to his throat, I started toward the foot bridge.

"No!" he quavered. "Don't—"

I ignored his panting plea, his futile efforts to free himself. Thrusting him forward, I crossed the swaying structure, averting my gaze from the dank depths beneath and focusing vision and purpose on the opening ahead.

Passing between the flame-tipped teeth of the candles on either side, I dragged Sandor down into the sewer's yawning throat. I was conscious of the odor now, the odor of carrion corruption which welled from the dark inner recesses, conscious of the clang of our footsteps against the rounded metal surface, but my attention was directed elsewhere.

A dark bundle of rags lay across the curved base of the tunnel. Skirting it as we approached, I saw I'd been mistaken. The rags were merely a covering, outlining the twisted form beneath.

Bobo had made a mistake too, for it was his body that sprawled motionless there. The grotesque angle of his neck and the splinter of bone protruding from an outflung arm indicated that he had fallen from above. Fallen, or perhaps been hurled.

My eyes sought the rounded ceiling of the sewer. It was, as I'd estimated, easily twenty feet high, but I didn't have to scan the top to confirm my guess as to Bobo's fate.

Just ahead, at the left of the rounded iron wall, was a wooden ladder propped against the side of a long, broad shelf mounted on makeshift scaffolding which rose perhaps a dozen feet from the sewer's base. Here the candles were affixed to poles at regular intervals, illuminating a vast humbled heap of handluggage, rucksacks, attache cases, boxes, packages, purses, and moldy, mildewed articles of clothing, piled into a thieves' mountain of stolen goods.

And here, squatting before them on a soiled and aging mattress, amid a litter of emptied and discarded bottles, Le Boss squatted.

There was no doubt as to his identity; I recognized him by his mocking smile, the cool casualness with which he rose to confront me after I'd forced Sandor up the ladder and onto the platform.

The man who stood swaying before us was a monster. Forgive the term, but there is no other single word to describe him. Le Boss was well over six feet tall, and the legs enclosed in the dirt-smudged trousers of his soiled suit were bowed and bent by the sheer immensity of the burden they bore. He must have weighed over three hundred pounds, and the fat bulging from his bloated belly and torso was almost obscene in its abundance. His huge hands terminated in fingers as thick as sausages.

There was no shirt beneath the tightly-stretched suit jacket and from a cord around his thick neck a whistle dangled against the naked chest. His head was bullet-shaped and bald. Indeed, he was completely hairless—no hint of eyebrows surmounted the hyperthyroid pupils, no lashes guarded the red-rimmed sockets. The porcine cheeks and sagging jowls were beardless, their fleshy folds worm-white even in the candle light which glittered against the tiny, tawny eyes.

I needed no second glance to confirm my suspicions of what had occurred before my arrival here; the scene I pictured in my mind was perfectly clear. The coming of Bobo, the breathless, stammered story, his master's reaction of mingled disbelief and anger, the fit of drunken fury in which the terrified bringer of bad tidings had been flung over the side of the platform to smash like an empty bottle on the floor or the sewer below—I saw it all too vividly.

Le Boss grinned at me, his fleshy lips parted to reveal yellowed stumps of rotting teeth.

"Well, old man?" he spoke in French, but his voice was oddly accented; he could indeed be a yougoslave.

I forced myself to meet his gaze. "You know why I'm here," I said.

He nodded. "Something about a key, I take it."

"Your pack of thieves took it. But it's my property."

His grin broadened. "My property now." The deep voice rumbled with mocking relish. "Suppose I'm not inclined to return it?"

For answer I shoved Sandor before me and raised the knife, poising it against his neck. My captive trembled and made mewing sounds as the blade pressed closer.

Le Boss shrugged. "You'll have to do better than that, old man. A child's life isn't important to me."

I peered down at Bobo's body lying below. "So I see." Striving to conceal my reaction, I faced him again. "But where are the others?"

"Playing, I imagine."

"Playing?"

"You find that strange, old man? In spite of what you may think, I'm not without compassion. After all, they are only children. They work hard, and they deserve the reward of play."

Le Boss turned, gesturing down toward the far recesses of the sewer. My eyes followed his gaze through the shifting candle glow, and for the first time I became aware of movement in the dim depths. Faint noises echoed upward, identifiable now as the sound of childish laughter. Tiny shapes moved below and beyond, shapes which gleamed white amid the shadows.

The yougoslaves were naked, and at play. I counted four of them, scuffling and squatting in the far reaches of the tunnel.

But wait! There was a fifth figure, slightly smaller than the others who loomed over it and laughed as they pawed the squirming shape or tugged at the golden hair. Over their mirth rose the sound of sobbing, and over that, the echo of Bobo's voice.

Hey, old man—you like girls? Fresh meat, only five, six maybe—

Now I could see only too clearly. Two of the boys held their victim down, spread-eagled and helpless, while the other two—but I shall not describe what they were doing.

Glancing away, I again met Le Boss' smile. Somehow it seemed more hideous to me than the sight below.

He groped for a bottle propped against the pile of loot beside him and drank before speaking. "You are distressed, eh?"

I shook my head. "Not as much as you'll be unless you give me back my key."

He smiled. "Empty threats will get you nothing but empty hands."

"My hands aren't empty." I jabbed the knife at Sandor's neck, grazing the flesh, and he squealed in terror.

Le Boss shrugged. "Go ahead. I told you it doesn't matter to me."

For a moment I stood irresolute. Then, with a sigh I drew the knife back from Sandor's throat and released my hold on his sweat-soaked collar. He turned and raced off to the ladder behind me, and I could hear his feet scraping against the rungs as he descended. Mercifully, the sound muffled the laughter from below.

Le Boss nodded. "That's better. Now we can discuss the situation like gentlemen."

I lifted the knife. "Not as long as I have this, and you have the key."

"More empty threats?"

"My knife speaks for me." I took a step forward as I spoke.

He chuckled. "I swear I don't know what to make of you, old man. Either you are very stupid or very brave."

"Both, perhaps." I raised the blade higher, but he halted my advance with a quick gesture.

"Enough," he wheezed. Turning, he stopped and thrust his

pudgy hand into a tangle of scarves, kerchiefs, and handbags behind him. When he straightened again he was holding the key.

"Is this what you're after?"

"Yes. I knew you wouldn't discard it."

He stared at the red stone gleaming dully from the crested handle. "I never toss away valuables."

"Just human lives," I said.

"Don't preach to me, old man. I'm not interested in your philosophy."

"Nor I in yours." I stretched out my hand, palm upward. "All I want is my key."

His own hand drew back. "Not so fast. Suppose you tell me why."

"It's not the ruby," I answered. "Go ahead, pry it loose if you like."

Le Boss chuckled again. "A poor specimen—big enough, but flawed. It's the key itself that interests you, eh?"

"Naturally. As I told Bobo, it opens the gate to my estate."

"And just where is this estate of yours?"

"Near Bourg-la-Reine."

"That's not too far away." The little eyes narrowed. "The van could take us there within the hour."

"It would serve no purpose," I said. "Perhaps 'estate' is a misnomer. The place is small and holds nothing you'd be interested in. The furnishings are old, but hardly the quality of antiques. The house itself has been boarded up for years since my last visit. I have other properties elsewhere on the continent where I spend much of my time. But since I'll be here for several weeks on business, I prefer familiar surroundings."

"Other properties, eh?" Le Boss fingered the key. "You must be quite rich, old man."

"That's none of your affair."

"Perhaps not, but I was just thinking. If you have money, why not conduct your business in comfort from a hotel in Paris?"

I shrugged. "It's a matter of sentiment—"

"Really?" he eyed me sharply, and in the interval before speaking, I noted that the sounds below had ceased.

My voice broke the sudden silence. "I assure you—"

"*Au contraire.* You do not assure me in the least." Le Boss scowled. "If you do own an estate, then it's the key to the house

that's important, not the one for the gate. Any locksmith could
open it for you without the need of this particular key."

He squinted at the burnished brass, the dulled brilliance of the
ruby imbedded in the ornate crest. "Unless, of course, it isn't a
gate key after all. Looks to me more like the key to a strongbox, or
even a room in the house holding hidden valuables."

"It's just a gate key." Again I held one hand out as the other
gripped the knife. "But I want it—now."

"Enough to kill?" he challenged.

"If necessary."

"I'll spare you that." Grinning, Le Boss reached down again into
a bundle of discarded clothing. When he turned to face me again
he held a revolver in his hand.

"Drop that toothpick," he said, raising the weapon to reinforce
his command.

Sighing, I released my grip and the knife fell, clattering over the
side of the open platform to the surface of the sewer below.

Impelled by blind impulse, I turned hastily. If I could get to the
ladder—

"Stand where you are!"

It wasn't his words, but the sharp clicking sound that halted me.
Slowly I pivoted to face the muzzle of his cocked revolver.

"That's better," he said.

"You wouldn't murder me—not in cold blood."

"Let's leave it up to the kids." As Le Boss spoke his free hand
fumbled for the whistle looped around his neck. Enfolding it in
blubbery lips, he blew.

The piercing blast echoed, reverberating from the rounded iron
walls beside me and below. Then came the answering murmurs,
the sudden thud of footsteps. Out of the corner of my eye I
glanced down and saw the four naked figures—no, there were five
now, including the fully clothed Sandor—moving toward the platform on which we stood.

Again I conjured up a vision of Hell, of demons dancing in the
flames. But the flames were merely candle light and the bodies
hurrying beneath were those of children. It was only their laughter
which was demonic. Their laughter, and their gleefully contorted
faces.

As they approached I caught a glimpse of what they held in
their hands. Sandor had scooped up the knife from where it had

fallen and the others held weapons of their own—a mallet, a
wooden club, a length of steel pipe, the serrated stump of a broken
wine bottle.

Le Boss chuckled once more. "Playtime," he said.

"Call them off!" I shouted. "I warn you—"

He shook his head. "No way, old man."

Old man. That, I swear, is what did it. Not the menace of the gun,
not the sight of the loathsome little creatures below. It was just the
phrase, the contempt with which it had been repeated over and
over again.

I knew what he was thinking—an unarmed, helpless elderly
victim had been trapped for torment. And for the most part he was
right. I was weaponless, old, trapped.

But not helpless.

Closing my eyes, I concentrated. There are subsonic whistles
which make no audible sound, and there are ways of summoning
which require no whistles at all. And there's more than human
vermin infesting abandoned sewers, lurking in the far recesses of
tangled tunnels, but responsive to certain commands.

Almost instantly that response came.

It came in the form of a purposeful padding, of faint noises
magnified by sheer numbers. It came in the sound of squeaks and
chittering, first as distant echoes, then in closer cacophony as my
summons were answered.

Now the yougoslaves had reached the ladder at the far side of
the platform. I saw Sandor mount the lower rungs, knife held
between clenched teeth—saw him halt as he too heard the sudden,
telltale tumult. Behind Sandor his companions turned to seek its
source.

They cried out then, first in surprise, then in alarm, as the gray
wave surged toward them along the sewer's length; the gray
wave, flecked with hundreds of red and glaring eyes, a thousand
tiny teeth.

The wave raced forward, curling around the feet and ankles of
the yougoslaves before the ladder, climbing and clinging to their
legs and knees. Screaming, they lashed out with their weapons,
trying to beat back the attack but the wave poured on, forward
and upward. Furry forms leaped higher, claws digging into
waists, teeth biting into bellies. Sandor pulled himself up the ladder with both hands, but below him the red eyes rose and the gray

shapes launched up from behind to cover his unprotected back with a blanket of wriggling bodies.

Now the screams from below were drowned out by the volume of shrill screeching. The knife dropped from between Sandor's lips as he shrieked and toppled down into the writhing mass that had already engulfed his companions. Flailing helplessly, their faces sank from sight in the rising waves of the gray sea.

It happened so quickly that Le Boss, caught by surprise, could only stare in stunned silence at the shambles below.

It was I whose voice rose above the bedlam. "The key," I cried. "Give me the key."

For answer he raised his hand—not the one holding the key, but the one grasping the gun.

His fingers were trembling, and the muzzle wavered as I started toward him. Even so, at such close range I realized he couldn't miss. And he didn't.

As he squeezed the trigger the shots came in rapid succession. They were barely audible in the uproar from the tunnel, but I felt their impact as they struck my chest and torso.

I kept on, moving closer, hearing the final, futile click as he continued to press the trigger of his emptied revolver. Looking up, eyes red with rage, he hurled the weapon at my head. It whizzed past me, and now he had nothing left to clutch but the key. His hands started to shake.

My hand went out.

Snatching the key from his pudgy paw, I stared at his frantic face. Perhaps I should have told him he'd guessed correctly, the key was not meant to open a gate. I could have explained the ruby in the crest—the symbol of a lineage so ancient that it still adhered to the old custom of maintaining a tomb on the estate. The key gave me access to that tomb, not that it was really needed; my branch of the line had other resting places, and during my travels I always carried with me what was necessary to afford temporary rest of my own. But during my stay here the tomb was both practical and private. Calling a locksmith would be unwise and inconvenient, and I do not relish inconvenience.

All this I could have told him, and much more. Instead I pocketed the key bearing the great flawed ruby that was like a single drop of blood.

As I did so, I realized that the squeals and chittering below had faded into other sounds compounded of claws ripping through cloth, teeth grating against bone.

Unable to speak, unable to move, Le Boss awaited my approach. When I gripped his shoulders he must have fainted, for there was only a dead weight now to ease down onto the platform floor.

Below me my brothers sated their hunger, feasting on the bodies of the yougoslaves.

Bending forward to the fat neck beneath me, in my own way I feasted too.

What fools they were, these creatures who thought themselves so clever! Perhaps they could outwit others, but their little tricks could not prevail against me. After all, they were only yougoslaves.

And I am a Transylvanian.

Bite-Me-Not, or, Fleur de Fur

TANITH LEE

I

In the tradition of young girls and windows, the young girl looks out of this one. It is difficult to see anything. The panes of the window are heavily leaded, and secured by a lattice of iron. The stained glass of lizard-green and storm-purple is several inches thick. There is no red glass in the window. The colour red is forbidden in the castle. Even the sun, behind the glass, is a storm sun, a green-lizard sun.

The young girl wishes she had a gown of palest pastel rose—the nearest affinity to red, which is never allowed. Already she has long dark beautiful eyes, a long white neck. Her long dark hair is however hidden in a dusty scarf, and she wears rags. She is a scullery maid. As she scours dishes and mops stone floors, she imagines she is a princess floating through the upper corridors, gliding to the dais in the Duke's hall. The Cursed Duke. She is sorry for him. If he had been her father, she would have sympathised and consoled him. His own daughter is dead, as his wife is dead, but these things, being to do with the cursing, are never spoken of. Except, sometimes, obliquely.

"*Rohise!*" dim voices cry now, full of dim scolding soon to be actualised.

The scullery maid turns from the window and runs to have her
ears boxed and a broom thrust into her hands.

Meanwhile, the Cursed Duke is prowling his chamber, high in
the East Turret carved with swans and gargoyles. The room is
lined with books, swords, lutes, scrolls, and has two eerie portraits, the larger of which represents his wife, and the smaller his
daughter. Both ladies look much the same with their pale egg-
shaped faces, polished eyes, clasped hands. They do not really
look like his wife or daughter, nor really remind him of them.

There are no windows at all in the turret, they were long ago
bricked up and covered with hangings. Candles burn steadily. It is
always night in the turret. Save, of course, by night there are particular *sounds* all about it, to which the Duke is accustomed, but
which he does not care for. By night, like most of his court, the
Cursed Duke closes his ears with softened tallow. However, if he
sleeps, he dreams, and hears in the dream the beating of wings.
. . . Often, the court holds loud revel all night long.

The Duke does not know Rohise the scullery maid has been
thinking of him. Perhaps he does not even know that a scullery
maid is capable of thinking at all.

Soon the Duke descends from the turret and goes down, by
various stairs and curving passages, into a large, walled garden on
the east side of the castle.

It is a very pretty garden, mannered and manicured, which the
gardeners keep in perfect order. Over the tops of the high, high
walls, where delicate blooms bell the vines, it is just possible to
glimpse the tips of sun-baked mountains. But by day the mountains are blue and spiritual to look at, and seem scarcely real. They
might only be inked on the sky.

A portion of the Duke's court is wandering about in the garden,
playing games or musical instruments, or admiring painted sculptures, or the flora, none of which is red. But the Cursed Duke's
court seems vitiated this noon. Nights of revel take their toll.

As the Duke passes down the garden, his courtiers acknowledge
him deferentially. He sees them, old and young alike, all doomed
as he is, and the weight of his burden increases.

At the farthest, most eastern end of the garden, there is another
garden, sunken and rather curious, beyond a wall with an iron
door. Only the Duke possesses the key to this door. Now he un-

locks it and goes through. His courtiers laugh and play and pretend not to see. He shuts the door behind him.

The sunken garden, which no gardener ever tends, is maintained by other, spontaneous, means. It is small and square, lacking the hedges and the paths of the other, the sundials and statues and little pools. All the sunken garden contains is a broad paved border, and at its centre a small plot of humid earth. Growing in the earth is a slender bush with slender velvet leaves.

The Duke stands and looks at the bush only a short while.

He visits it every day. He has visited it every day for years. He is waiting for the bush to flower. Everyone is waiting for this. Even Rohise, the scullery maid, is waiting, though she does not, being only sixteen, born in the castle and uneducated, properly understand why.

The light in the little garden is dull and strange, for the whole of it is roofed over by a dome of thick smoky glass. It makes the atmosphere somewhat depressing, although the bush itself gives off a pleasant smell, rather resembling vanilla.

Something is cut into the stone rim of the earth-plot where the bush grows. The Duke reads it for perhaps the thousandth time. *O, fleur de feu—*

When the Duke returns from the little garden into the large garden, locking the door behind him, no one seems truly to notice. But their obeisances now are circumspect.

One day, he will perhaps emerge from the sunken garden leaving the door wide, crying out in a great voice. But not yet. Not today.

The ladies bend to the bright fish in the pools, the knights pluck for them blossoms, challenge each other to combat at chess, or wrestling, discuss the menagerie lions; the minstrels sing of unrequited love. The pleasure garden is full of one long and weary sigh.

"Oh flurda fur

"Pourma souffrance—"

Sings Rohise as she scrubs the flags of the pantry floor.

"Ned ormey par,

"May say day mwar—"

"What are you singing, you slut?" someone shouts, and kicks over her bucket.

Rohise does not weep. She tidies her bucket and soaks up the spilled water with her cloths. She does not know what the song, because of which she seems, apparently, to have been chastised, means. She does not understand the words that somehow, somewhere—perhaps from her own dead mother—she learned by rote.

In the hour before sunset, the Duke's hall is lit by flambeaux. In the high windows, the casements of oil-blue and lavender glass and glass like storms and lizards, are fastened tight. The huge window by the dais was long ago obliterated, shut up, and a tapestry hung of gold and silver tissue with all the rubies pulled out and emeralds substituted. It describes the subjugation of a fearsome unicorn by a maiden, and huntsmen.

The court drifts in with its clothes of rainbow from which only the colour red is missing.

Music for dancing plays. The lean pale dogs pace about, alert for tidbits as dish on dish comes in. Roast birds in all their plumage glitter and die a second time under the eager knives. Pastry castles fall. Pink and amber fruits, and green fruits and black, glow beside the goblets of fine yellow wine.

The Cursed Duke eats with care and attention, not with enjoyment. Only the very young of the castle still eat in that way, and there are not so many of those.

The murky sun slides through the stained glass. The musicians strike up more wildly. The dances become boisterous. Once the day goes out, the hall will ring to *chanson*, to drum and viol and pipe. The dogs will bark, no language will be uttered except in a bellow. The lions will roar from the menagerie. On some nights the cannons are set off from the battlements, which are now all of them roofed in, fired out through narrow mouths just wide enough to accommodate them, the charge crashing away in thunder down the darkness.

By the time the moon comes up and the castle rocks to its own cacophony, exhausted Rohise has fallen fast asleep in her cupboard bed in the attic. For years, from sunset to rise, nothing has woken her. Once, as a child, when she had been especially badly beaten, the pain woke her and she heard a strange silken scratching, somewhere over her head. But she thought it a rat, or a bird. Yes, a bird, for later it seemed to her there were also wings. . . . But she forgot all this half a decade ago. Now she sleeps deeply and dreams of being a princess, forgetting, too, how the Duke's daughter died. Such a terrible death, it is better to forget.

"The sun shall not smite thee by day, neither the moon by night," intones the priest, eyes rolling, his voice like a bell behind the Duke's shoulder.

"Ne moi mords pas," whispers Rohise in her deep sleep. "Ne mwar mor par, ne par mor mwar. . . ."

And under its impenetrable dome, the slender bush has closed its fur leaves also to sleep. O flower of fire, oh fleur de fur. Its blooms, though it has not bloomed yet, bear the ancient name *Nona Mordica*. In light parlance they call it Bite-Me-Not. There is a reason for that.

II

He is the Prince of a proud and savage people. The pride they acknowledge, perhaps they do not consider themselves to be savages, or at least believe that savagery is the proper order of things.

Feroluce, that is his name. It is one of the customary names his kind give their lords. It has connotations with diabolic royalty and, too, with a royal flower of long petals curved like scimitars. Also the name might be the partial anagram of another name. The bearer of that name was also winged.

For Feroluce and his people are winged beings. They are more like a nest of dark eagles than anything, mounted high among the rocky pilasters and pinnacles of the mountain. Cruel and magnificent, like eagles, the sombre sentries motionless as statuary on the ledge-edges, their sable wings folded about them.

They are very alike in appearance (less a race or tribe, more a flock, an unkindness of ravens). Feroluce also, black-winged, black-haired, aquiline of feature, standing on the brink of star-dashed space, his eyes burning through the night like all the eyes along the rocks, depthless red as claret.

They have their own traditions of art and science. They do not make or read books, fashion garments, discuss God or metaphysics or men. Their cries are mostly wordless and always mysterious, flung out like ribbons over the air as they wheel and swoop and hang in wicked cruciform, between the peaks. But they sing, long hours, for whole nights at a time, music that has a language only they know. All their wisdom and theosophy, and all their grasp of beauty, truth, or love, is in the singing.

They look unloving enough, and so they are. Pitiless fallen angels. A travelling people, they roam after sustenance. Their sustenance is blood. Finding a castle, they accepted it, every bastion and wall, as their prey. They have preyed on it and tried to prey on it for years.

In the beginning, their calls, their songs, could lure victims to the feast. In this way, the tribe or unkindness of Feroluce took the Duke's wife, somnambulist, from a midnight balcony. But the Duke's daughter, the first victim, they found seventeen years ago, benighted on the mountainside. Her escort and herself they left to the sunrise, marble figures, the life drunk away.

Now the castle is shut, bolted and barred. They are even more attracted by its recalcitrance (a woman who says "No"). They do not intend to go away until the castle falls to them.

By night, they fly like huge black moths round and round the carved turrets, the dull-lit leaded windows, their wings invoking a cloudy tindery wind, pushing thunder against thundery glass.

They sense they are attributed to some sin, reckoned a punishing curse, a penance, and this amuses them at the level whereon they understand it.

They also sense something of the flower, the *Nona Mordica*. Vampires have their own legends.

But tonight Feroluce launches himself into the air, speeds down the sky on the black sails of his wings, calling, a call like laughter or derision. This morning, in the 'tween-time before the light began and the sun-to-be drove him away to his shadowed eyrie in the mountain-guts, he saw a chink in the armour of the beloved refusing-woman-prey. A window, high in an old neglected tower, a window with a small eyelet which was cracked.

Feroluce soon reaches the eyelet and breathes on it, as if he would melt it. (His breath is sweet. Vampires do not eat raw flesh, only blood, which is a perfect food and digests perfectly, while their teeth are sound of necessity.) The way the glass mists at breath intrigues Feroluce. But presently he taps at the cranky pane, taps, then claws. A piece breaks away, and now he sees how it should be done.

Over the rims and upthrusts of the castle, which is only really another mountain with caves to Feroluce, the rumble of the Duke's revel drones on.

Feroluce pays no heed. He does not need to reason, he merely knows, *that* noise masks *this*—as he smashes in the window. Its panes were all faulted and the lattice rusty. It is, of course, more than that. The magic of Purpose has protected the castle, and, as in all balances, there must be, or come to be, some balancing contradiction, some flaw. . . .

The people of Feroluce do not notice what he is at. In a way, the dance with their prey has debased to a ritual. They have lived almost two decades on the blood of local mountain beasts, and bird-creatures like themselves brought down on the wing. Patience is not, with them, a virtue. It is a sort of foreplay, and can go on, in pleasure, a long, long while.

Feroluce intrudes himself through the slender window. Muscularly slender himself, and agile, it is no feat. But the wings catch, are a trouble. They follow him because they must, like two separate entities. They have been cut a little on the glass, and bleed.

He stands in a stony small room, shaking bloody feathers from him, snarling, but without sound.

Then he finds the stairway and goes down.

There are dusty landings and neglected chambers. They have no smell of life. But then there comes to be a smell. It is the scent of a nest, a colony of things, wild creatures, in constant proximity. He recognises it. The light of his crimson eyes precedes him, deciphering blackness. And then other eyes, amber, green, and gold, spring out like stars all across his path.

Somewhere an old torch is burning out. To the human eye, only mounds and glows would be visible, but to Feroluce, the Prince of the vampires, all is suddenly revealed. There is a great stone area, barred with bronze and iron, and things stride and growl behind the bars, or chatter and flee, or only stare. And there, without bars, though bound by ropes of brass to rings of brass, three brazen beasts.

Feroluce, on the steps of the menagerie, looks into the gaze of the Duke's lions. Feroluce smiles, and the lions roar. One is the king, its mane like war-plumes. Feroluce recognises the king and the king's right to challenge, for this is the lions' domain, their territory.

Feroluce comes down the stair and meets the lion as it leaps the length of its chain. To Feroluce, the chain means nothing, and since he has come close enough, very little either to the lion.

To the vampire Prince the fight is wonderful, exhilarating and meaningful, intellectual even, for it is coloured by nuance, yet powerful as sex.

He holds fast with his talons, his strong limbs wrapping the beast which is almost stronger than he, just as its limbs wrap him in turn. He sinks his teeth in the lion's shoulder, and in fierce rage and bliss begins to draw out the nourishment. The lion kicks and claws at him in turn. Feroluce feels the gouges like fire along his shoulders, thighs, and hugs the lion more nearly as he throttles and drinks from it, loving it, jealous of it, killing it. Gradually the mighty feline body relaxes, still clinging to him, its cat teeth bedded in one beautiful swanlike wing, forgotten by both.

In a welter of feathers, stripped skin, spilled blood, the lion and the angel lie in embrace on the menagerie floor. The lion lifts its head, kisses the assassin, shudders, lets go.

Feroluce glides out from under the magnificent deadweight of the cat. He stands. And pain assaults him. His lover has severely wounded him.

Across the menagerie floor, the two lionesses are crouched. Beyond them, a man stands gaping in simple terror, behind the guttering torch. He had come to feed the beasts, and seen another feeding, and now is paralysed. He is deaf, the menagerie-keeper, previously an advantage saving him the horror of nocturnal vampire noises.

Feroluce starts towards the human animal swifter than a serpent, and checks. Agony envelops Feroluce and the stone room spins. Involuntarily, confused, he spreads his wings for flight, there in the confined chamber. But only one wing will open. The other, damaged and partly broken, hangs like a snapped fan. Feroluce cries out, a beautiful singing note of despair and anger. He drops fainting at the menagerie-keeper's feet.

The man does not wait for more. He runs away through the castle, screaming invective and prayer, and reaches the Duke's hall and makes the whole hall listen.

All this while, Feroluce lies in the ocean of almost-death that is sleep or swoon, while the smaller beasts in the cages discuss him, or seem to.

And when he is raised, Feroluce does not wake. Only the great drooping bloody wings quiver and are still. Those who carry him are more than ever revolted and frightened, for they have seldom seen blood. Even the food for the menagerie is cooked almost black. Two years ago, a gardener slashed his palm on a thorn. He was banished from the court for a week.

But Feroluce, the centre of so much attention, does not rouse. Not until the dregs of the night are stealing out through the walls. Then some nervous instinct invests him. The sun is coming and this is an open place, he struggles through unconsciousness and hurt, through the deepest most bladed waters, to awareness.

And finds himself in a huge bronze cage, the cage of some animal appropriated for the occasion. Bars, bars all about him, and not to be got rid of, for he reaches to tear them away and cannot. Beyond the bars, the Duke's hall, which is only a pointless cold glitter to him in the maze of pain and dying lights. Not an open place, in fact, but too open for his kind. Through the window-spaces of thick glass, muddy sunglare must come in. To Feroluce it will be like swords, acids, and burning fire—

Far off he hears wings beat and voices soaring. His people search for him, call and wheel and find nothing.

Feroluce cries out, a gravel shriek now, and the persons in the hall rush back from him, calling on God. But Feroluce does not see. He has tried to answer his own. Now he sinks down again under the coverlet of his broken wings, and the wine-red stars of his eyes go out.

III

"And the Angel of Death," the priest intones, "shall surely pass over, but yet like the shadow, not substance—"

The smashed window in the old turret above the menagerie tower has been sealed with mortar and brick. It is a terrible thing that it was for so long overlooked. A miracle that only one of the creatures found and entered by it. God, the Protector, guarded the Cursed Duke and his court. And the magic that surrounds the castle, that too held fast. For from the possibility of a disaster was born a bloom of great value: now one of the monsters is in their possession. A prize beyond price.

Caged and helpless, the fiend is at their mercy. It is also weak from its battle with the noble lion, which gave its life for the castle's safety (and will be buried with honour in an ornamented grave at the foot of the Ducal family tomb). Just before the dawn came, the Duke's advisers advised him, and the bronze cage was wheeled away into the darkest area of the hall, close by the dais where once the huge window was but is no more. A barricade of great screens was brought, and set around the cage, and the top of it covered. No sunlight now can drip into the prison to harm the specimen. Only the Duke's ladies and gentlemen steal in around the screens and see, by the light of a candlebranch, the demon still lying in its trance of pain and bloodloss. The Duke's alchemist sits on a stool nearby, dictating many notes to a nervous apprentice. The alchemist, and the apothecary for that matter, are convinced the vampire, having drunk the lion almost dry, will recover from its wounds. Even the wings will mend.

The Duke's court painter also came. He was ashamed presently, and went away. The beauty of the demon affected him, making him wish to paint it, not as something wonderfully disgusting, but as a kind of superlative man, vital and innocent, or as Lucifer himself, stricken in the sorrow of his colossal Fall. And all that has caused the painter to pity the fallen one, mere artisan that the painter is, so he slunk away. He knows, since the alchemist and the apothecary told him, what is to be done.

Of course much of the castle knows. Though scarcely anyone has slept or sought sleep, the whole place rings with excitement and vivacity. The Duke has decreed, too, that everyone who wishes shall be a witness. So he is having a progress through the castle, seeking every nook and cranny, while, let it be said, his architect takes the opportunity to check no other window-pane has cracked.

From room to room the Duke and his entourage pass, through corridors, along stairs, through dusty attics and musty storerooms he has never seen, or if seen has forgotten. Here and there some retainer is come on. Some elderly women are discovered spinning like spiders up under the eaves, half-blind and complacent. They curtsy to the Duke from a vague recollection of old habit. The Duke tells them the good news, or rather, his messenger, walking before, announces it. The ancient women sigh and whisper, are left, probably forget. Then again, in a narrow courtyard, a simple boy, who looks after a dovecote, is magnificently told. He has a fit from alarm, grasping nothing, and the doves who love and understand him (by not trying to) fly down and cover him with their soft wings as the Duke goes away. The boy comes to under the doves as if in a heap of warm snow, comforted.

It is on one of the dark staircases above the kitchen that the gleaming entourage sweeps round a bend and comes on Rohise the scullery maid, scrubbing. In these days, when there are so few children and young servants, labour is scarce, and the scullerers are not confined to the scullery.

Rohise stands up, pale with shock, and for a wild instant thinks that, for some heinous crime she has committed in ignorance, the Duke has come in person to behead her.

"Hear then, by the Duke's will," cries the messenger. "One of Satan's night-demons, which do torment us, has been captured and lies penned in the Duke's hall. At sunrise tomorrow, this thing will be taken to that sacred spot where grows the bush of the Flower of the Fire, and here its foul blood shall be shed. Who then can doubt the bush will blossom, and save us all, by the Grace of God."

"And the Angel of Death," intones the priest, on no account to be omitted, "shall surely—"

"Wait," says the Duke. He is as white as Rohise. "Who is this?" he asks. "Is it a ghost?"

The court stare at Rohise, who nearly sinks in dread, her scrubbing rag in her hand.

Gradually, despite the rag, the rags, the rough hands, the court too begins to see.

"Why, it is a marvel."

The Duke moves forward. He looks down at Rohise and starts to cry. Rohise thinks he weeps in compassion at the awful sentence he is here to visit on her, and drops back on her knees.

"No, no," says the Duke tenderly. "Get up. Rise. You are so like my child, my daughter—"

Then Rohise, who knows few prayers, begins in panic to sing her little song as an orison:

"Oh fleur de feu
"Pour ma souffrance—"

"Ah!" says the Duke. "Where did you learn that song?"

"From my mother," says Rohise. And, all instinct now, she sings again:

"O flurda fur,
"Pourma souffrance

"Ned ormey par
"May say day mwar—"

It is the song of the fire-flower bush, the *Nona Mordica*, called
Bite-Me-Not. It begins, and continues: *O flower of fire, For my misery's sake, Do not sleep but aid me; wake!* The Duke's daughter sang it
very often. In those days the shrub was not needed, being just a
rarity of the castle. Invoked as an amulet, on a mountain road, the
rhyme itself had besides proved useless.

The Duke takes the dirty scarf from Rohise's hair. She is very,
very like his lost daughter, the same pale smooth oval face, the
long white neck and long dark polished eyes, and the long dark
hair. (Or is it that she is very, very like the painting?)

The Duke gives instructions, and Rohise is borne away.

In a beautiful chamber, the door of which has for seventeen
years been locked, Rohise is bathed and her hair is washed. Oils
and scents are rubbed into her skin. She is dressed in a gown of
palest most pastel rose, with a girdle sewn with pearls. Her hair is
combed, and on it is set a chaplet of stars and little golden leaves.
"Oh, your poor hands," say the maids, as they trim her nails.
Rohise has realised she is not to be executed. She has realised the
Duke has seen her and wants to love her like his dead daughter.
Slowly, an uneasy stir of something, not quite happiness, moves
through Rohise. Now she will wear her pink gown, now she will
sympathise with and console the Duke. Her daze lifts suddenly.

The dream has come true. She dreamed of it so often it seems
quite normal. The scullery was the thing which never seemed real.

She glides down through the castle, and the ladies are astonished by her grace. The carriage of her head under the starry
coronet is exquisite. Her voice is quiet and clear and musical, and
the foreign tone of her mother, long unremembered, is quite gone
from it. Only the roughened hands give her away, but smoothed
by unguents, soon they will be soft and white.

"Can it be she is truly the princess returned to flesh?"

"Her life was taken so early—yes, as they believe in the Spice-
Lands, by some holy dispensation, she might return."

"She would be about the age to have been conceived the very
night the Duke's daughter d—— That is, the very night the bane
began—"

Theosophical discussion ensues. Songs are composed.

Rohise sits for a while with her adoptive father in the East

Turret, and he tells her about the books and swords and lutes and scrolls, but not about the two portraits. Then they walk out together, in the lovely garden in the sunlight. They sit under a peach tree, and discuss many things, or the Duke discusses them. That Rohise is ignorant and uneducated does not matter at this point. She can always be trained. She has the basic requirements: docility, sweetness. There are many royal maidens in many places who know as little as she.

The Duke falls asleep under the peach tree. Rohise listens to the love-songs her own (her very own) courtiers bring her.

When the monster in the cage is mentioned, she nods as if she knows what they mean. She supposes it is something hideous, a scaring treat to be shown at dinnertime, when the sun has gone down.

When the sun moves towards the western line of mountains just visible over the high walls, the court streams into the castle and all the doors are bolted and barred. There is an eagerness tonight in the concourse.

As the light dies out behind the coloured windows that have no red in them, covers and screens are dragged away from a bronze cage. It is wheeled out into the centre of the great hall.

Cannons begin almost at once to blast and bang from the roof-holes. The cannoneers have had strict instructions to keep up the barrage all night without a second's pause.

Drums pound in the hall. The dogs start to bark. Rohise is not surprised by the noise, for she has often heard it from far up, in her attic, like a sea-wave breaking over and over through the lower house.

She looks at the cage cautiously, wondering what she will see. But she sees only a heap of blackness like ravens, and then a tawny dazzle, torchlight on something like human skin. "You must not go down to look," says the Duke protectively, as his court pours about the cage. Someone pokes between the bars with a gemmed cane, trying to rouse the nightmare which lies quiescent there. But Rohise must be spared this.

So the Duke calls his actors, and a slight, pretty play is put on throughout dinner, before the dais, shutting off from the sight of Rohise the rest of the hall, where the barbaric gloating and goading of the court, unchecked, increases.

IV

The Prince Feroluce becomes aware between one second and the next. It is the sound—heard beyond all others—of the wings of his people beating at the stones of the castle. It is the wings which speak to him, more than their wild orchestral voices. Besides these sensations, the anguish of healing and the sadism of humankind are not much.

Feroluce opens his eyes. His human audience, pleased, but afraid and squeamish, backs away, and asks each other for the two thousandth time if the cage is quite secure. In the torchlight the eyes of Feroluce are more black than red. He stares about. He is, though captive, imperious. If he were a lion or a bull, they would admire this "nobility." But the fact is, he is too much like a man, which serves to point up his supernatural differences unbearably.

Obviously Feroluce understands the gist of his plight. Enemies have him penned. He is a show for now, but ultimately to be killed, for with the intuition of the raptor he divines everything. He had thought the sunlight would kill him, but that is a distant matter, now. And beyond all, the voices and the voices of the wings of his kindred beat the air outside this room-caved mountain of stone.

And so Feroluce commences to sing, or at least, this is how it seems to the rabid court and all the people gathered in the hall. It seems he sings. It is the great communing call of his kind, the art and science and religion of the winged vampires, his means of telling them, or attempting to tell them, what they must be told before he dies. So the sire of Feroluce sang, and the grandsire, and each of his ancestors. Generally they died in flight, falling angels spun down the gulches and enormous stairs of distant peaks, singing. Feroluce, immured, believes that his cry is somehow audible.

To the crowd in the Duke's hall the song is merely that, a song, but how glorious. The dark silver voice, turning to bronze or gold, whitening in the higher registers. There seem to be words, but in some other tongue. This is how the planets sing, surely, or mysterious creatures of the sea.

Everyone is bemused. They listen, astonished.

No one now remonstrates with Rohise when she rises and steals down from the dais. There is an enchantment which prevents movement and coherent thought. Of all the roomful, only she is drawn forward. So she comes close, unhindered, and between the bars of the cage, she sees the vampire for the first time.

She has no notion what he can be. She imagined it was a monster or a monstrous beast. But it is neither. Rohise, starved for so long of beauty and always dreaming of it, recognises Feroluce inevitably as part of the dream-come-true. She loves him instantly. Because she loves him, she is not afraid of him.

She attends while he goes on and on with his glorious song. He does not see her at all, or any of them. They are only things, like mist, or pain. They have no character or personality or worth; abstracts.

Finally, Feroluce stops singing. Beyond the stone and the thick glass of the siege, the wing-beats, too, eddy into silence.

Finding itself mesmerized, silent by night, the court comes to with a terrible joint start, shrilling and shouting, bursting, exploding into a compensation of sound. Music flares again. And the cannons in the roof, which have also fallen quiet, resume with a tremendous roar.

Feroluce shuts his eyes and seems to sleep. It is his preparation for death.

Hands grasp Rohise. "Lady—step back, come away. So close! It may harm you—"

The Duke clasps her in a father's embrace. Rohise, unused to this sort of physical expression, is unmoved. She pats him absently.

"My lord, what will be done?"

"Hush, child. Best you do not know."

Rohise persists.

The Duke persists in not saying.

But she remembers the words of the herald on the stair, and knows they mean to butcher the winged man. She attends thereafter more carefully to snatches of the bizarre talk about the hall, and learns all she needs. At earliest sunrise, as soon as the enemy retreat from the walls, their captive will be taken to the lovely garden with the peach trees. And so to the sunken garden of the magic bush, the fire-flower. And there they will hang him up in the sun through the dome of smoky glass, which will be slow murder to him, but they will cut him, too, so his blood, the stolen blood of the vampire, runs down to water the roots of the fleur de feu. And who can doubt that, from such nourishment, the bush

will bloom? The blooms are salvation. Wherever they grow it is a
safe place. Whoever wears them is safe from the draining bite of
demons. Bite-Me-Not, they call it; vampire-repellent.

Rohise sits the rest of the night on her cushions, with folded
hands, resembling the portrait of the princess, which is not like
her.

Eventually the sky outside alters. Silence comes down beyond
the wall, and so within the wall, and the court lifts its head, a
corporate animal scenting day.

At the intimation of sunrise the black plague has lifted and gone
away, and might never have been. The Duke, and almost all his
castle full of men, women, children, emerge from the doors. The
sky is measureless and bluely grey, with one cherry rift in the east
that the court refers to as "mauve," since dawns and sunsets are
never any sort of red here.

They move through the dimly lightening garden as the last stars
melt. The cage is dragged in their midst.

They are too tired, too concentrated now, the Duke's people, to
continue baiting their captive. They have had all the long night to
do that, and to drink and opine, and now their stamina is sharpened for the final act.

Reaching the sunken garden, the Duke unlocks the iron door.
There is no room for everyone within, so mostly they must stand
outside, crammed in the gate, or teetering on erections of benches
that have been placed around, and peering in over the walls
through the glass of the dome. The places in the doorway are the
best, of course; no one else will get so good a view. The servants
and lower persons must stand back under the trees and only imagine what goes on. But they are used to that.

Into the sunken garden itself there are allowed to go the alchemist and the apothecary, and the priest, and certain sturdy
soldiers attendant on the Duke, and the Duke. And Feroluce in the
cage.

The east is all "mauve" now. The alchemist has prepared sorcer-
ous safeguards which are being put into operation, and the priest,
never to be left out, intones prayers. The bulge-thewed soldiers
open the cage and seize the monster before it can stir. But drugged
smoke has already been wafted into the prison, and besides, the
monster has prepared itself for hopeless death and makes no
demur.

Feroluce hangs in the arms of his loathing guards, dimly aware the sun is near. But death is nearer, and already one may hear the alchemist's apprentice sharpening the knife an ultimate time.

The leaves of the *Nona Mordica* are trembling, too, at the commencement of the light, and beginning to unfurl. Although this happens every dawn, the court points to it with optimistic cries. Rohise, who has claimed a position in the doorway, watches it too, but only for an instant. Though she has sung of the fleur de fur since childhood, she had never known what the song was all about. And in just this way, though she has dreamed of being the Duke's daughter most of her life, such an event was never really comprehended either, and so means very little.

As the guards haul the demon forward to the plot of humid earth where the bush is growing, Rohise darts into the sunken garden, and lightning leaps in her hands. Women scream and well they might. Rohise has stolen one of the swords from the East Turret, and now she flourishes it, and now she has swung it and a soldier falls, bleeding red, red, *red*, before them all.

Chaos enters, as in yesterday's play, shaking its tattered sleeves. The men who hold the demon rear back in horror at the dashing blade and the blasphemous gore, and the mad girl in her princess's gown. The Duke makes a pitiful bleating noise, but no one pays him any attention.

The east glows in and like the liquid on the ground.

Meanwhile, the ironically combined sense of impending day and spilled hot blood have penetrated the stunned brain of the vampire. His eyes open, and he sees the girl wielding her sword in a spray of crimson as the last guard lets go. Then the girl has run to Feroluce. Though, or because, her face is insane, it communicates her purpose, as she thrusts the sword's hilt into his hands.

No one has dared approach either the demon or the girl. Now they look on in horror and in horror grasp what Feroluce has grasped.

In that moment the vampire springs, and the great swanlike wings are reborn at his back, healed and whole. As the doctors predicted, he has mended perfectly, and prodigiously fast. He takes to the air like an arrow, unhindered, as if gravity does not anymore exist. As he does so, the girl grips him about the waist, and slender and light, she is drawn upward too. He does not glance at her. He veers toward the gateway, and tears through it,

the sword, his talons, his wings, his very shadow, beating men and
bricks from his path.

And now he is in the sky above them, a black star which has not
been put out. They see the wings flare and beat, and the swirling
of a girl's dress and unbound hair, and then the image dives and is
gone into the shade under the mountains, as the sun rises.

v

I t is fortunate, the mountain shade in the sunrise. Lion's blood
and enforced quiescence have worked wonders, but the sun
could undo it all. Luckily the shadow, deep and cold as a pool,
envelops the vampire, and in it there is a cave, deeper and colder.
Here he alights and sinks down, sloughing the girl, whom he has
almost forgotten. Certainly he fears no harm from her. She is like a
pet animal, maybe, like the hunting dogs or wolves or lam-
mergeyers that occasionally the unkindness of vampires have kept
by them for a while. That she helped him is all he needs to know.
She will help again. So when, stumbling in the blackness, she
brings him in her cupped hands water from a cascade at the pool-
cave's back, he is not surprised. He drinks the water, which is the
only other substance his kind imbibe. Then he smooths her hair,
absently, as he would pat or stroke the pet she seems to have
become. He is not grateful, as he is not suspicious. The complexi-
ties of his intellect are reserved for other things. Since he is exhausted he falls asleep, and since Rohise is exhausted she falls
asleep beside him, pressed to his warmth in the freezing dark. Like
those of Feroluce, as it turns out, her thoughts are simple. She is
sorry for distressing the Cursed Duke. But she has no regrets, for
she could no more have left Feroluce to die than she could have
refused to leave the scullery for the court.

The day, which had only just begun, passes swiftly in sleep.

Feroluce wakes as the sun sets, without seeing anything of it. He
unfolds himself and goes to the cave's entrance, which now looks
out on a whole sky of stars above a landscape of mountains. The
castle is far below, and to the eyes of Rohise as she follows him,
invisible. She does not even look for it, for there is something else
to be seen.

The great dark shapes of angels are wheeling against the peaks,
the stars. And their song begins, up in the starlit spaces. It is a

lament, their mourning, pitiless and strong, for Feroluce, who has died in the stone heart of the thing they prey upon.

The tribe of Feroluce do not laugh, but, like a bird or wild beast, they have a kind of equivalent to laughter. This Feroluce now utters, and like a flung lance he launches himself into the air.

Rohise at the cave mouth, abandoned, forgotten, unnoted even by the mass of vampires, watches the winged man as he flies towards his people. She supposes for a moment that she may be able to climb down the tortuous ways of the mountain, undetected. Where then should she go? She does not spend much time on these ideas. They do not interest or involve her. She watches Feroluce, and because she learned long ago the uselessness of weeping, she does not shed tears, though her heart begins to break.

As Feroluce glides, body held motionless, wings outspread on a down-draught, into the midst of the storm of black wings, the red stars of eyes ignite all about him. The great lament dies. The air is very still.

Feroluce waits then. He waits, for the aura of his people is not as he has always known it. It is as if he had come among emptiness. From the silence, therefore, and from nothing else, he learns it all. In the stone he lay and he sang of his death, as the Prince must, dying. And the ritual was completed, and now there is the threnody, the grief, and thereafter the choosing of a new Prince. And none of this is alterable. He is dead. Dead. It cannot and will not be changed.

There is a moment of protest, then, from Feroluce. Perhaps his brief sojourn among men has taught him some of their futility. But as the cry leaves him, all about the huge wings are raised like swords. Talons and teeth and eyes burn against the stars. To protest is to be torn in shreds. He is not of their people now. They can attack and slaughter him as they would any other intruding thing. *Go*, the talons and the teeth and the eyes say to him. *Go far off.*

He is dead. There is nothing left him but to die.

Feroluce retreats. He soars. Bewildered, he feels the power and energy of his strength and the joy of flight, and cannot understand how this is, if he is dead. Yet he *is* dead. He knows it now.

So he closes his eyelids, and his wings. Spear-swift he falls. And something shrieks, interrupting the reverie of nihilism. Disturbed, he opens his wings, shudders, turns like a swimmer, finds a ledge against his side and two hands outstretched, holding him by one shoulder, and by his hair.

"No," says Rohise. (The vampire cloud, wheeling away, have not heard her; she does not think of them.) His eyes stay shut. Holding him, she kisses these eyelids, his forehead, his lips, gently, as she drives her nails into his skin to hold him. The black wings beat, tearing to be free and fall and die. "No," says Rohise. "I love you," she says. "My life is your life." These are the words of the court and of courtly love-songs. No matter, she means them. And though he cannot understand her language or her sentiments, yet her passion, purely that, communicates itself, strong and burning as the passions of his kind, who generally love only one thing, which is scarlet. For a second her intensity fills the void which now contains him. But then he dashes himself away from the ledge, to fall again, to seek death again.

Like a ribbon, clinging to him still, Rohise is drawn from the rock and falls with him.

Afraid, she buries her head against his breast, in the shadow of wings and hair. She no longer asks him to reconsider. This is how it must be. *Love* she thinks again, in the instant before they strike the earth. Then that instant comes, and is gone.

Astonished, she finds herself still alive, still in the air. Touching so close, feathers have been left on the rocks, Feroluce has swerved away and upward. Now, conversely, they are whirling towards the very stars. The world seems miles below. Perhaps they will fly into space itself. Perhaps he means to break their bones instead on the cold face of the moon.

He does not attempt to dislodge her, he does not attempt anymore to fall and die. But as he flies, he suddenly cries out, terrible lost lunatic cries.

They do not hit the moon. They do not pass through the stars like static rain.

But when the air grows thin and pure there is a peak like a dagger standing in their path. Here, he alights. As Rohise lets go of him, he turns away. He stations himself, sentry-fashion, in the manner of his tribe, at the edge of the pinnacle. But watching for nothing. He has not been able to choose death. His strength and the strong will of another, these have hampered him. His brain has become formless darkness. His eyes glare, seeing nothing.

Rohise, gasping a little in the thin atmosphere, sits at his back, watching for him, in case any harm may come near him.

At last, harm does come. There is a lightening in the east. The frozen, choppy sea of the mountains below, and all about, grows visible. It is a marvellous sight, but holds no marvel for Rohise. She averts her eyes from the exquisitely pencilled shapes, looking thin and translucent as paper, the rivers of mist between, the glimmer of nacreous ice. She searches for a blind hold to hide in.

There is a pale yellow wound in the sky when she returns. She grasps Feroluce by the wrist and tugs at him. "Come," she says. He looks at her vaguely, as if seeing her from the shore of another country. "The sun," she says. "Quickly."

The edge of the light runs along his body like a razor. He moves by instinct now, following her down the slippery dagger of the peak, and so eventually into a shallow cave. It is so small it holds him like a coffin. Rohise closes the entrance with her own body. It is the best she can do. She sits facing the sun as it rises, as if prepared to fight. She hates the sun for his sake. Even as the light warms her chilled body, she curses it. Till light and cold and breathlessness fade together.

When she wakes, she looks up into twilight and endless stars, two of which are red. She is lying on the rock by the cave. Feroluce leans over her, and behind Feroluce his quiescent wings fill the sky.

She has never properly understood his nature: Vampire. Yet her own nature, which tells her so much, tells her some vital part of herself is needful to him, and that he is danger, and death. But she loves him, and is not afraid. She would have fallen to die with him. To help him by her death does not seem wrong to her. Thus, she lies still, and smiles at him to reassure him she will not struggle. From lassitude, not fear, she closes her eyes. Presently she feels the soft weight of hair brush by her cheek, and then his cool mouth rests against her throat. But nothing more happens. For some while they continue in this fashion, she yielding, he kneeling over her, his lips on her skin. Then he moves a little away. He sits, regarding her. She, knowing the unknown act has not been completed, sits up in turn. She beckons to him mutely, telling him with her gestures and her expression *I consent. Whatever is necessary*. But he does not stir. His eyes blaze, but even of these she has no fear.

In the end he looks away from her, out across the spaces of the darkness.

He himself does not understand. It is permissible to drink from the body of a pet, the wolf, the eagle. Even to kill the pet, if need demands. Can it be, outlawed from his people, he has lost their composite soul? Therefore, is he soulless now? It does not seem to him he is. Weakened and famished though he is, the vampire is aware of a wild tingling of life. When he stares at the creature which is his food, he finds he sees her differently. He has borne her through the sky, he has avoided death, by some intuitive process, for her sake, and she has led him to safety, guarded him from the blade of the sun. In the beginning it was she who rescued him from the human things which had taken him. She cannot be human, then. Not pet, and not prey. For no, he could not drain her of blood, as he would not seize upon his own kind, even in combat, to drink and feed. He starts to see her as beautiful, not in the way a man beholds a woman, certainly, but as his kind revere the sheen of water in dusk, or flight, or song. There are no words for this. But the life goes on tingling through him. Though he is dead, life.

In the end, the moon does rise, and across the open face of it something wheels by. Feroluce is less swift than was his wont, yet he starts in pursuit, and catches and brings down, killing on the wing, a great night bird. Turning in the air, Feroluce absorbs its liquors. The heat of life now, as well as its assertion, courses through him. He returns to the rock perch, the glorious flaccid bird dangling from his hand. Carefully, he tears the glory of the bird in pieces, plucks the feathers, splits the bones. He wakes the companion (asleep again from weakness) who is not pet or prey, and feeds her morsels of flesh. At first she is unwilling. But her hunger is so enormous and her nature so untamed that quite soon she accepts the slivers of raw fowl.

Strengthened by blood, Feroluce lifts Rohise and bears her gliding down the moon-slit quill-backed land of the mountains, until there is a rocky cistern full of cold, old rains. Here they drink together. Pale white primroses grow in the fissures where the black moss drips. Rohise makes a garland and throws it about the head of her beloved when he does not expect it. Bewildered but disdainful, he touches at the wreath of primroses to see if it is likely to threaten or hamper him. When it does not, he leaves it in place.

Long before dawn this time, they have found a crevice. Because it is so cold, he folds his wings about her. She speaks of her love to him, but he does not hear, only the murmur of her voice, which is musical and does not displease him. And later, she sings him sleepily the little song of the fleur de fur.

VI

There comes a time then, brief, undated, chartless time, when they are together, these two creatures. Not together in any accepted sense, of course, but together in the strange feeling or emotion, instinct or ritual, that can burst to life in an instant or flow to life gradually across half a century, and which men call *Love*.

They are not alike. No, not at all. Their differences are legion and should be unpalatable. He is a supernatural thing and she a human thing, he was a lord and she a scullery sloven. He can fly, she cannot fly. And he is male, she female. What other items are required to make them enemies? Yet they are bound, not merely by love, they are bound by all they are, the very stumbling blocks. Bound, too, because they are doomed. Because the stumbling blocks have doomed them; everything has. Each has been exiled out of their own kind. Together, they cannot even communicate with each other, save by looks, touches, sometimes by sounds, and by songs neither understands, but which each comes to value since the other appears to value them, and since they give expression to that other. Nevertheless, the binding of the doom, the greatest binding, grows, as it holds them fast to each other, mightier and stronger.

Although they do not know it, or not fully, it is the awareness of doom that keeps them there, among the platforms and steps up and down, and the inner cups, of the mountains.

Here it is possible to pursue the airborne hunt, and Feroluce may now and then bring down a bird to sustain them both. But birds are scarce. The richer lower slopes, pastured with goats, wild sheep, and men—they lie far off and far down from this place as a deep of the sea. And Feroluce does not conduct her there, nor does Rohise ask that he should, or try to lead the way, or even dream of such a plan.

But yes, birds are scarce, and the pastures far away, and winter is coming. There are only two seasons in these mountains. High summer, which dies, and the high cold which already treads over the tips of the air and the rock, numbing the sky, making all brittle, as though the whole landscape might snap in pieces, shatter.

How beautiful it is to wake with the dusk, when the silver webs of night begin to form, frost and ice, on everything. Even the ragged dress—once that of a princess—is tinselled and shining with this magic substance, even the mighty wings—once those of a prince—each feather is drawn glittering with thin rime. And oh, the sky, thick as a daisy-field with the white stars. Up there, when they have fed and have strength, they fly, or, Feroluce flies and Rohise flies in his arms, carried by his wings. Up there in the biting chill like a pane of ghostly vitreous, they have become lovers, true blind lovers, embraced and linked, their bodies a bow, coupling on the wing. By the hour that his first happened the girl had forgotten all she had been; and he had forgotten too that she was anything but the essential mate. Sometimes, borne in this way, by wings and by fire, she cries out as she hangs in the ether. These sounds, transmitted through the flawless silence and amplification of the peaks, scatter over tiny half-buried villages countless miles away, where they are heard in fright and taken for the shrieks of malign invisible devils, tiny as bats, and armed with the barbed stings of scorpions. There are always misunderstandings.

After a while, the icy prologues and the stunning starry fields of winter nights give way to the main argument of winter.

The liquid of the pool, where the flowers made garlands, has clouded and closed to stone. Even the volatile waterfalls are stilled, broken cascades of glass. The wind tears through the skin and hair to gnaw the bones. To weep with cold earns no compassion of the cold.

There is no means to make fire. Besides, the one who was Rohise is an animal now, or a bird, and beasts and birds do not make fire, save for the phoenix in the Duke's bestiary. Also, the sun is fire, and the sun is a foe. Eschew fire.

There begin the calendar months of hibernation. The demon lovers too must prepare for just such a measureless winter sleep, that gives no hunger, asks no action. There is a deep cave they have lined with feathers and withered grass. But there are no more flying things to feed them. Long, long ago, the last warm frugal feast, long, long ago the last flight, joining, ecstasy and song. So, they turn to their cave, to stasis, to sleep. Which each understands, wordlessly, thoughtlessly, is death.

What else? He might drain her of blood, he could persist some while on that, might even escape the mountains, the doom. Or she herself might leave him, attempt to make her way to the places below, and perhaps she could reach them, even now. Others, lost here, have done so. But neither considers these alternatives. The moment for all that is past. Even the death-lament does not need to be voiced again.

Installed, they curl together in their bloodless icy nest, murmuring a little to each other, but finally still.

Outside, the snow begins to come down. It falls like a curtain. Then the winds take it. Then the night is full of the lashing of whips, and when the sun rises it is white as the snow itself, its flame very distant, giving nothing. The cave mouth is blocked up with snow. In the winter, it seems possible that never again will there be a summer in the world.

Behind the modest door of snow, hidden and secret, sleep is quiet as stars, dense as hardening resin. Feroluce and Rohise turn pure and pale in the amber, in the frigid nest, and the great wings lie like a curious articulated machinery that will not move. And the withered grass and the flowers are crystallised, until the snows shall melt.

At length, the sun deigns to come closer to the earth, and the miracle occurs. The snow shifts, crumbles, crashes off the mountains in rage. The waters hurry after the snow, the air is wrung and racked by splittings and splinterings, by rushes and booms. It is half a year, or it might be a hundred years, later.

Open now, the entry to the cave. Nothing emerges. Then, a flutter, a whisper. Something does emerge. One black feather, and caught in it, the petal of a flower, crumbling like dark charcoal and white, drifting away into the voids below. Gone. Vanished. It might never have been.

But there comes another time (half a year, a hundred years), when an adventurous traveller comes down from the mountains to the pocketed villages the other side of them. He is a swarthy cheerful fellow, you would not take him for herbalist or mystic, but he has in a pot a plant he found high up in the staring crags, which might after all contain anything or nothing. And he shows the plant, which is an unusual one, having slender, dark, and velvety leaves, and giving off a pleasant smell like vanilla. "See, the *Nona Mordica*," he says. "The Bite-Me-Not. The flower that repels vampires."

Then the villagers tell him an odd story, about a castle in another country, besieged by a huge flock, a menace of winged vampires, and how the Duke waited in vain for the magic bush that was in his garden, the Bite-Me-Not, to flower and save them all. But it seems there was a curse on this Duke, who on the very night his daughter was lost, had raped a serving woman, as he had raped others before. But this woman conceived. And bearing the fruit, or flower, of this rape, damaged her, so she lived only a year or two after it. The child grew up unknowing, and in the end betrayed her own father by running away to the vampires, leaving the Duke demoralised. And soon after he went mad, and himself stole out one night, and let the winged fiends into his castle, so all there perished.

"Now if only the bush had flowered in time, as your bush flowers, all would have been well," the villagers cry.

The traveller smiles. He in turn does not tell them of the heap of peculiar bones, like parts of eagles mingled with those of a woman and a man. Out of the bones, from the heart of them, the bush was rising, but the traveller untangled the roots of it with care; it looks sound enough now in its sturdy pot, all of it twining together. It seems as if two separate plants are growing from a single stem, one with blooms almost black, and one pink-flowered, like a young sunset.

"Flur de fur," says the traveller, beaming at the marvel, and his luck.

Fleur de feu. Oh flower of fire. That fire is not hate or fear, which makes flowers come, nor terror or anger or lust, it is love that is the fire of the Bite-Me-Not, love which cannot abandon, love which cannot harm. Love which never dies.

The Lost Art of Twilight

Thomas Ligotti

I

I have painted it, tried to at least. Oiled it, watercolored it, smeared it upon a mirror which I positioned to rekindle the glow of the real thing. And always in the abstract. Never actual sinking suns in spring, autumn, winter skies; never a sepia light descending over the trite horizon of a lake, not even the particular lake I like to view from the great terrace of my massive old mansion. But these *Twilights* of mine were not merely abstraction, which after all is just a matter of technique; a method for keeping out the riff-raff of the real world. Other painterly abstractionists may claim that nothing is represented by their canvasses, and probably nothing is: a streak of iodine red is just a streak of iodine red, a patch of flat black equals a patch of flat black. But pure color, pure light, pure lines and their rhythms, pure form in general all means much more than that. The others have only *seen* their dramas of shape and shade; I—and it is impossible to insist on this too strenuously—I have *been* there. And my twilight abstractions did in fact represent some reality, somewhere, sometime: a zone formed by palaces of soft and sullen color standing beside seas of scintillating pattern and beneath sadly radiant skies; a zone in which the visitor himself is transformed into a formal essence, a luminous presence, free of substance—a citizen of the abstract. And a zone (I cannot sufficiently amplify my despair on this point, so I will not try) that I will never know again.

Only a few weeks ago I was sitting out on the terrace, watching the early autumn sun droop into the above-mentioned lake, talking to Aunt T. Her heels clomped with a pleasing hollowness on drab flagstones. Silver-haired, she was attired in a gray suit, a big bow flopping up to her lower chins. In her left hand was a long envelope, neatly caesarianed, and in her right hand the letter it had contained, folded in sections like a triptych.

"They want to see you," she said, gesturing with the letter. "They want to come here."

"I don't believe it," I said and skeptically turned in my chair to watch the sunlight stretching in long cathedral-like aisles across the upper and lower levels of the lawn.

"If you would only read the letter," she insisted.

"It's in French, no? Can't read."

"Now that's not true, to judge by those books you're always stacking in the library."

"Those happen to be art books. I just look at the pictures."

"You like pictures, André?" she asked in her best matronly ironic tone. "I have a picture for you. Here it is: they *are* going to be allowed to come here and stay with us as long as they like. There's a family of them, two children and the letter also mentions an unmarried sister. They're travelling all the way from Aix-en-Provence to visit America, and while on their trip they want to see their only living blood relation here. Do you understand this picture? They know who you are and, more to the point, where you are."

"I'm surprised they would want to, since they're the ones—"

"No, they're not. They're from your *father's* side of the family. The Duvals," she explained. "They do know all about you but say," Aunt T. here consulted the letter for a moment, "that they are *sans préjugé.*"

"The generosity of such creatures freezes my blood. Phenomenal scum. Twenty years ago these people do what they did to my mother, and now they have the gall, the *gall*, to say they aren't prejudiced against *me.*"

Aunt T. gave me a warning hrumph to silence myself, for just then Rops walked out onto the terrace bearing a tray with a slender glass set upon it. I dubbed him Rops because he, as much as his artistic namesake, never failed to give me the charnel house creeps.

He cadavered over to Aunt T. and served her her afternoon cocktail.

"Thank you," she said, taking the glass of cloudy stuff.

"Anything for you, sir?" he asked, now holding the tray over his chest like a silver shield.

"Ever see me have a drink, Rops," I asked back. "Ever see me—"

"André, behave. That'll be all, thank you."

Rops left our sight in a few bony strides. "You can continue your rant now," said Aunt T. graciously.

"I'm through. You know how I feel," I replied and then looked away toward the lake, drinking in the dim mood of the twilight in the absence of normal refreshment.

"Yes, I do know how you feel, and you've always been wrong. You've always had these romantic ideas of how you and your mother, rest her soul, have been the victims of some monstrous injustice. But nothing is the way you like to think it is. They were not backward peasants who, we should say, *saved* your mother. They were wealthy, sophisticated members of her own family. And they were not superstitious, because what they believed about your mother was the truth."

"True or not," I argued, "they believed the unbelieveable—they acted on it—and that I call superstition. What reason could they possibly—"

"What *reason?* I have to say that at the time you were in no position to judge reasons, considering that we knew you only as a slight swelling inside your mother's body. But I was actually there. I saw the 'new friends' she had made, that 'aristocracy of blood,' as she called it, in contrast to her own people's hard-earned wealth. But I don't judge her, I never have. After all, she had just lost her husband—your father was a good man and it's a shame you never knew him—and then to be carrying his child, the child of a dead man. . . . She was frightened, confused, and she ran back to her family and her homeland. Who can blame her if she started acting irresponsibly. But it's a shame what happened, especially for your sake."

"You are indeed a comfort, *Auntie,*" I said with now regrettable sarcasm.

"Well, you have my sympathy whether you want it nor not. I think I've proven that over the years."

"Indeed you have," I agreed, and somewhat sincerely.

Aunt T. poured the last of her drink down her throat and a little drop she wasn't aware of dripped from the corner of her mouth, shining in the crepuscular radiance like a pearl.

"When your mother didn't come home one evening—I should say *morning*—everyone knew what had happened, but no one said anything. Contrary to your ideas about their superstitiousness, they actually could not bring themselves to believe the truth for some time."

"It was good of all of you to let me go on developing for a while, even as you were deciding how to best hunt my mother down."

"I will ignore that remark."

"I'm sure you will."

"We did not *hunt* her down, as you well know. That's another of your persecution fantasies. She came to us, now didn't she? Scratching at the windows in the night—"

"You can skip this part, I already—"

"—swelling full as the fullest moon. And that was strange, because you would actually have been considered a dangerously premature birth according to normal schedules; but when we followed your mother back to the mausoleum of the local church, where she lay during the daylights hours, she was carrying the full weight of her pregnancy. The priest was shocked to find what he had living, so to speak, in his own backyard. It was actually he, and not so much any of your mother's family, who thought we should not allow you to be brought into the world. And it was his hand that ultimately released your mother from the life of her new friends, and immediately afterward she began to deliver, right in the coffin in which she lay. The blood was terrible. If we did—"

"It's not necessary to—"

"—*hunt* down your mother, you should be thankful that I was among that party. I had to get you out of the country that very night, back to America. I—"

At that point she could see that I was no longer listening, was gazing with a distracted intensity on the pleasanter anecdotes of the setting sun. When she stopped talking and joined in the view, I said:

"Thank you, Aunt T., for that little bedtime story. I never tire of hearing it."

"I'm sorry, André, but I wanted to remind you of the truth."

"What can I say? I realize I owe you my life, such as it is."

"That's not what I mean. I mean the truth of what your mother become and what you now are."

"I am nothing. Completely harmless."

"That's why we must let the Duvals come and stay with us. To show them that the world has nothing to fear from you, because that's what I believe they're actually coming to see. That's the message they'll carry back to your family in France."

"You really think that's why they're coming?"

"I do. They could make quite a bit of trouble for you, for us."

I rose from my chair as the shadows of the failing twilight deepened. I went and stood next to Aunt T. against the stone balustrade of the terrace, and whispered:

"Then let them come."

II

I am an offspring of the dead. I am descended from the deceased. I am the progeny of phantoms. My ancestors are the illustrious multitude of the defunct, grand and innumerable. My lineage is longer than time. My name is written with embalming fluid in the book of death. A noble name is mine.

In the immediate family, the first to meet his maker was my own maker: he rests in the tomb of the unknown father. But while the man did manage to sire me, he breathed his last breath in this world before I drew my first. He was felled by a single stroke, his first and last. In those final moments, so I'm told, his erratic and subtle brainwaves made strange designs across the big green eye of the EEG monitor. The same doctor who told my mother that her husband was no longer among the living also informed her, on the very same day, that she was pregnant. Nor was this the only poignant coincidence in the lives of my parents. Both of them belonged to wealthy families from Aix-en-Provence in southern France. However, their first meeting took place not in the old country but in the new, at the American university they each happened to be attending. And so two neighbors crossed a cold ocean to come together in a mandatory science course. When they com-

pared notes on their common backgrounds, they knew it was
destiny at work. They fell in love with each other and with their
new homeland. The couple later moved into a rich and prestigious
suburb (which I will decline to mention by name or state, since I
still reside there and, for reasons that will eventually become apparent, must do so discreetly). For years the couple lived in con-
tentment, and then my immediate male forbear died just in time
for fatherhood, becoming the appropriate parent for his son-to-be.

Offspring of the dead.

But surely, one might protest, I was born of a living mother;
surely upon arrival in this world I turned and gazed into a pair of
glossy maternal eyes. Not so, as I think is evident from my earlier
conversation with dear Aunt T. Widowed and pregnant, my
mother had fled back to Aix, to the comfort of family estates and
secluded living. But more on this in a moment. Meanwhile I can
no longer suppress the urge to say a few things about my ancestral
hometown.

Aix-en-Provence, where I was born but never lived, has many
personal, though necessarily second-hand associations for me.
However, it is not just a connection between Aix and my own life
that maintains such a powerful grip on my imagination, a lifelong
idée fixe which actually has more to do with a few unrelated facts in
the history of the region. Two pieces of historical data, to be exact.
Separate centuries, indeed epochs, play host to these data, and
they likewise exist in entirely different realms of mood, worlds
apart in implication. Nevertheless, from a certain point of view
they can impress one as inseparable opposites. The first one is as
follows: in the seventeenth century there occurred the spiritual
possession by divers demons of the nuns belonging to the Ursu-
line convent at Aix. Excommunication was soon in coming for the
tragic sisters, who had been seduced into assorted blasphemies by
the like of Grésil, Sonnillon, and Vérin. De Plancy's *Dictionnaire
infernal* respectively characterizes these demons, in the words of an
unknown translator, as "the one who glistens horribly like a rainbow of insects; the one who quivers in a horrible manner; and the
one who moves with a particular creeping motion." There also
exist engravings of these kinetically and chromatically weird beings, unfortunately static and in black and white. Can you believe
it? What people are these—so stupid and profound—that they
could devote themselves to such nonsense? Who can fathom the

science of superstition? (For, as an evil poet once scribbled, super-stition is the reservoir of all truths.) This, then, is one side of my imaginary Aix. The other side, and the second historical datum I offer, is simply the birth in 1839 of Aix's most prominent citizen: Cézanne. His figure haunts the landscape of my brain, wandering about the Provençal countryside in search of his pretty pictures.

These, then, are the two aspects of my personal Aix. Together they fuse into a single image, as grotesque and coherent as a pan-theon of gargoyles amid the splendor of a medieval church.

Such was the world to which my mother reëmigrated some decades ago, this Notre Dame world of horror and beauty. It's no wonder that she was seduced into the society of those beautiful strangers, who promised her an escape from the world of mortal-ity where shock and suffering had taken over, driving her into exile. I understood from Aunt T. that it all began at a summer party on the estate grounds of Ambroise and Paulette Valraux. The Enchanted Wood, as this place was known to the *hautes classes* in the vicinity. The evening of the party was as perfectly temperate as the atmosphere of dreams, which one rarely notices to be either sultry or frigid. Lanterns were hung high up in the lindens, guide-lights leading to a heard-about heaven. A band played.

It was a mixed crowd at the party. And as usual there were present a few persons whom nobody seemed to know, exotic strangers whose elegance was their invitation. Aunt T. did not pay much attention to them at the time, and her account is rather sketchy. One of them danced with my mother, having no trouble coaxing the widow out of social retirement. Another with labyrin-thine eyes whispered to her by the trees. Alliances were formed that night, promises made. Afterward my mother began going out on her own to rendezvous after sundown. Then she stopped com-ing home. Térèse—nurse, confidante, and personal maid whom my mother had brought back with her from America—was hurt and confused by the cold snubs she had lately received from her mistress. My mother's family was elaborately reticent about the meaning of her recent behavior. ("And in her condition, *mon Dieu!*") Nobody knew what measures to take. Then some of the servants reported seeing a pale, pregnant woman lurking outside the house after dark.

Finally a priest was taken into the family's confidence. He sug-gested a course of action which no one questioned, not even

Térèse. They lay in wait for my mother, righteous soul-hunters.
They followed her drifting form as it returned to the mausoleum
when daybreak was imminent. They removed the great stone lid
of the sarcophagus and found her inside. *"Diabolique,"* one of them
exclaimed. There was some question about how many times and
in what places she should be impaled. In the end they pinned her
heart with a single spike to the velvet bed on which she lay. But
what to do about the child? What would it be like? A holy soldier
of the living or a monster of the dead. (Neither, you fools!) Fortunately or unfortunately, I've never been sure which, Térèse was
with them and rendered their speculations academic. Reaching
into the bloodied matrix, she helped me to be born. I was now heir
to the family fortune, and Térèse took me back to America. She
was extremely resourceful in this regard, arranging with a sympathetic and avaricious lawyer to become the trustee of my estate.
This required a little magic act with identities. It required that
Térèse, for reasons of her own which I've never questioned, be
promoted from my mother's maid to her posthumous sister. And
so my Aunt T. was christened, born in the same year as I.

Naturally all this leads to the story of my life, which has no
more life in it than story. It's not for the cinema, it is not for novels;
it wouldn't even fill out a single lyric of modest length. It might
make a piece of modern music: a slow, throbbing drone like the
lethargic pumping of a premature heart. Best of all, though, would
be the depiction of my life story as an abstract painting: a twilight
world, indistinct around the edges and without center or focus; a
bridge without banks, tunnel without openings; a crepuscular existence pure and simple. No heaven or hell, only a quiet haven
between life's hysteria and death's tenacious darkness. (And you
know, what I most loved about Twilight is the sense, as one looks
down the dimming west, not that it is some fleeting transitional
moment, but that there's actually nothing before or after it: *that
that's all there is*.) My life never had a beginning, so naturally I
thought it would never end. Naturally, I was wrong.

Well, and what was the answer to those questions hastily put by
the monsters who stalked my mother? Was my nature to be souled
humanness or soulless vampirism? The answer: none of the above.
I existed between two worlds and had little claim upon the assets
or liabilities of either. Neither living nor dead, unalive or undead,
not having anything to do with tedious polarities, such tiresome

opposites, which ultimately are no more different from each other than a pair of imbecilic monozygotes. I said no to life and death. No, Mr. Springbud. No, Mr. Worm. Without ever saying hello or goodbye, I merely avoided their company, scorned their gaudy invitations.

Of course, in the beginning Aunt T. tried to care for me as if I were a normal child. (Incidentally, I can perfectly recall every moment of my life from birth, for my existence took the form of one seamless moment, without forgettable yesterdays or expectant tomorrows). She tried to give me normal food, which I always regurgitated. Later she prepared for me a sort of puréed meat, which I ingested and digested, though it never became a habit. And I never asked her what was actually in that preparation, for Aunt T. wasn't afraid to use money, and I knew what money could buy in the way of unusual food for an unusual infant. I suppose I did become accustomed to similar nourishment while growing within my mother's womb, feeding on a potpourri of blood types contributed by the citizens of Aix. But my appetite was never very strong for physical food.

Stronger by far was my hunger for a kind of transcendental fare, a feasting of the mind and soul: the astral banquet of Art. There I fed. And I had quite a few master chefs to plan the menu. Though we lived in exile from the world, Aunt T. did not overlook my education. For purposes of appearance and legality, I have earned diplomas from some of the finest private schools in the world. (These, too, money can buy.) But my real education was even more private than that. Tutorial geniuses were well paid to visit our home, only too glad to teach an invalid child of nonetheless exceptional promise.

Through personal instruction I scanned the arts and sciences. yes, I learned to quote my French poets,

> Gaunt immortality in black and gold,
> Wreathed consoler hideous to behold.
> The beautiful lie of a mother's womb,
> The pious trick—for it is the tomb!

but mostly in translation, for something kept me from ever attaining more than a beginner's facility in that foreign tongue. I did master, however, the complete grammar, every dialect and idiom of the French *eye*. I could read the inner world of Redon (who was almost born an American)—his *grand isolé* paradise of black. I could effortlessly comprehend the outer world of Manet and the Impressionists—the secret language of light. And I could decipher the impossible worlds of the surrealists—those twisted arcades where brilliant shadows are sewn to the rotting flesh of rainbows.

I remember in particular a man by the name of Raymond, who taught me the rudimentary skills of the artist in oils. I recollect vividly showing him a study I had done of that sacred phenomenon I witnessed each sundown. Most of all I recall the look in his eyes, as if they beheld the rising of a curtain upon some terribly involved outrage. He abstractedly adjusted his delicate spectacles, wobbling them around on the bridge of his nose. His gaze shifted from the canvas to me and back again. His only comment was: "The shapes, the colors are not supposed to lose themselves that way. Something . . . no, impossible." Then he asked to be permitted use of the bathroom facilities. At first I thought this gesture was meant as a symbolic appraisal of my work. But he was quite in earnest and all I could do was give him directions to the nearest chamber of convenience in a voice of equal seriousness. He walked out of the room with the first two fingers of his right hand pressing upon the pulse in his left wrist. And he never came back.

Such is a thumbnail sketch of my half-toned existence: twilight after twilight after twilight. And in all that blur of time I but occasionally, and then briefly, wondered if I too possessed the same potential for immortality as my undead mother before her life was aborted and I was born. It is not a question that really bothers one who exists beyond, below, above, between—triumphantly *outside*—the clashing worlds of human fathers and enchanted mothers.

I did wonder, though, how I would explain, that is *conceal*, my unnatural mode of being from my visiting relatives. Despite the hostility I showed toward them in front of Aunt T., I actually desired that they should take a good report of me back to the real world, if only to keep it away from my own world in the future. For days previous to their arrival, I came to think of myself as a certain stock character in Gothic stories: the stranger in a strange castle of a house, that shadowy figure whom the hero travels over long distances to encounter, a dark soul hiding his horrors. In short, a medieval geek perpetrating strange deeds in secret sanctums. I expected they would soon have the proper image of me as all impotence and no impetus. And that would be that.

But never did I anticipate being called upon to face the almost forgotten realities of vampirism—the taint beneath the paint of the family portrait.

III

The Duval family, and unmarried sister, were arriving on a night flight which we would meet at the airport. Aunt T. thought this would suit me fine, considering my tendency to sleep most of the day and arise with the setting sun. But at the last minute I suffered an acute seizure of stage fright. "The *crowds*," I appealed to Aunt T. She knew that crowds were the world's most powerful talisman against me, as if it had needed any at all. She understood that I would not be able to serve on the welcoming committee, and Rops' younger brother Gerald, a good seventy-five if he was a day, drove her to the airport alone. Yes, I promised Aunt T., I would be sociable and come out to meet everyone as soon as I saw the lights of the big black car floating up our private drive.

But I wasn't and I didn't. I took to my room and drowsed before a television with the sound turned off. As the colors danced in the dark, I submitted more and more to an anti-social sleepiness. Finally I instructed Rops, by way of the estate-wide intercom, to inform Aunt T. and company that I wasn't feeling very well and needed to rest. This, I figured, would be in keeping with the façade of a harmless valetudinarian, and a perfectly normal one at that. A night-sleeper. Very good, I could hear them saying to their souls. And then, I swear, I actually turned off the television and slept real sleep in real darkness.

But things became less real at some point deep into the night. I must have left the intercom open, for I heard little metallic voices emanating from that little metallic square on my bedroom wall. In my state of quasi-somnolence it never occurred to me that I could simply get out of bed and make the voices go away by switching off that terrible box. And terrible it indeed seemed. The voices spoke a foreign language, but it wasn't French, as one might have suspected. Something more foreign than that. Perhaps a cross between a madman talking in his sleep and the sonar screech of a bat. I heard the voices chittering and chattering with each other until I fell soundly asleep once more. And their dialogue had ended before I awoke, for the first time in my life, to the bright eyes of morning.

The house was quiet. Even the servants seemed to have duties that kept them soundless and invisible. I took advantage of my wakefulness at that early hour and prowled unnoticed about the old place, figuring everyone else was still in bed after their long and somewhat noisy night. The four rooms Aunt T. had set aside for our guests all had their big panelled doors closed: a room for the mama and papa, two others close by for the kids, and a chilly chamber at the end of the hall for the maiden sister. I paused a moment outside each room and listened for the revealing songs of slumber, hoping to know my relations better by their snores and whistles and monosyllables grunted between breaths. But they made none of the usual racket. They hardly made any sounds at all, though they echoed one another in making a certain noise that seemed to issue from the same cavity. It was a kind of weird wheeze, a panting from the back of the throat, the hacking of a tubercular demon. Having had an earful of strange cacophonies the night before, I soon abandoned my eavesdropping without regret.

I spent the day in the library, whose high windows I noticed were designed to allow a maximum of natural reading light. However, I drew the drapes on them and kept to the shadows, finding morning sunshine not everything it was said to be. But it was difficult to get much reading done. Any moment I expected to hear foreign footsteps descending the doubled-winged staircase, crossing the black and white marble chessboard of the front hall, taking over the house. Nevertheless, despite my expectations, and to my increasing sense of unease, the family never appeared.

Twilight came and still no mama and papa, no sleepy-eyed son or daughter, no demure sister remarking with atonishment at the inordinate length of her beauty sleep. And no Aunt T., either. They must've had quite a time the night before, I thought. But I didn't mind being alone with the twilight. I undraped the three west windows, each of them a canvas depicting the same scene in the sky. My private *Salon d' Automne.*

It was an unusual sunset. Having sat behind opaque drapery all day, I had not realized that a storm was pushing in and that much of the sky was the precise shade of old suits of armor one finds in museums. At the same time, patches of brilliance engaged in a territorial dispute with the oncoming onyx of the storm. Light and darkness mingled in strange ways both above and below. Shadows and sunshine washed together; streaking the landscape with an unearthly study of glare and gloom. Bright clouds and black folded into each other in a no-man's land of the sky. The autumn trees took on the appearance of sculptures formed in a dream, their leaden-colored trunks and branches and iron-red leaves all locked in an infinite and unliving moment, unnaturally timeless. The gray lake slowly tossed and tumbled in a dead sleep, nudging unconsciously against its breakwall of numb stone. A scene of contradiction and ambivalence, a tragicomedic haze over all. A land of perfect twilight.

I was in exaltation: finally the twilight had come down to earth, and me. I had to go out into this rare atmosphere, I had no choice. I left the house and walked to the lake and stood on the slope of stiff grass which led down to it. I gazed up through the trees at the opposing tones of the sky. I kept my hands in my pockets and touched nothing, except with my eyes.

Not until an hour or more had elapsed did I think of returning home. It was dark by then, though I don't recall the passing of the twilight into evening, for twilight suffers no ostentatious finales. There were no stars visible, the storm clouds having moved in and wrapped up the sky. They began sending out tentative drops of rain. Thunder mumbled above and I was forced back to the house, cheated once again by the night.

In the front hall I called out names in the form of questions. Aunt T.? Rops? Gerald? M. Duval? Madame? Everything was silence. Where was everyone? I wondered. They couldn't still be asleep. I passed from room to room and found no signs of occupation. A day of dust was upon all surfaces. Where were the domestics? At last I opened the double doors to the dining room. Was I late for the supper Aunt T. had planned to honor our visiting family?

It appeared so. But if Aunt T. sometimes had me consume the forbidden fruit of flesh and blood, it was never directly from the branches, never the sap taken warm from the tree of life itself. Yet here were spread the remains of just such a feast. It was the ravaged body of Aunt T., though they'd barely left enough on her bones for identification. The thick white linen was clotted like an unwrapped bandage. "Rops!" I shouted. "Gerald, somebody!" But I knew the servants were no longer in the house, that I was alone.

Not quite alone, of course. This soon became apparent to my twilight brain as it dipped its way into total darkness. I was in the company of five black shapes which stuck to the walls and soon began flowing along their surface. One of them detached itself and moved toward me, a weightless mass which felt icy when I tried to sweep it away and put my hand right through the thing. Another followed, unhinging itself from a doorway where it hung down. A third left a blanched scar upon the wallpaper where it clung like a slug, pushing itself off to join the attack. Then came the others descending from the ceiling, dropping onto me as I stumbled in circles and flailed my arms. I ran from the room but the things had me closely surrounded. They guided my flight, heading me down hallways and up staircases. Finally they cornered me in a small room, a dusty little place I had not been in for years. Colored animals frolicked upon the walls, blue bears and yellow rabbits. Miniature furniture was draped with graying sheets. I hid beneath a tiny elevated crib with ivory bars. But they found me and closed in.

They were not driven by hunger, for they had already feasted. They were not frenzied with a murderer's bloodlust, for they were cautious and methodical. This was simply a family reunion, a sentimental gathering. Now I understood how the Duvals could afford to be *sans préjugé*. They were worse than I, who was only a half-breed, hybrid, a mere mulatto of the soul: neither a blood-warm human nor a blood-drawing devil. But they—who came from an Aix on the map—were the purebreds of the family.

And they drained my body dry.

IV

When I regained awareness once more, it was still dark and there was a great deal of dust in my throat. Not actually dust, of course, but a strange dryness I had never before experienced. And there was another new experience: hunger. I felt as if there were a chasm of infinite depth within me, a great abyss which

needed to be filled—flooded with oceans of blood. I was one of
them now, reborn into a hungry death. Everything I had shunned
in my impossible, blasphemous ambition to avoid living and dying, I now had become. A sallow, ravenous thing. A beast with a
hundred stirring hungers. André of the graveyards.

The five of them had each drunk from my body by way of five
separate fountains. But the wounds had nearly sealed by the time I
awoke in the blackness, owing to the miraculous healing capabilities of the dead. The upper floors were all in shadow now, and I
made my way toward the light coming from downstairs. An im-
pressionistic glow illuminated the wooden banister at the top of
the stairway, where I emerged from the darkness of the second
floor, and this sight inspired in me a terrible ache of emotion I'd
never known before: a feeling of loss, though of nothing I could
specifically name, as if somehow the deprivation lay in my future.

As I descended the stairs I saw that they were already waiting to
meet me, standing silently upon the black and white squares of the
front hall. Papa the king, mama the queen, the boy a knight, the
girl a dark little pawn, and a bitchy maiden bishop standing behind. And now they had my house, my castle, to complete the
pieces on their side. On mine there was nothing.

"Devils," I screamed, leaning hard upon the staircase rail. "Devils," I repeated, but they still appeared horribly undistressed, perhaps uncomprehending of my outburst. "*Diables*," I reiterated in
their own loathsome tongue.

But neither was French their true language, as I found out when
they began speaking among themselves. I covered my ears, trying
to smother their voices. They had a language all their own, a style
of speech well-suited to dead vocal organs. The words were
breathless, shapeless rattlings in the back of their throats, parched
scrapings at the mausoleum portal. Arid gasps and dry gurgles
were their dialects. These grating intonations were especially disturbing as they emanated from the mouths of things that had at
least the form of human beings. But worst of all was my realization
that I understood perfectly well what they were saying.

The boy stepped forward, pointing at me while looking back
and speaking to his father. It was the opinion of this wine-eyed
and rose-lipped youth that I should have suffered the same end as
Aunt T. With an authoratative impatience the father told the boy
that I was to serve as a sort of tour guide through this strange new

land, a native who could keep them out of such difficulties as
foreign visitors sometimes get into. Besides, he grotesquely concluded, *I was one of the family.* The boy was incensed and coughed
out an incredibly foul characterization of his father. The things he
said could only have been conveyed by that queer hacking patois,
which suggested feelings and relationships of a nature incomprehensible outside of the world it mirrors with disgusting perfection.
It is the discourse of hell on the subject of sin.

An argument ensued, and the father's composure turned to an
infernal rage. He finally subdued his son with bizarre threats that
have no counterparts in the language of ordinary malevolence.
After the boy was silenced he turned to his aunt, seemingly for
comfort. This woman of chalky cheeks and sunken eyes touched
the boy's shoulder and easily drew him toward her with a single
finger, guiding his body as if it were a balloon, weightless and toy-
like. They spoke in sullen whispers, using a personal form of address that hinted at a long-standing and unthinkable allegiance
between them.

Apparently aroused by this scene, the daughter now stepped
forward and used this same mode of address to get my attention.
Her mother abruptly gagged out a single syllable at her. What she
called her daughter might possibly be imagined, but only with
reference to the lowliest sectors of the human world. Their own
words, their choking rasps, carried the dissonant overtones of another world altogether. Each perverse utterance was a rioting opera of evil, a choir shrieking psalms of intricate blasphemy and
enigmatic lust.

"I will not become one of you," I *thought* I screamed at them. But
the sound of my voice was already so much like theirs that the
words had exactly the opposite meaning I intended. The family
suddenly ceased bickering among themselves. My outburst had
consolidated them. Each mouth, cluttered with uneven teeth like a
village cemetery over-crowded with battered gravestones, opened
and smiled. The expression on their faces told me something about
my own. They could see my growing hunger, see deep down into
the dusty catacomb of my throat which cried out to be annointed
with bloody nourishment. They knew my weakness.

Yes, they could stay in my house. (*Famished.*)

Yes, I could make arrangements to cover up the disappearance of the servants, for I am a wealthy man and know what money can buy. (*Please, my family, I'm famished.*)

Yes, their safety could be insured and their permanent asylum perfectly feasible. (*Please, I'm famishing to dust.*)

Yes, yes, yes. I agreed to everything; everything would be taken care of. (*To dust!*)

But first I begged them, for heaven's sake, to let me go out into the night.

Night, night, night, night. Night, night, night.

Now twilight is an alarm, a noxious tocsin which rouses me to an endless eve. There is a sound in my new language for that transitory time of day preceding the dark hours. The sound clusters together curious shades of meaning and shadowy impressions, none of which belong to my former conception of an abstract paradise: the true garden of unearthly delights. The new twilight is a violater, desecrator, stealthy graverobber; death-bell, life-knell, curtain-raiser; banshee, siren, howling she-wolf. And the old twilight is dead. I am even learning to despise it, just as I am learning to love my eternal life and eternal death. Nevertheless, I wish them well who would attempt to destroy my precarious immortality, for my rebirth has taught me the torment of beginnings, while the idea of endings has assumed in my thoughts a tranquil significance. And I cannot deny those who would avenge the exsanguinated souls of my past and future. Yes, past and future. Endings and beginnings. In brief, Time now exists, measured like a perpetual holiday consisting only of midnight revels. I once had an old family from an old world, and now I have new ones. A new life, a new world. And this world is no longer one where I can languidly gaze upon rosy sunsets, but another in which I must fiercely draw a full-bodied blood from the night.

Night . . . after night . . . after night.

Blood Disease

❧❦❧

Patrick McGrath

This is probably how it happened: William Clack-Herman, the anthropologist (popularly known as "Congo Bill") was doing field research on the kinship systems of the pygmies of the equatorial rain forest. One afternoon he was sitting outside his hut of mongongo leaves, writing up his notes, when a mosquito bit him. It is only the female that makes the blood meal, for she needs it to boost her egg output. From the thorny tip of her mouthparts she unsheathed a slender stylus, and having sliced neatly through Bill's skin tissue, pierced a tiny blood vessel. Bill noticed nothing. Two powerful pumps in the insect's head began to draw off blood while simultaneously hundreds of tiny parasites were discharged into his bloodstream. Within half-an-hour, when the mosquito had long since returned to the water, the parasites were safely established in his liver. For six days they multiplied, asexually, and then on the morning of the seventh they burst out and invaded the red blood cells. Within a relatively short period of time Congo Bill was exhibiting all the classical symptoms of malaria. He was delirious; he suffered from chills, vomiting, and diarrhea; and his spleen was dangerously enlarged. He was also alone —the pygmies had deserted him, had melted deeper into the gloom of the rain forest. An essentially nomadic people, they could not wait for Bill to recover, nor could they take him with them. So there he lay, shivering and feverish by turns, on a narrow camp bed in a dark hut in the depths of a chartless jungle.

How he made it back is a fascinating story, but not immediately relevant to the events that concern us here. Make it back he did; but the Congo Bill who docked at Southampton one morning in the summer of 1934 was not the vigorous young man who'd left for Africa a year previously. He was haggard and thin now, and forced to walk with a stick. His flesh was discolored, and his fingers trembled constantly. He looked, in short, like a man who was dying. When at last he stepped gingerly down the gangway, one steward was at his elbow and another close behind, carrying a large bamboo cage. Huddled in the corner of the cage was a small black-and-white Colobus monkey that the anthropologist had befriended before leaving the Congo for the last time. He intended to give it to his son, Frank.

Virginia Clack-Herman was considerably shocked at her husband's frailty; and the fact that he could speak only in a hoarse whisper certainly added pathos to their reunion. Frank, then aged nine, did not recognize his father, and accepted with some unease the monkey; and then the three of them, with the monkey, made their way very slowly through the customs shed and out to the car. There were at the time no strict regulations regarding the quarantining of monkeys.

The journey from Southampton was uneventful. Virginia drove, and Bill sat beside her with a rug over his knees and slept most of the way. Frank sat in the back; the bamboo cage was placed on the seat beside him, and the little monkey sat hunkered inside it, alert but unmoving. From time to time the boy's eyes were drawn to the monkey's; they were both, clearly, perplexed and slightly alarmed. Congo Bill muttered as he dozed, and Virginia, stony-faced, kept her eyes on the road.

It was a warm day, and in the sunshine of the late afternoon the cornfields of Berkshire rippled about them like a golden sea; and then, just as Virginia began to wonder where they would break the journey, from out of this sea heaved a big inn, Tudor in construction, with steeply gabled roofs and black beams crisscrossed on the white-plastered walls beneath the eaves. This was the Blue Bat; since destroyed by fire, in the early Thirties it boasted good beds, a fine kitchen, and an extensive cellar.

Virginia pulled off the main road and into the forecourt of the inn. Servants appeared; suitcases were carried in and the car taken round to the garages. Some minutes later, a cream-colored roadster pulled in beside it. The owner of this car was Ronald Dexter. He was traveling with his valet, an old man called Clutch.

Ronald Dexter was a gentleman of independent means who had never had to work a day in his life. He was an elegant, witty chap with sleek black hair, parted high, brushed straight back from his forehead, and gleaming with oil. Half-an-hour later he stepped out of his bathroom and found Clutch laying out his evening clothes. He slipped into a dressing gown, sank into an armchair, lit his pipe—and sighed, for Clutch was running a small silver crucifix with great care along the seams of his garments. A curious-looking man, Clutch, he had a remarkable head, disproportionately large for his body and completely hairless. The skull was a perfect dome, and the tight-stretched skin of it an almost translucent shade of yellowy-brown finely engraved with subcutaneous blue-black veins. The overall impression he gave was of a monstrous fetus, or else some type of prehistoric man, a Neanderthal perhaps, in whom the millennia had deposited deep strains of racial wisdom—though he wore, of course, the tailcoat and gray pin-striped trousers of his profession. He was stooped and frail now, and Ronald had long since given up interfering with the bizarre superstitions he practiced. When he was finished, he tucked the crucifix into an inside pocket and turned, nodding, to his master.

"Do you imagine, Clutch," said Ronald, "that I shall be set upon by vampires?"

"One cannot be too careful," replied the old man. "We are not in London, sir."

"No indeed," said Ronald, as the put-put-put of a tractor came drifting across the cornfields. "This is wild country."

"Will there be anything else, sir?"

Ronald told him there was nothing else, and Clutch left the room, closing the door softly behind him. At precisely the same instant, just down the corridor, Virginia Clack-Herman, who was a tall, spirited woman with a rich laugh and scarlet-painted fingernails, was sitting before her mirror clad only in stockings and slip, the latter a silky, sleeveless undergarment with thin shoulder straps and a delicate border of patterned lacework at the breast. A cigarette burned in the ashtray beside her, its tendril of smoke coiling away through casement windows thrown open to the warmth of the early evening. She was plucking her eyebrows with a pair of silver tweezers, and in the bathroom that connected their rooms she could hear her husband shuffling about and talking to himself. With her head close to the glass, the fingers of her left hand splayed upon her forehead, she clamped the twin pincers about a hair. Her lips were parted, her teeth locked; all at once she plucked out the hair; her eyes fired up and a single tear started from the left one. Simultaneously, Congo Bill dropped his hairbrushes, and as they bounced on the tiles Virginia cast a glance at the bathroom door. She turned back to the mirror and prepared to pluck a second hair. Bill's mumble rose and fell like the distant drone of public prayer. Oh, to come back to her so utterly ruined, like one of the walking dead! Out came another hair; the eyebrows arched thin as filaments, flaring a fraction as they neared the nose. Satisfied, she dabbed at her left eye with a small handkerchief and then, still facing the glass, she closed her eyes and clenched her fists and sat rigidly for a moment in an attitude of bitter mortification. But when Congo Bill came in, several minutes later, with his shirt cuffs flapping pathetically about his wrists and asked her to fasten his links, she displayed only warm concern. "Of course, darling," she murmured, as she rose from her dressing table and pecked his cheek, leaving a very light impression of red lips upon the yellowing skin.

"I wonder," whispered Congo Bill, "how that monkey's doing."

In point of fact the monkey was not doing at all well. Even as his father asked the question, young Frank had his face pressed flush to the bamboo cage, in a corner of which the monkey lay curled up and very still. "Are you sick?" he whispered. He inserted a finger through the bars. "Little monkey," he cooed, poking it. There was no response. Frank straightened up and turned away from the cage with his lips pressed tight together. From the public bar below came a sudden gust of laughter. He opened the door of the cage, reached in, and retrieved the monkey. It was dead. He laid its little head against his shoulder and stroked the matted, scurfy fur for a moment. A flea hopped onto his wrist and bit him. He opened a drawer and took out the sheet of tissue paper lining it; in this he wrapped the little corpse, then tucked it down the front of his shirt, crossed the bedroom, and opened the door. The corridor was deserted, and he stepped out.

*   *   *

Ronald Dexter had already ordered when the door of the Blue
Bat's shadowy, wood-paneled dining room swung slowly open
and an attractive woman entered with a shuffling figure whose
evening clothes hung like shrouds upon his wasted body. Ronald,
who hated to dine alone, assumed they were father and daughter,
and wondered if he could tempt them to join him. There were no
other guests in the dining room; in fact, there were no other guests
in the Blue Bat at all.

"Excuse me," he said, rising to his feet with a charming smile.
"Good lord! Virginia!"

Bill and Virginia paused, turned, and scrutinized him. "Ronald!" cried Virginia at last. "Ronald Dexter! Darling, you remember Ronald Dexter?"

Congo Bill did not remember Ronald Dexter, with whom Virginia had been friendly before her marriage. The two were in fact
very distantly related, on her mother's side, and in the few moments of theater that followed, Virginia recapped the rather tenu-
ous blood relationship they shared. Congo Bill participated mini-
mally in all this, his appetite for "extraordinary coincidences"
much dampened by the malaria. Ronald was altogether delighted,
and his pleasure was shot through with an undeniable charge of
sexual excitement—for despite their consanguinity the two were
instantly, and strongly, attracted to each other.

There was no question now but that they must eat together, and
so, in a flurry of small talk, and continuing expressions of pleasure
that they should meet again in such odd circumstances, they sat
down. Behind Congo Bill's chair the empty fireplace was hidden
from view by a low woven screen, and above the mantelpiece the
eyes of a large stag's head with sixteen-pointed antlers glittered
glassily in the gloom of the encroaching dusk. Food arrived, and
wine, and Ronald proposed a toast to homecomings and reunions.
Congo Bill's hand trembled as he lifted a glass of claret to his
bloodless lips. They drank, and there followed a brief, slightly
uncomfortable silence. Ronald turned to Congo Bill, fishing for a
conversational gambit. "See much cricket in Africa?" he said.

"None at all," whispered Congo Bill, dabbing his lips with a
starched white napkin and staining it with wine.

"I don't suppose they have much time for cricket, do they darling?" said Virginia, brightly, "what with all the hunting and gath-

ering they have to do." She turned to Ronald. "They're quite primitive, you know; practically living in the Stone Age."

"That must have been refreshing," said Ronald. "One grows so weary of decency and good manners, don't you agree, Virginia? Don't you sometimes wish we could indulge our impulses with unrestrained spontaneity, like savages?" His eyes flashed in the candlelight; Virginia took his meaning all too clearly.

"Oh, but we must have manners," she said; "otherwise we'll return to a state of nature, and I don't think we'd do terribly well at it."

"Bill would," said Ronald. "He can cope in jungles."

"You must be mad!" cried Virginia. "Just look at the state of him! I'm sorry, darling," she added, laying slender, red-nailed fingers on Congo Bill's bony wrist. "But you must admit, equatorial Africa did get the better of you this time."

"Malaria," began Congo Bill; but Ronald cut him short. "On the other hand," he reflected, "I suppose even the savages have manners, don't they? Rather different from ours, of course, but the same principle—which wife you sleep with tonight, who gets the best bit of the elephant—"

"Pygmies," whispered Congo Bill, but Ronald had not finished. "Manners are what distinguish us from the animals," he said, "so I suppose the more of them we have the better. What?"

Virginia laughed aloud at this. She opened her mouth and gave full, free tongue to an unrestrained peal of mirth that rang like clashing bells through that dusk-laden dining room. How lovely she was! thought Ronald. Exquisitely made up, perfectly at ease. Her dress was of dead-white satin and cut extremely low. She was wearing a rope of pearls; her face was as white as her pearls, and her lips a vivid scarlet. Quite spontaneously, as her laughter subsided, she leaned across the table and pressed Ronald's hand. At the touch of her fingers his blood turned hot and rapid. He promptly suggested that they take their brandy in the saloon bar. Virginia agreed, rose gracefully, and linking one arm in her husband's and the other in Ronald's, shuffled them off toward the door.

Clutch, meanwhile, having left his master's room, frowning, uneasy, conscious of some subtly malignant influence at work in the inn, had made his way downstairs and into the public bar. He took a seat at a small table in the corner and nursed a bottle of Guinness. There were perhaps twenty people gathered in the bar—local farm laborers they appeared, fat, sallow people, many with a yellowish tinge to their pallor. They were clustered about a wooden trapdoor in the center of the flagged floor, a trapdoor which stood upright on its hinges, a chain on either side stretched taut to hooks in the opening. The ceiling was low, and spanned by thick black beams, and though the air was thick with tobacco smoke a rising moon was visible through the uncurtained window. And then a weak and ragged cheer erupted as from the cellar beneath appeared the head of the landlord of the Blue Bat, Kevin Pander, a young man but, like his customers, very fat, and pale, and sallow-skinned. Wheezing badly, he ascended the cellar stairs with a hogshead of ale on one shoulder and a wooden crate containing two dozen bottles of beer dangling, clinking, from his white and hamlike palm. His wrists and ankles were bagged and swollen with accumulated body fluids, but he came up like a god, an asthmatic Bacchus ascending from the netherworld, and paused, breathing heavily, at the top of the steps. Then he kicked the trapdoor down behind him and it slammed shut with a great bang. Congo Bill, sunk in a black leather armchair in the saloon bar, sat up in considerable distress. "Darling, what is it?" said Virginia.

"Must go up," he whispered. "The noise . . ." Clearly, the sounds from the public bar had awakened some African memory, a memory profoundly disturbing to the fragile nervous system of the debilitated anthropologist. Virginia, glancing at Ronald, helped her husband to his feet and led him off toward the stairs. At precisely the same instant, Clutch realized with a thrill of horror what was wrong with the people in the public bar: pernicious anemia.

Frank tiptoed out of his bedroom with the wrapped dead monkey stuffed down his shirt. He did not make for the main staircase, for he was quite sure that his parents would veto the ceremony that he had decided privately to conduct. Instead he went to the other end of the corridor, to a door with a large key protruding from the lock. He turned the key and pushed open the door, and found himself on a dusty, uncarpeted back stairway. A small high window filmed over with cobwebs admitted what dim light was still to be had from the day. He crossed the landing and began to descend the stairs, which were steep, narrow, and, in the gloom, quite treacherous. Reaching the lower floor, he found a long passage at the far end of which stood another door. But barely had he begun to advance along the passage when he heard footsteps on the stairs he had just descended. He stood for a moment frozen in an agony of terrified indecision. As luck would have it, the wall of the passage was not entirely without a place of concealment: there was a shallow, rounded depression, no more than two feet high and two feet deep, quite close to where he was standing. He rapidly squeezed himself into this depression and huddled there like a fetus in a womb, with the dead monkey tucked in his lap like a second fetus, a fetus of the second order. Thus he waited as the descending step grew louder on the stairs.

It reached the bottom and paused. It was like no ordinary footstep; rather, a slow, heavy clump-clump-clump. To the small boy crouched in his womblike hiding hole, with his little heart hammering fit to burst, it was a very terrible sound indeed. It began to advance along the passage. Clump-clump-clump. Closer and closer. Eyes wide, fists clenched, Frank waited. He needed to go to the bathroom very badly. Clump-clump. Go past! Hurry! screamed a voice in the boy's head. Clump. It stopped. Frank glanced sideways in terror. He saw an orthopedic boot, an ugly big black one with a pair of metal braces ascending either side of a slim white ankle to a stout belt buckled halfway up the calf. And then a head, upside down, dropped into view, its red hair fanning out in waves upon the dusty boards. "What are you doing in there?" it said from an upside-down mouth.

"I'm hiding," said Frank.

"What from?"

"You."

Late that night, when Congo Bill lay heavily sedated in sleep, and the moon hung suspended like a silver ball over the black bulk of the Blue Bat, and a susurrus of night breezes whispered through the palely gleaming cornfields like a ghost, Ronald Dexter, in silk pajamas, rustled softly along the corridor and tapped on Virginia's door. Farther along the corridor, in the deep shadows, another door creaked open just a crack; it was Frank's. "Come," came a voice, and Ronald slipped into Virginia's room. Frank frowned, and then tiptoed away in the opposite direction, to the door at the end of the corridor. He carried in his trouser pocket the large key that opened that door. A moment later he was on the back stairs, and lit by the moonlight glowing through the cob-webbed window over the staircase, he quickly descended.

He was on his way to meet the girl in the orthopedic boot. She was eleven years old and her name was Meg Pander; she was the landlord's daughter. "What's that?" she had said, earlier, pointing at the lump under Frank's shirt as he scrambled out of the depres-sion in the wall of the passage. Frank had pulled out the bundle and folded back the wrapping to show her the dead monkey. She had taken it from him and cradled it in her arms, cooing gently.

"I want to bury it out in the fields," said Frank.

"I know a better place," said the girl.

"Where?"

"In the cellar."

Frank thought about this. "All right," he said.

"We can't go there now. Meet me here at midnight."

"All right."

"You better let me keep the monkey," she said.

Frank was not the only one to see Ronald Dexter enter his mother's bedroom. Two men from the public bar, flabby men with waxy skin and big, soft faces as round and pale as the rising moon, and a predisposition to breathlessness, were lurking in the shad-ows. They said nothing, as the minutes passed, but they were not silent: the corridor was filled, like a living thing, with the wheeze and gasp of their laboring lungs. Nearby lay Congo Bill, who had returned in the depths of his sleeping mind to the eerie twilight of the rain forest, where huge trunks of mahogany and African wal-nut reared two hundred feet over his head to form a densely woven canopy that effectively blocked out all sunlight, while un-derfoot, moldering gently, the forest floor deadened all sound, and a heavy, ominous silence clung to the place, a silence broken only occasionally by the manic chatter of a troop of Colobus monkeys . . . But even as Congo Bill relived in dream his last fevered jour-ney through that dim and silent forest, Ronald Dexter was rising from his (Bill's) wife's bed and slipping on his silk pajamas. With a few last whispered words, a few last caresses, he left Virginia's bedroom and with a soft click! carefully closed her door. The soft click was succeeded by a crisp crack! and a brief ringing sound, as one of the fat men emerged from the shadows and hit him very hard on the back of the head with a length of metal piping. The pipe bounced off the skull and Ronald wobbled for a moment and then collapsed into a limp heap on the floor. The first man lifted him by the armpits, the second from under the knees, and then they shuffled rapidly off down the corridor, panting heavily, as Ronald's head lolled on his shoulder and his fingers dragged limply along the carpet.

Meg had finished dressing the body of the dead monkey when Frank reached her room shortly after midnight. It was a small, low-ceilinged servant's room, massively dominated by the bedstead, a vast Victorian contraption of dark, lacquered wood with an extremely thick mattress and a Gothic headboard all crockets and gargoyles. High in the wall above the bed was set a single small window, and upon its broad sill burned a candle by the wavering flame of which Frank could see, on the bed, the monkey stretched out in a tiny gown of white lace such as an infant might have worn for its christening or, as in this instance, burial. Meg herself was sitting very straight in a hard-backed chair beside the bed with her hands folded on a small black prayer book in her lap. She turned to Frank with a solemn face.

"God took your monkey away," she whispered.

Frank grinned, rather uncertainly.

"He's in Jesus' bosom now."

Frank absently scratched his wrist where the flea had bitten him. A small crusty scab, reddish-black in color, had begun to form there. On Meg's washstand stood a large jar full of clear fluid, and something floated in the fluid that he could not quite identify in the candlelight, but it looked organic.

"We have to go to the cellar now," said Meg. She stood up and stamped her orthopedic boot four or five times on the floor. "My leg keeps going to sleep," she said. "Will you get the candle down?"

So Frank climbed onto the bed and retrieved the candle from the windowsill while Meg laid the monkey gently in a cardboard shoe box lined with the tissue Frank had taken earlier from the drawer in his bedroom.

They made their way to the door at the end of the passage, then out into the yard at the back of the inn. Clinging to the shadows,

they crept around the building; the walls and out-buildings of the
Blue Bat glimmered in the fullness of the moonlight, and from far
across the fields came the muted barking of a dog on a distant
farm. Meg held Frank's hand firmly in her own as she edged down
a flight of worn stone steps at the bottom of which damp grass and
moss struggled up through the cracks between ancient paving
stones. Directly before them stood a very low green door with
peeling paintwork and rusting studs. Meg lifted the door on its
hinges and it slowly scraped inwards; a moment later the pair
were crouched in the musty darkness of the cellar, the door
pushed firmly closed and the candle flickering on the ground between them and throwing up a strange light onto their pale, excited faces.

Congo Bill meanwhile was blindly crashing through the jungle
in a state of deep delirium. He had lost his quinine in an accident
on the river two weeks previously, and now the fever roiled and
seethed unchecked within him. Delicate screens of misty lichen
hung from the branches, and through these he clawed his wild
way as brightly colored birds shrieked from the foliage high overhead, and the Colobus monkeys chattered derisively from dappled
tree trunks wreathed with vines. On through the damp gloom of
the forest he charged, till his strength at last started to flag. It was
then that he saw Virginia. She was standing beside a sunlit pool
some thirty or forty yards from him, wearing a simple summer
frock and waving a large straw hat with a tilted brim and a cluster
of bright fake cherries fastened to the band. Congo Bill stared at
her for a few seconds, clutching the thick tendril of a climbing
liana that twisted about a huge-trunked ebony tree smothered in
flowering orchids. Upon the pool the few shafts of sunlight that
penetrated the foliage overhead picked diamonds of light which
trembled and shimmered in such a way that Virginia seemed to
evanesce momentarily and then rematerialize, more clearly than
before, still slowly waving her straw hat at him. Then she turned
and moved round the pool and into the trees, and Congo Bill,
stumbling after her, cried "Wait!" as her dappled form danced
away among the shifting shadows of the forest. "Wait!" cried
Congo Bill, as he staggered toward the pool.

And even as he did so, Virginia was drifting into sleep, her
limbs languid and heavy, her whole drowsy being suffused with
the lingering glow of deep and recent sexual pleasure. She sank

into sleep, dreamless sleep, and as the curtains stirred slightly in the warm night breeze, a single broad shaft of moonlight drifted languidly across her bed and touched with silvered fingers the ridges and hummocks of the white sheet spread over her now-slumbering form.

Frank and Meg had penetrated the membrane of the cellar. With their feebly glimmering candle they crept forward from post to post toward the center, where they could hear a low murmur of human voices. Toward the source of the murmur the two children crept with stealth and trembling. They extinguished the candle; Meg still carried the dead monkey in its cardboard coffin. They ascended a shallow wooden staircase and squirmed forward along a damp planked platform between big-bellied barrels reeking of tar and ale; reaching the edge of the platform, they gazed down upon the men and women from the public bar, who were seated about a screened lamp, waiting. Barely had the children settled, side by side on their bellies with their chins cupped in their hands, to watch, when the trapdoor in the cellar roof was hauled open and voices were heard from the public bar above. For a moment there was confused bustle in the cellar; and then, with fresh lamps lit, two men descended carrying between them a supine form in silk pajamas.

"What are they going to do with him?" whispered Frank.

"I expect Daddy wants his blood."

"Oh, crikey!" breathed the boy, and in his mind a series of images rapidly unfolded of opened sarcophagi and ghoulish creatures neither dead nor alive. In fact, the explanation for the events in the cellar was quite straightforward, in scientific terms. Clutch was right: these people suffered from pernicious anemia, a disease which, if untreated, produces a chemical imbalance in the organism that can manifest in a craving for fresh blood. It has this in common with malaria, that in both diseases there is disintegration of the red blood cells, though malaria for some reason has never produced a sense of group identity among its victims. This is not true of pernicious anemia. The Blue Bat was in fact both haven and refuge to a small cell of untreated anemics, and had been for five years, ever since Kevin Pander had watched his wife sicken and die of the disease. This trauma had brought about what is clinically termed an *iatrophobic reaction* in the young innkeeper, a

pathological dread of doctors, with the result that when he detected the first symptoms in himself he did not seek treatment, but
instead began to gather about him a cadre of anemics who, like
him, were prepared to live and die beyond the pale of contemporary medical practice; beyond, indeed, the law. For five years these
committed anemics had maintained a sporadic supply of fresh
blood in the cellar, and there they were to be found, outside normal licensing hours, sipping the good red corpuscles their own
bodies so desperately lacked. The Blue Bat's clientele being what it
was, almost all of this blood came from members of the upper
classes. The fall of the Roman Empire has been attributed in part to
malarial epidemics, and also to the effects of pernicious anemia
caused by lead in the plumbing. Whether these facts played any
part in Pander's elaborate delusional system is not known; the
psychopathology of that disturbed young man is fortunately beyond the scope of this narrative.

And so the limp Ronald Dexter was stripped of his pajamas, and
then—after his pale, naked body had aroused a spontaneous gasp
of appreciation from the assembled company—his ankles were
lashed together with a length of stout twine, and the twine slipped
into an iron ring attached to a rope which ran to a pulley block
fixed to a hook set into a thick beam overhead. Several of the men
then took up the rope hanging from the pulley block, and with no
small effort managed by a series of heaves to hoist Dexter aloft,
and there he hung, quite comatose, and twisting gently, as Kevin
Pander lashed the end of the rope to a pair of thick nails driven
into an upright post for that purpose. A trellis table was then
positioned beneath the dangling man, and upon the table was set a
wooden keg bound with hoops of steel.

All this work had produced a greatly intensified respiration
among the anemics, and even those who had not participated
were panting in short, hoarse, shallow gasps, such was the excitement that now crackled almost palpably in the depths of the body
of the inn. To young Frank, on his platform, the whole nightmarish
scene had assumed a distinct patina of unreality; as the bulky
figures moved about in the lamplight, their shadows against the
stacked barrels and massy beams took on huge, monstrous proportions, and he watched like a spectator of cinema, suspended in
the darkness in wordless captivation. He was barely conscious of
the mounting excitement in the girl beside him as she followed her

father's activity. Then Kevin Pander suddenly seized Ronald by the hair and sliced open his throat; and as the young man's blood came pumping out, young Meg trembled all over and rose onto her knees and gazed with wide, shining eyes, her palms pressed together at her breast as if in prayer. Kevin Padner released Ronald's hair and stepped back, lifting high the dripping razor then bringing it to his lips while two of the other men took hold of the violently convulsing body so as not to lose a drop, and the rest looked on with little piggy eyes that gleamed in the lamplight, the only sound now the hiss and pant of their flaccid lungs.

At length Ronald ceased twitching, and the spurts dwindled to a thick drip, faintly audible amid the wheezing. The keg was tapped, and now, his gestures inflected with theatricality, Kevin Pander drew off a small amount of the contents into a glass and, to a subdued murmur of approval, held it up before him. In the obscurity the blood was black. He tossed it down his throat; then, his heavy eyelids sliding over his eyes until he resembled a latter-day satyr, lacking only hoofs and horns, and his blood-smeared lips parting in a voluptuary's grin, he said something that produced a perceptible twitch of ardor in the assembly's collective body. And where, you may wonder—though now, of course, it was too late for him to be of any assistance to his master—was Clutch all this time?

A cell without a nucleus is a ruin, and when Congo Bill stumbled into an abandoned pygmy camp there was nobody there to greet him but a ghost; and the ghost in the ruin was Virginia. She smiled shyly at him from the entrance to one of the huts, then disappeared into its dark interior. He managed to drag himself in after her, and collapsed in the cool gloom onto the floor. Illness, according to the pygmies, passes through the following stages: first one is hot, then feverish, then ill, then dead, then absolutely dead, and finally, dead forever. When a small hunting group came through late the following day they found Congo Bill dead. He was not, however, dead forever, nor even absolutely dead, and they set about nursing him with medicines derived from plants growing wild in the forest. At this time, the 1930s, these people enjoyed an existence which to most Westerners would seem utopian. Utterly at peace with the forest that sustained and sheltered them, they lived without chiefs and had no need of a belief in evil

spirits. The state of nature was, for them, a state of grace—a functioning anarchy within a benign and generous environment. Not
surprisingly, they sang constant songs of praise to the forest that
provided for them with such abundance. They were singing these
songs when, having seen Bill through his crisis, they carried him
into the *Station de Chasse* on a litter, and handed him over to the
resident Belgian colonial.

Had he known what was occurring in the depths of the Blue Bat,
Congo Bill would doubtless have wished to return to the paradise
he had briefly known among the people of the forest. By this stage
Ronald Dexter was no more than a desiccated envelope of flesh, an
empty thing—*bule*, as the pygmies would have said; but the
anemics were by no means satisfied. When, some time later, Virginia was awakened by the sounds of heavy breathing, she opened
her eyes to find herself surrounded by large pale women whose
eyes glittered at her with an unnatural brilliance. Without further
ado she was dragged screaming from her bed; Congo Bill, deeply
sedated and ignorant of her plight, slept on in the next room,
reliving the happiness and innocent plenty he had known among
the pygmies. Help was in fact on its way, thanks to Clutch; the
only question was, would it get there in time?

Yes, Clutch had known the anemics for what they were after
only a few minutes in the public bar. He was an old man, and he
had seen many strange things in his long life. He doubted he
would have been listened to if he'd raised the alarm earlier; so he
had hiked off toward Reading, where somebody at the Royal Berkshire Hospital, he felt sure, would take his story seriously. By a
stroke of good fortune the physician on duty was a man called
Gland who'd once read a paper on iatrophobia and sanguinivo-
rous dementia (bloodlust) in pernicious anemia, and within minutes a small fleet of ambulances was racing through the moonlit
countryside, klaxons wailing, toward the Blue Bat. But even as
they did so, Virginia, in a filmy summer nightgown, was being
hustled across the public bar toward the yawning trapdoor, where,
in the darkness below, Kevin Pander awaited her with horrible
relish.

It was when he saw his mother being manhandled down the
cellar steps that the bubble of suspended disbelief in which young
Frank had witnessed the atrocity perpetrated on Ronald Dexter

was finally punctured. His whole body stiffened; he turned to Meg, and she immediately gripped him hard by the wrists. "Don't make a sound," she hissed, "or they'll drink your blood too."

"That's my mother," he hissed back. "I must help her."

"You can't."

"I must!"

"They'll cut your throat!"

"I don't care—"

Then suddenly Frank broke off, his gaze burning on the shoe box. Meg's eyes followed his; in stupefied amazement they saw the lid move. Then it was still. Then it moved again, and this time it rose slowly, then slid off, onto the planks, and the dead monkey in its white gown sat up stiffly and turned its little head toward them. The two children were barely conscious of the scuffling, of the muffled screams, that issued from the cellar beyond, where the anemics were leering at Virginia and making vulgar remarks. She was not a person in their eyes, merely a blood vessel, a blood bank, to be plundered and consumed like all her kind. The monkey (which was dead but not, clearly, dead forever) rubbed its eyes with tiny paws, and with a small sob Meg seized it up and clutched it to her chest.

Frank saw his chance; he was on his feet and down the stairs, and running at the assembled anemics. "You leave my mother alone!" he screamed. "You take your hands off her!" Kevin Pander, chuckling hoarsely, seized the child, then passed him to another man, who held him still and smothered his mouth with a fat white hand. There was jocular murmuring among the anemics about this, all conducted in a rich, slurry Berkshire dialect, while Kevin Pander began stropping his razor on a stout strip of leather nailed to a post. Virginia had also been muzzled by her captors; her limbs jerked and her eyes blazed with desperation as she struggled in vain to get close to her son.

Then the trellis was being hauled over and a number of men took hold of the two Clack-Hermans to steady them over the keg when their bodies began the series of involuntary spasms that predictably ensue when the carotid arteries are sliced. Close by, Ronald turned slowly on his hook. Kevin Pander touched the razor's edge to his tongue. Apparently satisfied, he stepped forward. He was not smiling now. It was a tense moment, for it very much looked as though Clutch had failed, that he was going to be too late.

Congo Bill was in pretty bad shape when they brought him out of the forest, and it was generally agreed that a few more hours would have seen the end of him. He had the pygmies to thank, then, for saving his life. Fortified with quinine, he was shipped down the Congo to Léopoldville (as it was then called), where he rested up for some weeks before going on to the coast to board a liner for home. It was in Léopoldville that he bought the monkey. His prognosis was somewhat gloomy—periodic relapses were predicted, accompanied by general enfeeblement and, because of the large number of red blood cells destroyed in the successive paroxysms of fever, a chronic anemic condition. In fact, he could look forward to the life of a semi-invalid, and how Virginia would adapt to that was a cause of some anxiety to him as he crossed the Atlantic—though, as matters stand at this point, the question may well have been academic. He was also filled with deep regret that he would never again do anthropological fieldwork, never again set foot in the equatorial rain forest. Curious irony, he reflected, that the forest in which he had known his deepest tranquility was the same forest in which he had contracted the disease that drove him out forever.

An hour later Dr. George Gland stood in the public bar of the Blue Bat with a small man in a gray raincoat. This was a detective from the Berkshire County Constabulary, a man called Limp, and he was smoking a pipe. The trapdoor was up on its chains, and policemen and forensic experts moved silently and purposefully up and down the cellar stairs. The anemics had already been led away to waiting ambulances, bound, first, for the Royal Berkshire Hospital, where they would begin a course of painful injections of liver extract, which was how the disease was treated in 1934. The two men were watching Clutch, who sat at a table nearby with his great brown head in his hands, mourning the death of his master, whose drained corpse lay on the floor beneath a white sheet. Sad to say, Ronald was not the only corpse on the flagstone floor of the public bar; beside him lay Virginia, also sheeted, and beside her lay the pathetic remains of little Frank. Clutch had, in fact, come too late, and the three white sheets bore silent and tragic testimony to his failure. Suddenly Limp removed the pipe from his mouth and, turning to the doctor, pointed it at him, wet stem forward. "He had a girl!" he exclaimed.

"Who?"

"Pander," said Limp. "Pander had a little girl—a cripple—she wore one of those boots."

"An orthopedic boot?" said Gland. "A girl in an orthopedic boot?"

Upstairs, a uniformed policeman was knocking on Congo Bill's locked bedroom door. Slowly the anthropologist was roused from his dream, which was almost over anyway. "Who is it?" he cried, irritably, in a hoarse whisper.

"Police. Open the door please, Dr. Clark-Herman."

Congo Bill sat up in bed, his withered, yellowing face pouched and wrinkled with annoyance and sickness and sleep. "What do you want?" he mumbled.

"Open the door please, Doctor," came the voice.

"Wait." Slowly he eased himself out of bed, sitting a moment on the edge of the mattress to get his breath. What on earth would the police want, in the middle of the night? He reached for his stick, and slipped his feet into a pair of slippers. His dressing gown lay tossed on a chair beneath the window. He levered himself up off the bed and shuffled across the room. Picking up his dressing gown, he glanced through the curtains. The moon had gone down, and it was the hour before the dawn, that strange, haunted hour between the blackness of the night and the first pale flush of sunrise, and the sky had turned an eerie electric blue. His eye was caught by a movement in the fields, and he saw that it was a girl, a young girl, far out among the glowing cornstalks and limping away from the inn toward a copse of trees that bristled blackly against the blue light on the brow of a distant low hill. Tiny as she was in the distance, he could make out, on her shoulder, the little black-and-white Colobus monkey. He frowned, as he tied the cord of his dressing gown. Why was she taking Frank's monkey to the trees?

"Doctor."

"I'm coming," whispered Congo Bill, turning toward the door, faintly disturbed; "I'm awake now."

Midnight Mass

⭒❉⭒

F. Paul Wilson

I

It had been almost a full minute since he'd slammed the brass
knocker against the heavy oak door. That should have been
proof enough. After all, wasn't the knocker in the shape of a
cross? But no, they had to squint through their peephole and peer
through the sidelights that framed the door.

Rabbi Zev Wolpin sighed and resigned himself to the scrutiny.
He couldn't blame people for being cautious, but this seemed a bit
overly so. The sun was in the west and shining full on his back; he
was all but silhouetted in it. What more did they want?

I should maybe take off my clothes and dance naked?

He gave a mental shrug and savored the damp sea air. At least it
was cool here. He'd bicycled from Lakewood, which was only ten
miles inland from this same ocean but at least twenty degrees
warmer. The bulk of the huge Tudor retreat house stood between
him and the Atlantic, but the ocean's briny scent and rhythmic
rumble were everywhere.

Spring Lake. An Irish Catholic seaside resort since before the
turn of the century. He looked around at its carefully restored
Victorian houses, the huge mansions arrayed here along the beach
front, the smaller homes set in neat rows running straight back

from the ocean. Many of them were still occupied. Not like Lakewood. Lakewood was an empty shell.

Not such a bad place for a retreat, he thought. He wondered how many houses like this the Catholic Church owned.

A series of clicks and clacks drew his attention back to the door as numerous bolts were pulled in rapid succession. The door swung inward revealing a nervous-looking young man in a long black cassock. As he looked at Zev his mouth twisted and he rubbed the back of his wrist across it to hide a smile.

"And what should be so funny?" Zev asked.

"I'm sorry. It's just—"

"I know," Zev said, waving off any explanation as he glanced down at the wooden cross slung on a cord around his neck. "I know."

A bearded Jew in a baggy black serge suit wearing a yarmulke and a cross. Hilarious, no?

So, *nu?* This was what the times demanded, this was what it had come to if he wanted to survive. And Zev did want to survive. Someone had to live to carry on the traditions of the Talmud and the Torah, even if there were hardly any Jews left alive in the world.

Zev stood on the sunny porch, waiting. The priest watched him in silence.

Finally Zev said, "Well, may a wandering Jew come in?"

"I won't stop you," the priest said, "but surely you don't expect me to invite you."

Ah, yes. Another precaution. The vampire couldn't cross the threshold of a home unless he was invited in, so don't invite. A good habit to cultivate, he supposed.

He stepped inside and the priest immediately closed the door behind him, relatching all the locks one by one. When he turned around Zev held out his hand.

"Rabbi Zev Wolpin, Father. I thank you for allowing me in."

"Brother Christopher, sir," he said, smiling and shaking Zev's hand. His suspicions seemed to have been completely allayed. "I'm not a priest yet. We can't offer you much here, but—"

"Oh, I won't be staying long. I just came to talk to Father Joseph Cahill."

Brother Christopher frowned. "Father Cahill isn't here at the moment."

"When will he be back?"

"I—I'm not sure. You see—"

"Father Cahill is on another bender," said a stentorian voice behind Zev.

He turned to see an elderly priest facing him from the far end of the foyer. White-haired, heavy set, wearing a black cassock.

"I'm Rabbi Wolpin."

"Father Adams," the priest said, stepping forward and extending his hand.

As they shook Zev said, "Did you say he was on 'another' bender? I never knew Father Cahill to be much of a drinker."

"Apparently there was a lot we never knew about Father Cahill," the priest said stiffly.

"If you're referring to that nastiness last year," Zev said, feeling the old anger rise in him, "I for one never believed it for a minute. I'm surprised anyone gave it the slightest credence."

"The veracity of the accusation was irrelevant in the final analysis. The damage to Father Cahill's reputation was a fait accompli. Father Palmeri was forced to request his removal for the good of St. Anthony's parish."

Zev was sure that sort of attitude had something to do with Father Joe being on "another bender."

"Where can I find Father Cahill?"

"He's in town somewhere, I suppose, making a spectacle of himself. If there's any way you can talk some sense into him, please do. Not only is he killing himself with drink but he's become quite an embarrassment to the priesthood and to the Church."

Which bothers you more? Zev wanted to ask but held his tongue.

"I'll try."

He waited for Brother Christopher to undo all the locks, then stepped toward the sunlight.

"Try Morton's down on Seventy-one," the younger man whispered as Zev passed.

Zev rode his bicycle south on 71. It was almost strange to see people on the streets. Not many, but more than he'd ever see in Lakewood again. Yet he knew that as the vampires consolidated their grip on the world and infiltrated the Catholic communities, there'd be fewer and fewer day people here as well.

He thought he remembered passing a place named Morton's on his way to Spring Lake. And then up ahead he saw it, by the railroad track crossing, a white stucco one-story box of a building with "Morton's Liquors" painted in big black letters along the side.

Father Adams' words echoed back to him: . . . *on another bender* . . .

Zev pushed his bicycle to the front door and tried the knob. Locked up tight. A look inside showed a litter of trash and empty shelves. The windows were barred; the back door was steel and locked as securely as the front. So where was Father Joe?

Then he spotted the basement window at ground level by the overflowing trash dumpster. It wasn't latched. Zev went down on his knees and pushed it open.

Cool, damp, musty air wafted against his face as he peered into the Stygian blackness. It occurred to him that he might be asking for trouble by sticking his head inside, but he had to give it a try. If Father Cahill wasn't here, Zev would begin the return trek to Lakewood and write this whole trip off as wasted effort.

"Father Joe?" he called. "Father Cahill?"

"That you again, Chris?" said a slightly slurred voice. "Go home, will you? I'll be all right. I'll be back later."

"It's me, Joe. Zev. From Lakewood."

He heard shoes scraping on the floor and then a familiar face appeared in the shaft of light from the window.

"Well I'll be damned. It *is* you! Thought you were Brother Chris come to drag me back to the retreat house. Gets scared I'm gonna get stuck out after dark. So how ya doin', Reb? Glad to see you're still alive. Come on in!"

Zev saw that Father Cahill's eyes were glassy and he swayed ever so slightly, like a skyscraper in the wind. He wore faded jeans and a black Bruce Springsteen *Tunnel of Love* Tour sweatshirt.

Zev's heart twisted at the sight of his friend in such condition. Such a mensch like Father Joe shouldn't be acting like a *shikker*. Maybe it was a mistake coming here. Zev didn't like seeing him like this.

"I don't have that much time, Joe. I came to tell you—"

"Get your bearded ass down here and have a drink or I'll come up and drag you down."

"All right," Zev said. "I'll come in but I won't have a drink."

He hid his bike behind the dumpster, then squeezed through the window. Father Joe helped him to the floor. They embraced, slapping each other on the back. Father Joe was a taller man, a giant from Zev's perspective. At six-four he was ten inches taller, at thirty-five he was a quarter-century younger; he had a muscular frame, thick brown hair, and—on better days—clear blue eyes.

"You're grayer, Zev, and you've lost weight."

"Kosher food is not so easily come by these days."

"All kinds of food is getting scarce." He touched the cross slung from Zev's neck and smiled. "Nice touch. Goes well with your zizith."

Zev fingered the fringe protruding from under his shirt. Old habits didn't die easily.

"Actually, I've grown rather fond of it."

"So what can I pour you?" the priest said, waving an arm at the crates of liquor stacked around him. "My own private reserve. Name your poison."

"I don't want a drink."

"Come on, Reb. I've got some nice hundred-proof Stoly here. You've got to have at least *one* drink—"

"Why? Because you think maybe you shouldn't drink alone?"

Father Joe smiled. "Touché."

"All right," Zev said. *"Bissel.* I'll have *one* drink on the condition that you *don't* have one. Because I wish to talk to you."

The priest considered that a moment, then reached for the vodka bottle.

"Deal."

He poured a generous amount into a paper cup and handed it over. Zev took a sip. He was not a drinker and when he did imbibe he preferred his vodka ice cold from a freezer. But this was tasty. Father Cahill sat back on a crate of Jack Daniel's and folded his arms.

"Nu?" the priest said with a Jackie Mason shrug.

Zev had to laugh. "Joe, I still say that somewhere in your family tree is Jewish blood."

For a moment he felt light, almost happy. When was the last time he had laughed? Probably more than a year now, probably at their table near the back of Horovitz's deli, shortly before the St. Anthony's nastiness began, well before the vampires came.

Zev thought of the day they'd met. He'd been standing at the counter at Horovitz's waiting for Yussel to wrap up the stuffed derma he had ordered when this young giant walked in. He towered over the other rabbis in the place, looked as Irish as Paddy's pig, and wore a Roman collar. He said he'd heard this was the only place on the whole Jersey Shore where you could get a decent corned beef sandwich. He ordered one and cheerfully warned that it better be good. Yussel asked him what could he know about good corned beef and the priest replied that he grew up in Bensonhurst. Well, about half the people in Horovitz's on that day—and on any other day for that matter—grew up in Bensonhurst and before you knew it they were all asking him if he knew such-and-such a store and so-and-so's deli.

Zev then informed the priest—with all due respect to Yussel Horovitz behind the counter—that the best corned beef sandwich in the world was to be had at Shmuel Rosenberg's Jerusalem Deli in Bensonhurst. Father Cahill said he'd been there and agreed one hundred per cent.

Yussel served him his sandwich then. As he took a huge bite out of the corned beef on rye, the normal *tummel* of a deli at lunchtime died away until Horovitz's was as quiet as a *shoul* on Sunday morning. Everyone watched him chew, watched him swallow. Then they waited. Suddenly his face broke into this big Irish grin.

"I'm afraid I'm going to have to change my vote," he said. "Horovitz's of Lakewood makes the best corned beef sandwich in the world."

Amid cheers and warm laughter, Zev led Father Cahill to the rear table that would become theirs and sat with this canny and charming gentile who had so easily won over a roomful of strangers and provided such a *mechaieh* for Yussel. He learned that the young priest was the new assistant to Father Palmeri, the pastor at St. Anthony's Catholic church at the northern end of Lakewood. Father Palmeri had been there for years but Zev had never so much as seen his face. He asked Father Cahill—who wanted to be called Joe—about life in Brooklyn these days and they talked for an hour.

During the following months they would run into each other so often at Horovitz's that they decided to meet regularly for lunch, on Mondays and Thursdays. They did so for years, discussing religion—Oy, the religious discussions!—politics, economics, philosophy, life in general. During those lunchtimes they solved most

of the world's problems. Zev was sure they'd have solved them all
if the scandal at St. Anthony's hadn't resulted in Father Joe's removal from the parish.

But that was in another time, another world. The world before
the vampires took over.

Zev shook his head as he considered the current state of Father
Joe in the dusty basement of Morton's Liquors.

"It's about the vampires, Joe," he said, taking another sip of the
Stoly. "They've taken over St. Anthony's."

Father Joe snorted and shrugged.

"They're in the majority now, Zev, remember? They've taken
over everything. Why should St. Anthony's be different from any
other parish in the world?"

"I didn't mean the parish. I meant the church."

The priest's eyes widened slightly. "The church? They've taken
over the building itself?"

"Every night," Zev said. "Every night they are there."

"That's a holy place. How do they manage that?"

"They've desecrated the altar, destroyed all the crosses. St. Anthony's is no longer a holy place."

"Too bad," Father Joe said, looking down and shaking his head
sadly. "It was a fine old church." He looked up again, at Zev.
"How do you know about what's going on at St. Anthony's? It's
not exactly in your neighborhood."

"A neighborhood I don't exactly have any more."

Father Joe reached over and gripped his shoulder with a huge
hand.

"I'm sorry, Zev. I heard how your people got hit pretty hard
over there. Sitting ducks, huh? I'm really sorry."

Sitting ducks. An appropriate description. Oh, they'd been
smart, those bloodsuckers. They knew their easiest targets. Whenever they swooped into an area they singled out Jews as their first
victims, and among Jews they picked the Orthodox first of the
first. Smart. Where else would they be less likely to run up against
a cross? It worked for them in Brooklyn, and so when they came
south into New Jersey, spreading like a plague, they headed
straight for the town with one of the largest collections of yeshivas
in North America.

But after the Bensonhurst holocaust the people in the Lakewood
communities did not take quite so long to figure out what was

happening. The Reformed and Conservative synagogues started
handing out crosses at Shabbes—too late for many but it saved a
few. Did the Orthodox congregations follow suit? No. They hid in
their homes and shules and yeshivas and read and prayed.

And were liquidated.

A cross, a crucifix—they held power over the vampires, drove
them away. His fellow rabbis did not want to accept that simple
fact because they could not face its devastating ramifications. To
hold up a cross was to negate two thousand years of Jewish history, it was to say that the Messiah had come and they had missed
him.

Did it say that? Zev didn't know. Argue about it later. Right
now, people were dying. But the rabbis had to argue it now. And
as they argued, their people were slaughtered like cattle.

How Zev railed at them, how he pleaded with them! Blind,
stubborn fools! If a fire was consuming your house, would you
refuse to throw water on it just because you'd always been taught
not to believe in water? Zev had arrived at the rabbinical council
wearing a cross and had been thrown out—literally sent hurtling
through the front door. But at least he had managed to save a few
of his own people. Too few.

He remembered his fellow Orthodox rabbis, though. All the
ones who had refused to face the reality of the vampires' fear of
crosses, who had forbidden their students and their congregations
to wear crosses, who had watched those same students and congregations die en masse only to rise again and come for them. And
soon those very same rabbis were roaming their own community,
hunting the survivors, preying on other yeshivas, other congregations, until the entire community was liquidated and incorporated
into the brotherhood of the vampire. The great fear had come to
pass: they'd been assimilated.

The rabbis could have saved themselves, could have saved their
people, but they would not bend to the reality of what was happening around them. Which, when Zev thought about it, was not
at all out of character. Hadn't they spent generations learning to
turn away from the rest of the world?

Those early days of anarchic slaughter were over. Now that the
vampires held the ruling hand, the bloodletting had become more
organized. But the damage to Zev's people had been done—and it
was irreparable. Hitler would have been proud. His Nazi "final

solution" was an afternoon picnic compared to the work of the vampires. They did in months what Hitler's Reich could not do in all the years of the Second World War.

There's only a few of us now. So few and so scattered. A final Diaspora.

For a moment Zev was almost overwhelmed by grief, but he pushed it down, locked it back into that place where he kept his sorrows, and thought of how fortunate it was for his wife Chana that she died of natural causes before the horror began. Her soul had been too gentle to weather what had happened to their community.

"Not as sorry as I, Joe," Zev said, dragging himself back to the present. "But since my neighborhood is gone, and since I have hardly any friends left, I use the daylight hours to wander. So call me the Wandering Jew. And in my wanderings I meet some of your old parishioners."

The priest's face hardened. His voice became acid.

"Do you, now? And how fares the remnant of my devoted flock?"

"They've lost all hope, Joe. They wish you were back."

He laughed. "Sure they do! Just like they rallied behind me when my name and honor were being dragged through the muck last year. Yeah, they want me back. I'll bet!"

"Such anger, Joe. It doesn't become you."

"Bullshit. That was the old Joe Cahill, the naive turkey who believed all his faithful parishioners would back him up. But no. Palmeri tells the bishop the heat is getting too much for him, the bishop removes me, and the people I dedicated my life to all stand by in silence as I'm railroaded out of my parish."

"It's hard for the commonfolk to buck a bishop."

"Maybe. But I can't forget how they stood quietly by while I was stripped of my position, my dignity, my integrity, of everything I wanted to be . . ."

Zev thought Joe's voice was going to break. He was about to reach out to him when the priest coughed and squared his shoulders.

"Meanwhile, I'm a pariah over here in the retreat house. A goddam leper. Some of them actually believe—" He broke off in a growl. "Ah, what's the use? It's over and done. Most of the parish is dead anyway, I suppose. And if I'd stayed there I'd probably be dead too. So maybe it worked out for the best. And who gives a shit anyway."

He reached for the bottle of Glenlivet next to him.

"No-no!" Zev said. "You promised!"

Father Joe drew his hand back and crossed his arms across his chest.

"Talk on, oh, bearded one. I'm listening."

Father Joe had certainly changed for the worse. Morose, bitter, apathetic, self-pitying. Zev was beginning to wonder how he could have called this man a friend.

"They've taken over your church, desecrated it. Each night they further defile it with butchery and blasphemy. Doesn't that mean anything to you?"

"It's Palmeri's parish. I've been benched. Let him take care of it."

"Father Palmeri is their leader."

"He should be. He's their pastor."

"No. He leads the vampires in the obscenities they perform in the church."

Father Joe stiffened and the glassiness cleared from his eyes.

"Palmeri? He's one of them?"

Zev nodded. "More than that. He's the local leader. He orchestrates their rituals."

Zev saw rage flare in the priest's eyes, saw his hands ball into fists, and for a moment he thought the old Father Joe was going to burst through.

Come on, Joe. Show me that old fire.

But then he slumped back onto the crate.

"Is that all you came to tell me?"

Zev hid his disappointment and nodded. "Yes."

"Good." He grabbed the scotch bottle. "Because I need a drink."

Zev wanted to leave, yet he had to stay, had to probe a little bit deeper and see how much of his old friend was left, and how much had been replaced by this new, bitter, alien Joe Cahill. Maybe there was still hope. So they talked on.

Suddenly he noticed it was dark.

"Gevalt!" Zev said. "I didn't notice the time!"

Father Joe seemed surprised too. He ran to the window and peered out.

"Damn! Sun's gone down!" He turned to Zev. "Lakewood's out of the question for you, Reb. Even the retreat house is too far to risk now. Looks like we're stuck here for the night."

"We'll be safe?"

He shrugged. "Why not? As far as I can tell I'm the only one who's been in here for months, and only in the daytime. Be pretty odd if one of those human leeches should decide to wander in here tonight."

"I hope so."

"Don't worry. We're okay if we don't attract attention. I've got a flashlight if we need it, but we're better off sitting here in the dark and shooting the breeze till sunrise." Father Joe smiled and picked up a huge silver cross, at least a foot in length, from atop one of the crates. "Besides, we're armed. And frankly, I can think of worse places to spend the night."

He stepped over to the case of Glenlivet and opened a fresh bottle. His capacity for alcohol was enormous.

Zev could think of worse places too. In fact he had spent a number of nights in much worse places since the holocaust. He decided to put the time to good use.

"So, Joe. Maybe I should tell you some more about what's happening in Lakewood."

After a few hours their talk died of fatigue. Father Joe gave Zev the flashlight to hold and stretched out across a couple of crates to sleep. Zev tried to get comfortable enough to doze but found sleep impossible. So he listened to his friend snore in the darkness of the cellar.

Poor Joe. Such anger in the man. But more than that—hurt. He felt betrayed, wronged. And with good reason. But with everything falling apart as it was, the wrong done to him would never be righted. He should forget about it already and go on with his life, but apparently he couldn't. Such a shame. He needed something to pull him out of his funk. Zev had thought news of what had happened to his old parish might rouse him, but it seemed only to make him want to drink more. Father Joe Cahill, he feared, was a hopeless case.

Zev closed his eyes and tried to rest. It was hard to get comfortable with the cross dangling in front of him so he took it off but laid it within easy reach. He was drifting toward a doze when he heard a noise outside. By the dumpster. Metal on metal.

My bicycle!

He slipped to the floor and tiptoed over to where Father Joe slept. He shook his shoulder and whispered.

"Someone's found my bicycle!"

The priest snorted but remained sleeping. A louder clatter outside made Zev turn, and as he moved his elbow struck a bottle. He grabbed for it in the darkness but missed. The sound of smashing glass echoed through the basement like a cannon shot. As the odor of scotch whiskey replaced the musty ambiance, Zev listened for further sounds from outside. None came.

Maybe it had been an animal. He remembered how raccoons used to raid his garbage at home . . . when he'd had a home . . . when he'd had garbage . . .

Zev stepped to the window and looked out. Probably an animal. He pulled the window open a few inches and felt cool night air wash across his face. He pulled the flashlight from his coat pocket and aimed it through the opening.

Zev almost dropped the light as the beam illuminated a pale, snarling demonic face, baring its fangs and hissing. He fell back as the thing's head and shoulders lunged through the window, its curved fingers clawing at him, missing. Then it launched itself the rest of the way through, hurtling toward Zev.

He tried to dodge but he was too slow. The impact knocked the flashlight from his grasp and it went rolling across the floor. Zev cried out as he went down under the snarling thing. Its ferocity was overpowering, irresistible. It straddled him and lashed at him, batting his fending arms aside, its clawed fingers tearing at his collar to free his throat, stretching his neck to expose the vulnerable flesh, its foul breath gagging him as it bent its fangs toward him. Zev screamed out his helplessness.

II

Father Joe awoke to the cries of a terrified voice.

He shook his head to clear it and instantly regretted the move. His head weighed at least two hundred pounds, and his mouth was stuffed with foul-tasting cotton. Why did he keep doing this to himself? Not only did it leave him feeling lousy, it gave him bad dreams. Like now.

Another terrified shout, only a few feet away.

He looked toward the sound. In the faint light from the flashlight rolling across the floor he saw Zev on his back, fighting for his life against—

Damn! This was no dream! One of those bloodsuckers had got in here!

He leaped over to where the creature was lowering its fangs toward Zev's throat. He grabbed it by the back of the neck and lifted it clear of the floor. It was surprisingly heavy but that didn't slow him. Joe could feel the anger rising in him, surging into his muscles.

"Rotten piece of filth!"

He swung the vampire by its neck and let it fly against the cinderblock wall. It impacted with what should have been bone-crushing force, but it bounced off, rolled on the floor, and regained its feet in one motion, ready to attack again. Strong as he was, Joe knew he was no match for a vampire's power. He turned, grabbed his big silver crucifix, and charged the creature.

"Hungry? Eat this!"

As the creature bared its fangs and hissed at him, Joe shoved the long lower end of the cross into its open mouth. Blue-white light flickered along the silver length of the crucifix, reflecting in the creature's startled, agonized eyes as its flesh sizzled and crackled. The vampire let out a strangled cry and tried to turn away but Joe wasn't through with it yet. He was literally seeing red as rage poured out of a hidden well and swirled through him. He rammed the cross deeper down the things' gullet. Light flashed deep in its throat, illuminating the pale tissues from within. It tried to grab the cross and pull it out but the flesh of its fingers burned and smoked wherever they came in contact with the cross.

Finally Joe stepped back and let the thing squirm and scrabble up the wall and out the window into the night. Then he turned to Zev. If anything had happened—

"Hey, Reb!" he said, kneeling beside the older man. "You all right?"

"Yes," Zev said, struggling to his feet. "Thanks to you."

Joe slumped onto a crate, momentarily weak as his rage dissipated. *This is not what I'm about*, he thought. But it had felt so damn good to let it loose on that vampire. Too good. And that worried him.

I'm falling apart . . . like everything else in the world.

"That was too close," he said to Zev, giving the older man's shoulder a fond squeeze.

"Too close for that vampire for sure," Zev said, replacing his yarmulke. "And would you please remind me, Father Joe, that in the future if ever I should maybe get my blood sucked and become a vampire that I should stay far away from you."

Joe laughed for the first time in too long. It felt good.

They climbed out at first light. Joe stretched his cramped muscles in the fresh air while Zev checked on his hidden bicycle.

"Oy," Zev said as he pulled it from behind the dumpster. The front wheel had been bent so far out of shape that half the spokes were broken. "Look what he did. Looks like I'll be walking back to Lakewood."

But Joe was less interested in the bike than in the whereabouts of their visitor from last night. He knew it couldn't have got far. And it hadn't. They found the vampire—or rather what was left of it—on the far side of the dumpster: a rotting, twisted corpse, blackened to a crisp and steaming in the morning sunlight. The silver crucifix still protruded from between its teeth.

Joe approached and gingerly yanked his cross free of the foul remains.

"Looks like you've sucked your last pint of blood," he said and immediately felt foolish.

Who was he putting on the macho act for? Zev certainly wasn't going to buy it. Too out of character. But then, what *was* his character these days? He used to be a parish priest. Now he was a nothing. A less than nothing.

He straightened up and turned to Zev.

"Come on back to the retreat house, Reb. I'll buy you breakfast."

But as Joe turned and began walking away, Zev stayed and stared down at the corpse.

"They say they don't wander far from where they spent their lives," Zev said. "Which means it's unlikely this fellow was Jewish if he lived around here. Probably Catholic. Irish Catholic, I'd imagine."

Joe stopped and turned. He stared at his long shadow. The hazy rising sun at his back cast a huge hulking shape before him, with a dark cross in one shadow hand and a smudge of amber light where it poured through the unopened bottle of Scotch in the other.

"What are you getting at?" he said.

"The Kaddish would probably not be so appropriate so I'm just wondering if maybe someone should give him the last rites or whatever it is you people do when one of you dies."

"He wasn't one of us," Joe said, feeling the bitterness rise in him. "He wasn't even human."

"Ah, but he used to be before he was killed and became one of them. So maybe now he could use a little help."

Joe didn't like the way this was going. He sensed he was being maneuvered.

"He doesn't deserve it," he said and knew in that instant he'd been trapped.

"I thought even the worst sinner deserved it," Zev said.

Joe knew when he was beaten. Zev was right. He shoved the cross and bottle into Zev's hands—a bit roughly, perhaps—then went and knelt by the twisted cadaver. He administered a form of the final sacrament. When he was through he returned to Zev and snatched back his belongings.

"You're a better man than I am, Gunga Din," he said as he passed.

"You act as if they're responsible for what they do after they become vampires," Zev said as he hurried along beside him, panting as he matched Joe's pace.

"Aren't they?"

"No."

"You're sure of that?"

"Well, not exactly. But they certainly aren't human anymore, so maybe we shouldn't hold them accountable on human terms."

Zev's reasoning tone flashed Joe back to the conversations they used to have in Horovitz's deli.

"But Zev, we know there's some of the old personality left. I mean, they stay in their home towns, usually in the basements of their old houses. They go after people they knew when they were alive. They're not just dumb predators, Zev. They've got the old consciousness they had when they were alive. Why can't they rise above it? Why can't they . . . resist?"

"I don't know. To tell the truth, the question has never occurred to me. A fascinating concept: an undead refusing to feed. Leave it to Father Joe to come up with something like that. We should discuss this on the trip back to Lakewood."

Joe had to smile. So *that* was what this was all about.

"I'm not going back to Lakewood."

"Fine. Then we'll discuss it now. Maybe the urge to feed is too strong to overcome."

"Maybe. And maybe they just don't try hard enough."

"This is a hard line you're taking, my friend."

"I'm a hard-line kind of guy."

"Well, you've become one."

Joe gave him a sharp look. "You don't know what I've become."

Zev shrugged. "Maybe true, maybe not. But do you truly think you'd be able to resist?"

"Damn straight."

Joe didn't know whether he was serious or not. Maybe he was just mentally preparing himself for the day when he might actually find himself in that situation.

"Interesting," Zev said as they climbed the front steps of the retreat house. "Well, I'd better be going. I've a long walk ahead of me. A long, *lonely* walk all the way back to Lakewood. A long, lonely, possibly *dangerous* walk back for a poor old man who—"

"All right, Zev! All *right!*" Joe said, biting back a laugh. "I get the point. You want me to go back to Lakewood. Why?"

"I just want the company," Zev said with pure innocence.

"No, really. What's going on in that Talmudic mind of yours? What are you cooking?"

"Nothing, Father Joe. Nothing at all."

Joe stared at him. Damn it all if his interest wasn't piqued. What was Zev up to? And what the hell? Why not go? He had nothing better to do.

"All right, Zev. You win. I'll come back to Lakewood with you. But just for today. Just to keep you company. And I'm not going anywhere near St. Anthony's, okay? Understood?"

"Understood, Joe. Perfectly understood."

"Good. Now wipe that smile off your face and we'll get something to eat."

III

Under the climbing sun they walked south along the deserted beach, barefooting through the wet sand at the edge of the surf. Zev had never done this. He liked the feel of the sand between his toes, the coolness of the water as it sloshed over his ankles.

"Know what day it is?" Father Joe said. He had his sneakers slung over his shoulder. "Believe it or not, it's the Fourth of July."

"Oh, yes. Your Independence Day. We never made much of secular holidays. Too many religious ones to observe. Why should I not believe it's this date?"

Father Joe shook his head in dismay. "This is Manasquan Beach. You know what this place used to look like on the Fourth before the vampires took over? Wall-to-wall bodies."

"Really? I guess maybe sun-bathing is not the fad it used to be."

"Ah, Zev! Still the master of the understatement. I'll say one thing, though: the beach is cleaner than I've ever seen it. No beer cans or hypodermics." He pointed ahead. "But what's that up there?"

As they approached the spot, Zev saw a pair of naked bodies stretched out on the sand, one male, one female, both young and short-haired. Their skin was bronzed and glistened in the sun. The man lifted his head and stared at them. A blue crucifix was tattooed in the center of his forehead. He reached into the knapsack beside him and withdrew a huge, gleaming, nickel-plated revolver.

"Just keep walking," he said.

"Will do," Father Joe said. "Just passing through."

As they passed the couple, Zev noticed a similar tattoo on the girl's forehead. He noticed the rest of her too. He felt an almost-forgotten stirring deep inside him.

"A very popular tattoo," he said.

"Clever idea. That's one cross you can't drop or lose. Probably won't help you in the dark, but if there's a light on it might give you an edge."

They turned west and made their way inland, finding Route 70 and following it into Ocean County via the Brielle Bridge.

"I remember nightmare traffic jams right here every summer," Father Joe said as they trod the bridge's empty span. "Never thought I'd miss traffic jams."

They cut over to Route 88 and followed it all the way into Lakewood. Along the way they found a few people out and about in Bricktown and picking berries in Ocean County Park, but in the heart of Lakewood . . .

"A real ghost town," the priest said as they walked Forest Avenue's deserted length.

"Ghosts," Zev said, nodding sadly. It had been a long walk and he was tired. "Yes. Full of ghosts."

In his mind's eye he saw the shades of his fallen brother rabbis and all the yeshiva students, beards, black suits, black hats, crisscrossing back and forth at a determined pace on weekdays, strolling with their wives on Shabbes, their children trailing behind like ducklings.

Gone. All gone. Victims of the vampires. Vampires themselves now, most of them. It made him sick at heart to think of those good, gentle men, women, and children curled up in their basements now to avoid the light of day, venturing out in the dark to feed on others, spreading the disease . . .

He fingered the cross slung from his neck. *If only they had listened!*

"I know a place near St. Anthony's where we can hide," he told the priest.

"You've traveled enough today, Reb. And I told you, I don't care about St. Anthony's."

"Stay the night, Joe," Zev said, gripping the young priest's arm. He'd coaxed him this far; he couldn't let him get away now. "See what Father Palmeri's done."

"If he's one of them he's not a priest anymore. Don't call him Father."

"*They* still call him Father."

"Who?"

"The vampires."

Zev watched Father Joe's jaw muscles bunch.

Joe said, "Maybe I'll just take a quick trip over to St. Anthony's myself—"

"No. It's different here. The area is thick with them—maybe twenty times as many as in Spring Lake. They'll get you if your timing isn't just right. I'll take you."

"You need rest, pal."

Father Joe's expression showed genuine concern. Zev was detecting increasingly softer emotions in the man since their reunion last night. A good sign perhaps?

"And rest I'll get when we get to where I'm taking you."

IV

Father Joe Cahill watched the moon rise over his old church and wondered at the wisdom of coming back. The casual decision made this morning in the full light of day seemed reckless and foolhardy now at the approach of midnight.

But there was no turning back. He'd followed Zev to the second floor of this two-story office building across the street from St. Anthony's, and here they'd waited for dark. Must have been a law office once. The place had been vandalized, the windows broken, the furniture trashed, but there was an old Temple University Law School degree on the wall, and the couch was still in one piece. So while Zev caught some Z's, Joe sat and sipped a little of his scotch and did some heavy thinking.

Mostly he thought about his drinking. He'd done too much of that lately, he knew; so much so that he was afraid to stop cold. So he was taking just a touch now, barely enough to take the edge off. He'd finish the rest later, after he came back from that church over there.

He'd stared at St. Anthony's since they'd arrived. It too had been extensively vandalized. Once it had been a beautiful little stone church, a miniature cathedral, really; very Gothic with all its pointed arches, steep roofs, crocketed spires, and multifoil stained glass windows. Now the windows were smashed, the crosses which had topped the steeple and each gable were gone, and anything resembling a cross in its granite exterior had been defaced beyond recognition.

As he'd known it would, the sight of St. Anthony's brought back memories of Gloria Sullivan, the young, pretty church volunteer whose husband worked for United Chemical International in New York, commuting in every day and trekking off overseas a little too often. Joe and Gloria had seen a lot of each other around the church offices and had become good friends. But Gloria had somehow got the idea that what they had went beyond friendship, so she showed up at the rectory one night when Joe was there alone. He tried to explain that as attractive as she was, she was not for him. He had taken certain vows and meant to stick by them. He did his best to let her down easy but she'd been hurt. And angry.

That might have been that, but then her six-year-old son Kevin had come home from altar boy practice with a story about a priest making him pull down his pants and touching him. Kevin was never clear on who the priest had been, but Gloria Sullivan was. Obviously it had been Father Cahill—any man who could turn down the heartfelt offer of her love and her body had to be either a queer or worse. And a child molester was worse.

She took it to the police and to the papers.

Joe groaned softly at the memory of how swiftly his life had become hell. But he had been determined to weather the storm, sure that the real culprit eventually would be revealed. He had no proof—still didn't—but if one of the priests at St. Anthony's was a pederast, he knew it wasn't him. That left Father Alberto Palmeri, St. Anthony's fifty-five-year-old pastor. Before Joe could get to the truth, however, Father Palmeri requested that Father Cahill be removed from the parish, and the bishop complied. Joe had left under a cloud that had followed him to the retreat house in the next county and hovered over him till this day. The only place he'd found even brief respite from the impotent anger and bitterness that roiled under his skin and soured his gut every minute of every day was in the bottle—and that was sure as hell a dead end.

So why had he agreed to come back here? To torture himself? Or to get a look at Palmeri and see how low he had sunk?

Maybe that was it. Maybe seeing Palmeri wallowing in his true element would give him the impetus to put the whole St. Anthony's incident behind him and rejoin what was left of the human race—which needed him now more than ever.

And maybe it wouldn't.

Getting back on track was a nice thought, but over the past few months Joe had found it increasingly difficult to give much of a damn about anyone or anything.

Except maybe Zev. He'd stuck by Joe through the worst of it, defending him to anyone who would listen. But an endorsement from an Orthodox rabbi had meant diddly in St. Anthony's. And yesterday Zev had biked all the way to Spring Lake to see him. Old Zev was all right.

And he'd been right about the number of vampires here too.

Lakewood was *crawling* with the things. Fascinated and repelled, Joe had watched the streets fill with them shortly after sundown.

But what had disturbed him more were the creatures who'd come out *before* sundown.

The humans. Live ones.

The collaborators.

If there was anything lower, anything that deserved true death more than the vampires themselves, it was the still-living humans who worked for them.

Someone touched his shoulder and he jumped. It was Zev. He was holding something out to him. Joe took it and held it up in the moonlight: a tiny crescent moon dangling from a chain on a ring.

"What's this?"

"An earring. The local Vichy wear them."

"Vichy? Like the Vichy French?"

"Yes. Very good. I'm glad to see that you're not as culturally illiterate as the rest of your generation. Vichy humans—that's what I call the collaborators. These earrings identify them to the local nest of vampires. They are spared."

"Where'd you get them?"

Zev's face was hidden in the shadows. "Their previous owners . . . lost them. Put it on."

"My ear's not pierced."

A gnarled hand moved into the moonlight. Joe saw a long needle clasped between the thumb and index finger.

"That I can fix," Zev said.

"Maybe you shouldn't see this," Zev whispered as they crouched in the deep shadows on St. Anthony's western flank.

Joe squinted at him in the darkness, puzzled.

"You lay a guilt trip on me to get me here, now you're having second thoughts?"

"It is horrible like I can't tell you."

Joe thought about that. There was enough horror in the world outside St. Anthony's. What purpose did it serve to see what was going on inside?

Because it used to be my church.

Even though he'd only been an associate pastor, never fully in charge, and even though he'd been unceremoniously yanked from the post, St. Anthony's had been his first parish. He was here. He might as well know what they were doing inside.

"Show me."

Zev led him to a pile of rubble under a smashed stained glass window. He pointed up to where faint light flickered from inside.

"Look in there."

"You're not coming?"

"Once was enough, thank you."

Joe climbed as carefully, as quietly as he could, all the while becoming increasingly aware of a growing stench like putrid, rotting meat. It was coming from inside, wafting through the broken window. Steeling himself, he straightened up and peered over the sill.

For a moment he was disoriented, like someone peering out the window of a city apartment and seeing the rolling hills of a Kansas farm. This could not be the interior of St. Anthony's.

In the flickering light of hundreds of sacramental candles he saw that the walls were bare, stripped of all their ornaments, of the plaques for the stations of the cross; the dark wood along the wall was scarred and gouged wherever there had been anything remotely resembling a cross. The floor too was mostly bare, the pews ripped from their neat rows and hacked to pieces, their splintered remains piled high at the rear under the choir balcony.

And the giant crucifix that had dominated the space behind the altar—only a portion of it remained. The cross-pieces on each side had been sawed off and so now an armless, life-size Christ hung upside down against the rear wall of the sanctuary.

Joe took in all that in a flash, then his attention was drawn to the unholy congregation that peopled St. Anthony's this night. The collaborators—the Vichy humans, as Zev called them—made up the periphery of the group. They looked like normal, everyday people but each was wearing a crescent moon earring.

But the others, the group gathered in the sanctuary—Joe felt his hackles rise at the sight of them. They surrounded the altar in a tight knot. Their pale, bestial faces, bereft of the slightest trace of human warmth, compassion, or decency, were turned upward. His gorge rose when he saw the object of their rapt attention.

A naked teenage boy—his hands tied behind his back, was suspended over the altar by his ankles. He was sobbing and choking, his eyes wide and vacant with shock, his mind all but gone. The skin had been flayed from his forehead—apparently the Vichy had found an expedient solution to the cross tattoo—and blood ran in a slow stream down his abdomen and chest from his freshly truncated genitals. And beside him, standing atop the altar, a bloody-mouthed creature dressed in a long cassock. Joe recognized the thin shoulders, the graying hair trailing from the balding crown, but was shocked at the crimson vulpine grin he flashed to the things clustered below him.

"Now," said the creature in a lightly accented voice Joe had heard hundreds of times from St. Anthony's pulpit.

Father Alberto Palmeri.

And from the group a hand reached up with a straight razor and drew it across the boy's throat. As the blood flowed down over his face, those below squeezed and struggled forward like hatchling vultures to catch the falling drops and scarlet trickles in their open mouths.

Joe fell away from the window and vomited. He felt Zev grab his arm and lead him away. He was vaguely aware of crossing the street and heading toward the ruined legal office.

V

"Why in God's name did you want me to see that?"

Zev looked across the office toward the source of the words. He could see a vague outline where Father Joe sat on the floor, his back against the wall, the open bottle of scotch in his hand. The priest had taken one drink since their return, no more.

"I thought you should know what they were doing to your church."

"So you've said. But what's the reason behind that one?"

Zev shrugged in the darkness. "I'd heard you weren't doing well, that even before everything else began falling apart, you had already fallen apart. So when I felt it safe to get away, I came to see you. Just as I expected, I found a man who was angry at everything and letting it eat up his *guderim*. I thought maybe it would be good to give that man something very specific to be angry at."

"You bastard!" Father Joe whispered. "Who gave you the right?"

"Friendship gave me the right, Joe. I should hear that you are rotting away and do nothing? I have no congregation of my own anymore so I turned my attention on you. Always I was a somewhat meddlesome rabbi."

"Still are. Out to save my soul, ay?"

"We rabbis don't save souls. Guide them maybe, hopefully give them direction. But only you can save your soul, Joe."

Silence hung in the air for awhile. Suddenly the crescent-moon earring Zev had given Father Joe landed in the puddle of moonlight on the floor between them.

"Why do they do it?" the priest said. "The Vichy—why do they collaborate?"

"The first were quite unwilling, believe me. They cooperated because their wives and children were held hostage by the vampires. But before too long the dregs of humanity began to slither out from under their rocks and offer their services in exchange for the immortality of vampirism."

"Why bother working for them? Why not just bare your throat to the nearest bloodsucker?"

"That's what I thought at first," Zev said. "But as I witnessed the Lakewood holocaust I detected the vampires' pattern. They can choose who joins their ranks, so after they've fully infiltrated a population, they change their tactics. You see, they don't want too many of their kind concentrated in one area. It's like too many carnivores in one forest—when the herds of prey are wiped out, the predators starve. So they start to employ a different style of killing. For only when the vampire draws the life's blood from the throat with its fangs does the victim become one of them. Anyone drained as in the manner of that boy in the church tonight dies a true death. He's as dead now as someone run over by a truck. He will not rise tomorrow night."

"I get it," Father Joe said. "The Vichy trade their daylight services and dirty work to the vampires now for immortality later on."

"Correct."

There was no humor in the soft laugh that echoed across the room from Father Joe.

"Swell. I never cease to be amazed at our fellow human beings. Their capacity for good is exceeded only by their ability to debase themselves."

"Hopelessness does strange things, Joe. The vampires know that. So they rob us of hope. That's how they beat us. They transform our friends and neighbors and leaders into their own, leaving us feeling alone, completely cut off. Some of us can't take the despair and kill ourselves."

"Hopelessness," Joe said. "A potent weapon."

After a long silence, Zev said, "So what are you going to do now, Father Joe?"

Another bitter laugh from across the room.

"I suppose this is the place where I declare that I've found new purpose in life and will now go forth into the world as a fearless vampire killer."

"Such a thing would be nice."

"Well screw that. I'm only going as far as across the street."

"To St. Anthony's?"

Zev saw Father Joe take a swig from the Scotch bottle and then screw the cap on tight.

"Yeah. To see if there's anything I can do over there."

"Father Palmeri and his nest might not like that."

"I told you, don't call him Father. And screw *him*. Nobody can do what he's done and get away with it. I'm taking my church back."

In the dark, behind his beard, Zev smiled.

VI

Joe stayed up the rest of the night and let Zev sleep. The old guy needed his rest. Sleep would have been impossible for Joe anyway. He was too wired. He sat up and watched St. Anthony's.

They left before first light, dark shapes drifting out the front doors and down the stone steps like parishioners leaving a predawn service. Joe felt his back teeth grind as he scanned the group for Palmeri, but he couldn't make him out in the dimness. By the time the sun began to peek over the rooftops and through the trees to the east, the street outside was deserted.

He woke Zev and together they approached the church. The heavy oak and iron front doors, each forming half of a pointed arch, were closed. He pulled them open and fastened the hooks to keep them open. Then he walked through the vestibule and into the nave.

Even though he was ready for it, the stench backed him up a few steps. When his stomach settled, he forced himself ahead, treading a path between the two piles of shattered and splintered pews. Zev walked beside him, a handkerchief pressed over his mouth.

Last night he had thought the place a shambles. He saw now that it was worse. The light of day poked into all the corners, revealing everything that had been hidden by the warm glow of the candles. Half a dozen rotting corpses hung from the ceiling—he hadn't noticed them last night—and others were sprawled on the floor against the walls. Some of the bodies were in pieces. Behind the chancel rail a headless female torso was draped over the front of the pulpit. To the left stood the statue of Mary. Someone had fitted her with foam rubber breasts and a huge dildo. And at the rear of the sanctuary was the armless Christ hanging head down on the upright of his cross.

"My church," he whispered as he moved along the path that had once been the center aisle, the aisle brides used to walk down with their fathers. "Look what they've done to my church!"

Joe approached the huge block of the altar. Once it had been backed against the far wall of the sanctuary, but he'd had it moved to the front so that he could celebrate Mass facing his parishioners. Solid Carrara marble, but you'd never know it now. So caked with dried blood, semen, and feces it could have been made of styrofoam.

His revulsion was fading, melting away in the growing heat of his rage, drawing the nausea with it. He had intended to clean up the place but there was so much to be done, too much for two men. It was hopeless.

"Fadda Joe?"

He spun at the sound of the strange voice. A thin figure stood uncertainly in the open doorway. A man of about fifty edged forward timidly.

"Fadda Joe, izat you?"

Joe recognized him now. Carl Edwards. A twitchy little man who used to help pass the collection basket at 10:30 Mass on Sundays. A transplantee from Jersey City—hardly anyone around here was originally from around here. His face was sunken, his eyes feverish as he stared at Joe.

"Yes, Carl. It's me."

"Oh, tank God!" He ran forward and dropped to his knees

before Joe. He began to sob. "You come back! Tank God, you come back!"

Joe pulled him to his feet.

"Come on now, Carl. Get a grip."

"You come back ta save us, ain'tcha? God sent ya here to punish him, din't He?"

"Punish whom?"

"Fadda Palmeri! He's one a dem! He's da woist a alla dem! He—"

"I know," Joe said. "I know."

"Oh, it's so good to have ya back, Fadda Joe! We ain't knowed what to do since da suckers took ova. We been prayin fa someone like youse an now ya here. It's a freakin' miracle!"

Joe wanted to ask Carl where he and all these people who seemed to think they needed him now had been when he was being railroaded out of the parish. But that was ancient history.

"Not a miracle, Carl," Joe said, glancing at Zev. "Rabbi Wolpin brought me back." As Carl and Zev shook hands, Joe said, "And I'm just passing through."

"Passing t'rough? No. Dat can't be! Ya gotta stay!"

Joe saw the light of hope fading in the little man's eyes. Something twisted within him, tugging him.

"What can I do here, Carl? I'm just one man."

"I'll help! I'll do whatever ya want! Jes tell me!"

"Will you help me clean up?"

Carl looked around and seemed to see the cadavers for the first time. He cringed and turned a few shades paler.

"Yeah . . . sure. Anyting."

Joe looked at Zev. "Well? What do you think?"

Zev shrugged. "I should tell you what to do? My parish it's not."

"Not mine either."

Zev jutted his beard at Carl. "I think maybe he'd tell you differently."

Joe did a slow turn. The vaulted nave was utterly silent except for the buzzing of the flies around the cadavers. A massive clean-up job. But if they worked all day they could make a decent dent in it. And then—

And then what?

Joe didn't know. He was playing this by ear. He'd wait and see what the night brought.

"Can you get us some food, Carl? I'd sell my soul for a cup of coffee."

Carl gave him a strange look.

"Just a figure of speech, Carl. We'll need some food if we're going to keep working."

The man's eyes lit again.

"Dat means ya staying?"

"For a while."

"I'll getcha some food," he said excitedly as he ran for the door. "An' coffee. I know someone who's still got coffee. She'll part wit' some of it for Fadda Joe." He stopped at the door and turned. "Ay, an' Fadda, I neva believed any a dem tings dat was said aboutcha. Neva."

Joe tried but he couldn't hold it back.

"It would have meant a lot to have heard that from you last year, Carl."

The man lowered his eyes. "Yeah. I guess it woulda. But I'll make it up to ya, Fadda. I will. You can take dat to da bank."

Then he was out the door and gone. Joe turned to Zev and saw the old man rolling up his sleeves.

"*Nu?*" Zev said. "The bodies. Before we do anything else, I think maybe we should move the bodies."

VII

By early afternoon, Zev was exhausted. The heat and the heavy work had taken their toll. He had to stop and rest. He sat on the chancel rail and looked around. Nearly eight hours work and they'd barely scratched the surface. But the place did look and smell better.

Removing the flyblown corpses and scattered body parts had been the worst of it. A foul, gut-roiling task that had taken most of the morning. They'd carried the corpses out to the small graveyard behind the church and left them there. Those people deserved a decent burial but there was no time for it today.

Once the corpses were gone, Father Joe had torn the defilements from the statue of Mary and then they'd turned their attention to the huge crucifix. It took a while but they finally found Christ's plaster arms in the pile of ruined pews. They were still nailed to the sawn-off cross-piece of the crucifix. While Zev and Father Joe worked at jury-rigging a series of braces to reattach the arms, Carl found a mop and bucket and began the long, slow process of washing the fouled floor of the nave.

Now the crucifix was intact again—the life-size plaster Jesus had his arms reattached and was once again nailed to his refurbished cross. Father Joe and Carl had restored him to his former position of dominance. The poor man was upright again, hanging over the center of the sanctuary in all his tortured splendor.

A grisly sight. Zev could never understand the Catholic attachment to these gruesome statues. But if the vampires loathed them, then Zev was for them all the way.

His stomach rumbled with hunger. At least they'd had a good breakfast. Carl had returned from his food run this morning with bread, cheese, and two thermoses of hot coffee. He wished now they'd saved some. Maybe there was a crust of bread left in the sack. He headed back to the vestibule to check and found an aluminum pot and a paper bag sitting by the door. The pot was full of beef stew and the sack contained three cans of Pepsi.

He poked his head out the doors but no one was in sight on the street outside. It had been that way all day—he'd spy a figure or two peeking in the front doors; they'd hover there for a moment as if to confirm that what they had heard was true, then they'd scurry away. He looked at the meal that had been left. A group of the locals must have donated from their hoard of canned stew and precious soft drinks to fix this. Zev was touched.

He called Father Joe and Carl.

"Tastes like Dinty Moore," Father Joe said around a mouthful of the stew.

"It is," Carl said. "I recognize da little potatoes. Da ladies of the parish must really be excited about youse comin' back to break inta deir canned goods like dis."

They were feasting in the sacristy, the small room off the sanctuary where the priests had kept their vestments—a clerical Green Room, so to speak. Zev found the stew palatable but much too salty. He wasn't about to complain, though.

"I don't believe I've ever had anything like this before."

"I'd be real surprised if you had," said Father Joe. "I doubt very much that something that calls itself Dinty Moore is kosher."

Zev smiled but inside he was suddenly filled with a great sadness. Kosher . . . how meaningless now seemed all the observances which he had allowed to rule and circumscribe his life. Such a fierce proponent of strict dietary laws he'd been in the days before the Lakewood holocaust. But those days were gone, just as the Lakewood community was gone. And Zev was a changed man. If he hadn't changed, if he were still observing, he couldn't sit here and sup with these two men. He'd have to be elsewhere, eating special classes of specially prepared foods off separate sets of dishes. But really, wasn't division what holding to the dietary laws in modern times was all about? They served a purpose beyond mere observance of tradition. They placed another wall between observant Jews and outsiders, keeping them separate even from other Jews who didn't observe.

Zev forced himself to take a big bite of the stew. Time to break down all the walls between people . . . while there was still enough time and people left alive to make it matter.

"You okay, Zev?" Father Joe asked.

Zev nodded silently, afraid to speak for fear of sobbing. Despite all its anachronisms, he missed his life in the good old days of last year. Gone. It was all gone. The rich traditions, the culture, the friends, the prayers. He felt adrift—in time and in space. Nowhere was home.

"You sure?" The young priest seemed genuinely concerned.

"Yes, I'm okay. As okay as you could expect me to feel after spending the better part of the day repairing a crucifix and eating non-kosher food. And let me tell you, that's not so okay."

He put his bowl aside and straightened from his chair.

"Come on, already. Let's get back to work. There's much yet to do."

VIII

S un's almost down," Carl said.

Joe straightened from scrubbing the altar and stared west through one of the smashed windows. The sun was out of sight behind the houses there.

532 F. Paul Wilson

"You can go now, Carl," he said to the little man. "Thanks for your help."

"Where youse gonna go, Fadda?"

"I'll be staying right here."

Carl's prominent Adam's apple bobbed convulsively as he swallowed.

"Yeah? Well den, I'm staying too. I tol' ya I'd make it up ta ya, din't I? An besides, I don't tink the suckas'll like da new, improved St. Ant'ny's too much when dey come back tonight, d'you? I don't even tink dey'll get t'rough da doors."

Joe smiled at the man and looked around. Luckily it was July when the days were long. They'd had time to make a difference here. The floors were clean, the crucifix was restored and back in its proper position, as were most of the Stations of the Cross plaques. Zev had found them under the pews and had taken the ones not shattered beyond recognition and rehung them on the walls. Lots of new crosses littered those walls. Carl had found a hammer and nails and had made dozens of them from the remains of the pews.

"No. I don't think they'll like the new decor one bit. But there's something you can get us if you can, Carl. Guns. Pistols, rifles, shotguns, anything that shoots."

Carl nodded slowly. "I know a few guys who can help in dat department."

"And some wine. A little red wine if anybody's saved some."

"You got it."

He hurried off.

"You're planning Custer's last stand, maybe?" Zev said from where he was tacking the last of Carl's crude crosses to the east wall.

"More like the Alamo."

"Same result," Zev said with one of his shrugs.

Joe turned back to scrubbing the altar. He'd been at it for over an hour now. He was drenched with sweat and knew he smelled like a bear, but he couldn't stop until it was clean.

An hour later he was forced to give up. No use. It wouldn't come clean. The vampires must have done something to the blood and foulness to make the mixture seep into the surface of the marble like it had.

He sat on the floor with his back against the altar and rested. He didn't like resting because it gave him time to think. And when he started to think he realized that the odds were pretty high against his seeing tomorrow morning.

At least he'd die well fed. Their secret supplier had left them a dinner of fresh fried chicken by the front doors. Even the memory of it made his mouth water. Apparently someone was *really* glad he was back.

To tell the truth, though, as miserable as he'd been, he wasn't ready to die. Not tonight, not any night. He wasn't looking for an Alamo or a Little Big Horn. All he wanted to do was hold off the vampires till dawn. Keep them out of St. Anthony's for one night. That was all. That would be a statement—*his* statement. If he found an opportunity to ram a stake through Palmeri's rotten heart, so much the better, but he wasn't counting on that. One night. Just to let them know they couldn't have their way everywhere with everybody whenever they felt like it. He had surprise on his side tonight, so maybe it would work. One night. Then he'd be on his way.

"What the fuck have you *done?*"

Joe looked up at the shout. A burly, long-haired man in jeans and a flannel shirt stood in the vestibule staring at the partially restored nave. As he approached, Joe noticed his crescent moon earring.

A Vichy.

Joe balled his fists but didn't move.

"Hey, I'm talking to you, mister. Are you responsible for this?" When all he got from Joe was a cold stare, he turned to Zev.

"Hey, you! Jew! What the hell do you think *you're* doing?" He started toward Zev. "You get those fucking crosses off—"

"Touch him and I'll break you in half," Joe said in a low voice.

The Vichy skidded to a halt and stared at him.

"Hey, asshole! Are you crazy? Do you know what Father Palmeri will do to you when he arrives?"

"*Father* Palmeri? Why do you still call him that?"

"It's what he wants to be called. And he's going to call you *dog meat* when he gets here!"

Joe pulled himself to his feet and looked down at the Vichy. The man took two steps back. Suddenly he didn't seem so sure of himself.

"Tell him I'll be waiting. Tell him Father Cahill is back."

"You're a priest? You don't look like one."

"Shut up and listen. Tell him Father Joe Cahill is back—and he's pissed. Tell him that. Now get out of here while you still can."

The man turned and hurried out into the growing darkness. Joe turned to Zev and found him grinning through his beard.

" 'Father Joe Cahill is back—and he's pissed.' I like that."

"We'll make it into a bumper sticker. Meanwhile let's close those doors. The criminal element is starting to wander in. I'll see if we can find some more candles. It's getting dark in here."

IX

He wore the night like a tuxedo.

Dressed in a fresh cassock, Father Alberto Palmeri turned off County Line Road and strolled toward St. Anthony's. The night was lovely, especially when you owned it. And he owned the night in this area of Lakewood now. He loved the night. He felt at one with it, attuned to its harmonies and its discords. The darkness made him feel so alive. Strange to have to lose your life before you could really feel alive. But this was it. He'd found his niche, his métier.

Such a shame it had taken him so long. All those years trying to deny his appetites, trying to be a member of the other side, cursing himself when he allowed his appetites to win, as he had with increasing frequency toward the end of his mortal life. He should have given in to them completely long ago.

It had taken undeath to free him.

And to think he had been afraid of undeath, had cowered in fear each night in the cellar of the church, surrounded by crosses. Fortunately he had not been as safe as he'd thought and one of the beings he now called brother was able to slip in on him in the dark while he dozed. He saw now that he had lost nothing but his blood by that encounter.

And in trade he'd gained a world.

For now it was his world, at least this little corner of it, one in which he was completely free to indulge himself in any way he wished. Except for the blood. He had no choice about the blood. That was a new appetite, stronger than all the rest, one that would not be denied. But he did not mind the new appetite in the least. He'd found interesting ways to sate it.

Up ahead he spotted dear, defiled St. Anthony's. He wondered what his servants had prepared for him tonight. They were quite imaginative. They'd yet to bore him.

But as he drew nearer the church, Palmeri slowed. His skin prickled. The building had changed. Something was very wrong there, wrong inside. Something amiss with the light that beamed from the windows. This wasn't the old familiar candlelight, this was something else, something more. Something that made his insides tremble.

Figures raced up the street toward him. Live ones. His night vision picked out the earrings and familiar faces of some of his servants. As they neared he sensed the warmth of the blood coursing just beneath their skins. The hunger rose in him and he fought the urge to rip into one of their throats. He couldn't allow himself that pleasure. He had to keep the servants dangling, keep them working for him and the nest. They needed the services of the indentured living to remove whatever obstacles the cattle might put in their way.

"Father! Father!" they cried.

He loved it when they called him Father, loved being one of the undead and dressing like one of the enemy.

"Yes, my children. What sort of victim do you have for us tonight?"

"No victim, father—trouble!"

The edges of Palmeri's vision darkened with rage as he heard of the young priest and the Jew who had dared to try to turn St. Anthony's into a holy place again. When he heard the name of the priest, he nearly exploded.

"Cahill? Joseph Cahill is back in my church?"

"He was cleaning the altar!" one of the servants said.

Palmeri strode toward the church with the servants trailing behind. He knew that neither Cahill nor the Pope himself could clean that altar. Palmeri had desecrated it himself; he had learned how to do that when he became nest leader. But what else had the young pup dared to do?

Whatever it was, it would be undone. *Now!*

Palmeri strode up the steps and pulled the right door open— and screamed in agony.

The light! The *light!* The LIGHT! White agony lanced through Palmeri's eyes and seared his brain like two hot pokers. He retched and threw his arms across his face as he staggered back into the cool, comforting darkness.

It took a few minutes for the pain to drain off, for the nausea to pass, for vision to return.

He'd never understand it. He'd spent his entire life in the presence of crosses and crucifixes, surrounded by them. And yet as soon as he'd become undead, he was unable to bear the sight of one. As a matter of fact, since he'd become undead, he'd never even *seen* one. A cross was no longer an object. It was a light, a light so excruciatingly bright, so blazingly white that it was sheer agony to look at it. As a child in Naples he'd been told by his mother not to look at the sun, but when there'd been talk of an eclipse, he'd stared directly into its eye. The pain of looking at a cross was a hundred, no, a thousand times worse than that. And the bigger the cross or crucifix, the worse the pain.

He'd experienced monumental pain upon looking into St. Anthony's tonight. That could only mean that Joseph, that young bastard, had refurbished the giant crucifix. It was the only possible explanation.

He swung on his servants.

"Get in there! Get that crucifix down!"

"They've got guns!"

"Then get help. But get it *down!*"

"We'll get guns too! We can—"

"*No!* I want him! I want that priest alive! I want him for myself! Anyone who kills him will suffer a very painful, very long and lingering true death! Is that clear?"

It was clear. They scurried away without answering.

Palmeri went to gather the other members of the nest.

X

Dressed in a cassock and a surplice, Joe came out of the sacristy and approached the altar. He noticed Zev keeping watch at one of the windows. He didn't tell him how ridiculous he looked carrying the shotgun Carl had brought back. He held it so gingerly, like it was full of nitroglycerine and would explode if he jiggled it.

Zev turned, and smiled when he saw him.

"*Now* you look like the old Father Joe we all used to know."

Joe gave him a little bow and proceeded toward the altar.

All right: He had everything he needed. He had the Missal they'd found in among the pew debris earlier today. He had the wine; Carl had brought back about four ounces of sour red babarone. He'd found a smudged surplice and a dusty cassock on the floor of one of the closets in the sacristy, and he wore them now. No hosts, though. A crust of bread left over from breakfast would have to do. No chalice, either. If he'd known he was going to be saying Mass he'd have come prepared. As a last resort he'd used the can opener in the rectory to remove the top from one of the Pepsi cans from lunch. Quite a stretch from the gold chalice he'd used since his ordination, but probably more in line with what Jesus had used at that first Mass—the Last Supper.

He was uncomfortable with the idea of weapons in St. Anthony's but he saw no alternative. He and Zev knew nothing about guns, and Carl knew little more; they'd probably do more damage to themselves than to the Vichy if they tried to use them. But maybe the sight of them would make the Vichy hesitate, slow them down. All he needed was a little time here, enough to get to the consecration.

This is going to be the most unusual Mass in history, he thought.

But he was going to get through it if it killed him. And that was a real possibility. This might well be his last Mass. But he wasn't afraid. He was too excited to be afraid. He'd had a slug of the Scotch—just enough to ward off the DTs—but it had done nothing to quell the buzz of the adrenalin humming along every nerve in his body.

He spread everything out on the white tablecloth he'd taken from the rectory and used to cover the filthy altar. He looked at Carl.

"Ready?"

Carl nodded and stuck the .38 caliber pistol he'd been examining in his belt.

"Been a while, Fadda. We did it in Latin when I was a kid, but I tink I can swing it."

"Just do your best and don't worry about any mistakes."

Some Mass. A defiled altar, a crust for a host, a Pepsi can for a chalice, a fifty-year-old, pistol-packing altar boy, and a congregation consisting of a lone, shotgun-carrying Orthodox Jew.

Joe looked heavenward.

You do understand, don't you, Lord, that this was arranged on short notice?

Time to begin.

He read the Gospel but dispensed with the homily. He tried to remember the Mass as it used to be said, to fit in better with Carl's outdated responses. As he was starting the Offertory the front doors flew open and a group of men entered—ten of them, all with crescent moons dangling from their ears. Out of the corner of his eye he saw Zev move away from the window toward the altar, pointing his shotgun at them.

As soon as they entered the nave and got past the broken pews, the Vichy fanned out toward the sides. They began pulling down the Stations of the Cross, ripping Carl's makeshift crosses from the walls and tearing them apart. Carl looked up at Joe from where he knelt, his eyes questioning, his hand reaching for the pistol in his belt.

Joe shook his head and kept up with the Offertory.

When all the little crosses were down, the Vichy swarmed behind the altar. Joe chanced a quick glance over his shoulder and saw them begin their attack on the newly repaired crucifix.

"Zev!" Carl said in a low voice, cocking his head toward the Vichy. "Stop 'em!"

Zev worked the pump on the shotgun. The sound echoed through the church. Joe heard the activity behind him come to a sudden halt. He braced himself for the shot . . .

But it never came.

He looked at Zev. The old man met his gaze and sadly shook his head. He couldn't do it. To the accompaniment of the sound of renewed activity and derisive laughter behind him, Joe gave Zev a tiny nod of reassurance and understanding, then hurried the Mass toward the Consecration.

As he held the crust of bread aloft, he started at the sound of the life-sized crucifix crashing to the floor, cringed as he heard the freshly buttressed arms and crosspiece being torn away again.

As he held the wine aloft in the Pepsi can, the swaggering, grinning Vichy surrounded the altar and brazenly tore the cross from around his neck. Zev and Carl put up a struggle to keep theirs but were overpowered.

And then Joe's skin began to crawl as a new group entered the nave. There had to be at least forty of them, all of them vampires. And Palmeri was leading them.

XI

Palmeri hid his hesitancy as he approached the altar. The crucifix and its intolerable whiteness were gone, yet something was not right. Something repellent here, something that urged him to flee. What?

Perhaps it was just the residual effect of the crucifix and all the crosses they had used to line the walls. That had to be it. The unsettling aftertaste would fade as the night wore on. Oh, yes. His nightbrothers and sisters from the nest would see to that.

He focused his attention on the man behind the altar and laughed when he realized what he held in his hands.

"Pepsi, Joseph? You're trying to consecrate Pepsi?" He turned to his nest siblings. "Do you see this, my brothers and sisters? Is this the man we are to fear? And look who he has with him! An old Jew and a parish hanger-on!"

He heard their hissing laughter as they fanned out around him, sweeping toward the altar in a wide phalanx. The Jew and Carl— he recognized Carl and wondered how he'd avoided capture for so long—retreated to the other side of the altar where they flanked Joseph. And Joseph . . . Joseph's handsome Irish face so pale and drawn, his mouth drawn into such a tight, grim line. He looked scared to death. And well he should be.

Palmeri put down his rage at Joseph's audacity. He was glad he had returned. He'd always hated the young priest for his easy manner with people, for the way the parishioners had flocked to him with their problems despite the fact that he had nowhere near the experience of their older and wiser pastor. But that was over now. That world was gone, replaced by a nightworld—Palmeri's world. And no one would be flocking to Father Joe for anything when Palmeri was through with him. "Father Joe"—how he'd hated it when way the parishioners had started calling him that. Well, their Father Joe would provide superior entertainment tonight. This was going to be *fun*.

"Joseph, Joseph, Joseph," he said as he stopped and smiled at the young priest across the altar. "This futile gesture is so typical of your arrogance."

But Joseph only stared back at him, his expression a mixture of defiance and repugnance. And that only fueled Palmeri's rage.

"Do I repel you, Joseph? Does my new form offend your precious shanty-Irish sensibilities? Does my undeath disgust you?"

"You managed to do all that while you were still alive, Alberto."

Palmeri allowed himself to smile. Joseph probably thought he was putting on a brave front, but the tremor in his voice betrayed his fear.

"Always good with the quick retort, weren't you, Joseph. Always thinking you were better than me, always putting yourself above me."

"Not much of a climb where a child molester is concerned."

Palmeri's anger mounted.

"So superior. So self-righteous. What about *your* appetites, Joseph? The secret ones? What are they? Do you always hold them in check? Are you so far above the rest of us that you never give in to an improper impulse? I'll bet you think that even if we made you one of us you could resist the blood hunger."

He saw by the startled look in Joseph's face that he had struck a nerve. He stepped closer, almost touching the altar.

"You do, don't you? You really think you could resist it! Well, we shall see about that, Joseph. By dawn you'll be drained—we'll each take a turn at you—and when the sun rises you'll have to hide from its light. When the night comes you'll be one of us. And then all the rules will be off. The night will be yours. You'll be able to do anything and everything you've ever wanted. But the blood hunger will be on you too. You won't be sipping your god's blood, as you've done so often, but *human* blood. You'll thirst for hot, human blood, Joseph. And you'll have to sate that thirst. There'll be no choice. And I want to be there when you do, Joseph. I want to be there to laugh in your face as you suck up the crimson nectar, and keep on laughing every night as the red hunger lures you into infinity."

And it *would* happen. Palmeri knew it as sure as he felt his own thirst. He hungered for the moment when he could rub dear Joseph's face in the muck of his own despair.

"I was about to finish saying Mass," Joseph said coolly. "Do you mind if I finish?"

Palmeri couldn't help laughing this time.

"Did you really think this charade would work? Did you really think you could celebrate Mass on *this?*"

He reached out and snatched the tablecloth from the altar, sending the Missal and the piece of bread to the floor and exposing the fouled surface of the marble.

"Did you really think you could effect the Transubstantiation here? Do you really believe any of that garbage? That the bread and wine actually take on the substance of—" he tried to say the name but it wouldn't form "—the Son's body and blood?"

One of the nest brothers, Frederick, stepped forward and leaned over the altar, smiling.

"Transubstantiation?" he said in his most unctuous voice, pulling the Pepsi can from Joseph's hands. "Does that mean that this is the blood of the Son?"

A whisper of warning slithered through Palmeri's mind. Something about the can, something about the way he found it difficult to bring its outline into focus . . .

"Brother Frederick, maybe you should—"

Frederick's grin broadened. "I've always wanted to sup on the blood of a deity."

The nest members hissed their laughter as Frederick raised the can and drank.

Palmeri was jolted by the explosion of intolerable brightness that burst from Frederick's mouth. The inside of his skull glowed beneath his scalp and shafts of pure white light shot from his ears, nose, eyes—every orifice in his head. The glow spread as it flowed down through his throat and chest and into his abdominal cavity, silhouetting his ribs before melting through his skin. Frederick was liquefying where he stood, his flesh steaming, softening, running like glowing molten lava.

No! This couldn't be happening! Not now when he had Joseph in his grasp!

Then the can fell from Frederick's dissolving fingers and landed on the altar top. Its contents splashed across the fouled surface, releasing another detonation of brilliance, this one more devastating than the first. The glare spread rapidly, extending over the upper surface and running down the sides, moving like a living thing, engulfing the entire altar, making it glow like a corpuscle of fire torn from the heart of the sun itself.

And with the light came blast-furnace heat that drove Palmeri back, back, back until he had to turn and follow the rest of his nest in a mad, headlong rush from St. Anthony's into the cool, welcoming safety of the outer darkness.

XII

As the vampires fled into the night, their Vichy toadies behind them, Zev stared in horrid fascination at the puddle of putrescence that was all that remained of the vampire Palmeri had called Frederick. He glanced at Carl and caught the look of dazed wonderment on his face. Zev touched the top of the altar—clean, shiny, every whorl of the marble surface clearly visible.

There was fearsome power here. Incalculable power. But instead of elating him, the realization only depressed him. How long had this been going on? Did it happen at every Mass? Why had he spent his entire life ignorant of this?

He turned to Father Joe.

"What happened?"

"I—I don't know."

"A miracle!" Carl said, running his palm over the altar top.

"A miracle and a meltdown," Father Joe said. He picked up the empty Pepsi can and looked into it. "You know, you go through the seminary, through your ordination, through countless Masses *believing* in the Transubstantiation. But after all these years . . . to actually *know* . . ."

Zev saw him rub his finger along the inside of the can and taste it. He grimaced.

"What's wrong?" Zev asked.

"Still tastes like sour barbarone . . . with a hint of Pepsi."

"Doesn't matter what it tastes like. As far as Palmeri and his friends are concerned, it's the real thing."

"No," said the priest with a small smile. "That's Coke."

And then they started laughing. It wasn't that funny, but Zev found himself roaring along with the other two. It was more a release of tension than anything else. His sides hurt. He had to lean against the altar to support himself.

It took the return of the Vichy to cure the laughter. They charged in carrying a heavy fire blanket. This time Father Joe did not stand by passively as they invaded his church. He stepped around the altar and met them head on.

He was great and terrible as he confronted them. His giant stature and raised fists cowed them for a few heartbeats. But then they must have remembered that they outnumbered him twelve to one and charged him. He swung a massive fist and caught the lead Vichy square on the jaw. The blow lifted him off his feet and he landed against another. Both went down.

Zev dropped to one knee and reached for the shotgun. He would use it this time, he would shoot these vermin, he swore it!

But then someone landed on his back and drove him to the floor. As he tried to get up he saw Father Joe, surrounded, swinging his fists, laying the Vichy out every time he connected. But there were too many. As the priest went down under the press of them, a heavy boot thudded against the side of Zev's head. He sank into darkness.

XIII

A throbbing in his head, stinging pain in his cheek, and a voice, sibilant yet harsh . . .

" . . . now, Joseph. Come on. Wake up. I don't want you to miss this!"

Palmeri's sallow features swam into view, hovering over him, grinning like a skull. Joe tried to move but found his wrists and arms tied. His right hand throbbed, felt twice its normal size; he must have broken it on a Vichy jaw. He lifted his head and saw that he was tied spread-eagle on the altar, and that the altar had been covered with the fire blanket.

"Melodramatic, I admit," Palmeri said, "but fitting, don't you think? I mean, you and I used to sacrifice our god symbolically here every weekday and multiple times on Sundays, so why shouldn't this serve as *your* sacrificial altar?"

Joe shut his eyes against a wave of nausea. This couldn't be happening.

"Thought you'd won, didn't you?" When Joe wouldn't answer him, Palmeri went on. "And even if you'd chased me out of here for good, what would you have accomplished? The world is ours

now, Joseph. Feeders and cattle—that is the hierarchy. We are the
feeders. And tonight you'll join us. But *he* won't. *Voila!''*

He stepped aside and made a flourish toward the balcony. Joe
searched the dim, candlelit space of the nave, not sure what he was
supposed to see. Then he picked out Zev's form and he groaned.
The old man's feet were lashed to the balcony rail; he hung upside
down, his reddened face and frightened eyes turned his way. Joe
fell back and strained at the ropes but they wouldn't budge.

"Let him go!"

"What? And let all that good rich Jewish blood go to waste?
Why, these people are the Chosen of God! They're a delicacy!''

"Bastard!"

If he could just get his hands on Palmeri, just for a minute.

"Tut-tut, Joseph. Not in the house of the Lord. The Jew should
have been smart and run away like Carl."

Carl got away? Good. The poor guy would probably hate himself, call himself a coward the rest of his life, but he'd done what he
could. Better to live on than get strung up like Zev.

We're even, Carl.

"But don't worry about your rabbi. None of us will lay a fang on
him. He hasn't earned the right to join us. We'll use the razor to
bleed him. And when he's dead, he'll be dead for keeps. But not
you, Joseph. Oh no, not you." His smile broadened. "You're
mine."

Joe wanted to spit in Palmeri's face—not so much as an act of
defiance as to hide the waves of terror surging through him—but
there was no saliva to be had in his parched mouth. The thought of
being undead made him weak. To spend eternity like . . . he
looked at the rapt faces of Palmeri's fellow vampires as they clustered under Zev's suspended form . . . like *them?*

He *wouldn't* be like them! He wouldn't allow it!

But what if there was no choice? What if becoming undead
toppled a lifetime's worth of moral constraints, cut all the tethers
on his human hungers, negated all his mortal concepts of how a
life should be lived? Honor, justice, integrity, truth, decency, fair-
ness, love—what if they became meaningless words instead of the
footings for his life?

A thought struck him.

"A deal, Alberto," he said.

"You're hardly in a bargaining position, Joseph."

"I'm not? Answer me this: Do the undead ever kill each other? I mean, has one of them ever driven a stake through another's heart?"

"No. Of course not."

"Are you sure? You'd better be sure before you go through with your plans tonight. Because if I'm forced to become one of you, I'll be crossing over with just one thought in mind: to find you. And when I do I won't stake your heart, I'll stake your arms and legs to the pilings of the Point Pleasant boardwalk where you can watch the sun rise and feel it slowly crisp your skin to charcoal."

Palmeri's smile wavered. "Impossible. You'll be different. You'll want to thank me. You'll wonder why you ever resisted."

"You'd better sure of that, Alberto . . . for your sake. Because I'll have all eternity to track you down. And I'll find you, Alberto. I swear it on my own grave. Think on that."

"Do you think an empty threat is going to cow me?"

"We'll find out how empty it is, won't we? But here's the deal: Let Zev go and I'll let you be."

"You care that much for an old Jew?"

"He's something you never knew in life, and never will know: he's a friend." *And he gave me back my soul.*

Palmeri leaned closer. His foul, nauseous breath wafted against Joe's face.

"A friend? How can you be friends with a dead man?" With that he straightened and turned toward the balcony. "Do him! *Now!*"

As Joe shouted out frantic pleas and protests, one of the vampires climbed up the rubble toward Zev. Zev did not struggle. Joe saw him close his eyes, waiting. As the vampire reached out with the straight razor, Joe bit back a sob of grief and rage and helplessness. He was about to squeeze his own eyes shut when he saw a flame arc through the air from one of the windows. It struck the floor with a crash of glass and a *wooomp!* of exploding flame.

Joe had only heard of such things, but he immediately realized that he had just seen his first Molotov cocktail in action. The splattering gasoline caught the clothes of a nearby vampire who began running in circles, screaming as it beat at its flaming clothes. But its cries were drowned by the roar of other voices, a hundred or more. Joe looked around and saw people—men, women, teenagers—climbing in the windows, charging through the front doors. The women held crosses on high while the men wielded long wooden pikes—broom, rake, and shovel handles whittled to sharp points. Joe recognized most of the faces from the Sunday Masses he had said here for years.

St. Anthony's parishioners were back to reclaim their church.

"Yes!" he shouted, not sure of whether to laugh or cry. But when he saw the rage in Palmeri's face, he laughed. "Too bad, Alberto!"

Palmeri made a lunge at his throat but cringed away as a woman with an upheld crucifix and a man with a pike charged the altar—Carl and a woman Joe recognized as Mary O'Hare.

"Told ya I wun't letcha down, din't I, Fadda?" Carl said, grinning and pulling out a red Swiss Army knife. He began sawing at the rope around Joe's right wrist. "Din't I?"

"That you did, Carl. I don't think I've ever been so glad to see anyone in my entire life. But how—?"

"I told 'em. I run t'rough da parish, goin' house ta house. I told 'em dat Fadda Joe was in trouble an' dat we let him down before but we shoun't let him down again. He come back fa us, now we gotta go back fa him. Simple as dat. And den *dey* started runnin' house ta house, an' afore ya knowed it, we had ourselfs a little army. We come ta kick ass, Fadda, if you'll excuse da expression."

"Kick all the ass you can, Carl."

Joe glanced at Mary O'Hare's terror-glazed eyes as she swiveled around, looking this way and that; he saw how the crucifix trembled in her hand. She wasn't going to kick too much ass in her state, but she was *here*, dear God, she was here for him and for St. Anthony's despite the terror that so obviously filled her. His heart swelled with love for these people and pride in their courage.

As soon as his arms were free, Joe sat up and took the knife from Carl. As he sawed at his leg ropes, he looked around the church.

The oldest and youngest members of the parishioner army were stationed at the windows and doors where they held crosses aloft, cutting off the vampires' escape, while all across the nave—chaos. Screams, cries, and an occasional shot echoed through St. Anthony's. The vampires were outnumbered three to one and seemed blinded and confused by all the crosses around them. Despite their superhuman strength, it appeared that some were indeed getting their asses kicked. A number were already writhing on the floor, impaled on pikes. As Joe watched, he saw a pair of the women, crucifixes held before them, backing a vampire into a corner. As it cowered there with its arms across its face, one of the men charged in with a sharpened rake handle held like a lance and ran it through.

But a number of parishioners lay in inert, bloody heaps on the floor, proof that the vampires and the Vichy were claiming their share of victims too.

Joe freed his feet and hopped off the altar. He looked around for Palmeri—he *wanted* Palmeri—but the vampire priest had lost himself in the melée. Joe glanced up at the balcony and saw that Zev was still hanging there, struggling to free himself. He started across the nave to help him.

XIV

Zev hated that he should be hung up here like a salami in a deli window. He tried again to pull his upper body up far enough to reach his leg ropes but he couldn't get close. He had never been one for exercise; doing a sit-up flat on the floor would have been difficult, so what made him think he could do the equivalent maneuver hanging upside down by his feet? He dropped back, exhausted, and felt the blood rush to his head again. His vision swam, his ears pounded, he felt like the skin of his face was going to burst open. Much more of this and he'd have a stroke or worse maybe.

He watched the upside-down battle below and was glad to see the vampires getting the worst of it. These people—seeing Carl among them, Zev assumed they were part of St. Anthony's parish —were ferocious, almost savage in their attacks on the vampires. Months' worth of pent-up rage and fear was being released upon their tormentors in a single burst. It was almost frightening.

Suddenly he felt a hand on his foot. Someone was untying his knots. Thank you, Lord. Soon he would be on his feet again. As the cords came loose he decided he should at least attempt to participate in his own rescue.

Once more, Zev thought. *Once more I'll try.*

With a grunt he levered himself up, straining, stretching to grasp something, anything. A hand came out of the darkness and he reached for it. But Zev's relief turned to horror when he felt the cold clamminess of the thing that clutched him, that pulled him up and over the balcony rail with inhuman strength. His bowels threatened to evacuate when Palmeri's grinning face loomed not six inches from his own.

"It's not over yet, Jew," he said softly, his foul breath clogging Zev's nose and throat. "Not by a long shot!"

He felt Palmeri's free hand ram into his belly and grip his belt at the buckle, then the other hand grab a handful of his shirt at the neck. Before he could struggle or cry out, he was lifted free of the floor and hoisted over the balcony rail.

And the dybbuk's voice was in his ear.

"Joseph called you a friend, Jew. Let's see if he really meant it."

XV

J oe was half way across the floor of the nave when he heard Palmeri's voice echo above the madness.

"Stop them, Joseph! Stop them now or I drop your friend!"

Joe looked up and froze. Palmeri stood at the balcony rail, leaning over it, his eyes averted from the nave and all its newly arrived crosses. At the end of his outstretched arms was Zev, suspended in mid-air over the splintered remains of the pews, over a particularly large and ragged spire of wood that pointed directly at the middle of Zev's back. Zev's frightened eyes were flashing between Joe and the giant spike below.

Around him Joe heard the sounds of the melée drop a notch, then drop another as all eyes were drawn to the tableau on the balcony.

"A human can die impaled on a wooden stake just as well as a vampire!" Palmeri cried. "And just as quickly if it goes through his heart. But it can take hours of agony if it rips through his gut."

St. Anthony's grew silent as the fighting stopped and each faction backed away to a different side of the church, leaving Joe alone in the middle.

"What do you want, Alberto?"

"First I want all those crosses put away so that I can see!"

Joe looked to his right where his parishioners stood.

"Put them away," he told them. When a murmur of dissent arose, he added, "Don't put them down, just out of sight. Please."

Slowly, one by one at first, then in groups, the crosses and crucifixes were placed behind backs or tucked out of sight within coats.

To his left, the vampires hissed their relief and the Vichy cheered. The sound was like hot needles being forced under Joe's fingernails. Above, Palmeri turned his face to Joe and smiled.

"That's better."

"What do you want?" Joe asked, knowing with a sick crawling in his gut exactly what the answer would be.

"A trade," Palmeri said.

"Me for him, I suppose?" Joe said.

Palmeri's smile broadened. "Of course."

"No, Joe!" Zev cried.

Palmeri shook the old man roughly. Joe heard him say, "Quiet, Jew, or I'll snap your spine!" Then he looked down at Joe again. "The other thing is to tell your rabble to let my people go." He laughed and shook Zev again. "Hear that, Jew? A Biblical reference—Old Testament, no less!"

"All right," Joe said without hesitation.

The parishioners on his right gasped as one and cries of "No!" and "You can't!" filled St. Anthony's. A particularly loud voice nearby shouted, "He's only a lousy kike!"

Joe wheeled on the man and recognized Gene Harrington, a carpenter. He jerked a thumb back over his shoulder at the vampires and their servants.

"You sound like you'd be more at home with them, Gene."

Harrington backed up a step and looked at his feet.

"Sorry, Father," he said in a voice that hovered on the verge of a sob. "But we just got you back!"

"I'll be all right," Joe said softly.

And he meant it. Deep inside he had a feeling that he would come through this, that if he could trade himself for Zev and face Palmeri one-on-one, he could come out the victor, or at least battle him to a draw. Now that he was no longer tied up like some sacrificial lamb, now that he was free, with full use of his arms and legs again, he could not imagine dying at the hands of the likes of Palmeri.

Besides, one of the parishioners had given him a tiny crucifix. He had it closed in the palm of his hand.

But he had to get Zev out of danger first. That above all else. He looked up at Palmeri.

"All right, Alberto. I'm on my way up."

"Wait!" Palmeri said. "Someone search him."

Joe gritted his teeth as one of the Vichy, a blubbery, unwashed slob, came forward and searched his pockets. Joe thought he might get away with the crucifix but at the last moment he was made to open his hands. The Vichy grinned in Joe's face as he snatched the tiny cross from his palm and shoved it into his pocket.

"He's clean now!" the slob said and gave Joe a shove toward the vestibule.

Joe hesitated. He was walking into the snake pit unarmed now. A glance at his parishioners told him he couldn't very well turn back now.

He continued on his way, clenching and unclenching his tense, sweaty fists as he walked. He still had a chance of coming out of this alive. He was too angry to die. He prayed that when he got within reach of the ex-priest the smoldering rage at how he had framed him when he'd been pastor, at what he'd done to St. Anthony's since then would explode and give him the strength to tear Palmeri to pieces.

"No!" Zev shouted from above. "Forget about me! You've started something here and you've got to see it through!"

Joe ignored his friend.

"Coming, Alberto."

Father Joe's coming, Alberto. And he's pissed. Royally pissed.

XVI

Zev craned his neck around, watching Father Joe disappear beneath the balcony.

"Joe! Come back!"

Palmeri shook him again.

"Give it up, old Jew. Joseph never listened to anyone and he's not listening to you. He still believes in faith and virtue and honesty, in the power of goodness and truth over what he perceives as evil. He'll come up here ready to sacrifice himself for you, yet sure in his heart that he's going to win in the end. But he's wrong."

"No!" Zev said.

But in his heart he knew that Palmeri was right. How could Joe stand up against a creature with Palmeri's strength, who could hold Zev in the air like this for so long? Didn't his arms ever tire?

"Yes!" Palmeri hissed. "He's going to lose and we're going to win. We'll win for the same reason we'll always win. We don't let anything as silly and transient as sentiment stand in our way. If we'd been winning below and situations were reversed—if Joseph were holding one of my nest brothers over that wooden spike below—do you think I'd pause for a moment? For a second? Never! That's why this whole exercise by Joseph and these people is futile."

Futile . . . Zev thought. Like much of his life, it seemed. Like all of his future. Joe would die tonight and Zev would live on, a cross-wearing Jew, with the traditions of his past sacked and in flames, and nothing in his future but a vast, empty, limitless plain to wander alone.

There was a sound on the balcony stairs and Palmeri turned his head.

"Ah, Joseph," he said.

Zev couldn't see the priest but he shouted anyway.

"Go back Joe! Don't let him trick you!"

"Speaking of tricks," Palmeri said, leaning further over the balcony rail as an extra warning to Joe, "I hope you're not going to try anything foolish."

"No," said Joe's tired voice from somewhere behind Palmeri. "No tricks. Pull him in and let him go."

Zev could not let this happen. And suddenly he knew what he had to do. He twisted his body and grabbed the front of Palmeri's cassock while bringing his legs up and bracing his feet against one of the uprights of the brass balcony rail. As Palmeri turned his startled face toward him, Zev put all his strength into his legs for one convulsive backward push against the railing, pulling Palmeri with him. The vampire priest was overbalanced. Even his enormous strength could not help him once his feet came free of the floor. Zev saw his undead eyes widen with terror as his lower body slipped over the railing. As they fell free, Zev wrapped his arms around Palmeri and clutched his cold and surprisingly thin body tight against him.

"What goes through this old Jew goes through you!" he shouted into the vampire's ear.

For an instant he saw Joe's horrified face appear over the balcony's receding edge, heard Joe's faraway shout of *"No!"* mingle with Palmeri's nearer scream of the same word, then there was a spine-cracking jar and a tearing, wrenching pain beyond all comprehension in his chest. In an eyeblink he felt the sharp spire of wood rip through him and into Palmeri.

And then he felt no more.

As roaring blackness closed in he wondered if he'd done it, if this last desperate, foolish act had succeeded. He didn't want to die without finding out. He wanted to know—

But then he knew no more.

XVII

Joe shouted incoherently as he hung over the rail and watched Zev's fall, gagged as he saw the bloody point of the pew remnant burst through the back of Palmeri's cassock directly below him. He saw Palmeri squirm and flop around like a speared fish, then go limp atop Zev's already inert form.

As cheers mixed with cries of horror and the sounds of renewed battle rose from the nave, Joe turned away from the balcony rail and dropped to his knees.

"Zev!" he cried aloud. "Good God, Zev!"

Forcing himself to his feet, he stumbled down the back stairs, through the vestibule, and into the nave. The vampires and the Vichy were on the run, as cowed and demoralized by their leader's death as the parishioners were buoyed by it. Slowly, steadily, they were falling before the relentless onslaught. But Joe paid them scant attention. He fought his way to where Zev lay impaled beneath Palmeri's already rotting corpse. He looked for a sign of life in his old friend's glazing eyes, a hint of a pulse in his throat under his beard, but there was nothing.

"Oh, Zev, you shouldn't have. You shouldn't have."

Suddenly he was surrounded by a cheering throng of St. Anthony's parishioners.

"We did it, Fadda Joe!" Carl cried, his face and hands splattered with blood. "We killed 'em all! We got our church back!"

"Thanks to this man here," Joe said, pointing to Zev.

"No!" someone shouted. "Thanks to *you!*"

Amid the cheers, Joe shook his head and said nothing. Let them celebrate. They deserved it. They'd reclaimed a small piece of the planet as their own, a toehold and nothing more. A small victory of minimal significance in the war, but a victory nonetheless. They had their church back, at least for tonight. And they intended to keep it.

Good. But there would be one change. If they wanted their Father Joe to stick around they were going to have to agree to rename the church.

St. Zev's.

Joe liked the sound of that.

Son of Celluloid

CLIVE BARKER

Trailer

I

Barberio felt fine, despite the bullet. Sure, there was a catch in his chest if he breathed too hard, and the wound in his thigh wasn't too pretty to look at, but he'd been holed before and come up smiling. At least he was free: that was the main thing. Nobody, he swore, nobody would ever lock him up again, he'd kill himself rather than be taken back into custody. If he was unlucky and they cornered him, he'd stick the gun in his mouth and blow off the top of his head. No way would they drag him back to that cell alive.

Life was too long if you were locked away and counting it in seconds. It had only taken him a couple of months to learn that lesson. Life was long, and repetitive and debilitating, and if you weren't careful you were soon thinking it would be better to die than go on existing in the shit-hole they'd put you in. Better to string yourself up by your belt in the middle of the night rather than face the tedium of another twenty-four hours, all eighty-six thousand four hundred seconds of it.

So he went for broke.

First he bought a gun on the prison black market. It cost him everything he had and a handful of IOUs he'd have to make good on the outside if he wanted to stay alive. Then he made the most obvious move in the book: he climbed the wall. And whatever god looked after the liquor-store muggers of this world was looking after him that night, because hot damn if he didn't scoot right over that wall and away without so much as a dog sniffing at his heels.

And the cops? Why they screwed it up every which way from Sunday, looking for him where he'd never gone, pulling in his brother and his sister-in-law on suspicion of harbouring him when they didn't even know he'd escaped, putting out an All-Points Bulletin with a description of his pre-prison self, twenty pounds heavier than he was now. All this he'd heard from Geraldine, a lady he'd courted in the good old days, who'd given him a dressing for his leg and the bottle of Southern Comfort that was now almost empty in his pocket. He'd taken the booze and sympathy and gone on his way, trusting to the legendary idiocy of the law and the god who'd got him so far already.

Sing-Sing he called this god. Pictured him as a fat guy with a grin that hooked from one ear to the other, a prime salami in one hand, and a cup of dark coffee in the other. In Barberio's mind Sing-Sing smelt like a full belly at Mama's house, back in the days when Mama was still well in the head, and he'd been her pride and joy.

Unfortunately Sing-Sing had been looking the other way when the one eagle-eye cop in the whole city saw Barberio draining his snake in a back alley, and recognized him from that obsolete APB. Young cop, couldn't have been more than twenty-five, out to be a hero. He was too dumb to learn the lesson of Barberio's warning shot. Instead of taking cover, and letting Barberio make a break, he'd forced the issue by coming straight down the alley at him.

Barberio had no choice. He fired.

The cop fired back. Sing-Sing must have stepped in there somewhere, spoiling the cop's aim so that the bullet that should have found Barberio's heart hit his leg, and guiding the returning shot straight into the cop's nose. Eagle-eye went down as if he'd just remembered an appointment with the ground, and Barberio was away, cursing, bleeding and scared. He'd never shot a man before, and he'd started with a cop. Quite an introduction to the craft.

Sing-Sing was still with him though. The bullet in his leg ached, but Geraldine's ministrations had stopped the blood, the liquor had done wonders for the pain, and here he was half a day later, tired but alive, having hopped half-way across a city so thick with vengeful cops it was like a psycho's parade at the Policemen's Ball. Now all he asked of his protector was a place to rest up awhile. Not for long, just enough time to catch his breath and plan his future movements. An hour or two of shut-eye wouldn't go amiss either.

Thing was, he'd got that belly-ache, the deep, gnawing pain he got more and more these days. Maybe he'd find a phone, when he'd rested for a time, and call Geraldine again, get her to sweet-talk a doctor into seeing him. He'd been planning to get out of the city before midnight, but that didn't look like a plausible option now. Dangerous as it was, he would have to stay in the locality a night and maybe the best part of the next day; make his break for the open country when he'd recouped a little energy and had the bullet taken out of his leg.

Jeez, but that belly griped. His guess was it was an ulcer, brought on by the filthy slop they called food at the penitentiary. Lots of guys had belly and shit-chute problems in there. He'd be better after a few days of pizzas and beers, he was damn sure of that.

The word *cancer* wasn't in Barberio's vocabulary. He never thought about terminal disease, especially in reference to himself. That'd be like a piece of slaughterhouse beef fretting about an ingrowing hoof as it stepped up to meet the gun. A man in his trade, surrounded by lethal tools, doesn't expect to perish from a malignancy in his belly. But that's what that ache was.

The lot at the back of the Movie Palace cinema had been a restaurant, but a fire had gutted it three years back, and the ground had never been cleared.

It wasn't a good spec for rebuilding, and no one had shown much interest in the site. The neighborhood had once been buzzing, but that was in the sixties, early seventies. For a heady decade places of entertainment—restaurants, bars, cinemas—had flourished. Then came the inevitable slump. Fewer and fewer kids came this way to spend their money: there were new spots to hit, new places to be seen in. The bars closed up, the restaurants followed. Only the Movie Palace remained as a token reminder of more innocent days in a district that was becoming tackier and more dangerous every year.

The jungle of convolvulus and rotted timbers that throttled the vacant lot suited Barberio just fine. His leg was giving him jip, he was stumbling from sheer fatigue, and the pain in his belly was worsening. A spot to lay down his clammy head was needed, and damn quick. Finish off the Southern Comfort, and think about Geraldine.

It was one thirty A.M.; the lot was a trysting ground for cats. They ran, startled, through the man-high weeds as he pushed aside some of the fencing timbers and slid into the shadows. The refuge stank of piss, human and cat, of garbage, of old fires, but it felt like a sanctuary.

Seeking the support of the back wall of the Movie Palace, Barberio leaned on his forearm and threw up a bellyful of Southern Comfort and acid. Along the wall a little way some kids had built a makeshift den of girders, fire-blackened planks and corrugated iron. Ideal, he thought, a sanctuary within a sanctuary. Sing-Sing was smiling at him, all greasy chops. Groaning a little (the belly was really bad tonight) he staggered along the wall to the lean-to den, and ducked through the door.

Somebody else had used this place to sleep in: he could feel damp sacking under his hand as he sat down, and a bottle clinked against a brick somewhere to his left. There was a smell close by he didn't want to think too much about, like the sewers were backing up. All in all, it was squalid: but it was safer than the street. He sat with his back against the wall of the Movie Palace and exhaled his fears in a long, slow breath.

No more than a block away, perhaps half a block, the babe-in-the-night wail of a cop car began, and his newly acquired sense of security sank without trace. They were closing in for the kill, he knew it. They'd just been playing him along, letting him think he was away, all the time cruising him like sharks, sleek and silent, until he was too tired to put up any resistance. Jeez: he'd killed a cop, what they wouldn't do to him once they had him alone. They'd crucify him.

O.K. Sing-Sing, what now? Take that surprised look off your face, and get me out of this.

For a moment, nothing. Then the god smiled in his mind's eye, and quite coincidentally he felt the hinges pressing into his back.

Shit! A door. He was leaning against a door.

Grunting with pain he turned and ran his fingers around this escape hatch at his back. To judge by touch it was a small ventilation grille no more than three feet square. Maybe it let on to a crawlspace or maybe into someone's kitchen—what the hell? It was safer inside than out: that was the first lesson any newborn kid got slapped into him.

The siren song wailed on, making Barberio's skin creep. Foul sound. It quickened his heart hearing it.

His thick fingers fumbled down the side of the grille feeling for a lock of some kind, and sure as shit there was a padlock, as gritty with rust as the rest of the metalwork.

Come on Sing-Sing, he prayed, one more break is all I'm asking, let me in, and I swear I'm yours forever.

He pulled at the lock, but damn it, it wasn't about to give so easily. Either it was stronger than it felt, or he was weaker. Maybe a little of both.

The car was slinking closer with every second. The wail drowned out the sound of his own panicking breath.

He pulled the gun, the cop killer, out of his jacket pocket and pressed it into service as a snub-nosed crowbar. He couldn't get much leverage on the thing, it was too short, but a couple of cursing heaves did the trick. The lock gave, a shower of rust scales peppered his face. He only just silenced a whoop of triumph.

Now to open the grille, to get out of this wretched world into the dark.

He insinuated his fingers through the lattice and pulled. Pain, a continuum of pain that ran from his belly to his bowel to his leg, made his head spin. Open, damn you, he said to the grille, open sesame.

The door conceded.

It opened suddenly, and he fell back on to the sodden sacking. A moment and he was up again, peering into the darkness within this darkness that was the interior of the Movie Palace.

Let the cop car come, he thought buoyantly, I've got my hidey hole to keep me warm. And warm it was: almost hot in fact. The air out of the hole smelt like it had been simmering in there for a good long while.

His leg had gone into a cramp and it hurt like fuck as he dragged himself through the door and into the solid black beyond. Even as he did so the siren turned a corner nearby and the baby wail died. Wasn't that the patter of lawlike feet he could hear on the sidewalk?

He turned clumsily in the blackness, his leg a dead-weight, his foot feeling about the size of a watermelon, and pulled the grille door to after him. The satisfaction was that of pulling up a drawbridge and leaving the enemy on the other side of the moat, somehow it didn't matter that they could open the door just as easily as he had, and follow him in. Childlike, he felt sure nobody could possibly find him here. As long as he couldn't see his pursuers, his pursuers couldn't see him.

If the cops did indeed duck into the lot to look for him, he didn't hear them. Maybe he'd been mistaken, maybe they were after some other poor punk on the street, and not him. Well O.K., whatever. He had found himself a nice niche to rest up awhile, and that was fine and dandy.

Funny, the air wasn't so bad in here after all. It wasn't the stagnant air of a crawlspace or an attic, the atmosphere in the hidey hole was alive. Not fresh air, no it wasn't that, it smelt old and trapped sure enough, but it was buzzing nevertheless. It fairly sang in his ears, it made his skin tingle like a cold shower, it wormed its way up his nose and put the weirdest things in his head. It was like being high on something: he felt that good. His leg didn't hurt anymore, or if it did he was too distracted by the pictures in his head. He was filling up to overflowing with pictures: dancing girls and kissing couples, farewells at stations, old dark houses, comedians, cowboys, undersea adventures—scenes he'd never lived in a million years, but that moved him now like raw experience, true and incontestable. He wanted to cry at the farewells, except that he wanted to laugh at the comedians, except that the girls needed ogling, the cowboys needed hollering for.

What kind of place was this anyhow? He peered through the glamour of the pictures which were damn close to getting the better of his eyes. He was in a space no more than four feet wide, but tall, and lit by a flickering light that chanced through cracks in the inner wall. Barberio was too befuddled to recognize the origins of the light, and his murmuring ears couldn't make sense of the dialogue from the screen on the other side of the wall. It was "Satyricon," the second of the two Fellini movies the Palace was showing as their late-night double feature that Saturday.

Barberio had never seen the movie, never even heard of Fellini. It would have disgusted him (faggot film, Italian crap). He pre-

ferred undersea adventures, war movies. Oh, and dancing girls.
Anything with dancing girls.

Funny, though he was all alone in his hidey hole, he had the
weird sensation of being watched. Through the kaleidoscope of
Busby Berkeley routines that was playing on the inside of his skull
he felt eyes, not a few—thousands—watching him. The feeling
wasn't so bad you'd want to take a drink for it, but they were
always there, staring away at him like he was something worth
looking at, laughing at him sometimes, crying sometimes, but
mostly just gawping with hungry eyes.

Truth was, there was nothing he could do about them anyhow.
His limbs had given up the ghost; he couldn't feel his hands or feet
at all. He didn't know, and it was probably better that he didn't,
that he'd torn open his wound getting into this place, and he was
bleeding to death.

About two-fifty-five A.M., as Fellini's "Satyricon" came to its
ambiguous end, Barberio died in the space between the back of the
building proper and the back wall of the cinema.

The Movie Palace had once been a Mission Hall, and if he'd
looked up as he died he might have glimpsed the inept fresco
depicting an Angelic Host that was still to be seen through the
grime, and assumed his own Assumption. But he died watching
the dancing girls, and that was fine by him.

The false wall, the one that let through the light from the back of
the screen, had been erected as a makeshift partition to cover the
fresco of the Host. It had seemed more respectful to do that than
paint the Angels out permanently, and besides the man who had
ordered the alterations half-suspected that the movie house bubble
would burst sooner or later. If so, he could simply demolish the
wall, and he'd be back in business for the worship of God instead
of Garbo.

It never happened. The bubble, though fragile, never burst, and
the movies carried on. The Doubting Thomas (his name was Harry
Cleveland) died, and the space was forgotten. Nobody now living
even knew it existed. If he'd searched the city from top to bottom
Barberio couldn't have found a more secret place to perish.

The space however, the air itself, had lived a life of its own in
that fifty years. Like a reservoir, it had received the electric stares
of thousands of eyes, of tens of thousands of eyes. Half a century
of movie goers had lived vicariously through the screen of the

Movie Palace, pressing their sympathies and their passions on to
the flickering illusion, the energy of their emotions gathering
strength like a neglected cognac in that hidden passage of air.
Sooner or later, it must discharge itself. All it lacked was a catalyst.

Until Barberio's cancer.

The Main Feature
II

After loitering in the cramped foyer of the Movie Palace for
twenty minutes or so, the young girl in the cerise and lemon
print dress began to look distinctly agitated. It was almost three in
the morning, and the late-night movies were well over.

Eight months had passed since Barberio had died in the back of
the cinema, eight slow months in which business had been at best
patchy. Still, the late-night double bill on Fridays and Saturdays
always packed in the punters. Tonight it had been two Eastwood
movies: spaghetti westerns. The girl in the cerise dress didn't look
like much of a western fan to Birdy; it wasn't really a women's
genre. Maybe she'd come for Eastwood rather than the violence,
though Birdy had never seen the attraction of that eternally squinting face.

"Can I help you?" Birdy asked.

The girl looked nervously at Birdy.

"I'm waiting for my boyfriend," she said. "Dean."

"Have you lost him?"

"He went to the rest room at the end of the movie and he hasn't
come out yet."

"Was he feeling . . . er . . . ill?"

"Oh no," said the girl quickly, protecting her date from this
slight on his sobriety.

"I'll get someone to go and look for him," said Birdy. It was late,
she was tired, and the speed was wearing off. The idea of spending any more time than she strictly needed to in this fleapit was
not particularly appealing. She wanted home; bed and sleep. Just
sleep. At thirty-four, she'd decided she'd grown out of sex. Bed
was for sleep, especially for fat girls.

She pushed the swing door, and poked her head into the cinema. A ripe smell of cigarettes, popcorn and people enveloped
her; it was a few degrees hotter in here than in the foyer.

"Ricky?"

Ricky was locking up the back exit, at the far end of the cinema.

"That smell's completely gone," he called to her.

"Good." A few months back there'd been a hell of a stench at the screen end of the cinema.

"Something dead in the lot next door," he said.

"Can you help me a minute?" she called back.

"What'd you want?"

He sauntered up the red-carpeted aisle towards her, keys jangling at his belt. His T-shirt proclaimed "Only the Young Die Good."

"Problem?" he said, blowing his nose.

"There's a girl out here. She says she lost her boyfriend in the john."

Ricky looked pained.

"In the john?"

"Right. Will you take a look? You don't mind, do you?"

And she could cut out the wisecracks for a start, he thought, giving her a sickly smile. They were hardly on speaking terms these days. Too many high times together: it always dealt a crippling blow to a friendship in the long run. Besides, Birdy'd made some very uncharitable (accurate) remarks about his associates and he'd returned the salvo with all guns blazing. They hadn't spoken for three and a half weeks after that. Now there was an uncomfortable truce, more for sanity's sake than anything. It was not meticulously observed.

He about turned, wandered back down the aisle, and took row E across the cinema to the john, pushing up seats as he went. They'd seen better days, those seats: sometime around "Now Voyager." Now they looked thoroughly shot at: in need of refurbishing, or replacing altogether. In row E alone four of the seats had been slashed beyond repair, now he counted a fifth mutilation which was new tonight. Some mindless kid bored with the movie and/or his girlfriend, and too stoned to leave. Time was he'd done that kind of thing himself: and counted it a blow for freedom against the capitalists who ran these joints. Time was he'd done a lot of damn-fool things.

Birdy watched him duck into the Men's Room. He'll get a kick out of that, she thought with a sly smile, just his sort of occupation. And to think, she'd once had the hots for him, back in the old days (six months ago) when razor-thin men with noses like Durante and an encyclopaedic knowledge of de Niro movies had really been her style. Now she saw him for what he was, flotsam from a lost ship of hope. Still a pill-freak, still a theoretical bisexual, still devoted to early Polanski movies and symbolic pacifism. What kind of dope did he have between his ears anyhow? The same as she'd had, she chided herself, thinking there was something sexy about the bum.

She waited for a few seconds, watching the door. When he failed to re-emerge she went back into the foyer for a moment, to see how the girl was going on. She was smoking a cigarette like an amateur actress who's failed to get the knack of it, leaning against the rail, her skirt hitched up as she scratched her leg.

"Tights," she explained.

"The Manager's gone to find Dean."

"Thanks," she scratched on. "They bring me out in a rash, I'm allergic to them."

There were blotches on the girl's pretty legs, which rather spoiled the effect.

"It's because I'm hot and bothered," she ventured. "Whenever I get hot and bothered, I get allergic."

"Oh."

"Dean's probably run off, you know, when I had my back turned. He'd do that. He doesn't give a f—. He doesn't care."

Birdy could see she was on her way to tears, which was a drag. She was bad with tears. Shouting matches, even fights, O.K. Tears, no go.

"It'll be O.K." was all she could find to say to keep the tears from coming.

"No it's not," said the girl. "It won't be O.K., because he's a bastard. He treats everyone like dirt." She ground out the half-smoked cigarette with the pointed toe of her cerise shoes, taking particular care to extinguish every glowing fragment of tobacco.

"Men don't care, do they?" she said looking up at Birdy with heart-melting directness. Under the expert makeup, she was perhaps seventeen, certainly not much more. Her mascara was a little smeared, and there were arcs of tiredness under her eyes.

"No," replied Birdy, speaking from painful experience. "No they don't."

Birdy thought ruefully that she'd never looked as attractive as this tired nymphet. Her eyes were too small, and her arms were fat. (Be honest, girl, you're fat all over.) But the arms were her worst feature, she'd convinced herself of that. There were men, a lot of them, who got off on big breasts, on a sizeable ass, but no man she'd ever known liked fat arms. They always wanted to be able to encircle the wrist of their girlfriend between thumb and index finger, it was a primitive way to measure attachment. Her wrists, however, if she was brutal with herself, were practically undiscernible. Her fat hands became her fat forearms, which became, after a podgy time, her fat upper arms. Men couldn't encircle her wrists because she had no wrists, and that alienated them. Well, that was one of the reasons anyhow. She was also very bright: and that was always a drawback if you wanted men at your feet. But of the options as to why she'd never been successful in love, she plumped for the fat arms as the likeliest explanation.

Whereas this girl had arms as slender as a Balinese dancer's, her wrists looked thin as glass, and about as fragile.

Sickening, really. She was probably a lousy conversationalist to boot. God, the girl had all the advantages.

"What's your name?" she asked.

"Lindi Lee," the girl replied.

It would be.

Ricky thought he'd made a mistake. This can't be the toilet, he said to himself.

He was standing in what appeared to be the main street of a frontier town he'd seen in two hundred Westerns. A dust storm seemed to be raging, forcing him to narrow his eyes against the stinging sand. Through the swirl of the ochre-grey air he could pick out, he thought, the General Stores, the Sheriff's Office and the Saloon. They stood in lieu of the toilet cubicles. Optional tumble-weed danced by him on the hot desert wind. The ground beneath his feet was impacted sand: no sign of tiles. No sign of anything that was faintly toilet-like.

Ricky looked to his right, down the street. Where the far wall of the john should have been the street receded, in forced perspective, towards a painted distance. It was a lie, of course, the whole thing was a lie. Surely if he concentrated he'd begin to see through the mirage to find out how it had been achieved; the projections, the concealed lighting effects, the backcloths, the miniatures;

all the tricks of the trade. But though he concentrated as hard as his slightly spaced-out condition would allow, he just couldn't seem to get his fingers under the edge of the illusion to strip it back.

The wind just went on blowing, the tumbleweed tumbled on. Somewhere in the storm a barndoor was slamming, opening and slamming again in the gusts. He could even smell horseshit. The effect was so damn perfect, he was breathless with admiration.

But whoever had created this extraordinary set had proved their point. He was impressed: now it was time to stop the game.

He turned back to the toilet door. It was gone. A wall of dust had erased it, and suddenly he was lost and alone.

The barndoor kept slamming. Voices called to each other in the worsening storm. Where was the Saloon and the Sheriff's office? They too had been obscured. Ricky tasted something he hadn't experienced since childhood: the panic of losing the hand of a guardian. In this case the lost parent was his sanity.

Somewhere to his left a shot sounded in the depths of the storm, and he heard something whistle in his ear, then felt a sharp pain. Gingerly he raised his hand to his earlobe and touched the place that hurt. Part of his ear had been shot away, a neat nick in his lobe. His earstud was gone, and there was blood, real blood, on his fingers. Someone had either just missed blowing off his head or was really playing silly fuckers.

"Hey, man," he appealed into the teeth of this wretched fiction, whirling around on his heel to see if he could locate the aggressor. But he could see no one. The dust had totally enclosed him: he couldn't move backwards or forwards with any safety. The gunman might be very close, waiting for him to step in his direction.

"I don't like this," he said aloud, hoping the real world would hear him somehow, and step in to salvage his tattered mind. He rummaged in his jeans pocket for a pill or two, anything to improve the situation, but he was all out of instant sunshine, not even a lowly Valium was to be found lurking in the seam of his pocket. He felt naked. What a time to be lost in the middle of Zane Grey's nightmares.

A second shot sounded, but this time there was no whistling. Ricky was certain this meant he'd been shot, but as there was neither pain nor blood it was difficult to be sure.

Then he heard the unmistakable flap of the saloon door, and the groan of another human being somewhere near. A tear opened up in the storm for a moment. Did he see the saloon through it, and a young man stumbling out, leaving behind him a painted world of tables, mirrors, and gunslingers? Before he could focus properly the tear was sewn up with sand, and he doubted the sight. Then, shockingly, the young man he'd come looking for was there, a foot away, blue-lipped with death, and falling forward into Ricky's arms. He wasn't dressed for a part in this movie anymore than Ricky was. His bomber jacket was a fair copy of a fifties style, his T-shirt bore the smiling face of Mickey Mouse.

Mickey's left eye was bloodshot, and still bleeding. The bullet had unerringly found the young man's heart.

He used his last breath to ask: "What the fuck is going on?" and died.

As last words went, it lacked style, but it was deeply felt. Ricky stared into the young man's frozen face for a moment, then the dead weight in his arms became too much, and he had no choice but to drop him. As the body hit the ground the dust seemed to turn into piss-stained tiling for an instant. Then the fiction took precedence again, and the dust swirled, and the tumbleweed tumbled, and he was standing in the middle of Main Street, Deadwood Gulch, with a body at his feet.

Ricky felt something very like cold turkey in his system. His limbs began a St. Vitus' dance, and the urge to piss came on him, very strong. Another half minute, he'd wet his pants.

Somewhere, he thought, somewhere in this wild world, there is a urinal. There is a graffiti-covered wall, with numbers for the sex-crazed to call, with "This is not a fallout shelter" scrawled on the tiles, and a cluster of obscene drawings. There are water tanks and paperless toilet roll holders and broken seats. There is the squalid smell of piss and old farts. Find it! in God's name find the real thing before the fiction does you some permanent damage.

If, for the sake of argument, the Saloon and the General Stores are the toilet cubicles, then the urinal must be behind me, he reasoned. So step back. It can't do you any more harm than staying here in the middle of the street while someone takes potshots at you.

Two steps, two cautious steps, and he found only air. But on the third—well, well, what have we here?—his hand touched a cold tile surface.

"Whoo-ee!" he said. It was the urinal: and touching it was like finding gold in a pan of trash. Wasn't that the sickly smell of disinfectant wafting up from the gutter? It was, oh boy, it was.

Still whooping, he unzipped and started to relieve the ache in his bladder, splashing his feet in his haste. What the hell: he had this illusion beat. If he turned round now he'd find the fantasy dispersed, surely. The saloon, the dead boy, the storm, all would be gone. It was some chemical throw-back, bad dope lingering in his system and playing dumb-ass games with his imagination. As he shook the last drops onto his blue suedes, he heard the hero of this movie speak.

"What you doin' pissin' in mah street, boy?"

It was John Wayne's voice, accurate to the last slurred syllable, and it was just behind him. Ricky couldn't even contemplate turning around. The guy would blow off his head for sure. It was in the voice, that threatful ease that warned: I'm ready to draw, so do your worst. The cowboy was armed, and all Ricky had in his hand was his dick, which was no match for a gun even if he'd been better hung.

Very cautiously he tucked his weapon away and zipped himself up, then raised his hands. In front of him the wavering image of the toilet wall had disappeared again. The storm howled: his ear bled down his neck.

"O.K. boy, I want you to take off that gunbelt and drop it to the ground. You hear me?" said Wayne.

"Yes."

"Take it nice and slow, and keep those hands where I can see them."

Boy, this guy was really into it.

Nice and slow, like the man said, Ricky unbuckled his belt, pulled it through the loops in his jeans and dropped it to the floor. The keys should have jangled as they hit the tiles, he hoped to God they would. No such luck. There was a clinking thud that was the sound of metal on sand.

"O.K.," said Wayne. "Now you're beginning to behave. What have you got to say for yourself?"

"I'm sorry?" said Ricky lamely.

"Sorry?"

"For pissing in the street."

"I don't reckon sorry is sufficient penitence," said Wayne.

"But really I am. It was all a mistake."

"We've had about enough of you strangers around these parts. Found that kid with his trousers round his ankles takin' a dump in the middle of the saloon. Well I call that uncouth! Where's you sons of bitches been educated anyhow? Is that what they're teaching you in them fancy schools out East?"

"I can't apologize enough."

"Damn right you can't," Wayne drawled. "You with the kid?"

"In a manner of speaking."

"What kind of fancy talk is that?" he jabbed his gun in Rick's back: it felt very real indeed. "Are you with him or not?"

"I just meant—"

"You don't mean nothing in this territory, mister, you take that from me."

He cocked the gun, audibly.

"Why don't you turn around, son and let's us see what you're made of?"

Ricky had seen this routine before. The man turns, he goes for a concealed gun, and Wayne shoots him. No debate, no time to discuss the ethics of it, a bullet would do the job better than words.

"Turn round I said."

Very slowly, Ricky turned to face the survivor of a thousand shootouts, and there was the man himself, or rather a brilliant impersonation of him. A middle period Wayne, before he'd grown fat and sick looking. A Rio Grande Wayne, dusty from the long trail and squinting from a lifetime of looking at the horizon. Ricky had never had a taste for Westerns. He hated all the forced machismo, the glorification of dirt and cheap heroism. His generation had put flowers in rifle barrels, and he'd thought that was a nice thing to do at the time; still did, in fact.

This face, so mockmanly, so uncompromising, personified a handful of lethal lies—about the glory of America's frontier origins, the morality of swift justice, the tenderness in the heart of brutes. Ricky hated the face. His hands just itched to hit it.

Fuck it, if the actor, whoever he was, was going to shoot him anyway, what was to be lost by putting his fist in the bastard's face? The thought became the act: Ricky made a fist, swung and his knuckles connected with Wayne's chin. The actor was slower than his screen image. He failed to dodge the blow, and Ricky took the opportunity to knock the gun out of Wayne's hand. He then followed through with a barrage of punches to the body, just as he'd seen in the movies. It was a spectacular display.

The bigger man reeled backwards under the blows, and tripped, his spur catching in the dead boy's hair. He lost his balance and fell in the dust, bested.

The bastard was down! Ricky felt a thrill he'd never tasted before; the exhilaration of physical triumph. My God! he'd brought down the greatest cowboy in the world. His critical faculties were overwhelmed by the victory.

The dust storm suddenly thickened. Wayne was still on the floor, splattered with blood from a smashed nose and a broken lip. The sand was already obscuring him, a curtain drawn across the shame of his defeat.

"Get up," Ricky demanded, trying to capitalize on the situation before the opportunity was lost entirely.

Wayne seemed to grin as the storm covered him.

"Well boy," he leered, rubbing his chin, "we'll make a man of you yet . . ."

Then his body was eroded by the driving dust, and momentarily something else was there in its place, a form Ricky could make no real sense of. A shape that was and was not Wayne, which deteriorated rapidly towards inhumanity.

The dust was already a furious bombardment, filling ears and eyes. Ricky stumbled away from the scene of the fight, choking, and miraculously he found a wall, a door, and before he could make sense of where he was the roaring storm had spat him out into the silence of the Movie Palace.

There, though he'd promised himself to butch it up since he'd grown a moustache, he gave a small cry that would not have shamed Fay Wray, and collapsed.

In the foyer Lindi Lee was telling Birdy why she didn't like films very much.

"I mean, Dean likes cowboy movies. I don't really like any of that stuff. I guess I shouldn't say that to you—"

"No, that's O.K."

"—But I mean you must really love movies, I guess. 'Cause you work here."

"I like some movies. Not everything."

"Oh." She seemed surprised. A lot of things seemed to surprise her. "I like wildlife movies, you know."

"Yes . . ."

"You know? Animals . . . and stuff."

"Yes . . ." Birdy remembered her guess about Lindi Lee, that she wasn't much of a conversationalist. Got it in one.

"I wonder what's keeping them?" said Lindi.

The lifetime Ricky had been living in the duststorm had lasted no more than two minutes in real time. But then in the movies time was elastic.

"I'll go look," Birdy ventured.

"He's probably left without me," Lindi said again.

"We'll find out."

"Thanks."

"Don't fret," said Birdy, lightly putting her hand on the girl's thin arm as she passed. "I'm sure everything's O.K."

She disappeared through the swing doors into the cinema, leaving Lindi Lee alone in the foyer. Lindi sighed. Dean wasn't the first boy who'd run out on her, just because she wouldn't produce the goods. Lindi had her own ideas about when and how she'd go all the way with a boy; this wasn't the time and Dean wasn't the boy. He was too slick, too shifty, and his hair smelt of diesel oil. If he had run out on her, she wasn't going to weep buckets over the loss. As her mother always said, there were plenty more fish in the sea.

She was staring at the poster for next week's attraction when she heard a thump behind her, and there was a piebald rabbit, a fat, dozy sweetheart of a thing, sitting in the middle of the foyer staring up at her.

"Hello," she said to the rabbit.

The rabbit licked itself adorably.

Lindi Lee loved animals; she loved True Life Adventure Movies in which creatures were filmed in their native habitat to tunes from Rossini, and scorpions did squaredances while mating, and every bear-cub was lovingly called a little scamp. She lapped up that stuff. But most of all she loved rabbits.

The rabbit took a couple of hops towards her. She knelt to stroke it. It was warm and its eyes were round and pink. It hopped past her up the stairs.

"Oh I don't think you should go up there," she said.

For one thing it was dark at the top of the stairs. For another there was a sign that read "Private. Staff only" on the wall. But the rabbit seemed determined, and the clever mite kept well ahead of her as she followed it up the stairs.

At the top it was pitch black, and the rabbit had gone.

Something else was sitting there in the rabbit's place, its eyes burning bright.

With Lindi Lee illusions could be simple. No need to seduce her into a complete fiction like the boy, this one was already dreaming. Easy meat.

"Hello," Lindi Lee said, scared a little by the presence ahead of her. She looked into the dark, trying to sort out some outline, a hint of face. But there was none. Not even a breath.

She took one step back down the stairs but it reached for her suddenly, and caught her before she toppled, silencing her quickly, intimately.

This one might not have much passion to steal, but it sensed another use here. The tender body was still budding: the orifices unused to invasions. It took Lindi up the few remaining stairs and sealed her away for future investigation.

"Ricky? Oh God, Ricky!"

Birdy knelt beside Ricky's body and shook him. At least he was still breathing, that was something, and though at first sight there seemed to be a great deal of blood, in fact the wound was merely a nick in his ear.

She shook him again, more roughly, but there was no response. After a frantic search she found his pulse: it was strong and regular. Obviously he'd been attacked by somebody, possibly Lindi Lee's absent boyfriend. In which case, where was he? Still in the john perhaps, armed and dangerous. There was no way she was going to be damn fool enough to step in there and have a look, she'd seen that routine too many times. Woman in Peril: standard stuff. The darkened room, the stalking beast. Well, instead of walking bang into that cliché she was going to do what she silently exhorted heroines to do time and again: defy her curiosity and call the cops.

Leaving Ricky where he lay, she walked up the aisle, and back into the foyer.

It was empty. Lindi Lee had either given up on her boyfriend altogether, or found somebody else on the street outside to take her home. Whichever, she'd closed the front door behind her as she left, leaving only a hint of Johnson's Baby Powder on the air behind her. O.K., that certainly made things easier, Birdy thought, as she stepped into the Ticket Office to dial the cops. She was rather pleased to think that the girl had found the common sense to give up on her lousy date.

She picked up the receiver, and immediately somebody spoke.

"Hello there," said the voice, nasal and ingratiating, "it's a little late at night to be using the phone, isn't it?"

It wasn't the operator, she was sure. She hadn't even punched a number.

Besides, it sounded like Peter Lorre.

"Who is this?"

"Don't you recognize me?"

"I want to speak to the police."

"I'd like to oblige, really I would."

"Get off the line, will you? This is an emergency! I need the police."

"I heard you first time," the whine went on.

"Who are you?"

"You already played that line."

"There's somebody hurt in here. Will you *please*—"

"Poor Rick."

He knew his name. Poor Rick, he said, as though he was a loving friend.

She felt the sweat begin in her brow: felt it sprout out of her pores. He knew Ricky's name.

"Poor, poor Rick," the voice said again. "Still I'm sure we'll have a happy ending. Aren't you?"

"This is a matter of life and death," Birdy insisted, impressed by how controlled she felt sure she was sounding.

"I know," said Lorre. "Isn't it exciting?"

"Damn you! Get off this phone! Or so help me—"

"So help you what? What can a fat girl like you hope to do in a situation like this, except blubber?"

"You fucking creep."

"My pleasure."

"Do I know you?"

"Yes and no," the tone of the voice was wavering.

"You're a friend of Ricky's, is that it?" One of the dope fiends he used to hang out with. Kind of idiot game they'd get up to. All right, you've had your stupid little joke," she said, "now get off the line before you do some serious harm."

"You're harassed," the voice said, softening. "I understand . . ." it was changing magically, sliding up an octave, "you're trying to help the man you love . . ." Its tone was feminine now, the accent altering, the slime becoming a purr. And suddenly it was Garbo.

"Poor Richard," she said to Birdy. "He's tried so hard, hasn't he?" She was gentle as a lamb.

Birdy was speechless: the impersonation was as faultless as that of Lorre, as female as the first had been male.

"All right, I'm impressed," said Birdy, "now let me speak to the cops."

"Wouldn't this be a fine and lovely night to go out walking, Birdy? Just we two girls together."

"You know my name."

"Of course I know your name. I'm very close to you."

"What do you mean, close to me?"

The reply was throaty laughter, Garbo's lovely laughter.

Birdy couldn't take it any more. The trick was too clever; she could feel herself succumbing to the impersonation, as though she were speaking to the star herself.

"No," she said down the phone, "you don't convince me, you hear?" Then her temper snapped. She yelled: "You're a fake!" into the mouthpiece of the phone so loudly she felt the receiver tremble, and then slammed it down. She opened the Office and went to the outer door. Lindi Lee had not simply slammed the door behind her. It was locked and bolted from the inside.

"Shit," Birdy said quietly.

Suddenly the foyer seemed smaller than she'd previously thought it, and so did her reserve of cool. She mentally slapped herself across the face, the standard response for a heroine verging on hysteria. Think this through, she instructed herself. One: the door was locked. Lindi Lee hadn't done it, Ricky couldn't have done it, she certainly hadn't done it. Which implied—

Two: There was a weirdo in here. Maybe the same he, she or it that was on the phone. Which implied—

Three: He, she or it must have access to another line, somewhere in the building. The only one she knew of was upstairs, in the storeroom. But there was no way she was going up there. For reasons see Heroine in Peril. Which implied—

Four: She had to open this door with Ricky's keys.

Right, there was the imperative: get the keys from Ricky.

She stepped back into the cinema. For some reason the house-lights were jumpy, or was that just panic in her optic nerve? No, they were flickering slightly; the whole interior seemed to be fluctuating, as though it were breathing.

Ignore it: fetch the keys.

She raced down the aisle, aware, as she always was when she ran, that her breasts were doing a jig, her buttocks too. A right sight I look, she thought for anyone with the eyes to see. Ricky was moaning in his faint. Birdy looked for the keys, but his belt had disappeared.

"Ricky . . ." she said close to his face. The moans multiplied.

"Ricky, can you hear me? It's Birdy, Rick. *Birdy*."

"Birdy?"

"We're locked in, Ricky. Where are the keys?"

" . . keys?"

"You're not wearing your belt, Ricky," she spoke slowly, as if to an idiot, "where-are-your-keys?"

The jigsaw Ricky was doing in his aching head was suddenly solved, and he sat up.

"Boy!" he said.

"What boy?"

"In the john. Dead in the john."

"Dead? Oh Christ. Dead? Are you sure?"

Ricky was in some sort of trance, it seemed. He didn't look at her, he just stared into middle-distance, seeing something she couldn't.

"Where are the keys?" she asked again. "*Ricky*. It's important. Concentrate."

"Keys?"

She wanted to slap him now, but his face was already bloody and it seemed sadistic.

"On the floor," he said after a time.

"In the john? On the floor in the john?"

Ricky nodded. The movement of his head seemed to dislodge

some terrible thoughts: suddenly he looked as though he was going to cry.

"It's all going to be all right," said Birdy.

Ricky's hands had found his face, and he was feeling his features, a ritual of reassurance.

"Am I here?" he inquired quietly. Birdy didn't hear him, she was steeling herself for the john. She had to go in there, no doubt about that, body or no body. Get in, fetch the keys, get out again. Do it *now*.

She stepped through the door. It occurred to her as she did so that she'd never been in a men's toilet before, and she sincerely hoped this would be the first and only occassion.

The toilet was almost in darkness. The light was flickering in the same fitful way as the lights in the cinema, but at a lower level. She stood at the door, letting her eyes accommodate the gloom, and scanned the place.

The toilet was empty. There was no boy on the floor, dead or alive.

The keys were there though. Ricky's belt was lying in the gutter of the urinal. She fished it out, the oppressive smell of the disinfectant block making her sinuses ache. Disengaging the keys from their ring she stepped out of the toilet into the comparative freshness of the cinema. And it was all over, simple as that.

Ricky had hoisted himself on to one of the seats, and was slumped in it, looking sicker and sorrier for himself than ever. He looked up as he heard Birdy emerge.

"I've got the keys," she said.

He grunted: God, he looked ill, she thought. Some of her sympathy had evaporated however. He was obviously having hallucinations, and they probably had chemical origins. It was his own damn fault.

"There's no boy in there, Ricky."

"What?"

"There's no body in the john; nobody at all. What are you on anyhow?"

Ricky looked down at his shaking hands.

"I'm not on anything. Honestly."

"Damn stupid," she said. She half-suspected that he'd set her up for this somehow, except that practical jokes weren't his style.

Ricky was quite a puritan in his way: that had been one of his attractions.

"Do you need a doctor?"

He shook his head sulkily.

"Are you sure?"

"I said no," he snapped.

"O.K., I offered." She was already marching up the rake of the aisle, muttering something under her breath. At the foyer door she stopped and called across to him.

"I think we've got an intruder. There was somebody on the extension line. Do you want to stand watch by the front door while I fetch a cop?"

"In a minute."

Ricky sat in the flickering light and examined his sanity. If Birdy said the boy wasn't in there, then presumably she was telling the truth. The best way to verify that was to see for himself. Then he'd be certain he'd suffered a minor reality crisis brought on by some bad dope, and he'd go home, lay his head down to sleep and wake tomorrow afternoon healed. Except that he didn't want to put his head in that evil-smelling room. Suppose she was wrong, and *she* was the one having the crisis? Weren't there such things as hallucinations of normality?

Shakily, he hauled himself up, crossed the aisle and pushed open the door. It was murky inside, but he could see enough to know that there were no sandstorms, or dead boys, no gun-toting cowboys, nor even a solitary tumbleweed. It's quite a thing, he thought, this mind of mine. To have created an alternative world so eerily well. It was a wonderful trick. Pity it couldn't be turned to better use than scaring him shitless. You win some, you lose some.

And then he saw the blood. On the tiles. A smear of blood that hadn't come from his nicked ear, there was too much of it. Ha! He didn't imagine it at all. There was blood, heel marks, every sign that what he thought he'd seen, he'd seen. But Jesus in Heaven, which was worse? To see, or not to see? Wouldn't it have been better to be wrong, and just a little spaced-out tonight, than right, and in the hands of a power that could literally change the world?

Ricky stared at the trail of blood, and followed it across the floor of the toilet to the cubicle on the left of his vision. Its door was closed: it had been open before. The murderer, whoever he was, had put the boy in there, Ricky knew it without looking.

"O.K.," he said, "now I've got you."

He pushed on the door. It swung open and there was the boy, propped up on the toilet seat, legs spread, arms hanging.

His eyes had been scooped out of his head. Not neatly: no surgeon's job. They'd been wrenched out, leaving a trail of mechanics down his cheek.

Ricky put his hand over his mouth and told himself he wasn't going to throw up. His stomach churned, but obeyed, and he ran to the toilet door as though any moment the body was going to get up and demand its ticket-money back.

"Birdy . . . Birdy . . ."

The fat bitch had been wrong, all wrong. There was death here, and worse.

Ricky flung himself out of the john into the body of the cinema.

The wall lights were fairly dancing behind their Deco shades, guttering like candles on the verge of extinction. Darkness would be too much; he'd lose his mind.

There was, it occurred to him, something familiar about the way the lights flickered, something he couldn't quite put his finger on. He stood in the aisle for a moment, hopelessly lost.

Then the voice came; and though he guessed it was death this time, he looked up.

"Hello Ricky," she was saying as she came along Row E towards him. Not Birdy. No, Birdy never wore a white gossamer dress, never had bruisefull lips, or hair so fine, or eyes so sweetly promising. It was Monroe who was walking towards him, the blasted rose of America.

"Aren't you going to say hello?" she gently chided.

" . . er . . ."

"Ricky. Ricky. Ricky. After all this time."

All this time? What did she mean: all this time?

"Who are you?"

She smiled radiantly at him.

"As if you didn't know."

"You're not Marilyn. Marilyn's dead."

"Nobody dies in the movies, Ricky. You know that as well as I do. You can always thread the celluloid up again—"

—that was what the flickering reminded him of, the flicker of celluloid through the gate of a projector, one image hot on the next, the illusion of life created from a perfect sequence of little deaths.

"—and we're there again, all talking, all singing." She laughed: ice-in-a-glass laughter, "We never fluff our lines, never age, never lose our timing—"

"You're not real," said Ricky.

She looked faintly bored by the observation, as if he was being pedantic.

By now she'd come to the end of the row and was standing no more than three feet away from him. At this distance the illusion was as ravishing and as complete as ever. He suddenly wanted to take her, there, in the aisle. What the hell if she was just a fiction: fictions are fuckable if you don't want marriage.

"I want you," he said, surprised by his own bluntness.

"I want *you*," she replied, which surprised him even more. "In fact I need you. I'm very weak."

"Weak?"

"It's not easy, being the center of attraction, you know. You find you need it, more and more. Need people to look at you. All the night, all the day."

"I'm looking."

"Am I beautiful?"

"You're a goddess: whoever you are."

"I'm yours: that's who I am."

It was a perfect answer. She was defining herself through him. I am a function of you; made for you out of you. The perfect fantasy.

"Keep looking at me; looking *forever*, Ricky. I need your loving looks. I can't live without them."

The more he stared at her the stronger her image seemed to become. The flickering had almost stopped; a calm had settled over the place.

"Do you want to touch me?"

He thought she'd never ask.

"Yes," he said.

"Good." She smiled coaxingly at him, and he reached to make contact. She elegantly avoided his fingertips at the last possible moment, and ran, laughing, down the aisle towards the screen. He followed, eager. She wanted a game: that was fine by him.

She'd run into a cul-de-sac. There was no way out from this end of the cinema, and judging by the come-ons she was giving him, she knew it. She turned and flattened herself against the wall, feet spread a little.

He was within a couple of yards of her when a breeze out of nowhere billowed her skirt up around her waist. She laughed, half closing her eyes, as the surf of silk rose and exposed her. She was naked underneath.

Ricky reached for her again and this time she didn't avoid his touch. The dress billowed up a little higher and he stared, fixated, at the part of Marilyn he had never seen, the fur divide that had been the dream of millions.

There was blood there. Not much, a few fingermarks on her inner thighs. The faultless gloss of her flesh was spoiled slightly. Still he stared; and the lips parted a little as she moved her hips, and he realized the glint of wetness in her interior was not the juice of her body, but something else altogether. As her muscles moved the bloody eyes she'd buried in her body shifted, and came to rest on him.

She knew by the look on his face that she hadn't hidden them deep enough, but where was a girl with barely a veil of cloth covering her nakedness to hide the fruits of her labor?

"You killed him," said Ricky, still looking at the lips, and the eyes that peeked out between. The image was so engrossing, so pristine, it all but cancelled out the horror in his belly. Perversely, his disgust fed his lust instead of killing it. So what if she *was* a murderer: she was legend.

"Love me," she said. "Love me forever."

He came to her, knowing now full well that it was death to do so. But death was a relative matter, wasn't it? Marilyn was dead in the flesh, but alive here, either in his brain, or in the buzzing matrix of the air or both; and he could be with her.

He embraced her, and she him. They kissed. It was easy. Her lips were softer than he'd imagined, and he felt something close to pain at his crotch he wanted to be in her so much.

The willow-thin arms slipped around his waist, and he was in the lap of luxury.

"You make me strong," she said. "Looking at me that way. I need to be looked at, or I die. It's the natural state of illusions."

Her embrace was tightening; the arms at his back no longer

seemed quite so willowlike. He struggled a little against the dis-comfort.

"No use," she cooed in his ear. "You're mine."

He wrenched his head around to look at her grip and to his amazement the arms weren't arms any longer, just a loop of some-thing round his back, without hands or fingers or wrists.

"Jesus Christ!" he said.

"Look at me, boy," she said. The words had lost their delicacy. It wasn't Marilyn that had him in its arms any more: nothing like her. The embrace tightened again, and the breath was forced from Ricky's body, breath the tightness of the hold prevented him from recapturing. His spine creaked under the pressure, and pain shot through his body like flares, exploding in his eyes, all colors.

"You should have got out of town," said Marilyn, as Wayne's face blossomed under the sweep of her perfect cheekbones. His look was contemptuous, but Ricky had only a moment to register it before that image cracked too, and something else came into focus behind this façade of famous faces. For the last time in his life, Ricky asked the question:

"Who are you?"

His captor didn't answer. It was feeding on his fascination; even as he stared twin organs erupted out of its body like the horns of a slug, antennae perhaps, forming themselves into probes and cross-ing the space between its head and Ricky's.

"I need you," it said, its voice now neither Wayne nor Monroe, but a crude, uncultivated voice, a thug's voice. "I'm so fucking weak; it uses me up, being in the world."

It was mainlining on him, feeding itself, whatever it was, on his stares, once adoring—now horrified. He could feel it draining out his life through his eyes, luxuriating in the soul looks he was giving it as he perished.

He knew he must be nearly dead, because he hadn't taken a breath in a long while. It seemed like minutes, but he couldn't be sure.

Just as he was listening for the sound of his heart, the horns divided around his head and pressed themselves into his ears. Even in this reverie, the sensation was disgusting, and he wanted to cry out for it to stop. But the fingers were working their way into his head, bursting his eardrums, and passing on like inquisi-tive tapeworms through brain and skull. He was alive, even now, still staring at his tormentor, and he knew that the fingers were finding his eyeballs, and pressing on them now from behind.

His eyes bulged suddenly and broke from their housing, splashing from his sockets. Momentarily he saw the world from a different angle as his sense of sight cascaded down his cheek. There was his lip, his chin—

It was an appalling experience, and mercifully short. Then the feature Ricky'd lived for thirty-seven years snapped in mid-reel, and he slumped in the arms of fiction.

Ricky's seduction and death had occupied less than three minutes. In that time Birdy had tried every key on Ricky's ring, and could get none of the damn things to open the door. Had she not persisted she might have gone back into the cinema and asked for some help. But things mechanical, even locks and keys, were a challenge to her womanhood. She despised the way men felt some instinctive superiority over her sex when it came to engines, systems and logical processes, and she was damned if she was going to go whining back to Ricky to tell him she couldn't open the damn door.

By the time she'd given up the job, so had Ricky. He was dead and gone. She swore, colorfully, at the keys, and admitted defeat. Ricky clearly had a knack with these wretched things that she'd never quite grasp. Good luck to him. All she wanted now was out of this place. It was getting claustrophobic. She didn't like being locked in, not knowing who was lurking around upstairs.

And now to cap it all, the lights in the foyer were on the blink, dying away flicker by flicker.

What the hell was going on in this place anyhow?

Without warning the lights went out altogether, and beyond the doors into the cinema she was sure she heard movement. A light spilled through from the other side, stronger than torchlight, twitching, colorful.

"Ricky?" she chanced into the dark. It seemed to swallow her words. Either that or she didn't believe it was Ricky at all, and something was telling her to make her appeal, if she had to, in a whisper.

"Ricky . . . ?"

The lips of the swing doors smacked together gently as something pressed on them from the other side.

" . . is that you?"

The air was electric: static was crackling off her shoes as she walked towards the door, the hairs on her arms were rigid. The light on the other side was growing brighter with every step.

She stopped advancing, thinking better of her enquiries. It wasn't Ricky, she knew that. Maybe it was the man or woman on the phone, some pebble-eyed lunatic who got off on stalking fat women.

She took two steps back towards the Ticket Office, her feet sparking, and reached under the counter for the Motherfucker, an iron bar which she'd kept there since she'd been trapped in the Office by three would-be thieves with shaved heads and electric drills. She'd screamed blue murder and they'd fled, but next time she swore she'd beat one (or all of them) senseless rather than be terrorized. And the Motherfucker, all three feet of it, was her chosen weapon.

Armed now, she faced the doors.

They blew open suddenly, and a roar of white noise filled her head, and a voice through the roar said:

"Here's looking at you, kid."

An eye, a single vast eye, was filling the doorway. The noise deafened her; the eye blinked, huge and wet and lazy, scanning the doll in front of it with the insolence of the One True God, the maker of celluloid Earth and celluloid Heaven.

Birdy was terrified, no other word for it. This wasn't a look-behind-you thrill, there was no delicious anticipation, no pleasurable fright. It was real fear, bowel fear, unadorned and ugly as shit.

She could hear herself whimpering under the relentless gaze of the eye, her legs were weakening. Soon she'd fall on the carpet in front of the door, and that would be the end of her, surely.

Then she remembered Motherfucker. Dear Motherfucker, bless his phallic heart. She raised the bar in a two-handed grip and ran at the eye, swinging.

Before she made contact the eye closed, the light went out, and she was in darkness again, her retina burning from the sight.

In the darkness, somebody said: "Ricky's dead."

Just that. It was worse than the eye, worse than all the dead voices of Hollywood, because she knew somehow it was true. The cinema had become a slaughterhouse. Lindi Lee's Dean had died as Ricky had said he had, and now Ricky was dead as well. The doors were all locked, the game was down to two. Her and it.

She made a dash for the stairs, not sure of her plan of action, but certain that remaining in the foyer was suicidal. As her foot touched the bottom stair the swing doors sighed open again behind her and something came after her, fast and flickering. It was a step or two behind her as she breathlessly mounted the stairs, cursing her bulk. Spasms of brilliant light shot by her from its body like the first igniting flashes of a Roman Candle. It was preparing another trick, she was certain of it.

She reached the top of the stairs with her admirer still on her heels. Ahead, the corridor, lit by a single greasy bulb, promised very little comfort. It ran the full length of the cinema, and there were a few storerooms off it, piled with crap: posters, 3-D spectacles, mildewed stills. In one of the storerooms there was a fire door, she was sure. But which? She'd only been up here once, and that two years ago.

"Shit. Shit. Shit," she said. She ran to the first storeroom. The door was locked. She beat on it, protesting. It stayed locked. The next the same. The third the same. Even if she could remember which storeroom contained the escape route the doors were too heavy to break down. Given ten minutes and Motherfucker's help she might do it. But the Eye was at her back: she didn't have ten seconds, never mind ten minutes.

There was nothing for it but confrontation. She spun on her heel, a prayer on her lips, to face the staircase and her pursuer. The landing was empty.

She stared at the forlorn arrangement of dead bulbs and peeling paint as if to discover the invisible, but the thing wasn't in front of her at all, it was behind. The brightness flared again at her back, and this time the Roman Candle caught, fire became light, light became image, and glories she'd almost forgotten were spilling down the corridor towards her. Unleased scenes from a thousand movies: each with its unique association. She began, for the first time, to understand the origins of this remarkable species. It was a ghost in the machine of the cinema: a son of celluloid.

"Give your soul to me," a thousand stars said.

"I don't believe in souls," she replied truthfully.

"Then give me what you give to the screen, what everybody gives. *Give me some love.*"

That's why all those scenes were playing, and replaying, and playing again, in front of her. They were all moments when an audience was magically united with the screen, bleeding through its eyes, looking and looking and looking. She'd done it herself, often. Seen a film and felt it move her so deeply it was almost a physical pain when the end credits rolled and the illusion was broken, because she felt she'd left something of herself behind, a part of her inner being lost up there amongst her heroes and her heroines. Maybe she had. Maybe the air carried the cargo of her desires and deposited them somewhere, intermingled with the cargo of other hearts, all gathering together in some niche, until—

Until this. This child of their collective passions: this technicolor seducer; trite, crass and utterly betwitching.

Very well, she thought, it's one thing to understand your executioner: another thing altogether to talk it out of its professional obligations.

Even as she sorted the enigma out she was lapping up the pictures in the thing: she couldn't help herself. Teasing glimpses of lives she'd lived, faces she'd loved. Mickey Mouse, dancing with a broom, Gish in "Broken Blossoms," Garland (with Toto at her side) watching the twister louring over Kansas, Astaire in "Top Hat," Welles in "Kane," Brando and Crawford, Tracy and Hepburn—people so engraved on our hearts they need no Christian names. And so much better to be teased by these moments, to be shown only the pre-kiss melt, not the kiss itself; the slap, not the reconciliation; the shadow, not the monster; the wound, not death.

It had her in thrall, no doubt of it. She was held by her eyes as surely as if it had them out on their stalks, and chained.

"Am I beautiful?" it said.

Yes it was beautiful.

"Why don't you give yourself to me?"

She wasn't thinking any more, her powers of analysis had drained from her, until something appeared in the muddle of images that slapped her back into herself. "Dumbo." The fat elephant. *Her* fat elephant: no more than that, the fat elephant she'd thought *was* her.

The spell broke. She looked away from the creature. For a moment, out of the corner of her eye, she saw something sickly and fly-blown beneath the glamour. They'd called her Dumbo as a child, all the kids on her block. She'd lived with that ridiculous grey horror for twenty years, never able to shake it off. Its fat body reminded her of her fat, its lost look of her isolation. She thought of it cradled in the trunk of its mother, condemned as a Mad Elephant, and she wanted to beat the sentimental thing senseless.

"It's a fucking lie!" she spat at it.

"I don't know what you mean," it protested.

"What's under all the pizzazz then? Something very nasty I think."

The light began to flicker, the parade of trailers faltering. She could see another shape, small and dark, lurking behind the curtains of light. Doubt was in it. Doubt and fear of dying. She was sure she could smell the fear off it, at ten paces.

"What are you, under there?"

She took a step towards it.

"What are you hiding? Eh?"

It found a voice. A frightened, human voice. "You've no business with me."

"You tried to kill me."

"I want to live."

"So do I."

It was getting dark this end of the corridor, and there was an old, bad smell here, of rot. She knew rot, and this was something animal. Only last spring, when the snow had melted, she'd found something very dead in the yard behind her apartment. Small dog, large cat, it was difficult to be sure. Something domestic that had died of cold in the sudden snows the December before. Now it was besieged with maggots: yellowish, greyish, pinkish: a pastel fly machine with a thousand moving parts.

It had around it the same stink that lingered here. Maybe that was somehow the flesh behind the fantasy.

Taking courage, her eyes still stinging with "Dumbo," she advanced on the wavering mirage, Motherfucker raised in case the thing tried any funny business.

The boards beneath her feet were creaking, but she was too interested in her quarry to listen to their warnings. It was time she got a hold of this killer, shook it and made it spit its secret.

They'd almost gone the length of the corridor now, her advancing, it retreating. There was nowhere left for the thing to go.

Suddenly the floorboards folded up into dusty fragments under her weight and she was falling through the floor in a cloud of dust.

She dropped Motherfucker as she threw out her hands to catch hold of something, but it was all worm-ridden, and crumbled in her grasp.

She fell awkwardly and landed hard on something soft. Here the smell of rot was incalculably stronger, it coaxed the stomach into the throat. She reached out her hand to right herself in the darkness, and on every side there was slime and cold. She felt as though she'd been dumped in a case of partially-gutted fish. Above her, the anxious light shone through the boards as it fell on her bed. She looked, though God knows she didn't want to, and she was lying in the remains of a man, his body spread by his devourers over quite an area. She wanted to howl. Her instinct was to tear off her skirt and blouse, both of which were gluey with matter; but she couldn't go naked, not in front of the son of celluloid.

It still looked down at her.

"Now you know," it said, lost.

"This is you—"

"This is the body I once occupied, yes. His name was Barberio. A criminal; nothing spectacular. He never aspired to greatness."

"And you?"

"His cancer. I'm the piece of him which did aspire, that did long to be more than a humble cell. I am a dreaming disease. No wonder I love the movies."

The son of celluloid was weeping over the edge of the broken floor, its true body exposed now it had no reason to fabricate a glory.

It was a filthy thing, a tumor grown fat on wasted passion. A parasite with the shape of a slug, and the texture of raw liver. For a moment a toothless mouth, badly molded, formed at its head end and said: "I'm going to have to find a new way to eat your soul."

It flopped down into the crawlspace beside Birdy. Without its shimmering coat of many technicolors it was the size of a small child. She backed away as it stretched a sensor to touch her, but avoidance was a limited option. The crawlspace was narrow, and further along it was blocked with what looked to be broken chairs and discarded prayer books. There was no way out but the way she'd come, and that was fifteen feet above her head.

Tentatively, the cancer touched her foot, and she was sick. She couldn't help it, even though she was ashamed to be giving in to such primitive responses. It revolted her as nothing ever had before; it brought to mind something aborted, a bucket case.

"Go to hell," she said to it, kicking at its head, but it kept coming, its diarrheal mass trapping her legs. She could feel the churning motion of its innards as it rose up to her.

Its bulk on her belly and groin was almost sexual, and revolted as she was by her own train of thought she wondered dimly if such a thing aspired to sex. Something about the insistence of its forming and reforming feelers against her skin, probing tenderly beneath her blouse, stretching to touch her lips, only made sense as desire. Let it come then, she thought, let it come if it has to.

She let it crawl up her until it was entirely perched on her body, fighting every moment the urge to throw it off—and then she sprang her trap.

She rolled over.

She'd weighed 225 pounds at the last count, and she was probably more now. The thing was beneath her before it could work out how or why this had happened, and its pores were oozing the sick sap of tumors.

It fought, but it couldn't get out from under, however much it squirmed. Birdy dug her nails into it and began to tear at its sides, taking cobs of it, spongy cobs that set more fluids gushing. Its howls of anger turned into howls of pain. After a short while, the dreaming disease stopped fighting.

Birdy lay still for a moment. Underneath her, nothing moved.

At last, she got up. It was impossible to know if the tumor was dead. It hadn't, by any standards that she understood, lived. Besides, she wasn't touching it again. She'd wrestle the Devil himself rather than embrace Barberio's cancer a second time.

She looked up at the corridor above her and despaired. Was she now to die in here, like Barberio before her? Then, as she glanced down at her adversary, she noticed the grille. It hadn't been visible while it was still night outside. Now dawn was breaking, and columns of dishwater light were creeping through the lattice.

She bent to the grille, pushed it hard, and suddenly the day was in the crawlspace with her, all around her. It was a squeeze to get through the small door, and she kept thinking every moment that she felt the thing crawling across her legs, but she hauled herself into the world with only bruised breasts to complain of.

The abandoned lot hadn't changed substantially since

Barberio's visit there. It was merely more nettle-thronged. She stood for a while breathing in drafts of fresh air, then made for the fence and the street beyond it.

The fat woman with the haggard look and the stinking clothes was given a wide berth by newsboys and dogs alike as she made her way home.

Censored Scenes
III

I t wasn't the end.
The police went to the Movie Palace just after nine-thirty. Birdy went with them. The search revealed the mutilated bodies of Dean and Ricky, as well as the remains of "Sonny" Barberio. Upstairs, in the corner of the corridor, they found a cerise shoe.

Birdy said nothing, but she knew. Lindi Lee had never left.

She was put on trial for a double murder nobody really thought she'd committed, and acquitted for lack of evidence. It was the order of the court that she be put under psychiatric observation for a period of not less than two years. The woman might not have committed murder, but it was clear she was a raving lunatic. Tales of walking cancers do nobody's reputation much good.

In the early summer of the following year Birdy gave up eating for a week. Most of the weight loss in that time was water, but it was sufficient to encourage her friends that she was at last going to tackle the Big Problem.

That weekend, she went missing for twenty-four hours.

Birdy found Lindi Lee in a deserted house in Seattle. She hadn't been so difficult to trace: it was hard for poor Lindi to keep control of herself these days, never mind avoid would-be pursuers. As it happened her parents had given up on her several months previous. Only Birdy had continued to look, paying for an investigator to trace the girl, and finally her patience was rewarded with the sight of the frail beauty, frailer than ever but still beautiful sitting in this bare room. Flies roamed the air. A turd, perhaps human, sat in the middle of the floor.

Birdy had a gun out before she opened the door. Lindi Lee looked up from her thoughts, or maybe *its* thoughts, and smiled at her. The greeting lasted a moment only before the parasite in Lindi Lee recognized Birdy's face, saw the gun in her hand and knew exactly what she'd come to do.

"Well," it said, getting up to meet its visitor.

Lindi Lee's eyes burst, her mouth burst, her cunt and ass, her ears and nose all burst, and the tumor poured out of her in shocking pink rivers. It came worming out of her milkless breasts, out of a cut in her thumb, from an abrasion on her thigh. Wherever Lindi Lee was open, it came.

Birdy raised the gun and fired three times. The cancer stretched once towards her, fell back, staggered and collapsed. Once it was still, Birdy calmly took the acid bottle out of her pocket, unscrewed the top and emptied the scalding contents on human limb and tumor alike. It made no shout as it dissolved, and she left it there, in a patch of sun, a pungent smoke rising from the confusion.

She stepped out into the street, her duty done, and went her way, confidently planning to live long after the credits for this particular comedy had rolled.